By Joseph McElroy

LOOKOUT CARTRIDGE

LOOKOUT

CARTRIDGE

JOSEPH MC ELROY

 ALFRED A. KNOPF
NEW YORK   1974

THIS IS A BORZOI BOOK
PUBLISHED BY ALFRED A. KNOPF, INC.

I wish to thank my friend Dorothy Carrington for insights
into Corsican culture given in letters, in conversations in
Ajaccio and New York, and in her book *Granite Island:
A Portrait of Corsica* (Longman, London, 1971).

I am indebted to two other books in particular: John L.
Stephens, *Incidents of Travel in Central America,
Chiapas and Yucatan* with illustrations by Frederick
Catherwood, 2 vols. (Dover Publications, New York,
1969); Victor Wolfgang von Hagen, *F. Catherwood.
Architect-Explorer of Two Worlds* (Barre Publishers,
Barre, Massachusetts, 1968).

For grants of money I wish to thank the Ingram Merrill
Foundation and the National Endowment for the Arts.

Chapters I and II with the interchapter "Printed circuit
cut-in flash-forward" first appeared in *TriQuarterly* 29.

Library of Congress Cataloging in Publication Data

McElroy, Joseph   Lookout cartridge.

A novel.   I. Title.
PZ4.MI422LO   [PS3563.A293]   813'.5'4
74-7744   ISBN 0-394-49375-3

FIRST EDITION

TO BILL WILSON

LOOKOUT CARTRIDGE

It is a silent flash there in the city's grid, and as I happen to look down at that precise point I am thinking of real estate prices.

From my height the detonation noise is a signal of light only. My cabin responds by at once easing its forward motion so we're barely moving. We hover level with the 900-foot tower at 40 Wall Street, three quarters of a mile to our right. We have a new purpose.

We dip, and the controls alter the tilt of the rotor head's swash-plate ring, which is above my head out of sight in the open air.

Had I been watching left or right of where the flash appeared, I would have seen it more clearly still.

Up in the cockpit the flash has been seen and the man in the right-hand seat is reporting it. But something is happening to our prop blades, the cadence is gone. Something is wrong, we throb, we rock, we drop, we wait. The pilot is rubbing his head against the side window, he is peering up.

Helicopters are designed to wait, but can we? We hover lower, the props seem better, but if it is possible to swerve with no forward motion, that's what we're doing—or the cabin is now hung on the end of one of its own prop blades.

We have to get down, we can't just drop onto a roof. We tilt to go ahead toward the river, the heliport; therefore, the swash-plate hasn't come loose. But in a sensation that is not the vectors of revolution and is not sound, the blades feel less hinged. I know that if the

3

blades' lag-hinges have come loose, the blades can't feather and will take too much stress and will snap—the chopper loses its lift; and when it does, does it come down like a landing?

I can't make out the radio voice from headquarters.

I did not hear the flash, I saw it, just as I was contemplating real estate inflation, Peter Minuit and the Indians, and an American gentleman named John Lloyd Stephens buying a Maya city in the 1840's for twice what the Dutch gave for Manhattan—the flash just north of City Hall Park could have been a vehicle blowing up. But there was no shock up here.

Smoke came like a substance squeezed from the hole that now narrows following the flash. Not the quick sound of artillery.

And dark points come and move almost as if sound and speed have become identical, but not quite, for I can see them move. They are like genes in a microphotograph.

This light without sound is not the beginning.

Was there a beginning?

Sound without illumination maybe.

Such a field of noise was coming everywhere, from tile, concrete, the chill-blown street above, the tracks below, and even as if from the change booth where a black girl in blue-smoked cartwheel glasses pushed out tokens without looking up from her paper—that till I was through the turnstile and to the brink of the escalator and put my foot on it hearing behind me the click of steps closing fast yet seeming oddly slow, I didn't guess why the toddling graybeard in a herringbone with the hems drooping who'd preceded me through the turnstile had made for the stairs instead.

But about to put my hands on the escalator rails only to see they weren't running and clear to the bottom the escalator was stopped, I got a blind jarring shove in my back that jumped me three or four of those stationary steps over the brink just as I felt both my hands stuck in the tailored pockets of the trenchcoat I'd bought in London for this trip to New York. But legs and feet believing they could survive apart from the rest of me slowed their motion to fit the momentum of fall and frequency of steps so my four-steps-at-a-time made a metrobeat my limbs were marking like old times when my school friends and I took stairs three, four at a go and here again now years later no hands.

So I paced my plunge two-thirds of the way before slowing enough to do two, then one at a time, then stop, get the hands and fingers free, and twist to look back up to the top. But I saw only the

4

old man on the adjacent stairs who'd been ahead of me but was now looking down at me no doubt taking me for an escalator freak, not somebody who'd been pushed.

The old man had known the escalator wasn't running. The pusher perhaps had not.

I ran back up. The steps weighed as much by contrast as if going down the first time I'd been riding. In London they used to call it Moving Staircase.

I pushed through the gate. I could barely hear the change-woman when I said what had happened, but her tongue flickered out and I put her moist smile with her words: Enough to do watching nobody cheats the City.

How was it the steps behind me had been much slower than mine yet right on top of me?

She let me go back through the gate free like a transit worker or a cop, and I went back down the stopped escalator into a noise like the subway rails splitting and caught the train the old man had boarded.

A large black woman yawned without opening her eyes and I smelled her breakfast. Travelers on the London Underground do not as a rule sit with their eyes closed.

I had in my head somewhere why Dagger DiGorro's film got destroyed. I saw almost none of the film itself and shot only a few minutes of it; but no one saw more than I and I was there when Dagger shot the bulk of it.

Who knew better what was in that film? Only Dagger maybe. And he must have forgotten parts—to judge from what he once said in London and once in Ajaccio and once when we changed the Druid's tire on Salisbury Plain.

Just the one rush got processed at first. Rush may be rather big talk; we weren't exactly pros. You'd have thought Dagger cared more for the Beaulieu 16 he got hold of than the film we were supposed to be making with it. Alba took my hand the day Dagger and I left London for Ajaccio; she'd decided she was too pregnant and she was sorry because she'd never seen Corsica and she retains something of the metropolitan French condescension toward La Corse. She said, Cartwright, you take care of Dag, and she put a finger on a button of my shirt where my collarbone is. She wore rust-colored nail varnish. She wouldn't have expected much from this film idea we'd had that I'd spoken of as mainly his idea. But she loves him, and there was money in the bank and the promise of more in the autumn.

And she perhaps did not even want him to stay home; his absence excites her, and she's as glad as I am to live in London.

When I went to see the Druid south of the river weeks later about my breathing and my imminent trip to New York, the old man sitting there in his dark green business suit told me someday the destruction of Dagger's film would seem part of a large endless harmony. He asked if my trip would include Cape Kennedy. I said I was not after all a tourist, and he said at once though slowly, But you try to become one.

Which seemed not up to his usual standard so I opened my mouth to get us back to my breathing but the moment grew and the words stayed in my head and instead he spoke: You keep a diary.

I said, I don't just keep it. And I was about to say I give—or send—parts of it away now and then, but the interview seemed over.

Still, as I was showing myself out he said from the far end of his hall, But what *is* cinema? Evanescent no doubt. Years ago I went to see a film called *Breaking the Sound Barrier*.

I have in my head things I may not have exactly seen, just as you who read this have me.

A hand enters a lab's glass wall through large elastic lips sleeving a glove port.

You have seen this, don't think you haven't. Once the hand is into the sleeve it feels its way into a thick lightweight glove in order to get at pieces of who knows what on the other side of the glass—cans of bacteria, say.

You have this in your head. You have it from some grainy wire-service photo on the way to the editorial page or the fishing column or the real estate; or you have it moving live contained by your living-room television; or you've had it shown you in the enlarged privacy of a dark theater; or you have it from less pure sources, someone has told you it.

Or, as with me, the image emerged out of standard elements while you sat in a dark projection room during an intermission half-listening to a couple of computer-filmmakers argue whether one can compose more freely with plasma-crystal panels.

You may never be called to account for what you've seen, but you've seen the glove port and the white coveralls and some of the semi-automated gear on the other side; and you've seen, let us say, radioactive material the glove hand handles without contamination.

Like me, you have in your head things you may not have exactly seen.

6

Like a lookout cartridge.

Or the Landslip Drive-in Movie, whose monumental screen under clean and clement American stars and in front of you and a hundred other cars without audible warning one summer night began to lower, to tilt back hugely and drop as if into a slot in the earth.

The image became yours even more surely by disappearing. It disappeared with a distinguished rumble mixed with what still came out of the speaker draped over the edge of your car window. An actress and actor in the corrected colors of the spectrum had been touching each other's colossal faces and their breaths kept coming faster and more intimately loud to bring right into your car this whopping slide of mouths and fingers and nostrils inserted into the night-pines and sea-sky above the locally well-known clay cliffs that had just enjoyed their first clear day in two weeks. But now for the first time since before World War II a section of cliff gives way and the famous faces are swept as if by their camera right up off the monumental screen until you have only the upper half of the two torsos thrown onto the remaining upper half of the descending screen as it tilts back toward the sea; and now where's the movie? The drive-in screen's rear props fall with the clay cliff, and mouths and cheekbones and eyelids have tipped away under the projector's light.

Then you have before you ocean sky—not to mention an experience tomorrow's news won't do justice to—and you get your feet on the ground as your speaker with its static swings with the car door. You look to the rear of the drive-in and see many silhouettes doing the same as you.

You find the cone of light still projected.

Circuits in the head make the image feasible. These often bypass other printed circuits neater and newer. These newer circuits can ask questions not so sharp as the images streaming from older circuits but still of interest to me. Questions like: Is there an insurance group prepared to write a policy to cover Landslip Drive-in up to and including landslip itself? Would fissures appear well in advance of such a major landslip? What are the dimensions of such a cinema screen? How many outdoor drive-in screens one hundred by sixty feet exist in England?

The American girl said no to breakfast. She then shifted under the clammy-looking khaki blanket she'd tucked round herself in the deck chair sometime the night before and looked apparently through a break in the bushes toward the Thames and a barge pilot-house passing, and said well yes she would, then stared up at me and said after all no thanks, and instead of asking what I was doing in Embankment Gardens at seven, which is early for a commuter to be coming through Charing Cross, she said, How long you been over?

Most of them don't know a fellow American short of an Alabama twang or an American Express travelers check. I said I had a daughter almost her age who was born a year before we moved to England. The barge pilot-house had moved beyond the corner of my eye, pigeons walked along Brunel's Embankment wall, the girl smiled back up at me from her deck chair on the grass near the band stage and said, Lucky scrounger.

I thought, A girl doesn't have to shave first thing in the morning.

In the summer of '53 Lorna laughed and laughed when I couldn't zip our sleeping bags together because one track was half rusted out.

When I was a boy my grandfather wouldn't shave till after we came back for breakfast and cleaned our white perch. The loons the other end of the lake would toss out their watery laugh. No one else would be on the still surface. My grandfather would bob his rod a couple of times and so would I. If the Maine sky was gray he'd say, They love that sky.

The American girl's suede desert boots were propped on her knapsack. My hand on the top of her deck chair felt the drizzle beginning. She looked up and said, You homing on me? and I said, Scrounger.

In summer I let the odd bus conductor take me for a tourist. What does it matter? But also English people down from the North with their children for a weekend have asked me the way. I know London as only an American can. They'd say how long since you've been back to America, and I'd say I'm always going back.

If you are not sure where you are, you have me.

Lorna came with me to the airport when I went to Chicago in '64. Her perfume and her pallor went together. The cabbie when he let us out at the Departures Building said, Had a good time then? and Lorna quickly said, Oh we've lived here for years.

What do you mean, *always going back?* said the American girl. She worked the blanket up under her chin. You must be rich or you've got a racket. Spain's cheaper.

No surprise in any case to be once again entering a holding

8

pattern over Kennedy listening to the captain's baritone pass on to his passengers the commuterized forecast of an autumn cold front coming in from Ohio, which to a New Yorker is the Midwest.

No surprise to be held up getting into Manhattan from Kennedy.

No surprise in ocher twilight on the expressway to see slowed, outbound cars with their lone drivers float toward us over the rise.

No surprise to find New York hard to enter, though perhaps always a surprise to find New York.

No surprise to be on a sidewalk Wednesday morning walking north trying to use the Druid's advice.

Surprising only that this time I brought a venture whose principal product had been virtually ruined a month before. So instead of concentrating on letting my neck muscles ease into my lung mass, I was imagining that the Druid had secretly pondered Dagger's film and my diary of it.

I knew just how much I was going to tell Claire.

Twenty blocks north the mauve and amber air waited retreating before a glittering length of vehicles. Down into the deafening business of the avenue down through the late-morning film the dots of light thirty-six stories up gave alternately time and temp. The traffic here close was spaced and moving. On the small panel truck that passed me was my name.

To feel the sheaf of diary inside my jacket I put my hand to my breast like a hatless bigwig hearing a national anthem.

I knew roughly what I was going to do.

However, I could not know in advance that at an intersection in Manhattan I would abruptly have to think about a piece of equipment common everywhere but put now to unusual use.

On such an instrument the stabber will leave no usable prints: at most a few curves broken from a second, still more fugitive set of marks in his moist palm. Recompose the two sets if you can, but it won't be with an expert's dust and a police photographer's plate.

The stabber may reflect that given the instrument's diameter there could be no prints worth developing. But what he will not recall is what he did not see or feel in his skin gripping the instrument—to wit, the presence behind him of an old college classmate Cartwright whom he might have known if he'd turned around.

At the corner ahead, sandy hair and a tanned neck became now the profile of Jim Wheeler, who turned his head sharply as if to peer at the couple on his left who had stepped off the curb and stood looking at each other.

It was Jim, and he'd appeared in front of me during the few moments I was seeing my name on the panel. I turned to see if likewise someone had spotted me from behind.

The light was now green sharing its light with the green word GO. The couple went forward still looking at each other. Jim stepped off the curb.

But from his left a black car with bird-lime on the hood launched itself veering out of the northbound avenue into the eastbound street they were moving to cross, and it must have brushed the couple and would have swiped Jim with the tail end but his hand came up onto the rear radio aerial and so he was able to stop himself, but when the car did not instantly brake, the aerial snapped in his hand, which it is not supposed to be able to do, and this was what seemed to stop the car.

The driver was out fast. He came back along the far side of the car as I slowed my approach. He was a big man in a white T-shirt with a brown decal on the chest. Someone said, Jersey plates.

A woman's laugh was off to my right somewhere near a florist's doorway flanked by pussywillows in a black can and soft dark and bright pansies in tiers of flats.

The driver came round the rear of his car, his hands in front of him at hip level.

Jim stuck the length of aerial straight out.

The man in the T-shirt rushed onto it.

It went into his shirt well below the brown decal, which I now saw was a target of numbered rings.

The two words "License revoked" suddenly survived above the engines whose din swirled like a virtually immeasurable air conditioner killing itself yet letting off staggered signal horns to mark its decaying sequences.

The victim's mouth was open.

From the rise and fall of the woman's laugh I couldn't tell if she had seen the stabbing.

The driver had got his aerial back in one piece. The other man let go.

A few inches showed in front.

When the victim turned, as to avoid the aerial already in him, the rod could be seen to have gone clear through and pierced his back. But instead of puncturing his T-shirt again it tented it out as if he had a rolled tabloid in his back pocket sticking up under his shirt.

The stabber, Jim, stepped back onto the curb. He set out east finding his way into the clusters of early lunchtime strollers.

The driver, with the severed aerial through him, stood against his black fender not doing anything. The gathering mass of traffic pressed north. There was blood at the corner of the driver's mouth. His eyelids were pinched shut.

I was at the curb now. There was more than enough of the broken silver rod to get hold of.

Jim walking east was already half a block away if that was his beige suit.

A voice like the laughing woman's said, Call a cop.

The noise volume guarded by high buildings rose into a homogeneity like quiet; like a patient *Om*.

Back down the swarming block I saw Claire; it had to be Claire because she still looked much like my Jenny, who is only seventeen.

At once she turned back and went into a corner camera shop. Even if she simply didn't want to meet me an hour before the time we'd agreed on as well as in a place other than her apartment, had she in any case seen the stricken man through the crowd?

At this point, then, the driver is several feet in front of me, Claire is in a shop a block south, Jim is now half a block east. The aerial is fixed in the driver's front and gleaming so cleanly the T-shirt is like a new polishing rag.

He went to his knees and the aerial sticking out his back scraped a line on the fender.

The pressure then must have increased his pain inside, but his eyes were shut and he was apparently silent among the vehicle horns and the revvings of diesel trucks pushing dark fumes out of side-stacks.

The kneeling man dropped his large hands from his stomach to the street, and one mashed a length of ocher turd, the other a dark circle of spit. So he was on his hands and knees, and his T-shirt had ridden above the two inches of aerial that came straight up out of his back red-sleeved.

Two Puerto Ricans pushing coats and dresses along left their four-wheeled racks at the curb and looked into the black car.

One of the driver's hands was missing part of the middle finger.

A siren that seemed in its low register as close as a speaking voice rose and swooped to rise again, a cop car in traffic a block and a half south.

There was clearly nothing to do for the man in the T-shirt till the ambulance came, certainly not disengage the aerial.

I felt I had been inserted into a situation.

I went back to the camera shop a block south but, being on the corner, it happened to have another door around on the crosstown street.

I entered and someone called behind me, I saw it.

I passed along the glass counter thinking to catch Claire in the crosstown street. The man said, What happened?

Jenny my daughter was in the market for a Leica IIIG box for a hundred dollars top, and if I could find one an Elmar f3.5 too.

I said over my shoulder, A man was stabbed.

Claire was out of sight.

Back through the door, the camera man said, Oi.

Could I get Jenny a reliable second-hand 200-millimeter automatic as cheap here in the camera capital as on the other side through Dagger?

It had been Claire, but she looked even more like my own seventeen-year-old Jenny now the difference in age was less.

My eyes stung as if blinking through chlorine. Eastward the way I thought Claire had gone, a Salvation Army hatband showed dull soft red moving toward me.

Did Jenny even want something from America this time? Why did I have the idea she was saying to me, Don't bother, I'll get it myself when the time comes.

In 1957 she was three and didn't yet object to *Ginny;* I said I'll bring you a present when I come back from America. She knew *present* but not *America*. A list of all I've brought her since would make a history.

If I told the camera man my problem too simply, he'd say, Look, all your camera prices are much higher in England, they got a very serious problem with their economy.

But when he got my point about the American PX or the continental duty-free shops Dagger had connections with, he'd turn right off; he'd say, Well we don't compete with those foreign prices— maybe you need some film? you take slides, try this Fuji color.

During this absence from my house in London that has almost no mortgage left on the freehold, I could be holed up in another part of London for a fortnight and not even be in America. Bringing a present from the PX in Ruislip on the outskirts of London or the Navy place near the Embassy was like bringing a present from the States. But Jenny wanted something else.

I cut back through the camera shop, I would meet Claire as arranged. The man was outside the other door looking up the block, but behind the counter now was evidently the proprietor, a white-haired broad swarthy man in very dark glasses.

A man in a stained apron came in behind me and put a lidless shallow cardboard box on the counter. The clerk came back in the other door. The ambulance is stuck in traffic, he said.

What's the ambulance? said the deli man.

On his forearm across a vein and barely visible in the hair were five blue numerals.

Claire's disappearance wouldn't have mattered if she hadn't first appeared. You see Jim Wheeler you haven't seen in years, or been aware of not seeing. You see him impale somebody without exactly meaning to and walk away down a lunch-hour street. You see behind you a young woman you're going to talk to in half an hour. She cuts back through a camera shop and you lose her.

My children aren't children any more. Not like the Kodacolor display ad propped high on this glass counter—a regular neighborhood snap enlarged and backed—five kids aged say six to ten: if I could draw them out from behind their u-v filter, slide away the health spectrum, leave them black and white, they'd hear the tale of my trip to America and dismiss it in none of the adult ways your own family can.

The weekend had been confusing. Jenny had picked an argument Friday night but dropped it until Monday night and then Lorna seemed deliberately to have stayed upstairs packing my bag when I knew she'd normally get into the act.

I hadn't told Lorna and Jenny and Will the trip was more than business, though Lorna unlike Dagger knew I had an appointment with Claire, and Lorna must have thought I wanted support for a second try on the film and wasn't just having a friendly lunch with Dagger's beautiful niece. And Lorna knew nothing of the Indian I thought might have slipped into Dagger and Alba's flat during the three hours when someone had broken in and ruined most of our film.

My son Will would not dismiss the trip's true purpose if he could understand it. But he'd think big, he'd imagine international manipulations.

Feed facts to wife, son, daughter: before you're through you're retrieving responses.

You take these little Americans in the Kodacolor blow-up who would be just as multiracial in black and white: whip them out of their crush of color-corrected health, polarize them into Tri-X prints, and they'd ask good questions.

About Dagger's film. They'd ask why and how. Maybe not when.

And *who* ruined the movie? And *why* did they?

Were the cops there—? The pigs, you mean, says the oldest, a ten-year-old black girl, her full lips moving in this still enlargement and my mind moving with her lips—let's say she had fish-fingers for lunch at her school on Ninth Avenue this noon—fish-*fing*ers! What's fish-*fing*ers? calls a nine-year-old oriental boy whose mother does not permit him to take advantage of the new hot breakfast how many New Yorkers in the highest-taxed city in America know is given at that same public school on Ninth Avenue—It's fish-*sticks!* And the rest giggle, and two little ones add their motion to this blow-up ad for Kodacolor and start wrestling saying Fish-*fing*ers! Fish-*fing*ers!—and I'd tell them that in London fish-sticks are called fish-fingers (hot, fish-fingers old, *which* little piggie stays home with a cold), and I'd remind them it was in London that the film was destroyed.

Yeah? Anybody get killed in it? What's it about?

I could be mysterious and the kids would take it. But if after I said, What would you rather do, see the film or hear me tell about it? and they said, See it, and I said, But it's ruined, wrecked, exposed, burnt up by the light of day, then they'd squint in the New York sun, shrug and maybe nod and say, Yeah you could tell about it.

Last year when Will was fourteen he asked for a book on analog computers. (Or did I suggest it?) This trip it was brochures from the Stock Exchange. He is thinking of opening a numbered account in a Swiss bank with a hundred pounds.

At my end of the display case under the glass were some used items. Cameras mostly Japanese, then four lensless boxes with lens cap covering the hole; then some lenses on their own, at waist level black barrels ribbed with white-numbered distance scale, depth of field, f numbers, cylinders so rich you could just reach through the display case's plate glass (avoiding the smudges) and lift out the heavy zoom and adjusting it to your eye and the subject snap without a box directly into your head like an act of thought. A 12–120 zoom with a crank and a little steel bar either of which turns the barrel. On sale also an Olympus-Pen just like Dagger's; the half-frame means on a thirty-six-exposure roll you get seventy-two shots, said Dag; and it was one of my bad days and I said to him, What if they're lousy?

At the avenue door through which I'd first entered, I was

14

weighed back by a thing in my eyes and chest like the damned sickness in my wrist when I fell off a ladder in Highgate and Lorna couldn't stop laughing and Jenny ran to me and cried. (My Maine grandfather died not in his boat casting for lake bass but in a hotel.)

A new breeze blew steam to the doorway of the camera shop, sewer steam was what I smelled looking out. A smell not of London.

When I had asked what she wanted this time, Jenny said Bring me back a memory. But maybe because Dagger had just been on the phone to me I didn't decide what she'd said and filed it away in my head as a request for a Memorex, which for a start was unlikely because you can buy them in London.

Outside I couldn't see through the crowd up at the accident. Two cops were backing them off, but you'd think the trick would be clearing a way for the ambulance.

Crosstown vehicles were now locked into the uptown traffic. The black car hadn't been moved. One cop was very tall and had a moustache.

In reply to my letter Claire couldn't see what there was to discuss: her Uncle Dagger's film as she saw the situation did not now exist even if it *had* been shot with a 16 that blows very well to 35, and Phil Aut doesn't exactly promote nonexistent films. Furthermore, Claire went on, Mr. Aut had only said originally that he'd look at it, you never know what you can sell to TV, it wasn't necessarily going to be a commercial proposition; he liked Claire, she said, and so he'd said he'd look at it when it was finished. What was there to discuss now?

If I'd wanted her just to hear my voice I could have sent her a cassette explaining myself.

How often had I seen her? What did I know?

She was in New York.

I was coming to New York anyway. I didn't write her that.

Did the appointment stand?

Forty-eight hours before my flight from London, there was a cable. WEDNESDAY NOON INSTEAD MY PLACE CLAIRE.

PRINTED CIRCUIT
CUT-IN
FLASH-FORWARD

England is not safe for me. Is that it? The tempered voices in Geoffrey Millan's living room above me as I pad up his stairs are past and future. I trail him into the long room that has at the street end some of his curious work and at the garden end some people. The round healthy face of the pediatrician and across the circle his sleek wife who has illustrated a children's book. A bearded grim intellect whom I don't know, with eyes either puffy or with an eastern fold at the corners. A splendid dark-haired woman not my wife who rises for some purpose. A girl named Nuala who once looked up my friend Sub in New York. A white-haired lady in a tweed suit who is a maths don and a vigorous violist and asks where my wife Lorna is tonight. A tall, long-haired boy of twenty named Jasper stretched in brown velvet trousers on his side on the rug between the chairs of Nuala and the woman who has risen, so he forms the one explicit arc of the circle.

The subject is not dropped on my entrance. It is a person— something he has done. The splendid woman is leaving. I've arrived even later than I knew. The pediatrician's wife is insisting to her husband that violence on the contrary can make one more authentic. Geoff embraces the woman who is leaving; she gives me a nod, disappears, and I acquire her chair. There comes a time, says Nuala, when one has to act. Nonsense, adds Jasper, and giggles.

I can't tell if everyone knows the person or no one.

The pediatrician is arguing that this man they're talking about would do better to consult the authorities, a man who has appointed himself a committee of one to attack and undermine an organization of potentially violent exiles by sowing confusion here and there among them. The mathematician argues that violence nullifies itself and that hewing to a line of moderation while less attractive particularly to people of certain temperaments and even more of certain ages is more delicate, difficult, and complexly responsive to the really human.

Around me are the years in London, years of evenings in which people listen and talk and do not drink too much, get a ride home after the Underground closes down or phone a cab that comes in seven minutes. The bearded man has been expatiating on American allegiances: what after all can one expect of Americans, they never reflected seriously upon their own revolution, they cared only to put it behind them. The mathematician interjects that Charles the First's last word before they chopped off his head was *Remember*.

The bearded man seems not to hear her. He says that indeed Americans confused the natural resources of their continent with their own ability to exploit those resources, even mingled those minerals and plants with the illusion of philosophical ideas, and now in the interest of holding violence down, whom does America back?

16

I am about to intervene, as I have on some other evenings with a glass in my hand on the side of ideas I do not hold defending, for instance, American internal security systems (for after all we do have something to be secret about!); challenging the standard of living here which for ten years the English middle classes have comfortably not let themselves inquire into; and gently (though later at home Lorna often says I was terrible) attacking . . . what was it? . . . the Truman Doctrine? Churchill, self-fulfilling Cold War prophecies? . . . the ease of friendly intercourse has buffered my memory—but I don't intervene now, for the bearded man is saying he's not sure what violence is and he can sympathize with the man in question. And Geoff Millan returns us to the man in question himself, an American resident here from whom now for lack of information the talk finds its exit into sex, and I have the odd sense that no one in the room in fact knows this mythical committee of one, and it turns out that Geoff doesn't know the name of the man.

I stay and stay.

When the other guests are gone, Geoff does not betray surprise when I ask if I can stay over. It's very late, a new stage of talk.

Who is Claire?

Claire is in New York.

Cartwright's contact.

For the film.

Yankee dollar.

You measure the pound by it.

You rely on the American connections.

My boats on the south coast were bought with money I made here in England. So were the French stoves, you have one yourself.

You bought into those young married boutiques, you started an antique bottle shop.

Was it money I wanted?

It was cordless electric carvers from the States at the time of the assassination. And who ever heard of exporting brass beds from here to Manhattan?

My margin was surprising.

And quilts from Maine and Appalachia, some old, some new, and antique stoves from France that aren't really antique. And then that University of Maryland education racket at your Air Force bases here.

I'm hardly involved.

And this film.

Which film?

Cartwright, international businessman.

Sounds like the title.

What did you hope for?

More than what we have.

Is it all a waste?

What can you do with several pounds of ruined film?

You're the American.

The English take photographs too.

Not so many.

Maybe they don't see so much.

They're not so busy snapping pictures.

They would know better than an American what to do with a load of ruined film.

You said some burnt. Well then, blow up the negative, silkscreen it, rephotograph the print, hang it over that flak hole in your study—

It's a crack—

Or just hang the blown-up negative.

Find me the negatives and we'll go into business. There *are* no negatives. Or just one.

But you had other prints. I don't understand.

You really don't. The point is, it hadn't been processed. So no negative. Dagger was taking most of it in on the Monday to someone he knows in Soho. When Dagger found it, it had been just yanked out of the cans, most of it.

Were you actually there?

He's my friend.

What was it all doing lying about?

When Dagger shot most of it he put off thinking about rushes. Anyhow a lot was shot in the boondocks.

Not exactly a home movie. Real art.

This was real. This was something.

Where was it lying?

On a table Dagger uses. For working, eating, talking. A big table by a window.

You said yanked out of the can. Was it burnt then?

There was a magnifying glass on the sill and a couple of inches of leader was trailing out of a cartridge.

You're not saying it was burnt by the English sun.

During a bright interval.

Is it so easy to pull film out of a cartridge?

Sixteen-millimeter comes in spools. This that was burnt by the magnifying glass was eight.

Did you plan on a mixture of eight and sixteen?

We planned to blow the whole lot to thirty-five. Eight doesn't blow to thirty-five, though we did have a cartridge of eight that Dagger'd been against using one evening when we were out of film, but I wanted to blow it to thirty-five so you'd see sprocket holes and frame lines.

This was what was incinerated.

No, the eight that was burnt by the magnifying glass was a baby movie Dagger's wife Alba took of a friend's baby.

What happened to the sixteen-millimeter film that was yanked out of the cans?

It was unspooled and exposed.

Ah. Burnt by light, as it were.

You should be endowed.

My father is entirely too old to have a thirty-five-year-old son on a permanent family fellowship. Why don't you take some money out of the Cartwright trust and endow me; sell some of that cheap land you bought in the Norfolk Broads, you'll never build there.

I'll let your father take care of you.

Let him give me what he's going to leave me, then leave me and disappear into his retreat in Sussex and if he lives long enough escape death duties or the added hazard of dying *before* he endows me, for then we might find that not having in the end to face me, he's posthumously endowed the retreat instead.

Someday Will and Jenny will sell my Millan originals for ten times what you let them go for.

No one knows what they are.

Admit they're hard to describe. Music, painting, sculpture, dolls, even in my humble view engineering.

Why describe?

It might help you finish things. Look out for yourself.

Look, *you* start things, others finish them. But how was the magnifying glass fixed? I should have thought sort of on end. That is to say, on its side. Was the sun burning through the glass when your friend came in?

This was later. When Dagger and Alba came back from shopping, there was a smell. The sun had gone in.

The smell of course was from the eight-millimeter baby film. Your vandal was indiscriminate.

He didn't get it all. But what he got is almost irreplaceable.

Why don't I know Dagger? I feel I know him.

Dagger DiGorro. Everyone else in London knows him.

American of course.

Irredeemably.

Now why should someone want to destroy your great American film?

I should have stayed in waterbeds.

Wasn't it water bumpers?

You do listen.

So do you.

Who was the American they were talking about tonight?

No name mentioned. Lana was the one who knew him—

The splendid dark-haired woman—

And she only knows through a friend of hers. But why did you say a moment ago *almost* irreplaceable? And if the baby film wasn't part of yours with Dagger DiGorro, then there must be some more eight-millimeter unaccounted for.

At least you listen. They don't always listen in New York.

2 | Looped London minutes with pink-faced Millan, I insert them in front of Claire even though they haven't happened yet. They come equipped with what I don't like about him—his automatic ironies—and what I do like—his attention. Once looped, those moments of friction will never run out of sprocket holes, the loop runs as long as you want, its hard data too hard a vita of me I cannot pause to understand for if I do I cannot, or not yet.

I forgot, said Claire, to ask about Lorna and Jenny and Billy.

He wants to be called Will.

That's wonderful.

He went on a school trip to Chartres.

That's great.

The long room held little in it—only beige and cream and pale orange and light lavender tones amid which Claire in a brown pants suit possessed the sinister vividness of the only painted thing in a drawing. Dark lip gloss thinned her mouth.

Newhaven, Dieppe, Rouen, Chartres, I said.

Imagine.

Coming back, Rouen, Dieppe, Newhaven.

Recently?

Oh no. A year ago.

But I've seen you since then.

The news has had time to age.

Claire wanted me to get on with it. She had avoided me forty minutes ago in the street, no question. It hadn't been my daughter Jenny who'd turned into that camera shop; Jenny was in London and she did not wear lipstick, though she looked a bit too much like Claire.

20

Claire was saying we'd arrived in Chartres.

On the table before me was an enamel cross, the colors irregularly partitioned by tiny strips of metal.

I thought I would press her further. I described the English guide, quite a young man, who lives in Chartres eight months a year and knows every one of the 176 windows inside out, and he told Will's group about things way high in Chartres meant only for God, and Will's friend Stephen said they weren't all that high.

Oh Christ, said Claire, I could throw it all up and go live in England.

But I want to know what Claire knows, however little that is, and I am fresh from London and in New York, and Dagger DiGorro's film is in my head.

Brighton, said Claire.

The Pavilion, I said.

All that campy orientalia, she said.

I said my mother's dentist who lives on Brooklyn's Park Slope had hosted a cocktail party at the Brighton Pavilion for an international group of dentists.

Claire drummed on the sofa arm.

I had come all the way from London. If she didn't want to talk she could have canceled. Fine by me: no film, no deal. Instead, I was here in her lunch hour in the pastel clarity of her flat which seemed oriental partly because of what hung horizontal behind her—a poster three times the size of its subject which in the grainy blow-up seemed slow-motion even more than enlargement, a slim arm—elbow to finger-tips—Claire's I sensed (though I do not know why)—and a free margin all round.

Granted, I'd have looked Claire up cable or no cable.

I told her how Will was half talking to himself one night in the kitchen and was muttering something about pulley blocks and hoisting yourself up in there to see some of that stuff meant only for God, and Lorna had reached into the fridge bent way over and Will had eyed her behind and the ceiling and without shifting his gaze had slid his arm off across *The Radio Times* to reach a chocolate digestive biscuit.

Claire did not get it. Maybe I was showing a very dull domestic scene.

Chartres made an impact on him, said Claire. She drummed on the sofa arm.

I explained that it was the engineering, I thought, more than any religious meaning, that for Will it was the hoisting and the getting up there more than the actual seeing, that for instance he would take suction boots to walk up the wall and didn't believe that that stuff way up there wasn't meant for people to see.

Claire dropped her wrist to see the tie. Where was I staying? I said Sub, and she said the man with the children, and I said an old friend.

From Brooklyn Heights?

And college.

And later life?

And he asks all the right questions and has an idea my life abroad is exciting.

Claire wanted to know what questions. I said, Not only about the film, and she said Oh, and I said, Like why you wanted to see me when I have no film to show, and why the cable.

Claire got up, and I said, He's about my only connection with college now. Claire sauntered around behind me and then in front swinging her wide, high-cuffed trousers. She stopped and took a deep breath and said softly didn't I understand she felt bad about Dagger's film. I said I wouldn't be surprised one way or the other.

She went and fell back into her sofa under the six-by-eight poster and said if I really wanted to know, she'd thought I was coming anyway on business and she'd felt kind of bad about Dagger and his film, she loved Dagger—and wasn't the film mine too?

She kept raising her voice slightly only to drop it, and there was a difference between her chic and the sound of her words.

I said that as for business, if she meant business Dagger's film was pretty much ruined and only me left to tell the story.

Claire said well no she'd thought I might bring Billy over again if I came on business.

She was filling in while she thought.

I said that once Will had asked me to bring him back a book on building a twenty-eight-bit computer, he even went out and got a big tin for a drum and some doweling for an axle and put on side supports, but it ended there. He was a great admirer of Brunel and Babbage. She didn't know Brunel? The famous engineer of French extraction Isambard Kingdom Brunel, I explained, who once in a nursery entertainment for his little nephew Ben happened to swallow a coin that stuck in his windpipe and thereupon in danger of choking designed a centrifugal pivot board on which he had himself strapped and swung round and round till the half-sovereign came up out of his mouth. The same Brunel that designed the Great Western Railway.

I said that last year I had gotten Will a digital computer kit through an American firm I occasionally represented complete with input sliders, circuit changing, and a read-out panel that lights up, but that now he was into shares and was planning a world stock exchange, which should not bore me but did.

You've always got Jenny, said Claire.

I thought I saw her go into a camera shop near here, I said.

Claire seemed to ease herself when I said that, as if it told her that she was in New York and I was not. She said, who is the fairest of the fair, is it Jenny or is it Claire? and I said the difference in looks was uncannily small and decreasing as Jenny approached twenty, and I wondered if Dagger and I were related.

You're not Jenny's uncle, said Claire.

I said Claire must be getting to know a lot about film distribution, and she said, Enough. I said didn't she ever want to *make* a film, and she said, Distribution's creative too, I should see what some of my experimental geniuses were ready to do for a buck. I said, Why *my*?

I grinned. She may have seen not the friendliness I know wasn't exactly there but rather the domestic male expatriate gently downing her by paying real attention to her, yet the guard I guess I had up worked almost accidentally, for such a guard was one thing she'd wanted to see, so for a moment now she stopped looking for something *else*. She burst out, Oh I could tell you a tale or two about your own London.

You sent that cable.

Only knowing you were coming anyway.

Claire pulled a foot up under her; she hadn't said quite what she'd wanted to.

I could have written you what I have to say.

Look, said Claire, I'm in business. Mr. Aut's got like all three phones triangulating on him in his office and in the outer office it's very complex—you don't know Monty Graf—look, last April I thought we might be able to do you a favor, that's all.

You look, I said, speeding things up but now splicing into some circle of which I was the center the stabbing I'd seen and the young woman who'd been behind me when I turned (namely Claire) —the film we shot is not lost just because people think it's destroyed.

Think? said Claire, and tapped the middle finger of her right hand on the sofa arm.

I recall it absolutely, you see.

I get your point, said Claire, and cast a look out the far window beyond her circular dining table as if fifteen floors up she might see a secretary if she had one waving an urgent message.

I said I recall it absolutely.

How do you promote a film that doesn't exist?

That's *my* line, I said.

The soft angles of my eyes were soiled with grains of the bright haze outside that either was the product of a sievelike process or was the sieve itself, and must be both the substance beyond which stood what you wanted to see and the abundant ground that was all you were going to see.

She kept looking and I said, So you see your Uncle Dagger's film isn't wholly destroyed.

Do you mean there's still you? Is that what you mean? I haven't heard a thing from him since it happened. Where were you shooting besides England and Corsica?

It began with a fire, you know that.

Claire shrugged. A helicopter sounded close enough to be outside her clean window. She said she couldn't care less how the film was destroyed, and I said I meant the bonfire, we'd wanted a bonfire and it was there in a foggy midnight field in Wales ready for us sooner than Dagger expected.

Claire got up again and went and stood looking out toward the East River and fuel storage tanks like giant drums beyond in Queens, and the sound down in the street seemed to increase. She said something about vandalism everywhere, even in London; and I thought, How sure am I the stabber was Jim? Very sure.

I went on through the foggy midnight field making it graphic for Claire, and the sun was in her long straight hair that seemed to have had a gray or heathery tone rinsed through it so it wasn't as sandy-bright as Jenny's. I was telling about the ditch, how Dagger switched off the lights fifty yards before he pulled over to the right side and how he half-tilted us into a ditch. He reached into the back, needed two hands, turned all the way round. He said he didn't know about the light. He hauled the Beaulieu out of the sponge-lined aluminum case. It had the 200-foot magazine screwed to the top. To find the mechanical button to unscrew so he could pistol-grip the light meter independently of actually running the camera, Dagger needed more light. So he pushed the door handle down but the dome light would have advertised us and I stopped him with my penlight. I said, Wait—we want eight frames a second for this light. Dagger was trying to make out the light meter's hair-line Maltese Cross. He said I'd been reading the wrong books, he was going to stick to twenty-four.

I flicked the overhead switch. He opened the door. The dome light stayed off.

Claire looked back from the window. In my light, I said, every black hair of Dagger's moustache was distinct, and the lowered eyelids when he looked from me down to that French camera in his hand showed some tiny red and blue dots from all the Beaujolais and the good times that just seemed to come to him the first years in those Hampstead pubs or later when he was married and pubs were too public for him and he wanted to know who he was drinking with.

He gets his way, said Claire, and I could tell she loved him.

Dagger was in profile against the fire in the field, and I turned off my penlight.

I was telling Claire an odd, graphic tale, yet some knowledge I hoped she had could put a secret pivot in my own story to which meanwhile she seemed indifferent.

He looked straight out the windscreen, the heavy nose, the cheek bone, the mouth a bit open on his overbite. He said he'd had enough trouble loading the Beaulieu why didn't we load it with color, here we were in the dark and a great fire and probably someone from Berkeley over there in the ring—they couldn't all be Welsh hippies—and what have we got but black and white. I said they probably weren't Welsh, they were probably from London, and I said overall we'll mix color and black and white, we'd be wasting color here, we need fast film.

Well even before we reached the hedge he was shooting, hand-held, and I said Steady. We stood in soft earth that gave but wasn't mud. The inevitable stone farmhouse must have been nearby but the inevitable dogs must have been friendly or deaf.

Where's yours? I said to Claire.

Hospital, she said, and came back from the window to the sofa.

Jenny's crazy about dogs. I guess she's quite English.

Manhattan's crawling with dogs, said Claire.

It's different, though, I said. You never see children.

I never do. *You* probably see plenty.

London's more of a family city.

You must be right.

You get the picture, I said. Fog damping the sound. The chanting soft, close. *Māyā Māyā.* Somewhere not in the circle a guitar drummed alternating chords like somebody learning. I couldn't see where it was. *Māyā Māyā Māyā* was one word. The others I didn't understand. Hell, I didn't understand *Māyā* either. Not then. But I could make it out and I said it in Dagger's ear. We're in South Wales. How we got there is plausible enough. I had business on the Dorset coast. Then we drove up past Bristol where we had a mutual actor-friend. So far, Dagger was the casual traveler. I was the one talking about the images we needed to go with what was then the third section of the film. But when we got into South Wales and night had come into the soft farm valleys above Newport and dew chilled the manure and sweet grass and we were running snug between hedgerows, Dagger was scooting around curves and shifting down and accelerating as if now he had a purpose. And now he's saying let's find a bonfire to film—which seemed right to me because I'd said in the beginning that we ought to find visions intermingling England and America so you wouldn't be able to tell. And here we were between villages hunting for a bonfire, though Dagger was also now saying he was looking for a roundabout that would get us onto the A-40 east to London.

Claire was looking at her hands wedged between her thighs.

The fog partly hid Dagger and me from these people. Claire didn't yet know I was recalling my diary. Fog stood here and there as far as the edge of the ring. But passing through the ring the fog became something else gassy and jumped and bent through the forms of those people into the inner circle where it passed into the fire but freshened and inflated the colors of their clothes, the woven oranges and denim blues, a brown cloak, some yellow, some olive green.

A baby's cheek flashed on a girl's back. Dagger tracked a little boy in overalls who as he walked stared at the blaze they were all circling. The camera's drive motor seemed loud, a softer or more musical dentist's drill, a buzz saw under water. Dagger switched off and focused on one corner of the ring and shot till they'd all gone by once. I whispered wouldn't it be funny if some were Americans. When he said, Recognize someone from Berkeley? he may not have been kidding, though he often speaks of his old bailiwick and feeding some friend who later became an official in Washington, for Dagger unlike me keeps up with the old Alma Mater. A big woman with a red and yellow blanket over her shoulders burst from her place and surged across the circle to hug and kiss the boy in overalls—and they all shouted something. And she, in a glad tantrum of head-wagging, stood aside till her spot in the circle came by.

My ankles were wet and torn. Sheep bleated. Dagger flipped the turret to get a closer shot of the fire.

What were they burning? They stopped circling and clapped. What was burning? I saw two branches sparkling and one gray label with letters that didn't mean anything.

Is that all? Claire murmured, staring at her hands.

They stopped circling and began to clap.

We didn't know about the Hindu group, said Claire.

Who didn't?

At the office.

You mean you did know other things we filmed?

Dagger I thought had written her a note in April answering the tentative encouargement he said she'd given him.

Dagger didn't mention Hindu to you, did he?

Māyā's the giveaway, said Claire. I mean, that's Hindu. Anyhow I think Dagger wrote me.

I let that pass. I told her that later an American whom Dagger and I know in London hearing me talk about the bonfire got worked up about looping zoom dissolves. He thought Dagger had *zoomed* in through the ring to the fire; but in May we had no zoom.

What was his name? said Claire.

Cosmo. And he had a friend from Delhi he wanted Dagger to meet who he said lives completely in the present. I said we weren't interested in technical tricks like looping zoom dissolves but he just kept talking at Dagger saying we ought to make a separate cartridge loop. Dag said he thought you could do that with eight but not sixteen, but Cosmo said when we got to projecting just insert the cartridge wherever we wanted and change the whole scene at will. Like, three, four loops, the audience couldn't tell if it was a repeat or the people in the ring were just being shot all over again round and round. Dagger said, No, you better check that out, that doesn't sound right.

Cosmo said to me, What else you got, man?

Once Cosmo got some high-priced audio equipment through Dagger and turned up one midnight waking Dagger and Alba and meaning to tape their entire record collection. Which is not quite the same thing as a friend dropping over in the middle of the afternoon to hunt up a magazine.

Did someone say anything to you? said Claire. Did you get close to the ring?

Here, I said, pulling out of my inside pocket a handful of diary pages.

Look, said Claire, I didn't shop for lunch, all I've got in is granola and Earl Grey tea bags from England. And honey, Greek honey. Like, how long are you in New York? I could return those pages to your friend's.

I said I didn't have time. I skipped to a passage way past what I'd read her, put all but ten pages back in my inside pocket and said I was skipping a sentimental part full of technical stuff on loading our 200-foot magazine when we used it.

She said, Eight doesn't blow, so it wouldn't have been any good to us. But that was Alba's film you said—how many 8 cartridges did you say?

But I began again.

Look, said Claire, but she sank back stiff into the pale cushions.

I said, There's some here you wouldn't care about.

We're well past the hedge, well past a young American Indian's challenge to us and Dagger's raucous I'm-from-Pathé-News-I'm-looking-for-the-United-States, wait! hold that! out of the pan into the can, I do my best work when the subject stays still, who's on guitar I got news for him there's a chord called the subdominant.

And well past the guy who when we approached got off into the dark to a small tall grove of trees; well past the Beaujolais I went back to the car for and we couldn't get this crowd to touch.

All the way a few minutes later to a tough little apple with hair to her buttocks. Dagger touched her fire-bright face with the back of his hand, he looked twice her size when he bent and gave her a one-arm hug and got shoved. The camera looked heavy then. He said, But it's you I've been looking for ever since I got onto this road. Because you are beautiful.

He raised the camera, the motor hissed, he started to pan, he said, Try to be loving, what do you get.

I said I didn't understand, why not just shoot some footage— and as for panning, it's overrated.

The Nagra unit was in the boot; no point intruding it. Too bad because against the snapping of the blaze the damping of the various voices sounded an odd turn of distances.

When Dagger swung to get the grove where the man had gone, he didn't switch off the motor. So it was an unintentional swish-

28

pan and hand-held at that, so you can imagine how it must have wobbled however strong the Dagger arm. The grove was just a shadow in the dark and thus almost as indefinite as the intervening blurs he swished through. Then the round-cheeked woman grabbed the arm supporting the pistol grip and Dagger switched off and listened to her.

She said they were finishing and we had no right to force it by entering their field.

A gaunt fellow said to me, It doesn't matter, you will come and break bread at the house and we will drink a glass of your wine. I said, Oh you drink.

But the little woman said they'd been combining a Hymn to Night with the little boy's initiation and she turned and informed me only three of them drank and the group was unusual in not excluding visitors from meals.

On the side of the fire toward the grove three men circled the boy chanting what sounded like *Rama Rama*. Several of the group were drifting away from the light.

Who's that in the grove, said Dagger, I think your guru's taking a breather.

There is no one in the grove, said the little woman, though she need not have answered, and as if continuing an instruction that had not been interrupted she explained that just as the group included different conditions of rebirth, so it included also different styles of practice, Tantric release, ascetic release.

Dagger moved away saying, What I want to know is who went into that there grove.

He was having trouble revolving his turret to find the 50 lens.

I said to the little bright-cheeked woman, Are there Americans here?

She said, Why do you ask? and pointed to the American Indian, who was saying to Dagger, I've been here four months, I mean in Britain, and I'm not looking back. I'm from Kansas City originally.

The woman pointed to the small circle chanting *Rama* and said, Also the boy—his father's American, his mother's English, they're in London.

Dagger was on the far side of the fire. The big woman in the blanket stopped him and embraced him so he had to drop his camera hand. She said, Anyone who enters as you entered is so lost he risks rebirth as a tortoise. She giggled.

The little woman called to Dagger across the fire, But I *know* you, I know you from London. The big woman said with more laughter, Elspeth *knows* you. The big woman held Dagger and his camera at arm's length: As the calf knows the mother, she said, you have not known the relation between your samsara and your karma.

Dagger very friendly said, Out of the karma, and the woman said, Into the camera.

I joined him near the grove. He was shooting. Sure enough I detected ahead a pale motion, though why he had to get (as he said) the complete picture puzzled me.

A skinny man in a hooded jacket stood with his arm around the young initiate: Come with us, brothers, he called, and Dagger called back, Just a minute, and the other fellow said, Throw away your machine, brother, you are filming as if you were pursuing your enemies.

Dagger called back, Don't know till I catch up with them.

But now, instead of the elusive character in the grove, out of it came at us in a brief, accidental charge a cow that cantered off into the fog-sifted night.

She is going to the river, said a man's voice behind us, and someone chuckled, and I said, Just some of the local fat stock (for that was no dairy cow), and Dagger said, Near the intersection of the River Usk and the Monmouth-Breconshire border.

The man in the grove—unnecessarily it seemed to me and almost as if to show us—stood clear of a tree and I saw him quite well in the light of the fire at my back. I saw him, and Dagger got a shot of him veering out of the grove and running after the cow.

The big woman captured Dagger from behind. As when a lute is played, she said with her cheek against his shoulder, one cannot grasp the eternal sounds but by grasping the lute or the player of the lute the sound is grasped.

I was talking to the fellow from Kansas City who was explaining how the Indians would not let Sir Walter Raleigh in on the secret of pot that they smoked in the peace pipe but gave him tobacco instead to take back to the white man in Europe.

The little woman at this distance not so ruddy was close to me talking across me low and rather fiercely to Dagger: This is *our* place, we rent it, we are here only a small part of the year. We prepare now for the cosmic dance of the Dancing Siva tomorrow evening and *no* one outside the group is allowed here, I don't know what you are doing to us.

And that, I said to Claire, looking up from a page of onion

skin, is the dance that celebrates the end of the world, and when I said this to the woman, Dagger said, Well I don't want to be here when it happens—he asked her name—a baby started crying—I said *Elspeth,* and he said, Do you go to the National Film Theater? Maybe you saw me there.

She only said, I do know you, and Dagger said, Dagger Di-Gorro, and this here is an untrustworthy merchant adventurer named Cartwright, a Common Market lobbyist. Now the cat chasing the sacred cow, is he dancing Siva tomorrow night?

She turned to go back to the fire. She seemed to sense we weren't sticking around. Dagger said, Oh hell.

He didn't like this after all, and I wasn't sure why.

Mind you, I said, getting up and leaving on Claire's table the onion-skin pages I'd had out, that was more than a cow-catcher, the piece of his face I did see.

Funny, said Claire.

In the bathroom Scotch-taped to the wall beside her beige toilet was a two-page glossy-spread of a stately mansion, Luton Hoo. To the viewer's right of the pillared portico and one of those English lawns so vastly level green they seem artificial (and in a sense are) and under Dr. Samuel Johnson's *This is one of the places I do not regret having come to see,* was an inset shot of the celebrated ivory casket whose deep surfaces hold twenty carved scenes from the lives of Virgin and Son.

Claire called out: Did you write down a description of him?

I reached for the silver flusher and then did not push it, and said without raising my voice, Somewhere.

And the phone rang.

On the inside of the bathroom door was a white felt heart and pinned to it a big button showing Claire in a floppy hat.

Peace, said Dagger, and we passed the fire heading for the hedge.

Why did I say to the newly initiated boy, Is it tomorrow you welcome the god?

The boy said, Every day.

Without thinking, I said, Every minute, and he said, Right.

Those few words weren't in my diary and Dagger didn't film them. The boy had a narrow face and a cowlick and sandy hair as light as Jenny's. And real overalls. I bore down with all my weight and gentleness upon the bathroom doorknob.

In her bedroom Claire was saying, I knew he *might* be—that's all.

My onion-skin pages in the living room were neater now. The enamel cross lay beside them.

Monty, I didn't *know*, said Claire from the bedroom; then not so loud, That's what I said.

The receiver rattled but she did not come out.

I had the diary pages stuffed back into my inside pocket with the others when she appeared in the bedroom doorway.

I picked up the cross.

Cloisonné, she said. The Japs imitate cloisonné but they cover up the metal.

She put her hands in her jacket pockets to cheer herself, and said, I'm afraid I have to make another call.

(If no, keep looping; if yes, proceed.)

I said, You still haven't explained why I saw Jenny behind me today and then she turned into a camera shop and gave me the slip.

Claire took heart. I strengthened her. She shrugged and said, What do you want? You're not going to believe this, but I didn't know what to say to you seeing you there. I mean we had a date for half an hour later.

I asked what Outer Film was interested in at the moment, and she said a little bit of everything. I said I couldn't think who would want our film destroyed. Claire said, Maybe a competitor who was making a film on the same subject. I said, Very funny. She said, We'll go to the theater in London next time I'm there. I said I must go see Cosmo's Indian, maybe he'd know what happened.

Oh don't do that, said Claire ironically.

I let her feel she was making me go.

She asked me for Sub's number and address. She said it was better than staying in a hotel, and I said my grandfather from Maine died in a hotel.

That fire, she said, and came away from the bedroom as I went to the front door. I put my hand on the knob.

That was the third part, I said. The first was in Hyde Park two weeks before. Too bad you never got any idea of all this.

But the fire, she said.

We'll never know if Dagger got a good shot of what they were burning, I said.

I meant when the film got burnt on his table.

Oh it only got Alba's Super-8 baby film.

32

But your film was destroyed there too, right?

Not burnt. Except by the light of day. Exposed. No, I meant the fire might have spread.

I held the front door. Poised concern in the tilt of her head, cigarette in her fingers, some melancholy immobility in the cheeks which next to my Anglo-American Jenny's seemed bloodless.

I meant the film they missed that wasn't *on* Dag's table, I said. That's what I meant.

How is he? said Claire, keeping me.

Older, well-covered, very strong, keeps open house, magical, more American than ever, a father now at last as you know. And in that film never mind how clumsy we were, we really saw something.

So did we, said Claire. I mean, we thought there was something in it.

I was over her threshold and let the door slip.

Too bad, said Claire softly. What's Jenny up to?

Dying to try America. Has a new boyfriend. Plans to take A-levels in Latin, I hope.

Now Claire let *me* wait. What'll you do with the film they missed?

Who's *they*?

My chat with Geoff Millan recircuited Fast Forward; I heard nothing new.

Claire smiled: It's your life; how would I know who *they* is? Going to make any more films?

I'm still working on this one. It's all written down.

Who reads any more? said Claire.

VACUUM INSERT | Show an American girl London the day before the young bodies of Schwerner, Goodman, and Chaney are missing in Mississippi—which makes it summer solstice years ago. She rang you at home in Highgate, got your wife Lorna who passed the phone instantly to you even though you were twenty feet away.

Now you hear the girl again when the bearded desk clerk hands you the housephone. She's running behind schedule, she says, would you like to come up.

OK, but what's with her? It's too early for a drink even if she had a bottle in her room. You don't know her. Surely she doesn't want you to listen to her brush her teeth.

The lift's ornate ironwork opens each floor as you and the

attendant rise past. It's a lovely machine, ride all day, not a cage. You catch the eye of a chamber maid passing along a hall her arms full of last night's sheets, then she's out of sight below you.

Your college friend Sub's wife's former roommate this is: you forget the first name as you take her hand crossing the threshold, it's a double room. A harpsichord steady and copacetic is coming from a little transistor on a plaid suitcase. Not a stitch of clothing adrift, not a half-slip, not a passport on the bureau's glass top or a collection of change. Her bed is turned right down and a London A to Z is on the night table by a half full tumbler with bubbles at the bottom and up the side. She takes the tumbler into the lav.

She's tall and dainty, her page-boy newly trimmed. She gives you a lifesaver. She stops the transistor, and her name comes back: Connie—Constance. She makes references to her parents and the job she's just packed up, and a play she got a ticket for at the last minute last night. She puts a hand to her cheek thinking. She puts the transistor on the bed, opens the suitcase and carefully tears out two travelers checks. When you ask how Sub and his wife are, she locks the case, comes very close to you and says, Not good.

She's better being solemnly shy in the slow elevator. She thanks the attendant, who thanks her, and doesn't volunteer additional information when I answer her question about the big orange globes on posts at crossings. Belisha Beacons. Belisha. Someone during the war.

You cross Oxford Street and in the busy seclusion of Soho Square she turns the talk from your awe-inspiring expatriation to the church on the left which you find you don't know anything about though you've sat on these benches reading *The Evening Standard* waiting for Lorna. You say it's Huguenot you believe, let's look.

Anon, leaving the far side of the Square you point out the film companies and for some reason say you want to make a film. About England sort of. When she asks if you have any experience, she seems quite alone.

To reach Blake's house you cut through quiet St. Anne's Court where, nodding at the male window-shoppers, you ask if she wants a little bedside reading, and she giggles. At the corner of Broadwick and Marshall down the block and across the street from the pub named for the pioneer anesthetist Dr. Snow, there is the sign on the small house, and you both read it. She says, Blake's wife was totally uneducated. Let's see, what would *he* have said about pornography?

You tell her a hat-designer friend of yours is just round the corner, and Carnaby Street's a few steps further down Ganton, but she asks if St. Paul's is near Aldermanbury Square, she promised to say hello to an associate of Daddy's. You say, That's getting down into the City; she says, Where are we now then? and you explain the City with a capital C.

Her father's associate is of course a broker. He is plugged into a New York Stock Exchange computer but of course when he plays with it to show what it can do the quotation on the read-out panel is yesterday's closing because it's only 6:30 A.M. in New York. He cashes a travelers check for Connie.

Children roam St. Paul's. They pass under arches and look up into Wren's Roman dome. Leave the Whispering Gallery to them. You show your guest the gold American chapel from the war, and she says she sometimes forgets if Churchill is dead yet or not and you say he wouldn't appreciate that in his present state, and she says, Of course I wouldn't say it to him, and giggles as if she's chilly. She wants to see John Donne in his winding sheet and you tell her where it is and say you'll wait.

In a small antique pub where every varnished line seems out of plumb you buy her a late lunch. You tell how Wren couldn't get his way after the Great Fire, the Parisian unity of radiating axes offended the English mind, so London remains neighborhoods. Yes, instead of a baroque wheel (you say, wondering about another pint and about Connie), or for that matter say a grid like Manhattan, you say—but then you say Oh Christ and with a smile raise your mug and she touches and says, Thanks for riding down in the elevator with me, and she means it. You say she could have walked down, and she says she has several times.

You bear two halves of best bitter back to your lanterned nook thinking that Lorna said, Don't you dare bring her home for dinner.

Connie asks if you have money of your own.

You return to the elevator. She says they just terrify her, that's all there is to it, it's her only neurosis.

She wants to see the London Stone, she isn't sure why. The *what*? you say. We're quite warm, she says, her finger on square 2B page 62 of her *A to Z*.

You say, Something to tell my English friends about, I mean who ever heard of the London Stone?

It's stuck, in fact, into the outside of the Bank of China. The Cannon Street traffic grinds by, and she reads the plaque out loud, you watch her lips pucker on a couple of *w*'s and the tip of her nose takes a delicate dip—and plaque and *A to Z* mingle in the mind—this relic moved here 1962 from Church of St. Swithun's south wall where it had been since 1798 (whip out your box and snap it onto Kodachrome), piece of original limestone once fronting Cannon Street Station, something about 1188 Henry Son of Elwyn de Loudenstone later Lord Mayor, this hunk is the stone the Romans used to measure all distances from London.

She's a real walker, but when you find a little church she seems glad to go in and sit. She says things are so bad with Sub and Rose she doesn't like to visit them; Sub gets a second wind and is charming to Connie and Rose accuses Connie of taking sides. Too bad Rose is pregnant again.

You suggest tea at Connie's hotel. Can't I buy you a drink? she says.

Pubs aren't open till five thirty.

And I've got my train to catch, she says.

You think, Well that's that.

Salisbury by dusk, she says, maybe wear myself out so I can sleep.

Can't sleep?

Not in the normal course of things, she says.

You push a bit: the *normal course* of things?

She turns in the pew and contemplates your lapel before dismissing you.

I could have given you Raymond Chandler, you say, *The Big Sleep*.

Travel books, she says, they're wonderful drugs.

You ask if *they* put her to sleep, and she says almost but not quite.

So, out of bed tomorrow morning in Salisbury; meet friends, drive to Stonehenge, get ahead of the crowds. Do you believe the Druids used it? she says. Why not? they use it now. Well, do you believe they sacrificed human people there? she asks. Maybe. Have you been? Never. The raincoat has parted over her thighs, are those patterned stockings tights? Two black copies of the Book of Common Prayer stand in the rack. You put your hand on hers and look her in the eye and say, Do you believe Merlin was buried alive under one of those megaliths at Stonehenge?

I'll have to see, she says.

At her hotel she declines your help saying she's got to get organized.

You wonder if Lorna rang up the garage, they've had the bloody car ten days. You buy an *Evening Standard* at the tube.

. . .

3 | Before I could wait for Outer Film I had to make sure they'd take action. Under the timeless tungsten of the tenth-floor hall, I felt in my pocket through English and American change for the key that Sub had given me, but then Myrna let me in. Her dark face broke the momentary glare of a living-room window which for a second took even her eyes into blackness. She must have heard my steps and looked through the peep hole. She scuffed back to Sub's room. Her stockings were laddered each in exactly the same way. She'd had her hair conked but then fluffily curled so it looked like an Afro I'd seen on a white girl in Claire's elevator.

On Sub's bedpost hung a towel or two maybe still damp after the drier. Wash quilted the big bed, a week of Sub's and his children's things. Over a bunched sheet lay what looked from where I stood in the hall like the Johann Sebastian Bach sweatshirt I'd brought Billy from the States the spring JFK beat Humphrey. When Billy outgrew it Lorna passed it back across the Atlantic.

I would phone Outer Film.

Between the fridge and the kitchen table the ironing board had been set up and on it was a blue glass of water and the iron on end, its cord taut across the adjacent counter to the plug. Water in a saucepan had come to a bubble; I turned the flame off, found a glove-potholder and poured, and the teabag label popped into the mug. I phoned the charter man to see if he wanted to have a drink, though we could have settled our business on the phone—it was the England holdovers on New York-to-Sidney charter flights: people had complained. I asked him to speak up; he said it was the connection. Myrna stepped around me to rescue her tea.

I phoned Outer Film and there was a voice talking before the ring could start. I asked for Mr. Aut, my gamble worked, and I settled for asking a woman to tell him I'd called and then as if as an afterthought added that I'd left part of a diary at Claire's flat and would Claire mind mailing it on. I said I'd just got in from London and was in a rush. I hung up.

Suspicion is a comfort. I was able to like Claire even less having made this phone call, though now again infused with that uncertain languor I'd felt as I came from the lav and visualized her lying along or across her bed on her belly or her back. But she might almost as well have been talking to some Man from the Moon as

37

talking about me to the Monty Graf who'd inspired inarticulateness in her earlier.

Myrna's tea mug was on her *News*. She was older than when I'd seen her in April, it was her smart hair—but there was her long, very bare neck sustaining the brown eyes, and her forearms lay smooth and rich. She sighed and slowly without looking up said, Mr. Cartwright you a regular globe-trotter.

Just another commuter, I said, and she sighed with a little tittering catch in her throat.

The second before I'd hung up, the secretary hadn't tried to pass me on to Claire, which might mean Claire hadn't got back there yet. I had to allow for the chance that Phil Aut might not get the message I'd left for Claire, but then again he might.

I wrote one for Myrna to give Claire if she phoned. She might any minute.

Myrna pushed her chair back and said she had her ironing. The phone rang and I handed her my message telling her who it might be and what to say.

But it was Sub. Myrna passed me the receiver. Sub had a late appointment at the dentist, would I pay Myrna eighteen ten. I said, What about the children. Sub said, There's a slight though tantalizing chance Rose will take them tonight, she knows I have to be in Washington this weekend so this week she wants them on a week night. But Myrna's there when they get home and I'll be home no more than an hour after she leaves no matter what happens. It's exciting, said Sub. He wanted to know if I'd be in for dinner. Myrna was scanning my note.

At a drug store I bought some 3-D cards, the Americana Hotel, Empire State, George Washington Bridge, World Trade Center, Grant's Tomb. One I sent to my family adding that I'd forgotten what I was to bring home for Jenny. At the soda fountain counter recalling all those lemon cokes after Scout Troop meetings Friday nights, I was so near recalling what she'd asked for that I at least knew it was peculiar and I imagined now that so had been her tone and I suspected I'd done something peculiar *with* her request, I had my finger almost on it but the thin, heavily made-up elderly woman behind the counter came toward me drying her hands and said, Yes? and I thought and said BLT on white toast, forgetting about American bread.

On my way back to the scene of the accident I stopped in a record shop and looked through the bins of cassettes all tumbled together on sale. An old gent in a camel's hair overcoat asked me the difference between a cassette and a cartridge—but a girl in a khaki cape and blue-smoked glasses spoke up and said a cassette gives half an hour on each side, an eight-track cartridge means you can flip from the middle of one track to the start of another. When he said he didn't know why his niece would do *that*, I added that cartridge and cassette were alike in that you inserted both into solid state systems, and the girl said to the old man, I get it mixed up myself sometimes. He had a drooping white moustache.

A recording ended that I'd barely noticed; rock you'd have to call it, with southern accents and a lot of falsetto—the girl touched the old gent's sleeve and told him the group was English.

Now *You Are Everything and Everything Is You* came on and like a sacred loop awaiting release repeated the title words and repeated. And I left the shop convinced the gift I'd forgotten wasn't anything to do with cassettes.

Halfway down the block I knew Lorna wanted the new Joni Mitchell record.

A trip like this can get away from you and in the middle of a giant traffic that, unlike Lorna, I'd never left though never lost because never gained, you believe that there in a Manhattan avenue, as if at the bottom of some poor type-compositor's dream surrounded by three- and four- and five-hundred-foot sticks of type, the trip's idea has been by some regulatory betrayal fed back to your point of departure. But the idea wasn't just there back in London, any more than you have to come to New York to shop to the music of cassettes. Any more than Dagger's movie began as we drove across Waterloo Bridge in the middle of the night after a marathon showing at the National Film Theatre, and Dagger said as he often had said, Let's make a film: and I said, I've got an idea.

I know what it is for a trip to drift away from you. I wasn't exactly showing myself around New York this trip. It's always a less clear place than the New York of the English papers where key statistics lurk well behind crisp narratives of snipers and rapists and the junky whose luck it was to pinch a wallet full of hot bills.

Sub had to go to Washington this weekend, a rush call to design a program for a new client. I didn't know what he was doing about the children.

On Third Avenue a library looked ready to open where a car park had been; a carton labeled Encyclopedia Americana was stacked on other cartons in the dusty vestibule. At a sidewalk taco counter next door to a bar I looked the Puerto Rican proprietor (if he was Puerto Rican and the proprietor) in the eye and decided instead to get a bite when I met the charter man.

The scene of the stabbing when I arrived was just another intersection. People brushed past me when the light changed. In the florist's I asked what had happened to the victim's car. The proprietor said the man was dead by the time the ambulance got through, they'd covered him up. The phone rang and turning toward it he said, You didn't think they're going to leave a car in the middle of the street. I said, I'm in the aerial business, I want to know why that one broke. But the proprietor had picked up and was talking. There were a few deep red sweetheart roses in the refrigerator case and I wanted to take some.

But now a woman with a handful of dark green leaves was standing next to the refrigerator, and some pom-poms behind the glass were the same rusty orange as the enamel butterfly on her breast.

I asked *who* had covered the man up.

The sweetheart roses were tight and alive.

The woman's cheekbones were abnormally wide, her chin narrowed nearly to a point. Her gray-black hair was parted in the middle and drawn down close upon her temples and over her ears. She might be thirty-eight, she wore no rings, her lips broke with a light exhalation and her laugh was not only happy it was the laugh I'd heard just after someone said Jersey plates and just as the driver was coming around his car to have it out with the man I was certain was Jim.

You laughed just before the accident, I said.

Call the precinct if you want to know about the car, she said, but they'll want to know why. You can tell *them* you're in the aerial business.

The woman couldn't help smiling again. She turned her profile to me. In profile you might have thought her face narrow.

The proprietor was saying, But Father Moran, that's *been* our price.

The woman said, It was no accident. She reached to close the door she'd come through from the dark storeroom.

Neither blood nor skid tracks marked the site of the stabbing. A garter snap was imbedded in the tar street just beyond the curb. I figured the woman in the florist's would do something.

A cab waiting at the light had a black rubber-looking bumper with buttonlike plugs all along it and a woman driving. The cab moved on, and a little girl in a blue coat kneeling on the back seat waved to me. My eyes came back to the garter snap and the tar.

The woman was next to me and I was exactly where Jim had been before he stepped into the street. She didn't talk like a gossip.

Someone brought a piece of canvas out of one of these buildings and covered him, but not his face. The man who killed him just stuck the aerial out not even in self-defense, you know what I mean? He didn't seem shocked. And when he turned and walked away I saw you and you looked like you saw something over your shoulder and you turned around and got out of here in a hurry. It didn't seem like it was just to miss the crowd. I remember you. That raincoat.

You saw the man's face.

He turned right at me, he walked past the window, and I looked him over. Good-looking man.

The florist was in his doorway by the pussy willows calling her. Her name was Gilda.

You'd know him again?

Got a picture? She put a hand on my arm. You're not police and you're not an aerial salesman. You don't feel like insurance either.

You'd know *me* again, eh Gilda?

Now I would.

I stepped off the curb and looked to see if a car was turning. But my light was now red and a crosstown car blew past. I stepped back onto the curb; the woman Gilda was reentering the florist shop. Instead of crossing I turned and walked the way Jim had gone, and Gilda smiled at me in the window.

I was walking as if that handsome woman had put into my head that I could catch up to Jim even here two and a half hours past the stabbing. For—as if it were somewhere in my body—I felt a tissue of collaboration between Claire and Jim. The trenchcoat snug across my shoulders, I would go to meet the charter man on foot rather than hop a bus stopping every other block or relax in the back seat of a cab held in midafternoon traffic. A flag out over the sidewalk signaled a post office and I dropped off my postcards. Our more observant neighbors in London would have been interested to see Lorna clipping rose bushes today as she'd told me she would, for our garden was notorious not only for its roaming tortoise but also for its untended growth. The London County Council man who called on us unexpectedly during the summer after I'd failed to answer letters wished us good morning and asked to see the garden behind the house, and when he'd done so he said they'd have the grass cut at our expense if I didn't have it done. At the front door as he was going and the hall clock rattled as if about to disintegrate, and began to chime, he mentioned the tortoise. Its lawn-droppings had been reported by neighbors who cited our erratic fencing, but must have seen the tortoise as something from the States when in fact a couple of years ago Lorna had simply come upon it solid and headless, a brown and patterned stone, in a permanently spongy portion at the far end. The L.C.C. man as he left hesitated in our front doorway in late-morning light, I halfway between him and Lorna, Lorna at the other end of the marble-floored front hall on the first step of the curving stairway whose pale oak we'd scraped layers of white paint off and refinished up to the landing where there was a leaded red-and-yellow-stained floral window that kept one from seeing the disgraceful garden in back. He wondered if the tortoise could be contained. Then he said, You've been over here now for . . . ? And in response to his breathing I said, Let's call a turtle turd a turtle turd, and behind me Lorna laughed. He reemphasized that the lawn was the first priority; it was eleven, the final stroke had been flung out, and as the door scraped gently to, I turned toward Lorna and my eye passed a large photo of Jenny and Billy running downhill in Waterlow Park ten years ago but I wasn't thinking exactly that at this moment they were in school. I felt in the old way American, American with Lorna—who now asked me if I would like to come upstairs.

The sun was on the bed, the bed was unmade but quite neat.

Claire had wanted me at her flat probably because I'd be trouble at the office. But who there knew me? And Phil Aut wouldn't have had to see me.

I detoured seeking a record shop to get the Joni Mitchell for Lorna.

What if Claire had been told to do nothing more with this film matter but had felt she had to see me? Hence, the Friday cable. Lorna had ripped it open—Aha, Claire likes older men.

After I'd read it Lorna sat on the piano stool and read it again, languidly young in her white nightgown. She said nothing about the film.

Midafternoon Manhattan pressured my eyes so stepping off the curb at Park and Fiftieth looking into the blue fish-eye sky bordered by hard-edged tops of buildings and farther north a penthouse tree, I was sensitive to the words of a blind man whom I'd just stepped around: Could you help me? But a girl was already there with her hand on his arm asking if he wanted to cross. He said would she let him feel her. She nodded, and looked at me. Then he asked again, and she said Sure.

He held her shoulder, touched her cheek and hair and ear. He said Yes, and she said OK? and I followed them west across Park to the traffic island where because of their slow pace they ran out of green light and she stopped. He held on.

It would be different in the dark, for there the girl wouldn't see either. To be blind making love in the light with someone not blind.

Quite different from being a lookout prevented from communicating what you see.

The girl put her free hand over his face and as she drew the fingertips down, she spread her thumb and little finger to miss his eyes. He gave her index a peck as it came by.

She looked at me, at the light, at me, and took the man across the rest of the way. She disengaged herself and said Bye, looked unsmiling at me, and swung off down the block toward Madison.

A frail, white-haired woman spoke to the man and passed on.

A girl was at the curb and they talked and then he touched her. They went east right back across Park but made it all the way in one light because she hurried him as if they had a mutual appointment. She didn't touch his face, but she did look at me. With compassion. For him.

Being three blocks from the New York branch of the scientific hobby firm for which I periodically acted as U.K. sales scout reminded me I'd put off till later in the week my visit to them. I had to look over for the English Yuletide an enlarged 1500-watt three-channel color organ that turns sound into light and can operate two hundred Christmas tree lamps and three 50-watt spots simultaneously.

I looked close into the blind man's eyes and whether he smelled Claire's soybeans in my teeth or had activated that spatial sense blind heads are known to possess; he said, So what are you looking at, pal? and was not about to feel my nose.

I said I'd just made the round trip across Park Avenue and wondered how far *he* usually got.

In an undertone so his eyes seemed to be putting up a front

for an audience he didn't want to hear this, he said, You know what you can do with your round trip.

God knows what flashback he saw when I looked into his pale squint. He was blind all right.

But what was I doing—I wasn't here seeing sights—this round trip of mine was not routine and I seemed to be having a time getting uptown to my charter man whom I'd never met face to face. On the other hand, I wasn't sure the drink with him was quite the casual drink he'd let it seem, even though he would continue to need someone at the London end. His predecessor, a portly youth, had graduated from City College and split to Hamilton, Ontario, and a part-time job at a travel agency run by a Genoese immigrant capitalizing on the considerable Italian community.

I told the blind man I'd stop by again if I was in the area if he didn't mind and he said he did—and on the point of remembering what Jenny had asked me to bring back this trip, I set out again. But there were cloudy screens at many distances and all around in more directions than Gotham's old grid seems to permit, and I myself a projection out of focus unless aimed at the right screen.

An oriental with a good camera snapped a dozen pictures from curb to curb crossing Park at Fifty-second and kept snapping even after a car honked him into a jump shot that I stepped back out of.

If I didn't get to the charter man, I was still less than twenty-four hours past that twilight holding-pattern at Kennedy and if this throbbing horizontal gravity kept me from getting uptown to see the charter man today, I still had two or three weeks.

I could not know naturally that today was not the day I was going to be shoved down a dead escalator, as if some private-spirited mechanic at wit's end were trying to prime those stopped steps with living feet. I couldn't know for sure that Jim and Claire weren't linked—hell, the people you know tend to do the same things as you—in New York you see a French bloke you haven't seen in three years suddenly in the lobby at a festival of horror films contemplating popcorn through the glass counter, his hand detached below a leather sleeve; or in London at the end of a bad day you catch an Arts Council Show and in the first of its series of American interiors you sit down in a Vegas madam's 1943 parlor that's traveled from California to Germany and now here to London on the way back home and you listen to the authentic jukebox and you cross eyes with a blue-uniformed guard who looks away as you wonder if he ever heard

"Don't Fence Me In" during the Blitz, but now at eyelevel from Roxy's seedy armchair where you're sitting two new knees materialize and they turn out to be knees that followed yours at the Cinderella Ball in Brooklyn Heights a year later in '44, for you move up past them to a Lincoln green wool hem and thence in a rush to Renée's russet shag that is not russet now but hot San Francisco copper: Renée—for Christ sake *Renée*—opens her bright mouth, moans, and reaches at you and as you incredulously get up almost falls into your lap there in the easy chair of your traveling brothel but a moving lap is hard to find and as Renée says quite loud, Missed it in L.A., had to see it here, the russet hair you mouthed on Brooklyn Heights flies back in your face here half a mile from Buckingham Palace at this summer show (where in Days of old, Knights were bold) and the same low-pitched voice you once kissed gives you a twenty-five-year résumé and when the Crosby changes in the bright dome of this jukebox that transcends nickles and dimes, the mouth takes a breath, its breasts rise, and it asks where you're staying—and you don't know where to start, here in Merry England, where Knights were bold and ladies not particular. You shrug (as if amused): I'm making a film—and she says, Oh you're on location, and you say, No I mean I live here. She says, We're going to Stratford tomorrow, and you say be sure and go over to Warwick Castle to see the peacocks.

What's your film called? she says, and when you ask for ideas she says, Murder in Murmansk.

Where does time pass on a day in New York? Is that what my eyes were bucking? all that time-waste recycled as dirty air thus dense enough to be like the looking glass in some tale I read Jenny who was then Ginny in which if you wish you can see what's happening somewhere else? I walked east and south and east again, I was between the first opening which had been mine and the next which had to be Outer Film's.

I had cut back to Goody's record store. I was shot at the entrance by a toy pistol that fired actual wooden cartridges. Downstairs I found the section and looked for the *M*'s. One of the big bands was into a fox trot of "I Remember You" but got rejected, and in the lesser noise of voices speaking, a German accent with the authority of a root canal specialist was lecturing a customer: *Keep* then your monaural but you ruin your stereo records if you don't buy a stereo pickup. The customer was saying something, but now a crash of strung steel covered the ceiling and at once lowered itself upon us like a lid drummed by our own ears at a 4-8 shake tempo so established that the group seemed to have been playing sound-proofed till some Goody employee hunting a disc opened their door. This siege of feeling may have been the Stones, I didn't ask, but Jenny gets *Rolling Stone*, and between the instants at which I spotted the dark blue edge of Lorna's album *Blue* and put my fingers on it and drew out the blue-gloamed face, I knew again that all my daughter had asked me to bring her back was a goddamned memory, she'd come upon the words Monday night while Lorna was upstairs packing for me. A farewell dispute—and Jenny knew her words *bring me back a memory* orphaned her in my eyes and lessened me. We had more than an argument. It was the first time Jenny—christened Virginia, called by us Ginny, changed by her to Jenny—hadn't asked me to bring her something from the States and I gave myself so little leeway I pressed her hoping to calm her, but she held on to a signal she'd found in her just-uttered words, yet now not with a very young woman's clear, spiky sex but a late adolescent girl's subtler uncertainty as to how much she might have to hurt herself: as if the five words she'd come upon in cruel delight—*bring me back a memory*—had become a venture she must see through. Then with a friendliness I didn't like she said, You and that film.

You can't help, I said.

If I could only get away to my plane and to New York Jenny would be safer in London free of this nonsense about postponing A-levels and taking a job in San Francisco, where she'd never been, or New York, which she stuck in only so I'd think of her seeing her grandparents.

I paid Goody's by check using an old Shell credit card and a New York driver's license in whose fold a snap of Will had got stuck. The woman took card, license, and picture, turned my check over onto the cash register's little counter, poised her pen and asked me my address as if she'd forgotten it, and I automatically gave Sub's, the one on the license. Will had on a bikini and below his snorkel mask his mouth was grinning.

Back on Third I bought a pack of absorbent rings which give off sandalwood scent when the light bulbs they fit onto are lighted. How near the Outer Film office was I; I got out my wallet, my Manhattan address-locater, and as I finished dividing the first three figures by 2 and subtracting 12 for Avenue of the Americas I was accosted by a heavy-set black man in a lumpy overcoat and no socks who asked me for a dollar, and when I automatically said, Sorry I don't have any change, he looked at my address-locater torn from some host's Yellow Pages long ago, his hair was cropped close to his skull, he shrugged and I felt I had earned him his dollar and in the breeze carefully took it out of my wallet and handed it over. He didn't thank me and as I looked at his splayed nose I got a spread of adrenalin in my face: I hadn't paid Myrna the eighteen ten.

He said, Don't go too far downtown, man, the wind is blowing the high buildings and they got these flakes of asbestos coming down like first snow.

I asked if he knew that at Mt. Sinai they'd found asbestos in someone's uterus. His eyes followed my address-locater back into my wallet and he said, I believe you, man, that's the important thing. Hard-hat fell thirty floors, you hear? I just got into town, I said, I've been away. I believe you, man, so you didn't read it in the papers— fell thirty floors through a steel grate, some other cats are standing there but this hard-hat he just went right through, nothing left on the platform, only his helmet, right?

Right, I said, and he nodded and turned away.

The hem of his coat was coming down. He said over his shoulder, Got my back to the wall.

At the corner of one of those phone booths that expose you as if to single you out, I tried Myrna. I listened but heard only the traffic and wondered if these booths ever got hit. Two taps came on the glass, I listened some more and the tapping got heavy and there was a face close to me and I left the booth and left my quarter in the broken box unreturned.

If Tris and Ruby still liked bedtime stories I could tell them one tonight. How Sub and I when we were kids in Brooklyn Heights once burrowed a tunnel through a thirty-foot-long snowdrift and took our lunch in there and a friend of ours tried to wall us in; or how Sub got concussed in a doubles match against Brown, or how the Great Train Robbery got pulled off, or how Dagger got his name.

Instructions repeat: If something from Outer Film, go on through new open circuit.

If nothing, get looped.

I could tell them Beauty and the Computer.

Ruby wouldn't like it.

If Myrna had gone and Ruby and Tris were spending the night with their mother Rose, and Sub was at the dentist, I could be freer with the phone.

When I got home Myrna was in the hall with her coat on.

I entered to the tune of a commercial in the living room and Sub's angry voice. Myrna called, I'm going now.

I said, I have your eighteen ten.

The TV stopped and Sub's voice was saying, If this room isn't picked up there will be no TV *period*. I'll take this discount portable which has proved its portability between here and the premises of our gifted repairman who specializes exclusively in new discount sets and I will drop it out of this living-room window.

Sub came into the hall, he had on a white T-shirt and bore a pile of folded laundry just high enough to touch his shaggy beard. Myrna said to me, Got my money right here in my bag.

I paid her, said Sub.

What if it hit somebody, said Tris offstage.

They'd put Daddy in jail, said Ruby.

Tris said, In the Tombs.

I wouldn't let them, said Ruby.

Myrna left and Sub was facing me and in the light from behind him his dark glasses seemed darker. He needed to speak, and to an intelligent white adult roughly of his background; but I wanted to ask about phone calls and I saw myself waiting for a phone call and saw the two of us over the midnight hill and deep into late late time watching on TV *King Kong* we saw together during the Korean War about the time I entered the Coast Guard.

Facing me Sub was nonetheless addressing Tris and Ruby who were still out of sight in the living room so his voice was loud: Myrna gets two-fifty an hour plus carfare for, among other things, cleaning up this apartment, and you come home from a private school that's costing me five hundred dollars a month and not only spread your printing press and uncapped magic markers over the indestructible rug your gifted mother bought when we moved in but also the caran d'ache Swiss modeling dreck with guaranteed highly perishable gouache colors she was good enough to buy you today.

We didn't want to mess up *our* rooms, said Tris.

You were at the dentist, said Ruby.

Myrna had gone. When the panhandler had accosted me outside the record store I hadn't quite reached the result of my division and subtraction but I thought it was forty-nine.

Sub hadn't budged and now he was addressing me too.

My hands came out of my trenchcoat.

I phoned the dentist for two solid hours, he said. I couldn't get in between the busy signals.

You were calling him? I said.

Rose phoned Myrna she *was* taking the children, so I wanted to come home and give them some money and see that Ruby had her

48

asthma medicine, so I've got to put off the dentist, right? But I couldn't get him, and rather than pay for a missed appointment I find a gifted cabdriver who immediately gets stuck in traffic, and I reach the dentist's just as his girl's getting a busy signal at *my* office or so she says, she's been phoning patients half the afternoon, Doctor Wall went home at lunchtime with a colitis attack. When I get home I find Myrna tried to reach me at the office to say Rose *won't* be taking Tris and Ruby after all—if you want to know why I'm suffering from brain damage—Rose came over earlier in the day with the caran d'ache for them and would have left it with the doorman because she is a mysterious fairy goodmother but we haven't had a doorman this week because he had some trouble getting into his own apartment house uptown the other night, but Rose was in luck, only Myrna was here because the children's bus was delayed at the garage getting new shocks according to Tris. And meanwhile you, I suppose, have signed a contract for another film.

Sub disappeared into Ruby's room so I was alone in the front hall. Sub behind me to my left, the children around a threshold to my right, rustling, straightening, fitting.

Any messages? I said.

Sub's voice was as if he'd put his head in a closet. All *I've* achieved today is provide a setting for you to receive phone calls.

They were on a pad in the kitchen next to a package of chopped meat the color of crushed strawberries.

The charter man had only been able to wait half an hour.

The other call had been a woman who said if I wanted the diary I'd called about, phone this number. Myrna had written it down. It wasn't Claire's flat or her office.

Who then is Monty Graf? Sub leaned into the kitchen, hands on the doorway.

I held up the pad.

It's not there, said Sub, Myrna was in the john when he called, Ruby turned up the TV, my head was full of broken glass. But I know he said he'd meet you tomorrow night about the film and it would be in your interest to deal directly with him and you'd know what he meant. I think that's right. It's been a day.

Where did he say to meet?

Someone will call. Is this *another* film?

If anything happens, I said (and took a deep breath thinking in London *call* can mean *come* but here it means *phone*), remember the name Monty Graf.

Sub listened.

Two weeks ago tonight—which is just a week after the film was ruined—this American Cosmo who lives in Ladbroke Grove with a lot of other people tells Dagger that an Indian he'd mentioned Dagger to is still looking to borrow a movie camera. Cosmo'd phoned a week before, and Alba, who is Dagger's wife, said Dagger and I were through filming. Cosmo told his Indian and the Indian said *he'd* phone Dagger the next day about the possibility of using his camer—

Hold it, said Sub, this is *three* weeks ago now.

Right. But the next day—which turned out to be the day the film was ruined—the Indian according to Cosmo forgets to phone Dagger, Cosmo says the Indian has no memory because he lives only in the present though he has a big white file cabinet and a big white flat in Swiss Cottage and works in a gallery in Knightsbridge so he can't be *so* dumb—

Hold it, said Sub, who's Cosmo?

An American who's always over at Dagger's eating little round slices of special Austrian wurst that Dagger buys at the Air Force PX. Well now a week after the film was ruined the Indian asks Cosmo to inquire about the camera. Dagger says sorry he gave the Beaulieu back, it was a liability after last week. So you can see I wondered if the Indian wanted just information, and I wondered if the Indian had phoned Dagger's the morning the film was destroyed while Dagger and Alba were at the PX shopping.

I hope my brain damage isn't catching, said Sub, and something was happening in the living room.

I looked at the pad. The woman would not be Claire. But was she phoning for Claire, or did Claire at least know about the call, or had Claire herself not received my bait?

I'm trying to entertain you, I said to Sub, but heard in the dark side of my head looping at too few revs per moment in my first words, *if anything happens*. So listen, I got the name of the Knightsbridge gallery and went. I didn't see any Indian. I liked a picture signed Jan Graf. Wondering where the Indian was, I asked the girl at the desk who Jan Graf might be.

Monty Graf's grandma, said Sub.

Who but the wife of the gallery owner. And the owner is Mr. Aut, an American. Not *Phil* Aut, said I. Yes indeed, said the girl. But the visit isn't over. For on the way out I bump into an Indian or Pakistani—probably *the* Indian; and I am sure I've seen him before only he looks bigger now in the gallery.

Ruby screamed and started to cry, and Sub jumped.

I have written too much. I have moved too slowly. If only I could have reduced my talk with Sub to a single picture framing say diary pages of mine lying in an open suitcase on a couch recomposed by Myrna and a cluttered corner of Sub's desk with his personalized checkbook open beside the portable radio he gave Rose for her birthday once which this very morning I had been able to reach without getting out of my day bed.

Tris was saying in the living room, Now you're a member of the secret group, and Ruby said, Look what he put on my hand.

Sub said, I told you to put away the printing set.

He sounded calmer.

I asked if he got our college alumni review. He said he threw it away instantly.

I heard again the urgency of Dagger's words phoning in the middle of Jenny being difficult Monday night: Let Claire alone, she's got her job. Our film made trouble for her. She doesn't know all that's going on.

I could have told Dagger about Claire's cable. But I didn't.

YELLOW FILTER INSERT

Between Ruby and Tris on Ruby's bed, I am also between them and their father, who is in the living room on the day bed couch having a stiff whiskey.

Ruby in a canary nightgown and broad-brimmed white straw hat with cornflowers round the crown wants me to tell about when Sub and I were children. Tris, who goes to bed later and would not normally be in Ruby's room at this hour, wants to hear how Dagger got his name. Really Tris wants some extensive conversation he can't quite envision. He has heard that Dagger is the one I made the film with, that Dagger was a police reporter in California, a beachcomber in the Bahamas, and in the Med a dealer in certain articles including semipriceless eighteenth-century French maps of the Thames estuary. Tris leans back against the bedside wall, his hiking boots of unfinished hide crossed just beyond Ruby's blanket; on his lap is a king-size paperback open at diagrams of home-made booby traps.

Ruby says, I want how you and Daddy hid in the snowdrift.

No, says Tris. How Dagger got his name.

No. Daddy.

My mom has the best camera you can buy and she has a

darkroom and develops her own pictures. Do you know a lot about photography?

Dagger DiGorro knows all about it. I just take pictures. I don't develop them.

Does Dagger develop his?

Tell about Daddy when you were little.

Dagger develops his own, yes.

Do movies get developed too? You have a yellow lens for your camera. I saw it. Is that like wearing sunglasses?

It's a filter, not a lens. OK, one story for Ruby, one for Tris.

Did someone else develop your movie? But I thought you lost it.

We had a bit developed. Almost all the rest was ruined before we could process it.

Why do you live in England?

I just do.

Tell about the snowdrift, complains Ruby.

Tris while talking stares at cartoon-scrawl diagrams of booby traps.

Ruby's got to go to bed, he says. It's eight-thirty.

I do not.

Sweet dreams, Ruby.

She reaches across my lap for Tris's hand and punches his book.

Well, Ruby, it used to snow a lot in New York in those days and we lived in Brooklyn Heights which is still the nicest part of Brooklyn, quiet streets of houses, children playing outside but not so many now. The snowdrifts along the sides of the street got even higher when the snowplow came through trying to clear the street. The snowdrifts were long and high and thick, and we tunneled out the insides of the drifts and sat in there snug as a squirrel in a tree trunk and listened to cars come slushing down our dead-end street.

What's a dead-end street? said Tris.

You know what a dead-end street is. In England it's called a cul-de-sac. It doesn't go through to another street, you have to turn around at the end and come back.

Oh.

A car, maybe a truck, would come by and park further on, or turn around and come back, or it might stop right by us, but parking was hard because of the snowdrifts.

Ruby rubs closer to me, hand on my leg, scraps of bright red nail polish, a clean leg soft through the pale yellow nightie. I like children and this isn't the first time in England or America I've intro-

52

duced this snowdrift intact into a child's room. Jenny and Will have heard this one more than once. There's really nothing to it. Think of what I leave out—the lunch Sub and I took into the tunnel was toasted cheese-bacon-and-tomato sandwiches, we had dark blue corduroys on for we'd refused to wear snowsuit pants this year, and Boyd, who played with us, still wore snowpants, maroon they were, but that was why we left him out that January day so cold it seemed to still the traffic in other blocks and the warning honks in the harbor where there floated in close to our Brooklyn docks great floors of ice which we said we'd use as rafts or aim like icebergs at the Queen Mary or the Normandy when one of those famous lengths appeared between the Statue of Liberty and the tip of Manhattan and as if by scale more than size cut off the gray waterfront of Jersey City. I haven't stopped talking, I'm telling about Boyd coming up to us wiping his nose on his mitten and sleeve and saying, Hey are you guys my friends?

We looked at him over our sandwiches and looked at each other and at our sandwiches, and I said, Gee I don't know, Boyd, and Sub shrugged and said, Let's have our lunch in the tunnel, and when Boyd asked if he could come—which was just as foolish to ask as about being friends, because we *were* sort of friends and Boyd had helped dig the tunnel—we said Sorry, Boyd, we got to discuss a plan, we'll see you later.

We climbed over the drift to get to the entrance which was on the street side so we could be private from people walking by on the sidewalk. We crawled in on two knees and one hand, holding our sandwiches and finished them in no time with Boyd squatting at the tunnel mouth watching. Then we decided to close the entrance and we dug into a mound we'd left inside the entrance when we were lengthening the tunnel.

Tris and Ruby don't want to hear how stony-hard the crust of that pile was so that at first we couldn't get hold of enough snow to block the entrance but then, with both pulling, the whole piece came away like a boulder and we jammed it perfectly into the hole and our den was a bluish dark yet shadowy white too, shutting out Boyd's dripping red nose and damp yellow mittens.

I wish *I* had a snowhouse.

It was cold in there. Boyd kept saying, Hey come on, you guys, you discussed your plan, lemme come in there now, can I? And we said Not yet, Boyd, and tried not to giggle because if he'd heard that, he'd have tried to bash his way in, and he was bigger.

How old were you? said Tris.

Eight. Just a year older than you, Ruby. I guess the drift was small inside but it seemed big. Well, Boyd wasn't there after a while, and I was cold and thinking my mother could make us some of her special hot chocolate with marshmallow, but we were discussing whether we'd join the Boy Scouts when we were eleven going on twelve.

A truck rolled down the block, it seemed slow but then it was on top of us, the motor still running though the truck had stopped. Then it seemed to move and stop again and move and stop. Then some man was yelling, Come on back you got plenty room, come right in here, and before we knew it a great blind crunch shook us where we sat, and then some yelling and talking I couldn't understand, and another crunch and this time the street-side wall moved right in on us and Sub said, Get the roof, and rammed his hands up but didn't have enough room and the snow was hard and the wall on the sidewalk side was too hard and thick and we got scared because we couldn't see what was happening to us.

The motor idled down and a man yelled, Come out of there, and we hauled on our boulder, got it away from the entrance, and crawled out into bright daylight right face to face with the tail-lights of a green delivery truck. Well, big Boyd was on the sidewalk crying. The man said, Lucky your friend told us you were in there.

Boyd was really crying, you know.

That's a crazy story, says Tris, who turns the page to a new set of bomb diagrams. He turns to me sharply—I bet there would have been a lot of blood in the snow.

Is it over? asks Ruby.

No. The funny part is that Boyd got up on our snowdrift and cursed the truckdriver and the man in the cab with him saying they had no right to drive like that, and you wrecked our tunnel, what'd you have to go bust up all our work—and Boyd called them names, then the helper got out of the truck and came over and reached for Boyd to grab him and shake him or hit him but just then when Boyd staggered, his weight got too much for the roof and he dropped through the drift up to almost his waist, and the man laughed and Sub and I on the sidewalk laughed too.

Was Boyd your friend? says Ruby.

Hey look at this, says Tris. A bomb you make out of a book—look, you hollow it out, stick in a dry-cell battery, stick in your TNT—but how do you hook up this wedge that keeps the contact points apart?

Simple, I say, the wedge is attached to your bookcase, someone pulls the book out, the wedge stays on the shelf, the contact points in the book close completing the battery circuit activating the primer detonating the charge.

Look at the bomb made out of a loose floorboard, says Tris.

His father calls from the living room, You got one thing wrong: Boyd came up to us and said are you my friend to *you* not to both of us.

Maybe so, I call back to Sub, but I know we all went up to my apartment and my mother made us hot chocolate with marshmallow.

Ruby says, You didn't live in England then.

Of course not.

What's your job? says Tris. When did you leave America?

A year or so after Charlie Chaplin.

Who's he?

A funny man in the movies.

Why did he leave?

Some people told him not to come back.

Did you ever get divorced?

I want to go to bed, says Ruby.

What does a yellow filter do?

Darkens the blue of the sky so you get a sharp contrast to clouds.

Between blue and white.

No, it's black and white. With color film a yellow filter keeps strong blue rays in the light from getting to the red and green layers. Cuts down blue.

Cuts down blue but darkens blue. I don't get it.

I'm going to bed, says Ruby. Sub's paper crackles in the living room.

I think of isolated elevators. A map stolen. Challenges from children. Lust in a capsule. A clear explanation pigeon-holed and lost.

Can you make gelatin dynamite? Tris has lowered his voice.

Will you color with me tomorrow? says Ruby.

4 It was the second morning, soon the second afternoon. It would be the third evening. At Sub's desk I went through his bills and some personal letters. I read a few pages of my diary. The New York sky was deep and bright. I watched a bearded man washing tenth-floor windows across the street, stretching for the top of the top pane, squatting to get the bottom pane so his harness made his shirt ride up leaving his lower back bare.

Noon images in those panes stirred with the wind.

If it hadn't been that the window-washer's building kept going up far beyond his floor, I might not have felt so keenly his height above the street. Even so, I could fire a baseball at him across the sixty or so feet between us and he could burn it back. He turned so as to miss the ledge, and spat.

He unhooked his terminal from the right-side anchor and swooping it under the left-side strap of his harness which remained hooked he stretched around the stone post to hook his free terminal on to the right-side anchor of the next office window on his left; then he released the left-hand terminal from its anchor in the window he'd finished, swung his left foot around the post to the ledge of the new window and reining his life belt close up to the new anchor he brought the rest of his body around so he was now standing on the next ledge. He gave upper and lower halves a swift wet swipe with his large brush, then got his rubber blade out of its belt loop and ran the water off back and forth, then a radial turn to finish.

A girl in the office was smiling quite close to him probably at him and I felt her hair was a special color but the brilliant window reflections of brick and sky through which I saw her secreted her colors from her. The window-washer turned and threw me a grin as if he'd known I was watching through Sub's gray-specked glass.

Baseball isn't cricket. Will fancies himself a spin-bowler at school and he's amused that when we put up the wicket in the garden and I bat he can't bowl me out. I don't get many solid hits off him, yet he reminds me it's the runs that count, but I know what I mean, I mean a clean pull-hit to left field even if it's only a single, with none of your stylish slices off a wittily angled cricket bat which there'd be no point in anyway because there's only the two of us. Jenny came out before supper—neighbors clicking tools and tidying nearby gardens—and she'd play (as she said) Silly Mid-on right on top of me when I was batting. Sunday she went with me to Hyde Park to the American softball game where I play shortstop to Dagger's first. Sometimes Dagger rather than get on the train to London after an evening stint teaching at one of the less accessible U.S. bases like Alconbury will stay the night in officers' quarters and play hardball the next day; he has a cap from the old San Francisco Seals. But what I am saying is that I waited for a phone call, and I looked through Sub's glass at a window-washer about as far away as

56

pitcher's mound from home, and while fingering some pages of my diary I got into a baseball game played from perilous individual towers ten stories high and each hit ball that dropped to the ground was merely a foul.

Yet the phone did ring in that apartment and I went toward it and turned off Sub's FM which had modulated from a gallant lunchtime suite for clavecin into news as if the set's selectivity or frequency control failed to hold station. The Bach sweatshirt lay on the threshold of the bathroom. What with shrinkage Alba's baby could wear it in four or five years.

If the charter man was calling, it wouldn't be to break news about some alteration in our arrangement, for he'd sooner do that by mail. I put my hand on the smudged white wall phone in the kitchen within reaching distance of the supper and breakfast dishes I'd said I'd do—but maybe instead of Monty Graf it was Dagger from London in my imagination announcing that the fugitive footage we'd had a rush of weeks ago and that had escaped destruction had now vanished from behind the Acoustic Research turntable and he figured it would be dumped in some north London dust bin in the next few hours all seven minutes plus of it and so we were dead.

Not quite, said my imagination. I took the receiver and recognized Rose.

If I phoned Dagger in London to warn him, why was there more danger now than two weeks ago when his flat had first been visited? That fugitive footage was in my notes too and some of the pages were right here at Sub's in my suitcase. Why, in this imaginary transatlantic call, had I not asked him where he'd stashed the 8-millimeter cartridge of ours that he'd been against shooting. Was I afraid that if I asked, the cartridge would be gone.

Rose accepted my presence. Myrna there today? Rose was calling to say the kids could come tonight, Thursday, and did I know when they'd be home from school because yesterday they were late. Rose has the fine, rather long English face that can make the switch from literate sparkle to sharp sexual sobriety, not that she isn't in her view a sex object either way. Her call seemed one of many she was making, and so her message to Sub sounded recorded though also unrehearsed, you could practically hear the beeps. I said why didn't she call him at work and she said she had a hard time getting through to him, she couldn't just hold. And oh yes she wanted to say hello to me anyway, and she thought Myrna was there today. She asked if I'd shown any unsuspecting American girls around London lately. I said, Women, not girls. She said Sub had told her all about my film and ah well maybe something like that would happen to Sub. I said did she mean have his film destroyed, and she laughed and said abruptly So long, and hung up.

I phoned Sub. The children were going to a school friend's until Sunday night.

Maybe phone Dagger at that. From me Claire now knew there was more film. How many people in London and New York were thinking about our film? Anyone but me? Could Claire have deceived someone she was so fond of?

I could just see the Empire State very close from an angle of Sub's bedroom window. But what if they did find out about the print and break into Dagger's again and take it?

But I'd forgotten the negative! There was that.

Dagger hadn't said where it was. His friend in the Soho lab was unknown to me. But someone could get to the negative there too.

My card to Cosmo, in quivering 3-D, had the Empire State in color like tin syrup.

There was something going on near the top, two figures at the base of a boom, then one straddling it, inching backward, the hundreds of tiny red window frames caressed my eyeballs.

Sub's bed looked like a stage set of rough terrain. I should leave the apartment as if the call from Monty Graf would take care of itself, whip down to the Stock Exchange to pick up the things for Will though it had already occurred to me he could have written. Stop off for a strong Szechwan lunch on the way back, be here again by two.

The ring now came, but when I went to the kitchen the stupid oversight I suddenly saw in my house-bound meditations nearly distracted me from the mild voice speaking.

So as soon as Messrs. Graf and Cartwright had taken tonal soundings and he'd said he was in the film business from time to time, and said he'd like to know more about the footage we still had, I told him that some of what had been destroyed had been on negative film but this rush we still had that had been developed was reversal film.

For this, you see, was what I'd remembered on the way to the phone.

I didn't add that, rather than workprint the original, Dagger had saved the money for the time being and so the reversal print he

58

had was our only print. The earlier bonfire scene had been on negative film, and the day after we got back to London Dagger and I had a little dispute about it. I said let's try projecting the negative itself, and he said the faces would come out masked, and I said so what, the snowy look would be haunting, and he said well anyway he wasn't going to get it processed yet. But Cosmo arrived and I said We'll talk about it later.

Monty Graf seemed uninterested to hear that what was left was a single reversal workprint. He called the conversation to a halt and said 8 P.M., gave me an address, and as a sort of afterthought asked where we had shot this particular footage. I skipped the question and thanked him for the address. But, he said, what did I *think* he was calling for.

I dialed last night's number on the pad. A man answered. I couldn't think and hung up. But I couldn't think because the man's voice had for an instant completed some circuit which could not tolerate further contact and so while my inability to think seemed to save me from something, the successful impulse to hang up broke the new circuit and shunted away its idea. Unfortunately, to be between does not necessitate being constantly connected with what one is between.

By the time the hot tap was running even lukewarm, the water was rising around the pans and plates and dishes and mugs. I inserted my hand under a leaning stack passing two fingertips along a submerged blade and opened the drain to let out the cold.

The oatmeal saucepan should have had cold water in it soaking the pasty remains. I hadn't got out of my living room day bed till Sub and the children had left. The supper dishes should have been at least rinsed.

Under two plain bone-china dinner plates was the black rim of Tris's white but smaller though thicker plate. The water had reached the rim just as I twisted the drain. Under and around these three plates were assorted silver, and on its side lay Tris's milk glass from last night.

Against the stack leaned like a big-hubbed wheel a blue-and-white cereal dish on which in turn leaned a child-size plate I knew had a faded pink and brown view of the Three Little Pigs and the Big Bad Wolf. Sub said Ruby was too old for it. She wasn't.

The water came steaming hot now and some of the pink gook I squeezed in gathered in a chipped cavity in the lip of a cheap old mug whose mineral and dilute pale-green took me along secondary blacktops in southern Maine and back streets of Bridgeport and Flat-bush and brought me from a drippy spigot at the base of a steel coffee urn that bitter worn liquid whose black-brown surface on a cool roadside night floats fine-sheened splotches of grease reminding you you are in a greasy spoon. This mug, framed by glistening space and multiplied by time, at once overflowed into the cereal dish it sat in which then overflowed suds around the base of the center stack. This was the mug I had poured water into for Myrna. Three others were in the sink, the large willow-pattern mug Sub used, Ruby's red-green-and-blue alphabet mug which had been a baby present, and Tris's gray, gravelly textured mug which Rose had made in a pottery class the last winter she lived with Sub and which Tris had had hot chocolate in last night. A fourth mug was in the living room on a large blotter next to the diary pages I'd been looking at on Sub's desk a few feet from the open day bed.

Whoever left the number would phone again. But what would happen when I found out who it was and where, and then said Sorry, I was mistaken about the diary, I didn't leave it at Claire's after all.

In the sink there was steam but little water. I'd left the loose old drain open, and the detergent water had mostly found it. I reached to close the drain and burnt my knuckles on a plate. I turned on hot and cold taps and squirted soap.

I should have told Dagger to shoot a sinkful of dishes. But film could not have seen what I saw. We could have used Lorna's unidentified hands reaching for a white plastic bottle of suprana-tional Lux though her brand is Fairy Magic—her skin over each pair of delicately raised wrist bones so fine there seem no creases from pore to pore. The blue sponge I pushed across the top plate swept off the dried catsup that marked it as Sub's and but barely eroded some sandy particles of bone and gristle tracked in congealed chop-fat leading into saffron crust which a green fleck revealed as broccoli butter.

Sub's plate I stood up in the water against the stack it had been part of and lifted out Ruby's with its three-fold fable licked clean last night but speckled now with greaselets launched by sink-water. Sub said Rose made fun of Ruby's bone-phobia; Sub, when he took the chops out of the oven and Ruby said she was having no bones on her plate, told Tris to put away his comic and get the bread and butter out of the icebox. Sub cut pieces of dry pork off Ruby's bone, arranged them on her plate, and kept her bone to chew on himself. I asked if I could dish out the broccoli.

60

But today where *was* that copper-bottomed broccoli pot? Not in the sink with the rest of last night's dishes or on the stove or on the windowsill by the ashtray with the filter-stub of my own cigarette yesterday. When I picked Tris's overturned milk glass out of the new submerged chop pan, my fingers found a slippery strip of fat the detergent hadn't had a chance to cut but couldn't have cut anyway without spreading the grease around the sinkwater. I lifted the pork pan out emptying the water. I found a spatula and shoveled up paths of fat which with my hand under to catch water drips I bore one by one to the garbage. Then I squirted detergent into the pan and ran water into it and placed it carefully again on the sink counter.

Yes I phoned the number.

The same man said he didn't know where Claire was but I should come now to an address downtown. When I asked if he worked for Aut he said Who's Aut? Then he said, quite finally, OK.

I said Sorry, I was mistaken, I didn't leave my diary at Claire's.

The man said as if it were a complete assertion, If you don't want these two pages.

And hung up.

I was feeling I hadn't learned much by this ruse of yesterday. When he rang off, the idea that had been shunted away when I'd hung up before circuited now in a neat eight-by-ten-inch rectangle the very size of that pile of my diary Claire had neatened on her table when she'd gotten up to answer her phone—and I'd come from her lavatory and had seen the pages had been neatened, and felt my hints had been heeded.

Now I rushed out of the kitchen through the hall to the living room. I clipped my shin on the steel corner of the day bed frame. I tore through the sheets on Sub's desk and at once found, yes, two pages missing that I knew I'd had at Claire's and that were not with others in my suitcase atop my wife's compact packing.

I took a bus downtown undecided.

If I chose not to go to the peremptory man who'd hung up on me, I could go all the way to Wall and get the brochures for my son. The bus was almost empty.

The pages must have been copied by now so I'd have no difficulty obtaining them. They might make Aut want to see the rest. Claire might not have had the chance to tell him she'd picked these two virtually at random having to run to answer the phone and knowing I'd be coming out of the bathroom. But if Aut thought these two pages were the best I had to offer, he might not care about others. But for him—if he was even involved—what in these pages mattered?

It was a rough bus ride. We started and stopped and I slid left and right on the seat's molded plastic. A pale-faced black-haired woman with blood-red lipstick dropped her fare into the machine and spoke to the black driver. I didn't see him speak, and as she spoke again the bus broke forward as if something had rammed it and the woman lost her hold on the fare machine and was inertially thrust toward the rear of the bus, but she lifted her knees in such a lucky slow-motion she didn't fall until, halfway down the length of the bus, I reached out.

I caught her so that she seemed about to learn to swim. She regained her slim long-calved legs and so involved herself in a magic smile to me and the immediate issue of whether to remove herself from me by sitting across from me or on my side and thus out of my normal line of sight, that she forgot the driver's behavior. She settled on my side toward the rear, slung one leg over the other, and looked straight ahead. The driver was answering a radio call, giving his position.

But what did Aut want with the diary pages? That is, what there in my words might equal what had been thought to be in the film? Almost the first words were Dagger's.

We were two miles east of Stonehenge among the great green and sand-pale grasses of Salisbury Plain, and Dagger slowing down nodded at the brown car on the shoulder ahead and said, Speak of the Devil, here's our volunteer for the final scene, let's change his tire.

But in fact we hadn't *been* discussing this Druid whose flat tire we now changed.

We'd been reviewing the raw stock we'd used in the Beaulieu up to now. A motley lot, I grant—but Dagger of all people should have recalled that the camera was lighter without the magazine one very bright morning the second day in Corsica, for we'd used a roll of black and white that was only a 100-footer. I said it had been between the petrol station and the fortress, around the corner from Place Napoléon, and the glare and shade decided Dagger to use instead the less inherently contrasty black and white. He'd had a hundred feet of Anscochrome in the camera when we came into Ajaccio on the Marseilles car-ferry the day before and he'd let it all go on the white, pink, yellow, and sky-blue crowd watching from the

pier; but at once he'd said he should have waited, the contrasts would
have been clearer in black and white, though he added I hadn't yet
sold him on mixing color with black and white. In London I'd given
him £12 to pay for six hundred feet of Anscochrome. He'd said
Claire's boss would foot that expense and gas to and from Corsica.
But it was black and white he was using when the two men and a girl
came up the street that crossed the end of ours. The fortress wall left
almost no pavement to walk on—*sidewalk* is the word in America,
not that *pavement* is exactly the word in Corsica, where the language
is French.

They were coming slowly up from the port in single file like
tourists who've had their café crème. The girl pointed at us, her
midriff blouse stark white. The blond man stepped off the pavement
toward us but was recalled by the other young man, bony brown and
bald. The three continued quite quickly along the fortress wall, the
bald man now with his hand on the girl's back where it was bare. We
were less than fifty yards from the end of our street where theirs
crossed coming up from the port, and Dagger who had been feeling
into his pocket for a pack of Tums gave up and went down to the end
of our street to look up after them. He wasn't shooting. They turned
into Place Napoléon out of sight. The blond man ambled behind. It
was this incident we were disagreeing about on the road from Stonehenge a month later. Dagger insisted now on confusing that black-
and-white footage with some Anscochrome we'd used the following
day. We'd shot a naval encounter off the beach just three blocks from
the École Normale where our American academic friend was putting us up. Aquamarine sea, three Corsicans in bikinis in one yellow
inflated landing raft, three Americans in cut-off jeans and bright
headbands in the other. And on the road from Stonehenge Dagger
seemed to have forgotten the black and white he'd used to shoot the
two men and the girl at the fortress in Ajaccio. I'd pointed out
that the b & w he shot there was almost the last of the single-perfora-
tion b & w he'd bought cheap by mail order from Freestyle Sales in
L.A. I described in detail the faces and clothes of the threesome, and
how he had complained about his stomach and the École coffee and
I'd said he obviously needed to change his diet. I reminded him they'd
not wanted to be filmed and tried to get away fast, but when we went
diving next day the same blond man was sitting with another girl in a
port café and as soon as we were in the gray rubber raft that looked
like French Navy surplus, I and the girl and the man who was taking
us out, with our suits on and the air tanks yellow alongside our fins

and masks and under the thwarts weighted belts like a sound-man's power pack, and Dagger and the boy who worked for the boss got in and the boss got the outboard going, the blond man got up from the table and walked across the cobbles and stepped inside the trailer with something-*Plonger* painted on it, presumably to engage the boss's wife in conversation about Dagger and me. The b & w in question was negative film, which is less adaptable to poor light than reversal film because if you're using a lab that will push it, negative unlike reversal usually can't be pushed in the developing to a higher emulsion speed as graded by the American Standards Association (ASA), whose system dating from 1943 was, I'm glad to say, adopted by the British in 1947, though the British use a logarithmic scale by degrees. In any case the last lot of b & w Dagger had had shipped from L.A. was ASA 200 but not with the magnetic stripe. The base price was $11.25 for four one-hundred-foot rolls, a saving of less than fifteen cents a roll at the single-roll price but much more if compared to prices elsewhere. Dagger and I, as we sighted the Druid and pulled over to help with the tire, had been disagreeing not about Freestyle, or perforation, or magnetic stripe, or price, but about whether we'd used black and white for those three people Dagger didn't recall having seen. So when he said, Speak of the Devil, I guessed that during our discussion he'd been thinking not of Ajaccio but of our dealings at Stonehenge minutes before with the very Druid we were now slowing down to help.

The woman with blood-red lipstick recrossed her legs. I looked over my shoulder at lower Broadway to see where I was. A door in a brown commercial building was shutting, but like a circuit for an instant open a hall was visible and a second doorway full of white, and a truth reached me: what I'd been recalling was more than the gist of the two pages Claire must have lifted; it was so closely aligned with those words as to be virtually verbatim.

In truth I had these pages by heart.

So what did it matter if the man on the phone gave them back or had something else in mind?

I had them in my head.

And so I reached over my head for the cord and bent a magical smile toward the dark and leggy woman who without really catching my eye smiled back less magically.

I took a step toward the exit and was staggered by the driver braking for my stop.

I was in Soho going east on Spring. I reached Crosby and

knew I was wrong. I turned back west along Spring. A small Chemical Bank branch was out of place among the loft buildings and drab commerce muted despite the trucks cramming the southbound street ahead. At Mercer I turned right and there were not only the trucks moving down the center but parked trucks tilted solid either side up onto the sidewalk and taking over the sidewalks with thigh-level roller-tracks running to basement loading windows or platforms— wool stock, nightgowns, leather. There were green pillars and posts on the east side, a lingerie firm was by a sheet-metal machinery firm and almost next to that I found my address halfway up the block toward Prince.

But the verbatim alignment between diary and memory had come not only without my trying; I wondered as I pressed the top button beside a nameless slot if I'd have been even capable of other words when I recalled the Corsica we'd discussed on the road from Stonehenge.

The latch clicked in answer and I pushed through.

Somewhere above as I started up the stairs, "Let the Sun Shine In" sang forth like an old chorale.

No one came as I passed the dark landings. The music which had been building leveled off, and then dropped away just as a door at the fourth or fifth landing swung open, but the song seemed to be from somewhere else.

Cartwright.

Over the man's shoulder to one side of the metal rim of his large round spectacles, two television sets in the room behind him faced each other a yard apart. Beyond them, across what must be the width of a loft, a workbench was against the wall with two green-glass pool-table lamps hung coolly above some tools, a generator, the uncovered tubes of a tuner, two or three small, cheap printed-circuit boards, a red box with a greasy-toothed gear leaning on it, and a tangle of looped wires arching up from a panel that lay flat.

What are the pages worth to you? the man said.

You've got the question turned around, I said.

The man backed into the loft and I stepped over the threshold and saw how long the loft was.

He snickered and said, No, man. Would *I* make you pay for your words?

I asked if I'd had any phone calls, I'd left word at the place I was staying that I could be reached here. The man snickered again and said, No phone calls, not even any mail.

The loft seemed to go clear through from Mercer to the next street west. At that far end was an extensive rig with a long track connecting a camera and some kind of focusing-plate gear. Areas around this imposing rig seemed in shadow because of the light on it from ceiling spots hung from two parallel socket-tracts.

I felt a third person but I didn't look around. I didn't have to see the man with the steel-rimmed glasses who'd greeted me with the voice I'd heard on the phone. The loft, the lights—the equipment I saw at once and the equipment I made out when I looked away from the lights—plus something genuine which seemed at odds with my teasing reception—all absorbed our words to spread their quotable sound into meanings I find now but found even then I could describe but not quote. But you who read this have me even though here I admit there are things I have heard that I didn't have in my head exactly. Do not withdraw your hand from the glove port, you haven't yet found what you imagine you're not looking for.

I asked if Claire was here and when the young man in the glasses asked who Claire was, the third voice said to him, You never met her.

The voice seemed so young I turned toward it and saw a child, virtually a child.

Or at most a fifteen-year-old, a boy with shoulder-length hair combed to a billowing sheen—and I checked the ceiling along which I realized I'd sensed transverse waves eight or ten inches deep flowing the length of the loft. God knows why they built those cement-and-plaster waves fifty years ago, but it was as strong and right as all the powder-smooth New York walls laid on by a generation of Italian immigrant plasterers.

I asked where my pages were. I asked again and sounded just anxious enough. Above a workbench was a poster showing formulaic sequences. Someone had written in the lower right the word NAND, which in computer logic means NOT AND—or, input signal zero, output one (which sounds like you get something for nothing).

The man in the glasses said my diary was . . .

I asked what kind of films he made and the boy said Original, original.

I said, Joined the filmmaking revolution, have you?

To you it's a revolution maybe, he said.

I said my diary wouldn't interest them if they were pros. The man said I seemed very into it, like the description of those two dudes and the chick in Ajaccio. I said there wasn't any description of them

66

in the two pages I'd left at Claire's, there was merely reference to my having described *in intimate detail to Dagger,* right? The boy cut in that it was good to keep a diary, he wished he'd started when he was young, he'd lost so much. I asked if either of them knew someone named Cosmo, and they said no.

The man in glasses mentioned a cup of tea. I said thanks. I looked at the far end of the loft and said, What's with the screen?

The man said it was going to be a slit scan when they got it finished, but it wasn't really what he was into.

The boy asked what we thought we were trying to do making that film. Get something together, I said. Christ, said the man from over by a table where he'd switched on a hot plate, how much diary had I written about it? I said maybe thirty thousand words. The boy said, Those two pages make the diary sound better than the film—I thought he was high—and the man said how much did I bring to New York, and I said thirty pages about, I thought, and he said did that mean twenty-eight back where I was staying—but tried to interrupt himself with a semblance of enthusiasm saying were they about Corsica too. I said I wasn't sure if it was twenty-eight or more, I sometimes got confused after they were typed up. The man dropped tea bags into two mugs and said why did I bring the pages to New York. I said I wanted to tell Phil Aut what had been in our film, so I wanted to be able to check my facts. The boy hummed.

The man said over his shoulder as he was pouring water that he'd show me the slit scan, he didn't have the camera yet, he needed a sixty-five mill for a job but he had some good interesting panels behind the screen slit. I wasn't in a hurry? This kind of film wasn't really what he was into, he said.

The big metal door closed behind me. I took out my wallet and I murmured, Let's see, how do I get to Graf's from here. I returned my wallet to my inside pocket which wasn't bulging as it bulged when I visited Claire. The big door scraped again and closed. There was the sweet smell of pot. I said what about the two pages I came for. The boy now surprisingly close behind me said, The great Phil Aut doesn't know shit about film, he'll quote you a price and tell you you're not commercial, that's Phil.

The man lifting two cups turned and said, Shut up, Jerry, and sloshed tea onto the floor. He grinned. I said, Jerry you've got principles.

Jerry said to our host, I've seen you put in your pretty contacts and go off to work as happy as . . .

I asked Jerry if he could get me an appointment with Aut.

I never go near him. I don't even know where his office is.

The door wasn't bolted.

If someone was busting into Sub's looking for more diary pages, at least they wouldn't find Sub or Ruby or Tris.

I got the door open. The boy took a drag on his joint. A bit close, I said. The boy said what did I mean I got confused when they were typed up, and the man said Hey your tea.

I said my daughter in London made a carbon usually, if she was doing the typing, so I sometimes thought of all those pages doubled.

The man with the metal-rimmed glasses had stopped but now moved my way again. He said, Your pages. Just take your cup, I'll get them.

I said no thanks, I knew them.

What did I come down here for, then? the man was saying as he bent over to put the cups on the floor.

I was going to be detained. I couldn't tell how clear the boy was.

I said, I don't know much yet that's going on here but I know we haven't been disagreeing about Freestyle, or perforation, or magnetic stripe, or price, and I know that—to quote myself again—I have no wish to engage the boss's wife in conversation about Dagger and me, but you tell your boss Mr. Phil Aut that whether or not he foots our gas from London to Ajaccio and back, it will be of interest to deal directly with me.

I was taking the stairs two at a time and steps came after but then stopped, then started, but far off.

I called up, I want you to explain your camera track to me.

He'd said it was not really what he was into. There had been something genuine up there, but nothing to do with my diary pages, which were also genuine. That music from *Hair* that Lorna used to play and play had stopped.

I was back on the street. Warehouse space, light industry, and in the area more and more artists, filling space, displacing industry.

Did the man in glasses know the name Monty Graf? If so he probably didn't know that I had six hours till that appointment.

A girl in jeans with a knapsack came along looking up at the buildings as if for something in one of those loft windows. She was smiling, like a blind person or as if she knew something good. My neck itched but I wouldn't find a chemist's this far south of the Village and north of Canal. Lorna's packing had been flawless, of course, but the Wilkinson dispenser was empty of new blades and the one in my razor was ready to be retired. When I visited the Wilkinson lab in Newcastle I asked a young engineer in a long white coat if the profit motive might not lead Wilkinson to relent and make a blade that didn't last so incredibly long. He said this was not a prime concern.

Wilkinson want their American people resident.

My only mistake had been to mention Cosmo just now. That was giving too much away. I didn't know if the Indian had mentioned my visit to the Knightsbridge gallery.

And the mistake seemed then doubled by my having sent that Empire State 3-D yesterday to Cosmo, who knew we weren't friends.

Well where had I seen the Indian before?

And why should Claire care if I'd put in writing what the man looked like who came running out of the grove in Wales?

What I wanted was not a trip to Wall Street but a cheeseburger and a malted and the early afternoon edition of the *Post*.

SLOT INSERT | Witness a different cartridge: not a thing solidly instated in a slot, rather a slot inserted in a thing.

What happens? Shift a something to make room for an emptiness.

This slot, then—has it identity unfilled? Maybe only so. I.e., if as appears to be true this slot is, say, the place where (not to be too specific) motives for making the DiGorro-Cartwright film can be found, isn't it true that when these appear in the slot thus filling it or causing it to cease to be empty, it thus ceases to be itself?

What appear to be such motives? Each one, as it fills the inserted slot, is also transparent. Through the motive may be seen the lack it is aimed to fill, as if the motive were a picture thrown not upon a screen but upon a volume, the motive thus even in its nagging transparency quite whole and plastic. A slot if like this one insertable is not only a place for a cartridge, and where inserted this slot is a cartridge of the future, of unknowns, or the unknown.

Are these statements themselves slots obscuring what's in them?

Forget the slot and give it content. One motive for doing the film was that an American named Constance had been told in so many words that the film was in fact projected. Another motive was that the partners both and each thought it high time to get something together. A third was to mingle England and America. A fourth was to permit accident, say a couple of pompous hippies swapping recipes for gelatin dynamite, but no joke, as Will did not quite see when he suggested a New York tycoon blowing up his own building to collect the insurance.

For years it was possible to bring back to Lorna, Will, and Jenny American gifts. These can be recalled like a roll of events reminding one that three-dimensional Scrabble predated tie-dye jean jackets, and Peter, Paul, and Mary came after the new ultra-thin polyester sandwich bags sticky with static electricity. *Bring back a memory* Jenny snidely said, but it was often a future. If America was to popularize the universe she must be given a chance.

There was indeed one motive unvoiced to pragmatical Dagger. This was that the film under the guise of documentary daydream (and early associated with the chance that Chaplin might appear in an interview) would express some way two decades of America. The Bonfire in Wales threw into contour this possibility—here, for instance, the trend toward eastern modes, organic community, dislodging from city. The Unplaced Room, which of course had not been Dagger's contribution, could show the American's increasing disjunction in his environment and the need and arresting capacity to assert an existence and a self in a departicularized setting; it would be helpful to insert into such a setting Americans; and Dagger, even had he intended to, could not have made an apter contribution to this Unplaced Room than the unknown deserter who came with his friend and talked for several minutes. The Hawaiian-in-the-Underground playing his guitar would help to include race, national integrity, and the signal sweep of new folk musics and all they have been able, even unable, to express, Dylan and Mitchell and Newman and Stills. Hints here and there that the film was originating somehow outside America served to cool the focus.

Motives that did not get voiced to Dagger included, for instance, the power of spoken words to make even more magical the merest objects of daily life—seen, say, in the scene designated Suitcase Slowly Packed: the laying of a black Marks and Spencer sweater upon a white-and-green plastic bottle of medicated shampoo, the insertion and removal of hands, the documentary account of each thing given in one voice as Dagger wished against his partner's alternative but impracticable plan that each thing going into the one gray case go with a new voice to live distinct and separate, though

70

Dagger, as he assured his partner and his partner's son one day in the park, would not automatically say no to any idea.

One summer there was one gift for the whole family from America—the one and only lost Cartwright family flick found in a large Whitman sampler—for God's sake take it, my mother had said, the kids might enjoy it.

That was a past all right but barely a remembrance even for those who shot it, certainly not for the stars. These were the two Cartwright children, a curly blond three-year-old boy named Me in light-colored jersey shorts that came out stony gray, and a five-year-old girl my sister in nothing but a rubber life-ring, the frames in those days so few per second that the pretty little girl in the film's grainy snow hops into and out of a shallow canvas lawn-pool like a swallow dipping its beak and wings in a birdbath. The little boy jerks down his elastic-waisted shorts, he pushes them to his ankles, stands free and bends menacingly at the camera, then erect turns profile and with a dynamic faraway look like a lookout but looking merely at his pretty sister, he forgets his hobble and starting off falls flat on his elbows.

The film (released from New York now) seemed a waste. Lorna said, A manly boy. Will said, There's no sound. Dagger, stationed at his projector, said, A remarkable film for its period. Alba said, You were enchanting, I recognized you right away. Jenny said, It's raised a lot of new questions, I must say.

Everybody laughed when Jenny said that. But her pleasantly insignificant quip with the film still running set some new deadline the meaning of which must come clear before the reel ended, and then it raced on and the leader whipped off and flapped clear leaving on Dagger's screen a glare without clear scale, and like a deadline set just on principle the thought came, with the end of these images of the thirties that weren't after all so distinctively of the thirties, that this film should not have been taken away from the creaky, spider-inhabited American attic, for someone would have to pay for its removal. The canvas pool is an ancestor of today's collapsible vinyl-lined Doughboy pools that have their indispensable counterparts in England and can even be heated from the point at which the pool's filter cartridge is located.

Unlike the three-year-old Virginia who said Daddy bring back a present, the seventeen-year-old Jenny said something else killingly sophisticated to her international businessman father: Bring back a memory.

Motives? Others would come after the film was done, even

later—even now—leaving or holding out possibility like a lunar depression or one of a series of superimposed transparencies, even that ultimate form, the shape of that slot-space visible through various contents.

5 | Let me convey Monty Graf's face, confirm his rather still voice. A mixed face and a dark mild voice that doesn't so much confide as pass on to you some prior confidence reached with someone else. Between nostril and upper lip an area very ample, sensitive, and ambiguous. Absolutely black eyebrows, thick and trimmed. And a vocabulary.

When he spoke to me his zinc-gray eyes widened sharply on certain words—*Stratford, Soho, Handel, Coventry, brain-drain.*

To see what it was like I widened my eyes the same way on two of mine—*Knightsbridge* and *Stonehenge.*

The narrow healthy nose and the eyebrows and eyes so vitally differed from the rest of his face they seemed a section jammed down to fit the rest as if that were a receptacle—pocked sallow cheeks, a pudgy, brief though not recessive chin jabbed by a mole at the fork of a center cleft, which was less an event than a surplus fold.

Dagger's camera could glibly sum up this face: a wary, half-sensual indeterminately beat-up forty-six soon to be much older.

Three deep lines cross Monty Graf's forehead no matter what happens lower down. The second stops midway across, but your eye goes on as if drawn between the upper and lower wrinkles to the far temple and its softly combed swell of gray and black hair, and my eye went still further to the ash blonde with her back to me in the next booth and to the right of her hair and above the back of the booth the eyes of the man she was with.

Monty Graf went through Coventry during the war and still knew someone in munitions there; the new modern cathedral was a great experience I should be sure not to miss—bitter experience, Coventry, but of course the English were pretty reserved—but I must know all about that, having lived there.

You said it, I said, they're so reserved there's a postman none of his coworkers have spoken to in three years.

Monty Graf picked that right up, said not he thought in Coventry but someplace else, it was due to a strike the postman hadn't joined, and did I know where that phrase sending to Coventry came from.

I did not know.

Coventry jail, Civil War, he said, the citizens of Birmingham sent a passel of Royalists away to Coventry; I'm an Anglophile, he said. He asked me what I'd drink. I was thinking it wasn't quite true that the English were reserved. How can you live so long there and not know if they're reserved or not? Think of the stranger, the bank clerk who came up behind you at Stonehenge and gave you a little talk unsolicited complete with weights and measures.

I said by the way I had indeed seen the new Coventry Cathedral, but speaking of Anglophilia he wasn't the one who phoned yesterday afternoon, was he?

He didn't seem to make the connection of Anglophilia with the phone call, but he did shake his head.

I asked if he was with Outer Film; he said No though he'd heard of them. Our film didn't include Coventry, did it—or had I said I knew someone in Coventry.

An engineer, but I don't think I mentioned him to you.

Automobiles?

I nodded.

Monty Graf sipped through a short straw a New Orleans gin drink made with milk and fresh-cracked ice, sugar, and white of egg.

He'd come in from London this morning, he said.

I said I'd guessed that.

He took another sip and said he'd learned—in London—that a film I'd made was very interesting and that I hadn't sold it yet.

I said we'd lost most of it so there was virtually nothing to sell.

He said according to his information we still had some significant footage.

I said what could you do with a few minutes of 16 mill?

Monty Graf drew gently on his gin and milk and looked beyond me phrasing the next move.

I asked if he had a settled place of residence, and he smiled and said sure he had a house south of the Village, I could come and stay any time; he mentioned the address.

Two fish platters came by and were placed before the ash blonde and the man. I'd been brought a dark beer by mistake. I said I didn't realize the kitchen was back there—and I turned around and saw light through the swinging door opening for the other waiter also in white shirt and white apron and as my eye further along the bar and off by the door thought it found the profile of the man in glasses who'd tried to serve me a cup of tea, I became aware of the jukebox playing later Dylan, and Monty Graf said he didn't know if I'd eaten but this was just a neighborhood place but pretty good pot luck and he could recommend the osso buco and the stuffed bluefish.

Who had he heard about the film from? I asked.

He passed right through that question and said (headed toward me like a devoted skin doctor), I'd like to hear about your film from *you*.

I wondered how Dagger would take the question. Lately Dagger didn't seem to care, though I will say for him that he seemed deliberately to want *not* to talk about the loss. He was considering the States, he had even assembled a job-application vita.

The truth was that there were in a way two films—his and mine.

That would be of little interest to this man waiting across the table in a black double-knit blazer.

You decide to reach, and before you're half into it the thing you want has taken you in hand and said wait here keep an eye out while we get through the window and look around inside, we'll be out in ten minutes unless you whistle.

Or your wife says to some visiting American who's asked if she'd like to go back to the States, By now it's six of one, half a dozen of the other, but it would be a change—though you think that when she looks over at you she remembers you inside her, recalls looking forward and backward to it, looks forward to it. (Why are English not called expatriate when they settle in the States?)

Or you say to your friend Dagger, We'll make a film, and you tell him what's on your mind. But later the film seems not yours, not his either, but just to have happened—and it's not what you dreamed of, but it's something.

You get an inkling one day that the ruination of the film was something someone decidedly reached out to effect: and you get on a plane to New York, leaving behind an encounter with your seventeen-year-old daughter and looking ahead beyond the East where you'll be to a California she says she is settled on going to perhaps even before she takes her A-levels.

But you were coming anyway on business, and the last time you made love to Lorna it rose through your head in clear blue-green bubbles of smiling sound that that amateur film had not after all been necessary.

But life is not so disappointing as such passages of consolation seem to conceal. You've spent forty-eight hours in New York and

74

someone is coming to you wanting to know what you have, though who is hand in glove with whom is hard to say. You haven't picked up those Wall Street brochures for your son or was it a *book* about the market—then over your cheeseburger you saw Will hadn't made it clear, maybe was just giving you something to do. Your frothy vanilla malted flowed down and was gone—such a malted.

You haven't had your cigarette today.

Monty Graf waited and now broke his lips to speak but I was in ahead of him: There are two films really, what my friend Dagger DiGorro wanted and what I wanted. He's good on the hardware. I mean, he never made a serious film but when we shot the naval engagement in Corsica in slow motion he knew it wasn't just a matter of turning the frame knob up to 64, there was the little power switch below and the ASA gauge above.

Could I have heard about him on the grapevine? said Monty Graf.

I turned to wave at a waiter and look the man in glasses in the corner of his profiled eye. He was the one who'd made me a cup of tea all right.

The idea was this, I began. But I couldn't mention Claire. Graf must be the Monty that Claire was talking to on the phone, for she'd already mentioned Monty Graf to me. I had slipped into other circuits, and Graf must know Aut too if Jan Graf was any relation, but if he knew Claire he must at least know *of* Aut; but Graf would not know Dagger, for Dagger would have mentioned him—still, through Claire Dagger must have become known to Graf, though what Claire could have told Monty Graf remained to be seen and Claire knew only what Dagger had told her plus my bait yesterday; but if Jan Graf was a relation, did Monty therefore know the Indian who worked in the Knightsbridge gallery, or even Cosmo? But that kid in the loft Jerry might know Claire, the way he said You never met her to the man in glasses.

So to be at least myself, I decided to tell Monty Graf what the idea had been and still in some form was. Graf widened his eyes as I said *Bluefish* to the waiter, who raised his eyebrows when I said beets or carrots instead of french fries, and as he was going away I said *light* beer.

For example, said Monty Graf, the footage that survived the fire, why a rush of that? Was that the beginning of the film and you wanted to see how you were doing? You shot that in London? Someplace else, I forget.

You didn't forget, I said, you were never told.

The waiter brought a coffee-colored dark beer with a thick head like rusty marshmallow. I pointed to my companion's milky champagne glass and the waiter said Right, and went away.

No, I said to Graf, it wasn't the beginning. I'll tell you about the beginning; we never did see it printed; but this is what happened.

I did not describe my effort to get Chaplin to let us film an interview with him and it would have been too hard to explain to Graf what I'd had in mind vainly urging Dagger to shoot a hundred frames or so of a letter lying, say, on Dagger's worktable that I in fact wrote to Chaplin.

No, I said, the beginning would have been a bare room and the only things on the film besides a couple of straight chairs and a vivid blue-red-and-umber Turkish floor cushion were the two guys we were shooting, plus whatever Dagger got of me with the mike: just a quick cut, then back to the faces.

We told them to go ahead, maybe not mention England, just say for example *"here,"* so the room as I conceived it with plain plaster walls that we'd depictured would be just an unplaced room. Dagger went along with this.

Who were they? said Graf.

One's an American corporal from Heidelberg, skipped to Sweden, later crossed into Norway, stopped off with his sister's girl-friend who's teaching at an English Institute in Trondheim. Well, then he shipped on some American's yacht looking for sanctuary perhaps and wound up in the Faeroe Islands between Iceland and the Shetlands and waited while his employer, a dilettante geologist, fished for trout. But our deserter apparently couldn't wait. He made it to the Hebrides with a fisherman and there I happen to know he lived in a hut near Mount Clisham.

The other? said Monty Graf.

Friend of the first, according to Dagger.

How did Dagger know? said Graf.

Most of what I told Graf was in a desk drawer in Highgate. Earlier today London time Lorna rested her arm on that desk writing a check for her yoga class and would look up with that blank eye when Jenny came in the living room having descended from her own desk upstairs where she might well have been studying A-level Latin. And being asked by Lorna how it had been going, Jenny tossed her head and blew hair out of her eyes which comes right back down again over her cheek like Claire's.

Does Jenny stay in the living room with Lorna or cross to the kitchen or go back upstairs to Will's room to borrow a quid if he's home, or go back to her room? Or go across the road to the new Americans she's friendly with who she says are so interested in her? It's suppertime. But why then is Lorna sitting at the desk?

I've been hard on Claire, maybe she was serious about throwing up her job and moving to England.

Graf sipped, then spoke with patient elocution. An unplaced room and you took the pictures down before you shot the scene. And a blue, red, and umber Turkish floor cushion. What did they talk about?

In my ear my voice seemed loud, though I kept hitting on the idea that Graf didn't exactly hear me, but this was perhaps his New York eye, not me.

The film's aim, I said, was a sort of power.

Over who?

No. Power shown being acquired from sources where it had momentum but not clarity.

What does that mean, said Graf.

Preying on power. Saving power from itself.

Did it have a story? said Graf.

For me it had. For Dagger I don't know. For him it was a documentary, he said, and he said it would come clear in the end, which was what I thought myself but from my angle.

Political power, said Graf, returning to my other remark. He was looking into his glass, an ice cube had a fog of milk over it.

Any power in the right sequence, I said.

The fire now, said Monty Graf.

Power with momentum but not clarity, I said. The fire? Imagine filming that, filming the dissolution of the film, the burning, filming the burning of even the raw stock running through your own gate, the fire from Dagger's table leaning out toward the camera you've got running in your hand.

There'd be no film then, said Monty Graf. But I didn't mean that fire; I meant the bonfire.

Plenty of energy there, I said. But the membership was pretty shifting, and from what we saw there were five or six religions there, not one. But we took the whole image.

Was this film of yours about a quest for identity?

Chewing my bluefish, I closed my eyes as if looking for a bone. I remembered many things. I swallowed, smiled, drank half my beer.

Interesting idea, I said. There was a man in the trees there who thought our film was a quest for him.

Did you preserve him for posterity? said Monty Graf.

You know I did, I said.

So that's the footage that didn't get burnt.

No.

Let's move on, said Graf. What's your next scene?

We might have shuffled the order in the editing.

But it got burnt first.

Right, I said.

Monty Graf wanted a rundown of scenes. That was nice. And as I forked out the stuffing rich with onion, damp with blackened mushroom, separately so I didn't get a bone, I wondered what I'd achieved in the time since I landed at Kennedy, which seemed long because it had been short but full—but full of what? There was green in the stuffing. I ate some more preceded on the prongs of my fork by a vinegary beet slice (in England called beet-root and sold in the greengrocer's already boiled but why?). Why would Monty Graf care what had been on a film that no longer existed?

Well, he said, could you take what you rescued from the fire and start over and make a similar film? I mean with expenses.

I chewed.

He was still hoping, but maybe not for the diary. The blonde in the next booth gave me her profile, I could almost smell the orange and blue-green eyeshadow. Monty had talked of the film, not the diary. Preserved for posterity? or from.

The man in the grove had come from the darkness of trees not really into my sight but into flickering shades, and Jenny had typed the page that told how when he broke from the grove he seemed to come from behind a tree much too slender to hide him, so he seemed to unroll from its trunk. I dabbed a parsley fleck off the silver side of my fish with a fork prong and a bit of chive off the plate.

I could forget the film. And Cosmo's Indian. And someone named Jan Aut. And Claire. And the camera jamming when we didn't allow enough loop in the left-hand side of the film feeding from the sprocket-wheel around into the slot between the film gate and pressure plate.

Back over my shoulder I found the man in the steel-rimmed glasses who'd made me a cup of tea looking our way.

Would he be here if Monty was in with Aut? Could I be sure

the man in glasses worked for Aut? The boy Jerry had opinions on Aut, and as for the man watching me here from the crowded bar, hadn't he told Jerry to shut up?

I looked; he seemed to be smiling, but he was alone; I'd seen several people around Manhattan walking along smiling for no outwardly visible reason, not only the blind man—the toucher—also the knapsack girl on Mercer Street smiling up at the lofts.

It was after nine. There was a waitress I hadn't seen, and she was laughing while she wrote on her order pad. There wasn't a table or booth vacant.

OK, I said. For what it's worth. A softball game in Hyde Park, a bonfire in Wales, a Hawaiian hippie and his girlfriend from Hempstead, Long Island, playing guitar in the London Underground. A suitcase slowly packed. People in a marvelous country mansion doing things inside and outside and ignoring a moonshot on a television set under a table umbrella out on a rainy patio. A Corsican montage featuring an international seminar on ecology. Toward the middle of August, Stonehenge. In the end a U.S. Air Force base. A quick 8-mill. cartridge of some pals of Dagger's the night we got back from shooting at the base.

You left out the beginning, said Graf.

OK, I said.

The two men in the Unplaced Room. Do they come in again?

No. But yes. They do come in again. They were at Stonehenge.

Sounds a peculiar film. *Power,* you said?

Power poached on when it had momentum but not focus.

In England.

Some bits maybe had focus. Objects, cuts, quickies, objects for music and voices. A bridge I like.

Objects? What about the pictures in the Unplaced Room?

Brunel's Clifton Bridge, for instance. We shot it on the way to Wales. Isambard Kingdom Brunel. And hands laying out TNT like a xylophone and then standing each stick up carefully, and fingers dismantling a kitchen timer. The times we live in.

Faces?

Some negative stills too. I was planning to splice them in, printed *as* negatives. People with black faces and white hair. Stills with voices. Ever think of the sound that goes with a snapshot?

Did you mean a *movie* sequence using stills?

A few. It's destroyed.

That negative stuff is a cliché of course.

The black and white might have had a point.

Was this to be a picture of American life abroad?

That may have been Dagger's idea, I said.

He was in charge of equipment, said Graf.

I was the one who wanted to use slit-scan screening.

I leave the hardware to the filmmaker, said Monty Graf. My thing is collaboration, sort of a mating of the aesthetic and the financial.

You might be of help, I said.

What about Speaker's Corner in Hyde Park? said Monty—he was being humorous. He sensed something wrong and knew it wasn't the bleeding beets or glistening bluefish fast disappearing, or my distrust of him. His own task was too tricky for him to see the simple truth that my table of contents had depressed me. I thought of the death camps, of Belsen, of certain photographs—and knew that as an issue or concern in my heart all the dead Jews were cold—what was the matter with me?

What happened at Stonehenge?

Just before the Stonehenge scene, I said, we were going to cut in an elevator down a coal mine in Wales; shoot the sky from a hundred feet down. You have to cut in a shot of a pile of slag or a coal trolley underground, a miner with a headlamp, else that shot of sky could just as well be the end of the Severn Railway Tunnel.

Monty Graf had gotten the waiter to bring a third gin and milk. I imagined dripping a beet into his wide, pure glass. I hadn't thought until now about the deserter's reappearance in the unpleasant Stonehenge scene at the end of the film. He and his friend just seemed like the usual supernumerary acquaintances who turn up at Dagger's parties; I'd noticed them and accepted them.

You said momentum, before, said Monty Graf—so where's the momentum in the coal-mine shaft?

I don't know, I said. You want too much consistency.

Just interested. It sounds different. I mean, you never know where you're going to find the real thing. Always on the lookout. I had a piece of a Swedish film. I promote an annual exhibition at the Coliseum. I do a little real estate.

I'd finished my fish and Monty Graf wanted to know what footage we'd actually had developed. Maybe there was a point of departure there, he was saying; and I was on the point of asking if our friend with the steel-rims was still at the bar, when Monty Graf said, Seven minutes is a lot, you know, even unedited, possibly quite a substantial basis in terms of what you can show on film in terms of time.

He sipped, and I wasn't sure if I would need him.

I was about to ask where he'd heard seven minutes, but he said, Look I really like the England mingled with America idea, I mean it's got possibilities right now what with the war and the recession and as it were the decline of America.

I said, I didn't say anything about seven minutes.

The top part of Monty Graf's divided face seemed to command the rest to fade and though I was even less sure who he was I believed now that he was convinced the film was worth knowing about but that he knew no more than what Claire chose to tell.

I had an impression of New York, but it passed.

I did not say to Monty Graf, What's Phil Aut to you?

Instead I said wearily, There were two films.

That I know, said Monty Graf.

Oh you know that, do you? Well do you know that also there *are* two films? The film and my recollection of it.

All right, you mean your diary, said Graf. But I'm afraid I meant two *real* films. That is, before yours got burnt.

What's the other?

Don't you really know?

I put a ten-dollar bill on the table and Monty Graf reached and pushed it into my lap and I took it and got up.

Let me see the print, Mr. Cartwright, I'm with *you*, he said.

I lifted my coat off the hook and walked between two tables toward the bar wondering what would happen and wishing I'd waited for a coffee. Monty Graf was right behind me.

The man who'd made me a cup of tea was still at the bar. I said hello and as Graf arrived I looked at the two of them, but Monty didn't seem to know him. He wore a fringed pale buckskin jacket and a dark purple neckerchief and a dark denim shirt with pearl snaps.

He held out an envelope. Your diary, man, all two pages. I know it by heart.

A delicate rain settled down, and I spotted an Off-Duty cab light coming. Monty Graf said I seemed to get around, and would I at least sleep on the prospect of a proposition and phone him tomorrow.

I said I was sure Dagger would show him the print. Dagger could borrow a projector.

If you, said Monty Graf, gave me an introduction. When are you back in London?

But he's Claire's uncle, I said, and waited. He hadn't known I connected him with her. Just tell Dagger you're a friend of Claire's.

All right, I know Claire, said Monty Graf. Then he said, You know you're in trouble, you know that.

I put the envelope in his hand. Give these pages to Claire; I told her they were technical sentiment, but she might be interested.

I was getting into a cab pointed downtown when I wanted to go uptown. Inside the restaurant the man in glasses peered through the glass door and for a second in the amiable light behind him everyone seemed to be turning away toward the interior.

I wanted to ask about Jan Graf, but expected Monty to speak; but he didn't. So I said, Do you know a painter named Jan Graf?

He smiled, to make me feel he knew something. He stuck out his hand. I bent up into the cab and through the opposite window saw two headless bike-riders flick past. I fell into the seat and reached and pulled the door.

I gave the driver Sub's street.

Monty rapped on the glass. My God, he said, the *sound,* the *sound!* They didn't get *that!* Where is the *sound?*

He may not have heard me say, Filmless.

Two films? Which two had he been talking about? Monty Graf was on the lookout for prospects that were started and had momentum so he could tune in on the energy.

Was the energy mine and Dagger's? If so, was there something in my own film, my own diary, that I didn't know about?

I didn't want to talk to Sub I wanted to end the evening right there in the cab, and wake tomorrow with new thoughts.

But Sub was waiting.

Why not?

My eye looking at someone I've known since we were eight saw someone seated on a couch that could not change into a bed until he absented himself. I wasn't tired, I just wanted either Sub's place to myself or something new to happen.

Two films, Monty Graf said.

OK he didn't mean two views, mine and Dagger's, or camera versus words in a diary. He meant two films, unless he was in the dark and merely holding on.

So I was in trouble, was I.

The camera never wearies. But apart from its inserted film

that comes and goes, a camera is unremembering. Granted it can break—which is memory of a kind; still, the lens is dumb.

I had in my head I felt sure why they destroyed our film. In my head or on paper. I could probably remember most of what I'd put down. Most of it Jenny had typed.

I hadn't needed to say I had those two pages in my head.

Well, I asked Sub what sort of day it had been. He stretched, and said Rose had been livid. I shook out a cigarette and wondered if Jenny had thought about the pages she'd typed. She might be able to help after all.

Sub got up and turned off the telly. Rose was fit to be tied, he said, she came for Ruby and Tris and nobody was here. Almost.

You said you'd phone her, I said.

I almost meant to and forgot. Talking to Ticketron about going to work for them, Rose went right out of my head.

Rose keeps in touch, I said.

She's not threatening a comeback, said Sub.

She have a key?

That's almost what I wanted to ask you.

You said she was livid.

By phone and in the note she scrawled me.

Sub was leaning back on the couch that turned into my bed. I looked for an ashtray. On a bookshelf stood some old coffee tins painted purple.

Who'd you give your key to? said Sub.

I let myself in, didn't you notice?

The labels on the coffee containers read PENCILS, PENNIES, BUTTONS, SHELLS, STRING, MISC. There was a slit in the plastic top of the PENNIES tin. My ash dropped on the carpet. I found an ashtray between two glass candlestick holders.

You see, said Sub, a man said to Rose you'd lent him your key.

To *Rose*? I said—which lucky for me was just about what I'd have wanted to say.

Rose came here expecting to find the children, said Sub, and when she didn't find them she phoned me but couldn't get through. So she phoned the school and found out what had happened. She was writing me a note when the buzzer went. She asked who it was and the man said a friend of Cartwright's and he had your key but didn't want to startle anyone if there was anyone in the apartment. Rose let him in. He said you'd been tied up at a studio and were meeting him later and had asked him to get something out of your suitcase. Rose couldn't care less.

Perhaps, I said, I shouldn't have.

She said he had a suede fringe outfit and big round glasses.

That's him, I said. Steel-rim.

And said he was in films, that was how he knew you.

I've been running around all day, I said. New York confuses me. I didn't think you'd mind.

Sub had gone into the kitchen. The fridge door smacked.

Want a beer? I got Heineken's.

I said no thanks.

They might never tell me what it was they wanted in my pages.

Sub leaned against the doorway. He was tired. He tipped the bottle up.

I hoped he would say something else. I got my suitcase up onto the couch and got my pajamas.

I said I appreciated this—it was much more than a place to crash.

Saying the words I found them true.

But I'd begun to say them because Sub had had another lousy day; and he might say something else about the man, and I couldn't very well ask without weakening my position. But the uttered words brought up the real feeling and real years. I was sorry Sub's marriage had busted up. But why?

Sub nodded.

He turned toward his bedroom and I mentioned that Will had got interested in Babbage. Sub had once written something for a house organ on that peculiar English genius and his proto-computers. Sub murmured, Drain Babbage, brain *dommage*.

But then from his bedroom he said, Rose asked who he was, and he said Monty Graf. But you know it was Monty Graf.

My fingers were on my diary but from some lower layer of packing an odor as of Lorna reached me; I felt and found a waxy ball of her pine soap; it was American.

Sub came back: But didn't this man with the suede fringe tell you he ran into Rose?

It was a good question and I kept my hands moving.

The pages were all there except the two I'd had in the envelope an hour ago. I said, He left the key for me in an envelope so I didn't see him to talk to.

84

Sub turned away toward his room and I grabbed my trench-coat pocket and to my relief found Sub's key. But why not?

Imagine the man in glasses taking it when I was in the loft; imagine him cutting a duplicate and returning mine to me in the envelope I then passed on to the real Monty Graf. But what would I have let myself in with just now?

Monty might be right. About my being in trouble.

Sub came back. He said, It's not so much your life I envy as the changes in it. Hell, I said, you're going to Washington tomorrow. Sub said he had watched a mystery movie tonight which had had little enough suspense and they had a trick of showing you shots of the big scenes before the thing started.

Dagger had just sent in a vita to Washington. He had given me the envelope with Health, Education, and Welfare on it to mail one day. Out of sight, out of mind, he said.

Much later I put my pages in my case.

I had an unmemorable dream but I know that as my thoughts were dissolving in the perpendicular laps of some Black and White Panther concubines, I was about to tell Ruby a bedtime tale of how her dad got the name Sub.

DAGGER-TYPE CASSETTE

At signal read vita: One winter Dagger camped on a Bahama beach. One Sunday morning some black boys who sometimes played on the beach came racing out and pretended to crucify one of their number near Dagger's lean-to.

Read slowly but not so slowly it is not clear: Dagger was known on the Bahama isle as a colorful character from California. He said, I fill a need here.

At signal, read vita; begin with latest position, work backward: Dagger lived on the beach at the bottom of an incline of tough-bladed dune grass that was the seaward end of a strip an eighth of a mile wide that lay between Sea View, a hotel, and Spindrift, a guest house with motellike units below the main building.

At night he sat cross-legged before his fire. He borrowed a rubber raft from the lady who ran Spindrift and with a snorkel-mask spear-fished a hundred yards offshore where there were rocks and a barrier reef. Once from a boat he caught a thirty-pound grouper and sold it to the proprietor of Sea View, who had been in films and displayed on a wall by the desk a photo of himself on a date with

Elizabeth Taylor. At Christmas and then occasionally after that Dagger filled in as bartender at Sea View.

Some nights cross-legged before his fire he'd open a cube of over-priced Spam, and if the island schoolmaster was there they'd look at the sizzling mold of browning pink meat and the schoolmaster would tell what a treat Spam had been in England during the war. Dagger took his supper off the coals and offered the schoolmaster some Bacardi and told him about folk life in New Jersey when he was growing up. He'd just missed War II and had matriculated his way out of the Korean. The schoolmaster, a burly man in shorts who was strong in maths, Empire history, and games, would allow that he too had missed the war in that sense of having been just too young to serve; he'd been evacuated north and still recalled looking down over his chin at his identity badge. His wife had been evacuated too and the separation from her mother and father had left in her something permanent she couldn't quite put her finger on. The schoolmaster was at present much concerned about the British government's renewing his two-year contract.

Read vita at signal; list positions in reverse order beginning with most recent: One warm February morning before he was awake enough to switch on his transistor to get the Bahama Islands weather and the Nassau news, he heard (as if all around him) the boys' familiar cries and a clattering of wood muted by open air, and for a second—for he saw he was still dreaming of California—he thought the boys were hammering up something out of all the driftwood he had looked at but never picked up off the beach in California when he was busy reading political theory in the San Francisco bay area, yet simultaneously had the thought that dreams are a species of sleep-teaching with a key difference that Dagger unfortunately lost just as he found it in his retreating dream. But he rubbed the sand from his eyes and dug at the salt in his bushy dark eyebrows thinking of two girls from Philadelphia in the hotel bar last night to whom he said he would be constant.

He saw that the boys were making a cross.

List education beginning with most recent institution and working backward: He had told his friends he was bound for the Gulf of Honduras because he wanted to find a long-lost schoolmate from Monmouth County, New Jersey, who was reputed to be down there diving for bullion, a fraternity brother. But he'd ended by answering an ad in an Oakland paper and driving to New York, where he encountered a Brooklyn cabdriver who was selling out and heading for the Virgin Islands to put his money in a boat and go into the moving business, and Dagger said he'd worked on charters out of New Orleans so when he left New York for the South Dagger had a loose arrangement with the cabdriver. But after transporting a car to Florida Dagger met a young painting contractor who'd just bought his first plane which he said he needed in his work; so Dagger flew with the contractor and his wife to Eleuthera, but then, being on principle opposed to round trips, he moved on across the bay to a smaller island when the painting contractor after an eventful week returned to his various commitments.

Give dates of each: there were eight hundred blacks on the island and two hundred resident whites. The Mayor of New York City once rented a beach house here for ten days. The schoolmaster did not visit Dagger often at night, for his wife disapproved; but he offered Dagger their porch swing in case of rain. The schoolmaster's father had been a Liverpool docker before the war and claimed to have played baseball with American sailors.

Dagger said to the schoolmaster, I'm between jobs you might say.

The schoolmaster wore a full moustache. He said he had never in fact believed his late father's claim to have played baseball in Liverpool. Dagger said, I believe him.

The lady at the guest house bawled Dagger out but liked him. He had told her the trouble with her station wagon was the differential. She did not like what was happening in Nassau but thought there still would never be a takeover. Her brother was in the glass business. She went to Miami to shop twice a year. The Anglican vicar Mr. Ash with a vintage tan over his face gave Dagger a nod when they met along the bright, hibiscus-scented streets. The real estate agent, who was always stamping out a cigarette, always asked Dagger if he was in the market for a house, and laughed loudly at his joke. Dagger would stroll across the island at lunchtime and sit under the fig tree by the combined ferry-ticket, ice cream, and clothing shop and discuss Harlem, which he had never actually been to, with two natives, one of whom had but had come home and now worked at the hotels. Dagger would discuss the future of the islands with these two. He would ask if they were ready for freedom from exploitation and they'd laugh and say It's OK if you got the money, and turn the talk back to cricket or English and American football because that would get Dagger going on some mad thing like the strangeness of a ball game where you had to keep hands off—so English, so un-American.

87

Dagger wanted to start a seminar on the beach. He was visited at his lean-to by natives and vacationers alike, a Toronto lawyer, a girl who had just quit her job in Chicago, a New York broker, the local Gospel preacher who tried in vain to get Dagger to play cornet Sunday night.

Date of birth, name of father, living, deceased. One Sunday in February after a night tending bar and a dream about dreams, Dagger woke to shouts and clatter, wood hammering wood. He kept his eyes tight shut. He knew it was his friends the little black boys from the bay side who had evidently not found any fallen coconuts in the road to sit down and crack and so had come the three-quarters of a mile across from their side of the island.

They were crucifying one of their number, tying his hands with seaweed and rotten twine to the crosspiece which had been nailed to an upright Dagger through one eye identified by its half-stripped white and black paint as a plank of driftwood he had set on the east side of his lean-to to keep sand from blowing.

Two little girls in bikinis who were at the hotel Dagger worked at were watching from the brink of a trench as deep perhaps as long, from which some of the boys were pelting their happy sacrifice with sand. One little girl jumped into the trench and could barely be seen as she began pitching sand too while the victim loosely strung upon the cross gave exaggerated yells of agony.

It was a good sight and Dagger looked under his plastic poncho for some fig newtons to give out but found a can of beer and sat up and opened it.

Most recent position: his knees cracked comfortably as he crossed his legs.

After he introduced himself into the University of Maryland operation in England some months later and thus gained access to low-priced audio equipment, he became interested in cassette collage, still later in the technical implications of semigratuitous switch-back and switch-forward juxta-sequences using eight-track cartridges, and he planned to work out his own way of cutting to an earlier or later track without having to start at its beginning.

When accused by one of his older U.S. Air Force students of being a closet-radical coming on as a professional discussion-provoker who was in reality a hired conflict-monger, he replied that he was designed to fit most systems.

Name (last name first): Who wants to know? said Dagger, rising when the father in his maroon Bermudas marched the little girls over to the lean-to and demanded to know Dagger's name.

When Dagger said, Who wants to know? the man said, Never mind who *I* am, just you explain how come you just sat there in your hobo jungle and let my little girls be subjected to God knows what. Dagger sat down again. But she liked it, he said.

The father said, If I didn't have these kids with me.

Keeps you out of trouble, said Dagger.

Do you think you own this beach, said the man.

List institutions, looking backward and forward: The little girl was being lifted out of the trench. She was screaming and laughing. She helped the black boys heap up sand for her to stand on to be high enough to have her arms properly tied to the cross. On the ocean side of the trench her sister was jumping up and down.

Date, place of birth: February 1928, Freehold, New Jersey.

Part-time, University of Maryland, U.K. Division, 1963 to present.

But possessed of a full-timer's card. Which, to his unofficial captain's status, added access to U.S. Government stores—cameras, liquor, booze, or for instance groceries (which he and eventually his wife Alba with him put in a supply of as a rule one morning toward the end of each week).

6 | The silent softball game came first. But five or six weeks after we shot it Dagger said let's put the Softball Game between the Hawaiian-in-the-Underground and the Suitcase-Slowly-Packed. This left the Unplaced Room first.

Opening our film with a silent softball game might have made us look like Super-8 weekenders, and I pointed this out. But the Unplaced Room had an austere dimension. And a real live U.S. deserter. And something genuine I felt Dagger had helped create without quite knowing what he was doing.

Not that the softball game wasn't genuine. T. R. Ismay, our retired Wall Street lawyer who lived nearest of any of us to Hyde Park, umpired. Dagger got bats and balls and bases through his Air Force connections, not to mention a catcher's mask. The bases were the regulation softball distance apart, and the Hyde Park grounds-keepers maybe had never thought about why our bases stayed put, namely with long anchoring spikes. Maybe they didn't care. Maybe they were thinking of the next tea-break. Or do they work on Sunday?

This Sunday, what with the camera, Dagger didn't play first.

He could use a higher *f*-number than he'd expected, and hence increase his depth of field, because light under these pleasant English overcasts can turn out to be broader or more solid than you think putting it up against the high blue heavens of New York. But the overcast broke and the clouds that made the sky all the bluer would come and go across the spring sun so suddenly you might have felt that an umbrella was being passed back and forth over our part of the park.

I was at short for an inning, came up once and doubled down the right-field line. I stood on the bag and talked to the second base-man about where he lived—he said he was here and there—I found Dagger getting a long shot of me. I had told him to leave me out of the film.

He did some hollering at Cosmo to watch the side-arm de-livery and wrist snap, for Cosmo was pitching. When I left the game and joined Dagger in foul territory between first and home, the Beaulieu was on the tripod ready. The camera seemed alive and way ahead of us.

Jenny stood over the guerrilla-theater boy from Connecticut who'd been playing second when I got my hit. He was waiting on one knee to bat. He stood up, she giggled. He started to turn away, she slapped him on the upper arm. He danced away from her and she ran him up the imaginary third-base line, and Dagger tracked them for four or five seconds. When Jenny tried a few moments later to get into the game in the outfield, Cosmo puffed and frowned and said, Wait three innings.

But then Jenny disappeared.

But my son Will stayed and even got into the film. For when Cosmo unloaded his fastball, a black man from the Bronx who some-times played if he was down from Oxford for the weekend lifted a foul straight back over the head of Cosmo's catcher.

This, as anyone would know who recognized the saber scar on the cheek or for that matter the red tan and blue flag on the bulging right arm with forty-eight infinitesimal pricks, or for that matter the depigmentation on the back of his horny right hand, was Savvy Van Ghent, Xavier Van Ghent, the UPI correspondent—and he didn't push off his mask but turned and plunged after the ball all the way to a pedestrian path and a bench where an elderly couple, kerchief and cap, sat smoking. Dagger panned behind home, then halted, didn't follow Savvy or the ball. I realigned my eyes to approxi-mate the lens direction. It was a long shot of two men with black hair and white shirts and a woman with apricot hair and a green blouse sitting on the grass ignoring the game—nice touch, Dag—and since my son Will was kneeling near us, Dagger must have caught the crest of his chestnut hair the same shade as Lorna's when Will turned toward me to point out that in cricket this shot behind the wicket keeper couldn't have been foul and might have gone for four, and through some narrowing accent forced by the camera I heard my boy's clear London English instead of—what?—the whole known person I live with who echoing down the stairwell or lecturing us at the kitchen table may seem no more English than American.

We were in color, so my sense of what we shot that opening Sunday is all the closer to what might have emerged from the emulsion had the reel ever been developed. The camera is like a pure glove reaching untouching to the thing it takes. Hyde Park London would not have been anybody's identifiable turf unless, say, you picked out a policeman's (or, as American visitors say, a bobbie's) black helm above a blond beard, or letters on a distant vendor's white pushcart spelling *ice lollies* or *cornet* (which is English for *cone*). Dagger never once aimed at three small boys playing cricket, bowler batsman wicket-keeper, and if he did once flick over two veering white triangles you'd have to know Hyde Park well to know they were toy yachts sailing the Serpentine, and I suspect his depth of field wasn't great enough to pick them up clearly.

Even with inflation the life most of us had here was good. You didn't need our umpire's great blocks of Telephone stock, Corning Glass, or Standard of New Jersey. You didn't have to send your children to expensive schools and commute twice a week to your American firm's new offices in Geneva. You didn't have to play poker Friday nights with some smart Fleet Street bachelors, or drink at the French pub in Soho with a relative of Freud's, and you didn't have to be a poet from Kentucky living off a BBC actress. You didn't have to do what I did, or what Dagger did, or like the right-fielder on the side opposing Cosmo's, sit under the British Museum Reading Room's cloudy skylight (or in the warmer North Library when the age or rarity of the book required, though as Savvy Van Ghent's researches claimed, the quality of the girls was not so high) week after week studying the elusive artist-engineer Catherwood till you almost thought you were Catherwood.

No, you might enjoy decent obscurity in your neighborhood watching the postal service decline, your English friend Millan's work get bigger, BBC TV show movies without the interruption of commercials, the London air get cleaner but hold in its smell the same stony tonic that came into the house the first year when Lorna's char at five bob an hour threw open all the windows in any weather. You take the wife to the theater and in the lobby at intermission hear an American explain that this is Shakespeare's only real-time play in which fictive time almost equals our time, Prospero's alchemical time almost equals the time we spend watching. You come to know Millan's friends, and their friends; but after a bad period in the fifties Lorna has made some friends of her own and you begin to move around, begin to make these carefully aimed returns to the States; you get a second London like some second wind, and instead of going home to America on the evening brink of J. F. Dulles's death and its advance lamentations, you stay: you get off the red double-decker two steps early and cut through a park always unexpectedly large and secret and sloping: you answer your parents' letters, for this is long before your mother on one of her visits brings a cassette recorder so you and Lorna and especially Jenny and Billy (with their accents that have a Cockney force their grandparents can't hear) can send cassettes instead of air letters—Billy at the word-game stage. You read the American news in the *Guardian*. One night years later you and your closest American friend cook up a film sort of: you've begun to think about London and England again, but you are comfortable, you live here in one way or another; but the altercation that now stops the Sunday softball game and draws the players in around the pitching rubber seems outlandishly to come from your own fear here in the third inning that there is something wrong about the film you and Dagger DiGorro are beginning; Dagger's camera is singing its gnatlike note at the Connecticut actor who's now standing on second and pounding his glove; Jenny's nowhere in sight, and the actor, as Cosmo raises his voice to the batter who has approached him from home plate and whose name eludes me as I watch the actor, moves idly around the disputants and keeps going and crosses the imaginary third-base line and without telling anyone walks away from the weekly American softball game. Dagger has unscrewed the camera base from the tripod, and now like my own head wandering from what we were there for that Sunday into the issue of whether or not the motorbike that brought Jenny home at 3 A.M. was the Connecticut guerrilla-theater actor, who indeed rides a motorbike, Dagger seems to let the man crossing behind the group at the pitching rubber draw his focus off over the third-base line into foul territory, which for the Connecticut actor is no longer even that, for he's stepped out of the game. When I murmur in Dagger's ear, Hey I wonder where that guy thinks he's going, Dagger takes his finger off the thumb button at the top of the pistol grip, hands me the Beaulieu, and heads for the pitching rubber where Cosmo is loudly claiming the batter was crowding the plate, and as the batter lowers his voice to a new intensity his left hand which has never dropped the bat tightens and through the midst of the group the blond bat with its meat end resting on the English grass seems a sinister and potential pole the mere people there depend on.

That Sunday night I wrote an account of that first filming and though that first scene the softball game was silent I included Dagger's words and Cosmo's and Will's but could not recall the batter's name, and having faithfully recorded the filmed origin of the dispute about Cosmo's low and inside smokeball, I found in the corner of my eye the Connecticut actor, a slight figure in tie-dyed jeans, passing behind the others at the center of the diamond, then emerging alone, strolling on and on as if the softball game were in another time, ambling off toward a pedestrian path and looking beyond it distinctly *at* something, though what I couldn't tell. There was a woman maybe fifty yards beyond the walk and she seemed shadowed by the tree she leaned against and at that instant Dagger called to me not to go crazy now—for I'd raised the Beaulieu just to follow the guerrilla actor through the viewfinder for the hell of it—thinking what prospects a boy like that could have acting antiwar skits on street corners in Battersea with an undergraduate group from Oxford—and I lowered the camera and the thought of Jenny sobered me too much so I called back Christ I'm not shooting!—I had suddenly registered that the woman off by the tree was indeed what the guerrilla-theater actor was aiming for; but Dagger's jibe was itself now interrupted by new words between Cosmo and the batter he'd dusted with his fastball. But now it wasn't You fat blowfish, where'd you learn to play ball, the only way you going to get me out is keep me ten feet away from the plate, and chawing tobacco out there won't help—

Nor Cosmo's ordinary noise: You so close to the plate I got to pitch behind you to get it over, take the shades off, man, you'll see better.

It was something else now, a new ball game they were speaking to each other: Got nothing better to do than hang around the park, the batter said, and I registered his words but still at that moment not exactly him, for way off to my left, though I wasn't exactly looking at them, the guerrilla-theater actor was moving with

93

a glow around him toward the woman at the tree. And then Cosmo, holding the white softball up so you could see the black seams and turning it this way and that the way he always did before his whirlwind double-three-hundred-sixty-degree windup, all of which Dagger had caught in the second or third minute of shooting, but now no windup, just the turning of the ball up near Cosmo's jaw, a sort of screwing toward his new words, Cosmo said, Listen I did my time back home, man, my number came up, I quit the collegiate power structure and I did my two years in the army, man, and I been here long enough to know a free-loader when I see one so don't shit me, man, you don't like it here go back to Copenhagen, those sixteen-year-olds you been picking up.

The woman turned as if to stand behind the tree, but I think she was moving off ahead of the actor, but what happened now made it hard to follow her out of the shadow of the tree, for the batter—the same one Dagger had shot his first time up the first inning, big orange and silver and cherry-colored rings on his fingers, his body wiggling up and down trying—and successfully then—to get a walk off Cosmo—came right back at Cosmo now: Cosmo, a vet like you is just another poor pig, you're a veteran of like Fort Dix, you never got to California much less Vietnam, and you're over here because it's a soft touch—the batter increasingly nameless the more I reached directly for his name, lifted his bat and there was Dagger taking it with both hands.

Back of third an English schoolboy in gray cap, gray knee-socks, monogrammed gray jacket, and dark blue shorts had a box camera over his eyes. He snapped us and turned away. I felt Jenny somewhere close, as if I were confined to a viewfinder's tunnel-window ruling her out below and above.

Cosmo said, What you doing in the Underground all day, moving hash? The batter left his Louisville slugger in Dagger's hands and lunged at Cosmo who with a wrist flick released the ball over-hand and hit the other assailant in the bridge of the nose. I almost had his name.

Why did the batter not retaliate? He carried his bumped nose away toward Umpire Ismay.

I saw the hit just as exactly as in the second inning our Beaulieu caught the Indian-head patch on the seat of the right-fielder's jeans and the drag bunt he laid down letting the bat give slightly with such finesse that the camera must have caught that instant of cushioned impact when the ball's substance tried to melt

94

back upon the curved wood of the bat and the right-fielder seemed to bear the ball around with him magically so my eye believed that if he hadn't dropped the bat to head toward first he could have carried the softball indefinitely on the front of the bat by the sheer force of attention, like what he gave his long-time British Museum subject Catherwood. I said to Dagger as the camera stopped that it reminded me of the time in college when I'd put down a bunt, the third baseman overthrew first so I went to second, the first baseman overthrew second and I went to third, the shortstop overthrew third and I ran home only to be denied a bunt home run when the third baseman nailed me at the plate. Dagger said hold onto that, we can use that.

He had given up on peacemaking, but the batter, having walked away holding his nose and his bat, had been persuaded to play ball again by Umpire Ismay and was going to resume with a 3 and 0 count. Tempest in a teapot. Umpire Ismay had been rolling a cigarette and Dagger at the Beaulieu caught the concluding lengthwise lick.

Dagger with the camera on the tripod again showed his toothed grin beneath the moustache like a silent-film villain's. I said, We could tape me telling that about the bunt homer and make it our sound track here.

The next pitch jumped straight through like a white weight —give Cosmo credit, he had a fastball. I said in Dagger's ear, When we edit we'll slow it down there and run a few stills to fix the ball. Dagger murmured, Depends on the lab.

Cosmo walked his man on the next pitch. But Dagger fooled me, he wasn't focused on the plate but a bit to the right across the third-base line. The batter—whose name, Nash, came to mind when Jenny typed my notes—dropped his bat and trotted off, while Savvy Van Ghent complained to Ismay that Cosmo's letup should have been strike two, while Cosmo as if he couldn't resist called out to Nash, If you got to blow up the subway go do it in New York.

Nash turned at first base, shrugged as if at Cosmo but his face had blanched. But Cosmo may have sensed the shrug was aimed beyond him, for he turned toward third and behind third stood an Indian or Pakistani in a white shirt who was looking at Cosmo, who himself now shrugged.

I believe that I, rather than the camera, got the full gaze of this new figure just before he turned his back and put his hands in his pockets and went off. But Dagger panned around to a medium shot of Nash leading off first—just as Nash's nose began to bleed as if the camera's focus had drawn the blood.

My boy Will called, You're bleeding. And when Nash touched knuckle to nostril, Cosmo threw to first and caught him off.

Dagger had every bit of this, and now switched off. I took the camera gingerly and through the viewfinder observed the Indian. He turned again and stopped and when I opened my other eye he seemed to make Cosmo look at him. Dagger said, Let's see what's left.

Reviewing all this now weeks, months later late at night in Sub's New York flat high above a woman's streetcorner soprano delivering a demented oration, I knew with a new natural ease as if I'd often known and it were somewhere among the luminous inhalations of my head, that this man, yes this man in the white shirt, had been the Indian I was later to see in the Knightsbridge gallery. He was Cosmo's Indian.

Godlike I said, Get a long shot of these girls pushing the push-chairs (*strollers* you say in American).

Right, said Dagger, and swung toward right-centerfield and ran through a hundred frames or so as one of the tots lurched up in his harness and tried to fall out. Dagger said, That's it. Two hundred feet.

We had another spool but didn't want the hassle of loading it in the light and threading it through those sprocket wheels so the divider would go in just right.

Our first footage was finished and the game was only into the third inning. The sequence was too full of nothing and I had missed something, yet something possibly not on the film; however, like some roving sense I hadn't controlled, Dag's focus had shifted with such natural drift I would have to watch it next time.

I couldn't see opening the film with that softball game, and later I couldn't see anything wrong with Dag's idea that it should go between the Suitcase and the Hawaiian.

I woke to coffee deep in my nostrils and saw through my narrowed lids the smell standing in the air's bright dust and listened to Sub in the kitchen taking a step here, a step there, having breakfast this third morning of my stay, and of all things Monty Graf's remark last night about *two* films seemed now, as I awoke, to fill the long evening of that inaugural Sunday we shot the softball game, for Jenny didn't come home till one and Lorna was off singing the Fauré Requiem with her chorus and Will had shut himself in, and as I wrote the opening record of the film, I needed family sounds around me. Our road in Highgate is by a quiet square, and on a Sunday evening you'll hardly hear a car or a passing laugh until the pubs let out at ten thirty, the kids who go by don't live in Highgate many of them, they come from around North London to the old courtyard pub called The Flask at the end of our road. Lorna came into the house at midnight with her music in her hand, a flush on her cheek, and her eyes dark, and I put down my pen. Her head snuggled down next to mine. Her hair covered her profile, I didn't see her eyes but smelled her vanilla scalp. She was reading my page and it seemed from the tilt of her head the last lines not the top lines.

So what I think she read was this: that after Jenny chased the actor up toward third base he circled and made it back to the plate ahead of her just as the batter struck out on a rising pitch that Savvy had to go up for. The actor grabbed the bat and Jenny stopped short at the umpire's elbow and she turned as if in a continuous motion and sank down cross-legged but so close that Ismay asked her to move and she got up with her head and long light hair dipping for an instant to the green grass, then interrupted Cosmo's full-circle windup to the actor asking if she could play now.

Sub seemed to know I was awake. He asked from the kitchen if I wanted a cup of tea.

Lorna mouthed my lower lip. She said, Is Jenny in?

I said I hadn't seen her since suddenly not seeing her at the game, and I blamed Cosmo because he needn't have said she had to wait three innings to get into the game. Lorna said it wasn't Cosmo who brought her home on the motorbike last night. I said, That actor's at least twenty-five.

Dagger phoned just as Jenny was coming in at 1 A.M. He'd lined up two surprising guys, he said, and we would let them sit at a table and rap. I said I hoped he could get hold of a Nagra unit and an omnidirectional mike and he said he didn't know about a Nagra but we'd do a tape, never fear, and he said he'd known from the beginning I was a born sound-man and he thought it was great that I'd dreamed up this idea of the Unplaced Room, and he told about his Uncle Stan in Yonkers who got one of the old wire recorders before the war and when he heard his voice on it he got a whole other idea himself, grew a moustache, and left his wife and went to live in New Jersey where he became a phone salesman for encyclopedias. Dagger asked if Jenny had come home and I said Why and he merely said, We'll put her in the outfield next Sunday, I think she's got ability. I wondered what made our filmed softball game either typical or on the other hand one particular softball game and not another.

Jenny was in bed, lights out, by the time I hung up and went upstairs, though I wasn't so sure what I wanted to ask about the Connecticut actor, just sure I should speak to her, whatever came out. I didn't put the upstairs hall light on.

I opened Jenny's door (I never do) and she said in the dark, Did you know Reid's from Ridgefield, Connecticut? His father's in real estate. Oh, I said, his name's *Reid*—you mean the actor. I've never been to Connecticut, said Jenny.

I looked into the dark, my daughter wasn't waiting for me to speak.

Reid built a dome on his parents' property. I want to see it. He never studied acting.

She wasn't waiting for me to speak, she was contemplating probably a number of things, how he swung a bat, or walked, or stepped down on the starter pedal, or stood when speaking lines onstage though I'd heard guerrilla theater was something else—how he listened to her, or took off her shoes, pulled off her American bluejeans that I'd paid for. I said goodnight and shut the door, turning the knob not to make a sound as if that would smooth a cut to some new footage of our film.

Lorna was near the doorway of our room in a blue bra, her near thigh in shadow, the light behind her setting the skin aglimmer beneath her Venus hair. She said, You're betting your soul on this film. Why?

I went to her and murmured something to the effect that she was my Connecticut, my California, my Hawaii. I undid the top hook but she turned away and moved swaying to the cupboard, and reached over her shoulders to get the other hook.

Was I asleep? I felt the knob and lock of Sub's front door turn so finely he could have been entering, not leaving.

What did he do weekends?

The Beaulieu, as I had hoped, had caught the name of Umpire Ismay's tobacco tin just as a flake of leaf fell to the English grass. If I knew these things and had even for mood's sake recorded in my diary what Savvy Van Ghent had said to Dagger after the game, still I did not know exactly what Claire was up to with Monty Graf, whether she knew of the 8-mm. cartridges we'd saved, what my man in glasses posing as Monty had hoped to find in my diary when he went through my suitcase, whether Cosmo's Indian who'd shown an interest in the Beaulieu had known Dagger and Alba's flat was empty the morning the film was destroyed, and how close Phil Aut's connection was with the Knightsbridge gallery he owned exhibiting his wife Jan Graf's work, and happening to employ the very same Indian. As for meeting Claire at the scene of the strange murder Wednesday—not to mention being for a moment bound *between* Claire and Jim—I'd decided I'd also know more about that.

The woman Gilda had seemed to locate me significantly at the event.

The charter man when I eventually got a phone call through to him had left a message to phone him at four. I had to be around for a call from Aut so I could turn down the inevitable lunch with my man Whitehead at the science-hobby firm. I called him and he talked nonstop about liquid crystals and a firm in Bristol that his file showed I had never mentioned, and now they'd written direct to New York for a wholesale price on Encapsulated Liquid Crystals in the sheets that show temperature variation by color, and the discs that do roughly the same but are advertised as a Wet Show. Whitehead had told them they should try also the Non-Encapsulated LC Kit which gives you great freedom in experiments with air density, friction heat, and thermal fingerprints. He couldn't quote them a wholesale price because he himself got the liquid crystals practically retail from a warehouse right in New York. He didn't see why the Bristol people hadn't gone through me. Evidently I hadn't gotten to them. The market over there wasn't looking so good; how did I explain that? Somebody'd said liquid crystals were revolutionary in the market, keeping pace with what was happening in several branches of science, he forgot exactly, it was a space spinoff. But like, think of those English kids in that famous school system, and the scientific tradition in Britain (*Breaking the Sound Barrier* had a rerun on TV), and all those kids with their insects and their microscopes and their three-inch reflectors ruining their eyes—liquid crystals for crying out loud were a natural for that market—well what did *I* think? vat vass der problem (he laughed), brain-drain? (He laughed.) Better joke than he knew—and he'd forgotten that that somebody who'd said LC displays were of revolutionary significance was me. But while Whitehead went on to retail to me as if I did not know then the practical applications and the fun things a boy could do with liquid crystals like testing the warmth of your fingerprint by the colors that emerged on the encapsulating plastic sheet, it was plain that Whitehead for all his happy LC slogan "DIGITAL COLOR CALORIZING!" had no feel for the real inner properties of liquid crystals: structure of a solid but mobility of a liquid, structure ordered clearly yet not rigid in the normal course of three dimensions, molecules bonded like a liquid's, other properties complex and marketable. Whitehead was saying again "So call me Red," and he was saying "So why you're so formal? You're in England too long."

I know where I am. And it is something of a mystery. His name's Whitehead like mine is Rap Brown. The New York "So call me Red" didn't fit the firmly modulated warning in what he said about Bristol. I was potentially redundant. But nothing seemed inevitable yet.

Or was I envisioning from my Sub-encapsulated headquarters a casting off of everything inessential to the film? I asked what was new. He said some audio-visual stuff for schools. I said did he know a Phil Aut. There were two rings and then he said, Can I put you on Hold, and I said, I'll be in touch.

But if Phil Aut phoned, what could I offer him in the way of a threat? Tell him what happened in the Unplaced Room and guess what it was he didn't want to hear? I became the film's sound, not at all an echo but (from a written diary) a delayed voice now printed on the original image's absence, though Aut could not know if the Unplaced Room had survived the fire. I was figuring he knew through Claire that a fraction of the film did still exist.

A lot had not happened.

It was well to be at last at the Unplaced Room. I must find its proper audience. You can't just recall something, like Savvy after the Softball Game telling Dagger he was afraid UPI might reassign him to St. Louis.

A lot never happened in England.

Jenny took Dagger to a shop near us one lunchtime to pick up a couple of emergency wine glasses—she liked to be baited by Dagger and she may have told him things she'd not tell Lorna—and the two proprietors of this smart shop with its window full of casseroles and design mugs and French vegetable choppers were locking up—a white man and a black girl—and they refused to make the sale—closed one to two—so Dagger said what would happen if they broke their rule and the man said, We couldn't have lunch together. But across our own lunch table Jenny afterward turned on Dagger saying, Fair enough, after all they've a right. Dagger got right to her saying, No one has any rights, Jenny, and as for fairness, that's the great empty virtue; and when Jenny said, But fairness is in fact why you like living in England, Dagger laughed and said she was so right, fairness was like loyalty, and Jenny got mad and said he didn't take her seriously. She took her glass and as she drank, Dagger said, I'll drink a toast to not taking you seriously, and he drank and I drank and Jenny drank her whole glass, which was an old-fashioned glass, and Will asked if Dagger could get some thunderclaps again this year for July 4th.

But Dagger's footwork, however prone to seasonal gout, seemed unconvincing when we lost our film. Look, he said, if we could get it back, then sure let's go after it, but we can't.

I said, We might get something—like what was the motive? —passing vandal breaks in when you just happen to be out, leaves I don't know how many camera lenses and a miniature telly and a hundred pounds cash in a cupboard he's taken the trouble to jimmy open, and three new Sony cassette-recorders unopened in their boxes—but wait, this fellow is a cinephobe, smells film in quantity, and passing your house that morning his crazy nostrils inflated scenting twenty-five hundred feet of movie film and up he came to your flat and, if I may reverse the likeness, saw like a tourist-vampire what he could smell.

Something may happen yet, said Dagger, but so we find out who did it, what then? Beat up on him? confiscate his wife?

Maybe my friend was getting tired. But hadn't he cared as much as I? Think how he'd darted from face to face at Stonehenge, from robes to giant stone to bluejeans, from one of the new Druids to the American mute with his green beret to the American Indian we'd dragooned through the little long-haired English woman at the bonfire in Wales—back to the midnight mumbo-jumbo which in some sentimental transcendence engrossed the lay cast into a scene not false, not trivially tourist, that through a luck like magic seemed then—and even now when I know some of what else was going on— to complete our film, so I almost thought Dagger's sense of it was like mine. Such intentness, the on and off of the Beaulieu motor, the certain passionate defensiveness of rhythm, the concentration of forehead, mouth, wrist, shoulder that framed Dagger off from all the others there who unlike him were, until the last invisible sprocket, potential for these last feet of our film. No, I could understand in his later resignation only fatigue, not reason. For he had been as much into that film as I.

At least he didn't say now, Well anyway we shot it.

Yet if I failed here now in New York, that's what I'd be saying: At least I tried.

But if I took the gloves off, my openings might disappear and there'd be nothing to get hold of.

Well, as I was checking to see if in the pages I'd brought there were any references to the Unplaced Room, Monty Graf phoned. Had I thought about his proposition? I said I thought I might sell the diary as a scenario for a feature film. He said Very funny, and said by the way I didn't expect him to believe we'd only had one small rush and the rest hadn't been processed. For why have that and nothing else?

It's certainly implausible, I said.

I think your film isn't destroyed, he said.

I would like to think that, I said.

And you and DiGorro are holding out for something.

If so, I said, why have I had no offer from Aut?

You haven't fed him enough of the diary.

Haven't fed him any of it.

The guy who gave you those pages works for Aut. But OK, how does the stabbing fit the pattern?

Claire can't have seen much of it, I said.

But you seem to have seen a lot in it, Cartwright.

I looked at the phone receiver by my chin thinking the gloves were coming off.

I was not speaking while thinking. I was only thinking, while there was either silence on the line or Monty Graf speaking, mentioning again that we were holding out for a big payday (but not suggesting we were blackmailing anyone), mentioning the time of the stabbing (but not mentioning the florist's). I was thinking Sub would be in the nation's capital till Sunday, and Monty Graf seemed to conceal more about my presence at and interest in the stabbing incident than I thought Claire (unless she had information beyond her own actual experience) could have given him to conceal.

So he had gotten to Gilda.

But her position had to be merely an accidental observer's.

Gilda, if Gilda, was an opening to an avenue opened only through other openings. Your vehicle passes at speed and one slot open shows another slot beyond so long as you glimpse at the instant your vehicle comes into line.

What opened Gilda to Graf?

All right, I said before summarily hanging up, you yourself said I was in trouble. So I need someone I can trust.

I phoned the florist's at the accident corner hoping Gilda would answer.

She said little except she'd drop up on the way home after work. I didn't think the florist was her husband.

I could no more have asked Graf how he'd arrived at Gilda

(as I was sure he in fact had) than I could quite explain why we'd
put off processing our exposed film except that we'd tacitly wanted to
get it all together first (maybe worried too about how good it was,
though to judge from the rush the focusing and light were right),
and twice Dagger's man in Soho whom I'd not met and who was
going to give us a break on price had said Hang on till Monday week,
and then besides we were on the move a bit, and on our own respective businesses in addition to the film, Dagger part-time teaching for
the University of Maryland at the U.S. base at Bentwaters, I among
other things arranging for five seven-foot leather chesterfields to be
made and shipped to the States, my price only a little more than a
third the New York retail for the same sofa—and all this made the
delay in processing the film seem natural enough.

In the diary pages I'd packed for the trip there were only the
two references to the Unplaced Room. One was the last-minute
thought that lavalier mikes round the neck might give more presence
to each speaker and even be easier to hide. But Dagger borrowed an
omnidirectional and we stuck it behind an earthen ewer, ran the
cable off the back of the table and around the outer legs of the
deserter's chair, which took the evidence pretty well off camera. We
told our principals please not to pour.

The other reference was in my record of an explanation some
weeks later to my son Will the night before our climactic Stonehenge;
he'd asked how the Nagra sound unit kept in phase with the Beaulieu
and I told him—albeit with mere terms—that the camera has in its
motor a sync pulse generator whose output frequency is exactly
proportional to the camera's optical record. But finding this second
reference on a diary page I found also something else and it was in
my head, not on paper: it was something I remembered: that in the
midst of this clear *abc* given to my serious son—in fact I believe
exactly *between* reflecting on the banality of what was said in the
Unplaced Room and on the other hand wondering (*a*) what even
Will whose electricity puts mine to shame would be able through
these technical terms to know in the moist isobars of his fingertips,
and (*b*) if my own idea for the Stonehenge scene would survive on
film—I had seen again (and now for more than that instant of actual
glimpse) a thing that the featured hands in Suitcase Slowly Packed
had slipped between the black V-neck sweater and the green-and-
white plastic bottle of shampoo which Lorna and I use: the thing was
a face, a snapshot of a man's face which had been apparently a
bookmark in a paperback that had been knocked off the adjacent

chair when the hands picked up a pair of red-white-and-blue beaded moccasins and the snapshot had fallen out. I'd been close enough to glance but not really look, for I was holding a mike just off camera close enough to catch the voice of the hands. The actor from Connecticut arrived just as we finished shooting and I forgot to ask Jenny about the snapshot—for it was Jenny whose hands packed that immemorial suitcase and who decided what to pack. Later when Dagger was praising her for a steady but unrehearsed-looking naturalness, I thought maybe he was thinking how when the book dropped the hands casually picked up the snapshot and packed it, then the shampoo, then the book. And days, weeks later the eve of Stonehenge the picture came back with Will in our garden and the technical explanation I reeled out for him as we both stared down at our tortoise in the twilight, its claws and snake-head withdrawn into the stone of its shell—for that afternoon Dagger had said we'd use the Suitcase Slowly Packed not on its own but as a cut-in shot in the middle of the following scene, the Marvelous Country House. I hadn't liked the idea, I guess partly because it subordinated Jenny's role, but I figured we could negotiate when we came to the editing. It was a dark snapshot but I wouldn't swear it wasn't color.

Gilda came early. Before she came I phoned Outer Film. I couldn't get Phil Aut and I passed on the message that one of his employees had broken into a friend of mine's apartment and I was getting the police on it through an influential person of my acquaintance named Monty Graf. The secretary said Mr. Aut was flying to London tonight.

I phoned the charter man at four and just as he was saying What else do you do to keep busy at that end? the doorbell went and before I could shelve the receiver I said, If I wanted to could you get me a charter-rate flight sooner than the return I've got?

Gilda wore a flowered raincoat. She looked all around her.

Back on the phone I said, I mean like a charter within a charter.

The charter man said, You could get to be my best customer.

He gave his home number and I said I'd be in touch.

Gilda's green-flowered mac lay between us on the brown couch which concealed inside its folded day bed mattress my blanket. I knew the blanket to be the same magenta as the fitted carpet Rose had paid a lot of money for. Gilda stared at it. Upon the carpet's magenta ground was a fine labyrinth of apricot lines that gave a kind of Moslem chic.

I don't have much time, she said. She was different today. We looked at each other's knees. I thought I was at last at the beginning, and I thought of the Unplaced Room which, if our film had not been destroyed, would have come first.

Listen, I said. I know.

She turned to me and when she spoke the rust-colored enamel butterfly glinted: You want to know what the insurance man asked me?

Yes.

He was insurance like you're the family doctor.

She described him.

She was talking about Monty Graf, who I'd thought must have found the accident scene through Claire but who Gilda said had come with a couple of plainclothesmen and a uniformed sergeant. Monty Graf had identified himself as an insurance investigator but not in the hearing of the policemen. Gilda had offered nothing about me at first and her brother-in-law the proprietor didn't recall me. But Monty Graf had asked if a bearded man in a trenchcoat with a small mole in the middle of his forehead had been at the accident and Gilda added to this that the man had come back again after lunch. She didn't know why she answered nor why her questioner had bothered to identify himself, she liked his soft voice, *it* seemed to be telling *her* things but afterward she knew little more that was new than the name Cartwright. She'd said I was concerned about the stabber, what he looked like, what happened to the car, and it sounded as if her questioner wanted to make sure I had not spoken to the stabber.

Did he tell you anything else besides my name?

What name?

Cartwright.

Oh, she had thought that was his, for he'd said so. She put her raincoat across her lap. She wasn't the same person as before in the florist shop and on the street corner. She wasn't amused, though not against me either.

My name is Cartwright, I said, and I don't know what the stabbing has to do with me. I believe it's important.

I went on: Because I've been making a film.

Gilda stared at the rug. Her eyes went relentlessly over it but her head did not move.

This film was destroyed before it was developed. Can you understand that? And I am finding out why. So I was on my way to see someone who's involved when I happened into this stabbing, but the person I was seeing—who was as I said involved in the film and maybe its destruction—appears down the block behind me and when I see her she turns around and disappears.

That's too bad about the film, said Gilda.

My voice said, What's it matter, nobody reads any more.

I do. Why'd you say that?

They read more in England where we made the film.

Why were you making it in England?

It's where I live.

You don't live here?

I come here, I don't live here.

Where am I, then? said Gilda.

She stood up looking toward the hall at an angle which if her eyes could have moved her would have led toward Sub's bedroom.

I said, A friend's.

Here I thought I was in your place. I saw the unmade bed.

Why did this man use my name, I said.

Gilda sat again and reached for my hand: What kind of film?

Why, if you want to know, it began with an Unplaced Room. Just a room that could be anywhere, that was the point, *a* point.

What kind of a point can you make out of that, said Gilda.

Well look at this room. What's New York about it?

When's your friend coming home?

My friend's in Washington for the weekend.

Gilda stood up and walked to the hall. If you ask me, he called himself Cartwright because he wanted me to tell someone else that a man named Cartwright came asking about the murder.

Tell who?

She slid her right hand into a sleeve, and I found Dagger's Beaulieu eye and at some key distance my naked eye triangulating upon a shimmering apex alternating into color and black and white as if between two ambiguously interesting lens focuses—and I went to Gilda instantly and held the other lapel so she could slip her left hand in.

She waited, not turning.

Helping you on with your flowers, I said.

Gilda still did not turn. You're American, right?

As if she might want to get off with me but, while staring at (or toward) the big unmade bed in Sub's room, wondering if I was circumscribed.

With my finger I drew a circle on her back beginning inside

106

one shoulder blade, touching the neck and her spine above the small.

In the hall her green flowers were dark.

OK, she said, and was at the door. This is interesting, I'm trying to figure if I know something about this that you don't.

She wanted Sub's phone number and I wrote it down for her.

I stood in the open doorway waiting for her elevator, and we didn't speak.

Have a good weekend.

I phoned Claire's answering service and left a question for Monty: Why had he wanted to know if I had spoken to the stabber? Didn't he know Wheeler as well as Claire and I did?

I had dinner alone out Friday and Saturday.

If you are, so to speak, in between people, New York can offer vintage solitude. Both nights I saw big frank films in color. One showed blood darting from a wound in a sheriff's neck. The other looked back only thirty years to an Unplaced Beach (if I may) seen through a 235-carat haze of clear sun and aquamarine to a pair of amber nipples.

When Jenny and the Connecticut actor left the place where the Suitcase had been Slowly Packed, he carried it for her. Four legs and a gray case the contents of which I knew—and a door closing upon our footage. Dagger said, Nice couple.

Alba came out of her kitchen and asked if I'd like some fish soup.

Jenny got home late, but not to the sound of a motorbike. Not a cab either and it was long after the Underground finished, even allowing for a long walk up Highgate Hill from Archway Underground station. I heard what had to be the gray suitcase being set down and then, like stereo, the front door opening from outside and inside. Naturally I had too much else on my mind to be thinking about the snapshot. I had been lying awake for a long time. Lorna facing away from me toward the window said as if out of a little dream, Go to sleep. She could not have known I was awake unless some tempo in my breath opened me to her dream or of course to her own sleepless thought.

Phil Aut's home number wasn't in the Manhattan book.

I went through my own address book in vain.

My diary pages lay on Sub's desk and I thought how sloppy and pompous the boys in the Unplaced Room were, swapping recipes for gelatin dynamite and Hong Kong hors d'oeuvres.

I think I straightened the pages and put my address book squarely on top as a paper weight for the night.

Sunday at 7 A.M. about a minute after I woke, Lorna phoned. Had I slept? What time was it in New York? She'd phoned twice yesterday. She was so tired, hadn't had much sleep. Will had just gone to Stephen's for lunch. My card had come and Jenny had laughed and said she'd in fact asked me to bring back a memory.

There was an expensive silence, the ocean-bed cable kept our pulses dry, Lorna didn't like these calls, coming or going.

Why couldn't you sleep? I said.

The house was broken into after lunch yesterday, she said. Jenny was out, Will was on his way home, I was at rehearsal. I feel so badly, the desk was rifled; what is happening?

They took the film diary?

The second drawer on the left is empty; I'm so sorry.

I did not tell Lorna what I felt. I saw her hair and her shoulders and heard her voice carry out of her eyes into my own voice, my mouth.

I said, I want you.

Lorna said, The young man, the second tenor I told you about who just joined us, he walked to the bus stop with me after rehearsal. He asked if I felt at home in England, I told him how long we'd been here. When I got home the door was open, there were snapshots on the rug and check stubs and letters and bills and stamps and stationery. My music on the piano hadn't been touched, I don't know why it would have been. The desk drawer you keep the diary in was empty. The police came. The lock was ruined and there are scrapes on the door frame. I thought of what that young man had asked me and I thought why the hell didn't we go back years ago. Stupid to think that. Forgive me.

I said, What about the carbon in Jenny's cupboard?

Lorna said, Oh thank God. I don't think they went upstairs.

I want you.

Lorna may have sensed my excitement. I said, Didn't Jenny mention the carbon?

She phoned last night to say she wouldn't be home. I haven't seen her since Friday.

Tell Dagger.

Lorna said, He phoned up. I told him. I said we'd had a card. He said Cosmo of all people had had one.

Did you get hold of a locksmith?

I finally got one through that young man the second tenor.

I didn't tell Lorna what I was going to do. But she said, There's no need to come back.

I said to go upstairs and look in Jenny's cupboard in the box-file on its side underneath her laundry bag. If the carbon wasn't there, phone back at once, screw the expense.

Lorna said, I miss you.

I said, I love you. I've got to think. I'll be in touch in the next few hours.

I shaved and showered with the door open. I made a pot of coffee.

At nine I started to go for my address book but found I knew the charter man's number. I phoned him. There was almost no time, as it turned out. I left my suitcase and day bed open and took only the Joni Mitchell *Blue*. I couldn't find its paper bag.

At Kennedy I thought of some of the people who didn't even know I'd been in New York.

On Cosmo's 3-D card of the Empire State Building I had written CLAIRE WANTS TO KNOW WHERE I SAW YOUR INDIAN FRIEND BEFORE.

The plane was like an Unplaced Room.

A beauty across the aisle had a new soft-yellow tea-rose stuck through her green pullover, the petals like a bud's tight-shut though with the merest flare at the top.

CARRIAGE | Your train like a tunnel draws you home to London from different times, to London from England, home from a small station destined to be defunct near an airbase where Dagger sometimes teaches northeast beyond Ipswich; home less recently from Axminster in the soft southwest coast; or still less recently from the seductive mid-sixties, from Liverpool north and west of London and in a second-class uncompartmented carriage where the cadence of the roadbed drags at the Beatle rock coming from somewhere in the car: your train takes you home to London, the switches up ahead pivot where necessary, bend your thrust so your train, your tunnel makes straight for its terminus, and an avenue is open to its end in Highgate, where your American family live and wait for their American father, a circuit even more open when your eyelids like NAND valves are shut and you are a tunnel in a tunnel.

The South African in his Liverpool bank by the thick waters

of the River Mersey was impressed with your care for detail and your ease about the future—you're one of his Americans—and he names two factory towns and two with new universities—if it's to be a group of, say, five or six bookshops. But dad in Capetown who likewise believes in the new reading public here in the mid-sixties puts up ten thousand pounds only if you deliver what you said, concessions Stateside and from two paperback distributors in London, one of whom you know through a friend of Millan's. But about the other business which your South African associate knows you were up in the Liverpool area for anyway, no questions asked and just as well; it was the subject of more than one letter to your own father back in Brooklyn Heights and easy to discuss in great detail and pleasant for your father to mention to his friends for it sounded so concrete; it was an American-style drive-in cinema, that's all your young South African banker knows. He doesn't know, as your train runs on to London, that the answer after weeks of possibility was negative. The English twilight did it, not the weather, not the thought of all those windscreen wipers sweeping away the rain like a scan on a radar scope so the audience could get through that out-of-focus shield to the adventure and emotion—no, not even the competition from the box, or even inertia (for Liverpool is not only the Beatles). No; after weeks of consideration, it was the long twilight. You are looking forward to a bottle of something Dagger got you from the U.S. armed forces cellars, and looking forward to joking with Lorna about this twilight because it does after all appeal to the imagination. There just are not movie projectors that can adjust to this long twilight. The Merseyside kids in the car park with their transistors in their laps would peer through a light too great for them to see what the projector cannot competitively convey onto the 100 by 60 screen, the American hero and heroine move as if in and out of a clear pastel substance that seems film itself but is the awkward light.

Famished (for there's no buffet on this train), you drowse through distance; there must be two transistors tuned to the same station, one in front, one behind you—and *you* are the station!—as you drowse, that word *film* becomes *flim* your son is at the word-game stage, tiresome, so you drowse toward Euston Station but your train like your son is not tired, nor is Euston, which the planners threaten to give a face-lift but now moves: it is the first railway station on wheels—the space it occupies has become interesting and strange and Cartwright is the one who thought it up and rubber tires at that—but the wheels backfire and the station recedes, and famished you will never get there, not till you (as the teacher once said) go out and come in again, not from Liverpool in the mid-sixties but from Axminster, 1968.

Is there then a River Ax, as at Exeter a River Exe (hence Exmouth, Exminster)? You have been driven through Axminster too preoccupied with other things to look or ask for the minster of Ax if there was one then or now. *Minster* (You will tell Will this August of '68 three months hence as you pass again through Axminster) comes from Latin for *monastery* and means a monastery church but may mean cathedral; hence the great cathedral at York is *Yorkminster*, which is also the name of the so-called French pub in Soho where Will's parents have a drink on a night out in a corner in front of an iron table among framed photographs of prize fighters. Whence cometh Munster cheese, asks Lorna in August crammed in a country taxi under a bag of beach things she couldn't get into any of the cases that are in the boot. Ah, also hence, say you: no doubt a clutch of German monks busied themselves in the crypts filling bags full of curd and punching them till they swung (back and forth) like dripping bells in the cool and sacred air—hence, Munster cheese. I don't believe it, says Jenny, looking out at the rounded seaside pastures of the Devon-Dorset border, but she doesn't care, we are all thinking of the pebbly strand and a lunch of fish and too many moist chips and the cold water English and damp even beyond its wetness and the great bay into which a prince once sailed hoping to overthrow a king, and thinking too of the boatyard that you suddenly by accident have a small piece of, which was why three months ago in May you visited that sea village with its senior citizens laboring up its lanes, one so steep there's a railing to haul your heart up hand over hand—and why, having settled £2500 in that boatyard you taxi back to Axminster through the warmth of May 1968 and take the return train. You lunch at a stand-up bar in the buffet car with a Lyons businessman who knows everything. The explosive events in Paris were inevitable, *les événements;* but De Gaulle must survive. You object: De Gaulle will not survive. The Frenchman has been to Bristol, has seen Brunel's suspension bridge above the Avon gorge at Clifton, *merveilleux,* from below it is very high, for its time ambitious, for any time beautiful. Its thrust, you say, is stunning. Correct, says your companion, though one must add that this span embodies engineering mistakes quite incredible for which he is glad to say his fellow-countryman Brunel never had to pay. It was (you point out) his father who was French, while Isambard Kingdom Brunel the son was

English, though perhaps arguably in the great line of nineteenth-century French engineers. That is correct, says your companion, whose moustache you become aware of. It was (you say) the father who built the Thames Tunnel that kept caving in. That is correct, says your companion, and with curled lip declines a thin white sandwich the barman imagined him to be looking at. The Revolution and the Napoleonic Wars cut into the program of French technology (you point out)—many engineers were on the wrong side at the wrong time. Your companion orders a second whiskey. Business is a taxing business. Will the Paris *événements* change anything? Your companion resolutely channels the talk to New York. He has been there last year—'67—and he will go again: for business, for pleasure— *formidable*. On the other hand (you continue, eyeing the siphon on the bar) the naval blockade in the 1780's that cut France off from the supplies of soda required in making glass and sundry other necessities stimulated the birth of chemical engineering in Le Blanc's soda process. Perhaps your undergraduates are true symptoms, not just trying something on. The Frenchman smiles mechanically: Liberty is the crime which contains all other crimes—that was one of their mottoes, correct?

Through the filmed glass, meadows and cricket fields and new towns and the unnetted bare white frames of soccer goals are seen as if from a breakneck canal. The Frenchman asks, For how many years have you lived in England? You don't quite answer, you are wondering if you could take Will up to see the Clifton Bridge in August when you and he and Lorna and Jenny come down to the seaside town where the boatyard is that you have a piece of. What do you think of Nixon? your French companion says, and with a finger and a nod decides to have that thin flat white triangle (called a round) after all. Going on fourteen years, you say, and ask for another can of Guinness.

In Victoria Station, the Gateway to the Continent, the schoolboys are copying train numbers neatly into their pocket notebooks. This is what Will did the whole of his tenth year. The man in a bowler carries himself well. Does anyone except you look up to the cast-iron and glass roof? It is a bridge for the light to rest on, though now begrimed. You have not enough time to make it worthwhile bussing home, bucking the early rush in the Underground or even turning toward the Thames and paying a quick visit to the Tate to look at Turner's tiny black train submerged in the artist's godlike steam of color, but almost too much time before you meet Lorna and friends in a pub, the Salisbury, before the theater; so wondering about the total effect of a bomb dropped through the vast delicacy of this roof, you decide to kill an hour, you feel like eating a bit of jellied eel. You may have to walk a ways for it.

Between engagements you have time in your hands. You would not say to one of those airmen in 1970 go out and come in again, even if you were really a teacher at the NATO first-strike base where the University of Maryland's worldwide contract with the Defense Department to supply college courses finds particular embodiment in the large and cheerful presence of Dagger DiGorro for whom you substituted this evening. He arranged it with the sergeant, who would in any case not tell the U.K. program-director, not that there is anything to tell except that Dagger and his French wife Alba are visiting her parents in La Frette near Paris this weekend, and you have nothing to do here at Bentwaters Air Force Base (having come by tube, train, and official car a considerable but enclosed distance) except discuss with the men (and one captain's wife) the effects of technology on government and then for the bulk of the period give Dagger's exam, for all of which he's paying you twenty-five dollars American plus expenses but you won't take it. A Bauer upright piano stands against the wall near the door behind you. You've done stints for him before but you have never felt a base as you feel this one tonight, the American security of a capsule suburbia with trees in the right places and prowling station wagons and street signs. The captain is taking his wife to Covent Garden to the opera next week, she is quiet and fluent and tough and content; three kids in the class are going home, with two years of college credit packed away somewhere. After class they were courteous and probably drew conclusions from your beard. You told them Mr. DiGorro would discuss their exams with them next period. The evening drew these people away to their duty-jobs, to barracks, to off-base housing, and then there was your Air Force station wagon and your driver, a black man who didn't say much coming and doesn't say much going, except that he's driving you to Ipswich not Wickham Market, which will be better for you, you won't have to change—and you imagine better for him in some unstated way too, though it is perfectly possible that he is sitting down passing time. He brakes smartly at the guard gate. You ask if he comes to London, how long he's been in, what he thinks of the war, and you get the briefest possible answer and chuckle to each as if he's been trained how to talk to spies. You do not ask him where he comes from, but he tells you New York and adds that he's got a mechanic's job waiting for him there. He calls you sir. He wants to talk now—but it's too late, your train is coming in.

Your train like a tunnel draws you home to London from England, from America, from nowhere, from another tube, from an official station wagon piloted by a Negro chauffeur. On the train you wonder how easy this easy life in England really is, and you wonder how on a couple of hundred feet of relentless film you could find the quality of American life at Bentwaters. Or, now you think of it, at Alconbury, where the U.S. Air Force has brought in falcons to countervent the starlings that threaten the flights.

7 | I had never come back so soon. Five days Stateside, less. I have come home to London in January and from the lower deck of a red bus have seen through shop windows tradesmen in their long, light brown workcoats or from the high-slung roominess of a taxi felt, like some intricate certifying of my own privacy, the route the driver's awesome knowledge of London zig-zags down unheard of residential streets but here (more often called *roads*) that curve into crossings I didn't know I knew where I've changed buses on the way home a hundred times or looked at a locksmith's or passed a medallion portrait of a glistening horse in the window of a betting shop, or contemplated a bank of Cox's at the sight of which like the mottling streams of rose down the pale honey skin, saliva springs under the tongue-roots, for Cox's Orange Pippins, however dry they sound when you shake them and hear unique among apples the rattle of seeds at the core, hold round each drop of fleshly sugar a sheen of tart no New York apple yellow red or even green as far back as those high-shouldered pale-streaked Red Delicious of the thirties and forties my mother chose on Hicks Street in Brooklyn Heights ever had—zags in, zigs out—the London cab corners up one spoke of the map, down another, and on from one to another of the city's interior circumferences as if swung into the next neighborhood—women queueing at a Request Stop, dun brick semidetacheds, an obscure shoe shop, a corner pub with a promising name in gold, a radio rental, then just before the inevitable Indian restaurant, a news agent who sells Cornish ice cream.

London villages, almost.

Once not long ago I came back from the other direction, from Dieppe, and at Newhaven it was as if everyone was on grass, a calm like slow-motion. Anything to declare? A wave of my hand, two hundred fags, a bottle of claret. Thank you. Thank you.

Then 'k you again, for even here at the Newhaven boat-train pier where after the watchful French these people seem Ruritanian, they don't want not to be the last to say thanks. And I let them. I like them. What is the matter with me?

Jenny falls to the ice of the Queensway rink and her hand splays out and Lorna calls from behind us, Her fingers!

I have come home to London in the spring. In spring rain. In St. Louis there was a rainbow when I left. Coming home I have heard the rain touching the leaves in our square, and when Lorna opened her mouth to kiss me and then sent me out again to the Express Dairy, the big wheezing Welshman didn't even know I'd been gone three weeks and when he put a packet of biscuits and a small marmite like a jar of dark brown ink out of my school past down on the counter he said, Well then, what do you hear from the States?

But now, though I knew that the burglary and Phil Aut's trip meant I had to be in London, I was aware of having been drawn away from an equal scene that made a demand that was equally immediate, and as I tried to have a few hours of sleep Sunday night in a bed-and-breakfast hotel in Knightsbridge and my teenage son Will was saying in my sleep, What English word has six consonants in a row? I counted 16-mm. spools on Dagger's work table, but they moved so I lost count but in the dark confusion of losing count of all those thousands of tangled frames a sound came clearly off the optical print repeating like some vehicular cadence (in nights of old when lays were cold and castles not particular, they lined her up against the wall and did her perpendicular; but can you be two places at once?). And just before the maid knocked at seven with my tea I woke muttering, Unless you're Phil Aut.

But listen to this. At ten I saw my daughter Jenny. I saw her come out of the Knightsbridge gallery. The door was held by the Connecticut actor Reid, but because of my angle across the road I didn't see in.

At the bus stop he kissed her and a bus came and he kissed her again and then she didn't get on and seemed to nod back down the block. They walked back slowly past the gallery and I window-shopped, and then Jenny kissed him quickly and as I expected entered the Knightsbridge tube station. Piccadilly Line to Holloway Road, 271 bus to Highgate Village. She might be going home.

Reid walked back toward the gallery. He went in. Then he

came out followed by a red-haired woman in a bright blouse, short suede jacket, and bluejeans whom I'd seen somewhere. At the bus stop they happened to stop. They were arguing. Reid kissed the woman and she gripped his hand. They were arguing. They moved on. When he talked he looked at her and she looked straight ahead. When she interrupted and·turned to him he looked straight ahead. He put an arm around her, she leaned on him, kissed his cheek or neck, then broke away and flagged a cab and left him at the curb with his hands up. She got in and the cab went on in the direction of the tube, and in an antique-shop window (so as to have my back to Reid) I saw Cosmo's Indian come out of the gallery and automatically flag the cab but then drop his shoulders, perhaps seeing that the yellow top light wasn't on, yet he seemed also with one now pointing finger to show he saw who was in the cab. Then it stopped and the red-haired woman I think hailed him and he ran and got in.

Reid watched, but as the cab pulled off for the second time and he turned to go on, his eyes crossed me and I turned to my shop window just in time to see that he looked my way an extra second.

The Indian had had on a heavy white turtle-neck, dark trousers; the woman inside the cab on the edge of her seat had become shadowy as if stripped of the flashing green of her blouse and the deep, once-washed look of her denim-blue and the flash of her hair. And my own Jenny, a quite gray delicacy in her light long hair, had had under her arm the black zippered portfolio I'd brought her from New York two years ago, but when she'd turned to be kissed her inky slicker opened to show a sky-blue high-neck mini-dress I'd never seen. As for her guerrilla-theater actor Reid, I know him as you can only know someone you've deliberately watched but never shaken hands with, never met except once in passing at second base. He'd spent two years at Carnegie Tech in Pittsburgh and he lived now in a Victorian square in Chalk Farm in the basement of a house scheduled for demolition, and the third thing I'd ascertained while standing on second base after my hit to right field and an instant before discovering that Dagger had broken his promise not to film me, was that Reid (who as you may recall was Cosmo's second baseman and who seemed somehow not to know I was Jenny's father) spoke of London with that tone of the American who's had a year maybe and knows the ropes and will tell you a few tricks and get off a remark about English laziness or the future of the Labour Party or if you mention the British Museum, not having gone there in ages, or (to show intimacy with London) this Camden Town pub whose Saturday night talent show (with a transvestite climax) where he'd taken two slumming Foreign Office friends and made the mistake of mentioning to a couple of hostel shoppers in the Underground who were living out of a guitar. Reid's long, slow strides gave the illusion of height. He seemed too swarthy for Ridgefield, Connecticut. He had the beginning of a pony tail. Where was his motorbike? He was the only one left to follow. When he turned back toward the art gallery once again—this time from the bus stop rather than the tube side—I thought maybe he was going to pick up a third female, say with lustrous silver hair dyed black. But he went on to the corner where he bought a paper, lit a cigarette, looked at the headlines, and suddenly entered the Knightsbridge tube station.

It was all as vivid as you could want, like a form—two becoming one. And like some imminent revelation that disarms us in order that we may then think we see it, it seemed not to require understanding. It was also like some future after you are dead and you see as if aesthetically. But you see, I knew who the woman was. She was the red-haired woman Dagger's Beaulieu paused upon when Savvy Van Ghent was chasing the foul.

If Phil Aut knew my face, was he in that gallery right now? It was his gallery.

I seemed to lose Reid on the Underground platform. I got into a car with the brandlike No Smoking red-circle-with-a-blue-bar across it in the windows. Hyde Park Corner. Green Park. The words open and close like ideas. Piccadilly. Leicester Square. Syllables more layered than pictures. Covent Garden, the ballet-stop when I took Jenny. Holborn, near the Home Office, where aliens renew visas and the stop also for my broker met by chance taking an American girl to see St. Paul's. Russell Square, where Cosmo's right-fielder in our film got off for the British Museum in quest of Frederick Catherwood. King's Cross, under whose acre of Victorian greenhouse roof Dagger entertained twice monthly when he taught at the U.S. base Chicksands. Then Caledonian Road, then Holloway Road. Ten nonsmoking Underground stops that made a clear avenue from Phil Aut's art gallery within striking distance of the Queen's preferred department store Harrod's to the broad jumbled itemized working-class life of the road that you associated both with Holloway Prison—not in fact in that road at all—and with Friday and Saturday's shopping list even if you were Lorna Cartwright coming down from Highgate or Geoff Millan, who lived closer, between Holloway and Highgate in the area called Archway (because of a high overpass further up Archway

Road preferred occasionally by suicides), an area like Holloway, though Geoff lived off a church corner in a road so cleanly hushed you might have been abducted through a tunnel of compressed atmosphere into a capsule as private as any residential English quintessence like where we lived on the west side of Highgate three-quarters of a mile on and three hundred feet higher past Whittington Hospital and the Singapore nurses from good polygamous families who used to babysit, and the railed little podium up the Hill enshrining the famous bronze cat.

I got off at Holloway Road. I waited for the lift rather than climb the long, spiraling stairs. I rode up thinking, Well I'm here, I may as well take my bus home to Highgate and see Jenny even at the risk of giving away too much.

But there boarding my 271 was Reid.

The bus had waited a few seconds for him as he ran out of the tube station, and this gave me the chance to catch it, but if he hadn't gone up to the top deck at once he might have turned and seated himself and seen me pay the driver and stare at his narrow black change-tray like a tourist who has learned shillings only to find a decimal system, or as if a power to which my brain is normally raised had been lowered and an avenue had not opened its usual alignment. I don't mean I was seeing nickels, dimes, and quarters, but I must have been tired; yet now another and tangential alignment opened and closed in the form of whether returning, say, as early as tomorrow to Sub's in New York would not only counter the drag between my body-clock and transatlantic time but pass me into a second, other New York. I at once recycled this thought, for it was not an avenue, at best an alley with the littered vividness only of dustbins upset, orange peel rocking, green wine bottles, and brown roses too ripe to get rid of their petals—and Reid was topside with his newspaper, and the bus's erratic motion had swung me right round the silver pole I held and I must sit where Reid wouldn't see me when (as I readily assumed) he came downstairs to get off at the last stop, the top of Highgate Hill, Highgate Village so-called.

It had not been Claire who'd come out of the Knightsbridge gallery. It had been Jenny. If Reid had nothing to do with the film, then neither had Jenny. But Jenny had something to do with the film. She had typed most of my diary. But that was not what I meant.

I know this route from Holloway tube past the great brown compound of Council flats, the ABC cinema, the branch of Sainsbury's fastidious supermarket where Lorna comes down once a week to shop, the branch of Marks and Spencer's which is for everyday clothes what Sainsbury's is for food and in whose bright aisles may be felt the M & S empire's grand auspices like a father's welcoming foreknowledge—and past the mile of shop fronts of this noisy domestic north-London thoroughfare off which down one street Lorna took Will for a National Health x-ray when he had bronchitis that wouldn't go away—yes, I know it so well that I was under the impression I did not think about what Reid and I passed in our bus. And yet it was important precisely for being taken for granted—though at this moment of my threatened life this didn't occur to me.

I am really here: this is what I saw when at our stop Reid had to wait, with his newspaper under his arm and his pony tail hanging outside his jean jacket collar which was of brown corduroy—while two old parties (in macs, in blue macs, and round white straw hats like snugger halos) stepped down; but he did not turn to my corner where I now took the precaution of twisting around as if to see something in the street and found myself looking at my unshaven cheeks above my beard, though in retrospect when I think hard about it I imagine people take my beard for granted and are thus able to see my whole face better, or then look at the mole in the middle of my forehead which for some reason I myself seldom see when I look in the mirror.

Then Reid was gone round the greengrocer's corner into the traffic and business of Highgate High. Mine was the other way. Yet there were more than two ways.

The buildings seemed low.

It was Monday. At the cash register in the window of the dairy in an ample white coat was Mr. Jones, who believed me no more surely when I said they didn't eat marmite in the States than Tris and Ruby believed me when they tasted on Pepperidge Farm whole wheat this spread like undiluted beef bouillon cubes and were told that English kids have marmite for tea.

Between two elms in the square a child's large ball was at rest, yellow in the autumn sun.

At other entrances to the square I saw no Reid. My house seemed forbidden. I had not made up Sub's day bed. Lorna would sit in her nightgown at the piano and work out another Charles Ives song she was performing at a local benefit. I had to admit I liked melody even (or especially) when being washed in the blood of the Lamb; the Ives songs were too intelligent, as if some old American strains were interrupting each other so as to break down into their comparative frequencies, so you got their true neural meanings only to find that after all you didn't really want these explicit.

The West Indian attendant sat on the black railing by the Public Convenience looking across toward a downhill lane whose opening gave a sight of central London silently rising through its own air but as if nearer and nearer rather than higher and higher—or this seemed the direction in which the West Indian attendant was looking.

I was not going to call Dagger.

It was eleven twenty-five, and several retired persons of genteel aspect would be settled into the Reading Room of the Highgate Literary and Scientific Institution across from the square. A sports car whipped in, gunning down for the turn. A sycamore leaf with its five limbs out like a rough star or some bundled human abstract lay on the pavement in front of a bench I had often passed.

A man and a girl were on the courtyard wall of a pub waiting for it to open. As I looked, it did.

I met no one I knew.

When it rains you don't think of the leaf shapes.

One should stay in one place.

My house seemed unusually close to the square. I came uncertainly abreast of the steps and the door lock cracked and I automatically decided not to arrive. I wanted to touch Lorna's spine.

Walking on, I crossed the road and stopped by a tree to light my cigarette of the day.

My angle of observation was poor so I saw only Lorna's arm. Her cardigan.

Perhaps you have not been here and so don't know what my eyes, my feet, my feelings took for granted, standing in, seeing through. But I have in my head things I may not exactly have seen, just as you who read this have me.

Lorna said, You really can go now, and then she said something I missed.

I moved dangerously far and she had her back to the street. I moved further and bent away lighting another match.

Lorna was facing into the hall, facing a man blond, young, and clean-shaven. Above his head at the landing above the rear end of the hall, light from the garden smudged the leaded compartments of our florid stained glass.

He would be the second tenor, but Lorna's lock was fixed.

I could not tell if the second tenor looked past Lorna. There wasn't a picture of me in the house.

He was there to reassure her. He liked her. She was alone and had been burglarized.

He came and kissed her on the forehead. She was wearing trousers.

She could not have had eyes in the back of her head.

Between my eyes or in my throat a space spun so slow I could barely code its message that to pass through Lorna to reach this other person whom I desired to erase from my hall might open something else again behind him.

Which was Jenny. Or what lay behind her.

You can understand my state.

Under the hall table next to Lorna's visitor was the three-dimensional noughts and crosses I'd constructed out of my head that in spite of the illuminated variations on O and X I'd drawn on the little four-by-four placards like options on a typographer's chart tended, Lorna said, to look like someone's three-tiered sandwich-server. For teas we'd never got in the habit of.

The door had closed, and the second tenor was still inside.

I took a turn down the block. Again I heard a door shut. I saw the second tenor turn away toward the bus.

Looking at me before she hugged me, she said, Marriage is an act of faith.

Her cheek against mine seemed to bear in to wear away the flesh. She smelled of pine soap that she said smelled like her parents' camp in Maine, and when she said, Say something, I could think only—in rapid sequence—of the white candles during the power cuts—white as marble in our dark, cheerful, chattering rooms—of the brown turtle in the green garden, of Jenny's dress, and Lorna's record I'd left in the Knightsbridge B & B this morning.

I'm glad after all, said Lorna. I thought I didn't want you to come.

You didn't phone back, I said.

Lorna's dark hair parted in the middle fell softly down each temple. She spoke with a new readiness and simplicity: It's all there, I'd say.

She stepped back and looked at my feet and my raincoat. I'd left my suitcase, which Lorna had slowly packed.

Lorna said, I even started reading it.

We went and sat in the gray velvet medallion sofa in the

shadow of the piano and held hands. Everyone knows something, but not enough, and still we wear gloves. Why did I not go right upstairs to Jenny's room?

Lorna and I held hands and talked quietly as if to be private and looked at each other and I thought her face even more like Will's than I usually do. Pale and dark with Will's blue Celtic eyes. If I had shut my eyes I could not have told you just then what color cardigan she had on. It was one of those heavy-smooth-knit English cardigans, dark brown with a pale brown trim at the collar.

After she asked if I thought she was afraid, and I shook my head thinking her question and its tone erased the second tenor and her not mentioning him, and I recalled her state of mind in the late fifties—how afraid I was, and how fearfully far she had drifted past what I would know as fear—she now asked if all that background was actually in the film, she'd looked at the pages in Jenny's closet and almost couldn't stop.

I said, Well you see I had to explain some of what the film couldn't have shown. Also, the film couldn't have been shown in words without all that explanation.

It was the middle of the night. I'd phoned you and you weren't in. Billy was asleep. He'd looked at the new lock and said no lock is fool proof. Then he went to bed.

Proof against a fool, I said, and kissed Lorna's cheek, and thought that Jenny could not know how she was involved in the theft. I wanted to stay with Lorna. I wasn't sure how to go on to Jenny. I looked back over my shoulder at the door from living room to hall, for the old pendulum clock had begun hissing and shifting getting ready to strike.

Come on, she said. It was the middle of the bloody night and I felt like a burglar in Jenny's closet and so I stayed there reading by that little light you put in rather than bring the pages out into the room. And being in the closet must have done something to the acoustics because I heard a door unlatch and couldn't tell if it was up or down.

Will.

Of course, but I didn't know that, and he'd heard me and thought it was someone in Jenny's room because I'd told him the carbon was in the closet. So he had a tennis racket and a flashlight he was going to switch on only at the last moment, holding it out from his side so the burglar wouldn't know where he was. Well, after all that, my heart was really going; he'd had his racket up for a serve, but all I saw was a glare and his voice saying, Lucky I've got my torch.

What with my call to you, and Billy after me with his new tennis racket, and I'd been reading that strange account of the room you filmed, which is stranger reading it in a closet in the middle of the night, why I stayed awake till I heard the church clock strike five and five minutes later the hall clock so I could see every inch of the hall, and I was tired of actively not worrying about Jenny, you know what I mean, and I kept seeing that hideous warped old racket that you won't throw away but this wasn't a dream.

Lorna stopped abruptly and said nothing for some time. I looked at our things in this room where we live—shells, flowers, two pewter ashtrays, stacks of magazines, a dark gold guitar leaning in a corner behind a shapeless low wide soft deep, now too deep uphol-stered armchair, then a pastel chalk self-portrait of my sister that makes her look like a million other eighteen-year-olds and not espe-cially of 1945, and then over above the other Victorian sofa a 1759 French map of the Thames estuary with the Suffolk, Essex, and "Comte de Kent" coasts in blue, yellow, and red with the sandbars pricked out like live shadows—and I listened to a car rev past and then another and thought what after all was American or English or anything else here except the rectangular plugs with the tiny fuses inside and three prongs, that you won't see in America and seem big but are better made. Lorna was scared. I looked over my shoulder again as if the old clock would go on beyond twelve. I wondered why Jenny didn't come downstairs. Since Lorna had got into the Unplaced Room, I'd go on and tell her what had been said; but then the penny dropped, as they say in England—or *a* penny—and there was that bare table Dagger and I had set between two windows that gave light but were not on camera, and over that bare table the U.S. deserter, speaking of the northern islands to his friend, said, Listen, I almost stayed up there, I mean you know how he is: and the deserter's friend at once said, These rich sailors they're all the same, and the deserter protested that wasn't what he meant and the friend whose control I now felt in my monitoring ears (even more than the Beaulieu could have seen in his almost too quiet hands palms down upon the table) interrupted blatantly, Of *course* I know how it is. And as I recalled that exchange now in a room holding hands with my wife, I could not be sure if he had stressed the word *it*—for if so he might have been trying with the most insidious rhythm of natural-ness to cancel out whatever the deserter's previous *he* had stood for.

Monty Graf would never believe I'd done nothing about the sound track after the film was destroyed. But *I* could hardly believe that Dagger had not brought it up. But like that other New York that I now sensed as a new circumstance from which I necessarily followed, a medium other than our white-and-black phone dial was what stood between me and Dagger, and I would not ring him up yet.

At last Lorna said, What was on that film? What's my friend Tessa got to do with your Marvelous Country House? I was reading the scene you call Marvelous Country House, right? And suddenly I'm in the middle of my friend Tessa. But then Billy went bump in the night and I didn't go back to the closet.

Oh, it was the Marvelous Country House, I said.

The dining room was strange in your description, was it like that? Jenny told me once you'd surprised yourself. But Tessa? You went into her life. But she wasn't there.

If it's dynamite they're looking for, they won't find it in what I say about Tessa.

Is that why you went to New York?

I'm in New York right now, I said; but I heard an old signal in Lorna's questions.

She drew her legs up and crossed them and kept my hand. Tessa Allott was Lorna's friend and our friend. First, Lorna's. From the bad time in the fifties.

That was when we lived day to day like a blind couple who know they blame it on each other, as if blame were the solid furnishings of the rooms they move about in. And Lorna then was buried somewhere parallel to me, which during that eerie period in her life was still stranger because we didn't really stop making love.

What it was—it was that she'd been telling herself for these first three or four or five years it was OK in England; and while she did miss the States (which means nothing phrased that way—missed the East, missed New York, missed Maine), in London the cost of living, the calm, the church music at Temple Church among many others, the magic nearness of the Continent, the informality of a shopkeeper who gives you the radio someone else left to be repaired even though you've lost the receipt and the tradesman doesn't know you; the privacy of private life, the trousered legs sticking out from under a small car on a Saturday morning along some garden street, the café that will not serve you a sandwich five minutes before noon; privacy haunted by the straight unbending, hence averted eyes she

124

felt she passed shopping in the Village, so on an unlucky day she might feel like Lorna in Underland wondering if indeed it was privacy that was being preserved—all these seeming amenities and the lush parks and theater tickets at a dollar and less apiece (theater which we made a point of going to at first, Shaw, Shakespeare), and a foreign country where you spoke the language—and something else whose vagueness I hesitate to let into this Chinese box reflection (Tessa within Lorna within the American Cartwrights abroad), to wit a rich option of returning home which if we'd been living in Portland, Maine, and thinking about New York we could never have entertained in the same grand style—all these things settled us—we even felt we were or had become superior Americans.

Lorna when she shopped felt she earned our dinner choice by choice; it was those little paper bags she acquired at the various Highgate Village shops (apples, runner beans, new potatoes, small ripe Guernsey tomatoes, hunks of pale yellow or dull orange English cheese), bags so full you couldn't hold them by the top even if you had hands enough to hold them all and so you left the top twisted closed at either side and held the bag under the bottom. Lorna placed them all with a pound of newspaper-wrapped mincemeat (in the seventies at last sometimes called *hamburger* and now wrapped in plain white butcher's paper) in her then recently acquired string bag which when you set out shopping next day you carried folded up in your hand.

But during the bad time in the late fifties, if I offered to cook she said it was one of the things she actually did. When Jenny and Will were in bed—Jenny the messy sleeper, Will neat, both snugly small asleep in bed—Lorna would stare at the blue air letter on the kitchen table or at the honey-varnished oak surface, or at an alumni review I never read which she might read, and if I came in for coffee she'd give me an ironic smile. Said I was keeping an eye on her.

She said her hair came out. I couldn't see it. It was long, it was dark, it seemed thick. She had it cut and had a rat of her own hair made saying she expected to need it in a couple of years.

She said why did I begin my letters home *Dear Mother and Dad* when I didn't write *Mrs. and Mr.* on the envelope.

She took her underwear off and stood at the mirror. She ran her hand along the pearly stretch-marks above her groin and said she was finished. I told her she was twenty-eight, she wouldn't hit her prime for ten years. Holding her, I felt protective in my clothes. (A touch of porn too whole for film.) I said, You're small—it was what

I'd felt from the first. She said, Oh I'm not, I've never felt I was small. I squeezed her: But you are, and the only reason you don't think so is that you were tall for your age till you were twelve.

All this is not the present point. Which is that into this ungrounded but so slowly spinning wheel came Tessa. She was not a friend of anyone we knew, though later I found that her American husband had known someone at the Embassy who knew Dagger.

Lorna met Tessa one Sunday at Kew. The ducks pedaled in toward Billy who had crawled near the water, I can barely see him he's so small, though I was not there. Then Jenny who was then Ginny was trotting off toward two boys who were throwing grass and sassing a fat groundskeeper who seemed to be equipped with a slow fuse, while a third, in an attempt to hew down a tree, was hitting its trunk with a wooden sword. I was at home in Highgate. An elderly woman in a little round hat was saying—as if to anyone or to herself though in hopes of Lorna—that weren't those boys terrible, got no respect—and instead of replying as she'd normally do no matter how she felt, Lorna turned away and spoke to a woman on her other side—asked what she was reading—and the woman said it was about a man who had collected 267 cowbells. But she said it without looking up from the book, so it came with the eeriest intimacy, neither English matter-of-fact friendliness nor anything else Lorna could think of except that Tessa—for this was Tessa—was a close friend (Lorna examined her), or a sister, with whom Lorna had come to Kew today. But after a while Tessa did look up; she looked at Jenny and Billy off playing, but not at Lorna; then she said, I'll tell it you when I'm finished.

What passed between them that day I think I never learned. When Lorna came back she seemed less aware of me, indifferent though in a casual family way as she hummed through two stacks of music looking for something. And through her preoccupation which seemed to express a feeling she'd come home with, I saw she was elated. Whatever I don't know, I know when she's miserable and when she's not. I took Jenny upstairs to wash and bandage her arm where one of the grass throwers had scratched her rather badly. When I came downstairs Lorna was empty-handed in the middle of the living room, behind her my sister's photograph just above her shoulder, and the house seemed to be trying to return Lorna to the state she had seemed to be released from by the event of the afternoon, which as I've said was Tessa Allott. Lorna said she'd been repelled by the first woman trying to start a conversation in Kew

Gardens and as soon as Lorna had turned to speak to the other person, a woman with the palest brown eyes—and indeed as if it could not happen *until* Lorna stopped watching Jenny—she got thrown down by one of the boys, thrown down again with some swiping motion that dug nails into her soft arm so it bled, and no doubt dirty nails.

There was apparently no place in my account of the Marvelous Country House for any of this—like later when Lorna was way past that trouble of the late fifties her remark that for her to meet Tessa, Jenny had to suffer that infected arm—*septic*, the English say—for it became infected—who knows where a nine-year-old's nails have been?—Jenny would peel up the bandage to show Billy the scab crusting and would inform us over our lasagna that there was some white around the blue and the bloody-red—the tracks of the scratches were like whip-welts—Jenny was absorbed: She picked and picked, and the little disk of scab pried away too soon and what was left itched and she scratched it till it bled and Lorna had to take her back to the doctor.

Which is again not the point. The link of Tessa with the Marvelous Country House thirteen years later was too strong to omit in my diary. The meeting in Kew was May 1958. Ronald Colman died a year later in California—my mother devoted a letter to him. If you had told Tessa that Ronald Colman was born in Richmond, Surrey, she would have looked away with a wild smile and said with a quiet quiver you might mistake for a put-down, My goodness.

In June Lorna took Tessa to Royal Festival Hall to hear Menuhin—our neighbor in Highgate whom Tessa's father had known for years—play Mozart and Bach concertos with the Festival Chamber Orchestra. On June 21 they took Billy and Ginny to the West End to *South Pacific* at the Dominion Cinema. I know, because summer solstice brought Stonehenge to mind—which we hadn't even known was in Wiltshire—and with it all the other wonders of Britain that after four years' residence we still had not seen. Ask a New Yorker if he's seen the Chrysler Building lobby or any American tourist abroad if he's been nearer the brink of the real Grand Canyon than an insurance company calendar. Well, in the paper next day was a report of Druid daybreak observances which Geoff Millan says have as little to do with Stonehenge as Welsh chapel services or Geoffrey of Monmouth's erroneous account of the Dance of the Giants—though Geoff Millan can describe for me from New York Franz Kline's great black forms against white canvas which seem some secret cross between ancient wood growths and the magic lintels in Wiltshire.

That June 21, 1958—scarcely a month after Lorna and Tessa had met at Kew—Tessa's husband joined them at the movie and had a fit of sneezing in the middle of "Bali Hai." The British Museum is only four blocks from that St. Giles Circus intersection where Tottenham Court Road, Charing Cross Road, and Oxford and New Oxford streets end and begin—and that was one of his Reading Room Saturdays at the BM. So after lunch instead of going somewhere to draw an old building in his sketchbook, Dudley Allott met them at the Dominion, and Lorna described him to me that evening. She was not sure what was between the Allotts, but she had this odd feeling Tessa was pregnant.

Not the point either; but maybe I'm thinking that Lorna never in any way described Tessa. Instead she would say—which was quite true when I had been with Tessa—that while Tessa sitting knees together and seeming in her narrow high shoulders tense or formal would never seem to do the talking, you might sometimes feel after she got up and went home that it was she who had moved the conversation—from Jews in New York, say, to Jews in London and the Brooklyn College girl who stayed with the Allotts one summer in the sixties who was surprised to find Tessa, a Jew, speaking with an English accent; yet Tessa brought *us* out—yet sometimes I discovered in myself, even in words I was using to tell anecdotes arising out of Tessa's easy transitions, an idea that our lives had been parallel and what I was telling had happened to Tessa, who sat listening till Lorna would go to the piano and ask her to sing.

Tessa and the film—not just parts of one's life sensing one another in that spirit of exhilaration called manic in someone deranged. Yes: Tessa and, in particular, the Marvelous Country House. But in the abbreviated form in which Lorna began but then was kept from finishing my section, the link with Tessa may be clear only to me. And what I now tried to tell the person who sat beside me, her soft dry hand half-closed in mine, was part what she'd read, part what she hadn't reached, and part what I added out of courtesy. I looked at her—at all except her eyes, the governing powers of her face which gave person to her bones, though in themselves those eyes if you forgot everything else and saw only them were impersonal, both mechanically animal for all their flecked textures, and wildly opaque —and then I looked right at two things in our room as if I could look at them both at once—and thinking of Tessa and the tiny fold at the inner angle of each of her eyes, I thought why didn't I include in my account of Tessa's connection with the film these two things. One is a cigarette burn in the northwest quadrant of our carpet. The other is a jagged blue-green hunk of rock salt Tessa brought from the Bavarian Alps when she at last brought herself to visit Germany in 1963.

The second came to us accompanied by the remark that this was the color Tessa had wanted her eyes to be instead of watery pale brown. I pointed out that in black and white her eyes looked blue. She said Dudley had told her to buy herself some of these new colored contacts, just as he had once told her to go ahead and get another cat—she smiled and shook her head, and Lorna said, You don't wear glasses, and Tessa said, I'd rather long for the eyes than have the contacts, it isn't that Dudley misses the point, he gets the point but he thinks why say so, though he's probably right that the rock salt must have come from Saxony, not where we were.

Tessa's cigarette burn occurred in 1970, just a year before Dagger and I began shooting. She would hold her cigarette for a minute or two as if she'd forgotten it, then take a deep stabbing drag and as if in the same motion sweep her cigarette away and tap it—but this time she tapped off a sizable coal, but more interesting than what it did to the carpet was her interest in what it did, the calm, the objectivity which in me and in Lorna and in three others in the room seemed to come from Tessa's—we sat and watched the spot smoke and settle out into a smudge of burnt nap and as if it were a nostalgic winter blaze or a hypnotic peephole we looked and looked until Lorna laughed and said, Tessa you bloody cow!

Beside me on the newly resprung couch as I troubled to show Tessa's place in the Marvelous Country House, Lorna seemed now incapable of such a frank outburst.

Why did you read the diary?

I thought it was about time.

I listened for Jenny who was still upstairs. After Reid had seen me across the street in Knightsbridge he might have told Jenny (no doubt also saying Don't look)—and now she was not sure what to do next. But I was sure I had to settle with Lorna before going on. Celibacy was one thing in Manhattan, another in Knightsbridge.

Lorna shook her head but held my hand. She wondered what the three moments I'd put in had to do with the film, and she said even if Will hadn't surprised her in the dark house and she'd read through the second and third of these "moments," she still would not have understood.

In the first of these moments, I come home to find not Lorna alone at stove or piano or with Jenny or Will, but at the kitchen table with Tessa, who taps ash onto a blue willow-pattern plate in the center of which is an uncut red-waxed Edam cheese. Someone has just said something; I think Lorna. Smiling silence ensues because of me. It might be just Her Beloved Man Arrives, but I don't take it quite that way. Lorna pours me a drink from what's left of the bottle. Dagger got me the case. Lorna doesn't ask how things went in Liverpool. Tessa now continues, and I'm stupidly thinking, Tessa is English, what the fuck am I doing here—dumb things to think when you are dealing with a mind and body as tenuously demanding as Tessa's. Yet she was German. And her mother had been Rumanian, and the shape of her eyes was east of Rumania.

So to make a long story stop (she says), my uncle woke up blind—woke up *being* blinded—and never saw the dawn of that day, and he was, as I've already told you, unaccustomed to opening his eyes before ten in the morning. But to the day of his death he was as filled by the dreams he had just before waking as if the new house they entered several years later had been really the house he'd dreamt of that night—which was only one of his dreams asleep in that bed before the accident—as influenced as if he'd been seeing that future home and thinking about it just as he was (say) killed—and dying seemed never to end but to be an endless continuation of that. So there. That's immortality: just concentrate hard enough when you're dying but you have to know you're dying. Uncle Karl still dreamed, of course. But the dreams that night were to him like the last things he saw.

Tessa rested. It was precise and seductive. But I did not ask for what I had missed of the story. How, for instance, had her uncle been blinded? Which uncle was this one? Most of her uncles were cousins or old refugee friends of her father. Had a burglar groped her uncle's eyeballs?

*Dud*ley (she said) had said that it merely showed how we must keep our eyes open as it might be our last look. But, picking up her intonation though I still hardly knew *Dud*ley, I asked did she mean *Dud*ley had no real right to this truth he spoke. And Tessa at once said, Anyone has a right to it, don't you think? I said enforcement was one thing, right another, and no I didn't think just anyone had a right to it, her story was a good one, I said, I'd once dreamt I was making love to Lorna and woke up and I was—but she was only just beginning to wake up.

130

Tessa said, Maybe *you're* the one that needs the shrink.

Tessa's uncle I said must have been able to find his way around that house he later bought even better than his wife or whoever he was living with, even though he was blind and they weren't.

Tessa at once said, Ah but you've hardly a right to that yourself, having not heard the whole story; and she put her cigarettes in her bag, put a hand on my wife's wrist, and said, as if in thanks: Lorna.

But I had already risen. I said I was tired and hungry and was going up to wash my hands. Tessa murmured, Americans are so explicit, as if she didn't know me pretty well. Jenny called me overhead as I put a foot on the stairs, and Lorna called that there was shepherd's pie in the fridge, and Tessa said—just audibly—You know your place, darling, and Lorna said, I do not.

There had been a nasty pale brown cigarette mark on the cheese plate. I thought, Tessa is a European, she would not normally think of eating cheese with an apéritif, much less Dutch cheese.

The second "moment" described in my film diary, because it seemed to me to bring Tessa into the Marvelous Country House, was in Tessa's flat. In her bedroom. And it should have been no more difficult for Lorna seven years later sitting on our resprung couch holding hands to understand why I'd associated that moment with my film, than it was for me to guess why Jenny still did not come down from her bedroom even though she must be curious why I'd come back from New York like this.

The second "moment" is 1964. Tessa packs her third or fourth suitcase, stops to add to a list for the Belgian couple who are going to be living there with her pictures and furniture for the next year while she and Dudley and Jane are in New York. She is into her packing, but in her references to Dudley she makes me feel she is more waiting for him (for he and Jane are not here) than packing for America: Lorna on the bed curled around a corner of the suitcase Tessa is filling: I upright in a straight chair holding a peculiar grayish stone that was on the night table on a Michelin Guide to New York City—and Tessa asked me to feel it and see if I liked it, and when I grinned stupidly at her she said, Go and take it.

I in my manner express maybe a trifle too much sympathy for Tessa, who does not want to leave London and says there must be something wrong to be going to New York where she knows no one and leaving here in London a New Yorker who is her best friend.

It was 1964, because that autumn I saw them when I passed through New York and I had a ride with a cabbie who said what if Goldwater did escalate, better be blown sky high than find the Chinese sailing their junks under the Golden Gate one morning. Tessa brought me a beautiful aquamarine drink in an overblown glass constructed like a tulip or rose blown with overlapped petals, and murmured flatly, I suppose we'll see *you*. Lorna lay on her side, elbow on the bed, palm under jaw; she said she would hate to be leaving her house to strangers, Tessa said she wouldn't have anyone *but* strangers, but said it in a way that made me feel that of all people I was the one making her live out of England—as if some oceanic conspiracy of refractions so multiplex as to render the person who was fascinated by them in fact passive had got hold of her who was not fascinated by them, and it was my fault, I had let it happen. We heard the front door of their spacious flat unlock and open, and Tessa's little girl call Mummy, and heard Dudley her father say something to her; and Tessa on some blinding impulse came at me as if falling on me from far away and at a long low angle—and plucked the gray stone from my hand that was loosely pleasurably holding it, flew it into Lorna's hand, said it was a very special present, and then put her hand on Lorna's hair and said, I mean if you were living here I'd hate to think of you here in this flat without me—you see that's not something you would feel about a stranger.

But now in 1971 on a resprung couch and holding a hand and not waiting for miracles because I was always beyond that, I found a thing I hadn't written down which might seem immaterial since Lorna in Jenny's closet last night hadn't read beyond the first "moment," and it was that at that other moment in August of '64 less than twenty-four hours before they boarded a Holland-America ship at Southampton, the intimacy Tessa's flat had for Tessa seemed located in Lorna, her lap curved about an angle of the suitcase. Dudley entered the bedroom with his fingers up in a V, and Tessa said, Of course *Dud*ley wants a house in the country when we come back to England, and Lorna said, teasing, If you come back.

I recall we talked about the three bodies unearthed in Philadelphia, Mississippi, and Dudley predicted there would be indictments but no convictions; he had been talking to an American at the British Museum.

Dudley said that in New York Tessa must have a cat again, and Tessa said he wouldn't be able to breathe and she didn't want to go through the same old disappointment.

What could a camera show; what for that matter could Jenny see if Lorna and I right now in the fall of '71 were exposed together holding hands on a resprung couch in Highgate? What could a camera know of that stone Tessa gave Lorna that was in fact a rather special piece of spotted dolerite from Wales?

Lorna took her hand away and patted my leg. She laughed: You didn't seriously think Tessa and I had something going? But why would anyone want to break into this house to steal one of those *moments*?

I said I was going to find out. I said I was glad we had been able to sit quietly like this; I said she mustn't be afraid. She said heaven knew our life had always been pretty quiet. I asked if the young second tenor had been helpful, and she said Very.

She asked about the third "moment." I asked where Jenny was. Lorna seemed relieved. Then the doorbell rang.

She can't get in now the lock's changed.

I thought Jenny was upstairs, I said, which seemed to wish Jenny there, for a moment later when Lorna let her in, there she went, and on the run; I'd risen as Lorna went into the hall, and through the doorway, as if only by watching Lorna vanish would I see it, I saw on the hall wall the old enlargement of my children that I hadn't looked at since that mellow morning at eleven just after the County Council man left and just before I followed Lorna up to bed.

Now Lorna had said, Daddy's here.

But Jenny must be checking her closet or going to the lavatory or avoiding me, for she hadn't stopped.

Lorna was in the doorway again, saying quietly, Jenny stayed with the actor this weekend, she phoned last night, she was upset about the break-in but she didn't come home.

Did you mention her carbon in the cupboard?

Strange I didn't. Neither did she.

Lorna seemed to lose me again; she leaned her head on the door post and stared at me as if I were some bloke who'd just presented a staggering estimate on a domestic repair whose importance suddenly escaped her. She looked at my knees. She said I didn't think the burglar was after my recollections of Tessa, did I?—and thereupon giggled. It's been quite a life, she said, hasn't it. Friends dropping in. Dagger dropping in when you were out, poking around our magazines, borrowing a couple. It's been a good life here.

But Jenny came downstairs.

She asked if the phone man had come and Lorna said no.

Jenny pushed past Lorna and reached for me. She was slighter than Claire in the high short blue dress, her hair was in my eyes, she wore no scent, her scale felt smaller than Claire's. I could trust Jenny; but to do exactly what? Her emergence from Aut's Knightsbridge gallery had passed parts of my body into sheer sheathing of unknown mass, I felt things I could see yet with a touch and sight unknown to each other.

Her excitement seemed love. And love was in her arms. But she let that excitement too naturally accept my homecoming. After all, my homecoming was abortive, or not a homecoming at all, and here she acted as if I'd gone through with my trip and been away a long time.

Yet I could not reason myself into believing that Jenny was in with those who seemed to be trying to liquidate the film Dagger and I had shot.

Maybe there were bad miracles too.

If Dagger was right when he kidded Jenny that time at lunch—though maybe without a right to be right—maybe loyalty was just a code waiting for a message. Suppose Jenny had told someone about the film diary in the desk drawer.

London you depend on. Lorna and I sometimes went to the Camden Town area to a Cypriot family restaurant with a telly and had a drink first in an Irish pub full of men who looked either out of work or temporary. We never felt known there. The young bartender was sometimes drunk at seven, which is fairly strange for London. Three young workingmen in brown suits and no ties huddled at the table, another approached and nodded and disappeared downstairs to the men's loo. Two of the huddlers followed. After a time a new one came up from the loo and nodded curtly to the one at the table who joined him, and the two disappeared downstairs. Lorna and I holding our rich dark halfs of draft Guinness decided they were I.R.A. We amused ourselves. We wondered why the I.R.A. didn't blow up an Underground station—maybe they just didn't want to—we amused each other softly—two men came up out of the loo, talked together seriously for a moment, then one returned downstairs—we almost believed our speculation that they were I.R.A. The leather bench cushions seemed luxurious, the Irish bartender tipped over a shot glass and a big black man at the bar stood up to avoid being dripped on, we didn't think he was a regular. Our Cypriot restaurant was less than thirty seconds away. We might take American visitors there but not here. The second hand of the big clock jumped. One of the

Irishmen came up out of the loo, his hair standing up all over his head, and without looking at anything but the door he walked out.

What did you bring me back, said Jenny, and released me.

Something happened to my face as I recalled forgetting Lorna's Joni Mitchell *Blue* in my hotel room, and then Jenny, seeing whatever it was in my face—fatigue, gloom, madness—said, No no I'm kidding, and she seemed about to cry as I heard right on top of her words Lorna saying, My God the poor man's had things to do.

Which had a warmth that made me grin. I said to my daughter, I brought you a memory but it's not exactly a present.

Is it your memory or mine?

Mine, maybe yours. It was on our softball film, but it's not in the diary.

What is it?

It's a red-haired woman. She was at the softball game we filmed. She was sitting nearby. She got up and walked away. Later your friend the actor walked away in her direction. Then I lost them both behind a tree.

That's possible, said Jenny.

Have you seen a red-haired woman? I asked.

No, of course not.

Lorna was in the kitchen, I heard her.

Your diary is safe, said Jenny.

There's some more of it in my head, I said.

I can't help you there.

You could.

Jenny had the same patient look I've seen, and it is mainly patience with herself and it meant she was containing herself. Now if she'd come out of the gallery just before the red-haired woman, it stood to reason she had encountered this red-haired woman. But I might lose what Jenny could tell me if I told her now that I'd seen the red-haired woman walking intimately with Reid the actor.

Does anyone know you've got that carbon up in your cupboard?

How would anyone?

At the door Jenny gave a bad imitation of an afterthought: What brought you back so soon?

I'm not really back. I'd prefer you not to tell anyone. Not even Reid.

Would he care?

Are you staying with him these days?

Not really.

Lorna was behind Jenny and instead of asking Jenny if she'd met a red-haired woman this morning, I said, Does Reid know an Indian?

I wish you'd leave my private life alone. Jenny got past Lorna into the hall and went upstairs.

Lorna said, You know Reid's dome that he built on his parents' property in Connecticut? He's shingling it with old LP's.

Lorna held her hands out to me. She dropped her hands. I saw something so obvious I couldn't believe I hadn't seen it before, as obvious as the sloppy paint splotches along the edge of white traffic lines in New York streets—you assume the line, so you don't see the splotches, till suddenly you look.

What I saw now when I looked at my wife Lorna was that the Indian, Cosmo's Indian, the Knightsbridge gallery Indian, had been one of the two men with dark hair and white shirts sitting on the grass with the red-haired woman when we filmed the softball game. Yet having expressed this I was now not sure.

I turned away from Lorna, and on the table with Tessa's hunk of rock salt was a bowl of apples, not Orange Pippins but Sturmers that are like small ordinary rough orchard apples you see by the bushel in the fall in New England.

Lorna said, There must be an awful lot on the film only you could know.

UNPLACED ROOM

Both ask anonymity. Anscochrome color will make the drab hues here threatening, like a strangely rich black and white. Windows in our Unplaced Room symmetrically on either side of and behind the table are not quite on camera; they give a light other than our overhead globe. Dagger thinks the effect may be expansive. Globe? says the deserter. Bulb to you, says his costar.

The deserter's hair is fair and long, down over his slanting neck as he stares at his hands on the table. In front of the table a blue-red-and-umber floor cushion. His friend's dark hair is longer than its clutching kinkiness indicates. Dagger has a tripod this morning; I didn't know he had one. He says he'll be ready to move laterally but wants, as we agreed, to keep it if possible still and at most play with focus, like on the near hands (deserter's left, friend's right) which are in a plane closer than the heads whose plane is not so delicate really because Dagger's distance gives a depth of field that easily includes in focus ear and nose.

My headset on, the mike hidden on the table, the Nagra spool spinning, I hear the first exchanges and see no significant movement.

I don't mind, says the deserter apparently in reply to something his friend asked just as I got the phones on before switching in the voices.

The friend, who must have said, Where were we? now says to the deserter Shoot.

I can hear the Beaulieu all too clearly.

The deserter tells a considerable opening tale; much of it I recall.

This boy—he is twenty-one tomorrow—moved out with his company from Fort Dix when he had just been best man in a wedding at the beautiful modern chapel, and they were all relieved to be going to Germany.

Why'd you let yourself get drafted? snapped his friend.

Everybody gets drafted, it's what you do with it that makes the difference.

You're just beginning to know your own power. You have to be shown. For example, you got drafted; I didn't.

You cut your finger off.

My face.

The deserter says No wonder—but the dark-haired one waves his hand as if to say get on with it.

The deserter says with a bit of lonely drama in his voice that all this is like months and years ago, another time, and the dark-haired one says evenly, It's the same only more so.

The deserter tells how the belly-aching black soldiers at the base bugged him with their challenges about nothing, so the news from Nam got on his nerves and letters came from his mother about chapel attendance and from his sister who he is hung up on and she was splitting from her husband and had a good job as a computer programmer, and a guy in quartermaster said the bombing in Southeast Asia would go on till 1980 till we were just touching up our own craters and it looked like the moon, and our deserter heard of an underground antiwar paper being put out by two GI's in England but it wasn't pushing counter-action like Roger Priest's *Om*, and he didn't at the time know why he did it but a black first lieutenant who'd never been channeled into vocational school like him gave him an

137

address up north in Kiel—clean-cut liberal black (both laugh at this), ROTC, scholarships, did card tricks and read palms, the whole bit but now getting out—and before our costar knew it he'd extended a furlough, slipped the Danish Coast Guard, landed on the east Swedish coast south of Kalmar (which is not much of a secret any more), and was hitching toward a lake three hundred miles north where there was a community—

OK. OK—

A land-reform lab in beautiful Sweden and when he got there he saw this TV broadcast he said, and he knew he'd done the right thing. No words for it. It was of a South Vietnamese officer hustling this wiry bare little VC along by the arm like some farmer who got drunk and disorderly on market day, and yelling at him and getting worked up, then in the middle of the street headed for the lockup or interrogation pulling a pistol and bombing that little VC just like that at right angles, bumping him off literally, a sideways bump in the head, the VC tipped over.

I'd been building this fence all day with—you know them—

Of course.

The girl. The guy. The other girl.

Right, right.

You know their names.

They don't matter.

But it was *them,* you see.

The black-haired one whispers something with the word *forget.* And Dagger for a moment has cut around to me I don't know why, the second unit on my shoulder strap, mike held out, dumbly alert I guess I look.

But, says the deserter, it was a good afternoon. We built that fence together and it was for us and the girl Joan—

Cool it. It was Joanne, wasn't it? It doesn't matter.

You kidding?

The deserter mouthed something, then said OK. To *me* it matters. We knew each other from the start and we came back after work and went down and swam in the cold lake, and we got off, and we had supper and then we saw the news on TV, and I knew I'd made the right move because I'd been more scared than I knew, worse than Vietnam, scared of white armbands in the night—but the TV news made me see.

In Sweden.

In my head, which is anywhere!

OK, baby.

That TV news changed my head.

The deserter is playing with his fingers. He looks at the camera and back at his friend, and says, What are we doing here?

They exchange formulas for gelatin dynamite, kidding. Big issue: do you use woodmeal with gun cotton or gun cotton alone? Let's ask Mr. Johnson in Senior Chem.

The black-haired one says, Where were we?

Here.

They laugh.

The black-haired one very composed in the midst of his laughter as his friend also laughing is not, says, A friend of a friend is making an experimental film.

More laughter.

The black-haired one says, Therefore talk. How come you left a good set-up? Affluent Sweden.

It was a visit only to a girlfriend of the deserter's sister who was in Norway. Trondheim. Some institute. Walked north and overland to cross into Norway south of the railway line that runs from Östersund in Sweden right over to Trondheim, but had to stay north enough to miss the higher mountains so they were in some uplands between the railway and the bad mountains. And well in Trondheim, you know what happened then. Joan decided to go back to the States and the deserter got in with an American like nobody he'd ever seen who said he was a geologist but he was a water freak working on his sixth or seventh boat, it was a broad-beamed converted trawler fitted up with the works, he had the bread.

The black-haired one says, This is all meaningless, you know.

We're off to the Faeroe Islands then, where the skipper wants to look at some curious rock formations, and in the Faeroes I started not being able to remember what happened to me, just knew I had to keep going on, and I got in with a fishing crew from the Hebrides who'd lost a man who'd gone off to the Orkneys to haul seaweed—like those northern islands are something else, no words for it.

The Hebrides are called the *western* isles.

So I came down to the Outer Hebrides and lived in a hut north of Mount Clisham, bleak and Puritan. I could have stayed there. Just stayed. You know the rest.

You found us.

But listen, I almost stayed up there. I mean you know how he is.

The deserter's voice has dropped on these last words and just as suddenly his friend says, These rich sailors they're all the same.

But the deserter says, I didn't mean—and his friend cuts in No, I *do* know how it is.

Why?

In a military situation you learn what to say and what to leave out.

More I think of it, it's a meaningless war. But where does that leave me? (The deserter wants to give with some on-camera dialogue, and coming up with some comes up with a genuine thought:) I mean, I made it mean something in my life.

You weren't in it, man, says the black-haired one. You were in Heidelberg. You were signed up for a course with University of Maryland at the base. I knew it long before you knew I knew and long before you knew me. And don't forget, the Visiting Forces Act says the English police can pick you up.

The deserter shrugs his shoulders in embarrassment, seems stumped: You saying I'm Visiting Forces?

You got away, man, what do *you* know?

I'm a Vietnam vet, man.

Why you don't know a thing about the war.

I know what you know.

Less, much less.

What do you know?

The correlation between this war and the nature of unearned income.

What about Billy Smith at Bien Hoa? This is a race war. Vietnam is the cheap Chink cunt.

Who's Billy Smith?

He's black. They charged him with fragging an officer's barracks.

What's fragging, soldier?

Fragmentation bombing. They say he tossed a grenade that killed two lieutenants.

That's fireworks, not ideology, says the older one, then raises a hand. I'm bugging you, I don't mean to bug you, not here.

There's a contradiction in what you said. (The clear simplicity of force in the words seems to have been drawn from the deserter by our scene.)

There is no contradiction.

Anyway, Smith may get off.

140

It's irrelevant.

Right—and all contradictions will be resolved, right? including the struggle of the individual, right? that's what your boss said.

Others have said it.

I glance at Dagger; the distance between us is secret; I might learn something seeing these blokes as he sees them.

Mao for one, says the deserter.

The dialogue has a strangely official spontaneity.

Got enough? asks the black-haired costar.

Dagger has switched off now; my sync unit is off.

You fellows are so good I've never in my career had less directing to do.

They laugh.

I'm going to let you have another minute, how's that?

They relax again, having been ready to get up. There is a bridge during which nothing happens but the sound of the Beaulieu and the phone ringing once. Dagger turns the camera on me: its sound almost visualized in my headset and preoccupations, the camera goes lower to my hands, my feet.

The deserter says, Well there it is.

The black-haired man bursts into a spiel, surprisingly exasperated, something has gotten to him. The war, he says, is ultimately a good thing because it significantly accelerates the decline of the democracies. The British filled the vacuum after the Japanese left, and this let something happen that would have delayed this process of decline for generations. What it did was keep Ho Chi Minh from moving in, and instead the French took over; and when the Americans filled the vacuum later when the French got out it was the same thing. So Ho didn't become what it would have been in the interests of the western capitalist democracies to have him be, namely a Southeast Asian Tito. The war had been a good thing, yes.

Hey, said the deserter, war's not that good. Think of all the things the POW's missed. And think of those kids with their backs skinned. But nothing's going to come out of this war.

No, something. (Dagger must have caught the contempt in the black-haired face.)

At that moment the room, unplaced in word or light or sign, resumes a power it first had had in the bare tableau like a still. So place is felt to be not always or at least visibly the one of national coordinates or crystallized history. The pictures we removed from view lean against a wall, off camera.

The black-haired one has to make a phone call. Dagger tells him where it is.

Not on camera perhaps is at the end a sense that the principals depart less friends than they arrived. But even as I make these words, the truth loses contour, though it will have more authority in Jenny's type.

8 I entered the Knightsbridge gallery Monday afternoon. The girl with the posh lisp that made *r* into *w* (*really* into *weally*) was at the desk and didn't seem to know me. She had a deep tan this time and her loose orange-and-magenta blouse put the pictures to shame.

When I asked for Mr. Aut, she said I'd just missed him, he was on a plane to New York. When I asked who had painted the pictures on the wall to my right, the girl said it was Jan Graf.

But then I looked, and there were two new ones up. One was very likely of the red-haired woman, though the hair had been left unpainted. What you had was face and shoulders, neck and breast, predominating pale peach and silver-mauve, with the hair left the plain underpainted white that had been laid on the canvas. I felt that this was an abstract, a kind of wildly energetic abstract—I think I really don't know about these things; I hear a bit from Geoff Millan, but he prefers to talk to me about liquid crystals or West End plays I haven't seen. The peculiar thing here was I was simply seeing the face, no problem, as if the displacements and the riding, shedding planes of the work that made the flesh look like it was undressing didn't exist. Now this was a switch, at least for the likes of me. Also, I wanted to sit down on the girl's desk and tell her.

Instead I asked if in real life that woman had red hair.

The girl shrugged: In weal life? I mean, it's a work of art.

I said it might be a good likeness.

I was wondering if anyone was in the back room where through a door I saw bigger canvases leaning up against white walls.

I said I guessed leaving the hair unpainted made the picture art.

The girl smiled.

I asked Jan Graf's address and phone, the girl wouldn't give it out. She said if I was interested in buying, she would take my name. The artist would be in Wednesday.

I asked when the girl herself came to work. It wasn't as if I'd invited her to breakfast, but she didn't like my asking and said, When we open. I felt I was losing something and could get something else better only if I took advantage of being in New York and London at the same time or if I started asking the girl some wonderful questions: like, Is there an insurance group prepared to write a policy to cover the theft even of the carbon copy of my film diary that's hidden in Jenny's cupboard? What are the dimensions of such a carbon copy and would those dimensions fit into a lookout cartridge? But these questions are like the dreams I envision when waking but then don't have sleeping. On the 271 from Highgate Village to Holloway Road tube station after lunch with Lorna—some very hot and good leftover curry—I had imagined having such a dream some night soon, imagined perhaps in order to forestall. For the familiarity of that route had obviated my looking at it except the marquee of the ABC cinema and instead I envisioned having a nightmare in which I challenged Outer Film to a public audit. Phil Aut in an Aquascutum Super Burberry with silk labels streaming out of the tailored pockets lay on an exercise couch waterbed that was just water and dreamily asked the audit to proceed and the audit was of my film record and then many carbons, and with each new carbon the price rose until I couldn't pay and Phil Aut said we still had not found who was responsible for destroying the film but we might try another carbon.

Instead of wonderful questions like forestalled dreams, I asked the gallery girl if she knew Jenny Cartwright.

When she said this wasn't American Express, I said would she pass on a message from Jenny to Reid.

There was an alertness in the way she said *Reid?*

You know Reid, I said.

She had work to do now.

She got up.

I said, Will you take a message from someone you don't know to someone you do? From Jenny to Reid, it's this: there's a carbon of the film diary in her cupboard.

She backed away, got out from behind her desk, side-stepped toward the door to the back room.

Might I use her phone?

She said no. Then she said in a different measured tone that if I saw Reid, someone had been trying to phone him here and would he stop giving this number.

I said I was not in touch with Reid; sorry.

I preferred that Lorna not hear my call, so before returning home I found a kiosk. Cosmo wouldn't be in my address book, but my address book was back at Sub's. Now the third of the four London phone directories was missing that in the alphabetical sequence contained Cosmo's name. I was close to the Knightsbridge bed-and-breakfast hotel where Lorna didn't know I'd spent last night—long after she'd perhaps prepared that curry for the second tenor. The hotel would have all four phone books. But as I pushed open the glass door of my kiosk I recalled Cosmo's number—pure accident.

He said he'd got my card and Dagger had told him who Claire was but he didn't understand why *she* would want to know where *I'd* seen Krish.

Then Cosmo didn't say anything. After all we are not friends, he knows me only through Dagger and perhaps I don't like Cosmo.

He said, Yeah well.

I said, What are you doing?

He waited, maybe thinking. Then he said, Just sitting.

I said, I'm off to New York tonight.

He said, That's your line, man.

I got back to Highgate and Lorna wasn't home. Will wouldn't be home from school. I got into the garden along a walk past our black plastic dustbins. The Joni Mitchell *Blue* was in the Knightsbridge B & B. I was three miles or whatever it was away now. London is so large. It is as long as a life. Cosmo had been just sitting, probably reading the sports in the Paris *Herald.* He would phone his sinister Indian friend Krish who must know already I was in London. Say Krish *was* the one who'd ruined our film, what if I never found out why? But what if I did? If I did I could blow the whistle. But why?

Maybe Cosmo was just, as he said, sitting.

There are times when your sense of being between here and there, between people, between one thing and another, fades not even into absurdity but into something else, death or revelation, more likely death, as you sense that whatever they are (whom you are or were between), they are not near after all, not holding, don't know you, or just don't know.

The only ground-floor window that I could see from outside wasn't locked was in full view of the back of the house of one of our neighbors who had complained about the tortoise. It was not locked, but it was a while before I could ram it upward so my old paint-job unstuck.

144

Minutes it took me. The window was narrow, so rather than dive into this storeroom I got myself slowly around in order to lower my feet to the floor, and this took more minutes. The room was dark but even so I felt the long but now surely shortening twilight on its way. But it was really too early for it; furthermore, in New York, where my body clock perhaps still slowly turned inside my suitcase that Lorna had slowly packed the other night while Jenny and I argued, it was hardly 10 A.M. Maybe I should just sit. Maybe that was what Phil Aut was doing right now.

Jenny's cupboard smelled of her perspiration and soap. It was the first time I'd been upstairs since being home. There was an American science-fiction book on the floor. I was sitting on Jenny's bed checking the pages of my carbon when I heard the door downstairs.

The Mick Jagger poster was slowly coming down over her mantel; a corner was loose like a film wipe peeling a pale fold over the bright brow and toward one eye, the face Rembrandt-bright among the black, brown, blue, and purple of night and clothing, though split and lighted by bits and stripes of ornament that at a glance might as well have been in the audience or low on the sky horizon as on the singer's shirt and pants. I found I hated him and I tried to control this only to find that I hated him for giving concerts in America.

The gray suitcase Jenny's fingers had slowly packed for our film stood before the unplugged electric heater rather than in her cupboard where she usually kept it. If I had seventeen carbons of the film diary it would be satisfying to pack them in this suitcase for my getaway.

I heard no steps downstairs. If Will, the kitchen; if Lorna, living room; if Jenny, here; if an intruder, anywhere or here. The distant creak was the fridge; it didn't make much sound closing because its magnet had failed and we stuck a hunk of cardboard in the top of the door to hold it.

The water running was unusual for Will.

Maybe Lorna rinsing big pale green soft-seeded grapes purchased from our greengrocer by the bus stop.

The water continued to fall, and I took the ninety-odd sheets of typing paper and on impulse a magic marker standing on the windowsill like a mechanical candle, and I eased slowly down these stairs whose dynamics I discovered I had an intimate electric knowledge of, though I had never thought about these stairs except when we were refinishing the wood a long time ago.

Against the stained glass on the landing halfway down I felt exposed as if the color made some friendly demand.

The hall came fully into view and the water running was closer, the faucet needed a new washer.

Will began to sing. He didn't know I was in London. His voice had changed directly from soprano to a low tenor.

The athletic West Indian who was in charge of the Men's Convenience in our square greeted me. He leaned against the railing by the bushes, he was waiting for the neighborhood kids to come and play soccer there. On the brick wall near him stood three pint mugs; the pub had closed a few minutes ago until five thirty.

I took a bus to the bottom of Highgate Hill, the Archway, exhaust bad even inside but worse when I got off in Junction Road looking for a Xerox.

The diary would be ready at five. I would not have been followed.

I wondered what Will had been washing. I think I am a counter-puncher, I don't necessarily start things. It is a fault. Dagger spoke of a film; I made something of it. I did not, as I sat in the downhill bus, rightly know what Dagger had, or thought he had, made of it. I could not have proceeded differently these last few days. Dagger would be sitting at his big table pouring wine for a couple of friends and cutting sausages and discussing a revolutionary newsletter a Pole and an American we knew were putting out broadside. It was a joke, I thought. Dagger seemed more serious talking about L.A. and going back.

I read an *Evening Standard* on the bus and tube. There was nothing in it except an opinion poll from Middle America but I kept looking, kept turning the neat tabloid.

You don't leave your newspaper on the seat in London; maybe you find a trash can.

I was seeing nothing but the inside of the gallery as I made my way out of the Knightsbrige Underground and up the street.

The girl was standing near her desk with a yellow cup in her hand, no one else in evidence.

She tilted it over her nose to sip.

She nodded and turned to go into the back room where the big canvases were. A chair was pulled out in there and I may have heard her bottom settle just before the knock of her cup on wood.

I went to the Jan Graf picture of the woman. I could not say then how the painter's analytic design had let me see the red-haired woman; for one thing the abstraction didn't shift into something comfortable other than its tumbling cubic artily disheveled self, but she was there.

I would visit the homeopathic Druid. He'd known about my diary. He knew me. But he knew something else, even though it might turn out to be associated with his various respiratory and muscular knowledge.

I would like to take a cab home but I had almost nothing but dollars and anyway I didn't want to spend the money.

With Jenny's magic marker I colored in the hair of the woman a slick, dry, too orange rust-red. I did not move. The picture had changed. I wasn't so worried about Jenny. The hair had become too vital and the abstraction had become either more subtle or less strong, depending on your viewpoint.

Jenny could go to America if she wanted. San Francisco would be safer than New York. Even L.A. She could do what she liked with her remaining A-levels. Yet I would never tell her so.

I left the gallery. I was getting fairly close to rush hour, which I avoid.

In a later *Evening Standard* I bought at the tube the only thing different was a stop-press item down the side of the page at right angles to the main print, about a Rembrandt drawing. It had just sold in New York for a puzzling three thousand less than it had been appraised. No doubt no one had lost. The inflation has to stop someplace. I was in a smoker and women on either side of me were smoking purposefully and not reading. You do not pass from car to car in the London Underground, you get in a car and stay there. A boy and girl with high rucksacks on their backs stood swaying at the pole by the door; their packs were sewn all over with insignia.

At the Holloway Road tube stop I met in the elevator an acquaintance outside our circle. He's a pediatrician. His heavy round face seemed browner. He'd been to 2001 this afternoon all alone. He wanted me to know it at once. He smiled.

We were waiting for a bus, and the Holloway Road lorry traffic wouldn't let up.

What happened to your sick children then?

I share a surgery with three other doctors, I thought I would disappear this afternoon.

I knew I would remember the man's name.

I told him the facilities for disappearing were even better in New York. He asked when I was going again, my daughter wanted to go to the States he seemed to recall, to work (wasn't it?), I was in films he seemed to remember.

On the fringe, I said, if that.

He was quite a nice person.

He said, We know an American couple you must meet. You live in Highgate. I said I was traveling lately but we must be in touch.

Doesn't your wife paint? he said.

Not yet, I said.

My bus came and he stepped up behind me. I needed a cigarette but we sat downstairs. Some people do listen in England or seem to. It may be better than not listening and if you are the one listened to you sometimes feel good. But there can be something wrong in it. What?

He said he would give me his number and when my timetable was easier we'd get together.

He got my address and number.

I asked if he thought Dr. Spock would make a good President.

I pulled out my little notebook and with it a crumpled American air letter which fell to the floor of the bus. I asked him how to spell his name, I said I couldn't spell worth a damn.

He had to get up to press the Request button but we were nowhere near his address; I was thinking about his address, visualizing it, I knew the block. He said, I'm just going to take a long look at the work of our mutual friend, and he named Geoff Millan. He smiled again as if at a mystery divided between us. What had he said about New York that night? Nice place to live but dreadful to visit— the opposite of what one said.

Why couldn't I have asked the gallery girl point blank who the picture was of? Maybe because she wouldn't have known, or wouldn't have told. She'd be from a medium posh school on a green estate with stone walls and a sign. She'd be living now in a bed-sitter in South Ken part paid by Daddy and if she gave me her address I could drive there as directly as any licensed hack.

I had missed the rush hour.

The pediatrician's name was Stein.

But the traffic was thick and so slow even a passenger might tire, up Highgate Hill past the Whittington Hospital, past Waterlow Park where when I had plenty of time I'd get off and walk, past places I always used to point out to visitors, Nell Gwynne's Lauderdale rest house, Cromwell's (which was Cromwell's?), past the neat two- and three-story commercial buildings of the Village, the ceramic interior of the antique shop whose bearded proprietor waited for pub-opening time, the now stained long white coat of the butcher whose display of Scotch and Argentine beef seemed to sag in the light, the art supply shop whose well-preserved proprietress told Will and me just before I went to New York that the vibrations of the new traffic up Highgate Hill bound for the North Circular were weakening walls and foundations—past our bank, past a Chinese and not an Indian restaurant and to virtually the top of the hill, the last stop where my bus came to rest window-to-window with the greengrocer where there was a queue from inside out onto the pavement around the shallow wood cartons of something I did not note except some red and some yellow and where inside there was still an awful lot of produce considering the hour.

I cut quickly past the boys playing soccer in the square.

Will let me in. There was not that little surprise to pass through, for Lorna had told him I was back. He didn't even ask about the film, the suddenness of my return, what airline. He did give a succinct report of the robbery. He asked me to come at once to his room, he had found in Jenny's room an ordnance survey map that was fabulous, he'd never known about them, it was just that his maths master digressing from averages into applications of averages had spent the whole hour on how map elevations are shown and how you can stick pins at various heights and make a sculptural drape to give a perspective view of what the master called a smoothed statistical surface. I said to Will that I'd had ordnance survey maps around the house for years. In fact, didn't I recognize that one?

You said we could go up there camping, but we never did.

There?

Well, Scotland. And you said the people had a hard life up there and were very honest.

I could never remember.

Will said he'd come up the stairs from the kitchen figuring just what a burglar would look at coming into our rooms but not knowing what was there and where to begin—and on Jenny's mantel —Will liked Jenny's room because she was always changing it—he'd found this ordnance survey map.

Will had jumped ahead and was in his room saying, I'll show you what you can do.

But he made me think of the carbon. I called to him that I had to ring someone up.

I plunged three steps at a time back into the hall.

The Xerox shop didn't answer.

I had been on the landing in front of the stained glass, and I could have used the upstairs phone in the bedroom. But I had come down to this hall.

I rang again, I thought of finding the proprietor at home and getting him to come back and open up. But even if he lived on the premises, which in Junction Road I doubted, he was as English as anyone else and five thirty closing would be as final as lunch time.

Will would break in with me if I asked him.

It was out of the question.

There was nothing in this hall inconsistent with a thousand interiors.

I had had to come back.

When I put the receiver down the phone started ringing.

Will called to me.

The man's voice could be Reid's. It moved around behind my back, it tried to loop a tense smile about me but my son called again, *Come* on, Dad! I want you to look at this; and then the voice, having heard me answer rather than Jenny or someone else, seemed to stop before starting, maybe just take a breath.

I said Jenny was out. I thought, Maybe with you.

The voice said boldly that it had expected her to be in.

I said You might call in an hour.

That's true, the voice said—ask her if she left a message for Reid.

Are you Reid? I said, though the question didn't do for me what I was beginning to think coloring in Jan Graf's portrait had. If you're Reid, I said, the lady at the gallery wants you to stop using their phone number as an answering service.

I am Reid, the voice said, and smiled again I swear.

Yet if I were to go to the vastly empty center, vaster than its actual circuit could ever really enclose, empty I suspected of me— and say straight out, Who's the woman in the picture? What's your connection with Krish the Indian?—what would I do with straight answers if I got them?

Reid said, We met at second base.

I said, Well we played against each other more than once Sundays.

150

Right, said the voice further away now.

I'll give you her message, I said.

Wait. She can't phone me. I've moved.

Where are you?

There's no phone here, said Reid, and rang off.

Lorna was entering with two shopping bags hanging from either hand. Reid's last words aside, Lorna's entrance opened in me a desire to find a formula to express the day, the day had been a thought, and if I didn't say in a few words what the thought was I would loop forever about a fascinating capture that must be killed to be known.

What would I say if the Indian phoned to ask why I'd defaced Jan Graf's picture.

We had a list of numbers Scotch-taped to the table. I heard Lorna put her shopping down. I felt her hands on my shoulders but I didn't turn. I felt her breasts under my wing-bones.

The gallery wasn't in the phone book under Aut. In the second book out of curiosity I found Jan Graf. I put down the number. I knew the area, it was rough.

Come on, Dad, called my son above.

Come on, Dad, murmured my wife below.

Where is my daughter, I said, I have a message for her.

In his room Will was kneeling on Jenny's map.

If I could only get the film across to Lorna I would find something beyond her.

She was making stuffed pork chops and a ratatouille out of the *New York Times Cook Book*.

How do you gauge the height of someone like Will upon his knees and leaning over the hilly folds of this map? Three years and two months ago he had been a child. He and Jenny and Lorna and I had taken a rainy-day leave from the seaside village where we were spending August and I was considering what to do about my share of the hire-boat business; and we had driven east to the Giant of Cerne. Jenny had been our road-map reader. You're always looking after our education, Lorna had said to me when we got out of the car into a drizzle. She decided to get back in and leave us to make the ascent. The children scrambled and raced so it occurred to me they might expect to find at the top of the chalk slope a giant looming upright above them. But he was on his back, at least as we could see him; the turf was cut away from the lines of his white chalk form 181 feet long. He was hard to see, like the rugged coast of an island you spend two or three days hiking along, and you can't grasp the indentations with a clarity other than your small map's. I had shown Will the aerial picture in the Dorset guide but we'd left that in the glove compartment. When we reached the top, we were all alone; we walked the craggy slant of the giant's shillelagh, the valley of his rubbery, dipper-like right arm; we jumped from eye to circular eye, and below we paced the span between nipple and circular nipple; and then Jenny and I on either side of his torso crossed his three ribs like five-yard stripes on an American football field, and then found Will between us standing on the tip of the Giant of Cerne's upward lying cock, and Will, facing down its twenty-foot length to the twin coves at its root, said, Is this . . . ? And Jenny said, What did you think it was, stupid. And Will chased her, and she eluded him, all over the giant's genitals, deliberately stepping and stamping and contouring the marvelous marks in the deep earth, while I tried again to get an over-all view and wondered what the original incisers (Roman Britons or earlier cultists) had been able to see without the moving wand of a plane's aerial height.

The map that Will now kneeled on in his room in Highgate was almost half blue, the land area was coast, maybe island. The rest was white and tan, the tan mainly elevation contours.

He stopped talking as I entered, but began again as if we had a briefing deadline.

You see, he said, you have to think of each of these isarithms as if a plane has been passed through the land at a certain height. These are the z levels, Mr. Ogg said. He read maps during the war; he is going to retire soon. The x and y values are horizontal, see, and the z is vertical, I don't think we all understood that, but you should have seen Mr. Ogg, he got all excited drawing on the board, and Stephen laughed.

I knelt beside Will and felt the relative lightness of my beard against the darkness of his hair whose fineness didn't lie flat because he didn't give it a comb very often and our English water is hard.

He was getting better marks. I have encouraged him to take Spanish. He's always been good in maths, which his teacher in primary school said frankly was not much of an indicator at that age, but now he was as good in English as Jenny had been and also wrote impressively boring essays on world interest rates, the Boston Tea Party, and the history of tobacco that were a bit slow but were saved by a tone of authority. He considered himself an American but told his friends that he would visit but never live there, Americans were too interested in making money and the cities were too dangerous.

You see this, he said, running an index finger around a nest of contours and working inward but occupying too much space with his fingertip so I couldn't tell which level he was on—you see, he said, this distance between two z levels, one at two hundred feet, one at one hundred, well the distance between tells you the gradient.

I asked how from this map he'd tell the exact gradient.

Mr. Ogg hadn't told them that. He got onto maps from something else, by accident, he was talking about percentages and the income tax and got sidetracked; he didn't do that often, he stuck to the point and you could never get him off it, but today he drifted into averages and statistical surface and how you can put the pins in and drape plastic wrap over the pins and make a real topography and he drew a set of contours on the board getting smaller and smaller going inward and then he went silent and stared. Stephen was trying to catch my eye.

Were you scared when you heard someone in Jenny's room in the night?

I guess so. But I wanted to see.

Were you disappointed it was only Mummy?

No. But she thought I was the one breaking in. I didn't like that.

Why not? It's funny.

This is our house.

Could you find your way around in it blind?

Naturally!

Mr. Ogg.

Mr. Ogg stood looking at the board almost with his back to us and his ears sticking out and I looked at Scott because he might be inclined to burst into snickers and shake his head as if Ogg was bonkers, Scott's done that before; but he was interested and he didn't even look at me.

What did Ogg do then? I asked, and I smelled the first softenings of our dinner in pan and oven downstairs as if being on my hands and knees brought me closer.

Old Ogg drew this super thing on the board. It was an island, a hypothetical island all mountain, and on a little platform like. And he drew all the z levels like pieces of stiff cartridge paper sort of half cutting into the mountain at different heights and from the front edge of each cut he drew dotted lines which were *traces* he said. But the best thing was it was three-dimensional, you could see it like a model on the desk.

Is he going on with it?

I don't think so but I don't know. He was saying at the end that this imaginary intersection, the plane that looks like a piece of paper, must intersect the land surface at all points having that z value, and he lost me there and when he said the *trace* will be a closed line and then he drew some more contours as if you were seeing them from above and he said you see these lines are closed. The hour was over. He just stood looking and I thought for a second he couldn't move. He was thinking. Then he just gave us the next lesson in the book for tomorrow but we were all left hanging and he was too. He wanted to go on.

Will stared down at Jenny's map. I pointed out other informations; archaic characters locating a "Chambered Cairn" or "Stone Circle" and at one spot there was a circle drawn around the designation "Standing Stones." It seemed a long way from bedtime stories. Through level upon level of Mr. Ogg's cartilaginous contours his ears guided his words in to memories he would rather not bring back from the wartime garden of the noble beast where at least you knew where you were and what you must do—garden of night—plucked flak, hills of bombed houses, the late Victorian castle-keeps of Tessa Allott's London childhood, her hair below her waist—what would we have done without bombed houses I hear her saying to Lorna in another room.

And so we sat down without Jenny, and as we sat down—Lorna and Will and I—the phone rang. But no one spoke when I answered.

Will switched off the lights but before lighting the candles rather than after. He opened the wine for us. He complimented Lorna on the herb stuffing stuffed into pockets in the chops. He said to me, You're supposed to be in New York; does anyone know you're here?

I said apart from Jenny and present company it was hard to say, and by the way Jenny was touchy about things taken out of her room.

Will said he planned to put the map back. He said did I know the dome Reid built with a friend who was on his way to Africa and stopped off in Connecticut was elliptical.

Lorna asked if I wanted to go to Geoff Millan's Sunday night. I didn't know.

Will cleared the table and did the dishes. Stephen phoned to ask if Will could spend the night next weekend. Will had been going this past Sunday but though Lorna urged him not to worry about her he'd only had lunch at Stephen's and come home for supper.

Lorna and I talked in our bedroom. We looked each other over. Her cheeks had never developed that ruddiness that when you look close is a hatching of veinlets ruptured by years of tea-drunk tannic acid. She had put on lipstick for dinner; old times, new fashions. Tessa was after her to stop wearing a bra, but Tessa was built differently. Lorna had compromised on the soft contour of the new slipover that looked like a bathing-costume top.

What did you find out today? she asked.

After a moment, I said, A man who was in from the beginning and came here from New York over the weekend flew back this morning. I think of why we made the film, which may be vague in Dagger's mind but not in mine; then I think: Why let someone get away with this!

Do you think they're finished with this house?

Will your young blond second tenor come and stay with you when I'm not here?

Ah. Since when is he blond?

Since this morning when he left here, and you must be watching yourself pretty carefully if you remember you didn't mention his hair. Did he have curry last night?

Will your digestion be better if I say no?

My digestion is perfect. Say no.

No. He's a friend of Dudley Allott's. Tell me more about Tessa.

The film?

Tessa and the film.

Undress.

All alone?

No.

Maybe you shouldn't have brought Jenny that memory of the red-haired woman and Reid.

Maybe I shouldn't have come back.

I was feeling something even before the burglary.

What?

I phoned Dagger to ask how Alba was. You know how he is. He said he'd come over and keep me company.

You phoned *him*.

This time yes. He told me his brother——

His brothers range from twenty-five to fifty.

His brother the car salesman had to stand by and watch his alcoholic cousin let the business go down. They were on the edge of Watts. The cousin kept saying Negroes buy Cadillacs too, in fact that is what they buy. But they didn't buy that many and then they didn't keep up the payments and one of these Cadillacs disappeared and Dagger's brother had to fly down to Mexico to repossess it but by then the chief of police was driving it around and said they could have it for thirty-three hundred dollars.

But the car salesman doesn't work for the bank.

Anyhow it was funny.

Lorna always took her pants off before her bra.

I've heard that story before, I said.

She was sitting beside me. He asked if you'd take your film thing with you.

He was getting in touch with Claire, I said.

We listened to Will come upstairs. He walked around. From the head of the stairs to the hall beside my sister's ghetto photos, his doorway, the bathroom (light on but at once off), hall down toward our room, back to the head of the stairs, his room, bathroom (again light on, off), his room, Jenny's room, linen cupboard for some reason, and then his doorway.

He said, What's the great circle route, Dad?

I'll tell you in the morning.

OK.

I pictured the Cadillac dusting a village, shedding its muffler. Dagger had stories to get him from Casas Grandes to Chihuahua, from Tampico to Veracruz. Probably he'd been to Mexico. Lorna and I had not.

What must happen before anything else was that I must finish with Tessa's moments. Lorna curled herself around behind me where I sat upright in thought—she had only her bra on—and I reminded her of the drink we'd all had in '68. I'd had some jellied eel and three oysters in the street that afternoon, just passed a stall and had to have some. Then at six I got a stabbing pain below the belt just as we were sitting down with Tessa and Dudley to have a drink and wait for her father who was meeting us. It was one of those old pubs that have kept the three divisions, Public Bar, Private Bar, Saloon Bar. We were in the Private, a wedge of a nook that made you half recall a horse-drawn hansom you'd just pulled up in. In the normal course of accident and permutation, I'd never seen Dudley with his father-in-law, who had once so terribly opposed their marriage. Tessa's father was an unassimilated German enclosing an assimilated Jew. When Dudley and Tessa made it doubly definite that they were getting married and that Dudley could not convert to

Judaism, Tessa's father put him through scenes of prophetic frenzy —rising to agonies of blood no rabbi's indoctrination could have equalled, particularly for a young American scholar of modern European history, and descending to exhausted acknowledgment that Dudley was in fact circumcised. But before Tessa's father arrived at the pub, my vitals attacked, and I left to go downstairs to the Men's. The pain passed, but as I stood at the wash basin an old man with an enormous nose and hands and a baggy cloth cap and a louring face got hold of me to tell me his plan for a pub. He caught my arm as I reached for the paper towel and he wouldn't let go and I let my hands just drip. His plan would cater to everyone, mind—it wouldn't just be the jukebox and the rock-and-roll, there'd be a room for older people and then a room where you could bring a lady for a quiet talk and the dart-board room like the Public Bar now but no jukebox and there'd be room for the rock-and-roll records—I leaned gently away—and there'd be a family room where you'd bring the family for a sandwich and crisps of a Saturday, and maybe other rooms, but the plan would be radiating, see, radiating—you'd get your central bar in like a circle and all the rooms would radiate outward, see, like a wheel.

I said I'd think about it. He said, Right you are, Guv.

He didn't leave when I did.

At the door to the Private Bar I heard Tessa saying, What would we have done without bombed houses! Her father put down his wine glass of neat whiskey to shake my hand. Lorna and Tessa sat snugly together on the leather cushions. Dudley was tamping his pipe and smiling at no one in particular. He said, That's the trouble with London, no more bombed houses. Tessa's father shook his head, no no we didn't want any more bombed houses, no indeed, why when he came from Germany in '38 he took a janitor's job and every house on the other side of the road was demolished. When the planes came over, Tessa sat like an Egyptian cat in the Morrison Shelter. Tessa's father seemed to be talking toward Dudley's drink, a pint of beer; he described a Morrison Shelter, right-angle, dimensions—the density and strength of the steel mesh that hung down on all four sides like an oversize tablecloth.

It was Tessa, not her father, who'd told us about his law practice and the house in Munich and everything else that had been taken away except her mother, who had also been taken away. And about coming to England at nine and living for six months with a relation, not knowing till her father later told her that after she'd been sent to England he was picked up and would have died in a camp but as a World War I veteran he was excused so long as he left

Germany at once. But her father now gave us a gentler, smaller picture to entertain us—of all the German Jews in North London trying to avoid the authorities who would intern them. They would be sent out by their wives first thing in the morning, and it was a sight, Tessa's father said, all these German Jews with sandwiches in their long overcoats, hands behind them, aliens each on his own pacing Hampstead Heath all day till the coast was clear at home.

My pain stupidly returned and I was about to get up again, but Tessa cried out in something like a laugh and said, Guess what, sometimes they got home and the coast was *completely* clear—no house!

The barmaid put her head around the partition. Dudley lowered his pipe hand to the table: That was in bad taste, Tessa.

Tessa put her hand over Lorna's where it rested lightly on the edge of the table and said, If I'm lucky, Dudley darling will buy me my dream house.

I said, Where? in Middle America?

Tessa snapped back, New York's not Middle America—but we were all laughing, Lorna too, who several years before—though I'd not remind her now as she lay curled around behind my back with her knickers off—had been enough changed by her friendship with Tessa to find herself the following autumn, which would be '58, plunging into the purchase of the house we now lived in.

I leaned to pull off my socks and looked around at a space of Lorna's thigh that seemed tonight less routine and less real than the transoceanic clothes I was getting out of.

I said, I suppose the connection with the film scene wouldn't mean as much to you as to me.

OK, so we laughed at Tessa but maybe I did because she had my hand clamped down.

Of course we all laughed at her—Dudley too.

She'd had a hard day.

I opened my belt and unbuttoned my shirt, which was the same blue as the trim on my teacup this morning when the maid at the Knightsbridge B & B brought my tray and I turned my bare shoulders and chest toward her and raised myself on an elbow and looked beyond her leg to my jockey shorts on the nearly napless oriental rug where they'd landed a few hours before directly below the Joni Mitchell record on the chair.

Diary and film parted and came together, hiding one another, parted and came together like some flesh breathing, an organ like a creature, and I must turn only to the ruining of the film, who did it, who had it done, and why. I would not tell Dagger a burglar had taken the original of the diary.

I turned and put my hand behind Lorna to unsnap her but found no snaps and drew the back of the bra upward toward her head. But she rolled around on her back preventing me from going further in that direction but seeming too to open herself to my feelings. But she rolled toward me and so I reached again to raise the bra over her head. But the phone was ringing downstairs and the ghost of some bad gag tiptoed away down our long-ago refinished stairs and I jumped up and followed, and passed my son standing in his doorway with a ballpoint in his hand.

And I picked up the phone hoping it was Dagger, and heard the male overseas operator telling me something I'd been told for years which I didn't hear, then Sub's voice approaching and receding down some drowned cable. And I must go back to America tonight.

I phoned my charter associate. He said I hadn't a minute to spare.

I needed something to write with. The ballpoint in Will's hand was a very special one given me by a man I knew in NASA.

When I went up, Lorna hadn't moved. I didn't tell her precisely what had happened in Sub's apartment, only that I must go.

But, she said, what was so marvelous about this country house? What did it look like?

From about any angle except a helicopter the house looked circular; but in fact it was shaped like a squat egg with the ends sliced curved, and it had a circular stone wall around it. The odd thing was that I in fact had told Dagger I wanted a house that looked circular but wasn't and he found the exact thing.

Lorna simply lay curled on the bed. I did not want to say what the film was about.

I'm sorry, I said.

I'm thinking, she said. That Dudley found a house in the country just like that. And Tessa spoke of it at dinner here. She'd been in Scotland with her friend. You were here part of the evening. You left to meet Geoff Millan, he wanted you to meet an American.

When was it?

Lorna told me.

It had been way back in March long before we shot the Marvelous Country House.

But not long before we laid our plans.

OK, I was fallible. I did recall hearing the beginning of Tessa's account.

The three key moments moved among all those perhaps trivial pages that I'd written and Jenny had typed.

I remember Tessa's description of the house. Her having in some eerie way been waiting for me was the least of my worries at this point.

LOVE SPACE | Top-secret lips like a soft book closed. Random elation. I forget during, I forget after, almost. The skin of the back bends from a gloam like Attic honey—late sun behind—to a stretch beyond the couched shoulder blade blue and amber near gray. Does sound from the street in a current of day under the window shade color us? It is skin I finger, not hue, but I have forgotten her first name for a second, and remember that it was a lot like this before with her or someone else, do you remember how the memory slides out or you slip into it? I speak for myself, not for her, though—and for her ribs and a down above the knees and for her fleshly shoulders that are not what you would think from her tense figure clothed, the parts of her body I speak for still speak for themselves, but I can't speak for her, I have her, I breathe with her, have in my hands even what I wouldn't ever want to get at in her, like one of my whole memories I can't divide.

She is on her stomach, hair over wrist, her behind white with a red dot and a pale mole across the way, her legs just open to show a fold of sex puffed downward. This shifts as she lifts the small of her back, and now I comb my nails up either side of the gates that space her spine. She sits up like a dancer slowly, I am behind her in the Japanese position. She settles on me like part of a multiple exposure of bending forward or back. My fingers out of sight catch what they must have forgotten: that the hair coming three inches from her cunt up onto her abdomen is in three plantings, with some of the skin between so the lines don't feel trimmed. I raise a finger to her eye, it does not shut, it is lidless but there is a fold at the corner by her nose, I can see it.

Before, when we came in the apartment and emerged from our clothes and she stood on the soft bed and then pointed her elbows at me and unhooked herself, these plantings seemed elegant—a sign of truth. Now, kneeling back on my heels behind her, I recall them with a hand and with a hand I fit myself under across an isthmus to hook in her as she bows for a memorable moment forward angling opener, and leans back as I lean forward into her back like this, I look at small shoulders rising, lowering by my mouth, and I can't imagine her face and I move my hand from forking a nipple way down her belly to touch her slippery tab as big as her nipple seemingly and larger than some other memory told me, unlike a childhood place years later revisited that is smaller—but softer than nipple and without direction, and I put my other hand to her mouth and feel the mouth widen across dry teeth. A fingertip of each hand upon the tongues of two mouths. An eyelid shudders, it is mine; I think of the room as hers, but the bed's dark footboard and beyond it a chair with a manila envelope extending off its edge and beyond that a chest of drawers all do not belong to anyone, she's between me and them but I have nothing to tell them if she were a gate to them, they are not hers either. She has a pretty stone or two hidden under a sachet in the top drawer, for she has shown me. I lean back on my fists and I empty my head into my prick, this is this time more muscle than bright flood, for aimed up, and therefore I feel less sure of reaching her than if we are prone and she my horizon, though aimed up now and lifted over my inner ridge along my underside because I am behind her I feel she can't get off me sitting right down on my pelvis even if she were conscious of not wanting to get off or away. Yet aimed up and become one of her muscles veined and vesseled can I get away? It is not worth thinking, she is straining her neck, arms up, I reach round, she's looking blind toward the ceiling of this double bed, breast firmed upward, back now arched so for a time I am not so deep.

She says, Hold me, which I was doing and as if I or it mercurial might launch her into an outside.

Our being here hangs upon someone's absence in a like time that goes at like rate but other kind. Whose is that absence, how many occupy it? What is the name of this woman I force forward and turn onto her right side doing what you want before you know what your will (that's more at rest but more alive) does want, yet it is she your will who does what you didn't until you got it know you wanted, rolling a hip beyond gravity and drawing knees to chin in honor of your arching back so now you lie face-to-face having pivoted along her thread to get here, her fingers doing bump after bump of your spine as if she is making the phone ring which is breaking you both up because it stops and starts again.

Do you, she breathes lest the phone might find the bed, do you think of anyone else when you fuck me?

What is she made of inside? I don't answer her but begin

circling, I have not much of a self only the change through which I drop and afterward don't recall except in that other time zone parallel. Her question grips me and is answered as if later in that other time but maybe it is right now as my hardness is felt in these circles I describe.

Someone else? Sure. With one person, have others; wife, think of friend; friend, think wife. Enemies? heavy.

Tom cat, she says. She dabs with her tongue a point in my left hand where if the fingers were spread the thumb and index finger extended downward on two imaginary lines would meet. This touch for some beatific technical reason the Chinese have doubtless understood for centuries seems to trace a light fingernail up the longitudinal dividing line of my scrotum.

Now, if you are thus between, then that accounts for your weightlessness, extended between bodies. But are you in fact weightless because she says you taste like custard.

(I taste like custard.) She says or will say inside her you split her right up and she is real again. Hurt? Inner structure be damned; here's a soft slot only.

I am about to do something different, I feel it in my chest hairs, but as if again she is ahead and waiting she cries out or laughs or something, and is coming with a force like sound but as submerged as the words I didn't speak answering her a moment but what a moment before, and I am not circling, I have come into her and time has come and gone by, into her and out her nose's nostrils each now to be kissed. And her smooth knee.

The phone is ringing once and once and once. A child is somewhere perhaps.

Neither of us feels at home; we are thousands of miles from home.

Phone is ringing. We are listening together. A person somewhere is concentrating on something.

I can almost smell who that is, I say aloud.

Tom cat, she says.

I remember from a moment or a minute before that our hands came together for the first time when hers came up to clamp mine down, I think ah what if she were a doctor, think what those eyes and hands would know.

There's a Mexican restaurant a few blocks south. Not worth thinking about but it is there. Maybe the phone with its cartridges will feel like having a Mexican repast a bit later.

She says, We're going to Mexico in January.

Enjoy it, I say.

Plunging ahead, she says, you have to plunge ahead without thought.

If you're going to get what you didn't know you wanted, I say.

I rise over her and swing my beard down to the three lines of hair, look deep, close my eyes and think what if she were a lawyer, what would that be like? I remember when my daughter was born and when the doctor raised her by the feet her back to me and her genitals were puffed and I thought it's a boy, and when he said, A beautiful girl, water broke over my eyes, I had wanted a girl maybe, and a nurse said cheerily, Every man should have a daughter.

She was a young nurse, sexy but not beautiful I can attest to that, and I can't remember if there was one of her or two.

9 | This was not a return, except to my true whereabouts. And yet not wishing to go at once to Sub's I did not for a while know where to go. I had no suitcase.

It was a long time before I got to New York even though the time difference being what it is you could leave at ten and if the wind was right arrive at eleven, which would not have forced my own clock because Monday night I was still in that respect virtually *in* New York though in London. But my charter associate, who at 10 P.M. found himself grumpily discussing our future when all I wanted was a cheap seat on a New York plane, did get me on a Sydney-London-New York flight out of Heathrow, but it didn't get off the ground of course until five in the morning—which is the trouble with these less popular lines that keep charter agencies in business—and by the time I buckled my seat belt to take off for New York my body was almost in London, which was why seven hours later I sat in an early morning cab riding the Van Wyck Expressway through South Ozone Park and with the very early commuter traffic (onto the Long Island Expressway) unable to tell the bearded driver with his Afro-pik stuck in the side of his head where I was going.

Should I have been guilty about Lorna—regretted only what I'd missed? I'd seen us together, night, morning, my body clock going off every hour on the hour, heard in my daydream a phone ring, the second tenor calling a blind baritone's wife smelling curry on the hob—earlier hearing Jenny come in with her new key, run upstairs, stop and call Lorna—and call me—or earlier still, Will come out and wash and discreetly go down and get himself bacon and egg and fried bread and leave for school—earlier still touch a pearly scar on Lorna's shoulder in the first light of Highgate dawn but as my cab bends down to the Midtown Tunnel toll booth (which for anyone east or west who does not know New York is on the Queens side) I can't decide if I'm looking at Lorna's scar from front or behind, and I know the only thing my daydream would certainly have heard: namely Will my son, and now as my driver tossed money into the toll bin and waited for the green light and I became aware of his radio just before the tunnel snuffed it out playing what used to be called in the fifties modern jazz, Will on the floor of his room waiting for his father raised my memory to a new power of decision and I gave the driver an address.

Made up your mind sooner, I'd taken the Williamsburg Bridge. Six half dozen.

I envisioned Sub's apartment room by room by my remote closed-circuit telly till I reached his own set right near my suitcase, the window open, sounds entering Sub's high apartment like the sounds my cab was driving through. But we were on Second, Broadway, Bleecker, through Washington Square Village with its giant Pablo (guarding NYU faculty families), Little Italy to the south, the Washington Square statue of Garibaldi to the north, then down Downing into Varick with the early morning trucks shaking over the cobbles, and my spirit for an instant shot ahead to the bail bond places way downtown off Varick where I and a lawyer I'd dug up on my own because I didn't want to involve my father had gone to raise bail for Reb Needle, whom I'd not seen since we graduated from college and who'd given of all people *my* name sitting in jail in shock from having punched a fellow drinker half to death in an East Side bar—but my driver was finished with the Varick Street cobbles in a moment and was in King Street stopped in front of a fine brick house, four-story with a high stoop like the brownstones in Brooklyn Heights where I grew up.

Well, Monty Graf was not exactly out on the stoop waiting. He'd been in bed, but everything about him when he opened the door was awake, his deliberate smile above the stubble veiled a mole at the fork of his chin cleft and below the middle line in his forehead that stops halfway across leading your eye still to the hair, and awake in some communicated sense of what he thought I might think of his stubble lip and uncombed hair, whatever I thought of him, and I didn't know for sure, which was why I was zooming at all these surfaces. Awake enough to lead me past a half-open door to what was the dark living room and back to the white-tiled kitchen before he asked how I'd had the address, his phone was unlisted.

Claire, I said.

Well, he said, you've certainly been giving me the silent treatment.

He wasn't rushing things; he seemed to sense I'd come from far away; I did not know why I thought that, for I had no suitcase, only a raincoat and a toilet kit too big for my tailored pockets and I hadn't given any indication that I'd come from Sub's down here to Monty's by way of London and Highgate; he said he was glad I'd come, I said I'd been up all night and was tired, he said we'd speak later, he pulled out of the fridge some pale grapes plastic-sealed and a half-gallon carton of homogenized milk, and said, Anything else you want, and swept his hand out gently so a hairy forearm slid out of his jet silk kimono sleeve.

He gave me a garden room in the basement, there was a pad and pencil on the night table. I followed him back to the kitchen. He touched my arm and said Claire had not known Wheeler. I said, But you know him.

I only knew that you did—and that he was hired because of you. Monty betook himself then upstairs to what sounded like the third-floor (American). I wolfed an apricot yogurt and some tight-wrapped square slices of boiled ham. I heard voices above but it could have been the radio. But it could be TV, a sudden thought, for I'd come from a country where radio is still equal if not superior.

I did not go to bed.

I was within walking distance of Soho.

In the curtained living room on a desk I made out Jenny's typing on the two pages I'd passed to Monty and Claire that rainy bluefish night. Because of the number of large and small paintings and photos fitted into every available foot of wall, I took the dark living room for granted.

However, at ten o'clock after a shower and a shave down-stairs I was walking along Prince Street and was aware of something on those walls I ought to notice.

At Mercer I turned my attention south. But as I came abreast of the building where the man in glasses who had given me a cup of tea had his peculiarly genuine loft, I saw a phone far down the street and thought of the Xerox copies. If anyone had broken in while Lorna was asleep, there was no receipt to tell which Xerox shop had the copies of the film diary. It was difficult to phone transatlantic from a pay booth.

I pushed the button by the nameless name slot.

I passed through and upstairs as if someone was expected. I could not recall the trucks and their noise, and their mass tilted half on the sidewalk, but if Mercer Street had been as before full of trucks, I'd taken them for granted.

If I say so myself I had at this time begun to happen in another spirit. I reach as through a glove port into quiet for the words, no doubt some the wrong words, in order to say what was then hard to feel and is now hard to tell though if I had and have this sense that at that time I had begun to happen in a new spirit or stage, you at least who read this have me even if you cannot perhaps reach inside.

The young man in steel-rimmed glasses stepped back into his loft and I said I'd come back to hear about slit-scan screening. He moved toward the corner where the electric ring was, his hand stirred toward his kettle and electric ring six or eight feet to his left; the workbench was ten feet behind him to his right; the slit-scan track at the far end to my right and his left seemed altered, there was more equipment at the near end of the track, the camera end from which the camera would take off along the track toward the far end where the little screen was fixed through which the approaching camera received larger and larger and with infinitesimal displacement to one side or the other whatever tricks had been prepared behind the vertical slit in the screen.

And behind and above the screen and in front of a black curtain that I thought had not been there last week stood a tall black girl. She was under one of the spotlights down there in tight white trousers and a bralike white top, and a black wire trailed from her hand off toward the floor, and now a white foot was raised to a ledge or stand to one side of the little screen, and her dark elbow came down to poise on the raised white thigh, and her mouth beneath a colossal Beefeater's pile of dense hair lowered toward the hand, and her eyes widened toward me in a huge soft sound around me that carried a meaning irrespective of the words addressed into what she had in her palm—which was a mike, call it a princess mike.

Her words I LIKE YOU I LIKE YOU I LIKE YOU swept through my knees and under my feet and came around behind to hold me with some delicately smacking breaths of unvoiced laughter.

OK, June, said the man in glasses. I'll be in touch, have a nice weekend.

June smiled into her hand and said seductively, Baby it's only Monday.

She was enjoying playing with the public-address system.

June smiled into her hand. The man in glasses still watching me reached behind him below the poster that had NAND at the lower right and switched on an amplifier. June spoke again and her new voice made the loft vast and the interview ahead real.

He moved away toward her and I wandered to the bench and removed a pistol from behind a generator, and moved away from the bench.

When she passed me on the way out scuffing her white shoes and having acquired somehow on her languid route a white jacket with padded shoulders, she gave my arm a nice little grab and said she really, really did like me.

And when she was gone down the stairs outside I asked the man in glasses what he meant rifling my friend's apartment right down to the kids' toys and clothes, spreading crayons all over the place and mashing them into the carpet.

He moved to the electric ring and turned it on and asked with a little smile on his face like someone in the movies, what *else* he had done at my friend's.

I said he had smashed a television set. He said he had not smashed any television set, and then I noticed that the two sets that had been facing each other a yard apart had been moved somewhere.

I moved closer and told him that his boss Phil Aut had had him do this, that he'd asked last time Who's Phil Aut, but I knew he worked for Phil Aut, I knew he'd entered my friend's flat first Thursday and encountered my friend's wife, who let him in, and that some time Sunday between nine and four he'd got in again.

The man in glasses said he was making a cup of tea, OK? and I moved closer feeling like the game called grandmother's footsteps we played at Jenny's and Will's birthday parties where you move up when the person who's it isn't looking and the person turns around to catch you moving.

My host let sugar out of a small square envelope like what you get in a restaurant, and he said he was drugging me.

He offered me the cup and I said I didn't take sugar.

He handed me the other, I discovered a chair and set the cup down on it.

He said he'd been afraid of this, and when I said of what, he sipped his tea and lowered his cup just a bit from his lip and said quietly Oh please, man.

I said even more quietly that I didn't know what Aut's thing with Graf was, but getting into Gene Autry drag to impersonate Graf must have got him a bonus and if he thought I believed one guy went there Thursday and another guy Sunday he must be as dumb as he must have been mean to shake the pennies out of a recycled coffee tin's slot when you could just take off the plastic top.

He finished his tea in a gulp, put his cup down by the ring, approached me and said he thought he knew what had happened—

I said there'd been a window cracked too.

Who's Gene Autry? he said.

I had my eye on him. His patience seemed gratuitous. I felt again a solid value in this place of his work. It was as if his patience for which in flickering spasms of insight he could see utterly no reason nonetheless protected that work. Instead of two tellies facing, there was just one up on the bench beside a compact console which to judge from its wiring may have been a video synthesizer.

But now so quick it was like the glory of that black girl's voice coming out of the woodwork, I had his pearl-buttoned denim shirt in one fist and had whacked the side of his head with the other hand which was open but hard so it was more like an unfeathered chop than a slap which it was not, and his glasses were on the deck and he was blinking deeply from his cheeks up. He hit me in the chest with the heel of his hand and I found I hadn't let go of his shirt so he stuck to me when I staggered back. My raincoat was killing me. The best I could do was bring my free hand up in a fist and as he brought his arm on that side out for a hook my fist cut into his armpit and he gave a high-pitched grunt and his punch didn't come fast and I blocked it with the elbow of the arm I'd uppercut him with and let go his shirt as he dropped to a knee. It was a fight I now sensed I had almost had in Corsica with Dagger. The armpit, as my Druid adviser must have said some time, is one of those openings dangerously near the real circuits of the body. And as my host dropped and my fist dropped, he couldn't have said more persuasively than in half-nauseated pain he did say the word *pennies*—so it occurred to me that he had not been the Sunday one. He crawled away and reached for his glasses across a line of sunlight that had escaped through one corner of a window where the shade that had probably been drawn for something he had been doing with June hadn't quite blocked it.

I told him to pass that information (which must have meant what I'd done to him) on to Aut.

168

Still on the floor he said the word *information* the way he'd said *pennies*.

What are you really into?

He reached for his glasses. You wouldn't believe me, he said. The line of sunlight rolled along a sleeve that I saw was of purple, a light so brightly violet the hand going for the glasses seemed feeling for something in murky dishwater. Feeling for my Wednesday night promise that I would color with Ruby Thursday night. But then Thursday I'd been here and with Graf and not home till past her bedtime. On the other hand kids forget.

What wouldn't I believe? I said.

The man on the floor began panting.

He said, I'm blind without glasses.

He panted and stopped as if he might die. He said, Go?

I thought I had done something to him.

I asked what Aut had expected to find Thursday, but my host said all he knew was what I knew he knew and he was an artist and all this up here had nothing to do with—Aut—at last he had said the word the way I'd wanted. I did not approach him because the issue of my friend Sub and his kids' toys was over, and a new fight would be my host now in the right defending his real work. Whatever he knew about the Corsican Montage or the Unplaced Room, he wasn't about to tell me if his slit-scan contraption had anything to do with Outer Film, so I didn't try anything like, say, asking if he used a selsyn drive to shift panels of painted glass behind the screen slit—he must have been playing about with something behind the slit for the oncoming camera to take. I had again this strong sense that the slit-scan wasn't Aut's business.

What wouldn't I believe? I said.

There were steps rising and the man in glasses got himself to his feet.

Answer me, I said.

He stared at my chest so idly the continuing steps seemed to stop rising: Expanded real-time projection, he said, directly mind through console.

But indicating the door he said, Don't tell *him* about this, he's crazy.

A selsyn is a sort of analog computer in that it transfers angular rotation from one power source to another.

About what? I said.

Oh he's crazy, the man in glasses said.

Well he's not a god, I said.

It occurred to me I hadn't been in a fight since before I grew my beard. Now three years later as the big metal door scraped and for a second wouldn't open, I had less feeling than I should have had about Sub's being inconvenienced or Tris and Ruby's things being upset. And this touch of new weightlessness I'd experienced climbing the stairs was not opposite to but in collaboration with the straightening effect my elegant raincoat had connecting my shoulders and biceps and chest.

But crazy how? I said. Hell, you might be crazy too—you go around impersonating a guy named Graf.

The door came open and Jerry the fifteen-year-old-looking child with the lush shimmering hair raised his hand to me Hi, and went to the electric ring. He turned as if thinking again, and stared at his friend, and said, You might save a tea bag.

I might.

I do pay the rent.

Lucky I let you, said the man in glasses.

Jerry contemplated me.

Graf I heard?

He poured water on his friend's tea bag.

I said, You know a Graf?

Jerry stabbed color from the bag. The question, he said, is do *you* know a Graf?

I smiled parentally. I tried something; I said, Yes, a painter Jan Graf.

Jerry turned to me and stood straight on two feet, shoulders back, teacup held like a host. What had I seen and where?

I said I was quite, well, familiar with her, her current work at a London gallery; her abstracts were very interesting especially of faces; I said I couldn't think of anything else really to say, I didn't know how to talk about painting but I saw some and I liked Jan Graf what I'd seen of her.

Jan Graf herself? he asked.

I smiled I think and said I'd come in contact only with her work.

Jerry was like a boy I knew in school, less head and more hair. A private school in Brooklyn, what is called in England a public school. You never knew what thing you said would drive him mad with an insanity. And what happened then was quite exciting though sometimes tiresome. He would seem with his attention to whip in close to you and like a word in some elaborate memory system the numerical address so to speak of what you'd said was lighting up a new mile of gates and circuits, functions and paths, loops and levels, though in those days during the war when we didn't know about computers, I must have thought this reaction in him was more like the pneumatic message-capsules that flew through the tubes at some New York department store my mother had a charge at. Yet no—for to think of these, I'd have had to think of computers first.

I asked if Jerry knew this painter. He smiled at the man in glasses, and without once looking at me said, I know her work, she's a beautiful artist, the real thing not some prostitute hack.

He was excited drinking his tea.

I said I was interested in buying one of her pictures, and Jerry was so quick to say which one, that I said, A sort of abstract woman with white hair.

Jerry turned suddenly to the man in glasses and said, Where's June?

I said, Your friend can pick 'em.

His trick, said Jerry, is he doesn't make it with them and so they keep coming back for more nothing.

Just that one time, said John as if pretending to care.

Jerry asked when I'd seen that portrait with the hair.

I said I had to go, and he said he had me mixed up with someone else, and as I was pulling the door to behind me I thought I heard the man in glasses say, No you don't, and Jerry say, Watch it, John.

I was sorry to have had a fight with John, the man in glasses, because I knew Jerry knew Jan Graf. But after the fight—which I'd asked John to pass on to Aut—I believed I would now hear from Aut.

I was in New York, wasn't I?

In London I could have phoned Jan Graf Aut and gone to see her. She might well be estranged from her husband if she lived there. Wasn't not going directly to her like not going directly to Aut's office, or was it like not telling Lorna what the film was about last night London time?

Jerry felt something about June. What? She was taller. He'd named her in that precipitate way he had that reminded me of my classmate Ned Noble. I didn't want to go back, only ahead.

I had almost lost that sensation on the stairs before of happening into a new stage.

I went to the bank, I took the subway to Wall and walked up that deep aisle named for the wall built by their governor for the Dutch against the Indians but soon taken down plank by plank to house and heat themselves. Straight old Trinity Church rises at the head if you go that far where Broadway ends Wall, but just past the legendary bank where in 1920 the bombers missed their target J. P. Morgan and exploded instead thirty-eight lunchtime strollers who happened to be near the crucial cart. I turned left down Broad and visited the Stock Exchange where I picked up some disappointing literature for Will and stood in the visitors' gallery watching shirt-sleeved men on the floor drop ashes into their telephones.

I came down around along Broad past Fraunces Tavern where our American history teacher, a Son of the Revolution, met some of us for lunch the spring he retired and told us its first owner, Black Sam Francis, a French West Indian Negro, became Washington's steward in the first presidential mansion in New York, and was going on about Black Sam's daughter Phoebe who saved the Father of his Country from a bodyguard's poison, when Ned Noble who'd been brought here for lunch more than once by his father who was a broker interrupted to say that Washington had left his hat here, and we all laughed and later found it was true.

I had Will's literature in a big envelope and I wanted to put it somewhere. I was cutting back on Water Street to Wall and the subway.

Sight unseen, Will wrote a school essay about James Hamlet, whom I'd never heard of, who in 1850 worked for a Water Street firm right by the East River near the junction with Old Slip, and that autumn he was kidnapped to Baltimore under the Fugitive Slave Act and it stood up before the Commissioner who perhaps because of the federal fee of ten dollars was willing to believe that black James Hamlet belonged to Mary Brown. I asked Will to tell all this to Dudley Allott, who was a historian, and Will did.

I saw a Leica IIIG box but for $130, and after all, this was the same trip and I'd already brought Jenny something and she wasn't in my good books anyhow.

If my suitcase hadn't been stolen from Sub's, and there was little reason to think it had been, I'd put Will's stock exchange literature in it for safekeeping.

That had been a good half hour with Will yesterday on the floor of his room. I'd lost the weightless feeling now. The sun had spun a rainbow cartwheel in a flawed pane of Jenny's window.

The slave-catcher's last name was Clare.

I let myself into Sub's and saw my suitcase standing in the hall; and the penny dropped.

I sidestepped a shopping basket full of laundry at the entrance to the kitchen and put in a call to London. I got Will and told him the Xerox address in Junction Road and asked if he'd use his money and not let Lorna know, and tell her I'd called to say everything was all right and to give my love. Will said nothing had happened, no one had broken in, Jenny had not come home, Lorna would be home soon.

I hung up and the coordinate truck engines and fire sirens in the sound grid of Manhattan weighed silently on the miles between me and Highgate till that distance dropped like some scope trace.

Where had Dagger stashed the sound tapes? And what about the reluctant 8-millimeter cartridge we'd shot the night we came back from shooting at the air base. I could simply ask. But on the other hand, by asking I might lose what I sought.

You may have to forget anything even on the brink of remembering everything.

Lorna my beloved in her bad period prior to Tessa forgot even me, perhaps me first.

Dudley Allott himself, the cool scholar backing across the Atlantic in one direction and then the other from period to period, said for his Catherwood work he sometimes felt that contrary to the laws of preparation and intellectual maturity, he had to forget ten thousand modern European histories for some unknown duration in order to find his object and its central American space: for he it was, with an Indian-head patch he'd sewn himself on the seat of his jeans, who lumbered around right field that softball Sunday and had his place in Dagger's camera on a good sluggish bunt that he was too slow to beat out.

That game had been the first scene we shot, though Dagger (as I've explained) was for putting the Softball Game back between the Hawaiian-in-the-Underground and the Suitcase Slowly Packed, which if the film had survived would have left the Unplaced Room first with its second-hand Marx and third-hand combat experience.

Oh if the deserter's lift from Trondheim fjord to the Faeroe Islands was a dilettante geologist looking out more for trout than rocks and caring still more for boats, what the devil was I with my smattering of music from plainsong to Charles Ives's variations on "Washed in the Blood of the Lamb" picked up from Lorna, my guidebook Chartres from Will, Stonehenge from newspapers, even science from outside and inside, the outside often seeming to be little more than that hobby firm that up to now had paid me a few hundred pounds a year for little more than bearing messages.

I did a sinkful of dishes.

I strode abruptly to the living room threshold dripping detergent water. The pages left on Sub's desk were gone.

On the other hand, Will had picked up a lot from me about computers, space, England, trains, Vietnam, and about women I dare say, not that he lacked instincts, but I could point out to him that Lorna found it hard to ask for help so we must offer it before she got upset and you could sometimes tell she was on the edge when she hummed a Brandenburg—or that Jenny often lost a good picture because once again she had to get out her lens brush and squeeze the blower bulb to get rid of that last foreign speck.

She asked for an electric pencil sharpener one year and I got her one through Dag.

I packed Will's stock exchange literature and set the suitcase on the day bed.

I hadn't thought to pick up some duty-free whiskey last night but it was less than a week between trips and I suddenly didn't know the law. My charter associates on either side of the ocean seemed farther and farther away.

I went out and purchased for Tris and Ruby and Sub two small packs of magic markers and a bottle of Scotch.

There was a fresh TV in the living room, a small Sony portable.

I left a note in case Phil Aut called and for good measure my address and phone but not Monty Graf's name.

I thought of an answer if Monty asked about the sound track.

However, if I'd known for sure about the sound, then I'd have been between Monty and Dagger. But right now I felt between. Like a lookout, my eye peeled for a sign from my people or a sound from the enemy.

Instinct this morning had been right. Bar the outside chance Graf was in with Aut, either Monty was in my way in my effort to get to Outer Film, or I was in his.

I set out again, couldn't find a bus; I didn't want to pay for a cab, though I didn't really think I'd have to buy Lorna's *Blue* all over again. I envisioned the map of Lower Manhattan, my destination a grid come adrift in slipped parallels sieving into some one of the drags funneling noise toward the tunnels and bridges, and against that map in my head I ticked off like a tourist my list of things that at this stage were not inevitable.

It was not inevitable I would run into the asbestos-watcher again to whom I'd given a dollar outside the record shop, or the

174

touchy blind man, or Jim the stabber; it was not inevitable that Aut would phone, nor that my collaboration with the painter Jan Graf would get a rise; not inevitable that it meant anything my seeing my name on the panel truck just before the aerial stabbing; not inevitable Dagger would mention the sound track on his own without prompting, nor that I'd ever meet the schoolteacher who had lost his job in the Bahamas possibly through associating with Dagger and now lived in London or Paris, I forgot which. And not inevitable that Gilda would phone, nor that Jenny would come to the States, nor that Claire, newly bathed and happy, would be waiting with Monty Graf when I arrived, nor that Sub would be angry seeing the suitcase, or for that matter even care if I came or went. Not inevitable that the weightlessness I now felt again seeing my head in the window of an uptown Express bus would recur or have meaning.

But the Druid my sometime source says that in the current between lungs and shoulders, head and hand, breathing and pan-creas—or one's own breathing and that of others—the gate which a pulse finds open may then flip a whole future of gates; for the gods, to whom are proper certain provinces of possibility in the field of forces, know each other and know that Yes sometimes equals Yes and sometimes No, and my Druid agrees all this lore looks and is parallel to computer talk because in every age arise partial tongues that may do violence to some truth but that you learn to use to find the gods who themselves have given the tongues. Think but of the difference between the true (if flattened) globe we live in (says the Druid) and Gerardus Mercator's plane grid on which regardless of the deformation of sphere into flat map Raleigh unlike Columbus could plot a straight-line course to the New and virgin World and know he had a line of constant compass-bearing.

Which, as my Druid may not have known, is a *rhumb line*— really not straight at all, a gentle loop from one point of the great circle you were following to another, but in practice a plottable and constant bearing the wheel-watch could hold till you ordered a change. Look at Mercator's Greenland (said the Druid), it dwarfs your United States because the price of transformation is that as you move away from the Equator your scales change, latitude parallels widen, Greenland grows into a new space that both does and does not exist.

And is for my Druid more mysterious than at this stage of my film inquiry it could quite have been for me. Yet for the sailor seeking some calculated haven beyond guesswork, Greenland could grow and grow till it covered the pole—what mattered was that you could draw a line from Cape Farewell straight to Norfolk and allowing for drift and other measurable accidents actually get there.

But weighing my head in the glass of the wrong (the up-town) bus, and touched by some words above in an ad that ran the length of the bus, I asked a question more appropriate to London than New York, and it was this: What will you have in your hand if you do get to the bottom of your film mystery?

I run into people in midtown Manhattan. Old acquaintances. People in a hurry, sort of like me, people I now began to list as I walked south thinking I could better bear the full threat of that London question if I met a casual handshake creased with the off-spring of the years—and these you understand are many of them in my address book—people, not years, but years too in various colors of ink—and I phone them on some of my trips; but now what I wished was for one of these persons to happen without my dialing a num-ber—as if there were nothing odd about my trip or about its enclos-ing me as so many of those things are enclosed that we know but put separate in their slots or soft portable places. But I did not run into such friends from school, from college, from Brooklyn Heights, from London, from the systems of business and entertainment. And I stayed west of Claire's pastel flat and east of Gilda's florist, I was inevitably east of Outer Film, then south, and inevitably north and then at last west of the man in glasses and Jerry who claimed to pay the rent; and I was, in my course, several directions from Brooklyn Heights, where at this time of year my parents may or may not have been—the directions to begin with all relative (as my father might say about many matters) since Manhattan is thought of as a north and south grid only by convention, and in fact moving south in Manhattan (or one should say *most* of Manhattan) is moving south-southwest, take it from there.

A newsstand headline said PROBE—but the rest as I swung by was half blocked by an oblong iron weight marked LIFE. The names and hastening faces in the thick city had begun to come at me one after the other clearing me like a fence. I might be early to get into Graf's house. The day had turned warm. I passed south to Twenty-third and thus unintentionally missed one of my few chances for a diagonal through Madison Park, the south side of which I now traversed so I saw the statue with Lincoln's body and Seward's head. A bum was leaning forward gripping the railing as if being searched, and as I passed, thinking he was vomiting, I saw he was peeing into the scraggly grass inside the railing, no hands, and feeling my eyes he lifted his tan face and opened his mouth to say the words asking me for something but couldn't bring it off in that position and looked back down. Two blocks north on the park's west (or Fifth Avenue) side the Statue of Liberty's right forearm, hand, and torch once stood displayed as if the rest of her had been buried by time. For several years money was raised for the pedestal and then in 1884 the arm returned to Paris.

I'd passed the Seward-Lincoln story on to Will when he was studying the assassination, but now as I walked down lower Fifth Avenue thinking I'd just take a turn into Tenth Street to look at where one of the Allott aunts had found Tessa and Dudley a flat in '64, that bony bronze touched me. First executed as Lincoln for some middle American city that in the end would not pay for it, then capitally altered when New York wanted a Seward, the statue now seemed more curious than the bare fact featured in one of Will's pages for his history teacher. It followed me down Fifth and went into Tenth and I was finding like my Druid currents from the quill in Lincoln's right hand up to his Secretary of State's fine frowning brow or from the long right leg (crossed over the left knee) through Lincoln's lap up to Seward's cool shaven chin, but wondered too if I had Sub's brain *dommage* and was sinking forward after too many trips here from London into some incontinent tourism.

A penny dropped again, but one out of many, and though its slot took it with a snug cluck which is one of my minor pleasures in machines, its meaning was more potent than clear and all I had in my hand was Tessa's hand, yes my wife's best friend, and we were strolling across Union Square past black and white junkies doing their skits and old Jews who might have just come from the socialist book shop. Yes, autumn '64, seven years almost to the day—and she was saying, Well you can see I'm at least *trying* to become a tourist, but saying it not so disconsolately as you'd expect after a bare two months settled sleepless in New York.

And curiously that was what the Druid had said to me now a fortnight ago in 1971 before I set out for America again to make inquiries about the film: But you try to *become* a tourist.

I was telling Tessa about the first Negro volunteers in 1864 presenting their colors in Union Square; but she squeezed my hand, stopped me, and looked up into my face, her pale brown eyes deceptive and lucid, and said with a flick of her hand, New York squares aren't in fact square, I mean some of them are rounded.

She refilled a prescription on Sixth Avenue. She complained of the price but she couldn't sleep. She liked the mail chute on each floor of their apartment building on Tenth Street and she liked the shower. Dudley was beginning a second week practically living at the Museum of the American Indian way uptown examining an eight-foot drawing of Maya ruins by Catherwood. Tessa complained about the taste of the water. She had a *London A to Z* on the desk. Her daughter was going from school to a friend's house. Tenth Street wasn't as noisy as Tessa said.

Not even seven years later, now in '71. But the traffic was gathering when I turned south in Sixth. When I reached Graf's house south of the Village I was drained.

But what happened now seemed even better than an informant telling the whole story. I stood at Monty Graf's desk and beside me was Claire scenting the bright room with something liberatingly organic like the milked essences of safflower pistils, and in the kitchen Monty was fixing gin and tonic and I suspected getting ready perhaps in concert with Claire to make me an offer that would tell me even more than it promised me for my cooperation—and as Claire and I stared at Jenny's typing and were amused, I found in one of Claire's bare feet a new map that took me up to the Highgate room of Will my American son and his mother's dark hair and what he was kneeling on—and I said in answer to Claire's inquiry, No, I think Jenny will go north before she comes here if she comes here at all.

Black eyebrows, black alligator slippers (a gift from Claire), Monty came now in white crepe shirt and white bell-bottoms with a tray of glasses.

North? murmured Claire.

Monty passed glasses laced with bubbles. He raised his glass and said, To film.

Claire said to Monty, To make a long story short he spent part of one night with her and now she's calling him transatlantic.

Monty said, So father and son do talk after all. I can guess why Jerry likes to think his friend was impotent with that girl.

I wasn't going to tell Claire what I had found in her beautiful foot, which was what I had found all over again on my son's floor. But so that it may be taken for granted in what follows I will make it clear: the map of Jenny's that Will borrowed, and in which as if near-sightedly I'd seen merely Mr. Ogg's gradients and my pride in Will's grades, was mainly of the Isle of Lewis in the Outer Hebrides; and while Jenny after all was not likely to go trekking seven hundred miles up there herself, she was involved with Reid and Reid with the red-haired woman and the red-haired woman through the gallery was connected with the Indian and perhaps with Aut and through the Softball Game with the Indian and with us. Now whatever the meaning of the black-haired chap's whisper in the Unplaced Room that I had so attentively depictured before we began shooting, his friend the deserter whom he treated with increasing condescension which the camera must dramatically have caught, had explicitly lived in that northernmost part of the Hebrides that Jenny's ordnance survey map covered (or was it Reid's? Not mine because it was too well used and I was sure I'd never bought one of Lewis).

It was necessary now to talk. We had had our sips, and now I had given thanks for hospitality and said how different this room looked with the northwest light let in past the opened blinds, and Monty had said I must be eager to get back to London and Claire could *live* there and he and she had talked about it.

Claire said Dagger had had the right idea. I asked if she'd give up her job with Aut or work for him abroad. She smiled at Monty, who was a very good twenty years older, and he said to me gently looking back at her that Outer Film didn't do all that much in Europe.

I said, But Phil Aut.

Monty said Claire knew more than he about Phil Aut, but what he knew was simple: Phil Aut was his brother-in-law, he was doing OK but was having to support his operation increasingly with porn imports and educational films and Claire thought he had a new silent partner; Phil was younger than he looked, lived in Connecticut, had no contact with Monty, and had a cousin attached to the twelfth precinct.

Claire was looking like Jenny again, in a blue blouse and pale green jeans, her light hair parted in the middle and flowing down beside her eyes. Her feet were tucked under her and against the white couch she was more vivid than she had been last week, an autumn sacrifice plucked from the fingers of a god by Monty Graf, who knew how old he was now and how old he'd be in ten years.

He was talking oh so calmly, very quietly; King Street was as quiet as Highgate, a car ran by, Claire bent her head looking at nothing, Monty was explaining that she didn't know as much as I thought but did know more than he did, and that now on the basis of what she knew, she reckoned the time had come to change.

On what she knows about what? I asked.

I want to do something creative, said Claire.

Right, said Monty, also she thinks it's time for a change.

I asked if Aut was getting to be too much, and Claire had a sip and Monty opened his mouth but Claire said, Lately we haven't talked much.

Monty came to the point, though if it was the true point my name is Graf, his Cartwright. Well, what I'd said about the aim of the film that I'd made with *Dagg*er had stayed deeply imbedded in his *mind,* he said, brows scoring key words which may have been just sounds.

And had this, I asked, aroused our Claire's creative instincts?

She may not have liked the sound of my words; her only movement was to purse her lips.

Monty said he'd loved the ideas I'd outlined—and I heard something genuine in what he thought he was saying—and, he said, if I could give him a clearer picture, then he and Claire might be prepared to make me a proposal.

I said to tell me the proposal, I'd give him a picture to suit it.

But I felt I had to let go of something. I was tired.

Monty smiled and said all he could say was it had to do with beginning with the *rush* Dagger and I still had and the *sound,* and the 8-millimeter cartridge I'd mentioned we'd shot between air base and Stonehenge—was *it* destroyed? (no reply from me)—and then to build on the original purposes as uncompromisingly as Dagger and I had tried to the first time through.

Claire said, Did we ever pay your gas to Corsica?

I didn't like her tone. She was still working for Aut.

I said to Monty as far as I could tell we'd stuck to our guns whatever had gone on at this end, and I thought Dagger would agree. When Monty pressed me, I went beyond what Dagger would have been able to accept. I said yes: power poached on or tuned in on when it lacked direction but had momentum. The religious group circling the fire but not united on what they all surely believed and the agitation and energy which the camera called forth was also part of this power poached on. Likewise the Hawaiian with the steady guitar seen as if by a series of travelers who were moving down the corridor toward a ticket booth out of sight, toward stairs, the train platform—the camera passing again and again at different speeds to suggest different persons but going over the same stretch of corridor, bobbing, leaning toward the swelling cheekbones of the large-eyed boy and his girl from Hempstead, Long Island, in her wool sergeant's jacket over a plaid shirt with the tails out over her bluejeans rocking in the London chill clapping hands, swinging her long tangled wheat-colored hair—their energy spent on those passers-by but protected by Dagger's saving Beaulieu 16-millimeter camera. To see Claire's reaction I mentioned the color snap briefly seen in the Suitcase Slowly Packed, a flickering glimpse of a person then instantly packed between a black sweater and something else—well, the power angle was just part. But through all the scenes mingling England and America and deliberately unplacing the scenes, there was a cool theme of America itself—

Monty said Yes, yes. And the 8 between air base and Stonehenge?

—the softball, the space shot ignored on the rainy terrace, a NATO First-Strike Base in the English countryside. But Dagger, I said, didn't know that all or exactly this was coming into his camera, and it doesn't matter that he didn't know.

Claire had risen suddenly. She wanted a cigarette but she had risen because of me: And likewise, she said, there are things in the film that he knew and you don't. Right?

No doubt, said Monty, reaching her a cigarette like a wand and she fell back into the sofa and murmured, No doubt; *indeed* no doubt.

A new weightlessness was upon me, the circle of Claire's light body filming the strong square of mine, erasing without a trace so that attachments to our film or even Outer Film, wife or friend, pearl scar or narrow Jewish shoulders, went like a radar weather-scope, and came again and went. My heart beat hard and a sweat cooling the roots of my moustache brought my empty glass to my mouth and then Monty's hand to my glass.

Claire said, But is Stonehenge so American?

Somewhere a cartridge grew and melted into its system, and though I did not know where, I was glad. It might have been a unit of protected memory. It might. It might have been Connecticut, Jenny's Reid's Connecticut, which on the map seems so much smaller than its space when you hear of all the prosperous people who live there on their own land, though my gravity just now was shaky and my concern for Jenny raised Connecticut to some north-bound Mercatorized acre as great as Greenland; and my words to Claire and hers to me and my thirty-odd-block walk with too few diagonals weakened me, especially as it was toward some new strength I may not have had the equipment for and another longer way lay behind me that I could not quite recall and either that way itself or my unlikely hardship recalling it weakened me too, but in the direction of this new strength like a salmon finding that unlikely electric path upstream generated by the downstream rapid.

I said that long before the first night we seriously talked about doing a film, Dagger had wanted Stonehenge and had said if we couldn't buy it and ship it to Berkeley we could at least shoot it. But he was full of passing tricks and he forgot about Stonehenge. One July 4th he had got a box of fireworks through an air force friend and had set them off in Hyde Park to the delight of Will and some other children and played as background a cassette of "My Country 'Tis of Thee, Sweet Land of Liberty," which my son of course called "God Save the Queen" just as he called cherry bombs *thunderclaps*. I had first opposed including Stonehenge. I pictured a fed-up American couple having a public argument at the altar stone, I pictured a midwestern small businessman with rimless glasses (and gray suedette loafers and four children in bright shorts and a pretty wife) saying, Excuse me, sir, to a guard he was about to ask the age of the stones—it was the old tourist thing, and both too well known and too immeasurably dubious, what did it mean? And this was even before television commercials were showing Sunset through a Stone Age Doorway, Dawn at the Henge, the Beginning of Time Told Round an Ancient Clock, the Holy Slice of Druid Sacrifice, the Mystery of Life. A void.

But then I'd gone there on my own for the first time, with Jenny, with our cameras, staying the night in Salisbury across the road from the Cathedral Close, driving over to Stonehenge in the morning but not early enough to climb the barbed wire unobserved. I found it then. By myself. Without any but the unavoidable advance word you get over the years about sun worship and remains and calendars and, of late, computers. I let Jenny know more than I. Lorna had complained that I'd been unable to persuade Will to come.

What I found was a ground so old and powerful I could not be lessened by others' relation to it. In the midst of the partly ruined circle I knelt to draw my hand over a fifteen- or sixteen-foot-long gray-brown stone that must surely once have been standing; it was neither rough nor smooth, and there were glints of something else in it, and I let myself feel at peace touching it where there were no initials to be seen, a fresh touch upon a thing thus real, a feeling like one of those days in the fifties when I sensed that without being in any way exiled Lorna and I were going to stay in England. And when Jenny reappeared stepping inside a circle, her slender back to me, to take a picture outward through one of the linteled arches, and I heard but ignored the imprint upon the earth of steps behind me, I gently clawed this gray-brown rock and felt that Stonehenge had been planted here in my planet turning about the sun so as to use the constant-bearing energy of the earth-turn as if Stonehenge were a mind. And as the light footprint behind me coughed, my daughter wheeled to me radiant and excited and slightly vague of eye and said, It's a message! and I fancied the earth fading like your green-edged blue fingerprints on a dark sheet of encapsulated liquid crystals when you put it on a cool window—fading to leave, all by itself in space, Stonehenge and its revolutions as together as an orbiting station. But the cough cleared into a voice, a man in a plastic mac who wanted to tell me that they called this stone here that I was touching the Altar Stone, though without any reason in the world, it had probably been standing back there—he pointed to a huge trilothon arch near us on the far side from Jenny—and there were two horseshoes of stones where we were in the middle of the circle and the circle was really two circles though you couldn't easily tell unless you knew, the Sarsen Circle outside the Bluestone Circle, and the diameter across the Sarsen was ninety-seven feet, and most of the lintels of the Sarsen Circle were gone and only sixteen of the original thirty standing stones in the Sarsen were here now but they were ten feet apart if you measured from the centers and each was thirteen feet six inches high. The man gave us many more measurements, a high narrow face and full lips and a narrow red-veined nose, and before we got away he had altered my consciousness of what was here, and Jenny had giggled because as she later said I was nodding so much and all of that could be found in the guidebook and she wondered if he expected to be paid because of my American accent.

Dagger could see with his own mind. I need not protect Stonehenge.

Who from? said Claire.

Dagger? I said instinctively.

Don't knock him, she bridled again, he's sensitive, he's smart, you talk like it was all your idea.

Monty raised a gentle hand toward Claire.

When I was just his twelve-year-old niece he'd come up from Mexico and bring me a present. He always had a story. He showed us an old wheel-map worth a thousand dollars once when he visited us in Philadelphia. Once he told me the saddest story and when he laughed at the end I was crying, but I didn't mind. When I think of him now I feel like a child.

What was the story, said Monty.

He'd come in from L.A., he was going to see someone in New York, he said he was giving his friends in California a rest, he said friends can be dangerous, I remember him saying that, but it isn't the kind of thing a kid takes you up on but that's what he said and it was about his friends in Berkeley, and this from a man who has more devoted friends than anyone I know who is so frank, maybe that's why. He was staying in a tenement in L.A. just before he came east, and for several mornings he didn't do anything but look out a window and on the roof of another building just like half a floor higher than his. There was a black man who would come out on this roof in the sun and move around as if he was blowing his mind, looking down to his feet as if he'd once been a dancer, tossing his head, seeming to stagger, looking here, there, breaking into a run looking over his shoulder. Six or seven floors up with a four- or five-foot barrier. He would talk to himself and Dag wished he had binoculars because he once learned to lip read when he had a deaf girlfriend, I'm not joking, that's what he said. Well the fourth or fifth day the black man came up and did his thing like practicing for a part and after a while he stopped and was staring over at Dagger but it must have been too far to see Dagger sitting at the window. When suddenly the man dodged to one side there all alone in the middle of the roof and made a dash right at Dagger, I mean from a hundred yards away and all that space in between. And suddenly close to the barrier he stopped and a white dog appeared in the air landing on the narrow ledge that the man had been running toward, and he'd been playing with this dog and the dog couldn't get its footing, I can hear its nails scratching, couldn't stop its momentum, and over it went and the man fell down on the roof and must have crawled because Dagger saw his head again and then he was peering over the edge down all those floors to the street where his dog was. And Dagger laughed and laughed, I never saw him laugh so hard, tears came to his eyes. Is that the Dagger you know? I mean it's quite a performance, true or not, and then I thought the tears had come first.

What friends were those? I said. But Monty wanted to get something accomplished and he at once asked if Stonehenge was the scene we'd got a rush of.

Claire looking at me said, No no no, that was the last scene they shot, they had their rush long before that.

Oh of course, said Monty gently.

His power with Claire did not come from his knowledge of our film, though in some indirect way maybe from his being Phil

184

Aut's brother-in-law. But this wasn't the main hold on Claire. She liked Monty, liked the house and the couch. She had smiled at him after her first sip (it was only tonic) and had drawn her bare feet up under her like a daughter or wife.

I was losing Monty and Claire, the attachments here in this picture-lined room asserted their drab gravity, and my stomach complained and I smelled bluefish and lobster and fennel-stewed squid, and cheeseburgers, and I gulped my drink and schemed.

I decided to lie.

You asked about the rush. OK, it was the night scene originally number three, then two when we shifted the Softball Game.

This shifting, said Claire, it's all pretty much in your mind, right, because you never got a real print to cut.

But she was interested.

The night scene I told you about, the second day I got here. Wales and the fire. We had to see if it had come out. We couldn't be sure. The light, the dark. Silhouettes. And that grove.

Claire didn't blink.

So we took it next day to the man in Soho, you know the man.

I don't think so, said Claire.

Dagger said you knew him.

Monty watched Claire as he drank.

And the man who came out of the grove, we wanted to see if he was just another thing like the flank of a cow or a shape of shrubbery. Dagger probably wrote you about this scene, didn't he?

I stood up and stretched and yawned.

No, said Claire, he didn't write.

Then how did you know about all those Mayas?

Māyā's Hindu.

I told Claire we'd had this conversation last week and she better decide if Dagger had or had not written about the Bonfire in Wales. But, said Monty, that could be a marvelous beginning.

Near where the Usk crosses the Breconshire-Monmouth border, I said.

Is there any land for sale? said Claire. Let's live in Wales, Daddy.

First let's get to know our friend Cartwright better.

You knew me well enough to use my name the other day, I said, and pose as me.

Say that again, said Claire.

A little harmless cloak-and-dagger work, said Monty.

Sometime we'll have to discuss what you found out, I said, but I was thinking of what Gilda could have told him and what she looked like when she was telling him, but also what might be of interest in the Softball Game to anyone wishing to destroy our film—for the Softball Game was the footage we'd had developed, and I wished now that I'd seen another run-through before coming to New York—I didn't even know where Dagger had been lucky enough to have it stashed at the time of the break-in.

But now without any warning I wondered how he had known we were near the intersection (his word) of the River Usk and the Breconshire-Monmouth border. How in hell had he known that? No one there had told him, for I'd have heard. And outside the radial neighborhoods of our London Dagger is no geographer. He can make time on a main route, but he has no patience with maps. Yet he'd known this thing.

I was still standing. I looked at a wall at a photograph covered with glass that reflected my face. It was next to a painting that looked familiar.

Claire said, You look drawn.

I said, This painting by your sister?

Monty said, Yes.

Nice color, but messy. What's it of?

Monty asked if Commons was about to vote Britain into the Market.

In this picture she's trying to make the colors rise up against each other. So what?

Monty asked when I'd eaten.

I said no, really I thought she could use a few lessons in black-and-white drawing and she should learn not to use color so indiscriminately.

Claire came between us. Monty, she said, had wanted to be an engineer when he was a boy and he'd promised his sister he'd build a spaceship for the two of them.

Monty ignored Claire. He said he loved his sister and he loved her work. She'd been unlucky in more than one respect and he'd be obliged if I would not attack her work.

The word was too right, and Claire couldn't resist identifying herself and said, You've come a long, long way today.

I excused myself and went downstairs. I heard Monty say, what about all those Mayas?

The phone was ringing.

I got on the scales.

I had not questioned Monty on what he'd meant about *two* films last Thursday.

He had not pressed me about the sound track.

I couldn't hear anything upstairs.

I wondered if Sub had noticed the dishes were done.

I was now not sure of Dagger.

Somewhere in my system I knew that we devise motives for ourselves in order to supply their lack.

No. I was not sure of Dagger DiGorro any more.

THE MARVELOUS COUNTRY HOUSE

My idea. But what a day. Beaulieu magazine loaded with color in case we saw an elephant we could cut into the house after the footage was developed.

We'd focus on the inside of the house, Dagger thought. I believe we'd agreed that panning 180 degrees beyond the dining room to the window would not only give motion to the room itself but imply depth; and Dagger did get a shot of the patio through the rain streaming down the dining-room window and through the rain pelting down around the big striped table-umbrella covering the portable television someone had left on with the Apollo 15 jalopy on the screen or pointing the view. I never saw the Falcon module till lift-off the next day in Highgate.

But my idea. Flanked by green manurey meadows, neighbored by stone farms fixed in the earth and the yard mud and by the thick trees and past them the square tower of a parish church, the graystone country house was in a space of land we learned had shrunk under previous owners and been further hedged by the neighbors and by constables who had got into the habit of trying a polite bust on the odd weekend. The house of our film was in a way England, and you could imagine you heard a purling rill.

But the day was circuitous first and last.

Dagger had said we'd need a larger car. But he turned up with the old Volkswagen and I said we could have used my Fiat station wagon if I'd known. He was on time, for him. But then he said we had to make some stops. It was a real Sunday circuit of north and northwest London, four different bed-sitters; in one we picked up a couple, and at another we picked up no one but stopped to give the girl who looked like my sister twenty years ago a chance to change. So after a while we were six—two in front, four in back—and headed into Kent or Sussex. Dagger said the house was close to the Sussex border. Herma, the dark-haired American girl who had changed her clothes, said she thought it was wonderful we were making a film just like that. She had a single long plait. Elizabeth, who was so small she could sit upright on her boyfriend's lap without banging her head on the VW roof, said, What the middle class won't do to keep itself entertained. She was English. Dagger said, That's what a man needs behind him, a good woman. The boys who were English joked about someone they knew and after I'd seen a Canterbury sign left, Dagger turned right and soon stopped at a tidy bed-and-breakfast cottage in the middle of nowhere with a circle of hardy perennials at the center of an oblong lawn, and we acquired a seventh person, a tall Jewish boy named Sherman. He limped out with a high orange rucksack with bedroll on top and collapsed aluminum tentpoles sticking up like antennae and he set about lashing this rig to the luggage rack. Then he insinuated himself into the crowded back seat. Dagger said, Sherman's from St. Louis. I said my sister lived there and was married to the manager of a department store. Sherman said, I just came from Africa. Herma asked if he'd ever been in a movie and he said he'd been invited to be in a skin flick, and Dagger said how was his performance, and he said it would have been OK. Elizabeth's boy said his brother had been in a documentary on one of the Aldermaston marches by accident, and Elizabeth said, My father took me. Big deal, said Sherman quietly. Well as for me, said Herma, I've never been in a film. Elizabeth said, What do you mean, *big deal*. Dagger's circus car was getting fuller, I saw another Canterbury sign, then two busloads of tourists; the traffic was heavier, Dagger turned off the Canterbury road. What were you doing in Africa? said Herma. Seeing some friends, said Sherman. Did you get your rhino? said Elizabeth. That's not their scene, said Sherman. Still, said the English boy under Herma, you're pretty tough aren't you. Elizabeth said, For my father and for many of us it *was* a big deal. Liberals, said Sherman, the Jewish hiker from St. Louis. I said Let's get them to go through this again when we get to the house. Dagger said Yucatan was just as tough as Africa and the heads were even tougher, and he told about a Mexican Indian he'd run across down there, a dwarf. Perhaps there were unusually many cars on the road; but enclosed in his VW I had the feeling that Dagger was prolonging the trip to the Marvelous Country House in order to complete his story.

188

It shot back and forth at first between Yucatan and Freehold, but the story was about the dwarf's head and his mother. Dagger said over his shoulder, You know who it was the dwarf met, and Sherman said, Right, and Herma said, O wow, and I looked back to see her hand touch Sherman's shoulder.

The Indians revered this dwarf, Dagger said, feared him—a fellow Indian but set apart, a legend in his own lifetime. His mother had been an old woman miserably childless who mourned for the kids she didn't have as if they had lived and died. She had a dream, and it was of a deep well colored down as far as she could see with green and red and yellow shapes and the more she dreamt the more they became birds, then real birds, and she reached down the well mouth and found red eggs. A pair of green birds flew up out of the darkness and they took out her eyes and it didn't hurt, for now she saw even better but something else. And in thanks for the red eggs and the new vision, she baked on her hand-packed earthen griddle some *tortillitas* and sailed them down into the well.

Well she woke from this dream and she took an egg and covered it with a yellow cloth and set it in a corner. She left it alone but always thought about it but told no one.

This is in Uxmal, said Dagger, and asked if we knew Yucatan, and Sherman said Right, and Dagger said it was strange on the map, Yucatan, like an underground water-cave you go way down to get to and pass under water then come upward, and come to think of it if you've come down from Laredo through Vera Cruz, Yucatan *is* like that.

Well one day the old woman got hungry looking at the blue sky at dawn and made some *tortillitas,* which are wheat cakes, and gobbled them up like a pregnant lady and when she went to the corner and lifted the yellow cloth, the egg had hatched and a *criatura,* a creature, had hatched and the old girl was happy and called the thing her son and took good care of it, fed it lots of fried beans and at the end of a year and a day, so this Mexican Indian dwarf told me, and he should know because he was it—walked and talked like a man, but it stopped growing.

Well the old woman was thrilled and she told him he would be chief man around there. One day she sent him to the house of the *gobernador.*

The boy under Elizabeth said abruptly as if he wanted to identify himself, Who built those ancient cities, I mean Uxmal, Copan?

Dagger said, It's all connected, Egyptian pyramids and hieroglyphs, Hindu temples even carved out of the living rock—the point is there was communication.

Telepathy at most, I said.

From the orient, you mean, said Elizabeth to Dagger.

Both ways, said Dagger.

Rubbish, said Elizabeth.

I'm convinced of it, said Dagger. But the dwarf's old lady now you see sent him to the gobernador and challenged him to a test of strength. The gobernador scoffed and told him to lift a one-hundred-pound stone, so the dwarf ran back home crying but his mother sent him back to the gobernador to say if the gobernador lifted it he would too, and that's what happened. And they had other tests. Same thing—it was as if the dwarf tied into the gobernador's power that had an inadequate purpose and used that power for his own ends.

Is he still alive? said Herma, and I looked around at her to check if she did have that lovely imagination in the cheekbone and mouth that my sister once had and I thought I'd heard this tale before in different form and I let Dagger get away with the power-direction idea he'd recruited from me to help his story.

The gobernador, anyway, got fed up and told the dwarf he must in one night build a house taller than any other there or he'd have the priests cut out his heart on top of one of their pyramids which were only fifty feet high. So the dwarf raced home crying and again his mother said to cool it.

Now according to him, he woke next morning and found himself in this high, high building which I myself have seen and if only I hadn't dropped my Pentax in a swollen river back in the jungle, but what you remember is the best. So the gobernador wakes up and looks out thinking what a great day for a rite, and lo and behold here's this high, high stone building with the dwarf leaning out of a top window enjoying the view of the village, and the gobernador's wife looks over his shoulder and says what a white elephant *that's* going to be—but the gobernador put on his hat and went out and collected two bundles of the hardest wood and went to the dwarf and proposed the ultimate test. He would beat the dwarf over the head with the wood and then when that was over, the dwarf would have his turn.

The hiker from St. Louis, Sherman, asked when we were getting there, and I said, So the dwarf ran home crying.

Right, said Dagger. Well the old lady put one of her special tasty *tortillitas* on the crown of his head, a thin buckwheat cake, and back he went and all the bigwigs gathered round.

Well, the gobernador stepped up and he put the wood to him, whaled away for as long as it took to bust the whole bundle, and he never raised even a pea on the dwarf's head, much less an egg.

What next, for heaven sake! Well the gobernador naturally tried to get out of his deal but he couldn't because he'd made it in front of his officers and the town fathers who were pretty interested by this time in what was going to happen.

Too bad the Nagra's in the boot, I said, we could use this. We could even play you outside the Marvelous Country House on a loudspeaker—what equipment do they have there?—while inside we film.

Is Gene running this show? said Sherman.

Dagger said it was Gene's place we were going to but the film was ours. Now Dagger had been in more than good form, he was talking faster than usual and seemed half-surprised at how the tale revealed itself. And the others in the crammed car must have felt with me that we were almost at our filming location. There was a man striding along swinging a cane. There was a stucco-faced pub with people outside at trestle tables. I'll always remember them, brown beer in mugs, red tomato juice in wine glasses, a kid with a can and a straw, then high hedgerows, a tunnel of overhanging leaves, every hundred yards a slight widening where two cars could pass, and Dagger expatiated upon *tortillita de trigo*, the wheat flour that went in and how they pounded the paste, until I said get on with it, but Dagger kicked the brakes, the Beaulieu tipped forward and I reached down and tapped my head on the dash. Another car, a black Mercedes 300, was upon us and the passing place was on the left and Dagger had us nearly in a ditch. And as the Mercedes passed he said, You know the dwarf took a single swipe and smashed the gobernador's skull into a hundred bits and the people hailed the dwarf as the new gobernador.

We were on the road again; one of the English boys said, You've got excellent brakes, and Herma said, What then?

But we had turned into a drive through an acre of unmown lawn and approached the house as rain began to skid down the windscreen.

Dagger had entirely set up the Corsica trip three weeks ago. Yet when we got into it even though, having come such a way, we were shooting a lot of footage and the camera work was largely Dagger's, I felt in charge. Why?

However, here, as we piled out and I examined the low circular wall and turned to the bonnet as Dagger pulled the knob under the dash so I could open the boot and lift out the Nagra unit, and then as I touched the rusty sculptured figures which were the hinges of the ironwork gate through which we passed toward the house which was as much my idea as the Unplaced Room, I felt not at all in charge.

A thin woman greeted us without enthusiasm looking over the younger contingent. She knew Dagger and Sherman. She told Sherman that Gene had had to split. She went off by the stairs with Sherman and seemed to be catching up on mutual acquaintances— her hair was pulled back along her narrow skull, she had long bare bony dirty feet and she wore her Big Smith overalls as nicely as she'd pressed them. Sherman pulled one of her shoulder straps in front but it didn't snap. I heard him say Costume, and she laughed and thumbed a ride and said, Len says it's a cover, what the hell, and Sherman started upstairs and called back, Count me out, I'm covered already.

She drawled her East Coast American words so you felt it didn't matter what country she moved in, she'd immediately know what to do. The kind of woman Dudley Allott might have married if he'd been more worldly and more sensible and more evidently strong.

I asked Dagger who Gene was; Dagger said, The genius she's married to. She received us in the manner of a Radcliffe girl I once met who was rich on her own account but married to a staggeringly famous folk singer and was used to people all over the house playing harmonicas and guitars and was as undemonstrative toward them as if they'd been familiar workmen hired by the hour. She shook hands, said to Dagger, You know the problems, and asked what exactly he would want to shoot. Some children passed through the hall. There was music upstairs, oriental and baroque at once on dulcimers and xylophones I thought. We never got upstairs and the young woman in overalls was not the sort of person you ask Who's that upstairs?

Sherman appeared with his rucksack. You could not have told from inside that the house was egg-shaped, much less as circular as the wall outside falsely suggested, even though the dining room where three people were eating peanut butter and buckwheat spaghetti had decoratively rounded corners.

We were getting ready to film the old oak hall and from it the view through the width of the huge living room to the trees outside. After a while the children appeared again in red and yellow and olive green macs. They ran back and forth in front of Dagger's camera and giggled in front of it. Gene's wife had gone back into the dining room.

192

We shot a coat of arms and a little boy sitting in a great high-backed chair beside a tall pale-green porcelain pot that held umbrellas and knobby, gnarled walking sticks. The children went out again into the living rain and we shot them opening the door, and I asked them to do it again and I took the Beaulieu and turned the turret to the 50-mm. lens and they trampled back inside sheepishly and I caught their colors retreating onto the gray step with the grass a green blur beyond and the wall stones a gray haze.

We set up for the large dining room. The occupants didn't stop their talking, they took us for granted. A giant hearth with copper kettles hanging, a pink eighteenth-century gentleman in a frame above a dark cupboard where pewter tankards were ranged— and a deep chill the camera must have taken in. I had the headset over one ear, and the resulting mix, though without noticeable reception delay, was subtler than what got onto tape.

The three eaters were, from left to right: first, a fat, acid Englishman in a green tweed hacking jacket who somehow kept inserting into the curious conversation the American airports he had used in his two hundred-odd "invasions" of America, the most satisfactory being O'Hare in Chicago; second, a tan young bald-headed American who spoke of radio telescopes in New Mexico and worked as far as I could tell for some foundation in Taos that had a lot of cottages, and he addressed the far man (with a note of irritation in his voice) as John and was addressed by Gene's wife when she came in after a while as Lem or Len, and was of interest to me in another way I'll explain presently; third, the one person here I'd already met, in fact played ball with in Hyde Park, for whom this was the second appearance in our film—this was the black man Chad who'd been up at Oxford on a Rhodes, and he had lately finished his degree in Philosophy, Politics, and Economics. He said hello. He was from the Bronx but you might not guess unless you listened very hard or saw him dig in at the plate waving the bat high, because he had had tribal cuts opened into his cheeks, three on each side, though he may have been much less interested in magic medicine than in policy and maneuvers. Herma, the American girl, was at the end of the table on our right, Elizabeth and her boyfriend on the left. The other English boy was out with the kids and I saw him dash past the window and slip and fall on the patio near the café umbrella and TV set, get up and run away perhaps pursued by a child, but I didn't see. We rigged the omnidirectional mike on the long dining table behind the jar of peanut butter running the wire off the table at the side away from us and hiding it under the spread-out pages of the Sunday *Observer*. My idea was to use some of their talk when they weren't on camera (even though that talk would be synchronized with whatever else in the way of objects we were shooting) and use it as sound track behind what we already had of the children and the hall, thus an adult collage in insignificant accents like a kind of audible projection into the future of those rustling color-visions of children in their slickers, and I hoped the sharp close-up of the tough little boy no more than eight shoving his cheeks right into Dagger's lens would say a lot when behind that simple energy you heard the rambling drone of two men's voices touching upon nutrition, space, or ideology. At one point in our day, imagining we'd have more time than it turned out we did have, I said we must tape the kids talking, they could make up a round-robin horror story to cut in behind our discussing adult faces that we'd already begun filming, and Herma who paid me a lot of attention in the absence of Sherman called from the far end of the table that that would be beautiful. Dagger by then was inserting a fresh magazine. My plan was when we had it all together, say in a month, to splice in shots of the English landscape there, the Frisian bull black and white against the damp blue sweater of the bearded booted young dairy farmer tramping through his field, and then near the church the graystone vicarage discovered from the side showing a flat lawn and white croquet wickets—the vicar too, for Gene's wife said he'd been to America and looked like Hollywood's idea of a Church of England skypilot and she could see him with her parents caressing their sherry glasses—I say this was some of the plan, brief cuts into these outer visions to establish a context and transform it strongly, suggesting an environment at least English, possibly mingling England and America, subtly and firmly adding this to the bulk of our Marvelous Country House footage as you can add scale or emotion in a commercial film by cutting in music. Herma's soft sex might do something to the three plates of buckwheat spaghetti diminishing in front of the three different faces of the men upon whom we'd intruded, and Elizabeth might irritate someone. But my first sense was that no one was going to jump through the window, and the relation of the monumental dining table to the men sitting at it left to right, fat, bald, black, was not going to flash onto our Anscochrome spawning vectors of mortality or enclosing any notable sense of space or stasis. Something like that was what I wanted, there was no plot, or none so far, but in my heart I thought I knew what we were going to get and in some eerie anticipation Dagger was going to get what he really wanted through getting what I pushed him to get in the process of our film. I don't deny the editing later is crucial, but I don't like all this cutting-room crucialness you hear about. I once went to a film theater and sat in an enclosed booth-seat itself so dark I felt ensured by velvet, and so toned or reinforced by the quarter-canopy that came above the back of the seat I felt like a spy-king even to the extent of feeling the electric danger of palace assassins, and I sat as if alone there in New York one night though very conscious of a couple of girls now out of sight in their niches in the row below mine, and I saw an ancient film about Eskimos that I later heard had little or no editorial cutting and no retakes at all. I wondered what it would have been like if there'd been all that after-the-fact doctoring, and on this day of the Marvelous Country House I had begun outside at the wall and its allegorical gate and in the hall with its aloof young proprietress and a few live children growing before your eyes irrespective of where on earth they were and one little girl chirping to me We had the June monsoon this year. Which was what the tabloids had called it with that faint tropical echo at some firm musical remove connecting the English mind to the empire gone by. But coming into this room with a not disagreeable faint scent of vomit from the grated cheese sprinkled on the hot spaghetti and the warm smell of peanut butter shining up out of the open jar, I'd felt something wrong with the triumvirate. It was perhaps that they didn't acknowledge us, didn't object or joke, or act interested in the equipment, and Dagger out of character didn't get at them to make them laugh or get mad; he might well have been under the spell of Gene's wife somewhere else in the house who had said she'd rather we just filmed in the dining room or outside the house, and of course it was raining though not on the moon.

John the Englishman, who looked like Teddy Roosevelt, was talking with his mouth full as we entered. He was saying, I don't see how you get from one to the other, I grant the first but how does the second follow?

Chad nodded to Dagger and me; he was careful, but he would smile and then forget to drop it; he wound his spaghetti on his fork slowly as if he were understanding something through it. He was about to answer before raising his neatly wrapped fork to his mouth, but John who had now swallowed continued in the same vein so you didn't know what the subject was except that John was not going to be inhibited by us. Dagger said the light was going to be strange but OK with gray day outside and electric globes here. He had the camera on me as well as on the triumvirate while I placed the mike and brought the cable toward me and under the table and back toward the camera and our window, so the person nearest the cable coming out on the camera side of the table was Elizabeth's boyfriend but he was a few feet to our left. Herma said I'm Herma, when she came in, and John finished his rapid-fire points about the perfect mechanism, the given, being subject to accidents which you may call solutions if you like, accidents, yes—and just before he said *thermal* accidents (which made Len turn his head abruptly to look at John), the Nagra began recording—*thermal* accidents you know, perturbations.

Chad said, But these accidents can be anticipated and built into the mechanism.

He looked up at the camera, then to his left to Herma and grinned sheepishly; he was perhaps twenty-five. She smiled back, and shrugged happily as if to say I haven't a clue but it's nice to be here and I'd be happy to fuck soon.

Herma's sensational, said Dagger, who hadn't shifted his aim from the triumvirate; she's from Toledo and her father produces glass.

Oh, Daddy's incredible, said Herma.

Len burst into a loud laugh, but John burst out with more words: Glass? What kind? You say he *produces* glass? I was in Toledo last spring when I had an appointment in Detroit, do you know Lambertville, I've a friend there who's in the coal-shipping business in Toledo, what are they going to do about Lake Erie?

But Chad said, But if accidents happen to this perfect system you're talking about, they're a minor factor.

Randomness, said John (and the camera still had not moved, and Len pushed back his chair to rise), obviates a master plan, I don't care if you're talking about replicating molecules or gambling—

Len rose and asked Elizabeth if she'd like something to eat, and she said a glass of the wine, but I had the distinct impression Len had wanted to interrupt the ongoing John, who now said Stop gnashing your teeth, Len.

Chad said, We don't disagree all that much, just about sequences.

I whispered to Dagger to shoot the painting, the pewter, the curious molding where the room's corners rounded, the dartboard on our left oddly hung to the right of the kitchen door and beyond the left end of the sideboard; I suggested a shot through the kitchen (a mere distant brainstorm, the kitchen door wasn't open and I only imagined a shot through the kitchen window above the sink to an ancient branching farm implement, its oak fittings standing low against the stony sky).

The randomness, Chad said, might be said to *precede* a plan, but the plan can forestall all kinds of accidents.

Randomness *creates* purposes, said John before lowering a helping of spaghetti into his mouth like some shredded, limp-blooming cephalapod. Dagger I am almost certain missed this, he had cut to Len pouring Chianti for Herma, Elizabeth, and the English boy, Dagger and I declining.

Far off, I heard the sea, it was a recording that had replaced the music. I had a physical sensation like being forced to breathe compressed air from a tank on my back—preternaturally abstract language getting out of hand. I asked what in particular was random, there *was* no such thing as randomness—but I think Dagger may have switched off for a second to pivot from the 15- to the 25-mm. lens, which isn't all that close, but we wanted enough width to get a good stretch of table—and he had cut round to the hall door where Gene's wife had appeared.

John at once said, Your film is random, you speak, a woman comes, a hand opens, the rain might be raining or not, though within that accident *you* might *film* it or not—

Oh *shut* up, said Len, and took his plate out into the kitchen leaving the door open, but there was no window from where I stood. I turned to the window behind us here in the dining room with its rounded corners and its discussion and its cast all so awkward you felt it was perfectly spontaneous except it seemed rigged—and under the striped umbrella stood two children and Herma's English boy watching the moon tour so I couldn't see the screen. I remarked that this was the first trail of the lunar rover. Dagger pivoted the turret to 50 mm. for a shot of the kitchen through the open door. Len stopped on the way back from the kitchen, asked Elizabeth's boyfriend why he didn't turn around and look at the camera and seemed testy about something as he moved around the table to his chair, and Dagger moved with him. He said he was going to turn off those seasounds upstairs, but at the hall door blocked by Gene's wife he turned to Dagger who was still with him, and said What the fuck is the point of this?

There was a little physical business at the door with Gene's wife but Len didn't want to play and he pointed his index finger toward her chest as if to touch her but then pushed past and then his steps were on the hall stairs.

John said what *were* we up to, then quickly called out to Len not to be so bloody restless; and Dagger, who was back on 25 and was filming Chad with the pink gentleman in the portrait behind, said we'd know when we saw it all together.

And where have you been? said John, who seemed unaware that Herma was wandering behind the duumvirate hoping to be filmed.

I said we had borrowed a zoom in Corsica but they were very expensive to rent and we figured the three standard lenses we had would—

Turret mount? said John.

The sea sound continued.

Dagger was filming Gene's wife, who looked more and more like a model. It even made her smile for a second, and John and I went on talking, and when I said we'd been in Corsica filming and he asked what and didn't let me speak but quoted a long Corsican song about a dead dog that ended with a proudly irrelevant chorus about Napoléon Napoléon Napoléon, I knew he had his facts off, though all he'd done was put two truths into one instance.

I asked for the camera. I pivoted it on the tripod ball and focused through the window. The patio was deserted, the TV screen snowy, then clear; the landscape beyond Hadley Rille Canyon disappeared and there was a man in street clothes standing by a lunar rover, the child in the olive green mac chugged by and this green against the rain-flattened color of the field was a subtle moment of life. John was asking about Corsica, had we been to Calvi, Bastia, Filitosa. Dagger was saying we'd gotten good footage of a naval battle but we weren't sure what political context to put it in, and John narrowed his puffy eyes instead of smiling uncertainly.

We needed more film. Dagger unscrewed the camera and tried to put it in my hands, but I said I'd go for the spools in the hall and Dagger indecisively said maybe we should reload out there, there was less light.

Gene's wife had disappeared. I heard her talking to Len upstairs, it didn't sound good, her even sound sort of combing through his rising falling intensity. I thought, We've been unlucky, Dagger muffed it.

I wanted people we could know, but this complaint found no place in the diary pages I gave Jenny to type.

Eighteenth-century choral music came on upstairs.

Elizabeth was engaged in a discussion of ends justifying means. John knew one of her dons. John was himself a technological consultant. He spent half the year in America and owned a house near Portland, Maine.

Chad was on camera saying he had more to offer us as a ballplayer. The six scars, the paler palms opening and closing, the modest American demeanor cloaking muscle, and behind him someone's pink ancestor in the wall: a series full of energy, though whose energy? And had one of the portrait eyes now blinked back its two-hundred-year-old pigment in favor of the human pupil of someone on the other side, the ghost of some grandmother somnambulist: and for us—energy of others—look out!—a chance of some experimental revelation on film which the commercial sector would get hold of and shrink to a neat train of erring or psychotic behaviors—and where was Sherman! Maybe just sitting, taking a bath, reading, all of these, or solemnly removing every item in his pack, his other jeans (not mentioned), his Minox (mentioned by Dagger), a photograph? (not mentioned), not the portable butane-cartridge mini-stove because he had given that away to a poor Scots couple after a bed and some porridge and not much sleep listening to them most of the night fight out their poverty and unemployment at the kitchen table rather than in bed.

The English boyfriend of Elizabeth had moved to the hall doorway and was talking to Gene's wife about the effect of this room's shape; by rounding the corners you enlarged the space.

Herma and Chad were discussing radical diets friends had gone on, and Chad wrapped one tube of buckwheat spaghetti around the tines of his fork and leaned over and put it in her mouth.

The choral music stopped in the middle of a big note upstairs.

John seemed redder and fatter, I looked forward to seeing him on Anscochrome. He rose in the middle of Elizabeth's latest sentence saying thank God he wasn't an undergraduate any more, looked at me, weighed my worth, and said, What *were* you after in Corsica? You went to Filitosa of course, I once met the lady who discovered the significance of the menhirs there, she had a lot to say about a face sculpted by superimposed V's; you know all about that I suppose.

I said going to Corsica had been Dagger's idea and the only pure plunge of the whole plan, and Dagger had got expenses from a New York contact, and there was an ecology conference there with

Americans, and Dagger's wife Alba was French, and there are drugs up in Bastia and there was a little Franco-Italian contretemps we got onto film which takes you back to the wartime occupation and a little rumble involving French and American students which was too complicated to tell just with film, but nothing exactly political.

But I didn't ask about that, said John, I didn't say anything about that.

No one was talking and we heard steps coming down.

John called out, Going somewhere, Len?

I said I didn't care if he'd asked or not, and I had almost a thing to say inspired by his dense dark hair almost as dark as Chad's that made John's mottled puss and the stiff one-piece movement of his corpulent torso seem prematurely old by contrast, but the thing just missed the circuit of articulation and he was saying You can go to hell, why would anyone pay your expenses to go make a film in Corsica, and spare me your—or were you *in* the war? Why I could tell you about *real* things do you hear, real forces and Corsica too while you're at it.

Christ, John, said Gene's wife, but Len was in the doorway beside her raising a long-barreled pistol at John and saying OK what about a game of darts John, but Dagger's quick pan to Len bumped into my shoulder as I moved slightly and Len fired twice into the dart board. Chad, John, Herma, Elizabeth, and the English boy dropped to the floor, I smelled the after-sound. Gene's wife said, Christ, Len, who replied, Come on I want to talk to you.

And that was pretty well that.

I guess you could say that in professional parlance we got a few reaction shots.

I smelled the shots.

I wanted to be invisible and stay here and see what the relations really were, though film might have failed to do them justice. And what did Gene's wife behave like with Gene?

An American proverb says, Modest dogs miss much meat.

The film, if only what was missing in it, was bringing on the very feelings that lay behind it.

But we weren't finished, though Gene's wife preferred that we not use the living room.

John and Len disappeared. Gene's wife made buckwheat spaghetti with soy sauce and insisted we eat.

Now that we were going, Gene's wife touched Dagger and kissed him.

The rain was trying to stop.

Dagger got a ten-second wide-angle hand-held pan of house, patio, and grounds.

We had more film, and we turned in at the vicar's. He was a tall, thin, white-haired widower officially retired but serving as supply priest. His reversed collar gave his lean, loose old neck room and his gray serge hung on him gracefully. He gave us a tour of his mantel-piece, all the postcards and knickknacks ending with Marilyn, who had died while he was in America. He had brought this picture. He had given three sermons, one a year, on Marilyn Monroe, and they had been a great success because out here in the country we'd be surprised, he said, but people thought about America. The title of the last had been Marilyn Monroe and the Knights in Shining Armor.

He showed us his set of Mark Twain and asked if we'd read "The Stolen White Elephant"—we had not.

Dagger filmed him but we didn't have sound, but I'd never have been able to forget the love in his Nordic blue eyes above the thin unhurried mouth that had spoken its brief Communion sermon this morning, even if when we said goodbye out in the drive in the Scotch mist he hadn't told us—slipping the black-and-white postcard of Marilyn into his pocket—that he had a married daughter in Cin-cinnati and one here in a hospital.

Elizabeth on the way back to London was of the opinion that Len was envious of John and having it off with Gene's wife. And who was Gene?

Dagger said I had almost gotten something interesting out of the scene when I baited John.

I said I hadn't baited him, John was just a bumptious bright Englishman rolled into one big mouth connected to a larger bowel.

Someone made a *ts-ts* sound—English chiding—restrained condescension.

Elizabeth wanted to know how long I'd been over, I said long enough, Herma asked where Sherman was, Dagger said Back loading his pistol.

It was his? said Herma's boyfriend.

How does one know? said Elizabeth.

I wondered what was on our film. A minor room mainly. A space containing persons English and American, possibly containing the outer spaces of field and farm and church and children in their glimmering slickers.

Why *would* Outer Film pay us to go to Corsica? It had been

an even longer ride back from Ajaccio. Now two weeks later I saw the Corsican venture had had an effect on Dagger and me. We were both venturing a bit further into the somewhat chance material.

Or that had always been my idea.

But Dagger had now returned to Yucatan, as if what had passed through the Beaulieu lenses onto film feeding across the camera's gate had gotten him from the dwarf's elevation into power, to now the present—or as if the Marvelous Country House hadn't happened.

Lorna started using the word *marvelous* a lot in 1958. The time of the first quickening of the Tessa relation. And *terribly* in that English or Anglo-Wasp sense of *very*. These words from Lorna's mouth, whether describing what Dudley looked like when she met him the Saturday they all (except me) went to *South Pacific* at the Dominion Cinema, or reporting Tessa's facetious respect for Dudley's historical researches, grew round them a conundrum importance that placed me between two fates: to be right in the wrong spirit, and to be wrong in the right spirit. I am confounding what already was a swollen cartridge but now has still not burst but billows with soft insistence into the creases of many times. My father oddly then in '58 did not say Well as for me I'd sooner see the rest of America first, though he did imply Well what exactly are you doing there. My mother went further and wanted to know what she could tell two of her dear friends it was I was doing abroad. Staring through her tourist lens foreseeing transparencies (called slides in the States), she found an alien element in the invisibly circled square of lens-view and did not wish to pivot to something else, for what she wanted was right here: in background a band-shell and two hundred empty folding chairs, in foreground upright masses of gross red carnations and rain-fed green (the shrubbery that evoked country estate, the sward that threw up or unfolded in front of you English cathedrals, Lincoln, Wells, Salisbury—within smell of beer mugs and taste of Worcester in the tomato juice)—but there was son Cartwright with a new beard in '58 and '59 and his hands in his pockets pursing skeptical lips not setting the scene, not moving out of the way—I speak figuratively, in fact I have on occasion stepped to one side so a lady of some nationality in flat walking shoes could "get" what lay behind me. No, my father said, hell it makes sense for you. It's a good life. And he told business associates about that good life of mine and my family's, though my catch-as-catch-can methods of finding a living came out in his words as some culturally filtered mode of capital diversification.

Lorna spoke about a country house. First back in New England. Then later nearer to home, as we increasingly thought of it.

We had six hundred feet, mostly of that dining room. Over twenty minutes. Pretty extravagant I thought then and that night when I got started writing. But the film shrank and my diary account (which I had to stop working on when Lorna came in and I noticed I had a headache) began to seem a rightful decompression.

The dwarf had told Dagger that after he'd killed the gobernador his mother died. But at another village there is an immeasurable well leading to a cave that goes miles and miles to another town, and in this cave by an underground stream an old woman with a snake at her feet sells small portions of water in return not for legal tender but for a tender *criatura* to feed the snake. And that old woman is the dwarf's mother.

Dagger slapped me on the right arm and I tried to be companionable and said I bet he'd made half of this up.

A little editing, said Herma's boy.

One of the boys asked if Herma had read Vonnegut.

I said my daughter had read him for days at a go.

The dwarf when Dagger talked to him was pretty well off, but political changes had come and he was no longer top dog, but the locals were afraid of him and he is afraid to go down that well to see his mother because he is after all not much bigger than a *criatura*.

When Dagger dropped me off in Highgate the summer light was still with us.

Out of the back seat Elizabeth said, If you don't like it here, why don't you go live in America?

I reached back and touched her leg and said I'd phone her, we were shooting Stonehenge in two weeks. As I straightened up outside the VW, Lorna and Will pulled up in the Fiat and Dagger waved frantically.

Parting, I still had one big thing to myself. Dagger hadn't mentioned it and I didn't think he'd believe me. And the morning in Ajaccio when the three people passed the wall of the fort he hadn't had the 12–120 zoom we borrowed, and then the three didn't like being filmed and hurried away. If Dagger hadn't seen it himself, he wouldn't now believe me—that the skinny bald man in that threesome in Corsica had been Len—a face which (along with Tessa's "moments") I recorded early in the original diary of that day we shot the Marvelous Country House, but which now in this swollen uncartridge-like and maybe no longer so replaceable memory of day and diary I put practically last.

I lay at length in our high-sided tub. Lorna knelt on the mat resting her arms along the edge.

I watched my risen hair gather bubbles and thought how Will had likened Vietnam on the map to a somewhat misshapen seahorse and I had said it was even better if you threw in Laos and Cambodia. My fingers stirred under the water.

I told Lorna that in Hindu thought Māyā has opposing qualities. It is a force of illusion, and illusion is inferior to truth, and truth lies beyond the senses. But Māyā is also a force of illusion that helps us to believe in this same world the senses give us, and this makes Māyā a force powerful, even good.

Who told you that? Tessa?

Lorna released one of her arms and took my flesh in her hand and lifted it above the water. I took the soap from the dish that is in the aluminum frame that rests athwart the tub on opposite edges, and I rinsed off the gray that Will invariably leaves. Lorna let her fingers slide up, and then let me drop, larger.

No one told me, I said. I looked it up.

Do you think they'll get off tomorrow?

Irwin and Scott? I said.

It'll be worth watching, said Lorna. We saw some today. Jenny even took pictures of it and Will made her mad.

Lorna and Will had been to Kew with Tessa and Jane, who was now almost thirteen. To my surprise, Tessa and Dudley had had a long talk with Dagger and Alba, at a party the evening of the day Dagger and I got back from Corsica. Whose party Lorna didn't know. Dudley was quite animated for him and had embarrassed Tessa by asking out of the blue if Dagger knew someone called Nash.

Who was Mary Napier? Tessa said Mary knew Cartwright.

Someone I met in Corsica. But why did Will make Jenny mad? Tell her a shot of the telly screen wouldn't come out?

No. That she ought to watch what was happening in front of her eyes instead of transferring it to a camera.

I thought of our twenty-minute shot today and could not imagine it cut up, transposed, reduced.

Tessa came to mind today, I said. There was unexpected violence on the set. It would have amused her.

The bath ended, and the night began.

The Sunday after Apollo 15 Dagger and I played softball in Hyde Park. Chad didn't appear, but he seldom did. Our umpire Mr. Ismay had told me long ago that Chad had postponed his Rhodes to fulfill his ROTC contract, then had come to Oxford without returning home. Well, now he was an Oxford B.A. with an automatic M.A. to follow and maybe he had gone back to New York.

Dudley Allott was not in right field.

I gave Jenny the Marvelous Country House to type and said I had even surprised myself this time, there were people in it who were not on the film.

I told Dagger the Allotts were at Cape Cod. Dagger said Dudley had been in New York checking out letters supposed to be in the possession of a relative of Samuel Cabot. Cabot was the physician-ornithologist who had traveled in Central America with Frederick Catherwood.

I was surprised. Yet Dagger knows everyone eventually.

What Dagger would not have known was that Dudley was not only tracking the elusive character of this Englishman Catherwood in his own unique drawings and in the words of his sponsor and companion the American John Lloyd Stephens and of others. Dudley hoped as well to solve a mystery heretofore accepted as part of Catherwood's odd story. Destined to drown in a collision between the *Arctic* and the *Vesta*, Catherwood suffered a tragedy almost as great by fire. The night of July 31, 1842, at a rotunda in New York, Catherwood's Panorama of Thebes and Jerusalem, together with hundreds of sepia drawings from his recent Central American trip with Cabot and Stephens and a treasure of pottery, sculpture, dated wooden lintels, and on them certain glyphs that were a revelation and precipitated a revolution in Central American archaeology, all burned, leaving Catherwood only his determination to embark again.

But by now Dagger had more pressing interests. One of them was Alba. The week after the Marvelous Country House he took with his double-lens reflex a delicate nude of Alba in profile at the end of her eighth month.

10 | The basement bath offered the best shower spray money might buy. It needled my scalp and hung my beard in mats and revived my eyelids when I turned my nose to the nozzle breathing the water which for all I cared could have come underground through sewers, then to be washed up into Monty Graf's tanks by the free swing of interborough sludge. But under pressure the fine tines of water this Tuesday in October at 6 P.M. struck me like ozone, and I looked up into them.

We have never installed a shower in Highgate. A hand nozzle

and hose is what we have, and so we take longer to bathe but it is more relaxing, though on the other hand or knee we don't bathe so often.

I kneaded my buttocks and abdomen, there was an amber oval of Pears coal-tar soap, I did not care how deeply Monty Graf might be in conversation about me on the phone upstairs or if one call had ended and the phone had rung again and a new conversation about me or not about me had begun.

I did not care, and yet the weightlessness had passed.

And now I feared it I think.

But I was glad about a thing I'd decided under the water, and those against whom I would now move would be unlikely to forestall me. What was known of me? Even from the diary what would Phil Aut know of me beyond certain technical interests or a difference between Dagger and me drawn so faintly Aut might guess at most that Dagger was impulsive and casual, I reflective, also imaginative, also plodding. Jerry and his friend John, the fellow in glasses, had made up their minds we were a couple of hacks. Anything of use must follow from that.

I was half-dressed and toweling my hair when Claire came down to say we were eating Mexican tonight. She had had her black clogs on before, so I assumed her bag was in or near the living room, not in the upper reaches of the house where she had had her own bath.

Sub had phoned for me, she said, and Monty had called down but I'd been in the shower. I said I'd phone back.

She asked if I wanted the bedroom door open and when I kept rubbing my hair and let the towel hang half over my face, she closed the door as far as the latch but not all the way. There was a doomed impracticality in this and in some spirit of her behavior that made me half-expect her to say, We mustn't disturb Monty on the phone.

He was in fact on the phone, I had come from the bathroom and found his voice but far away like a crossed line whose voices interfere but aren't close enough to hear.

I put on my wrinkled shirt. I was ravenous.

Claire said, That story about Dagger, it gave the wrong impression.

I asked if she thought his laughing about the dead dog would make me think Dagger cruel—and she said she didn't mean I wasn't his friend.

I felt it wasn't just that story that had brought her down to

206

speak to me; yet, not to be too smart, I did think that that story was part of why she came.

I asked if she had quit Outer Film yet, and she said, Oh no, and please not to say anything about it—but then she grinned and receded into some cleft of herself saying, But who *could* you say anything about it to?

And so I opened my trousers to tuck in my shirt and I asked her if Dagger had known there were *two* films—after all, if Monty knew, Dagger must have known.

Claire ran that one through her vacuum tubes and decided as I hoped that last Thursday evening Monty had told me about the two films—surely if I said Monty, then Monty had *mentioned* two, and he would hardly have mentioned the two films and not explained what he meant.

Yet she said nothing and so either Monty had tossed out some menacing riddle for dessert or Claire found the real fact of two films impossible to talk about with me.

Instead she recurred to what I'd suspected was her real motive here, her rebuke upstairs when I impugned Dagger's sensitivity: You know Uncle Dag as well as anyone and he knows things and goes his way and what he knows and doesn't know is probably much more a mystery to me than you—right?

I let the two-film idea drop. I would check it out when I made the new move I'd decided on in the shower.

I discreetly opened my door and went back to the bureau where my necktie lay.

Claire was a very pretty girl who could be boring. I had her full attention now and she talked and talked while (like something else I couldn't quite lay my fingers on) Monty's voice continued upstairs giving me intimations of my own irrelevance that I did not exactly mind because I had Claire, though I had real feelings only in the shape of more Dagger. I did not regret bringing up Jenny in England. Not that she was going to be someone's helpmate-wife, and I can't imagine I ever wanted that for her; but she is succinct.

Dagger took Claire to Freehold. That's in Jersey, quite near the shore; and there's a track.

I said I knew.

She was thirteen, she'd never forget. Dagger was about thirty-five, he kidded her a lot and gave her the feeling he did anything she wanted to do but that wasn't so, but it didn't matter, only the impression. Her parents were breaking up and then not breaking up. Her father is a gum specialist in Philadelphia. They would talk behind closed doors so that she wouldn't hear, except what she heard was even worse because she only half-heard it. Then they would sit down with her, they were always sitting down with her. Dagger took her to Freehold one weekend and saved her another sitting-down session with her parents, who would be murmuring behind closed doors, then emerge and call her and they'd sit down on some of the plastic-covered decorator furniture and she would be told gently and boringly the problems her parents were trying to work out, but she didn't care or thought she didn't or knew she didn't know how, and she hadn't had her periods very long but they stopped and her mother took her to her own doctor who phoned a shrink, but her father put his foot down; but that didn't matter, she'd sit at these sitting-down sessions in which her parents would so patiently define some of their differences and like some kind of patient herself she could be told the true possibilities of the situation and all these months she never heard her parents fight. But for all their sitting down with her and opening up for her the problems, she'd have liked it better if her father had said I'm fucking someone else and I don't want to fuck your mother and I haven't for some time; but maybe she'd forgotten what it was like to be thirteen and all this was unfair to her mother in defense of her father with whom she knew she could take risks without spoiling what she felt for him. Still she always felt that this attention she was officially receiving was directed to some thing called Our Daughter Claire or called Claire, like from whom we will have no secrets, so she felt like really a thing instead of the mature person they stupidly hoped they were treating her as in their dull imaginations, and if everything was so out in the open why did she then not know what was happening? Were they splitting or weren't they? And she now saw that Dagger took her to Freehold that weekend to get her out of the house, though at the time it was just a big thing and this was worth something too, it was fun, he took her to the races and up close the turf the trotters ran in seemed deep and soft as a farm and Dagger explained trotters and pacers, and they went to dinner at the American Hotel with all these horse trainers and a cute antique rocking horse and stately prints of horses, and Dagger introduced her to the owner of the hotel who lived up on Main Street in a big house with a long porch, and Dagger took her to visit a mad old man, the father of one of his school buddies who had disappeared down around the Gulf of Honduras, and Dagger bought her an onyx elephant and took her to the local Walter Reade movies and fell asleep, but what she liked best was having griddle cakes with him Sunday morning in the dining room of the American Hotel even more than his incredible long story of bringing ancient maps out of France wrapped round his leg so he had to walk stiff-legged with a cane and in front of the English customs man got such an itch inside his knee the sweat started out all over his face and he told the man his leg made him nauseous so the man decided to search Dagger's suitcase.

Claire asked if I understood all this nonsense and before I could speak she said this was after Dagger had left New Orleans where he'd worked on a charter boat and lived with a girl who was on the *Times Picayune* and through her had sold to the paper a photo of a fishing accident in the Gulf and the picture won a prize. But the thing was that when they got back to Philadelphia Sunday, Claire's father had left for good, and when Claire told her mother what a great time she'd had with Uncle Dagger, her mother said he was really only a cousin by marriage, but after that Claire got her periods again.

She asked if I worried about Jenny. There was something genuine in Claire's asking, but something false in the moment of silence after.

Monty was on the phone. I asked how she'd met him. She said that was another long story. I asked why she'd asked about Jenny before, and Claire said No reason. I said You know the man in the Hebrides. Claire sat on the bed holding her breath. I said, If you remember I said Jenny had probably gone north.

Claire asked why I'd put in the technical stuff about 8 mill. in the famous two pages. On the pad on the bed table I jotted "Gulf of Honduras" and circled it.

I stood at the door and told Claire I wanted to show her something, wait there a second.

She was still holding her breath—a bad thing to do. She stayed where she was. I was on the move up the carpeted stairs.

Monty rang off. He was still at a distance. His lower face looked and perhaps itself was tired. I said I couldn't go to eat with them. He was concerned. I said, Is Claire upstairs? He said upstairs? He went out of the room, did not call upstairs. On the floor beside the couch I found Claire's roomy leather bag with its shoulder strap draped over it. I found a small ring of keys beside her money purse and I took the keys. A floor above me, Monty called to Claire, called down to Claire—so he wasn't outside this room listening for a call to Sub. Below me, Claire called back, I'm here.

I snatched the pages off the desk and belted back downstairs. Claire was at my door. I kept my voice low and she did not object. I said rather fast, Do you believe this about Dagger forgetting which scene in Corsica we'd used b & w for and which we'd used color for? Do you believe Dagger could forget a thing like that?

I was of course using the two pages Jenny had typed (which had gone from hand to hand) as a cover for having nipped upstairs. Claire was caught between purposes, to defend Dagger's intelligence or his honesty.

Having asked my question as cover, I heard again the cluck of coin in slot (or was it a thin-shelled New York egg breaking as my mind came down hard on it). There was indeed something else about one of those pictures upstairs, but all I could handle now was Jan Graf and the magic orange I had marked her London canvas with: if Dagger had ignored Savvy Van Ghent chasing the foul ball and instead paused as I thought deliberately upon the red-haired woman and the Indian who himself was a friend of Dagger's idiot friend Cosmo, might Dagger not also know Jan Graf, who I was all but certain had painted that woman we'd filmed at the softball game even if I had had (if not for art's sake) to supply her hair color not so very many hours ago on a Knightsbridge gallery wall?

Monty called again. Claire said she must go up. I asked why she'd been following Wheeler the first morning. She said, OK it was you, not Wheeler. She went up the stairs fast and preoccupied. I thought she was deciding how much to say to Monty.

If she was alarmed about what I might now be thinking of Dagger, then there was reason for me to think whatever I was thinking, though at this instant I was willing to unthink such dubious suspicions, for Dagger DiGorro was my friend. I only hoped Claire and Monty didn't have a fight, for then she might not stay here tonight as I was sure she had last night, and in that case she would be more apt to find her keys gone. I thought of going back upstairs and taking her purse as a cover but Monty and Claire were already there, they were talking above me.

I took my toilet kit, a gift from Will, and at the top of the stairs Monty saw it and said where did I think I was going. I said I'd call him, never fear, I needed him but I wasn't going to impose another night, I'd go to Sub's where my suitcase was.

Monty said, Don't you like Mexican food?

If Claire didn't go away and find herself, something was going to happen to her.

An American proverb, said Monty, has it that there are only twenty-four hours in a day.

Maybe Monty didn't know I'd been in London last night, yet he must.

I mentioned a Mexican place where I'd eaten with Tessa and Dudley Allott seven years ago.

Monty said he knew the place but knew a better place, more authentic.

Claire said, I know that name Allott.

I said I didn't think she did, Tessa was Lorna's friend and Dudley was here at the time working on the Maya or on someone who *had* worked on the Maya.

Maya? said Monty.

That's right, I said; but they live in London, though they were here for the month of August.

Here? said Monty.

I said I was going to Sub's. Monty suggested I return the phone call. But I didn't.

They were stranded in the hall watching me open the front door. In one hovering moment, as if the distance between us were vertical, I detected something genuine: Monty cared about Claire.

The two films, said Claire, were meant to be complementary. I don't know if Monty mentioned that. Yours was going to be part of Phil Aut's.

That doesn't sound complementary, I said, and saw Monty's eyebrows jam his forehead wrinkles without any words to serve.

Gates winked all about me, but I held to my plan. I would not deal with Sub on the phone.

I was closing the door.

Monty said, Mayas, and Claire said, No.

No one seemed to be following me.

My cabdriver, a long-haired youth with a headband, drove bravely but with small knowledge of Manhattan. There was no picture of him displayed in the slot beside the police permit.

No one followed us.

However, anyone could have been hanging around Sub's building when I got out. And there was no doorman.

It was six thirty. I'd give Outer Film another hour to be closed.

I had been deeper than I thought. Looking up into the shower had been like looking into the bottom.

The narrow keen smell of roasting lamb as I passed the lobby mailboxes gave way in the lift to my sweat and cigarette smoke. The circle of fluorescent light in the elevator roof was harder on the pallid leaden paint than on my transatlantic eyes shifting over the capital letters delivery boys had cut into the wall panels, one pair being my own initials. In the old open elevator that Ned Noble and I took slowly up to the fifth-floor stamp dealer in the early forties you looked through the gratings of the hinge-folding door and each floor's hoistway door that did not fold but opened normally, and saw each dusky passing floor of that downtown Brooklyn office building, and no matter how much there was to say, which with Ned was a lot, you'd fall silent foreseeing the glass-topped case and the stamp tongs being laid down upon it, and the faint official scent of paper touching off in us visions of lozenge perfs and pale pastel windows with oriental rulers or the delicately antlered national animal of some now defunct country; and, somehow, the twenty-cent envelope of one thousand transparent glued peelable hinges put a scent upon the wind and the stamps themselves as if the micro-printing had been done on a grid like a TV scan, and the colors beyond any standard odor of ink gave off advance word. There was a triangular stamp Ned and I both wanted, and when I mentioned this to Will a year ago, all I could think of was Tannu Tuva, and he looked it up in his Faber atlas and said it didn't exist, and in Sub's elevator now thinking I hadn't been much help to Sub in overcoming the distances and encroachments his life was weighted down with, the alternative name Will came up with fell into my head—Tanna, an island—and Will said that must be what I'd been thinking of and insisted with strange rigidity as if he wished to settle something and would settle it if need be by force; yet with that authoritative emotion that belongs to memory I knew that Tannu Tuva was the place all right, it wasn't an ideal destination ideally far and purely possible, and if it wasn't in Will's English atlas then the world had changed. The stamp man's elevator was different from Sub's, which was a fast capsule with a small glassed port and all around me those metallic initials knifing through its shield of bilious late-night green not to the hoistway shaft or the passing floors but to a prior color hard to tell, and as the capsule came open at Sub's floor and an old lady tried to get in before I got out, I saw inside the oblong Tanna Tuva frame a deer or gazelle with lyrelike horns, and a Costa Rican triangle but no color where I knew there had been color, and knew that Will's alternative name Tanna had occurred not only because it was and is in the New Hebrides east of Australia, and through Jenny's map of Lewis in the other Hebrides I continued to be at her mercy.

Now the smell was the bristling rough moist salt of pork chops, a smell that sneaks beneath the tongue unlike lamb whose essence winds among stomach, eyes, and sinus first, and Ruby was unlocking and opening the door as Sub was yelling Who is it and then was suddenly behind her, then abruptly six strides back into the kitchen to the stove and I was looking not at him but out past the hall into the living room where Aut's (if it was Aut's) burglar had been—and as I said No in answer to his question had I eaten, I stepped through an invisible gate into that living room and barely registered Tris engrossed in a new or at least smaller TV set because I was seeing something else near my suitcase and seeing it with such completeness you might have thought that I was in a position to take for granted the rest.

The thing was a Halloween jack-o'-lantern, fired up and grinning through its mad half-evolved teeth, fat and in its healthy meridian grooves seeming symmetrical, and it said to me that I must have lost a week or ten days somewhere in my flights. Mad but possible.

Ruby had one hand in mine and the other through my legs. She didn't want me to color, she wanted a story about me and her daddy. But though I loved her, the supple backbone the wide eyes taking whatever there was to take, the smudge of magic marker blue below one cheekbone, loved the flesh smell of a child (which was also Jenny's smell now she'd stopped using a spray) as I loved Tris for his tongue-between-lips arrest absorbed in what he was seeing and thus seeming tenderer in that force you feel even in an older boy that you imagine isn't in a more self-possessed girl, even a little girl, loved them because they were my friend Sub's children, loved them because they could be entertained quite simply, though in the circuits of the last few days I could not recall just what I had told them by way of a story, it had come out of my head unplanned and restored itself to its spot under a baffle in a corner of my head at once it was finished—loved them because they were my own children a few years back in the multiplied accelerations of alien time that no record can begin to measure of the presents brought home to them from America (even those encapsulated or nonencapsulated liquid crystal kits acquired for Will from my scientific firm that were a steal at the price, or black-and-white moiré patterns or kinetic-art-kit mobiles for Jenny in all the colors of English wildflowers). Love, yes: but not this time, not right now.

I could eat and get to Outer Film in an hour, and if I let it go till later there'd be a night watchman I imagined downstairs tilting back in his chair behind the glass street-doors of the building reading the *News* and drinking coffee out of a cardboard container; but if I went soon I could be still part of the working day.

There were calls for me, and this had no doubt been why Monty wanted me to phone Sub before I left. Gilda. Claire. Monty Graf. My mother. Monty Graf again. June. Monty again.

Sub, if I asked him about his work, said it would bore me and if I said I'd like to know what he knew about computers, he'd say don't waste your time they're unbelievably dumb, and I could not push it because I might not be competent to tell why I thought computers part of a strange, seductive chance that was beyond the useful, and in fact I had failed more than once to make this clear to Lorna and to Geoff Millan, yet always I felt not so much because I didn't know enough as because I had failed to make use of what I already had. I would like to give a compressed explanation to Tessa that she would not be able to anticipate with a look or a word and that would be as sly and lucid as she. And at this instant, hearing Sub come out of the kitchen and stand on the threshold of the littered living room and not speak, I found that though my power to prove my feeling about computers—about miles of memory, or abstract numbers switched out of the blue into the real angular turns of a machine or the actual relation of two electric currents—stirred inchoate though contained inside a circle of broken connections that could get long or short or acquire right angles and stern diagonals while being still this circle of known emotions and words and people, my power to turn that inchoate into a statement was, as if half unwilled, finding itself in the new movements after the ruin of the film that my pulses from moment to moment were deciding to make. I grant that if you let all this boil it might boil down to being selfish, spending money that wasn't only mine, using friends and their phones. But if there was a glinting mass I could not frame, it seemed now to be becoming an argument that was my life. If my life was becoming an argument my mind could not frame, at least I was in that argument. Tessa's lost mother played Schumann at night to her when she was going to sleep. After her mother wasn't there any more she didn't herself try to play. But she listened, she knew what was coming, she gave Lorna the letters of Clara Schumann, she loved to listen to Lorna because the sound communicated with the lost wandering sound waves of her mother's playing and in 1958 and 1959 this gave Lorna a reason to play. But there was music in Tessa's circle. Dudley said, The Jews own the violin. Tessa seemed not intimate enough with Dudley to say jokingly, You bigot.

214

For a second I could not recall if there was or was not Halloween in the land where after all I'd brought up my children and where anyway I knew there were no pumpkins. Sub explained that Rose had brought this pumpkin from the country yesterday together with the Indian corn for which, though it was still almost two weeks to Halloween, five weeks to Thanksgiving, and nine until Christmas, we should give thanks. Who cut the teeth? I asked. Sub said he had. Sub had explained over the transatlantic phone last night what had been done to this living room. I was going to pay for the TV of course, I said; and Sub, wishing to drop the subject now I'd said what I ought, made it obvious he wanted to talk further about what the burglar was looking for, but Sub did not want Tris and Ruby to hear. So we sat down and divided the four pork chops. Ruby had set the kitchen table. Sub got mad at Tris for not turning the TV off, then when Tris got up Sub strode out of the kitchen and turned it off himself. The pork chops were as good as English pork, though as I told my companions, chicken wasn't as good here. Sub gave Ruby's bone to Tris. Ruby said it was nice of Mommy to bring the pumpkin and could she take some Indian corn tomorrow for Show and Tell. Tris said, She's just making that up. Sub said she could if she wanted. Make it up? said Tris. No, take it in, said Sub. Tris asked why chicken was better in England.

Claire, Gilda, Monty, my mother, and June. Still no call from Aut. June could be operating for the man in glasses and she might not know it was really for Phil Aut. I had not told Sub of the stabbing and Jim. It had been Jim.

Sub asked if I wanted coffee or tea.

Sub mentioned an old movie on TV. Tris and Ruby said they wanted to watch it. Sub said it came on too late and they were going to bed. There was more talk about what was happening when. Sub told them to go to their rooms and give me a chance to make my phone calls.

Sub had begun automatically to do the dishes. He lowered his voice and said, That burglar wanted something.

I said I was sorry. I said I might be in trouble, I had to find my own way through it but in any case we'd gone beyond the stage at which certain interests would imagine they could oppose me by rifling Sub's apartment. Sub said he had repacked my case—but had the burglar gotten anything? and *what* interests?

I said some pages Jenny had typed, I had copies. I promised it wouldn't happen again (and thought this sounded more like making a promise to myself).

But—I didn't say the words—*the address book*. The address book. On top of the pages but not on top of the pages, for I had consulted it to call my charter man. But I had not consulted it because halfway to Sub's desk I'd remembered the number and didn't need the book.

They had the book. And the Highgate burglar had a copy of the diary.

But why smash the TV screen? said Sub, and held up a long dripping serrated knife.

Ruby punched me at the base of my spine and asked for a story. I told her to get undressed for her bath. Sub said she wasn't taking a bath tonight. She left the kitchen and was replaced by Tris.

I said, It must have been an accident.

Sub said, You should have seen the screen.

Tris said, You should have seen the aerial.

Sub said, The aerial is beside the point. The tubes in back weren't touched. It's just that from the beginning we never really knew when the set would go and when it would work.

Tris left the kitchen and Sub said Rose had been thoughtful enough to say they absolutely must get a new doorman here, it was dangerous for the children.

Ruby was in the kitchen with nothing on.

Why couldn't Mommy get an apartment in this building?

We don't have closed-circuit television surveillance.

We have television.

Sub took a breath and said slowly, Sometimes so many lines of communication seem available, if I just made the right adjustment in myself I'd be clairvoyant.

Ruby wanted to know what that was.

I remembered my address book and its erratic script or capitals, in all my hands, in the hands of others, in pen and pencil.

I said I'd finish the dishes but I had an errand and would be right back.

Sub asked if I'd forgotten my phone calls—my mother had told him he ought to get married again and had been surprised to hear he and Rose weren't divorced yet. She'd left four years ago. Time is a fast mover. The address book was an old one.

Sub asked if I was staying. Ruby and Tris asked for a story. I said, when I came back, they said Now. I said I'd tell them Beauty and the Beast when I came back. They said they'd heard it. Tris seemed now in spite of his age to be with Ruby, the two currents joined even though bedtime was also a divider because of their different ages. At an angle through the hall and her half-open white door with DADDY IS STUPIED marked on it in a slanted column thrice, I saw half of Ruby bent over something. She had forgotten me.

The children were glad to see me and so was Sub. Then Tris said, Did you and Daddy ever blow anything up?

Balloons, said Sub.

Fourth of July firecrackers, I said. In England they're called thunderclaps and because they don't have Fourth of July in England they explode them on Guy Fawkes Day.

Remember, remember, the Fifth of November, said Sub.

Dad's suing the TV people, said Tris.

I was, said Sub.

It was like a still shot with sound, I an alien element, moving too softly toward the front door.

Everyone stayed still while I moved. This was better than the other way around.

We'd never got round to some insert shots I'd had in mind of Lorna lying still: first, the mole on her left shoulder blade; second, up upon her shoulder the pearly scar my eyes and nose and tongue had crossed; third, the two clear mounds of pale cool buttock untouched by mole or spot though able to hold the nip of some passing teeth for upwards of three weeks, though by then you would need eyes peeled by lust or love that for their moments of search took other motions or the smell of flesh for granted and so saw only this month-old mark of blue. But what made thirty tripod seconds of Lorna's still behind a movie—no quivering hand, no tremor on the skin or current through the faint dark down that grows at the end of her spine, nor later in projecting the developed film any faulting flicker to blink the moving frames. What, apart from sound on the film or in the projector, stamped a shot like that a movie rather than one of Millan's slides? When I asked Lorna she said the movie shot would seem more alive no matter how still. This comment made the film more real and gave me a confidence I hadn't known I needed or made me wonder if I had secretly dismissed our film.

I bore into Aut's office building, the location of whose address I had again checked on the address-locater in my wallet, a crisp brown paper bag containing a container of coffee. The night man already on duty was leaning his chair against the empty newspaper and candy stand and stared straight ahead as if dreaming, and if so, not of dynamite.

It was not inevitable one of Claire's keys would fit, but it did, and the glass door with Outer Film on it opened and my feet were on carpet.

Best turn on the lights, two banks of fluorescents momentarily blinking in the dark. Half a dozen big gray-green desks, some hooded typewriters, a World War II *Uncle Sam Wants You* poster, and nothing to do with films but a few cans on two desks and against a wall the hexagonal carrying cases.

Voices came, and as they passed my door the Outer Film phone nearest the door on what must be the receptionist's desk started ringing and the steps stopped after a moment. But there was no reason to think the voices that happened now to stop weren't waiting at the lift, and since it would not be unthinkable for lights to have been left on or for someone trying to finish up to wish not to get stuck on the phone, I let it go. I identified Claire's desk by the glossy photos on the wall of Big Ben and Stonehenge. In her desk, not to mention stationery, pens, pencils, and the personals some nine-to-fivers feel more intimate with than anything in their bathroom cabinets at home, were two scripts, a modern Greek textbook, folders with invoices and letters, and in the center drawer notes, a notice from the dog hospital, and under a scattering of more letters, one from Dagger that felt in my hand like a look into the future meant for me. It was dated May 24 and it was typed on both sides and too long to recall in every detail. I could not decide whether to take it or not. I could have it copied but Claire would know. Steps echoed toward me, I thought from the elevator—someone who just might know it was unusual for lights to be on at this hour in an office, if in fact it *was* unusual, but might not know who worked for Aut and who didn't. The letter was warm and confusing. What a guy! Dagger devoted the opening long paragraph apropos of nothing to a story about his Uncle Stan who had lived in Yonkers and when he heard his voice on one of the old prewar wire recorders had grown a beard and left his wife and gone to live in New Jersey and signed up in radio school and cultivated his voice and later got into eastern mysticism. Then Dagger wrote about the film. The ball-game footage was fast and funny, he'd dropped to 8 fps once so the film would show Umpire Ismay rolling a cigarette like a madman, and there were three moments, two of them not strictly in the game, that Outer Film would want to use, namely certain (shall we say, he said) *arresting faces.* Don't worry, Aut will never hear about our initiative from me.

The steps stopped, a phone began to ring, the same phone, I couldn't tell from the steps or the watery shadow in the glass door if I had two observers or one. This empty office was surrounded by me, or by the trick I sought in its aisles and files, its desks, demented desks every one messy but the receptionist's, which was too clean on top not to be tidy inside even to some pattern of emptiness. Each desk had a bit of something. No desk had all. Not even Aut's. Where was Aut's? Claire I was sure had not been straight with Aut. Tessa had given confidence to Lorna who had given confidence to me. In a dim and unplaced room of recollection I believed I had given confidence to Tessa.

In one long shot of three people, Dagger went on in the second paragraph of his letter, he knew of course two but had to dig a bit to place the other Indian. No doubt, he said, I will run into him Friday. It's been fun using the Beaulieu, blows better to 35 but it's just a nicer little machine to hold than a Bolex though hell to load and with a few French shortcuts, but we might have to switch to a Bolex if I have to give back the Beaulieu. Advance some more bread, I'll rent an Angenieux zoom. We are getting good now. We had a little practice this morning, but nothing to write home about. So far it's been just the ball game Sunday, May 16, but we'll be running both burners from this weekend on.

The steps started again but proceeded slowly. The second was like two people with a shared limp. The steps stopped down the hall. I thought I picked up a whisper. But I couldn't have at that distance and through walls. The steps went off and then I didn't hear them. I thought a door latched.

When the phone started again I noticed that when the steps had continued it had stopped ringing.

I was not sure. I closed the drawer, keeping the letter. I slipped to the wall and doused the light. I found my way back to Claire's desk. I struck a match so I must have laid Dagger's letter down. I wanted to check the deep drawer right bottom again in case the DiGorro film-file was in another folder. My match burned my fingers. I hadn't found anything. I straightened up to strike another, I would try the last four or five folders, the names on them had meant nothing to me.

Steps, the same, came along again and stopped. It was two men very clearly. Would Phil Aut have come in, or called the watchman? The watchman had been unarmed.

The flame pricked my finger. I had taken it not even for

granted, I had forgotten it. The steps had gone away again. To soothe and cure the burn, I didn't know how long I'd stood there with Claire's bottom right drawer out. I struck a match and as my head turned down to the folders my eye stopped on Dagger's P.S. and I read, and my recollection is that it said, Don't worry about Aut, I will definitely be able to handle the group in Wales, having experienced my Uncle Stan from Yonkers and New Jersey who once said, Don't talk to *me* about the Stones and transcendental meditation!

The penny dropped—noiselessly—two pennies—a pound—an inflation of pounds blown up and dropped on the moon. But how can a paper pound drop into a slot. My brain was going soft. But so were the things that had been occupying its slots.

In shape or not, I was on the treadmill and couldn't get off but it was moving the way I wanted it to and I was adding my movement to it. Dagger's letter was May 24. So he'd already known about a group in Wales; but we didn't find them in their field (by accident) till Friday, May 28.

The phone was ringing on the receptionist's desk. I was receiving signals and the Cartwright-DiGorro enterprise looked like passing into receivership. Whole printed circuits sailed softly through the new soft-warped slots of my head. Micro-circs. Faster than a speeding bullet, slower than an old movie. Sub believed in messages; people who knew the precision of his professional mind and the inspired practicality with which he keeps his home going do not know about his messages—pain in the dentist chair (a message understood, hence liquidated); coincidence a section drawn from the map of one's force field; if he had considered his word *clairvoyant,* no telling what he'd make of it. Or of Jim and the aerial stabbing now so far back, yet not six working days from this present Monday night, 8:45, October 18, 1971.

But Wales was not Dagger's idea, it was mine. For Wales was passion and sorcery, heroes and deceptive mountains and music and boozing and hidden communes up behind a misty hill and lambs bleating in the gorges. There was the story of the hound-dog Gelert left by his master the warrior Llywelyn in a tent to watch over his infant son. When Llywelyn returned that night he found the tent collapsed and his dog calmly sitting beside it, his head and coat all matted with blood. Llywelyn in a frenzy of vengeance ran Gelert through with his spear, but hearing then a cry he pulled back the canvas and found not only his child safe in the cradle but a huge wolf ripped open and hideously dead. Gelert breathed his last licking

Llywelyn's hand and Llywelyn gave him a hero's burial in a tomb visible to this day, a great slab on its side and two upright stones, and the valley where the meadow lies is called Bethgelert. Dudley Allott would tell you of American place names in Wales; he made no more of Gelert, Ontario, than of Tessa's animal legends, he wasn't much on mystic tumuli or Arthur's knights, but Dudley knew where the stone castles had been that marked the lines of the River Wye and the River Usk and he was moderately interesting on a name like Gelliswick, which is Celtic *gelli* (hazel grove) and Norse *wick* (haven). And he knew who holed up at Harlech and what prince of Gwynedd held a mountain against strangers from the east by means of the canniest practical skill. *How Green Was My Valley* came from my parents' book club and I read it from cover to cover the weekend of Pearl Harbor and got 70 on my geography test Monday. There was the Welsh poet Dylan Thomas whom my immediate predecessor with Lorna took us to hear read at the Young Men's Hebrew Association before we left for England and who in '52 or '53 along the college circuit seemed like the Voice of America until he was consumed by an America in himself. Lorna read him, I could not; but I could listen. And there was a young Welsh conductor for whom Lorna had sung in a chorus who went to Cleveland and New York seeking his fortune, and Cincinnati and Florida, and who got sick of podium politics and came back to London though his wife stayed. Catherwood's friend Stephens records a theory that ascribes to the Welsh the first and original peopling of America. Ned Noble and my sister and I saw the movie of *How Green Was My Valley* and when the lights went up Ned taunted me that there were tears in my eyes, and Ned would have had a fat eye or a bloody nose if we hadn't by some magical incoherence shunted off into whether it was anthracite or bituminous coal the miners were mining in the picture and my sister sided with me because she was still clutching my bandanna handkerchief that she had borrowed dry. Tessa and Dudley spent some weekends in a converted schoolhouse in Wales that had been bought by a friend who Dudley said had had the DT's at one time, but he wasn't American. The Welsh "Bells of Rhymney" Pete Seeger made into an American socialist anthem and we heard him sing it in Royal Festival Hall with the changeless Dietrich his friend sitting in the same row with us and Tessa, which was some months before the Allotts went to America in '64. Wales, then, had been in my mind.

But this fact remained, that Dagger had known that on Friday, May 28, the day after the day we'd planned to be on the south coast where I had to see a man about a boatyard, on Friday the 28th of May, after passing through Bristol to say hello to a mutual friend an actor in the repertory and to take another look at Brunel's great suspension bridge on the Clifton heights, we would film a *group* in Wales which was to Claire *the* group. Had known as early as the 24th. Earlier.

I snapped out the match, moved toward the partitioned-off cubicle, wheeled about, found Claire's desk and retrieved Dagger's letter, didn't fold it lest it crackle, went again toward Aut's cubicle wondering what I would do if I found him sprawled in his swivel chair dead, put down the letter, struck a match, heard the steps approach like two people with one unnatural rhythm, doubtless the two who'd paused to look at Outer Film's door and the darkness on my side and might conceivably have seen my match.

They didn't stop. I was at what must surely be Aut's desk. It was full. I went through drawers that told me nothing. I was meant to be here, to have come here from Monty's via Sub's, to Aut's office, Claire's desk, Aut's.

The phone had been ringing and ringing. I fingered letters, folders, scripts. I accidentally pushed something off onto the rug.

I was holding the match so close to the files in a lower drawer that even though the fire flamed upward I may have singed a manila corner. My eyes still dumbly told me something. There was something looking at my eyes.

My God it was the Unplaced Room. The morning of May 24 we'd shot the Unplaced Room, and here was my old friend Dag saying we'd had some *practice* that morning but as of the 24th P.M. we'd shot only the May 16 ball game.

But this wasn't what my inkling eyes meant. There was something else staring. However, I would run out of matches if I had to go through all of Aut's stuff. I looked up from the lower drawer and just as the flame at desk-top level pricked my thumb, I found at the edge of this light what had been shadowing my attention.

On the cubicle wall to the left of the desk were four framed black-and-white photos. One was a close-shot of a woman caught smiling thoughtfully, lips parted enough to show strong, unevenly spaced teeth with an animal gap in the middle, lips resisting this as if the smile had been got out of her against her will. I couldn't have guessed her size if I had not known at once who she was: she was the red-haired woman who'd been talking to the Indian near our ball game and whom Dagger must have meant as one of the moments mentioned to Claire; and she was the red-haired woman who had seemed to my puzzled paternity yesterday morning in London to be competition with Jenny for Reid.

The second, smaller picture was of two full-length figures, one a woman plump and pretty and seemingly gray-haired, the other a boy with longish hair and bluejeans seeming to suffer her arm around his shoulder—and he was indubitably Jerry, the friend of John, the man in glasses from the Mercer Street loft.

The third picture was of the gray-haired woman now dark-haired and younger, full face close-up smiling almost to the point of laughing.

The fourth was of the red-haired woman and Jerry, and Jerry's fingers were peeking around her waist.

My match had flared out without burning me. The flame, like a desire in my will, had turned the woman's hair in the b & w photo red.

Aut knew the red-haired woman.

Aut knew Jerry, who I already knew disliked Aut.

These were intimate pictures, and so Jan Aut was probably here; but must she be the red-haired woman?

I lit a match and looked. A clank came in the hall. It was a bucket. I heard a key in a lock too close. I looked around my cubicle but saw nothing in the amber oblong. I memorized the face of the woman I didn't know. The char wouldn't know who belonged in the Outer Film office and who didn't. But I would have to explain what I was doing in the dark. I could just be sitting still, like Cosmo when he answered my call in London. I must leave. The singing was now near my door. It went back into where it had been. *You Are Everything and Everything Is You.* I stopped near Claire's desk thinking I might leave her keys. But I needed them to lock up. I got out into the hall and the doorknob was as quiet as a rheostat that turns light up or down as gradually as you want.

I was right, the next door down was open, a bucket stood in the hall. I was not going to risk the sound of a key. I rubber-heeled my way to the elevator.

At last the red light sounded its bell-note but a phone rang. The charwoman reached out for the bucket. Bending over, she turned her head and saw me. The phone was ringing. She stood up and took her key ring and said to me I wonder if I should answer that?

I wouldn't, I said, and my doors opened and I said goodnight and was inside, my heart swelling into a chill machine.

The night watchman wasn't dreaming. He looked me over.

I bought a ballpoint and a pack of too many envelopes in a drug store in Claire's block. I put her apartment number on one and with a question mark enclosed her keys. I watched the doorman from across the street. He talked on the intercom, the bill of his braided hat was importantly low on his forehead. He hung up the receiver on the cradle among the switchboard buttons. He disappeared. I went across the street and left the envelope on a stool by the three gray softly curved closed-circuit TV screens.

Sub's old movie went on in an hour.

If the red-haired woman were Jan Graf Aut, the picture I'd defaced was a self-portrait.

Sub asked if I would babysit, he'd changed his plans.

June had phoned again. Sub raised his eyebrows and asked what kind of business I was on.

I'd overlooked something, but I didn't know what.

In the P.S. about transcendental meditation, I saw the point of Dagger's opening story. Claire had written him about the religious group.

I did not like Dagger nullifying the Unplaced Room.

I had decided the 8-millimeter cartridge was important. It had not been on Dagger's table, and he hadn't said anything about it. And the night we shot it he was reluctant and his friends who were sitting around talking to Alba when we came back from the air base were strange.

Sub was ready to go. There was a humid scent of soap. I have not begun to suggest Sub. There hasn't been the chance. He is, for all his domesticity and somewhere between duty and delusion, a heroic mind. There hasn't been any need to show this. There is none now except that we are in his presence, or you are in mine and I in his, or his apartment. He once in Rose's presence told her friend Connie that Connie answered not what people said but what she heard in their minds—which foreshadowed a trait of Tessa's—and when Rose said Sub was speaking nonsense because he was just imagining what Connie did think was in other people's heads, Connie sided with Sub, and Rose got mad, and a queer fracas ensued lasting between Rose and Sub several days climaxed by Rose's admitting Sub *should* have said what he'd said not of Connie but of her, and Sub's retorting that it wasn't true of Rose, then Rose that this was simply because Sub wasn't interested in her to find out. Sometimes duty and delusion closed over whatever was between, and Sub summed himself up— but I might fall into a description of his friends, his mad aunt, his

224

mother, his father, for instance, who was the sort who'd be glad a school tennis match had been rained out or a museum closed unexpectedly on a Monday since it meant he'd missed nothing by not being there—Sub summed himself up with a swift delicate painful computation that would blind someone who did not know him to all he meant when he saw himself as someone who did what needed to be done. By which he meant getting Tris and Ruby to bed and to school, and listening to what they had to tell him when he came home, a lot of which concerned their mother. I convey none of this in these scenes with Sub, who now, bringing into the hall that scent of soap, said, May as well make yourself useful.

Where will you be? I said.

He wrote down a number. It's up in the air at the moment.

Sub locked the door from the outside, which saved me the trouble of going and turning the inside latch. You could lock or unlock from outside or inside. The lock wasn't automatic.

I knew what I'd overlooked.

I had left the letter on Phil Aut's desk.

CORSICAN MONTAGE | The crowd on the approaching pier is pink, mauve, and brown—red, white, and yellow—green as blood when it flows under the sea—and the crowd is also blue, cornflower, cobalt, navy, chinks of blue in the white shirts, black kerchiefs, wild prints closing on us as if to leave behind them there parked on the pier beside a gray truck, a gray Volkswagen newer than Dagger's belowdecks—but no blue is there on the pier quite like the space you call the sky, a blue you'd catch hold of only on film, where it still is nothing till processed and projected. But rewind the voyage back half an hour to where Dagger several miles offshore took a tilt shot of sky as if slowly raising a face to something prime and new, moving the 50-mm. lens from sun-silvered whitecaps up past the hazy earth of Corsica that's sending out now white flecks which will come forward to become the brick and plaster of Ajaccio: he tilts the lens up into the Mediterranean sky whose blue unlike the sea leaves me full of blissful suspicion that thought matters no more than Napoleon, who does not come out in a launch one hand inside his greatcoat to meet us, matters no more than the random seabird that cuts through Dagger's shot, survives, and is gone.

Dagger has shot the Gulf of Ajaccio and, nearer in, a small

beacon on the low extension of the breakwater that's like a rampart. Then to the left he caught lines of white-hulled powerboats parked from the inner smallcraft dock by the cafés out toward us along the jetty to the breakwater. Gold letters on mahogany sterns tell my sharp sight that the girl who might be Claire basking above a bowsprit has come from Cannes, and the man in shorts pouring tea amidships for the man in jeans has probably sailed like our car ferry from Marseilles, and there's Nice and scandalous St.-Tropez, Genoa and Palma de Mallorca, even Malmö, Sweden, and of course Algiers whence seventeen thousand *pieds-noirs* came to Corsica after the '62 liberation. I see also a yacht from Cagliari and from the look of its striped awning aft and the gilt flash of its brass it could care less if Corsicans look down on Sardinians, for don't mainland French of whom Dagger's wife Alba is one look down on *les Corses*?

Corsica is a *département* of France.

This film is for the masses, murmurs Dagger.

I mention only what we film. And now the crowd.

The engines are turning us away from the crowd behind its barricade. My eyes have changed since May because of our camera. A middle-aged woman offers her beautiful profile, she is not looking our way, but off toward the smallcraft dock; the tip of her tongue is thinking, and her hair is gathered behind into a single plait and this is what I see even if, having never done Jenny's hair when she was a child, I don't know if it takes two strands or three.

Dagger doesn't switch off.

I say to him, That's enough, isn't it?

His American friend wrote that he would take the bus into downtown Ajaccio from the école and drive back with us. Dagger sometimes seems to use a camera like a spyglass to see what he can't see with his own eyes.

Any familiar faces?

Dagger lays a hand on my shoulder. On the far side of the pier is a small van with something *plonger* on it, the local scuba man. Dagger says, Never know where you'll run into an old contact from Berkeley.

We go below for the car.

Dagger has used a hundred feet of Anscochrome approaching Ajaccio.

Calvi is said to be prettier.

I will tape some Corsican French tomorrow. It has an Italian sound, but since the war you watch what you say about that.

Dagger's purpose, which in my view those hundred feet of approach shots won't advance, is to parlay his entrée here, mix shots of Bastille Day observances three days hence and tourists lounging around Bonaparte's birthplace plus the American, French, and English students reconnoitering Corsican ecology—our expenses paid by Claire's boss. Family life is not a millstone round Dagger's neck; but he sees Alba's baby coming week by week and he is a forty-four-year-old male with quite a history and he is going to be a father, and a bit of distance just now gives a man a certain perspective he needs on the internal effects of such an event. Pudovkin said montage was linkage, Eisenstein collision.

In the école garden Dagger shoots rich pink rhododendron blossoms and the heavy oval dark green leaves; he shoots the black iron fence down the slope and through the fence the street whose bright traffic he gives the same focus for a moment that he gave the rhododendrons, then adjusts so the blur of shine and color turns clear and exact and leaves the black iron fence softened at the edges as if instead of adjusting the focus Dagger has zoomed, and that's something on the agenda, for we know—or he knows—a man who will lend us an Angenieux 12–120. Long shot of the street traffic through the école fence; I slip behind Dagger, who tracks right and through a pattern of leaves on our side of the fence to catch across the street a column of sea and sky between the pastel buildings at the foot of one of which is a greengrocer.

Dagger cuts to the space of dirt and grass in front of the main four-story institutional edifice that houses dorm, dining room, and kitchen; there is a game of bowls in progress played with a small steel target ball and several larger ones, a Marseillaise game I learn and the traditional taunts and protest and boasting precede and follow the arcing toss and the thud of the ball onto the dust and its hushed roll too strong or weak, too much right or left. I will find out the name of the target ball. This footage is silent but I make a note to tape for it some of those shrill, hard, anguished songs you hear about, a rhythm I might pulse into phase and out with the flight and fall of those shotput-like tosses, the red tile roof high behind.

The peace in the blue of the sky and the chalky hues of the pier crowd over the water comes again, a peace beyond Dagger's prodigality with the Anscochrome (a minute still left), comes again in the blossoms, the green, a girl's miniskirt, a maroon Renault broadside through the arcade hung with vines and blooms like New England wistaria mingled with tiny whites and yellows more like buds, the maroon of the car now sliding out of view leaving on the far side of the driveway a stone wall, but Dagger has switched off. Here comes his American friend with a tall woman. She is vivid, she has auburn hair and speaks with a Scots clip. I tell her I have a friend who goes up there all the time to visit a clan chieftain.

The peace is in the color, and in the hope of something beautiful in the growth between authentic black and white and the color living in that strongest thing of all, surface. One of the American boys here—the one with the Sony recorder—will back us up against the wall before supper saying we're crazy to mix color with black and white.

Cut to morning. Next footage, b & w.

Sublime morning, the sun has a smell, or compounds the sweet bark-burn of coffee and the thick breath of hot milk from the kitchen, last night's wine bottles fish bread bougainvillaea Gauloises, exhaust fumes and sea two blocks away, it is not garbage, or even drains, but it is an unsieved odor of natural use—I can't imagine Dagger caring to convey it.

I mean to include here only what we film.

We are in black and white, and side by side we shoot thirty seconds next door upstairs. An American girl, hair in rollers under a pink kerchief, bangs "Rhapsody in Blue" on an upright at the back of the classroom; there is on each desk a headphone-with-mike and a metal switch box; the simultaneous interpreter who is taking a six-week break from NATO is reading yesterday's Ajaccio paper—how the students can listen to a lecture here with island sun glimmering through the upper branches of the école trees and white boats winking in the gulf and the beachboys hanging around last night's café is beyond me, and bare legs morning-cool upon a metal and educational chair—the interpreter puts away his paper and with a wave at us spreads his headset, it's hooked into the room's system, and anything of him we pick up only through the omnidirectional I've placed on an empty front-row desk. The last students have wandered in after breakfast, they put on their headsets and switch on their boxes, the professor from the Sorbonne has appeared in shorts, the girl in curlers relents and leaves her ringing piano. The class is depleted by a field trip. Dagger ignores the professor sitting at the desk on the podium and gets a close shot of a French girl and the American boy Dagger happened to know through Hampstead friends and spent a while with last night in our beach café down the street—I explain too much—while a group of us left our tables and swam out into the night.

We swam far out, each stroke directly into darkness, though out ahead the lights across the bay seemed close; the phosphorescent life all round vanished to the touch, but I felt them holding me up, loafing, treading a hundred yards off the beach, girls' shoulders slick under moonlight.

When I came back with a sandy towel on one shoulder and the café was closing, the American boy (whose somber self-importance Dagger refused to be put off by) was saying he'd thought Dagger was someone else and Dagger asked if he'd been expecting someone; the American stood up and said No—as if he felt he'd talked enough or drunk enough cassis on top of the rosé we get at the école.

This morning the girl Dagger shoots with that American boy is self-conscious; she takes her headphones off (her French is good), she keeps trying to stare at the professor (who is invisible except in my untranslated tape) but she keeps breaking her gaze and smiling first to her right at the boy—he's around twenty—then left at us. Too late I think of using a spare headset to tape French and English simultaneously.

We have our footage and the students watch it as we pack up and get out of there. They are sorry to see us go. The professor says *L'année prochaine à Cannes.*

Cut to outside. Long shot of classroom windows, silent vines above.

Cut to last night's beach café this morning full of the same men. I remember we're in black and white when a woman in a black dress comes trudging by (stout calves, posture straight) with a tiny kid in pink shorts, and Dagger cuts to them but I don't know if the Beaulieu is running.

Cut to downtown Ajaccio, but I have to explain it's near noon, and we've acquired four young people: the American boy Mike whom Dagger talked to last night, the admiring girl next to him in class this morning, a French boy and a French girl with pigtails and a little face like a fairy. We find the historic alley near the port and the blank seventeenth-century edifice where Napoleon was born. There's a delicate tree in its courtyard that they light at night. The French boy says what has this to do with Corsica; he says it to impress. The French girl laughs but she is well brought up, a nice girl from Paris who gets A's at the Sorbonne, and she has not seen the interior and she takes the American girl's arm and draws her in along the walk.

Mike nods at the house and says to the French boy, You can see why Napoleon was a high-achiever, and the French boy nods rapidly and laughs. They stroll after the girls and enter the house.

Cut to them coming out: on film it will look as if they stayed about half a second.

Melanie the American girl we decide to let speak. I hook up and Dagger shoots her close with the Bonaparte house behind. She surprises me by reeling off straight-face a speech: Napoleon's father Carlo Bonaparte served as secretary to the great Republican leader Pasquale Paoli. Carlo was of Genoese and Florentine ancestry. When Genoa sold Corsica to the French, Paoli fled to England. The French subdued the Corsican patriots. When Carlo Bonaparte fled south over the mountains, his wife Letizia was six months pregnant with Napoleon. Carlo and Letizia traveled by mule over dangerous mountains. They made it to Ajaccio and Napoleon was born in this very house. Melanie turns, and in good guided-documentary style with a sweep of her long brown arm ushers the camera forward, but Dagger doesn't move, we are as yet zoomless, Dagger hasn't phoned his contact. Two ladies with cameras and floppy straw hats step from the house. One carries a Blue Guide, the other says quite loudly in an educated English accent that she hopes they haven't butted in. Dagger says, We'll call you if we need you again, what hotel are you staying in, and the woman with the Blue Guide comes back at him with the name so calmly it's as if she's telling him the hour their lithological expedition sets off tomorrow, or perhaps she's defending her relation with her friend.

Melanie continues, but she is not being filmed or recorded. At the time of the French Revolution Paoli returned to Corsica and set up an independent state. His supporters because of the late Carlo's disloyalty drove Letizia who was by now a widow out of this house with her children and plundered it. Napoleon restored his mother to the house but by then the family's feeling for Corsica had turned to bitterness.

We have already cut. We are at the market, the French boy saying Corsicans aren't the fishermen the Italians are, Dagger filming flanks of tuna the deep beefy shade of whale, but we are in black and white, and he's been busy talking to Mike and Melanie about women, art, poverty, identity, and revolution here and in Sicily, and he was swinging off on the one hand to Scotland and on the other to Poland, so he may have forgotten if we were in color or not.

The French students take us to a big café where a lot of scowling men are reading form sheets and placing bets at a counter where lottery tickets are also sold. Dagger pans across the round iron tables. The English tourist-ladies come by, walking toward Place Foch where there are shops and restaurants. The American boy Mike excuses himself, he'll meet us at Hachette's book store say half an hour. This is not on film. Melanie tries to go with him but he raises a hand and shakes his head. The French girl's English is charming. Where do I live in America? I say I come from New York, I live in London. The French girl asks the difference between Pawnee and Sioux. The Sioux are a *group* of tribes; the Sioux came originally from Virginia—I surprise myself. The French boy wants to look at the Beaulieu. Dagger puts it in his hands. He squints through the rubber-lipped viewfinder. The girl met a man from New Mexico in the casino last night, he is a friend of Mike's, he told her how the government cheats Indians and the only thing in America is to make as much money as you can as fast as you can. Dagger wants to pick up a Paris *Herald* and he too will meet us in Place Foch in half an hour, why not make it that book shop—go ahead and shoot something on impulse.

The French girl is reading *Tender Is the Night*, do I like it? She thinks it is sublime. I confess I've never read it.

We shift to French and the French boy inquires why New York lacks effective air pollution control.

It's hot. I see us all separating: Mike, Dagger, Melanie, the French girl. The waiter comes. I am not writing well, Jenny. The French boy passes me the Beaulieu. The waiter goes, I answer in English that the landlords and entrepreneurs who schedule sneak pollution with their weekend cleanup crews burning incinerators they won't pay to have upgraded don't live in the central city so they don't care.

You live in Manhattan, the French boy says. He has a pallidly honest face.

No, London.

Dagger comes back a moment leaning over us, his hands on our shoulders. He wants to check the battery for the pistol grip, he'll just take the camera along. I can still see Mike up the street, he was looking in a window, he's taking his time. I'd like to follow Dagger.

Melanie is from Brooklyn, a big girl with a handsome head and a profile for a hero's bowsprit. Hippies are known to be out in the caves along the coast. Corsica is more than a hundred miles long.

The French boy asks if I've heard about the bomb that went off when an American cop jimmied open the window of an illegally parked car to let off the brake so the car could be towed away. The drinks have levitated from a dark corner of the bar and are approaching us. I say to Guy, the French boy, Next they'll work out a way of sending a charge along the chain to blow up the tow truck. The French girl says, I like the man from New Mexico; the French boy shrugs. Melanie pats me on the back; she says, Good boy. I reckon she has a doting dad. But, says Guy, it's not always police who do the towing, there are civilian tow trucks in America. I ask if he, too, is interested in American Indians. The French girl says the man from New Mexico tried out for the Olympic decathlon. Plenty of people try out, says Guy.

I have some malaria of the heart, and this young law student who's at the ecology seminar for a holiday finds my bad spots like a dumbly true X-ray camera. He is extolling the Corsican Resistance which was so tough the island was free by September 1943. Not even the Green Berets could subdue this crazy island, he says in English. The French girl says she thinks the man from New Mexico may be violent. Guy shrugs.

I have a friendly wave of dislike for Dagger, and it passes. Melanie says she loves it here but can't find anything made-in-Corsica that's creative to bring home to her parents. Guy now gleefully tells how the Yanks bombed the swamps on the east side of the island at the end of the war to get rid of the mosquitoes, and this is where the Algerian pioneers went to work in so un-Corsican a spirit and created an agricultural showspot, grapes, vegetables—reclaimed the swamps as they had reclaimed the North African desert—Egyptian cotton, Guy believes too.

I point out that those very emigrants were of Corsican descent. Guy guffaws and says do I know how their prosperity has been greeted here? (I don't think I put that in the pages Jenny typed. The Corsican capsule parts to let in which elements?) Sabotage, says Melanie. Correct, says Guy—certain unsavory elements blow up a power station over on that side of the island from time to time. Mike told me, says Melanie nodding reverently.

I raise my hands like a camera to frame a girl in a crisp flowered frock getting into a panel truck, and I murmur, The Egyptian cotton hasn't taken, by the way. *Taken?* says Guy, puzzled.

Cut to a new street a quarter of a mile away at the end of a section of hot fortress wall. My eyes throb. Our cast has split to buy the French boy a swimsuit. Yes, that is what Guy needs.

232

Copy of *Figaro* in Dagger's hip pocket. You can buy newspapers at Hachette's. Dagger conveys the heat shooting a second or two of a Chinese sweating in a laundry. We cross to the petrol-station side of the street. I cross back to look in a shop. My position matters here only in that I can now presently cross so as to be caught on film by accident after the minute or so of equally accidental comedy Dagger himself will track. Yet in turn my being caught is possible because in a moment Dagger himself will cross. But this might not be implicit enough in the finished film, so perhaps it doesn't belong in my diary; yet the *Corsican montage* has enlarged beyond the hours Jenny took to type it in London, the magazine opens to let in a future unphraseable there on a street in Ajaccio, never mind. My spine between my shoulder blades is wet, my temples hot. Dagger ambles powerfully along, and I have again this sense of introducing my motion into a field without motion, and now in my brain (that is suspended in fluid and has, they say, no sensitivity to pain) the amateur thought circles like a series of instructions performed repeatedly till some specified condition is satisfied whereupon a branch instruction is obeyed to exit from the loop—the thought that Dagger doesn't have a clue, maybe he knew once but he doesn't now know what he's doing. But I can't take the exit offered because Dagger has stopped and though I'm across the street and can't hear the hiss of the camera I know it's turning.

Is there a knob that turns visibly? I pan to what even from my acute angle I see he's shooting in the near-noon glare and the sharp shade here and there along the street fragrant of petrol and hot olive oil: his subjects are moving slowly up their street which crosses where ours ends, or up that portion of their street that's all we can see; they are three, a girl in a little white and black skirt and a white midriff blouse, a blond man in shorts and an orange terrycloth shirt, and a man also young but totally bald whose head seems to contain the deep brownness of the three of them—he's lean and bony and looks lithe and swift. They walk single-file like tourists who've had a drink in one of the fisherman's cafés and are now strolling toward the beach, except that the girl isn't carrying anything so maybe they are going somewhere else first. They are so slow they seem almost acting. The fort wall is glaring bright, the sidewalk is narrow. But now the girl points at Dagger, her midriff blouse stark white. The blond man steps off the curb toward us but is checked by the other young man who now jabs him in the ribs with his index finger. The three continue along the fortress wall, the bald man has his hand on the girl's back where it's bare. We are fifty yards from the end of our street where theirs crosses coming up from the port. I cross to Dagger's side. The three go almost out of sight to our right and he has the camera right on them. Dagger breaks to the left and is almost brushed by a car as he crosses the street to the side I was on in order to shoot a bit more of the three. I can't see them now, for I am still on the right side. Dagger trots to the end of the street, shoots again. They did not want to be filmed. The English have that sense of privacy, but the English would never so openly assert it and would suffer it and ignore it.

But I didn't give Dag £12 in London for film just to piss it away.

I cut across toward him, at an angle, for he's already at the intersection. I'm calling something to him, I cannot know what the three are doing, but now as if they are just part of a larger scene Dagger pans to me running toward him, switches off saying that I've run right out of focus. I don't know why I was running. I felt for a second almost between him and them. I turn again and the girl and the two guys are there almost out of sight up their street but turning out of it toward Place Napoléon, and the blond man looks back and then they're gone.

The exit from that loop swings by again and I don't quite make it out but I say to Dag (and feel this takes me part way, for maybe this is a soft exit), On film I'll look like I'm running at the cameraman to protect those people from him.

Dagger is at once, though with a certain casual slowness, into a tale about a New York friend who in the early fifties was doing a TV history-simulation called *See It Now*. So one day he was taping the show and put his eye to the viewfinder to check that he was getting what he wanted—and suddenly like a face from another dimension into the viewfinder comes an old college pal who owes him money and plans to borrow more and figures if he wanders onto the set he might even get a bit part.

Dagger's Beaulieu may have caught in my face some record of the French boy knocking America or Melanie touching me through my wet shirt and setting off a fatherly nerve that circles a memory that, because they grew up in London, I never had of taking my daughter fishing in Sheepshead Bay on a Sunday, my family to Lindy's in Coney Island for lobster, my children to see the sea lions and giant turtles in the aquarium that moved from the Battery to Coney Island the year Will was born in England.

Tourists, says Dag, tourists, against the wall of a fortress.

But I don't believe him, I don't believe he has a real idea.

But if he's using me—for what? fun and friendship? camera practice? Will Claire's boss pay our gas and film? I kicked in £12 in London for color stock Dagger ordered from L.A. I thought there was energy in his good nature as in the rechargeable power pack that drives the Beaulieu motor and can "transport" as many spools as we'll conceivably need. A chance plunge yields new power. My exit comes again and I find my branch instruction and leave the loop. I have seen how to use the Corsican footage. Between the silent Softball Game and the Marseillaise game of bowls with its arcing, thudding steel balls, there will have intervened the Unplaced Room with its barren venue and its military subject matter; the Bonfire in Wales with its burning branches and the Unknown Man running from darkness to darkness; the Hawaiian hippie (whose face will connect with that of the American Indian of the preceding scene) steadfastly drumming his guitar not on the road any more but in the great long pedestrian subway that leads to the South Kensington tube station; the colors and names of things going into the Suitcase Slowly Packed opening into the colors of the pier crowd here in Ajaccio. We will then cut ahead to footage not yet taken of the U.S. Air Force base in England but just for ten seconds of NATO first-strike bombers taking off silently against Guy's remarks about the bombing of the malaria swamps (which we'll get him to repeat at the casino tonight against the baccarat croupiers' calls). Then to Carlo and Letizia's house and Melanie's spiel, then use what she said when she wasn't being filmed or recorded (talking about Paoli's supporters driving Letizia out of her house) as sound track for the tourists against the fortress wall (though we'll have to establish that it is a fortress).

Cut to the fortress street from which the girl and the two men have just disappeared (though any potential justness in our finished film will hinge on how we edit). I ask Dagger to move up and shoot along the fortress wall to see down into the courtyard behind the wall— where they used to shoot the condemned.

Something newly sound and solid is coming. I'm excited. I do not know what the Marvelous Country House will yield—Americans, another fortress, a nice life perhaps shivered into montage with the air base and thus made to seem close to it in green England. We'll see when we get back from Corsica.

I decide we'll take a day's jaunt over to the west side of the island (where there's a Roman town at Aleria) and film that area where the U.S. Air Force bombed the fever mosquitoes.

Cut to Tuesday. The film will show the offshore battle of the landing craft. Across the Gulf of Ajaccio at a depth of forty meters are the shelves of coral the scuba man said he'd take me to for fifty francs. A gray outboard rounds a giant buoy. The eye-ear-nose-and-throat man from whom Dagger borrowed the zoom this morning lives in a large dusky apartment with heavy furniture and a calm beautiful blond woman. It is an Angenieux zoom with focal length variable from 12 mm. to 120 mm. Since one of our own prime lenses is 15 mm., our advantage with the zoom is at the long narrow end not at the short wide. It's not even the quick lens change between shots but the flexibility while shooting that turns Dagger on. But on the way back to the école for lunch he has said he's sorry we couldn't dig up a 12–240, and for less than eight inches long this here zoom is awful heavy and he's got to handle it like a China doll it's so expensive and he's not going to be able to do one combination he'd planned, moving the camera back while zooming at the same rate *toward* the boys in the yellow raft, because with a zoom the weight increases so much with the thing sticking out in front that you have to use a tripod; and he can't see holding the grip with his right hand, working the zoom crank with his left, to say nothing of pan zooms *and* going backward on sand stumbling over ladies and babies. I had nothing to say. Dagger said it was impossible to have anyone else turn the crank, it had to be the one looking through the viewfinder. I got his point. Dagger's American friend is on the beach with Dagger and wants to help out. The magazine is mounted on top so we won't have to reload for two hundred feet and its shape suggests cans of films. A giant soccer player in an ingenious bikini stands hand on hip, there are bare brown girls and boys discussing the camera and asking who is in the film. Dagger wears sawed-off jean shorts below his hairy torso, the San Francisco Seals baseball cap above. The Scotswoman wears two strips of black. The sand is molten. Dagger tries a five-second shot of her at ten feet. A tot is peeing in the water but perhaps not in focus. Out near the boys in their yellow rubber rafts a snorkler's yellow hose sticks out of his head like a periscope. Melanie is not in a swimsuit. She is watching the two teams a hundred yards offshore ramming each other with rubber-ended poles. She asks

Dagger if she can look, but he says the gear's pretty tricky; then he says Oh sure.

The Scotswoman charges the water—her long-legged run is slowed, she launches a flat dive.

Dagger has fixed the W-shaped crank in the Out position and is turning it.

I'm in the water way right of Dagger. I cup my hands to frame the boys in their yellow boats. The snorkler has come so close to their combat that one of them taps him on the head with the rubber end of a pole and he comes up suddenly as if he can't hold his breath any more. Words would not improve on Dagger's filming here. I could have held the mike near the camera to tape the observations of those at the observing end; instead I am out in the almost acidly salty water to the right of the naval encounter, which you can understand better if you know that it continues the dusty hostilities of last evening when the American and French boys at the école took on a bunch of locals in soccer.

The sky is a ground; I kick my toes to the surface, I fly at such a height I mark no progress overland. I rest my eyes, the salt sting when I close them also muscles my chest. Closed bodies like the Med build up higher salinity and the Med is one reason the Atlantic is saltier than the Pacific. Across my eyelids' apricot inside, quick dry intercuts occur—a collapsed and folded yellow raft on a shelf in a shop along the Cour Napoléon, three bright headbands displayed in a Greenwich Village window, bikinis in a haberdasher's drawer, pines contoured like children's mountains at dusk against a final brightness of sky after the sun has dropped—it would be too obvious not to say ludicrous to bring on a destroyer as backdrop for this naval engagement—my mind approaches a condition of music or more likely the phrase itself Lorna and Geoff Millan said back and forth one night and I deliberately failed to understand even when it became a branch of the conversation kindly directed at me, to wit that a formula, yes even a formula, say in engineering, might approach the condition of music—and months too late I retort that I'll take a mechanism over a formula any day; now take a servo-mechanism, in response to a control signal a servo like the sound of a dominant chord conveys to the control system the difference between a desired state and the actual state again and again until the difference is eliminated, like a marital grievance in a soap opera—my ears here below the surface catch tremors of warble and concussion, I drift nearer the combat; I turn back.

I let my ghostly legs drop. Something happens. In the stern of the American boat if these boats had sterns, Mike, upon seeing the Scotswoman Mary, reaches at her with his pole and just as one of the Corsicans on the far side from me dodges a pole but hangs on to its rubber end and pulls so the American boat jumps toward the Corsicans, Mary grabs hold of Mike's rubber end and pulls, and her move finds force in his move and weight. The sync is exact and like a thought proved. And into the water goes Mike and away goes his boat, a subtraction from the international event, an addition elsewhere. Yet Mike jabbed wantonly, and his may be a subtler judo still, as if, bored with battle in a suburban gulf, he looked at Mary and thought her emphatically worth not waiting any longer for.

Just two Yanks left, one drops his pole, grabs a paddle and maneuvers, leaving Mike still further off but Mike is wrestling with Mary. The Corsicans seem between the Americans and Dagger, a conjunction interestingly compressed by a zoom shot's diminished depth of field. I'm twenty-five yards from Mike and Mary; some U.S. or French firm must have thought up an underwater housing for a Nagra, but I have only ears. The mountains at my feet are brownly harsh green with maquis but the yellow blooms are past, we're too late except for postcards. The naval encounter turns serious, the Americans are in close, swinging their poles to hit the enemy with wood now, but except to Dagger at 120 mm. the hostilities will seem from the beach all in good fun. The Americans are now attempting to board the Corsicans. The two boats have drifted down the shore to a position opposite the café. Mary and Mike like a subplot discreetly spar. She says, I'll tell my brother. He says, I'll tell Melanie. She says, You don't need to. Mike and Mary are gasping and grappling. Mike says, Your brother I hear is a very bad influence on Paul. Where did you get that? says Mary. From Gene? Mike strokes over to the bobbing dark pink butt of his pole. Mary goes under, Mike twists round laughing, she's got his legs. He sees me as Mary surfaces and he is looking at me over her slim shoulder as she says, You didn't answer me.

Mike's look at me is blank. He says with a hand on Mary, *I'll* answer you, and dives. She screams while he's under. The fight is over. The yellow rafts are empty but being reboarded.

How do you know my brother? says Mary, and Mike's answer is too low, and she says, But how do you know *Paul*?

I can't hear Mike.

Halloween, says Mary I think, and becomes aware of me.

I swim in.

I wade out, firm and sleek.

Melanie meets me disconsolately. What were you doing out there? Aren't you making the film too?

Dreaming, I say.

Want to have a drink? she asks; and then: He stopped filming the boats when Mike fell in.

Good, that means more film left.

He dropped a reel on his instep and now he's limping around in agony, Melanie says, but he just went on shooting Mike and that Scotch woman.

She's old enough, I say.

Mike said he had to discuss something with your friend tonight. Do you know where?

Can't drape sea water over your toes like you can a blanket. Floating in the Gulf of Ajaccio, drape a line from eye to toe. Then one from toes to mountain like a suspension bridge. Document your daydream with fact.

Well here you talk about the condition of music whatever the hell that is, and let's say in a suspension bridge like Brooklyn Bridge there's as much melody heating up in its cables as in the formulas John Roebling used to arrive at just a couple of cables each 12½ inches in diameter and containing, helically wrapped with galvanized wire, almost as many wires as there are feet in a mile; what if we take it the other way round and, instead of finding beauty in calculations, make measurements *of* the beautiful, what about the cyanometer Ruskin devised to measure the blue of the sky?

Mad Ruskin.

I could no more have contained in its solid slot that Corsican *cartouche* than in the diary part I gave Jenny to type add to the after-all relevant dialogue a measure of the warm span of Melanie's breasts unbra'd beneath a spanking white T-shirt sporting a black Napoleon horsed at Waterloo, right hand inside his coat. Yet Jenny was to say next week that my style grew on her.

Once coming out of our Welsh dairyman Mr. Jones's I converged upon Tessa who was coming to have tea with Lorna, and right there in the middle of the road in Highgate Tessa gave me a book about the

Maya and told me to read the bit about physical characteristics, also Le Plongeon's theory that through their own colonists the Maya influenced the culture of Babylon, Syria, Asia, and Africa.

You have me. Even if you have not the book. I put it in my jacket pocket. I half read it the first night but to this day I have not returned it. I told Dudley I hadn't finished and he said the less of that we have around the house the better.

In Jenny's typescript of the Marvelous Country House the first week in August, the name *Gene* hit me, but the night we filmed at Stonehenge and I saw that the deserter from the Unplaced Room had turned up, I thought to ask Dagger how Mike in Corsica had known Gene. Through Cosmo, Dagger said; Mike was mainly in New York.

Place Foch: we dine outside.
　　　Back at the école they've finished dinner an hour ago no doubt and have grabbed their guitars.
　　　We are near the hips and elbows of promenaders. Stiff thick old palms stand around the square; flowers in the middle and a newsstand now closed where I bought postcards of sights I won't see. The strings of festival lights are not so fancy as the façade of lights hanging over Cour Napoléon that depict Napoleon's hat. Beyond, high above a side street off Place Foch a line of laundry sags near the light of a bare window. I put my hand on the Beaulieu where it lies on a chair between Dagger and me. A German was shot in a bar last night. In the leg from behind, in the foot from the front, in the buttock from the side—the tale circulates. They say every other car in Corsica has a gun in the trunk. Tonight the week has gotten away from us. But my prospect of ball games (soft and steel) and malaria bombs and rings of fire and glaring chalky walls with tourists plodding single-file holds as firm as the New Orleans I visited on business a fortnight after Mardi Gras once.
　　　We have shot footage of the seminar students sagely taking down names on mailboxes in the lower street of shops that runs parallel to Cour Napoléon, to determine the residents' ancestry, French, Italian, Greek. We have shot festival fireworks—no telling what explosively experimental fruit-storms have lathered our cellu-

loid skies. *Cartouche* means fireworks *and* cartridge. We've shot and taped the école youths feeding, drinking, singing *"Auprès de ma blonde"* and "Michael Row the Boat Ashore," and marching around the long tables but not like '68. (Corsica is too strategic for its own independence.) I want to go diving with the camera to deepen the Bonfire in Wales and the Naval Engagement. There's no way to take the camera down, I'll have to go alone.

We dine in Place Foch, giving the seminar's *bonhomie* a rest. A child is being force-fed yogurt, yogurt is good for the liver. We return the zoom tonight. I discuss the fish soup with a huge-nosed old waiter. People click by. You can see the pier. A bronzed foursome occupy a table near us. They're speaking Italian, I may have seen the dark girl on the Genoa boat. The older man who has a blue-and-gold captain's hat on holds the menu up to one side and talks from it to the obsequious girls and back, as if it describes them.

I ask Dagger what we have achieved here. He is putting away the rich peppery fish soup. The Italian in the hat claps his hands and calls out in French for someone higher up than the handsome waiter who stands by. Dagger says, We've got a lot of good stuff, the Naval Engagement, the market, the fortress. I say what about Mike and Mary playing games. I say I feel like we've been sleepwalking or waiting for something to happen when we should have been making it happen. Dagger is glad we ate out tonight—did I ever hear about the man who's been in a coma since early 1957? Dagger pilots a hunk of bread around his soup, sinks it, lifts it out, and puts it in his mouth: Well, this man wakes up from his coma and learns that Eisenhower is dead and says My God, then Nixon is President.

I propose shooting the east side of the island where the Algerians settled. Mussolini comes up at the Italians' table. Mussolini's son. Dagger agrees we might look at the east side of the island. I suggest we interview someone there who knows about the reactionary sabotage, for some of it may be anti-American. Dagger with his mouth full says, That's getting pretty wild.

This was not in what Jenny typed, though what she typed she said was the best I'd done. The Corsican cartridge has opened and spread, like the paper of gunpowder Dudley Allott told me of, that by joke or chance turned up instead of salt in the bread and eggs and fowl that Stephens and Catherwood had packed for a leg of their toiling trek through Guatemala seeking ruined cities. "It was," Stephens said, "the most innocent way of tasting gunpowder, but even so it was a bitter pill." But lucky for them they weren't cooking that night.

Our langouste comes, long narrow crayfish with spines. Paris fixes the market price.

The man in the captain's hat is at least sixty, and tough. The young man could be a film actor. The blonde inclines her head to our side and takes a relaxed look around.

We go to work. The wine is cool.

The Italian has sent a bottle back.

I put my hand on the Beaulieu—the business (or right-hand) side with knobs and a switch for frame-power and the two tiny windows over the footage gauges—the top with the vertical needle registering meters and feet, the bottom with horizontal needle registering frames 1   10   100. Dagger doesn't notice. OK, he says, you tell me: what *should* we be doing here? Here I thought I was looking after your health, education, and welfare—free grub at the école, girls on the beach, and you learned that there are five towns in the U.S. named after Pasquale Paoli.

The Italian with the hat does business with il Duce's nephew. I say Oh sure, Boswell got Ben Franklin interested, but Boswell got the Scots excited about the plight of Corsica, now what's that Scots lassie doing in Ajaccio with Mike?

The man in the captain's hat passes on to a Belgian ambassador named Duprat who is also a friend of his and who has been killed in a coup along with more than ninety dinner guests of King Hassan's. My Italian fails me so I don't get the link with Allende's copper coup the bad effect of which upon U.S. Anaconda the man in the captain's hat boasts can but be to his own advantage. My Italian fails me again and all I make out a moment later is It's just a matter of time, and then Mussolini is mentioned, and the dark-haired girl tries to put in an opinion but the skipper shut her right up saying he too was a partisan in '43 but no Red (he shakes a finger smiling).

He lifts his hat and he's bald. He runs his finger along a sculpted cleft where the Americans shot out a piece of bone and when he recovered he was a new man. He has stopped the conversation with his head but at the same moment the young handsome waiter has put down a big salad bowl full of shrimp. The skipper nibbles one, his full lips seem dyed purple on his burnished tan. He picks off a rib of shell, eyes the waiter, and chucks the shrimp back into the bowl. In Italian he says to the waiter, We always throw the babies back. His guests laugh, but that wasn't what the skipper

242

meant—he speaks to the waiter again in Italian, the others stop laughing, the waiter shakes his head with wary eyes that could mean he doesn't get the point or is implying Fuck You.

Our langoustes have been on a diet. Dagger is gnawing thoughtfully. I get hold of the camera. Dagger raises his eyebrows, a shard of abdominal carapace and a couple of spines in front of his moustache. No doubt what's happening. The Corsican is being told, now in French, to shell every last shrimp, and the girls are smiling.

The waiter goes away. The *patron* appears. The skipper is going to charm the *patron,* almost. The bottle of Château de Tracy '67 is almost finished, the skipper wants another, he talks French to the *patron.* The *patron* seems to charm the skipper, who in the way he looks up at the *patron* seems almost to be rising. The waiter goes away, the *patron* and the skipper (about the same age but in very different shape) discuss the shrimp and the size of the langoustes to come. I have the Beaulieu out of its case and without noting what lens we're on I focus quietly as the sullen *garçon* appears with a second misted bottle of Tracy '67 and a wood-handled knife which sticks out of his fist in the upward or number-one stabbing position. Dagger says, For Christ sake, and I let my thumb off the button. OK, he says, to get to Aleria on the east side you have to drive up to Corte in the middle where Paoli had his capital, didn't he?

Other tables have noticed. The waiter is shelling the shrimp. The event has lost its prankish magic. He has pulled the bowl to the edge and is using the wood-handled knife. The foursome are looking at each other but not moving. I'm shooting again. I haven't checked the light. We're on 50 mm., which is fine. Dagger says, I wouldn't. He might be Mafia.

The waiter is moving his hands as if he's trying to insert a tiny screw into a fixture at a bad angle. The blonde drinks, but the four are essentially motionless. The fruits of the sea accumulate on a plate.

I feel like a lookout looking opposite ways waiting to warn. Warn the waiter? The odious bigshot?

The bigshot has popped two babies into his mouth and has complimented the waiter, who is spilling tiny jets of rage as if from his ribs each time his elbow slightly rises or from his eyes each time he blinks. The energy is in an unstable state but feeding at a regular clip into the Beaulieu. The skipper spots me.

I switch off as he rises, and I have felt a new thing—that energy has been sent from me as well as received by me. My eye away from the viewfinder sees more. Dagger says, Watch it. The skipper asks in French what I think I'm doing. The waiter drops his knife into the bowl of unshelled shrimp. The skipper tells him he's not finished.

I call in English, We're doing a film on Corsica.

What *about* Corsica? the skipper demands, and when he turns eye-to-eye with the waiter and sees the shelling has again stopped and nods so sharply to the waiter it looks like the last OK to the executioner to go ahead, the waiter resumes performing his instructions and in spite of me is in even worse shape.

The Italian smiles with his purple lips, looks at his three guests, and says with a smug shrug, I am not exactly Onassis. He sits down and waves a hand at the waiter and says to me, Let him be the star, eh?

He *is,* I call.

Hello there!

Dagger's voice revolves me on the seat of my chair to Mary and Mike just a couple of close-ups away. She's in a pale sleeveless shift, her hair all over her shoulders.

The Italian calls: What is your film?

Revolution, I call. It's about revolution.

I raise the camera and shoot.

The Italian with a sweep of his hand over his table, stopping shy of the shrimp bowl above which the knife picks away, calls back in French this time, But there is no revolution here.

I cut. We can dub his words.

I'm reaching the Beaulieu back onto its chair but this is where Mike wants to sit.

Revolution? he says quietly to Dagger. You didn't *tell* me.

Dagger begins some tale about the passionate guitarist Prince Yusupov who assassinated the Tsar's favorite, Rasputin, escaped to New York, and later bought two houses up in Calvi.

Mike doesn't pursue my remark about revolution.

I post a card to Jenny: dark slender mules being loaded with cork bark, the unseen sun pumpkin orange in the inner trough of each chunk; my message: SOMETHING STRANGE GOING ON HERE.

To Will, a high stone viaduct and two neat white and red train carriages presumably moving from one dark blur of green foliage to the other while through the gray arches can be seen sky and cliffs in the distance; my message: TECHNOLOGICAL REVOLUTION COMES TO CORSICA.

To Lorna goes a postcard showing the buttercup-yellow bloom of the needle-furze, one of the hardy bushes generally called the maquis dotting the valleys and working up into the harsh slopes which are of the same granite as those unique statue-menhirs Mary described thirty miles and three millennia from where she and Mike and Dagger and I sat over our coffee, and the spiny grease of steaming fish soup and the crisp fat of fried batter and the rough local olive oil and Gauloise smoke and the acceleration of orbiting motorbikes kept out the green smell of the maquis that encroaches upon ancient menhirs and tilted dolmens, the blooms by now in July gone except on Lorna's card; its message, FILM HAS TAKEN UNEX-PECTED TURN.

In the bright morning I give the three cards to Melanie to mail. They aren't in what Jenny typed.

Revolution: spelled the same in French to mean also *revulsion,* but spelled *rivoluzione* in that obnoxious yachtsman's land where that other key English sense of *revolution* (for short, *rev* or plural *revs*) as *rotation* (e.g., as of an engine cycle or a satellite in space) is *giro* (as in *cento giri al minuto,* one hundred revs a minute). I said the word to impress Mary, maybe Mike; but also because I began then suddenly to think of our film as lurking on the margins of some unstable, implicit ground that might well shiver into revolution; yet the word I think arrived on my tongue from some dumb suburban meridian.

The girl's yellow tank through the bluing agency of the water is well below me like an insect torso, giant against her black rubber jacket. And as if we're starting the dive all over again and have just set our mouthpieces and ducked under the choppy sea of the gulf, I am once again inhaling the beat of my own breath.

Do not fill your lungs too full when you first put in your mouthpiece or you'll be overballasted and it will be harder getting down.

Michel is slowly showing me his wrist, and through the glass of my mask and the glass of what I don't see is his timer, it seems to say we are down thirty-five meters. The girl has gone below us to the floor of the gulf and from under a three-foot bivalve she is unearthing what looks like a piece of pottery. Now, if we've come down thirty-five meters I don't know where all that space has gone to. I figured us a while back for ten or twelve meters at the cleft where we leveled to cut brown-spined sea urchins off the rock and carve them open for the tiny orange meat at the center which we fed to the little light blue fish that hang around and dart at your palm. But from there, past the fifteen wheeling almost inter-cogged arms of three brick-red starfish stuck to a slanting ledge, we've angled down through the cleft to no more I would think than twenty meters; and I'm just headed off, hands at my sides, toward something pale thinking it may be the primrose-yellow coral called parazoanthus which you find at twenty meters in the Mediterranean but I've seen only in a book in a close-up stuck to a sponge at one end of the polyps' vegetal stalklet whose free end has opened into sharp, fragile feelers—when Michel taps my heel and pulls my fin, and when I turn back, cool and with my tank and my belt of weights weightless so I'm forgetting which is up and which is down, Michel extends his wrist for me to see.

The girl zooms slowly at us from the green gloom of what I'm thinking must be forty meters if Michel and I are thirty-five. (Dagger is sitting on the surface with the boss in a gray rubber raft, we are maybe fifty yards from the anchor line that seems to hold them down up there.) My room softens and opens, my cartridge does not get mushy, it swells out of capsule hardness to hear the never recorded words of the Bonfire night in Wales: What is here is elsewhere; what is not here is nowhere.

You think at first when you go down you will not have enough air, and you breathe too fast and your heart is as loud as the world. You die and live again. You are the only wind in this dusk. The limbs go free, but you must not swim your arms. No one you know in London has *plongé avec les bouteilles*. Not Geoff Millan, well ballasted as he is, whose work will no doubt achieve the condition of music. Not the three or four English couples who in their late thirties have taken up sailing. Not Dudley Allott, who still pursues that New York fire and perhaps can never be a friend but who tells you things which have become more interesting over the years as his life has become more clear. Not even formidable Mary who is from Inverness and whom you only met this week, who can show point by point why she sees in the male menhirs of southern Corsica an early outpost of the hero, bound out toward his patriarchal system away from the Majestic Mother, her terrible body, its sea of magic nights. I breathe

the water, I hear my other heart like a mechanical thing I'm learning to be further and further away from. The cartridge opens at a hundred gills. My mask has taken in three grains of water; Michel has shown us how to blow it clear even under water but I can wait, my nose and eyes like a brain sequestered from other functions is apart from my mouth to which my air hose runs. My window films a little.

Why film? Why not negative New York, blow her up into far-flung frames, detonate the notion of New York so it will go away and leave me alone in London with Lorna, an anesthetic TNT to soften New York into a mere remembrance of what the future used to seem. I breathe now a message from my tank and I make the adjustment, I reach back past my right shoulder for the valve understanding that it wasn't meters on Michel's left wrist-dial but minutes—now more than thirty-five. But now with an ache in my jaw I can't see where all that time went.

Michel unmouths his mouthpiece no hands, the girl's yellow tank like some ridable creature rises below me, and Michel is warbling the *Marseillaise* in tinkly bubbles. Up in the boat he said he'd sing it, it's part of your fifty francs plus a titillating encounter with the resident anemone of Ajaccio Gulf. The girl extends to me slow-motion her find—an ashtray from one of the cruise ships.

Michel undoes his rubber crotch-flap—the encased eyes the more ribald with his dimpled mouth transfixed by the hose. He signs to me do I want to do the same for some purpose?

We are not building the Brooklyn Bridge in 1872 in the watertight caissons so unintentionally menacing to all the sandhogs who risked "the bends" (so named by those very men after some Grecian pose then a ladies' fad in New York). Some came up too fast after ten hours raising cubic acres of muck to clear the bedrock for the towers which let you today admire on high, not think downward, to that dread dreck toil prey to pressure and flood and gas leak—days those immigrant workers did a century ago neither exactly brave nor at all crazy but needing work, and one victim of that so-called caisson disease (which has nothing to do with bullet boxes or artillery wagons) whose name alone survives was John Roebling's son and collaborator Washington, thus crippled, who watched the rest of the job through a telescope and cannot have found in the sandhogs' nickname for decompression sickness much of a joke.

The writing here is at least as good as the cartridge proper that Jenny typed and liked so much, perhaps even as good as the

Marvelous Country House about which when she typed it the first week in August she said not a word.

The girl rises before me. I reach for the back of her temperature-less thigh and in answer she puts her palm back on her butt where her rubber jacket-tail seals her neatly, even overlapping as well the fold or two of flesh, and fastening like mine in front with two plastic cotter pins. We rise through the gray-brown cleft at forty-five degrees, or do you translate that into some bomber-pilot's two-o'clock?, pass the three predator stars, and find the tall and luminous anchor line.

Slowly treading we follow the line up into a verdant slush of light and just before I slip into the surface there seems much more air coming through my mouthpiece though there isn't. But it is good to get my teeth out of it and get it off my gums. Dagger is saying so Rasputin ate the cyanide cupcakes and drank the glasses of cyanide wine and nothing happened when Yusupov's dog Nabosco came in and Rasputin handed him down the last of the poisoned cupcakes—I lift my mask up to my forehead and the man in the gray rubber boat with Dagger interrupts him, points at me, and says in French to blow the blood all out.

The girl is smiling beside me, I do not know her name. Michel's hair is as blond as that of the man who stepped off the fortress curb toward us and was recalled by the bald man and whom I saw watch us and enter the scuba trailer after the boss started our outboard and we were running out between the lines of power boats, and not only did I not call Dagger's attention to this but I did not tell him I saw he saw and wasn't telling me.

An English female voice—not the kind that has helped to keep me in England these many years—behind us in the evening (but of our group) asks what type of palm these are along the boulevard. They're date, replies an American male, but they've virtually given up bearing. From a distance by daylight the tops look like feathers slowly exploding from party tubes tricked up by a children's magician, but the trunks tonight are a formal avenue past the casino toward the center, stately or even to a tropical tourist stunning but, if one thinks also of the muscular indolence of Corsica, as idiotically official as Napoleon's hat in colored lights.

Close, as we stroll beside the dark glimmering gulf, the reptile bark and tough fronds seem fragrant, but the smell is not the palms

248

but the bougainvillaeas. Lights stand here and there against the dark shore across the gulf like bright thumb prints. There are corals there at forty meters, or so the scuba man promises if I dive another day.

I include our stroll because Dagger brought the Beaulieu after all. We thought we would not intrude into the famous café the Nagra unit—whose quarter-inch sync tapes are nonetheless (I learn only now from an école student) hell to match with the optical print when you come to editing. But unbeknownst to Dagger—why my secrecy? —I've begged a small Sony from the same student. In my hand now it's like a book, and its strap is discreetly wound about the black leather.

OK. Cut to famous café.

No, cut not yet.

A word more, first. Mike and Mary are again in our group. Dagger says to me OK we drive to the east side of the island tomorrow. Mike is interested why. I mention some possibilities—the American past dropping TNT in neat bombs on the mosquitoes over there in the malaria swamps, then the colonists settling there after leaving revolutionary Algeria, then *l'esprit de Corse* denied so many avenues of action, so they try a little home-grown sabotage more reactionary than revolutionary, opposed to change or just to *les colons* and secretly to their prosperous reclamation of that part of the island.

Mike doesn't say anything. Dagger says that nothing can take the place of the old cherry bombs they used to set off behind the Freehold Presbyterian Church on July 4.

I add, Of course it'll fit in with other footage.

Did he hear me depress the record button? Instead of an intro to him, I have as yet only myself faking a bit to draw him out.

But then Mike says, Would you kill?

Ah well, I say (thinking to see what the remarkable Mary sees in him, with her elegant legs—can she see with her legs?—and the wild-hawk turn in the bridge of her nose), you know we're just filmmakers, traveling eyes. But since you ask, would *you* kill?

Mike chuckles in the dusk.

Cut to famous café. We push in through sidewalk standees whom Dagger didn't have light enough to shoot, nor the darkening façades with a bright casement here and there, the isolated glare of a fish restaurant, two old women in black leaning toward each other in a doorway, adolescents near a corner ice cream shop, music down the street, but here is the music.

Dagger's American friend booked us what's now the last table in a far but public corner. Family people double up. We are watched across the packed room to our table. Dagger will use the 15-mm. lens, our widest angle now we've given back the zoom, and when he sits down he opens the aperture right up for maximum light.

His American friend is explaining a song. He says, Shepherds, lots of shepherds. Or used to be. But no artisan culture. Against the music I miss some words between Mary and Mike. I wish the American would stop explaining the song.

I do not know what Dagger is interested in. He asks Mary about her family because that's where she gets her archaeology and she's been telling him about the statue-menhirs. The great male faces are awesome, there are swords, the eyes are cavernous shadows carved back under plain eyebrow ridges, there's a head and not much more, the figure seems standing in the earth able to rise but only if there's a reason to rise, they're very dark and marvelous. Mary has been here before but this time she's on her way to Sardinia and stopped by to see this surly Mike who is a friend of her brother's. When she left Oxford she lost her passion for classical archaeology and is still torn, she says, between megalithic and Egyptian.

But your brother, says Dagger, and lets the sentence hang.

I reach toward Dagger: Hey isn't that the girl at the fortress?

Dagger says he doubts it, and I add, The one with the two guys who tried to get away from us.

My brother is changing, says Mary. She smiles and it's clear how much she cares about her brother.

Is Burns such a great hero where you come from?

> Amang the bonnie winding banks
> Where Doon rins wimplin' clear,
> Where Bruce ance ruled the martial ranks
> An shook his Carrick spear.

The Scots still hold out, I said.

Now *menhir*, she says, as a song ends and there's desultory clapping that declines oddly to a collective clap in near unison because the singers are about to take a break. Do you know what *menhir* means? Dagger is rising with the camera: just what it says: *men here*. Nonsense, says Mary, *men* (and you may learn from this, Michael) *men* means *stone* in Middle Breton, *hir* means *long*.

What could I learn? says Mike watching Dagger pan and cut and then get on up past the singer who because of the corner we're in has been standing with his back to us.

250

Now Dagger is moving. The singer doesn't mind. The big boss sits against the wall wringing his fingers over the steel strings of his guitar which lies snug between his belly and the table. Mike and Mary are between me and the singers. You get four or five. Mary has been here before and says the proprietor has to replace the singers because in the local style, furious, hard, and shrill, they kill their voices. Dagger is popping shots all over the room. The girl who looks like the midriff maiden at the fortress is with a dark-haired man. She is aware of Dagger but not watching him.

I have my elbow on the Sony and switch it on. Mary is talking to Mike, who is between her and the singers. Dagger's American friend is on the other side and Dagger is on the move.

That is surely the girl from the fortress. She had dark glasses on then. A mole above her upper lip moves when she smiles. Without looking at him she handles the dark-haired man's forearm. There is a cross-ways aisle behind them, then the door filled with standees.

I'm at the rear end of our table, facing the whole room. Dagger's American friend, whom I can't recall describing, is at my left, Mary and Mike in that order on my right. Mary talks despite the music, and Mike leans half around to be polite, then he gives up and turns in his chair to see her as she talks. Dagger's focus passes us and it occurs to me that he is filming the sound source—my recorder—though he doesn't know it, and in the developed print with, if possible, this tape integrated and synced, you'll see the singer and (until he suddenly moves to block us) our table with Mary facing the camera talking words which may well be salvageable on the final track.

In one song a dead dog tells a heavy tale. It's like one of Dagger's, tedious yet droll.

Then comes the shepherd. The lyrics are hard. I am listening to Mary as if I did not trust my machine.

Then a third singer: a bandit's lament sung by a wiry man who with his long slit of a moustache and passionate catlike indifference could have been a brigand. But there are no brigands in the mountains any more, Mary tells us.

Dagger roves.

You and your history, says Mike. Yet he is interested. Perhaps because she is interested in him. He looks like a long-haired quarterback from New Jersey. But I have never discounted him. You know, I say, that's precisely what I came to Corsica for.

I thought so, says Mary, and Mike looks at my glass and then up at me as if he's uncertain if I'm a dumb, horny over-the-hill flirt, or genuinely sinister.

Dagger bends near the portly guitarist, then straightens and turns, shooting (I think) Mary and Mike for a second, and Mike follows my eye, sees Dagger, and turns back to Mary hunching his shoulders. I'm not in the line of focus.

Here's Dagger shooting the crowd and the current singer, the brigand, and Mary and Mike; and if we ever get onto the Nagra an audible track from this cassette and then sync it in to this footage (for this isn't even what they call wild sync), we have a curious effect: people listening, singer singing—Corsica on the wall and the footage in montage—but the sound track will have the singer little louder than the crowd-murmur, and the principal track, the queer northern yarn Mary is telling, interspersed with my solicitous queries that deepen Mike's scowl as he glances about from time to time to see where Dagger is; perhaps that is the very reason she keeps on. Once he stares at me and says What do *you* care? and he stares at Mary's sharp bones of chin and cheeks and the most distantly menacing idea of a hawk in the bridge of that receptive nose and the faint golden rose that seems to illuminate her deep matte tan from inside her. She drinks her cassis; she is missing two joints of the fourth finger of her right hand.

My questions were not absolutely sincere. I enjoyed Mike's imitation.

The story almost bores me too.

Yet it proved to be the key development in Corsica.

Not that I care about her family per se, a nether branch of the famous Napiers. The heart of the tale which begins in 1650 though also much earlier is the magnetic Montrose, noble Scots royalist who landed on a cold March day in the Orkney Isles. Thence with a thousand unlucky local recruits and four hundred Danish troops including a dozen from the very Faeroe Isles nearby that you Mike mentioned when we were swimming—to invade the Scottish Highlands, raise support for the restoration of Charles the would-be Second, and press the practical Presbyterian government to that end toward which they were leaning in any event.

I was for Cromwell, said Mike.

But what happened was that Montrose was taken, the man MacLeod who had the stomach to turn him in got 5000 pounds of oatmeal, and Montrose for quite other reasons than the Orkney venture was put to death.

252

The singer tells of a reluctant fiancée. The people at the tables are grinning. The room is warm with smoke. Dagger has moved some more. He seems to be including in a shot the girl from the fortress scene; she either doesn't feel the lens upon her profile or doesn't care.

Montrose was hanged and then cut in pieces. Now the story starts.

Mike looks at me without pleasure and says, History can be fun; she leaves out the political position entirely.

The fortress girl is looking at me. The door with the standees is behind her. She may have said something, her swarthy escort eyes me across the room. Dagger is chatting up a tableful of locals—not shooting.

No, Michael, they didn't sew him back together and blow him up. His head they stuck on a pin above Edinburgh Toll Booth. His legs and arms were sent to four towns and hung up there for ten years. His trunk was interred in the common marsh graveyard.

Mike is looking about for the waiter. The Sony has fifteen minutes to run. Dagger is prowling again.

Lady Napier who revered Montrose like a god had his torso exhumed and had a surgeon named Callendar remove and embalm his heart. Pay attention, Michael. The same thing happened centuries before with Robert the Bruce who asked that his heart be taken after death to Jerusalem. (Mary's brogue thickens.)

Dagger has come almost behind the fortress girl and is photographing the standees, some of whom are less interested in this than others, for Dagger is between them and the singer who is contorting his insides up into a harsh high-pitched tragically calling climax.

That heart sealed in some unusual glue Lady Napier placed in a steel case made from Montrose's sword. The case she put in a gold box to be spirited off to his family in Holland where her own husband was also a refugee from Cromwell. But later the heart was lost there in the Low Countries, yet much later in a Dutch collection of curiosities this same gold filigree box was recognized by chance, for long before Lady Napier had it the Doge of Venice had given it to John Napier—and you know who *he* was?

Maybe Mary hasn't been boring us so much as dispersing herself in some strange irrelevance felt by Mike and passed to me.

We don't know who Napier was.

For Dagger is having words with a standee none other than the blond man from the fortress and the scuba trailer. He's asked

Dagger to move out of the way and he stands with one truculent shoulder well ahead of the other. Dagger lifts an arm in a great shrug as if to say, How do you talk to a shmoe like this. Now Dagger crouches in the aisle between the standees and the table. And I feel his focus on me—on the singer, Mike, Mary, and me like a staggered perspective expected to smile on signal.

Mary says, The inventor of logarithms. Didn't you know?

But the blonde with the mole turns smack into the camera's focal path, though much too close for clarity as her back view also was before. She objects. Her dark boyfriend gets up and speaks down to big Dagger who's still crouching.

The singer halts, and the big boss, who is a Corsican and knows what can happen if you drop the polite niceties, calls *Pas ici!*

Dagger elbows out the door, the burly back and black-gray hair somehow unchecked. And now as the boss picks out his intro like speedy mandolin bells lighting you into a festal and feminine harbor you've seen in the movies, Dagger and the Beaulieu lens appear over a modest standee shoulder, the angle is for a random moment ripe, though I am far from being close to it—the lens I'll bet has now been switched to 50—It's called *Lassie Go Home!* he shouts: the blonde at the table and the blond brown-eyed man ten feet in front of Dag automatically pivot: and in one through-shot whose depth of field is dubious, Dagger may just have caught them all, the two from the fort, the singer with a smoky swaggering deep breath, Mike, Mary, and (now for the second time at a circumference point oddly opposite to Dagger) *me.*

Which makes me glance behind, but there's just the wall, and as I see above my nose the familiar poster (labeled *Charmes de la Corse*) Mike is saying, That's too far, too far.

And Mary, calmly interested: That's that Marie person.

Meaning the blonde, who's pointing at us.

The blond man has gone out, it looks like after Dag. I imagine a smashed lens, dented magazines, stitches, discoloration, headlines—but I do not know their words because I do not know enough.

The singer tries again. A hush records my tape recorder's click-stop.

She asks who my friend is in Edinburgh. I say she visits there; I name her; Mary sips her cassis, puts the glass down, and her palm where I touch it is cool.

Mike is looking, but not at the recorder.

Suppose I've got the Montrose heart, I say; what would it go for?

Oh cut it out, says Mike.

Let's go swimming, says Mary.

The song sounds Italian. Who here ever knew the chronicle behind the lyrics? When Corsica was bartered back to Genoa in 1559 Sampiero came back to Corsica with eight men, raised 12,000, fought the Genoese, was betrayed, and died. He was the son of a mountain shepherd. His wife had taken a Genoese lover.

> *Evviva Sampiero*
> *E morti ai nemici*
> *Let us cleanse our sacred honor*
> *In the streams and in the fountains*
> *Il rumore della guerra*
> *A riscosso valli e monti.*

Sampiero your army included a squad of women with axes. You were betrayed by your best friend now known as the Corsican Judas. You were assassinated by your in-laws after you had strangled your wife.

> *Soni pieni li camini*
> *Delli veri patriotti*
> *E di buoni citadini*
> *Evviva Sampiero!*

Lorna accepted my explanation, but then on the Saturday night following my return from France came back from a rehearsal and started up again. Why had Dagger come back two days ahead of me?

I told you I went to Chartres.

Our Lady of Chartres.

In the morning I left for Hyde Park without speaking.

Dudley hasn't been to Corsica.

Dudley every chance he gets (though not fat) snacks on oily English peanut butter and grainy gray Scottish oatcakes in the pastel cylinders Tessa gets for him; Dudley staggers toward a sinking flyball in right field; Dudley after an emergency asthma refill at the Sunday chemist in Piccadilly stands with me watching marchers in summer '68 going Ho! Ho! Ho Chi Minh! as if gloating, and Dudley says flatly, By their lights I'm apolitical.

Dudley swims with me once a week at Swiss Cottage where on him the easily agitated water of the championship pool is like ballast that evens the straining cadence of his weighty limbs to a grace unlike his normal upright frame, strokes side by side with me, not racing, lazy in the kick like me—and Tessa flickers in the lane between us, though I think even at this late date he no more than Lorna or Jenny can know.

I set her to find those four lines of Burns, the bonnie winding banks, Bruce's martial ranks and Carrick spear.

And here is Dudley in the distended tropics of this Corsican cassette beyond Jenny's fingers on the family Royal portable (two carbons this time please), Dudley stating Montrose had German troops as well, but just might (as this woman of mine Mary said, though it was unlikely) have recruited from the Faeroe Isles, for though the Faeroes are off the main route they were Danish from the fourteenth century and by the sixteenth were often molested by English adventurers, which might but probably would not include the sober royalist Montrose who in any cassette was a Scot. I ask if drawing and quartering meant Montrose got castrated too.

Jenny, the following unfilmed untaped words have a place, believe me:

ME: Why was Mary here to see Mike?

DAG: To say hello from her brother.

ME: Who's he?

DAG: Scottish Nationalist Party. SNP for paranoid. Thinks his mail is opened.

ME: Don't tell me this kid Mike's in the SNP.

DAG: Neither is Mary's brother now. He was running a theater in Edinburgh last I heard.

ME: Must have been very special news for Mary to stop here.

DAG: She was going to Sardinia.

ME: This isn't the direct route.

DAG: Got any postcards left?

ME: I gave Melanie three to mail.

DAG: So Mike said.

ME: Mike?

And this too, Jenny, to explain why Corsica ends here:

Morning again. Dagger thought of Alba in his sleep. At breakfast Mike and Dagger stand at a table across the dining hall examin-

256

ing the Beaulieu. The girl from fortress and café—Marie—comes in and speaks to Mike; looks over the long breakfast tables; sees me. Dagger tries to talk to her but she speaks to Mike, who follows her out.

A half hour later I'm upstairs in the men's dorm floor writing, as always slowly, when Dagger comes and says, Here I was going to phone Alba to see how she was, and she's phoned me. She had false labor. She's kind of scared.

He thinks we have to leave.

I speak of the east side of the island, and the town where Paoli and Napoleon's father were; and down on the coast the ghosts of those mosquitoes are lost in the growing fields the Algerian *colons* reclaimed.

I could not settle down. I appreciate foreign shower equipment, but I'm not quite a transient. But just as you must not worry about your breathing when you first go under with a tank on your back, so now I must act evenly. My aims had found objects.

The letter left on Aut's desk would lead him to question Claire, who would then think of her lost and found keys and my running upstairs at Monty's with my beard damp and coming back down with the two pages she'd seen but not really with my excuse for momentarily leaving, namely to get something upstairs to show her. On May 24 Dagger had known of the group we found Friday night, May 28. Also three moments in the May 16 Softball Game showed *certain arresting faces*. Yet Aut, Dagger said, would not *hear about our initiative* from him—so Claire was acting on her own. And to judge from Monty Graf's hints about Claire, she wasn't acting on her own for Aut's sake.

I, a New York babysitter, switched on the small TV and presently a Stonehenge commercial appeared, which put me in mind of my effort all these years of London nights to dream certain preconsidered dreams when asleep, in order to explore them.

I hadn't turned up the sound.

I got up.

I went to the kitchen. By my list of calls was a stamped envelope addressed to Rose. The calls from Monty and Claire had preceded my drink with them, so no need to phone. Gilda and the stabbing seemed so far away I felt sad. My mother's call was as far outside my present problem as the packed envelope to Rose that Sub had overlooked when he left.

I would, however, phone June.

Lorna addresses her envelopes before writing the letters. In the late fifties she would not succeed in writing the letters. I might hear the fridge door smack open; the longer it stayed open the less likely she was to remove anything from the fridge. One night she bolted into the front hall and out of the house and when she didn't come back in the few minutes it would take to go to the pillar box at the end of the road, I went to the kitchen and found four empty red-and-blue-edged airmail envelopes addressed to the States—to her mother, her nephew, her one-time music teacher she still had a crush on, and the Metropolitan Museum of Art, and she hadn't written a word beyond those addresses, not even the order for Christmas cards from the museum.

I dialed June.

I hung up and returned slowly to the living room hoping to approach what had come into mind in such a way that it would not have vanished after all. But it was gone. Earlier today I'd noted only that those pages left Sunday morning on Sub's desk when I departed for the airport were gone, and in noting this I'd never thought what had happened to the thing I'd left on top of them as a paperweight and had last thought of when I'd got up to phone the charter man and had recalled his number and so had not needed my address book which I'd put on top of those pages Saturday night.

It wasn't anywhere.

I phoned June, who answered in the middle of the first ring. I said, You can tell them I have a list of all the addresses in that address book.

She didn't understand. She said would I meet her at ten tomorrow morning on a subway platform two stops past the stop near Sub's. She said she was worried. There was a pause. I heard Ruby moan, cry out; I heard covers whip, then a bump. At June's end there were men's voices; she said with put-on affection, OK darling the Film Archives at ten to ten, I don't know what they've got on tonight, think shorts by Léger, Genet, light and lively male shorts, darling.

I said, You don't mean tonight, do you? Of course not, darling, came June's voice, staying so cool her strength felt warm.

In the morning where you said.

I like you I like you. She hung up.

Something genuine there?

I was making things happen.

Monty Graf phoned to see if I'd meet him for lunch. Ruby swayed, squinting up. I drew her shoulder to me. Monty was saying Claire had gotten the day wrong for picking up her dog at the hospital, it had had distemper, it was all right, she'd found she could take it home tonight. Monty wanted to know who had told me about the two films, Claire had said I'd said *he* had, but we both knew that was a load of rubbish, eh?

I asked if Dagger knew about the second film Claire and Aut were going to use ours in.

She's coming out of the bathroom, said Monty, and I could hardly hear.

Your sister, Monty, I said, what's she like?

Claire's voice off phone asked who it was and Monty said, No, we're at Claire's. We brought the dog home.

Ruby went away from me and padded to the bathroom.

At Claire's! I said, and Monty hung up.

How big was the dog? If small, she might have been holding it; then Monty if *he* had a key to her place would pull it out and she wouldn't discover her own keys gone.

But there was the doorman. Yet now and then he disappeared leaving those TV scopes that were like stills except for a passing flaw in the scanning signal.

He might not have been there when Claire and Monty came in. Or if he had, Claire might figure she'd dropped the keys, but in her *house,* for else how could anyone have turned them in?

If Jerry was Aut's son, was Jan the red-haired woman or the gray? Ruby came from the bathroom holding up her pajama bottoms, and I embraced her gratefully and carried her back to bed. She was getting taller, I laid her down and she didn't answer me.

She wasn't awake long enough to tell me what she'd dreamt.

What I'd told June about addresses wasn't true; there you have me. Yet what mattered was not the addresses of some old American acquaintances who might well have moved on, but their names. And yet that didn't matter either.

I was looking at the moving picture of the TV screen that I was going to have to pay for. In London cinemas they put a series of commercials on the screen between features.

Sub when he got home stood in the hall in the dark as if deciding what to do and did not explain *what* had been up in the air, and I did not ask. I do not know how he handles women. A gap in my attention. And should they in that sense be handled? Once his trouble was he asked too much of them and too little; now he asked too little, which was, I later learned, too much for the woman he was seeing who wished to see him more.

Nor, when he came in, did Sub ask what it was that I had brought into his life, the smashed screen, the cracked window—red crayon crushed in the carpet.

We looked at a film we'd seen twenty-five years ago. No doubt if I gave a capsule glimpse of its action, you would find parallels. I wanted to get away. I couldn't phone Lorna now about the Xerox, it was too late in London.

I wanted to go to bed and dream about being a lookout between forces. I had known about the lookout for years and had often foreseen a night dream that would field me the formula; but I'd never dreamt that dream or some others I had been brought to think about. There are dreams and dreams, the lookout was one I'd hoped to explore.

But Sub talked on, on the couch–day bed. He had discovered the Small Claims Court. You could sue for $300 or less. Rose worked near the court downtown and if in initiating the suit you couldn't go yourself during working hours, any parent, relative, friend over twenty-one—or your wife—could go for you to plunk down the $3.01—$2.00 plus mailing fee. But Rose had forgotten, and then she claimed she'd originally begged off because she went to a gym most lunch hours. On a football team, said Sub, who had been watching only thrillers and the news he said, a good running game is to a good passing game *not* what on a baseball team good pitching is to good hitting. In any case, Sub ended by going down to Centre Street himself. If you won your case, the person sued sent you a check or money order. If he didn't you got a city marshal to collect for you, which cost $4.00 but cost the other person up to $15.00, but if a marshal asked for more, there was a number to call at the Department of Investigations. And after the marshal collected from the suee, you got your $4.00 back.

I was tired. I turned on the set.

We're too near the Empire State Building; we get a lot of interference, said Sub.

But that's where the TV comes from, I said.

Not all of it, said Sub.

Till he spoke I hadn't really seen the signal's quivering grain, for the news and TV were so much better and worse than in London. But Sub was right, you could discern a marginal outerlap like camera-shake in stills, and the picture-element scan-lines had noticeably emerged. So though you couldn't touch it except with your eyes, Sub's screen surface became what Cartwright was looking at much more than a zoom to a tenement cache of TNT, and Sub's words about a well-dressed minister with a ponytail spiriting two Bermuda onions into his dark green book bag at the supermarket ran like a U.N. translation over the commentator's comment near the close of which came the word *weather* yet also weather*men*, succeeded by a silent commercial which silenced Sub. The picture started to rise like frames on a reel and I reached to wave a hand across the screen and the imaginary wheel stopped turning.

I saw myself now having to find Jan Aut. She had nothing to do with the break-in here, but she was interested in Reid whom Jenny was chasing, and there were the Indians too.

You're a good citizen, I said to Sub.

What's the use? he said.

Did you win? I said.

It was over that TV that I had to get fixed every weekend. But now I can't blame a smashed screen on defective merchandise.

I'll write you a check for the Sony, I said, and as I then shuttled my slot in Sub's life outward to a margin, another coin dropped through my mossy tubes, a foreign object saucering in like the rear prop of a helicopter on the blade of which slow but mercurially revolving craft like great figures approaching by nonvehicular hydrofoil were the red-haired woman and Dagger.

Let's split it, said Sub.

It's my doing, I said, and got up as if to leave. Which made Sub rise, as though he thought I *were* going.

I asked if he trusted me, and he said, To do what?

But I was now thinking what Aut would make of Dagger's letter on his desk as an evidence that Dagger was between Jan and Claire. For Dagger had mentioned the three figures on the grass in Hyde Park and had said the one he hadn't known was the other Indian. So he did know the red-haired woman, and as if pressed by Monty Graf's will to close some deal with me and by my prematurely gray-bearded friend Sub's pollution-watch cards on certain window-sills (for on Manhattan nights you'll see like linear pressures the secret smokes from unupgraded incinerators of colorful old residence hotels or textile firms where, say, in a cutting room on one high floor past six windows one long unrolled bolt flashes its pigment) I kept catching myself assuming the red-haired woman was Jan Aut.

At nine forty-five the next morning I descended the subway

steps. It was turning cold. Again, I had not dreamt of the lookout, though for a moment in the night I'd seen Lorna smudged by black powder and pierced above the knee leaning negligently bare against our Highgate doorway watching for me I thought.

I did not know what day it was.

Escalators are common in the London Underground, less so in the New York subway. *Subway* in London means pedestrian underpass.

Hard to imagine now the adventure of building New York's subway. They had the Elevated, but when they went underground the El in Manhattan was doomed. And yet its scrapping much later might not seem to have cleared the skies to those who, like Tessa, come from London's low profile to live here in some towering closet where you can't decide if there's a lot of sky or none—for in New York Tessa did not like looking up, though one Friday and one Monday she did look up to me.

My father stands, two or three years after 1900, at Sixty-fourth and Broadway. For support they use a great extension girder at right angles to the Elevated where it crosses above the excavation trench. The first fifty-one-foot subway cars are to be four feet longer than the existing Elevated cars. Mahogany for the car doors, galvanized corrugated sheet iron for the bed on which is laid the fireproof flooring called "monolith."

Ah what happened to the wheels! So shining in 1903, steel-tired with cast-steel-spoke centers, now their gray gleam has turned to screaming space. I envision a constructive nightmare in which please find the formula for a new asbestos-veined synthetic tire, balance perfected as if in space, soft as rubber, softer-sounding than the London Underground, diamond-hard.

What Brunel would do with space! Run a vacuum bridge to Jupiter's lakes. Will, my son, asks about Skylab; I mention sun-sensors which from earth-orbit may learn how the sun turns hydrogen to energy, thus teach us a thing or two to solve pollution. Will tells his friends at school. They mention my accent, a sound I hear but not so loud as they.

I had a purpose. It was to see June in order to pass information to the Jerry-John cluster, thus to Outer Film. The London system tying Reid to the red-haired woman to the gallery and thus to the Indian and even to acts of a subversive sort aimed at removing our film from the DiGorros' flat lay parallel and (for today) secondary. The New York sequence had seemed to rule the field whose forces formed it, singled it out like a crescent or some other line, but as I came to the change booth (an oak original from 1903) the field seemed to equal the noise from the walls which in turn equaled the power whatever it was of our film destroyed unedited; and the noise came from the sidewalk concrete where I was born and then from deep under the tunnel the presumed bedrock above which, buried during construction, how many bodies will rise again when New York falls; and the noise was all those machines blowing past on the street above yet also on a dozen superimposed semipriceless maps of the Thames estuary Dagger juggled through customs, and on the tracks below (for a train was pulling out); and maybe the noise was some escalator ahead whose noise was also the breath of shyness in Rose's college friend Connie when I helped her ride the elevator; and the noise was rock from the change booth where a black girl stared at her newspaper through blue-smoked cartwheel glasses as big as Jenny's the once I saw her riding behind Reid in daylight with her knees out and she stuck out her arms as if Reid spinning past on his black motorbike built for two would turn two ways at once; and the retreating noise of the train that might have been mine was like ten tomcats and the noise above and below was not something you'd turn tail from because for one thing I thought that besides the black girl pushing tokens, there was no one but an old fellow in a herringbone with the hems drooping toward his ankles who preceded me through the turnstile and made for the stairs maybe because he didn't like escalators, which I see now made no sense, for the old do like escalators down or up.

But you've been here before and you're looking back and forward, so you know the escalator wasn't running. All those grooved steps dropping away in front in a noise like motion weren't moving, but the new steps behind me were, and their nature would have made me turn (for the clicks were at once close and slow, fast closing yet dream-slow like two rates simply merged), but I could look only ahead: for as you know I got a shove bang like a silent noise in my sacrificial shoulder-wings which when I told this before seemed *coincident* with my hands fast-stuck in the tight slash-pockets of my raincoat but now seems to have trapped my hands, and the rest you know as well as I, down to almost the foot of the fast-dragging grade all stopped as only an escalator can be stopped. I'd found a beat, so I kept myself from plunging head under hem, arms pinioned by hands socketed; and if I had fallen thus, no telling what I might have done to myself, my dry-mouthed momentum crashing into this moveless sequence of stairs. Yet when I began this story did I think this momentum mine? I think I did. But it was my pusher's first, then mine, which I see now is like what I, if not (no surely not) Dagger, saw us doing in the film, taking other energy in process and using it for our own peaceful ends. But was not the end there that of my pusher?

Plunging then up the dead escalator as if I had taken its energy, I reached the top again and would have run on up to the street but thought of June and stopped and asked the change-booth woman what she'd seen, but she mustered a moist smile with a new mild dreamy song for background on her transistor and she said how busy she was and in her glasses like a wide-angle fish-eye out of some bad movie about nerves and death I saw that the pusher had pushed me because I must have in some way pushed him; but I saw that I might not have in my head why my film got destroyed, I'd have to do more than just recall things. And I had better not go back. It may be a bad rule of detection, but the right way now had been don't go back. And as soon as I had thought this, I saw that the way to survive the pusher's push was to use its force to move on.

The pusher would not be at June's stop. I caught the old man's train just.

A pale brown woman next to me on the subway seat yawned, and I smelled on her breath a doughnut with coffee in the hole. Live in New York and you might have subway dreams. Of white men sitting and black men roaming. White men reading newspapers and engrossed in some inner page so they don't seem to notice the black men loping through the car as if it has no movement, the black riding between cars, returning to the head of your own car, batting his eyes for action, tramping through again patrolling his space station, not catching your glance which is like a blink, then passing into another car, leaving your door open sliding to and fro with the car's rushing lurch. A white woman with fat hands does her crossword with a white, company ballpoint. The black women do not look either.

June was where she'd said she'd be but was looking toward the other end of the train that I got off. Between a flight of steps and a post with a chewing gum machine she waited with her back to me, the highsprung ancient crown of hair independent as if turned also away. Two people moving toward either side of the platform crossed between us and at the point of my view where they crossed, June had turned and for that second hadn't seen me and then had, and I was like some expected surprise at the end of an avenue.

She was in color today, brown and gray and melancholy mauve, mid-thigh soft boots, a hot-pants suit.

She had hold of my arms, she leaned back smiling as if it had been a long time when in truth it had, for Corsica had come between us in the pica lines of Dagger's note to Claire which I'd left on Aut's desk, the space of that dubious isle emptying into our Beaulieu lens and the hours and days we'd exposed and lost.

June and I were arm in arm on a platform bench. She crossed her legs. The top rim of one mauve boot stuck up away from the dark thigh so one saw down in. Like a banner signing an interesting entrance, a label hung from inside the rim half unsewn. I'd seen it before.

She wasn't the same person as twenty-four hours ago, yet now seemed not to need the words *really really like you,* in order to show with the lean of her chic gray shoulder pad against me and the attentiveness of her whole eyes that moved all over my face as she spoke, that she really did need to act.

The matte softness of her skin could gather all her fear and brightness as if it were her person, at rest and accessible enough and still not different from the coasting flirting model who makes a white male feel unnecessarily good, but a firmer appearance of that person from yesterday. I could not help touching her lips with my own and she was friendly, no more, but eased from firm edges of curve to curve of the breathing space between us so the kiss did not seem unnecessary.

She said what she had to say with dispatch and grace and until I was safely on the plane to London I didn't stop to think she'd said it all without a single uptown or downtown local or express intervening.

I was in danger, she said. From Jerry. From his father. From some others. And from still others she didn't know. Did you always dream about being famous, baby? she asked.

Who are the others you don't know, I said.

Maybe I'll get to them, she said.

It seemed Jerry had been even madder to find that the person he'd wanted to get hold of had been standing right in John's studio that he, Jerry, paid rent on (with his dad's money, June added) and hadn't even known that this was that person; and he'd been mad too that this Cartwright had been in secret conversation with John, and (she thought) worst of all this Cartwright had been in the studio when *she* had been there with John—like if anyone's going to see

John and her together Jerry wants it to be him because from the top of his Clairol scalp down to the taps of his shoe-shoes he is jealous as hell.

When I asked which hole Jerry had come out of, June said she'd thought that I of course knew that Jerry was Phil Aut's son and knew about the hassle with Phil who wants Jerry in the business and Jerry's never been near the office and what Jerry wants is to make far-out films with John who does jobs for Phil and who Jerry thinks has been tainted by Phil and some silent partner, though John couldn't be corrupted by anyone, he's too crazy about his thing which was what her brother had said about John long before she'd met him.

June said, when I asked where she was in all this, that she was friendly with John and with a girl in Phil Aut's office, and a guy with an ocean-going-and-coming yacht who is interested in Phil Aut's wife, and with some others I wouldn't know.

I asked what else besides Jerry; and June talked straight through till we parted. One of her brothers coming through New York had read her palm and warned her a white man with a light brown beard might come from England asking questions and that she must absolutely say nothing, the white man would be taken care of, but answer none of his questions. She knew from John that I had come from England, but John didn't know her palm had been read with this warning any more than he or Jerry knew her brothers. Jerry was a brat; her brothers could be violent; she'd liked the feel of my arm when she gripped it in John's studio yesterday and felt an up-current trying to get through, and she'd liked how my smile was part of my face, and she was mad because her brother Chad used to be fun reading her palm and doing card tricks before he went away, but this time he took her hand and was very nice and suddenly started giving orders, but he had other long-range plans. There was a project, like five hundred people, organized by Berkeley and this university in England, a commune in Chile if the government approved, and it would be ecological and it would start in two to three years from now.

She had my hand, as if against the trundling waves of an approaching train. She got up and my hand followed and I.

How many brothers do you have? I said.

Many, many, she said, and leaned to me and kissed me. She turned then as if never to see me again, then turned back. Who is Allott? she said. He's in your address book, right? And they *have* your book—you know that?

266

Allott, I said, is a friend of mine. Do you know Gene and Paul?

Those words from Corsica released in the letter in Claire's desk that I'd left on Aut's had come automatically with a feeling that I had to use the space left before the train came in like a cartridge filling its place.

They are brothers, said June. She stepped back and a little girl bumped through between us. June was no genie out of a flask, she had a warm mouth openly fluent to belly and brain.

Wait, I said, I don't want to be the person your brother Chad warned you against, I mean asking questions. But where can I find this Paul? The platform was filling and June looked around her. Two people passed idly between us not seeing our conversation. June came close and said, I have heard that Paul is the most dangerous of all, he was supposed to be on an island off the coast of Scotland but they talk about him in New York and in London now like he was everywhere. He's not old. Two kids I met were just setting out to go see him. I didn't ask what it was about. One of these kids was a starry-eyed chick. I don't know if they had a message for him. I don't want to know.

Off the coast of Scotland? I said.

The Hebrides, she said. No one should go there, you understand me? No one.

The train was upon us and I couldn't see why she cared about my going to the Hebrides, maybe now she'd turned strange and wasn't thinking specifically about me. We had to talk loudly.

How did Aut get my address book?

He never had it.

She was gone in the crowd. I thought I heard men's voices angrily retreating as if beyond her but they may have been inside the train's noise.

Had June been in London? The white label with a gray oval inside a flat red triangle inside the rim of her boot was a London shop where Jenny had bought an expensive leather coat. I cared less what kind of brother Chad was than that he was the one I'd played ball with and the one at the Marvelous Country House where Gene and his wife and those kids in their olive and red and yellow slickers lived.

If Aut never had my book, then Jerry after breaking into Sub's had either kept it or given it to someone else. But would vandalism like that go with pinching the address book? The name Allott linked the book with Monty to whom the name had meant something as I left his house. I had never trusted Monty but had enjoyed not trusting him.

For a second as she went swiftly up the stairs, June was visible down an aisle that parted through the crowd of people.

The Hebrides was where Jenny was going.

Back at Sub's I put in a call to Highgate. Will answered, I asked what time it was there, he said five. What day? Wednesday.

I had a stitch in my heart, the time was getting away from me as if I were some tourist who'd spent a thousand dollars to arrive in Moscow or Osaka but hadn't planned what to do then.

Will said I must have been mistaken, the Xerox shop said the job had already been picked up and when he'd shown the receipt they'd said they really didn't know. I could imagine them saying they were sorry.

I'd been in New York thirty hours and I was going back to London.

Will read my mind: Dad, could we go camping in the Outer Hebrides?

During Easter hols, I said.

But I did not think to ask until I'd hung up what I then knew I need not ask and had I asked would have stated: You don't use pencil do you.

No question. My son's reply was in my head more intimately soon than if he had still been at the other end of our New York–London line, and the answer was a clean No.

I saw standing up on Jenny's windowsill in a jar with a Victorian black-and-white flower design the pencils she kept sharpened with the silly machine I'd got her cheap through Dagger.

You see, I'd also seen a penciled ring drawn I knew by her and her alone, and while I was willing to bet the map had gone with her, I knew that on a duplicate of that Ordnance Survey map I would find the site of those standing stones whose designation in archaic letters she had circled.

LOOKOUT | Think if I found the source of my undreamt lookout dream. And turned a profit too. Think if I grew soft hardware out of grain and could sell it in Middle America.

I had been looking for what had happened to the film, and now some who were concerned were looking for me, taking from me.

Dagger and Monty and I were looking out for ourselves. I did not know how much June knew; but as I went up the subway stairs forth into the street (which at once became not a roof of light but a walled floor) and crossed against the light and went down into the uptown side of the station, I knew that the film and my daughter's welfare had come together through June.

Someday a formula could be named for me.

A thrown ball snared by someone's instinct leaning way out of a fourth-floor window in Brooklyn Heights during the war does not come back down into the street. Much need not come back. Go ahead. That's what an old English upholsterer told me America was: go-ahead.

June's boots came from a London shop; had she gone to them or had they come to her? Her brother Chad had been in London; it was June who made me think he might be here instead. The starry-eyed chick—what if her last name was Cartwright and June knew? Did I trust June because I wanted to touch her under the label and she was warm?

A ceremonial plane slides into a corridor between New York and London, and I am on it.

My man Whitehead—my contact Red so call me Red!—at the scientific hobby firm that is growing and growing—pales into distance, an event whose key might not intrigue a young person enough to merit inclusion in a catalog offering Cartwright's Analog Formula Kit.

Tessa once flew over that extreme southwest frontier of California near the Colorado River, not very high but high enough to make out on the ground a man 167 feet tall. So long is he that he wasn't discovered till 1932 when an Air Force plane took his picture. Which was just thirty-three years prior to this Mexican trip of Dudley's that Tessa went along on. Dudley was the one who had stomach trouble, Tessa said because she upset him with her theory of the epicanthic eye-fold linking the ancient Maya with the east Asian psyche, though she followed Le Plongeon who in the last quarter of the last century argued that the earth's westward motion helped to account for the spread of Maya culture to the Nile and the Indian Ocean, the holy deserts and the Asian paddies, astronomy, art, words without prior roots—but, first and last, vivid violences disseminated over the earth until, like Maya language (falsely for example translated in one famous line, *My God, my God, why hast thou forsaken me?* when *Eli, Eli, lama sabachthami* is Maya for *Now, now, I am fainting; darkness covers my face*), these violences became diluted into the less vivid, more crude and calculated cruelties and routines and illusory surfaces of dominant East-West culture.

Maybe I'd find that the Picts—the tattooed people—planted evidences in some northern isle knowing someday someone named Paul would turn those evidences into power. I leave the Picts to Dudley Allott. Or more likely his wife, whose tabby cat Spirit proved so dangerous to Dudley's lungs that he was on a bottle of allergy pills a week until Tessa gave Spirit away.

No—I leave the Picts and the laws of their mysteries to Tessa and leave her also those iron files of prime tribes she saw (much against Dudley's judgment) trekking the top of the world by Bering's isthmus so that—lo!—a fourth-century Maya calendar follows an old habitual rhythm from Tibet. Dudley did not believe all cultures kin; but for reasons of love and fear he did not discuss Tessa's notions. Dudley tried to be more interesting than himself.

Reach into yourself even with kid gloves, you must find something. For instance, a ball that went up so accurately it didn't come down. Or a Tessa kiss rising from Lorna's dinner table.

Or Dudley's appendix. It went into Charing Cross hospital acute. But then they decided to observe him. And after forty-eight hours, Dudley said he was now surrendering his appendix only because he'd wasted so much time. But why was I there? You don't visit someone who's about to have an acute appendix out. Well, there was the two-day delay. So he was more visitable. And then, as it happened, I knew Tessa was stopping in to see Dudley on the way to meet her father and Lorna and Geoff Millan and an Irish mathematician who was doing a piece on Geoff's work, and me. So I turned up in Dudley's ward in time to see him stare at the other patients' supper trays—he was being operated on that evening.

Tessa wasn't there. Dudley accepted my *Evening Standard*. I was conscious of our accents, Dudley was the only patient with a visitor, and although it wasn't like visiting the boy who threw the ball during the war that did not come back down into the street, to wit Ned Noble in Brooklyn Hospital years ago when he had to let his roommate and his roommate's relatives crammed into the other side of a semiprivate hear his every acid witticism, Dudley was less alive than I to the fact that some of his ward-mates were listening with a certain digestive satisfaction.

A sister swished by, came with a thermometer and Dudley opened his mouth. She slipped it in, Dudley closed his eyes. The sister—she was oriental—went to another bed to plump the pillow of a pale old man with a sharp profile. Dudley, now mute, opened his eyes and Tessa appeared at the bedside dressed like a spy in tailored brown trenchcoat and brown floppy hat, a cigarette in her mouth. After a day in the open city you arrive at a hospital bed and feel the passive undress of the patient, as if your energy were ink entering a blotter. Tessa thrust her *Evening Standard* at Dudley and when he did not move she put it down beside his leg and touched his hand lying pale, hairy, and separate on the sheet where the edge had been turned down over his dark gray blanket. She gave him a letter from a New York lawyer Dudley had barely known until after they'd come back to England earlier this year of '66 who was curiously interested in the Catherwood holocaust and had in his possession a copy of Catherwood's 1844 portfolio of drawings. Tessa asked if Dudley was in pain; he shook his head. She'd left Jane with the Indian neighbors. Dudley nodded; she said there was a letter from his mother but she'd left it home, and Dudley nodded and smiled and the thermometer leaned with his smile; the sister called from the other bed to hold it in place.

There was a teardrop of some kind in the corner of Dudley's eye, and Tessa looked at me next to her as if just noticing me and gave me a kiss on the cheek.

We were going to an opening in the old Jewish quarter of Whitechapel Tessa's father once fervently described to me as a great early immigrant ghetto full of heroic poverty and vivid roots. Then we were going to Blum's which is almost next door to the Whitechapel Gallery.

The sister—Cambodian I recall—held the thermometer up, smiled at Dudley. Nothing, dear, she said. Dudley asked when it would be, and she said, Eight thirty.

She turned away and Tessa asked if there was a lav. The tailored trenchcoat made her taller and neater yet more fragile. The sister answered.

Tessa said to Dudley, At eight thirty we'll just be finishing the sweet and sour mackerel. Is the lady doctor going to operate after all?

Dudley did not smile; he was beyond objecting. He said, I cannot help it. He raised up on an elbow, had a spasm and doubled forward and lay back. He said he hadn't believed his feelings, he was a rational man, but if it was the case it was the case: he didn't want her going into his insides.

A big ruddy man two beds away said, You've got the best surgeons in the world in England. Still, it's all hormones.

The pale hawk next to Dudley said to the ruddy man, It's that she's a woman, that's what it is. You only came in today.

The old man had the beak and the post-mature sandy hair of my grandfather who died in a hotel bedroom.

Tessa and I stood above Dudley's bed. He said, I'm over it now. I simply didn't want a woman surgeon. Crazy. But I've got one.

The ruddy man said, I've known women doctors.

I've got to pee, said Tessa softly and strolled away.

Dudley had neatly torn open his letter. I asked why he'd ever got interested in Catherwood.

He said, I can't explain it—(and at once I knew he was not replying to what I'd said). It must be like killing, you don't know till you're face to face with it. I just could not stomach a woman surgeon sticking her rubber gloves into me.

He looked again at the letter from New York, read a bit and stopped. His eyes were glazed-looking. Nothing happened.

I missed you at the pool today, I said.

Dudley seemed to be talking low, not from discretion but fatigue.

Sometimes out of his bulky body and methodical mind he'd say something so frank it made my lack of naïveté seem immature. But he'd been lying in bed in front of me and his wife—and something had touched him, like a telephone ring you think you heard, or someone else's pain or pleasure that may be yours but you don't know.

He said, Do you ever think Lorna isn't experiencing as much pleasure in sex as she pretends?

How do you know she pretends? I said.

Actually, Tessa doesn't. Not now.

Dudley's cheek was lying on a corner of his letter and his eyes dropped from me to the lines of type as if at that slant he might turn up something.

I should have learned from my life, he said, but I didn't see how. I mean there I was. Till at last I was with the most fascinating woman you'd ever want to meet on the Orient Express and I suddenly felt odd and looked back. I was an only child, you know.

I said, My sister and I fought like hell, so what you missed may not have been better than what you had.

Did you ever want to have intercourse with her? (Unmediated first words from Dudley.)

272

We snuggled, I said.

What was she like?

My sister could sit like a cat staring away from me for a long time. She had a couple of beautifully placed moles.

So has Tessa, I think, said Dudley.

Sure, I said.

An only child feels a primacy, you see, said Dudley. But it can go either way. I felt alone, hence odd; I came to feel second-rate.

Tessa hadn't reappeared.

But, said Dudley, here was Tessa, here was I, from a good Episcopal school in Ohio, a couple of universities, here was her father who thought he'd wanted to be a scholar—and Tessa laughed at me first time we met when I said I'd be happy to stay in England. Later she said it was that she could tell I didn't say things like that. Which was true. When my mother came over and wanted to go to Windsor, Tessa took her on a canal boat from Little Venice to the zoo, and when they got there my mother said, *This* isn't Windsor. Tessa and I used to walk all night, did you know that? I had more stamina. It was what she'd done when she was eighteen and drifting into the University of London and not especially wanting to. It was before Aldermaston, not that she cared in that way.

My sister drifted like that, I said, only into marriage.

I don't understand Tessa, said Dudley, do you know that? I understand Catherwood better. Sometimes she seems to be replying not to what I say but to what's in my mind. Do you ever go to a college reunion? *I* don't, but I read my alumni reviews—people I never even knew to speak to.

I said as a matter of fact there were some alumni reviews in a stack somewhere at home but I never read them.

We heard Tessa's heels coming down the ward aisle's slippery lino. She took my arm.

She and I watched Dudley in bed.

We were about to leave. Tessa kissed Dudley on the forehead and patted that pale hairy hand that stirred then to grasp the letter from New York. I gave Dudley my hand. He said, Have a nice opening. Tessa said, Jane asked where an appendix is. Dudley said, Give my best to your father. Tessa said to me, My father thinks he's crazy about all those stuffed things at Blum's—stuffed neck, Kreplach, kishkes, I used to try to cook them but they don't agree with him.

He never gets fat, said Dudley.

Maybe, said Tessa, the lady surgeon will tuck some hormones into you tonight. I'll phone later. You'll probably be asleep.

Dudley gave a grin. Bring Janey tomorrow, he said. And to me he said slyly, What *did* you do with her?

Mainly dreamt of what I'd do, I said, knowing he meant my sister and wondering if she had come back to mind through Jane, whom I have not introduced seriously to you who have me—a humorous peculiar child just seven then, I think, and growing up between two unfairly married people from whom she seemed to try to learn (and reflect love) equally. When she was six she came into the bedroom one morning and lectured Tessa saying it was bad enough that she herself had to sleep alone but that with Daddy on the couch in the living room now all three of them were sleeping alone and something had to be done about it, and then she went into the huge living room and gave the same lecture with the same giggles.

But it was the twelve- or almost thirteen-year-old Jane whom Jenny thought of when typing the parts about the Hawaiian Hippie and the Suitcase Slowly Packed. For she and Reid had met Jane and Dudley in the half-mile-long pedestrian passage that leads from outside the Science Museum down under it to South Kensington Underground station (the dusky tunnel that makes Will think of Behind the Iron Curtain, echoing commuters from one part of the machine to another—I don't know where Will gets his anticommunism, maybe from me) but Jenny was in any case with Reid and so no doubt happy, but as she said the evening she finished typing Hawaiian Hippie and Suitcase Slowly Packed, earlier at 5 P.M. there approaching from the Science Museum end were the Allotts, father and daughter, and when Jane hailed them and they all came together, Dudley with a small plaid suitcase, Jane showing what she claimed was Dirk Bogarde's autograph on the cast on her arm and suddenly looking like a woman Jenny said in the calm attention her eyes gave you and she didn't walk from the shoulders any more like Dudley, and her legs seemed older and Tessa had bought her a pair of low-heeled Italian shoes which Jane wore without that slight pigeon-toed gauche schoolgirl shyness she'd had—though Jane did have her mother's figure—and the point was that when Reid took Dudley's ballpoint and Jenny introduced them all, Jane said *I* know *you*—in the boldest adult way—just as Jenny noticed under Dudley's raincoat, which Jane had undone the top button of to get a ballpoint, a V-neck sweater just like the one Jenny with her own hands had

274

packed in our filmed suitcase. Jane said, Don't I know you? Reid said, Not unless you're from Ridgefield, Connecticut (which, said Jenny, was nonsense because Reid in fact had masses of friends in London). But Jane said, In the park once and once in Regent Street—and she changed the subject to Jenny, whom she had to show the smashing moccasins her grandma had sent from Massachusetts, and Dudley like a magician's helper had to hold the suitcase in his arms while with her good hand Jane released the catches and without undoing the ruffled, garterlike ties neatly removed from under a green pleated kilt in one neat-packed side a red-white-and-blue-beaded moccasin like the moccasins in Suitcase Slowly Packed. But Jenny said anybody could buy those right in London. Jenny had been in Scotland with Tessa and had just flown in. Jane, resnapping the case, added that being at the Cromwell Road Air Terminal her father had thought of something he had to check at the Science Museum and so as Reid and Jenny found them here she, Jane, had just (you might say) taken her good boy to the museum—

But not, said Dudley, to press the buttons in the children's section in the basement. To which Jane retorted that there were buttons everywhere, not just in the basement—and Dudley in his sober way added that it was not for buttons that he'd wished to visit the museum today, and Jane said, Bye bye Jenny and Reid, though Reid hadn't been introduced except by his signature which from Jane's side was upside down.

At which point on the night Jenny finished typing SSP and HH, she stopped the story with a shrug—I still think because she'd let herself be frank to me about Reid, like letting me take pictures of her during this fugitive period when she said she hated her looks and took (she said) nauseating pictures (which was exactly what Lorna had once often said in the late fifties)—and Jenny said, well the tunnel and the sweater and the moccasins were just one of those coincidences and it wasn't as if a hippie'd been playing a guitar with his chick in the tunnel, though in fact two chaps were suddenly having a loud argument as they got further and further away which looked like developing into a fight, but as suddenly as their argument had blown up it subsided, and Jenny stopped abruptly again but no shrug. Reid had had a headache and she had come home.

Geoff Millan's Irish mathematician would have given me a formula for such a coincidence if I'd asked, for at that supper the night of Dudley's operation five years earlier, the Irishman had had something for everyone, was the star, carried his brain with such levity that when I asked (thick-tongued with the Moselle Tessa's father had ordered from next door) what university this Pythagorean savant taught at, he banged his head into his fist, and said he could not remember for the life of him the name of the insane place but there was a buttery and a brand new landscape laid on he believed by helicopter but as for him he would like to hear more about my boats on the south coast, if there were hire boats what could my margin be?

Formula for coincidence? Take a year off and study some system that makes the probable seem improbable. Oh the best I could do was add, to Jenny, that a book had been knocked off the chair when her filmed hands had snatched up those moccasins and that a bookmark had fallen from the book—and I couldn't recall the name of the book but did recall the bookmark.

Jenny said it was one of Reid's books and said it with such simple finality that the subject lapsed into the field of home conversation and Lorna practicing and Will on the phone; and anyway, at that stage—just June—I'd had no reason to quiz Jenny about the bookmark which she'd picked off the floor and slipped in the Suitcase Slowly Packed between the V-neck sweater and the green-and-white plastic bottle of shampoo she'd started using. A picture of Reid? I came to think it might be of someone important.

On the plane—where because Tourist had been overbooked by a Senior Citizens' group I'd at the last minute been installed for the same reduced rate in First Class—I made a small collection of Japanese slippers and chopsticks and plastic envelopes of duck and soy sauces (plus a couple of kimonos when the steward wasn't looking), to take to Sub's children when I got back to New York. Should I have worried about money? About how many gross of Red Whitehead's liquid crystal sets I could peddle? Being on a time that was neither American nor English I had tricked my body into a new exploratory line that might lead to intervals differing as the Maya sacred and solar calendars differ, the one holding within 260 days the full permutation of twenty day names and thirteen numbers, the other ordering itself into eighteen months of twenty days with five days at the end during which who knows what they did, perhaps meditated on what must have seemed in effect a cog-wheel (like an analog computer) fitting solar to sacred (tenon to mortise) so a rotation of 18,980 days or fifty-two true years would embrace all the variations or alignments of greater and smaller circles. The Irish mathematician would understand, for he seemed the night of Dudley's appendectomy to be free-floating between gravities.

In any case it was with this inter-time, like an expansible space inside my knuckles and eyes and the back of my shoulders—an organ time which must be in its sphere like a type of weightlessness—that I phoned home from the airport in London and got Will.

Lorna had spent the night at Tessa's.

I was between them all.

Lorna had wanted Will to go to his friend Stephen's. He couldn't believe Lorna was as disheartened about the break-in as she said. He said, rather importantly, In *fact,* Dad, I think Mummy misses you. I suspect that's all there is to it. Will had locked all the windows. In the front hall under an old black spread he had laid a complex field of pots and pans, and had rigged the small cassette recorder that was supposed to receive family letters from America so that if the intruder was for some reason hugging the wall he or she would rip a strong indirectly routed string yanking downward a bolt resting on the PLAY button releasing the National Anthem. Will was concerned only that he not be in a deep or bad dream from which he might wake ignorant and scared or which might itself naturally incorporate the kitchen clatter or "God Save the Queen" so he would not wake up at all. He had had nightmares.

Surely the humor of the music would have disturbed a burglar most.

I told Will I had his Wall Street literature, and asked where Jenny was.

He said off with Reid, she'd taken a bag.

There was a nearly final moment of silence in which a ghost stood at attention in our hall (and I thought, if you scare a ghost instead of being scared by the ghost, you double the event and pass through into a new field of force).

Did you ask who collected the copy and the original?

I asked if it was a man or a woman. They said they didn't know. Someone who knew the pages were there, I said.

Will asked if I had any enemies. I felt he was writing in his leather notebook. From train numbers he'd graduated to shares—now maybe detection.

I asked him why he asked.

Routine question, he said. Was I going to Mummy's concert?

I'd forgotten all about her chorus, but I said yes of course.

Will was going to Stephen's tomorrow night. I recalled Lorna had insisted he go even the night after the break-in, but Will would not leave her, and now he said she'd gone on about it and he almost felt obliged to spend the night at Stephen's.

I said, She just doesn't want to be a bother to you.

I said I'd see him when I saw him, and he agreed, and we hung up.

I was between Will and Lorna invisible. I was between June and Chad. I was between Dagger and Claire.

Jenny, however, was between me and probable northern danger, and that danger was not to me but to her, though her own damn fault.

Why had Tessa never really talked to me about the film? I was no longer between her and Dudley, or no more than anyone else was. She would take a drag and look at me and after a count of four or five say with languid finality, Oh everyone's making a film. But then to Lorna she suddenly said, Oh but can't you see Dudley in boots and breeches and flowing sleeves and tight cuffs marching around a set giving orders and checking historical details! And she and Lorna would laugh at that. And Dudley of course would not be present.

She and Dudley—this is not only during the time Dagger and I made the film but for a couple of years at least—didn't go away together much. A weekend in Wales was about the size of it. Dudley took Jane, or Jane Dudley, to the Bethnal Green dolls' house museum or a garden pub for Sunday lunch. Tessa took Jane shopping and to the cinema.

The three of them went to Tessa's father's for lunch on Saturday, or rather Tessa went early with a pot of chicken soup she'd cooked with a whole chicken, and spent two hours getting lunch while her father laid the table and talked to her and put out the chala with the white and gold cloth over it; and then Dudley and Jane came and at the end of the meal Jane and Tessa and Tessa's father sang the end of his grace more or less, and then the four of them went to the park, Jane hand in hand with her grandfather.

Will it be a cast of thousands? said Tessa in May—and in June, The plot doesn't have to be original, you know, and in August shortly after the Marvelous Country House, I bet if you looked around you I mean closely you could make a real documentary.

Tessa was in Scotland for a while in the spring and no one could figure how she'd come back with a tan, and she said a clan chieftain had spirited her off to Italy for two weeks. She was certainly in Scotland in July before she and Dudley flew to America to spend three weeks at Mrs. Allott's place on Cape Cod, because Jane just after she broke her arm was with her up in Scotland for a long weekend in late June when school still had a month to run. In August Tessa said she never seemed to see Jane any more, Jane was so busy visiting friends. Tessa had not lost interest in Mexico but didn't talk much now about the gods and their animate calendars and those primeval migrations Dudley could not listen to. According to her she sat around all day reading Wilkie Collins and old issues of *Galaxy* left by her Belgian subtenants six years ago. This is not quite accurate. She did ask to come along for the Stonehenge shooting and perhaps surprised me with her interest in the most hard and discrete information, some mine, some picked up from Jenny when she and I visited Stonehenge: the main large horseshoe within the circle is, or was, composed of five trilothons—i.e., two free-standing uprights topped by a lintel; *trilothon* means three stones and is not to be confused with the Sarsen Circle of thirty huge stones also originally capped by lintels but all connected; the western stone #56 of the central trilothon was 29 feet 8 inches, 50 tons, the largest at the Henge. It surprised me that Tessa knew some people who were going, but I must have assumed Lorna had told her. It did not surprise me that she at once said there must be a connection between the great stone's number, 56, and the number of Aubrey holes that make the far circle, out by the mounds and the ditch.

And now as I was about to drop a coin into a slot at Heathrow airport to call Tessa's to speak to Lorna if she was there, some god of true tourists interposed between the current that joined head and thumb some pancreatic pulse that eased breath into my shoulder-wings which had been tense since unknown hands three thousand miles down-range had launched me into a stalled escalator—and instead of the predictable thing I kept my coin and splurged on a big groaning cheerfully private cab.

Not to Highgate or Tessa's, but to the Druid's.

And not at random.

No such thing as randomness were five words on our sound track for the burned Marvelous Country House footage. Had Chad said them? No, I. I had wished for a formula to front the high abstract talk of Chad and the bumptious Englishman who looked like Teddy Roosevelt and in a recent unexpected dream of mine *was* Teddy, a brusque banal god following timetables full of ideas and audiences. He hadn't even looked at me, but to my *no such thing as randomness*, he'd said, Your *film* is random; look: you speak, a woman comes, a hand opens, the rain might be raining or not, your spacemen are taking their driving test—

My cab's dark leather cooled my hands, the cabbie asked if I was over for long; blue-gray-beige-medium-high-rises passed on the left, a green football pitch on the right browned at either goal-mouth; I said I didn't know how long I was over for. The Cockney cabbie had a pale thin neck and pale brown hair that started well above his ears—short back and sides. He might be fifty or he might be my age. I was going to the end of the predicament I had not yet formulated.

Do you believe in God? I said.

The missus handles that end, he said.

What's it the end of? I said.

The tether, Guv, he said.

The English, I told myself in the late fifties when Lorna went to pieces, are really not all that reserved.

If I could take the Beaulieu hardware, reduce its gates and motorized magazine and steel rims and the celluloid it was loaded with to software, to a program or a formula, I would sell it peacefully to myself alone. I would not be looping inside someone else's plan.

For it was someone else's plan.

Never mind how many projects there had been in the mind of Outer Film—Monty said *two*—never mind Claire and Dagger's collusion on the Wales footage; I'd find a formula that would be more than such half-knowledges as Chad's warning to June apparently about me, June's warning about Jerry, Jerry's feeling for Jan Aut, Phil's awareness of Claire, Dagger's acquaintance with Gene—and pray what has been the result of Mary's Scottish Nationalist brother's influence upon the mythical Paul? And why did June speak so of Paul?

And if you with your kid or canvas or asbestos gloves fixed in that lab wall have me, then you have also the riddles my film idea seems to have sparked.

I paid the cabbie. I stood on the Druid's step in the South London privacy of half a mile of brick semidetacheds.

I blinked, and a tiny red plump old woman stood in the doorway telling me Mr. Andsworth—which he says *on* as in *onward* but she pronounced as in *bound*—was not at home. And at once I saw the idea to film in Wales had not been mine any more than Dagger's. It had been my Druid's, for when I'd come to talk to him of what I imagined the film might make of my life and to ask speci-fically about using Stonehenge, he'd urged me in the most emphatic words to go to Wales first and see the mountain where they quarried the famous Stonehenge bluestones. But then we got on to physiology, breathing, divination from one's own living entrails no less, and the subject was dropped. I did not have to trust the Druid's motives for putting Wales in my mind, because I trusted other things in him, and unlike Dudley Allott and Lorna Cartwright I have come to doubt that probity and loyalty of the usual sort are the necessary grounds of personal power. Yet I *was* sure of one thing: The film idea was mine. No one had said, Do a film.

I was a cartridge myself. Yet as the slot softened like memories that one keeps separate and I found myself touched at all points and mildly engulfed by some sponge that dissolved as it engrossed me, I found myself also shrinking into independence, and though I could not yet frame a formula for my state, I looked through the little red fat woman (as if she were the NOT in a digital computer's NAND valve) forward to American futures as dark as the Druid's hall and the ruined film, but free in a field on which to delineate the hand that reaches at right angles out of a fourth-floor Brooklyn Heights apartment window as if to protect the glass but with an intimation of startled rebirth in having sliced between gravities to grasp a gift sphere with names in sundry scripts all over its white cover which is divided by red-stitched seams seemingly endless that you could only see if you skinned the sphere and laid out its cover. It was the week before Ned Noble first was in hospital and he seemed very well. He had come in to Brooklyn Heights from Flatbush to spend the day with Sub and me, and he had begun by recounting the little jokes by which last night without lifting a finger he had climaxed a day which included completing the construction of his personally designed crystal receiver set by going the limit with his sister's best friend in a Reformed synagogue's basement rec room and his sister was scared he'd tell their father. Ned and Sub had left me, for I had a bad cold, and they'd gone out into our street—one of the distinctively brownstone streets of Brooklyn Heights which are nonetheless if you look closely composed of several other materials as frequent—and the scene in that old Dutch street that was still elegant but year by year filled up with parked cars until just as it became virtually impossible to play there we found we had grown up so much that in fact we were playing even on Saturday afternoons on the athletic field elsewhere in Brooklyn of our private and so-called Country Day School—but the scene, this earlier scene, when we were fourteen you could not have conveyed on film and still caught that collusive vibration with which the mind saw the hand grasp. It was a baseball—what we called a hardball, as opposed not here to a softball (for we might play softball in Prospect Park in the shadow of the great triumphal arch in memory of the Civil War dead on a Sunday with a parent though never here on the discreet narrow streets of Brooklyn Heights) but rather to one of the white or dark pink rubber balls we played punchball or stickball with (though we played stickball also with old tennis balls so naplessly light if you hit one hard it would warp off in sharply unpredictable directions). Where did that rubber come from? From the latex-milk of whose trees? An official National League hardball in any case was what this was all about. With autographs. Of Dixie Walker, Carl Furillo. All the Brooklyn Dodgers. A birthday present from Sub and me to Boyd, who this afternoon brought it outside to show and Ned Noble had come down to the Heights for lunch and did not really accept Boyd who didn't believe Ned had experimented with gunpowder in the synagogue and who went to another school where they did not begin actual Latin grammar in the eighth grade. I was housebound with a cold and so when Sub and Ned went out and ran into Boyd I was not down there in the street with them. But I kept an eye on the four or five kids down there in one of those fairly serious conversations that might or might not lead to a ball game. Sub told me later that Ned was kidding Boyd he was going to put his own signature on Boyd's autographed ball, and someone who was looking at the ball flipped it on an impulse to Ned and Boyd shrugged keeping an eye on the clean autographed ball until he began to get a little mad and came after Ned, who backpedaled into the street regardless of cars and when Sub called for Ned to throw it to him—thinking to give it back to Boyd—Boyd cried out, No, it'll get scuffed, hey it'll get scuffed.

And as I ran up my window, Ned on the wings of his own private laughter had reached the curb below my window and said, Let's scuff it against the brick, and Boyd called out, Hey no! but instead of rubbing the ball against the building with his own hands, Ned turned toward my apartment house and unfurled a monumental throw almost straight up, but the ball never quite reached the bricks of my house, yet came so high it came just up to my level past the silence of the watchers but perhaps three and a half feet out from my window and as it came to rest in a moment of equality that I'll never forget, I lunged with one strange half of my body, and my mother who had felt a draft and come into my room shrieked behind me, and I took that white sphere out of the air at the instant it stopped rising and stopped spinning so it might have been a knuckleball in space and facing me as I took the ball was the name of Ed Head whose steady no-hitter one day was a mercurial once-in-a-lifetime he never survived.

Something had been interrupted and as I withdrew into my

parents' well-ordered apartment Boyd said, Goddamn Brooklyn Indian, and Sub said, Oh come on Boyd. But Ned may not have heard, for he seemed speechless.

For Ned knew he'd thrown the ball so nearly straight because he had not wholly wanted to scuff it against the bricks; and then at some interior angle of his act he had seen me behind a window and thought to throw to me. Later he said he'd thought of busting my window with all those dumb autographs Sub and I had given Boyd, but Ned said he'd had something else like prevision in his mind and now I feel it was like a prevision that he'd lost in the act but which averted time.

I felt I knew what it was, but I did not tell him, for Ned was quite possibly a genius.

When he mentioned the ball at school Monday he then dropped the matter with that electric or fanatic abruptness, and told of an experiment he was doing on his sister and father where he would speak so as to attract them to either side of what he was saying (that, for example, the rabbi might throw him out because he was playing with dynamite in the rec room but there *were* no synagogues on Brooklyn Heights) which resulted in what was for him a trance of power, like eyes independent of each other, or a balance of pulls—so he became free beyond the clear blackboard explanations of a physics teacher who ridiculed Ned's sci-fi magazines but gave him A's. But Ned's loss of that something else that had been in his head when he threw the autographed hardball out of a divided mind was, I felt sure, displaced by the energy transferred to my act of snatching the ball at its interval between thrust and fall—I mean Ned had acted, and the act had a velocity greater than any memory of its origin.

I've just come from America, I told the little fat red woman on the Druid's threshold, and she said in a polite and gently whining Cockney, Oh you're American, yes.

But I was way ahead of myself looking into the dark possibilities of our ruined film and into Dagger's idea broached to me August 4 or 5 that we better shift the Suitcase Slowly Packed and use it as a cut-in in the Marvelous Country House. The token dropped into a slot and on the chance that Jenny's mysterious bookmark snapshot was in fact of Gene's brother the great and notorious Paul, I said, Did he leave a message for me? I'm . . .

I paused, and she said, Mr. Andsworth's at the Community.

Ah, the Community, I said. It was the macrobiotic community where they breathed together. I could never go that far.

You're . . . ?

I'm Gene's . . . perhaps you know . . .

Oh, said the woman respectfully as if I'd reported a disaster in my family, oh yes. But then she seemed so knowing—that in retrospect I wondered if she didn't know enough to guess my ruse—she added, Oh, you'll be Jack from America.

Thinking this was enough work for the moment before the major journey upon which I was bent, I took a fingerful of my beard and smiled and said I had had reason to alter my appearance.

The little woman stepped back into the shadow suddenly fading into the face of someone I was sure I'd seen not long ago. She seemed to expect me to come in and wait, but I raised my hand and asked the address of the Community, I'd go there myself.

The Druid opened his door at the far end of the hall. I had presence of mind to forestall the woman's introduction by greeting the old man heartily and apologetically. I had just a question or two for him, I'd been experiencing difficulty in New York.

I nodded over my shoulder to the woman, having made my way past her. I told the Druid I regretted inserting myself so crudely into his schedule and not to blame the lady, for I'd been fully as insistent as he knew me capable of being—or *do* you? I added.

Yet now as I approached the old man through the dusk and the familiar untart scent of tangerines which brought to mind the French vegetable cutter I'd given him, I recalled that if Dagger had wanted in early August to shift Suitcase Slowly Packed because it contained a snapshot of Paul—and if the Marvelous Country House was occupied by Paul's brother Gene and his family—why had the Softball Game been shifted to between Suitcase Slowly Packed and Hawaiian Hippie? The time had come to phone Dagger.

With the distance between me and the Druid, as well as my growing need to trust fewer people with the weight of my private inquiries, this lookout cartridge narrows from the walls of its slot. But it enlarges too so that that which lies between, crowds that between which it lies.

Your breathing, said my Druid Andsworth, and stepped aside as if to reveal the thing I next saw in his tome-lined den, the phone on the desk.

You're back from New York. Was it a necessary trip?

I told him that once begun it had become necessary.

There was a fire in the grate. The phone receiver when I touched it was warm. (There was a copy of *English Country Life* open on the desk.) I took my hand off the phone and straightened up.

But I'd passed beyond Mr. Andsworth, having seen through that strangely familiar little woman in the front doorway that he was somehow involved with Gene and thus part of the network I had thought him authoritatively separate from. And if he could not yet know how I'd identified myself at the door, he knew either from reports or by the way I had walked into his study that I had knowledge which altered him.

I feared for you, he said, remaining at the open study door.

I let him talk—he said he'd sensed in me a need for cures that he could never satisfy, I might as well set off thunderclaps on Guy Fawkes night—he'd had only a handful of principles which might but only might be received in the body of my mind, he said, in such a way as to open currents between cell and cell, recollection and recollection, lungs and shoulders, head and hand, even (to let the fancy play a bit) between on the one hand America and England on a Mercator grid, and on the other America and England on some other representation—oh he'd sensed in me when I'd first come (in March, wasn't it?) a failure of collaboration with myself which he felt could not be especially helped by his macrobiotic community (which even if I'd been interested would have been inconvenient since I had a family I was devoted to way up in Highgate who incidentally—and he underscored the words—he *hoped* were *well*) but—

I interrupted to ask if I might use his phone.

He closed the door and continued.

I must have known, he said, that the film good or bad could hardly make a revolution in my life, and if it became an obsession might interpose itself between the Logos in me and the active instincts that, as Poseidonus tells us, must be organized by Logos. And if he did not hold dogmatically with the old arguments by which this control is articulated—as I myself must know from his efforts to associate the electronic idiom (which he thought closer to my personal interests) with the gods who are aspects of the one total Nature—any more than he necessarily believed with ancient Druids that the world is literally consumed from time to time by fire or water—any more than he disbelieved in the Norse gods—

I had begun to dial, begun amid my host's words as if only rudeness could roll me through (and I even whispered audibly the third number).

—any more than one would ever now talk seriously about human sacrifices at Midsummer Solstice.

Of my daughter Jenny? I shot out at him.

Or a substitute for her! he shot back, startled into automatic humor.

I dialed only two more numbers, for I'd decided a real Dagger on the other end of the line might cramp whatever now occurred to me. I held the receiver to my ear. Mr. Andsworth in retort raised his forearm so the sleeve of the dark green jacket of his suit pulled back to reveal his gold-banded Timex which he consulted with pursed lips.

To the phone (which began to crackle and then to whisper with one of those crossed connections one often overhears in the London telephone system) I spoke as if to Dagger.

Admit, friend, I said, you wanted the snapshot of Paul to appear in Suitcase Slowly Packed.

I waited. I said, I don't care what it would have looked like with the film slowed down. Why didn't you tell me in the first place? We might have saved our film.

I waited, then said, I don't care, Claire's told me what she and Graf have for their own film using our remains.

I paused for a long count, then said, I know all about that. They can pinch a dozen Xeroxes, they still have to find my original.

But pausing yet again—recalling Dagger's tales of summer stock in St. Louis and a screen test in which he had to talk on the phone, I saw (through this seeming irrelevance) that Dagger might often have been tracking and shooting people whose significance in this story he himself could only guess from what Claire had told him.

No, I said, when I finish here I'm going right back to New York. I've got to see Monty about his sister and above all I've got to see Claire.

Oh I paused, I paused! And you who have me, whatever is inside me, must imagine what energy I tapped from that almost dead phone. I said, Of *course* we're still pals, Dagger, but listen man, we got work to do on the Bonfire in Wales.

Mr. Andsworth was panting in an easy chair by the gilt-tooled encyclopedias and folios and some portfolios that might hold prints and maps. The color had so gone from his gaunt cheeks that last night's white stubble was now hard to see. I had been almost tired in the cab, but rather than lean too close to one time or the other I had kept my body buoyed in some gimbaled space, I'd passed through one gate, then another. And now through my *thoughts* about Dagger roused by an imaginary conversation with him, I'd found such energy that I could have rushed on foot eight London miles to take Lorna twice before tea.

Wales, said my Druid.

I know, I said, and taking a chance added, the meaning of the grove, the man in the grove whom you called a guru whom that lovely stern woman with the apple cheeks tried to shield—

I almost said *Elspeth!* as in my own talk I found the softening fade from present to past to present through the fat red little old woman at the door, some outer or other image of Elspeth herself beyond any difference between color and black and white.

I have to go, I said, hoping for what I now received (and wondering where my suitcase was). I hung up.

Mr. Andsworth looked ill.

Crazy Wednesday, I said.

I, he said, could see no reason why you should not film Stonehenge. It was what you wished. I knew your friend's acquaintance with certain people. You know my vision of a benign violence I will not live to see. I sincerely wished some new order for you yourself and for your dear wife—even a return to America. I did *not* know after all what I see I should have divined—that you would become involved in the violence that Paul in May was determined to sequester himself from once and for all. Believe me, I knew little, and know little more perhaps than you—it's Thursday not Wednesday—and maybe knew more then than now—only that these people are beyond me. I do not *want* to know what you know, do you see? I was concerned about Paul as I was about others whom I know in their individual contributions to—the continuum—even you, who were at best a marginal case. I was amused; yes, that's it, I was amused; and that is why I made my little remark about Cape Kennedy.

And about being a tourist? I said.

No. That was more serious.

Do you know Chad's brothers?

Not Chad's.

Who were you phoning? Your phone was warm.

Who were *you* phoning just now?

The Druid's door came toward me and I opened it. I bade Mr. Andsworth as gentle a goodbye as I could find in me.

But when I reached the front door and had my case in hand, he spoke again. He was at the end of the hall's twilight—*entre chien et loup* is the quaint French for twilight—and Andsworth said, Mr. Cartwright, someday the destruction of your film will seem part of a large endless harmony, believe that. Mary told me (and I enter it here like a stabbingly mysterious communication)—

The destruction, I replied, will be only one part.

I did not point out that he was repeating himself as if on a loop. But I was not particularly sorry for him.

Elsewhere in the field of the day I was lightly telling a girl on a train how right Jules Verne was to insert capsule lectures in *Twenty Thousand Leagues Under the Sea* on technical topics such as geology and the submarine isthmus which once joined and (in a literal sense Dudley would appreciate) still joins Europe to Africa.

And I found in what I said, like liquid crystals I sold in another life, an orderly solid, extremely firm yet also mobile or if you will nonrigid, through the normal course of three or four dimensions, reaching out east across the Lake District to the west coast and the declining town of Whitehaven where (as I told my companion) the parish church where George Washington's grandmother sleeps was gutted by a strange fire last August, east across the valley of the Eden River to the Yorkshire moors and the oil rigs of the North Sea where Dudley's appendix swam free, south (more or less) to Lorna in Highgate or the Druid in drab Wandsworth, until as I escorted the girl back three or four cars for a drink and the train slowed for one of those hushed operational reasons so the train's speed north suddenly equaled that of the girl and me stepping toward the buffet carriage, my own words retrieved the Druid's suddenly peculiar *your dear wife*.

I knew she knew his name and knew his address, for it was she who'd passed them on to me from some friend. But she had never visited such a man herself. Someone had mentioned his renown as an adviser on diet and psychosoma. He was a wise man who Dagger said had once treated a gigantic California politician by walking upon him. But I would have known if Lorna had gone to see the Druid personally.

Say Andsworth had talked to Lorna; what might he not have heard about the film?

The answer was, nothing; for Lorna would keep calm and friendly, and tell him nothing. But someone else?

At Glasgow I got off and phoned Tessa's flat in London.

I hadn't had time in London to pick up the Number 12 Ordnance Survey map I needed, so I decided to break my trip and took my case with me.

In a phone booth I dialed random numbers and let a look of preoccupation veil my survey of the immediate sector for anyone shadowing me. Across it men and women in dark-colored clothes passed, perhaps to places I knew the names of, to outskirts, Paisley, Renfrew, Barrhead—and because they came from my left and my right I could not easily think I was the one moving and they stationary.

A lookout stays in one place. But what of a moving lookout with a stationary trust?

If someone knew my destination—someone who knew what June had said to me in another old station not so many hours ago—why then have me followed? Why not wait for me instead?

If I knew anything about Jack the American (on whom I had grown my beard and into whose shoes I'd let myself be placed if not laced by the Druid's doorkeeper), then I'd be able to gauge the forces released by my impersonation. For her—at least for the time of my interview in Wandsworth—I *was* this Jack. For others I might be a moving core of knowledge about Jack the American. Though no superman.

You could shoot half a thousand feet of film here in this station of the British Railways—a girl running, weaving through the mass of people making connections, a grandma waiting on a bench with a green shopping bag, men with folded newspapers wearing rumpled suits and white shirts without ties. And the film would never show or know that you were in Scotland. You could cut in "Loch Lomond." A real sound track might yield grains of Gaelic or the sinewy joins of Glaswegian phrase to phrase tumbled and quizzical, not so curtly cadenced as other brogues. Or on your film a broad serious old man might pass, as in a fake documentary, in a pleated kilt, bound outward from this poor and difficult and deep city where joking young men who wait for a pub to open let the walking stranger calmly step over (like a fissure in the pavement) a vein of their danger felt in one column of thought—and where middle-aged men wait for ships to build in the yards along the sludgy Clyde back up whose inland reach in the 1840's the Navigation Trust steam dredgers lifted two million cubic yards of (as they put it) "matter" and dumped it in Loch Long, and along a few miles of whose outward reach from 1812 to 1820 the first steamer to ply regularly on any river in the Old World, the *Comet* with an engine of three horse, made the run between Glasgow and Greenock which there is no need for holiday-makers and tourists like me to know who contemplate taking a MacBrayne steamer out past Dumbarton Castle on the right then down left to the Firth of Clyde and the North Channel then up past the mouth of the Firth of Lorne on up to Mallaig on the west coast and across then to Skye where Boswell and Johnson deliberately walked and later beyond to the Outer Hebrides.

I wondered if no one would be there when I arrived.

In my glass kiosk like a functionary checking passengers, I listened for any loudspeaker that might betray over the phone where I was.

I dialed Tessa and was able before a voice answered to slot a two-shilling piece (which after all my years on the old scheme of sixes and twelves was no longer two bob but twenty new decimal pence).

The voice was not Tessa and it was not Lorna. It was Jane, and unlike my recent Jenny she did not at once abruptly say, Would you like to speak to my father, or, Would you like to speak to my mother—but addressed me directly and with what I can only call love, though it must have been a power already flowing from Jane in the home from which she spoke though the love in that home is not between the parents.

She might have been my own child glad to have me back and bursting to know what I'd brought, wanting my undivided attention, to tell me (as Jane did) that her grandmother was coming next month for Thanksgiving even though there is no Thanksgiving in England. And how were Jenny and her boyfriend? Jane had seen him once passing in the street when she was with Tessa having coffee at Yarner's in Regent Street and just before he passed behind the big bronze grinding wheel Tessa and the other woman Mrs. Flint who was an American had seen him and he waved and Jane had waved too though she'd never seen him before and then he was gone, a super chap neat and rather small with long hair. Jane wanted to know if we still taped letters to our family in America, she would like to try it. Her grandfather was going to Munich for three weeks and her mother was probably going to Scotland. Everyone was going somewhere, Jane said. Tessa had spoken of my film and Jane hoped I would show it to them. I asked when Tessa had mentioned it, and Jane said only yesterday or the day before. Daddy would love you to come over, said Jane, and then I heard sounds in the room from which she was speaking.

I asked if Lorna was there and Jane said, No, did she say she'd be?

I said, Only last night, but I thought I might find her there now.

Jane said maybe it was tonight, for Lorna hadn't come last night, Jane had played Go with Tessa till after midnight when Dudley came in, and there had been no Lorna that Jane could see.

Daddy doesn't like games, said Jane. Jane laughed off-phone and said off-phone, Oh Daddy.

Jane said wasn't I in New York though? Would I like to speak to Daddy?

I would, and I could see Dudley hauling himself out of a chair and leaning his bulk toward the phone from the other end of the high-ceilinged room as if the angle of inclination in the field of this powerful day of mine might equal what one experienced as movement on other days, and I wondered if Dudley knew he was in this field where static inclination as of mind might displace physical movement, yet again an energy quite other than any that movement bodes, embodies, or imparts. If so, Dudley's gravity whose center was, God knew, too low, leaving him topple-heavy, might find who could know what powers in process around him and convert them to his own uses. I had been at a moment of what Sub calls major illumination and felt the risk of even knowing so, for something threatened to recede as Dudley reached his receiver and raised it to one large ear never dreaming his American friend Cartwright was in Glasgow Central Station still fairly weightless in a giant wheeling field where distance and duration decay into fresh equation embracing Tessa's late blind uncle in Munich (where some of the stained glass in Glasgow Cathedral was made) being jarred awake near dawn in 1936 by the very waking agent that simultaneously stunned him back into dreamland from which his wife then roused him, having heard in her own sleep the concussion, and sensing something wrong with him there in the dark when in fact Tessa's uncle, delivered by that blow into a new weight of pain and limit, may yet (reroused) have felt shared between dream-space and wake-time yet in a field between, instantly swollen to power that was more than a headache and that absorbed those rules that wall our normal slot.

No, said Dudley, as I raised his saffron appendix on the grid of my fork at Blum's kosher restaurant in Whitechapel and inserted fork and forkload into my mouth knowing that while I chewed this sweet and sour most unkosher squidlike divination the tall bald festive waiter in the white coat would come to Tessa's ear (bared that night gracefully below the tight pull of hair combed back into a ponytail) and tell her she was wanted on the phone (where I foreknew she would learn that the lady surgeon had gone in and the offending appendix had come out); no indeed, said Dudley, Lorna hadn't been at the Allotts'. But Tessa never never tells me anything, said Dudley, she leaves me the odd message; today for instance someone called from New York to consult me about Maya glyphs but if Lorna were coming here for the night (which I'll stake my honor as a man of fact she didn't do) I wouldn't necessarily hear in advance.

We both waited for him to continue.

Weightlessness also tires. There has been research on this.

I suggested that Tessa might have answered the questions from New York herself, and Dudley said he'd have been glad if she had, for with her tales of the White Woman of Honduras and the Indomitable Dwarf of Yucatan she was much more interesting than he was and—

And then the operator asked for more money. And Dudley's end was accidentally suspended while I looked through shillings and sixpences and quarters and nickels and Lincoln pennies and Druid dimes and how many hard disks of black slate and white shell that are called "stones" in the game of Go that began in China four thousand and more years ago and then in some space between all these foreign coins there was that spotted dolerite from Wales which Tessa had told me to feel, to get the feel of, to see if I liked: and then as Dudley came at last preceded by their child into the bedroom where we were watching Tessa pack those suitcases, Tessa swooped at me almost in attack and took the stone from me and gave it to Lorna for a going-away gift: but I would not put that token into the slot, for one who like me finds in a Scottish phone kiosk that he has inserted himself into a dimensionless place Between, can refrain as naturally as act: I only knew later on that really I was previsioning myself a god and now like a tricky dream our systems use then let the light of day's exposure fade, I swiftly lost the thought of being a god which I know in my bones was the thing Ned Noble guessed in retrospect he'd foreseen when he hurled Boyd's autographed baseball against the elastic sheet of gravity aiming to put it (as in some perfect strike zone) exactly where I if I could instinctively risk my life could pluck it from between the two forces at the instant it had weight no longer.

I simply hung up.

If Lorna could play a game like that with her son, she was capable of having unknown traffic with the Druid. But Tessa was here somewhere too, having coffee with Gene's wife and, I was willing to bet, recommending Lorna to the Druid. I hadn't asked where Tessa was.

Yet was Lorna in danger the nature of which she'd disguised to Will as the possible reappearance of our burglar?

Why did I think of the Indian? If he'd broken into Dagger's place, he might have broken into ours. There were photo chemicals at Dagger's that might blow a hole in a wall.

Now that would be something to write home about to the City of Violence the London papers relied on so much that if New York were to suffer overnight some pacification plan Fleet Street would have to go out into Birnam Wood and catch a couple of hell's maidens sacrificing a Druid on a stump.

I hadn't the right change to phone home. I wanted to know where Lorna was. I needed that Number 12 map of the Islands of Lewis and Harris, in the Outer Hebrides. It occurred to me I could use a camera where I was going. I went through my wallet wondering if Monty Graf had been the New York call to Dudley Allott.

My phone rang—my operator or Dudley.

If Dudley, then with the help of the operator.

Perhaps Tessa. Perhaps Red Whitehead whose much reiterated "spectrum" of sales techniques I'd always taken with a grain of salt.

I pushed open the glass door.

I left the booth as the ring came again. A girl noticed.

I found a bookshop in Buchanan Street before closing. The map cost almost a dollar.

With a credit card and a little American warmth and tourist frankness I charged the following: two pairs of bluejeans, a dark green nylon rucksack like Lorna's and mine that was collapsed on top of some old blankets on the top shelf of a closet in Highgate, the aluminum frame for the rucksack, a pair of weatherproof leather boots on the heavy side, an olive green parka like Reid's hooded against the Hebridean rains (though I like the weather on my head), and a compass with a shock-proof window rimmed round with bright steel.

Leaving the name of my hotel with BEA, I charged a plane ticket to Stornoway for the following day; the only plausible alternative to this would have been a train to one of three points, then train and steamer or both over varying distances to reach that Calvinist town which at a latitude up above 58 degrees in October is turning down toward the dark period of its year. To wait a night and a morning in Glasgow and then fly would get me there sooner.

I unfolded my one-inch map on a hotel bed.

To get the same overhead feel as in Will's room I pulled the map off onto the carpeted floor and knelt above it.

I hung my right hand from my wrist, elbow, and forearm,

and let it go where it was drawn. Stornoway was off the map to the right. Most of Lewis shown on the map was swamped by the irregular perforations of hundreds of tiny lochs which in spots made the terrain look like a ragged sponge.

Jenny's pencil had circled a headland labeled (yes) Callanish, evidently the village contained in the headland which was itself an oval about a mile by half a mile; it extended like a button into the landward end of East Loch Roag which was a sort of Atlantic fjord. Across the lower part of the headland below the name Callanish was the label *Standing Stones*. I knew the name Callanish from somewhere; I roamed outward from it in all directions sensing I could recall it if I could half-mislay it in the corner of my eye. I had to keep moving forward toward the Hebrides and the Island of Lewis and that headland and Jenny and the danger she was in—but through that danger as if it were the entry to a new circuit to Paul. The names in that field of blue waters and white land lined with fine brown elevation contours like sinuously targeted or swelling islands might give an unsuspecting imagination Gaelic sorcery and old giants. My eye circled out from Callanish, past Loch na Gainmhich, Garynahine, Grimersta, Ben Drovinish, Loch Chulain, Feath Loch Gleaharan—eminence or brackish lake or hamlet whose syllables in print one had in one's possession without needing to say out loud correctly. But the heroes and wizards sleep in the tangled damp maxi-coats of black-face Hebridean sheep. And if the outlying poor in their tiny holdings called crofts seem less poor tomorrow when I trudge among them because they live in this landscape, they seem also *more* poor because there is before my experienced tourist eyes almost nothing, a few sheep, endlessly a few, no goats, rarely a cow, and over the rolling moor shallow-dug trenches of peat peeled out square by square, but no longer at this time of year propped against each other drying (so if you couldn't describe what you know to be the fact but wished to show it on film, you'd have to come back next year with your Beaulieu early enough to see those stacks and wigwams and card-houses before the men who took a comradely day from work to dig them came back to haul them home to burn on the grate).

Think of a revolution here in the northmost part of the Outer Hebrides.

What would you claim? How would you oppose London? Would you trap a tourist or two in the mountains to the south where Lewis becomes Harris? It doesn't happen. This isn't Corsica (where it doesn't happen any more either). True, the young leave for the mainland, for Glasgow and Liverpool and Manchester and London, and for America. But brigands in the Hebrides there never were; instead, some contentment, of privacy, of God-ruled small families, an island self-possession at which some nasty old lowland Scot may look across the water and call degenerate interbreeding—look at all those blue-eyed black-haired square-faced ruddy Celts, don't tell *me* they're Scots.

My eye (between places, between events) on the floor of a chilly hotel bedroom orbits Callanish and the Standing Stones that I now recall are well known; my eye turns about the circle my daughter made on that other map Will and I studied and Jenny took away when she went north with Reid; revolves below and above, bearing also only forward I hope not back into dragging average errors and the auras of nostalgia and weights of adolescent origins, the dull melancholy puzzles of those ancient mistakes that may profitably be left to mature in their time capsules and that if you wish can give you an average anchor on which to swing with the average yearly wind and current tethered. But it was now—as my stomach rumbled with hunger for the future blood of those who'd ruined my film and involved my daughter—that my eye circuiting stopped on Loch Cliasam Creag, the middle word doubtless kin to Clisham, Mount Clisham, a name I had last uttered in America which my Druid says is the future where things happen first—uttered across a restaurant table to Monty Graf, a businessman I could not trust, and with John, the man in steel-rimmed specs, somewhere behind—Mount Clisham I had said, in turn recalling words taped in the Unplaced Room—Mount Clisham as my blood-shot eye fell south on my Ordnance Survey to long Loch Langavat (a Great Lake on this one-inch map) and below to my left to the Forest of Harris (the Hebrides are nearly treeless), down then to the right to the rugged heights of North Harris so crammed with fine contours that this flatly mazelike legend of steepnesses was a fingerprint-life to be read by an infrared ranger—and at the center of one of these softened Chinese boxes I read 2622 *Clisham* and wondering if in that future America Monty Graf had been Dudley's caller from New York today, I recalled saying to Monty over my bluefish and his gin and milk that our deserter had shipped on a dilettante rock-hunter's yacht to the Faeroes and had made it to the Hebrides with a fisherman and for a time lived in a hut near Mount Clisham—my very words not a week ago recollecting a bare depictured room Dagger had borrowed from some friend—an old fellow-alumnus from Berkeley?—for what had then—on Monday, May 24—been our second scene, though, like an island he and I

295

had forked either side of, one thing to me but another to him to judge from his May 24 letter to Claire which Aut had read by now and which could cost Claire her job if she weren't packing it in in any case. The future of that letter hard to see. It could have more than one. Someone came down the hotel hall and stopped at my door. I stood up and stepped on the map which crackled. I looked away from the door past the open wardrobe where nothing hung but two hangers, one from the other—across the double bed to the night table where the phone was: there was a phone. The steps had not moved on.

Go open the door?

Wait?

The steps went on down the hall.

Should I phone Lorna? What future did we have?

The question, godlike, blinked open before you knew it was there.

I stepped off the map. Mount Clisham looked so far away. Gods didn't have incomes to live within, nor credit cards to buy extempore outdoor gear with either. Nor did they have to send their sons to private school.

The confused young deserter in the Unplaced Room had said: I started not being able to remember what happened to me, just knew I had to keep going on.

Wednesday nights Lorna had chorus rehearsal. I'd hung up on Dudley so some consciousness of power would recede instead of the power itself. I could have found change for the operator. I'd thought the circuit would take me the wrong way. But each fork finds new forks. When the booth phone rang I could have answered instead of exiting. The rich girl from Mississippi whom I'd told about Jules Verne I could have stayed with on that train; and continued to make my contribution to her year abroad. I bought her a gin and tonic and a flat, communion-white sandwich. Walking back to the buffet car we had equaled and canceled the then decelerated train's forward speed, a rate which, unlike that of the Down escalator Ned Noble and I once walked up, was not constant. But each of those equalizings is like a treadmill not like that signal escape through equalizing which was Boyd's ball's exit through a dimensionless chink between laws. Instead of boarding the Glasgow train to begin with I could have bought an apple in the station and gone home to worry about losing Red Whitehead's business in England. Instead of leaving my Druid's house and its smell of fennel and tangerine and dry spines of nineteenth-century cheap editions, I could have stayed to talk about my shoulders and lungs, head and hand—for I trusted him in these things at least. You must talk to people while you have them. I had not told him about the softening of the cartridge, and yet I thought he might understand, for he it was who had told me that the gate a pulse finds open may revise a whole future of gates, for the gods to each of whom are proper certain provinces of possibility in the field of forces, know each other—as through Tessa and me those two huge figures are mutually known, her pictograph giant 167 feet tall seen from the window of Dudley's chartered plane (and later described to me in New York), and my Giant of Cerne, 181 feet tall seen so close up I had to see him through my children's chase up and down him which I'd unsuccessfully photographed. Mr. Andsworth knew something, not everything. He could not map or remap my head, but his friend at the Cerebral Functions Research Group who did it with rats had found that cells deprived of input by injury are often taken over by other cells that sprout fiber-branches—which is growth, and therefore likely to be good, but may too often produce a retargeting of messages so that (to take my own willed or unwilled case of the softening cartridges) steps heard continuing down a hall could anesthetize a finger and thumb holding a match over Claire's desk drawer but at a later stage steps heard continuing down a hall could bring to my fingers the feel of a receiver phoning my wife and through Highgate a sensation about my future with Lorna that with gently tingling discomfort caressed my now giant eyes with the shimmering air of New York. It wasn't as if I'd have been asking my Druid why my head ached when I stepped on the map and it crackled, or why just before that great shove in my shoulder blades I should have received that sensation of the fast-approaching steps being both slow and close. But fork upon fork, fibers sprouting deltas, alternatives routed into huge parallel families ignorant of each other —and my only daughter Jenny chases Will into the private parts of the Giant of Cerne who looks out of chalk-rimmed popeyes of earth into a rainy sky.

I laid out my purchases on the bed. The phone rang. It was Lorna. Savvy Van Ghent had asked us for the same evening as Geoff Millan.

I asked if there'd been more trouble. She said Dudley had learned from the operator that my pay phone was in Glasgow and when she'd phoned BEA she found they not only had me booked but knew my hotel. I asked if there'd been any trouble.

Why didn't you come home? said Lorna. What did you tell Mr. Andsworth the Druid? I said. Tessa's the one who knows him, said Lorna, not me. Well he talks as if he knows you, I said. Do you think Tessa spilled the beans? said Lorna, being funny. I wasn't able to get hold of Tessa, I said. What did you want with her? said Lorna. Just as well I got Dudley, I said. Oh you'll be glad to know, said Lorna, Jenny and Reid picked up your Xerox. Who told them to? I asked. I did, said Lorna, I was in a hurry to get into the West End and they said they would.

Who told you, I said, Will?

Lorna paused. No, come to think of it Jenny mentioned it to me as I was rushing around collecting my music and keys and checkbook—this was our last rehearsal before the concert—and I said would you be a dear and collect it whatever it is, and she asked me for a receipt but I didn't have one, but I'm sure she and Reid didn't have any trouble.

That was an error, I said.

Oh fuck you, said Lorna.

Give me the number of Jan Graf, she's on the list on the table there.

Lorna gave it. She said, Lucky for you I'm at the downstairs phone.

Why didn't you sleep at Tessa's last night?

Why didn't you come home today—because you were in New York?

I hung up.

I phoned down to the desk leaving a call for the morning and asking that I not be disturbed no matter where the call was from.

I was too hungry to go to bed. I was not myself, but it was incredible.

Look out at the walls of your hotel room with its print of the four-story Venetian palazzo that houses municipal offices in Glasgow's George Square. Look out at the cheap Van Gogh flowers in the hotel off Boston Common or was it New Orleans or Baltimore, or Portland's Congress. Look at the watercolor cliffscape in the motel in Cincinnati where you lie eyes closed, English shoes still on, listening on black-and-white TV to the news of Kennedy's nomination campaign and thinking some English woman (in New York of course) told you American men go to conventions because they like a hotel room where they can masturbate in peace, and you woke up in the middle of the night to a bright ashy-blank screen and didn't know where you were except that it was a motel you didn't know how to get out of but as your father had said more than once in the fifties you hadn't burnt your bridges behind you, you kept a foot in the door while enjoying the advantages of life in London. And what are they? I asked the two sedately linked hangers in my wardrobe. State schools in England are mostly better than American public schools: but face it, your own Will happens to be attending a private school, else he wouldn't have had that group trip to Chartres whose 176 stained glass windows so exercised his engineering imagination. They stayed in the cathedral for four hours and saw the light change. They stayed in hotels down in the square where the traffic noise is dreadful. My grandfather whom I am like in looks died in a hotel.

In Stornoway tomorrow I did not look for a hotel and did not hop into a red rented Formula sports car but got my feet on the road at once and hitched almost to Callanish, then walked. In Callanish tomorrow I stayed in a crofter-widow's house and had a large tea and a peat fire and asked questions that might open my way to the next fork.

But tonight I dined in Glasgow, and Dudley's phone call from New York was on my plate. A man of fact, he hadn't hesitated to say that Lorna had not slept in his home last night. He was my friend not through Dagger-type laughs or warmth or in the usual way of shared concerns, but through my curiosity. But even in '66 in bed before Tessa and me, he was still just a stolid American living off and on in London whose wife had made her mark in our household. When at Blum's kosher restaurant she offered a toast to a vestige of Dudley, her father raised his glass with what was left of his Moselle and said, My son! and as Millan and Lorna and the Irish mathematician Christy Conn raised theirs, Lorna at last broke the day's ice between her and me with a pursed smile across the table. Millan was saying an operation is such a violent thing and Tessa's father vaguely demurred—oh no. Beyond Lorna in a line from me there was a couple at a table whom I knew but who did not seem to know me; Lorna opened up a real smile, then sensed that for an instant I was looking past her and she turned around only enough to see the pediatrician's wife who had a tan as deep as paint. Tessa's father was explaining why America would never have a Health Service like England's, but Tessa broke in to say that service of any kind was a problem where there was such a high standard of living, and having said that, she turned to her right and removed her tongue from her cheek and stuck it out at Christy who put a finger on the mole on his upper lip and said they'd be altering the sex of computers soon because women made better surgeons than men. But Tessa's father interrupted what promised to be a wild Irish aria to say to Tessa that that was what her mother had wanted to be before she'd married him. At which point we all sighed, even I think Christy Conn, who was the only one present who didn't know what had happened to Tessa's mother. Tessa's father shook his head and said, She was the image of my daughter. I sighted past Lorna's ear lobe and received from the pediatrician a faint mouth-twitch of recognition, and again Lorna turned and this time saw them both and turned back slowly surveying the room, and said their name to me quietly and I nodded (hoping she and I were friends again)—and the pediatrician's wife nodded back. Tessa's father was just saying that life is surprisingly rewarding when you look back; Christy had made Lorna laugh telling how his sister who taught the Irish harp in Armagh toured Florence in a nun's habit so as not to be hustled while she was trying to admire the sculptures. Tessa said directly to me in answer to her father who was on her left and my right at the end of the table, Rewarding when you look back if you've come through perhaps. I said I would be patient. Tessa's father said to Tessa in answer to me, Patient!—look what happened to Job. Tessa said if you can't have what you want, you have to want what you have. I caught Christy the mathematician's eye: Formula for a rainy day, I said, and he frowned and grinned as if I were mad, and said to Lorna, Where was I? and Tessa said to me, But it wasn't a rainy day, remember? but at once added, That wasn't what Father was speaking of.

The gallery show had been of very young painters, and Millan had walked away at one point when his Irish friend wanted to introduce a blond giant in corduroy overalls who was one of the exhibitors. Lorna had barely spoken to me and had made the rounds of the pictures arm in arm with Tessa's father. It was this—and the argument this afternoon that lay behind it about my sudden plan to fly to Pittsburgh to see a man about bringing Appalachian quilts into England—that had made me feel, among the white tablecloths and red cabbage and the plain munching stares we got from elder gentlemen in yarmulkas as we came into Blum's and made our way to a table for six against the wall at the back, as if I were standing in line to cash a check at Chemical Bank in New York about to be observed (as if by a light angled in a corner where wall met ceiling) by one of four closed-circuit TV cameras that did not know (any more than the senior teller or the new black girl who when I get to the head of the line asks me to endorse my own check) that I don't live in New York. (I heard Tessa say Of *course* I wasn't lonely in New York, no one is lonely in New York, of *course* I had gentlemen callers!) Dudley did not describe those early scenes with Tessa's father except to say that there was real passion despite its being also a formality; but Tessa had told Lorna that her father had shouted and wept and had let it be known through his confidante Mrs. Stone (who had lost two brothers and was living in Golders Green waiting for reparations) that Tessa was dead to him. Ned Noble's father said anyone brought up in Brooklyn, except Brooklyn Heights, was Jewish and Ned repeated it to me as an instance of his family's insanity. Tessa's father did not want any coffee; he was telling Millan about Dudley's achievements as a historian, speaking across me as if I weren't present; and Millan was nodding dimly while trying to hold on to Christy Conn's story of his sister's butch girlfriend the xylophone player in an Armagh orchestra who got a message in the middle of a concert that her xylophone would explode during a solo and who had been thrown off ever since and might go into social work.

And I was telling Tessa she would never be happy off in the country serving tea to the vicar's wife even if she did now want a piece of the land. What would Dudley do? Oh, Dudley would love it, said Tessa. He could run, said Tessa's father, the way I used to in Germany. Lorna laid her hand on Christy's hand. Tessa wanted to know when I was going to New York, and I said Pittsburgh in two days. Tessa's father was telling Millan the different fields his son-in-law had now published in and that he'd gone into Mesoamerican history with no background to speak of and had become an authority on the English artist and engineer Catherwood, and Millan with cherubic judiciousness said Catherwood's Egyptian drawings were better than the Central American stuff. But, said Tessa's father, the Maya work is the thing, and Millan smiled and said the camera lucida Catherwood had invented as a means of accurately drawing what he saw had met more curious problems in the Memnon monuments. Tessa's father said offhandedly, Oh no. Millan smiled, he liked Catherwood's temples on the island of Philae, especially now the new Aswan lake had covered them up except for a moment in July when you could still see the Temple of Isis emerge from the water. But, said Tessa's father, Dudley is going to publish an article on Catherwood.

Far away directly in the line of Tessa and me the waiter thought I was catching his eye and nodded and walked toward us taking out his pen. Tessa's father held his finger up to the waiter and called for the bill and they exchanged pleasantries about the sweet and sour mackerel and the stuffed neck and when they'd finished turned their attention benignly to Tessa who was telling how she and she alone had pushed her husband into Maya history by telling him all the Middle American stories that had come over from China—the beautiful white woman who came down from heaven to a town in Honduras, built a palace painted with magic cats and dogs and heroes, built a temple with a stone in the middle of it that because of the mysterious glyphs on three sides enabled her to kill her enemies, and though she was a virgin like the moon she bore three sons to whom she left her kingdom when she had her downy bed carried to the top of the palace and vanished into heaven—but Dudley of course cared more about exactly how high the Mayas set the stone ring for one of their ball games because if it was thirty feet high and they hit the six-inch rubber ball with their buttocks how could they get it in even with the ring perpendicular to the ground, and Dudley would tell you about the legal loopholes you could use to escape death for adultery.

At some point in this I had murmured that we should make a film about the White Woman and her three sons, but no one heard.

Tessa's father told the waiter his daughter's husband was a historian, a professor; and when the tall distinguished waiter said Professor! and tapped his temple, Tessa's father said Dudley was an American, and the waiter said his own son was an actor.

Oh darling, said Christy covering Lorna's knuckles (but his large lucid eye passed through me like a laser in a moment of recognition), adultery wasn't at all gay among the Maya.

I said very quickly, Think of what your sainted sister got away with in her nun's habit.

The businessman speaks, said Geoffrey Millan, a thing of quantums, quilts, and snatches.

And bottles, boats, and stoves, said Lorna, hearing Millan's tone—is there anyone *like* him?

The pediatrician rose behind Lorna, and I said putting my hand on Tessa's, You never know what I'll do.

But her father's hand was underneath hers, and we all laughed.

When we rose, Lorna brought her glass up with her and swallowed her wine. I said, shicsa is a goy, and Tessa's father grinned and gripped my elbow as I tried to get past him around the end of the table.

From a Glasgow hotel on a night in October 1971, that meal five years ago drew the straight line of my possible form through its field of talk and just beyond to the trip I'd had to the gallery with Tessa eight stops on the Underground from Charing Cross (and Dudley's hospital bed) to Whitechapel, but the input that was all I could add to Millan's insult was the talk she and I secretly had during our nonsecret trip. For Lorna that afternoon had not simply objected to my going so soon again to the States, she'd heard some new growth or insertion in my words when I said hell she wasn't jealous was she? and she said as if finding out something Yes, yes, maybe I am jealous, I'm going to ask Tessa what you were doing when she was there. But then she saw she couldn't laugh that off so she left the room.

These mean, mealy, missed moments in our unrevolutionary life on whatever side of the Atlantic thrust me out through a closed-circuit eye back or forth to the old lookout dream I'd never succeeded in having.

Tonight in Glasgow I thought I might have it at last. I wanted a woman, but not in a hotel other than my own. My thighs were cranked tighter than the whiskey I had not drunk could have undone. My toes were part of the same thing. My four-course à la carte had filled me full of shrimp and some kind of cream soup and roast pork and a dark pudding lathered with that yellow custard sauce designed to combat the weather.

The desk clerk said yes I could leave my suitcase tomorrow for a day or two. And he said I'd had a visitor, an Indian gentleman. Nothing more, no address.

I asked if he'd been in a white high-neck pullover and the clerk said, Yes, under his mac.

You could get up the stairs without the desk seeing so long as you could get into the lounge in the first place. Anyone coming in late would be spoken to and would find it impossible to sneak up. I checked the three corridors on my floor. A girl in a raincoat open on a short skirt was by a door and we stared.

I'd seen enough movies to check my window ledge on either side. It was inaccessible from other rooms.

I laid my map back on the bed where I could look at it comfortably. The stones of Callanish seemed days away from Mount Clisham to the south, and in Clisham's vicinity there was hardly a hamlet where I might learn exactly where Paul's hut was.

I lay back on the bed with my legs on the map. But that map was a one-incher, so the distance from Callanish to Clisham direct was less than twenty miles. I sat up to check.

The distances were not great. Yet cross-country there was no telling how much of the peat moor among the dozens of lochs was blanketed with that spongy sphagnum moss that over the millennia replaced the trees of an earlier drier climate. The alternative was a roundabout road that went back toward Stornoway then wound down thirty-odd miles into the mountains of Harris.

I took off everything and sat on the bed again. Jenny's circle must mean something. That was where Paul was or had been. What if no one was there now? What if they were all behind me when I got there? Or at the rim of a wheel, with me at the center and a few spokes gone.

Someone came by my door puffing.

The Indian wanted me. That meant someone was in Lewis or Harris whom I was to be prevented from encountering.

The Venetian Renaissance palace on the wall placed this room.

I didn't know what had been on the walls of the hotel where my grandfather died. Sub said one good thing now we were in our forties was that we couldn't die young. I heard steps coming back but no puffing. In Monty Graf's basement bedroom in the presence of Claire I had written *Gulf of Honduras* on a pad and circled it and then run upstairs on a pretext in order to pinch Claire's keys. I expected her to look at the pad and think I was chasing a lead to do with Dagger's missing school-friend whose deranged father she and Dagger had visited and if she thought what I wanted her to, she'd forget that a few minutes ago in Monty's living room we'd been looking guardedly toward the Hebrides.

This was a case for Ned Noble, who said at the time of his early death that he was designing a time machine. We were juniors in high school. Sub never liked him.

Just keep going, said the boy deserter in the Unplaced Room.

Ned's diagram of steps for assembling this time machine was less like a sequence than a map; I had a glimpse of isometric sections and formulas familiar but altered, then Ned folded it up closing between its folds a sheet of paper also folded where he said he had drawn the time machine's logo, which his father Hy Noble was going to get patented.

And (said Ned Noble with friendly contempt for my peace-making after I'd restored the autographed ball to poor serious Boyd four years earlier) you might find your little brain growing again— who knows?—so that whereas this time the hole in your left ear felt the draft of your mother swinging open your bedroom door and your right shoulder responded by launching you out the window to snare my shot, someday you will know how to turn your mind toward greater tasks.

I lay on my Glasgow bed, kicked the map off, felt myself all over counting forty-one years by fives, tried once more to will into my sleep the lookout dream I had thought out so often in vain but hoped to dream in order to find a power. But each part of the dream turns me out and away. A building site at night in a great American city: the steel frame is up, concrete forms have been poured—but unfortunately one of the upper unfloored rooms corrupts the dream, for it is Lorna in one of three scenes I think and it's afternoon not night (though no one is working at the site) and she has said I've no business traipsing out to Pittsburgh when she has a concert in four days and I was in the States just eight weeks ago. *Out* sounds like Australia, not Pittsburgh, and I try to get back to my housing site; but my word *jealous* turns the day up like a baring of light at one stopped point and next thing Lorna says she'll ask Tessa what Tessa thought I was up to when she and Dudley saw me in New York—as if I were some snake in the grass, not the husband of Tessa's best American friend. Which puts me between her and Tessa and returns me to my lookout dream where I am in another way between.

Between two dangers: and again the mind of my hotel bed disperses but now into love space where the outer glaze on a lady's eyes may also be a film on mine, I can't recall a single wall of her flat that Monday in New York except far, far away in this same city pictures of the gods and their ruined houses that her husband was making it his business to get acquainted with; and when I bring my thumb from her thighs to my mouth and then the same distance to her mouth she says with a nip that this city will be the ruin of her. I don't ask if I am better than a bombed house to play around, but I think it, and think of her mother whom Tessa will never settle, who was rolled into a concentration camp the week Tessa was eight, and never sent word: which returns me to my lookout site in a great American city through the gated areaways of Brooklyn Heights brownstones and pale gray clean old Dutch wood-planked town houses that were going in '38 for as little as $10,000—back through those grassy yards (now cut off by a two-level parkway) like the yard behind Sub's house that looked over Furman Street and its dock warehouses and the superstructures of freighters loading for the South American run, across the East River to a charmed range of

305

financial skyscrapers whose steel rose stonily out of the old wood-frame theme of those certain houses of our neighborhood Sub took for granted till years later he found himself working in New York, compelled to inhabit Manhattan because the quieter Brooklyn Heights where we grew up was too deep down the substance on which all the forkings of his first life seemed printed and grounded, gated through the northern rectangular faces of our mothers and fathers in their respective Persian lambs and dark velvet-collared or herringboned Chesterfields rising up the steps of a red-brick house on Cranberry Street to a dinner party whose guest list contains two cultured Quaker Jews, contains the house itself on which is super-imposed (like one of those dinner parties that traveled in evening dress course by course and drink by drink to different homes) a brownstone four blocks away where an eighteenth-century dinner table made in New Jersey by the host's ancestors is discovered in a candlelit back wing flanked like an ancient apron stage on three sides by high-window exposures to the huge flickering harbor upon which in daylight from the roof of my apartment house I'd look out to find around the Statue the patterns of a continent winding and rewinding back to my lookout site through a neat field where in addition Rommel's Egypt and Hitler's Jewish law and haggard flyers on a raft in the Pacific and Goering's nightly noise against England stood equal on some grid of weekly events to lone unlighted hands caught grabbing or waving out of a landslide of Polish rubble in a Saturday newsreel short at the St. George Playhouse on Pineapple Street and to my own boy voice assuring my sister who was sightreading bent tensely forward at the piano, that there would be bluebirds over the white cliffs of Dover: but I almost do not make it, and only long enough to see that at this night site of my undreamt dream where a building that's a keystone in a master American plan is going up by day, I am a lookout, I am a lookout between two forces, not between Dudley and Tessa, or Dudley and Lorna, or Jenny and Cosmo's Indian, but between forces: but they leave me so apart that my hotel bed concentration on the one hand or the other disperses as if over all the mustered parts of my open body to Tessa's lips on a Monday afternoon in New York saying to my thighs Oh ho ho! you are a bearded god Kokulcan and you have been released to come to me, oh ho ho! because Dudley is watching your temple, oh Kokulcan I have seen you before in other places, other beards, you were the snake that came to feather me and I will bite you back.

She played hide and seek in a bombed house, got a first kiss, hid one day all but the side-part in her hair and the pale brown eyes the only moving thing as her father's voice rose to a pitch she had not heard before which did not make her show herself but made her stay, a narrow face between textures of wrecked stone and as hard to see as I am on my lookout site keeping watch for those who have gone into the building's shadowy forms and are to be warned by me if the other forces come from the street outside, so I'm important but I'm struck stationary between the two motions of those inside and those outside but I do not know enough about the two sides, can't look at both at once; need power: to cope with (a) a wife who on the morning of my trip to Corsica called our film half-baked, and (b) my partner-friend whose view of our film was so haphazard that we had two films, my montage, his footage: yet a friend who, as with the 8-millimeter cartridge I somehow haven't inquired into, so with his changed plans first to put the Softball Game between the Hawaiian Hippie and the Suitcase Slowly Packed, and then August 4 or 5 instead to cut the SSP into the Marvelous Country House, seemed to know something I didn't, yet even now that I've found his collusive letter to Claire, Dagger seems not to know too much to be my friend. He must have wished to say something by means of that snapshot Jenny packed between the black sweater and the green-and-white plastic bottle of medicated shampoo in the filmed suitcase that I now see recalls uncannily Lorna's suitcase in a third scene in our bedroom, a suitcase that, like a poignant still picture invulnerable to the motions around it, remained half-packed on a chair for three days in 1958 when Lorna was leaving and not leaving, dreaming me with crystal clarity dead, not hearing what I said to her, wishing herself asleep for good: until on the third night (which was a week before she met Tessa) I lay on our bed preparing to dream the lookout dream and wondering what to do to the building-site watchman who is recovering consciousness after the blow on his head—and found that Lorna was now unpacking the case she'd half-packed three days before back into our less orderly life together.

But now in Glasgow wondering where Cosmo's Indian was spending the night, and whether the Druid through his connections had put Dagger in danger, and thinking what from my suitcase should I pack in my new rucksack, I knew that I would keep going and that if Cosmo's Indian who'd awed Cosmo by saying he lived only in the present turned up at this old hotel door in Scotland I would collar him and find a way back through his recent acts to my most practical course in the Hebrides tomorrow.

But I thought he'd wait. I jammed a chair under the door knob, killed the light, lay down, heard approaching my building site the quiet voices in the street of those who were opposed to the small squad at work inside for whom I was standing watch; and heroism seemed not so much unlikely as encumbered with tasks and time-tables, names and address books: the injured watchman stirs beside a long I-beam: Dudley corrects Tessa at a Mexican restaurant (Kokulcan did not simply arise in Yucatan as a Mayan god reborn from the Aztec Quetzlcoatl—Kokulcan arose quite probably through rumor collaborating round the figure of a bearded priest-ruler who took the name of Quetzlcoatl and as a result priests of a rival god Tetzcatlipoca expelled the impostor and he may have made his way to the sea and disappeared to the east on a raft, *or*—and we note a decisiveness in Dudley's very lack of certainty—this bearded Toltec exile may have detoured on the mainland instead, for about this time Kokulcan who has some but not all of Quetzlcoatl's characteristics first shows himself among the Maya of Yucatan).

I did not feel much like a god on my Glasgow bed. I found myself swelling to fill the spaces between me and the two forces, yet contracting too as to make some space between me and the rest. The squad inside were committing a subtle robbery and wiring a thunder-clap invented unknown to them by me, and they were taking too long about it. The watchman we'd coshed was reaching groggily to hold his forehead or rub his eyes, and for the first time in my mind he was a recently discharged veteran from a big Italian family in Brooklyn. Tessa's bombed houses were the third of those moments that placed her in my film diary if not in the Marvelous Country House where Dagger had found something to make him wish to cut into it the Suitcase Slowly Packed which would in my own vision of the film be as unplaced as the MCH or for that matter the Unplaced Room, or the pad of paper on which I'd written Claire the false lead "Gulf of Honduras" then circled it.

I was near sleep and near the end of my preparation to dream my lookout dream, and the bombers led by a man in a beard and a black sweater inside the shadowed geometries of the great unfinished building were in fact a revolutionary group. But, like an Indian rapping on my hotel door, the dim snapshot that had fallen from Reid's book and that Jenny had quickly packed turned into a picture hung in two places, and that picture was the oil of Jan Aut's that I'd noticed in Monty's living room because of the black-and-white photo next to it whose framed glass reflected my face and I'd disparaged the oil hoping to lure her brother into telling me something—and the other place I'd seen it was May 24 in a rough neighborhood of London in the Unplaced Room that Dagger and I had depictured and whose address I now saw congruent with an address I had written on our hall table in Highgate and now here on a scrap of paper in Glasgow, and it was the address of Jan: whom Dagger therefore knew.

But I placed my hand over my eyes and found a new detail of the lookout dream I was preparing to dream: the wakening watchman whom I might have to dispose of was one of three brothers, yes that was it: but as sleep reached to lock on my frequency for the night, Tessa's hand was on my body pulling hairs, stretching latitude parallels up a thigh with her middle three fingers so pinkie and thumb stuck out like my Jenny signaling left and right from Reid's motorbike (as if to say take a picture of anything but me) and Tessa was telling me the tale of the Moon and her three sons, and she sighed *Kokulcan* and I felt the wind and said if I am Gene's brother Jack, then I am also Paul's brother Jack.

And so as sleep did at last lock on and a breeze from Scotland crossed the sill onto my exposed feet, I had to end my preparing for the lookout dream as the unknown third brother Jack: and then I saw without preparation that I was going to be forced to kill the watchman.

But I was ready enough and felt in my relaxing shins and my collar of bone that if I didn't dream my lookout dream now I never would.

12 I left my case at the hotel desk and paid my bill early when the lobby was empty. After breakfast I told the desk I was expecting a call from London at noon and could be found in the lobby. I paid a boy to check my rucksack at the bus terminal. I could not recall what pages if any were in my case.

I consulted the classified. At 9:30 when I strolled out in jeans and parka I found a booth and phoned a gunsmith's and got the information I needed. I had the locker key and my compass in my pocket and nothing in my hands. I browsed at a news agent's. A vacant cab turned into the block and when I saw the light green ahead, I jumped in and we went toward George Square. I asked the driver how many fares he could expect during the working day. We weren't being followed so I asked for the bus terminal.

But an hour later when I appeared at the upper level of the

airport terminal having left my pack at the weigh-in counter, the Indian was ahead of me standing at a news agent's cash register reading a magazine. I didn't glance at him again, and when I boarded the plane I took a forward seat.

In the far north you feel close to the great cycles. You are close to the earth's flattened poles. A sunset especially if you see it from a mountain can show you the curve of the earth.

But west of Stornoway when I took the road with Krish the Indian somewhere in eyeshot behind me, I had for vantage points ahead only the earth-colored moors losing their heather purple as October waned and the dark cold lochs that seemed to have been purified of life by the withdrawal of the trees.

To a tourist, a dire land with a beauty of exile.

To a motion intent as mine, a place maybe potentially as static as the eastern Steppes.

According to my map Mount Clisham lay hazed way to the south; but to find my point on it I must go west to the stones Jenny had penciled at Callanish. Was there haze, then, on my map? I breathed breaths deep as a compressed dream. She could not have meant to give a false lead. But it might still be a lead. She had picked up that English interest in archaeology whose cachet is like that of anthropology in the States. Surrounded by the noise of a small city, English coeds ready to work like Trojans sign up for a summer of dusty sifting at the site hard by Exeter Cathedral, the way adolescent girls at genteel schools fall in love with horses.

Callanish was where I trusted to find the way on to Paul. I was alone and alert. I breathed out and in.

I knew nothing.

The pack focused my shoulders. I would walk all the way. I turned as a skier turning leans downhill, and looked back stiffly as if for a car, but really to see what I saw—which was the Indian.

He was at a quai-side fence looking at a boat basin. A long white trenchcoat tailored like my tan one now packed in my case in Glasgow. Nothing in his hands or on his back. He lived in the present, Cosmo said.

I was on the edge of Stornoway, the colorless sky low and long.

A drunk swung by and disappeared.

A car beeped. The driver of a bright red mini beckoned. The Indian was watching the empty boats.

I could still feel my pack after I'd dumped it in back.

My driver switched off the music.

We drove around the next corner and Stornoway lapsed. The man said I was from America. I thought him about my age; he looked younger; he had Irish in his voice; I'd seen nothing but black hair and blue eyes in Stornoway, but this man had brown hair and brown eyes. He said I was going to see the stones, and I said yes. He wasn't going all the way, he was turning off. I asked if this was dark for three o'clock in October. He said no, but this wasn't too bad a time to come.

A wind pushed a flicker of rain over the road and it was dry again. I asked about December, what was it like here. My companion laughed and said nothing.

I drew upon Stonehenge five hundred-odd flying miles somewhere to my left: I said the stones at Callanish might be worth visiting December 22, the winter solstice.

He didn't know.

He and some friends assembled for sunrise at summer solstice, drank a few pints, but did not dress up in robes or speak spells. I said he knew about the solstice . . . He said, the longest and shortest days. I said another way of seeing it was that the sun at those times appeared to stand still between northward and southward motion. He doubted if Stone Age man could have observed that.

I did not know what I would say next. It was a fact that once in Honduras Catherwood's American companion John Lloyd Stephens had dropped his dagger into the mountain mud and then had fallen off his mule almost onto the dagger which had stuck blade up. He passed a fork and he said that was where he'd been going to turn. I thanked him and asked if there had been Americans at Callanish. Americans were always writing books, he said.

He didn't come into this area, he lived several miles from here. Lewis was better than the mainland. In his view the stones were interesting, but no one would ever know what they really meant. It was lucky I wasn't up here on a Sunday because "the locals" he said might object to my doing the stones on the Sabbath. Stornoway was shut up and there were no buses or cars on the road, so be sure not to travel on Sunday. Many emigrated from the Hebrides to America.

I did not say, I am looking for my daughter.

Anyway, was I?

He asked where I was staying. I said I didn't know—I had an

address—a number with Callanish after it. A crofter's cottage. Maybe they would take me in.

He didn't comment.

I asked if the peat would ever give out.

No, he said, not unless the population drain were reversed, but maybe not even then.

Figures were cited.

Rain blew across the road more than once.

I wanted to say to this man that the film did not matter.

He did not speak of America. He spoke of peat.

America and Canada have forty million acres of it. It has to have special conditions, so you'd think it would yield something special. Now south of here—

Down by Clisham? I said.

Oh no. Down three islands to South Uist—there's a seaweed factory on the beach. They dry and pulverize seaweed and send it out to England. Process it for fertilizers, nylon, and some binding agent used in false teeth. A very special seaweed of huge plants like cables, and it comes by steamer from the Orkneys and takes two days to unload out of two holds. But what's peat good for? Burn it of course. The men make a party and go off digging on a Saturday. They spade up sods and stack them. The drying takes six weeks unless it's as wet as it was this summer (and you probably know, it's precisely wet weather coupled with poor drainage that encourages the formation of peat). Well elsewhere they may use excavators and heating chambers but in the Hebrides it is by hand, big square sods out there and you can see what the work is like right where you see the strip-trenches.

There's going to be an international commune in Chile, I said, ecologically based, self-supporting, recycling, all that, five hundred people.

They might make it, said the man.

Can you walk out there? I asked, say directly overland to Mount Clisham so as to cut the roundabout distance by road.

There are only three reasons to go out on the moor, said my driver: to find your sheep, to take a short walk for it's handsome country, and to cut peat. No good trekking; you run into high heather, and lochs, and bogs of moss that you'll go right down into.

My driver might have been an engineer or a schoolteacher. I wanted to ask if he had an independent income. I reviewed the air and steamer connections available to him (for instance the four-hour crossing from Stornoway to Kyle of Lochalsh). He could not easily or cheaply commute to the mainland; I had heard somewhere of a process of boiling peat in a weak solution of sulphuric acid, then neutralizing with lime, whereby a ton of peat could yield twenty-five gallons of alcohol for motor fuel. A Highgate neighbor had once, but only once, urged me over his fence to try peat on the stubborn rhododendron in one far corner of our garden.

My driver nodded ahead across three or four miles of road and field and moor. The stones, he said.

And as he continued his information on peat, I saw on a rise and blanched by the brightening but now later light a gathering of what must be quite high stones, some pointed like weapons with contours like heads, but more than in any of their single shapes they seemed from here more intelligible as a gathering. There was in the midst one greater than others.

They can make it into coke briquettes, said my driver. Pulp it, mill it, homogenize it, bake it, press it so it's like lignite—and the end product's a fuel as hot almost as coal with less sulphur. They can also convert the nitrogen in peat into ammonia.

I looked at the stones as they moved off to my left as if toward Clisham. You've studied chemistry, I said. And geology, he said. What about peat for caulking, I said.

But here, said my companion, they cut it; and when the dug peat dries, they burn it.

We stopped at a house on a rise: A red-faced heavy-set woman in a thick pink cardigan said hers was not the number I wanted and told me where to go, pointed across a valelike depression containing a loch, to a rise on the other side where a few cottages of wood frame or stone were scattered along a couple of miles of road from a church on the right or north to the neolithic site fenced off on the higher headland to the left above a considerable body of water.

I reflected upon further information received from my driver.

I went back and got in beside him, said I knew where I was going and would walk it from here; I thought I would like to arrive on foot; I thanked him for going out of his way. He did not ask what would happen if they couldn't take me in over there. He said it was a pleasure to talk to an American and asked what line I was in. I said business, a bit of this, a bit of that. Random enterprises. He said it sounded like I was quite free. I said that in fact I had a great untapped capacity for work. University of Lancaster had I said? The Chilean commune? Yes, I said, University of Lancaster. He said an

313

American firm had got into fish-processing in Stornoway, but he doubted it would keep people here. Did I know there was a factory in Michigan that used to turn peat into paper?

A breeze brought the rain racing across the loch and from the far cottages and over along the road and over the car, but the late sun on the headland lit the Callanish stones.

I decided there was nothing in his having picked me up. He made this run from Stornoway often on a weekday afternoon an hour or so after the Glasgow plane.

Peat fires, the man said, were an acquired smell; it was one reason he'd always planned to come back to Lewis, the smell was different in India.

But, I said, they use ox and camel dung there.

Yes, mainly, he said—but there is an Indian peat that forms from decaying rice plant material, it hasn't that brackish acrid odor of peat in the Western Isles.

You've traveled, I said.

He looked at me closely as I reached back for my pack and I was about to ask if he knew of an American in these parts named Paul (and it hit me I'd never asked Dagger Gene's surname), but the man (now looking through me as if out beyond the Callanish stones to the great loch from the sea, a meaning, a Norse source, an old sequence inspiring him) said the word *sphagnum* and said it again; yes, it was where some of this came from—amazing stuff, a moss that thrives on acid conditions, and grows at the top while it decays at the bottom so the heather is maintained above and the decayed matter sinks and settles in deposits that eventually form peat which if it were put under great subterranean pressures would in fact become coal. Ancient forests at different levels, he said.

He shook his head, and I nodded mine. I said, So there were trees here in Neolithic times. The Callanish stones look from here like old weathered trunks.

He hadn't heard of an American named Paul. He hadn't picked up any Americans going to or from Callanish in a year, the stones were probably a calendar, he said.

I felt his own words about peat had made him think. He shook his head again. I thanked him again. He said he'd expected to take me all the way. I hauled out my rucksack, and he said it didn't look very full.

I wanted to get away. I put up my hood. The landscape was bare and low and rolling.

He said I was going to get wet.

I shook hands, closed my door, hoisted the pack, and walked out ahead of the car. But I turned when his voice came again: Don't try walking far on the moors. You'll sink in.

He grinned behind the windscreen wipers which had started swinging again.

Time seemed far away. A thousand days passed in a blink of the eye. I knew nothing or tried to, except the man in front of me and the stones and the crofter's cottage across the vale behind me—and the cottage right here where the woman was watching through the vertical slit between the curtains. That was what I knew. The browns and faint rusts and purples fading into the firm fine gray of the rain seemed almost enough to die into, and a voice, my own, called suddenly, Who was that last American you picked up a year ago you said?

A beautiful woman, he called back. And she knew about the stones, she knew about the northward avenue—I forget what it was if she ever said. She had green eyes and she said the god Apollo used to visit the island every nineteen years, and she was most concerned about the Great Menhir, the big stone there in the center. Its shadow falls over the cairn which you'll see; she was concerned about that.

When does the shadow fall?

At the spring equinox, said the man, as if giving me something just because I deserved it.

So it was March, I said, passing around to his side where the window was open.

This year. And something about twenty days after the equinox, a constellation rising before sunrise. Mean anything? I don't know if she stayed twenty days.

I smiled at him and said without hesitation and beyond doubt, and hovering in the rain between truth and truth: And her hair—her hair was red.

The man looked up into my eyes and then he smiled and marvelously found no cause to say what we both knew. That I was right. And perhaps he guessed that I knew her name, though I knew I was far from sure.

I said, You know your peat.

I should, he said.

Which left something between us as I went away down across the vale.

The rain god received here a superfluity of propitiation and rained steadily if gently all year long, twenty days, twenty thousand days.

The crofter's widow I stayed with had the cheekbones of a Pawnee, and blue eyes deep as a skull's. She translated my queries and her answers into Gaelic for an old person who sat upright in a shawl snuffling at the fire of fibrous quiet peat-squares. The cells of the moss must hold plenty of water. But the water didn't get a chance to increase the dilution of the plant; the water impeded bacterial decay, the man had said: and the dead bottom of the plants sank to form peat. There was a cycle of mounds and hollows where a water-loving moss grew upward, got drier, gave way to slower-growing heather which became the new hollow now to be outgrown and over-grown by moss coming up from below to make new mounds. I went round and round trying to get straight how the water could spread downward, yet the osmosis, if it was osmosis, rather than diluting the system's capacity to do work, increased that capacity—through creat-ing peat. But maybe it wasn't a closed system. I had a great wish to know, to be thorough. A god could allow himself to be diverted by a study of this kind. I had to have more time, a year to myself, twenty thousand days, but instead as in a dream I had to settle for the things that were jammed together. The bog peat between Stornoway and Callanish wasn't all from sphagnum.

If there were messages in the stones they would not be magic-markered on the base of the Great Menhir or on some huge arrow-head stone of the avenue.

Yes, said my host, there was Thanksgiving in the Western Isles, it was going to be made earlier next year, she'd heard, on account of the weather. She knew of no recent Americans, but a boy and a girl had come on a motorbike the other day and had stopped up at the stones and then later came back down and before they went away, the girl came to the door and asked for a drink of water. Yes the girl had light hair, the boy dark. They had rucksacks.

The woman did not ask anything except when I would like my tea.

She said, You're American, and faintly smiled.

From my second-floor room, which seemed under its low ceiling to be bigger than my outside view of the cottage had made it look able to hold, I looked east over the bleak vale and moor along a black strip of trench to where the vacant road appeared. The light was lowering, but lowering slowly, respecting the great arc of the north.

316

It took me five minutes to walk past the few cottages and up through the gate to the stones, and then past a post with a Ministry of Monuments plaque which I did not read except the dates 2000–1500 B.C. and felt from the southerly direction in which I now followed the right or west-side of the two lines of stones forming the avenue, weak reminders of the British Museum and the Highgate Scientific Institution with its white paint and peaceful newspaper room visited each morning by a stocky gentleman in a white beard to whom I had nodded for years, and the musty library in the back rooms and a book Jenny had taken out once when she was doing biology that told of plant freaks such as the squirting cucumber that builds up in its interior against its elastic casing such osmotic pressure taking water that anything can set it off—the stalk pops like a plug, and seeds squirt thirteen yards. Not the same thing as a bog-burst where peat or swamp having been bound in by the roots of bushes builds up water pressure till it lets go as a kind of mud flow. Think of a peat bomb.

The gate had no lock, the site no watchman. Few came. For that matter, why guard Stonehenge? Against the Welsh nationalist splinter group planning to return the bluestones to where they were quarried.

I didn't have to be up in the air to see what I had here at Callanish.

A Celtic cross.

The long lower limb was the so-called avenue, a rungless ladder running roughly north to the arms, which were single lines reaching left or east and right or west. The top limb was another single line of stones pointing over the crest of the headland down toward the inland reach of the sea-loch that on the map looked so like a fjord—I stood here and a sodden paper cup caught my eye, and near it a flap of some plastic covering that seemed to have been half tucked under the next-to-last stone, probably a bag full of orange peel.

At the convergence of the four limbs was the circle of high irregular stones that may have stood for centuries before the cross was added, but more likely was itself added to efface some earlier system of heavenly worship using the avenue and perhaps the east and west single lines, which if true means that the upper limb of the cross was added with the circle. Yet looking at it and moved on a mood by Stonehenge much more even than by our strange scene of it, I couldn't believe the circle wasn't the basis. The circle was thirty-some feet across with the Great Menhir my peat man had named guarding the well-like cairn and standing more than twice my height like a freely sculpted quite flatly oblong headstone, its top blade canted upward north to south.

It was all meant. No question there.

Alignments east, west—and from what I'd heard about moonset seen from here over Mount Clisham I could now just make out its slopes as the weakening light and the dimly dissolving cloud left the peak an issue, one stone of the top limb of the cross was leaning east but the stones were remarkably upright.

Meant, however, by who knew what interlapping desires? The constellation whose rise the red-haired woman had said she would wait for I guessed might be the Pleiades to the east—and the link of this with the end of the nineteen-year cycle of lunar revolution. But that rising here would have been virtually invisible to the naked eye, not just the Electra star always invisible out of shame for having married a human, but the other six daughters too. I ran my hand over the gray speckled roughnesses and looked east. I had loved Jenny too much. But I was not looking for her now. It was the film. But I knew now I was not sorry someone had destroyed the film. But I must know why they had.

A figure was on the road two or three miles to the east.

A man at a distance has no eyes.

If he knew where the Callanish stones from there were he still could not see me standing near the Great Menhir with the ruined tumulus and its pit at my back. From a distance the stones may seem to lean toward one another.

The Indian had not walked all the way so soon.

Maybe my man had met him, turned around, and completed his disquisition on peat.

The Ministry's 2000 B.C. was doubtless conservative; I did not know if radio-carbon dating had been used at Callanish but I did know that errors in the application of its use to Stonehenge had inclined less conservative archaeologists to start thinking about Stonehenge as being in the vicinity of the Pyramids.

The Indian's pale trenchcoat was unmistakable if you knew to look for it. This was no time to ponder peat.

I looked toward Clisham, my tea was waiting. I turned back toward home. I reviewed what Krish might do.

Two children outside a cottage waved.

Lower down now I couldn't see the figure on the road.

The crofter's widow told me so readily and simply about the red-haired American woman when I sat down to my tea and about the man her husband who had met her here in March, that the news seemed old and meager. I said I knew her. I asked how long she had stayed. As I'd hoped, my host got out the book. It showed five days. The name given was Claire Wheeler, which despite my foresight in not saying the name Jan Graf or Jan Aut made me once more doubt she was Jan. But my host described the man her husband who met her on the fifth day as the same man who had come more than once before to Callanish over a period of a year and who had asked her questions she couldn't answer about the stones. Had Jenny drunk her water in here?

I looked out the window. I had not seen the Indian. I said, Claire is a painter and Paul is an archaeologist.

My host at once said, *Paul,* that was his name.

So the red-haired woman had spent the night here with Paul some time after the spring equinox.

The Indian was nowhere in sight when I had a look out the window.

I had had a succession of small courses, chalky white bread and butter, toasted spam and two sausages and a fried egg, biscuits and some kind of currant bread in wedges. It was dark now and a free fatigue was upon me.

The woman did not know where Paul lived. I was too tired for a bath.

I felt as if I had not been quite conscious since Glasgow.

There was no chink for me to float in. I was the means by which two bodies either side of me could merge.

But gods can live on carbohydrates and not get like this.

I was upstairs.

I took off my new shoes sticky and getting stiff.

And at once I woke to moonlight and rain.

I did not have my clothes on and I was in the crisp-packed fresh bed that made me feel as if I'd taken a bath.

I was at the window, and the Indian Krish stood in moonlight in the road outside the widow's gate and was looking right at me though he may not have seen me in the opacities of curtain and glass. It was as if his eyes had wakened me.

I dressed.

I looked again and he was still standing in the road but not in the same spot, as if he'd been moving till I'd looked.

I lit a match to see my socks and saw the wedding photo on the bureau that I'd seen in the hall upstairs and the room downstairs where I'd eaten. The men in their dark suits with the high shock of dark hair and skinned above the ears.

The front door when I got downstairs stuck as it opened, and I felt the widow's eyes deep in her room come toward me like the cat-eyes of the Indian in his white trenchcoat as I stepped outside.

I approached him in the road, and he said, Don't speak, you'll make a noise. He pointed toward the end of the road where the Ministry's fenced enclosure began and where the central stones on their eminence showed like negatives of shadows.

I saw, as I looked at Krish, that I'd been conscious only of his eyes.

I'd been the only one at the Callanish megaliths by day. I was with someone by night.

We passed the cottages, and then we were inside the gate and Krish set off to the left for the northeastern corner of the enclosure where the avenue—or, if you wish, the foot of the Celtic cross— ended a good hundred yards down the gradual grade from the circle; he motioned me to follow.

Instead, I kept walking toward the circle. The Great Menhir under the moonlight that seemed to breathe with the sighing of the rain looked as if it's head had sunk beneath its neck. I turned. Krish had stopped and had his hands in the pockets of his coat. I called to him. I asked if he did or did not want to know what I had come to find here at Callanish.

I went on and presently I heard the hissing concussion of his steps on the wet grass behind me. The water on Loch Roag shone flat in pieces of spheres.

We walked into the circle through its north arc—that is, the side facing downhill toward the crofting village from which we had come. By day I'd seen that the thirteen huge slabs surrounding the Great Menhir are not equidistant from each other—also that the circle is in fact an oval, flattened to the east—which it now occurred to me (thinking what to say and do, and wondering if Krish was as dangerous as I felt) might be because of the entrance to the sepulcher which appeared to be through that very east side.

I wheeled about and looked toward Krish's pockets.

So at last we meet, I said.

I had my back to the Great Menhir, and where he'd halted he was to the left of the cairn, his left and my left, but during our talk he moved to my right and his left so that at the point of peculiar violence at which our talk ended he stood between me and the cairn's open tomb, though as I have said it was at best a shallow pit. The pistol from the workbench in John's Mercer Street loft was in the left-hand slash pocket of my parka and my hand was on it; I hadn't thought about it till last night in Glasgow and then there was no time to do more than estimate by feel that there was something in the magazine—it was a Smith & Wesson 9-mm. automatic—and also by a phone call in the morning that if the last shot had been fired the slide would have locked open. My left hand was free.

Krish's hair glistened. I had about four inches on him but he looked quick and jumpy. His collar was up over the white neck of the heavy sweater he'd worn only a few mornings ago in Knightsbridge.

Your friend Dagger DiGorro, he said, must have a super hiding place for the two remaining pieces of your film because they were not found at his flat.

So Krish had been there again, but now with the knowledge that he'd missed the 8-mill. cartridge and the other reel which he no doubt thought was the Bonfire in Wales (but you who have me know was in reality the Softball Game in Hyde Park).

I said, You didn't fly to Glasgow and Stornoway and hike out here just to ask me what I can't tell you.

You are looking for your daughter.

Not now, I said, and looked around through the night at the high stones whose alignments shot off into bogs and lochs and to the west over the low resting backs of dim cattle in a field separated from this ancient area by a low stone wall—alignments that seemed at best unclear to me at this moment, while the stones themselves seemed more real than the dire mammoths fixed at Stonehenge on the clement plain of Salisbury. I voiced this feeling to Krish. He stood staring.

There is a link between this place and Stonehenge you think? he said.

Perhaps that's why I've come, and why we're standing at this point in the circle.

Krish's hand expanded in his left pocket. He said, I don't wish to do you an injury. I want two things. Information first, and second your presence though not your company on tomorrow's Glasgow plane. That is, you fly home tomorrow. To wherever your home is.

You have broken into my home, I said. Don't pretend you don't know where it is.

I do not pretend, he said. I do not need to pretend I have not broken into your house because I in fact have not done so.

You've conveniently forgotten because you live in the present —Cosmo is quite informative.

Cosmo talks too much.

Will your boss pay my fare home?

What boss?

The one who is concerned about the Bonfire in Wales.

Many may be.

And for these things I will be saved from injury? Is that all?

Your daughter too.

From injury.

Insofar as it is in *my* power. I cannot speak for others.

Others hired to watch me.

Cosmo talks too much.

My daughter, I said, does not have the sole copy of my diary.

We know that, replied the Indian, but that will not save her.

A cool wrinkle of recollection soothed my brain, a neutral tremor of technical device, a moonlight rainbow in b & w running the spectrum of visible grays between black and white which outdoes the color spectrum between red and violet, 200 to 160. Dagger had not used color for the Bonfire; that I knew because I'd seen him load.

I raised my left hand in a casual gesture to go with my next words—and Krish stepped backward: Krish, if you want some information, you might like to know that Paul stayed here with your friend whose painting was desecrated in the gallery.

Krish smiled faintly.

I couldn't tell what meaning I'd conveyed because I didn't yet know if the painting was a self-portrait. On the physical appearance of Jan I should have drawn Monty out.

For a moment I forgot that the only extant copies of the full diary were the original taken by the Highgate burglar, and Jenny's closet carbon with the Xerox she and Reid had picked up. What was the diary worth?

Did you know, Krish, that she was particularly interested in the shadow cast over the sepulcher behind you by the Great Menhir that stands behind me.

Ah, said Krish almost inaudibly, that was just Paul. I do not need that information. I have no use for it. I erase it herewith. I wish to know how in this crucial encounter you cannot pay the strictest attention.

322

For my eyes had lifted past him and around the circle north-ward. The rain was letting up. The rain god was nearby having a happy delayed-action dream of me thinking pleasantly of him many hours ago when I left my driver. The moon followed the rain into a cloud. I wanted to give thanks to the sun and moon and rolling moors and the mounds and hollows of peat forming and reforming in slow logics of energy down through the ancestors of the widow and her husband who had been a seaman and a crofter and the others here who came to church twice each Sunday, minister or no minister, for he moved from place to time dispersing his face and voice across the simple independences of their creed. I would not have wished to wake these living and dead ancestors from the nature of their past and present. I should have been afraid of this tense ungentle Indian who wore, and lived in, white.

I could not take him seriously. I reviewed with rapidity that should have astounded me Krish's known connections. His loop included Reid and Cosmo, the red-haired woman and Aut and Aut's wife and, hence, her brother Monty Graf (who might have heard from Claire and then told Krish I was headed for the Hebrides), and maybe Jerry who might be Jan Aut's son, not to mention the Druid Andsworth.

I recovered myself and murmured that I was rechecking alignments from the afternoon.

There is nothing here, said Krish.

An alignment pointing toward Mount Clisham, I said, nod-ding right.

There is nothing here, said Krish. A historic dump.

Except me, I said. And I will give you information if you will reciprocate. First, for whom did you break into DiGorro's flat and ruin our film? Second, how did you know I was in Glasgow? You didn't get that from the Druid. Third, why did you wait till we got out here?

In *reverse* order, said Krish, I wanted to see what your behav-ior here was. I knew you were in Glasgow because I phoned the Allott residence and was told you'd phoned from Glasgow, and learning yesterday that your daughter was in the Hebrides, I phoned BEA, said I was you though mumbling the name and asked if I could make it two reservations; they said yes, and checked the name by spelling it out, for which I commended them; so I knew you were on the plane. I asked if I had left my hotel phone number; they obliged by naming the hotel. The Scots are straight. As for your third or first query, I did not break into the DiGorro flat or destroy his film, nor do I need to oblige you by asking who *did* destroy it.

How did your source know Jenny was out here—if she *is* out here?

I believe my source was informed by Monty Graf. I myself saw him, but not to speak to.

Where?

In London of course. I do not believe in leaving London.

When?

Yesterday afternoon after I phoned Glasgow BEA.

Dawn would come late here. My watch said four but what time that was I couldn't tell.

I asked what he had in his left pocket and he said I could easily guess.

Oh here was the gentle Indian from overpopulated India the hope of the moral world I had once begun to think.

Our talk drops somewhere in the gaps of the Callanish circuit, and yields its sound; gains instead imagination or a dispersion of probabilities. But as soon as I think, looking through Krish to an avenue or an antenna, that a miracle won't be needed against him, my body gets heavy and uncoordinated the way it did one day near the end when I had a fight with Ned Noble, my muscle against the indifferent play of his mind.

Krish advised me to tell him at once where the Bonfire had been cached, why I'd come here rather than somewhere else, why I'd given the alias to Andsworth's housekeeper, and why I'd only pretended to phone Dagger DiGorro from Andsworth's. When I said oh indeed I had said to Dagger on the Druid's phone just what I'd wanted to say, Krish replied that after Andsworth had phoned he'd called Dagger himself and had almost missed him for he was leaving for a base where he had some business, but Dagger had said of course Cartwright hadn't phoned him, Cartwright was in New York.

I asked if Krish would trust Dagger before he would me; Krish said no, but Andsworth had had a feeling about the connection, how I'd held the phone too tight to my ear and jaw for real connection to be credible and hadn't looked far enough or vaguely enough away.

I said the Bonfire sequence was ruined as far as I knew, and when Krish said did I then *not* know, I said I really didn't except on Dagger's say-so, and by the way how did Krish know I *wasn't* Gene and Paul's brother Jack from America with a beard. Krish's hand stirred in the dangerous pocket and a breeze of rain came so light it seemed to have stopped above our heads and let go inertially the thinnest field of mist. Krish asked why Claire who had been so close to Dagger had said the Bonfire footage was extant—but Don't answer, said Krish, you know possibly less than anyone in this and are instigating a method by which we will all know less.

I asked to *whom* Claire had said the Bonfire had been saved and Krish, with a bored glance a third of the way round the circle of stones which would have scared me if I'd not regained my levity, shrugged and asked after all which of the brothers she *could* have said it to, and when I said Jack is *here*, Krish at once said, But as you know he was in New York two days ago but I assure you you will not get to him tomorrow.

Through these words I now believed that whoever had broken into Dagger's place twice and whatever was Krish's relation to Aut or Jan Aut through the Knightsbridge gallery, Krish was in fact working with Jack; and with the luck of his seeming acknowledgment of this, I took a chance: I said I began to see beyond the messages left here at Callanish an explosive—yes, explosive—equation I only half comprehended now but knew to be much more important than Jan Graf Aut's adopting here with Paul an alias which coupled her husband's beautiful assistant's given name with my old college friend Jim's surname. And the equation paired Callanish and the words of my film diary opposite Stonehenge and the film.

Krish spoke fast, to stop whatever was happening around him. OK. So Jim Wheeler, so what—our Stonehenge was dead, don't talk about explosive, likewise the absurd so-called Suitcase Slowly Packed with its photo of Paul (yes, Cartwright?) and the asinine baseball game in the park (which in any case lacked sound—right, Cartwright?) and the folly of spying in Corsica—and now, he said, answer please in one hell of a hurry the questions posed: Where is the Bonfire and why did you call yourself Jack? And where is the original of the diary?

I said the widow knew where I was and what I was doing right now, and so Krish had better watch it. I said I'd called myself Jack because I foresaw Krish would be working for me soon.

My mention of the widow may have encouraged him because with his right hand he reached and grabbed my parka and pushed me back to one side of the Great Menhir and past it. Dying seemed less awful than a passive life. The moon came out again and the rain increased. The place was too much for anyone not able to feel it. I had made Krish think I stood between him and something, and maybe it was true; but he had come after me to put himself between *me* and something, doubtless Jack and the brothers. And I had thought of Krish on one side and an object on the other, and of myself defending one against the other. But now I was not sure I was between.

Krish's left hand was in his tightly tailored trenchcoat pocket, his right was clutching my pack in front but not shaking me. I asked who said that in the Suitcase Slowly Packed it was a shot of Paul: and Krish unhesitatingly with the deepest watchful satisfaction said, Your friend Dagger on the phone yesterday.

But Krish's pleasure did not relieve him, and when I said, but Cosmo talks more than Dagger, Krish replied like an automaton: Wheeler was incompetent, he does not matter.

And so though I could not ask what talking Krish thought Cosmo had done, I knew I would handle Krish here. I felt at liberty in this wet earth and with these high stones, and I said, What would *you* know about Stonehenge?—and as for Callanish, I came here with much less information than, thanks to you, I now have, I came here because of a circle on a map and I came here really to find out *why* I came.

The Dravidians from South India! he cried or stuttered—*they* are the ones who built Stonehenge!

His fury seemed to shrink Krish.

Or was this my renewed sense of his left pocket as if far below?

For it transmitted itself through his arm to my chest.

I knocked his arm away with one hand and with the other pulled the pistol, and this so startled him—he being unable to assimilate any of *my* power—that he leapt backward, hit his head against the Great Menhir, and caroming on fell eastward half into the sepulcher.

His head and shoulders were over the edge. He was on his back but his head was turned so blood came down from his nose. But when I hauled him onto the ground blood welled from inside his brown ear. I could not tell if I had his pulse or mine. The head was bad but not bleeding as badly as one would have expected from the scalp area. He'd hit the stone as hard as if he'd been trying to. He might be dead. The eyes were half open, and the nose bleeding brought back the Softball Game when Cosmo had tossed off a remark about blowing up the subway (and, diary aside, Krish would have been glad we had no sound track that Sunday), and the guy standing off first whom Cosmo had said it to had sprung a nosebleed and then there had been Krish standing beyond the third-base line watching with potential ferocity. The name was Nash. That footage could bear another look. But the map came first, and Paul's hut, and a discreet sleep at the widow's.

If Krish were found here at the tumulus in the center of the famous Callanish circle that no one ever visited in the northmost of the Outer Hebrides with a crumb of the Great Menhir in his head, the tabloids would make enough noise to alert the very people I might need.

I got him to the east fence. He was surprising. It took all I had to get him up and over. The place had drawn his spirit down. I went over after him and hauled him to a boggy ditch where he was safe unless someone came looking. At least he was spared the sordid mess on his white raincoat. The left pocket held a leather-covered cylinder some six inches long, like a long lighter—and at one end it was a lighter. But when I put my thumb on a button to strike a light to see the wallet in my hand, something shot out of the other end by lucky chance parallel with my upturned sleeve rather than into me, for it was a ten-inch antennalike instrument sharp as an icepick; but the lighter had worked too, so I was able to see that what had sprung the blade was a release near the other end that the heel of my palm had depressed. Using the lighter end you'd take care with the rest of your hand; no doubt Krish didn't smoke. To retract the blade you pressed the release again. I pocketed the cylinder, first going through the wallet and taking the one thing I didn't understand, which was numbers on a strip of file card, plus Krish's money in case a false lead was useful. In an inside pocket of his coat I found a No. 12 Ordnance Survey map with, so far as I could tell in the light of the moon and the lighter, no marks. His ear had been bleeding but there was no cut to be seen.

Back in my room I hung my jeans on a chair and tilted my shoes against the baseboard of the wall. I looked at the numbers on Krish's file card.

If Cosmo had been capable of "talking" about "others" watching me, and this kind of information evoked from Krish the name Wheeler, what system of accident had brought Jim Wheeler into this far-flung sequence?

I had to know what the destroyers had wished to destroy. Had Krish been thrown off by the strange thought that Jack hadn't been straight with him? Krish acknowledged that Dagger's flat had been broken into this second time but said he had not done it. So it had been arranged by him for Jack or by Jack directly. Or indirectly.

The numbers were unspaced: 5758450815½.

My watch still said four. It was ticking. Had I just started it?

It was as if I hadn't been wakened by Krish's eyes. I was asleep again, awake again—the pale force of the morning sky spaced itself between the magic concussions of a hand on my door, and there came the murmur of the widow's voice saying it was nine o'clock, and when I opened my mouth to convert into energy the miles of peat between me and those numbers, and said, Latitude, the voice on the other side said, Yes in fifteen minutes, and I heard her creak lightly down the steep carpeted stairs.

My map open on the bed, the first six digits could be degrees, minutes, and seconds of latitude, a parallel which crossed the northern lowmost slopes of Mount Clisham if I read aright. The other numbers were not longitude, and as I drew my other pair of jeans on I kept looking back at these numbers as if they had a meaning in themselves.

South of Ardvourlie Castle heading down to Harris, I must turn off the road onto this parallel.

A ROUTE TO PAUL'S

What am I hungry for? What if I bought a bog? I might think up a revolutionary way to turn peat into tough elastic to shoe the wheels of a movable railway station. The soundlessness of rubber. Yet the cruel strength of steel like the metal-hard sapodilla wood the Maya whittled into lintel glyphs, not a few of which went up in poor Catherwood's New York holocaust of 1842.

What did I want to get my hands on? Some ready cash? Not really. The film? It might be sacrificed. But to what? Dagger and I the afternoon of May 26 paused at the foot of an insanely steep lane to look up after the slowly rising back of an old lady in a blue mac hauling her heart up the railing hand over hand. We were there on the south coast because I had to discuss with the boatyard man whose silent partner I was the possibility of my putting in another £500; he was determined to go beyond storing and repairing and into building, and he had two tentative orders, a 24-foot sloop and a 32-foot gaf-rigged ketch, from summer people who had inquired about bypassing a firm they'd heard of through friends who had taken up sailing, and my partner had encouraged them to have a boat made frame by frame right here in this yard.

He inclined toward fiberglass for the hull and he humored his grandfather, a small neat ninety-year-old countryman, who insisted that only wood would do, and when Dagger with great gentleness and good humor told of a friend of his family in Monmouth County, New Jersey, who had invented antipecking specs for chickens so they wouldn't be able to see each other directly enough to kill each other and these he manufactured by the thousands in plastic—tiny red pince-nez blinkers—the grandfather said that was America and what they did there was their own business. When I said the new ferro-cement hulls gave you as much as 12 percent more space because you did away with framing, Granddad said he could remember when tin pails took over from wooden buckets. He'd worked seven years to learn to be a wheelwright, when you made a wagon wheel in those days you didn't have nothing but your eye and your hands to go by, seven years wouldn't teach you all you must know, say, about elm and ash and a bone-hard butt of beech eight feet long six inches square for an axle but nothing would do for spokes but oak, for spokes must never be sawn lest you get a cross-grain, and a cross-grained spoke could snap, so you had to have a wood that could be cleft, and the wood was oak—and not just for spokes—you used nothing but heart of oak for the old harrows—a hundred years ago wheelwright shops made harrows and the finished harrow was fitted with a copse; now a copse was a wrought-iron loop let into the wood so you could harness your horse, and the copse was hooked in with a bolt (once made of wood, then of iron) called a whippance. Oh yes, but there was a lot to a wheel, you could cast the felloes out of ash or beech or elm as well as oak. And Grandfather (whose south-country speech despite the rolling *r*'s was not so different from my late grandfather's narrow dry Maine accent) bet we didn't know what part of the wheel the felloes were.

But he was interrupted by his grandson, and Dagger walked off down to the beach with the old man, while I finished my business with my partner whom I so rarely saw.

And next day when Dagger and I were on our way up to Bristol and Wales, Dagger recounted what the old man had told him about the parallel grain of the oak that made it ideal for spokes, and how it had to be cleft in the summer still full of sap so the split would run from end to end. The old man had changed jobs around the turn of the century and had gone to work in a coach-and-foundry shop where he'd done all right. Dagger said the old man had never himself made harrows, for by the time he got into the trade harrows and ploughs were being made of cast iron, though wagon and cart wheels were still made largely of wood.

At Clifton near Bristol we parked in the gorge far below the marvelous bridge and Dagger consented to take some quick cut-in shots of the high limestone cliffs and the Giant's Cave and the woods and the river cutting through to Bristol Channel, and above all Brunel's bridge—with the 15, then rotating to the 25, then to the 50—from crag to crag across the sky famous as a spectacle and known to students of Brunel for his original drawings which are art in their own right. And as if I were sound-tracking what the Beaulieu filmed, I told Dagger how despite numerous flaws in Brunel's calculations the bridge had beautifully survived, and he murmured getting his viewfinder-focus right how easy it would be to blow it up. I enumerated what in that case would be found under the first foundation stones—a plaque, some coins, a China plate bearing a picture of the bridge, and a copy of the Act of Parliament enabling its construction. The Egyptian towers Brunel had first designed were never built and because his sketches for them were lost we know of his projected tower-base plaque designs (for instance, men carrying one of the links of the chainwork) only through a friend's memoirs.

No doubt much is better lost. I should like to make a conveyance. A conveyance may be a deed. I doubt I'll ever get around to peat wheels. When I referred on May 24 to the Unplaced Room as a title of the footage we'd shot that morning, Dagger said Great, you make up the titles.

Will Dudley find out why Catherwood's Jerusalem panorama burnt? (Thebes, too.) The New York lawyer he corresponded with about it he consulted also on the question of an American divorce for an English marriage.

Why did I wish to share Tessa with Lorna? Did Dudley know about Tessa and me? Do I? One bright warm day that Tessa and I got together in New York was a Monday, and she later told me that contrary to her information the Museum of the American Indian was closed Mondays but Dudley who was supposed to be there never mentioned this.

Did Dudley know why he was taking up the study of Catherwood? If he didn't at first, he came to know. For he told me on the tiled edge of the Swiss Cottage public swimming pool.

Immediately after the New York holocaust Catherwood began the illustrations for his second Maya book with Stephens.

Dudley's hypothesis that an exponent of a rival archaeological theory had set the fire touched Tessa more than Dudley; he said there had been two hundred gaslights in the Rotunda the night of the fire, a considerable risk.

But Tessa, who had come to think herself part Maya because

of her East Asiatic fold—the epicanthic fold—at the inner corner of each eye, decided it was a Catholic continuing the work of the six-teenth-century priest Diego de Landa who had made good his revulsion at Maya religious practices by incinerating a number of codices containing Maya history.

Felloes, said Dagger in the early hours of May 29 driving home to London from Wales, were the wooden sections of the rim of a wheel.

We had discussed at length the strange man who had made a dash from the grove either into the dark and the fog or into a thicket.

I said, We've got to get this footage developed Monday.

It's possible, said Dagger.

13 | On the road it felt like Sunday. I might have been just another hiker. I observed the roadsides.

When I left the widow's and was still in sight of Callanish, I used my map to find three other sets of Standing Stones, some fallen. All three sites, but notably the largest and nearest, seemed now to me to look toward Callanish. Having been to those great crude contours on the headland, I wanted to tie to them these three other sites genuinely primitive in their present state.

The first, in a spongy, rising field and above and behind a crofter's house, seemed to communicate with Callanish, to share from its roughly equal elevation the signals of some observance. Here there were eight stones—I did not know why I studied them, I knew I had done with Callanish, knew where I must go, yet I paced and estimated, and could not believe it an accident that in one westward alignment two stones on opposite sides of the circle with one of the central cairn stones between them made a perfect pointer some three-quarters of a mile to the Great Menhir at Callanish. I slipped my compass back in my parka pocket and it rattled against the smaller of my borrowed weapons.

At the second of these minor sites it was hard to tell if the marshiness or the original construction of the central cairn or perhaps some modern excavation had pitted out the center; again the stones were large and strangely intentional; but inescapably Callanish was there almost two miles off, and this site with the eight-stone circle a mile away and to the right of Callanish created a triangle so vivid in the solitary breeze that I saw here three points of one community where ancient forms were buried to dissolve upward to the sky or outward in the earth that, if not so brackish then, may have had trees.

But I'd detoured already, though on a southwest road that would soon have brought me to where I could have set off cross-country on that direct (and, as my driver in the red car had said, foolhardy) route to Clisham. So I turned back to the road that went first toward Stornoway and met the southward road that would best take me where I wished to go. But there were no cars. And then one came up over a hill behind me and was gone as if accelerating at the sight of my thumb. And then I found I was off the map.

On a map you move faster, though often only somewhat faster. But each time you're again in the actual place that holds your feet, the trick-contraction of the map seems to have been someone else's thing you've poached on like a power not yours.

Dagger had smuggled maps of the French eighteenth century around his legs and maybe something less antique between his skin and the cartographer's parchment. But put him between Woking and Stonehenge, Lyme Bay and Bristol Channel, Monmouth County in Wales and the edge of Middlesex coming home to London, and he could not read a map to save himself.

He said he'd been at the barricades in Chicago in '68—I'd never been clear why—and had been picked up by Mayor Daley's cops with a couple of Yippie friends because they'd had maps of the city on them. One of these friends had come to stay with the Di-Gorros in January. He had spent a lot of time in a Haverstock Hill pub with UPI newsman Savvy Van Ghent, who liked to ripple his muscle under the American flag tattoo. He had come to one softball game in April and left (now I think of it) with the sensitive and surreptitious Nash—and I'd never seen this former Yippie again and I'd been then a bit sorry because, whatever Lorna thought of him with his large tattoo of a snake-handled knife extending concavely from under his chin down over his Adam's apple disappearing into the heavy hair on his chest and well below the opening of his shirt, I had wanted Will to meet him—because (to carry us one backward jump further) Will had seemed to show a strange lack of appetite for visiting America and I wanted him to see someone of this sort. I mean someone free. Unbound by ambitions. Though you can't tell these days—the most mystical Hawaiian drop-out when you look inside his guitar proves to be all business with a master plan set like a charge to launch him when the break comes. If no, keep looping; if yes, proceed.

I had always had a purpose in others' eyes. But it was a quality, not an object, and the quality was prudence, or the look of it. My father phoned me from New York to ask if I thought he should build a second cottage at the summer place. He'd had his martinis. Geoff Millan came and wept one night and when it was over and he was finishing the brandy Lorna had poured him and she was in the kitchen heating frozen pizza, he blinked out some sort of smile and said, Moral stability, yes, that's what you've got—moral stability.

A car flew by.

I walked sideways across a cattle grid to avoid slipping my toes through the widely spaced bars.

I was back on my Ordnance Survey map, now that my way had curved back south and west. So I could identify the cleanly delimited grove of trees on a hill to my right as a deliberate plantation.

Later I stopped by a black chilly loch where the land was more rugged and hills were becoming mountains as if by dropping their lower slopes abruptly, for I was getting down into Harris. I had the sandwiches the widow had made for me. I was in someone else's system. But certainly I knew some things that others did not.

Some gods saw all time at once.

I wished only to see—no, merely go—beyond where I was.

In order not to be between.

I had killed a moving watchman perhaps, if only through the threat of a pistol probably loaded.

A motorbike with two peasants in leather and helmets came up under the hill—forty miles off the coast of the Scottish mainland—and flew over the crest with revs to spare where I sat on a rock.

It was not Sunday, for I found a place open in a village and bought bread and milk and sardines. The old man asked if I was going to Tarbert, which I knew to be the steamer stop in Harris fifteen or twenty miles south of here through the mountains.

Why had I not asked him for Paul's hut? The question yielded an answer to another. The other numbers I now saw were hundred-meter grid references, 08 north, 15¼ east.

I had a light but if I found myself—as indeed I preferred—approaching the hut in the dark, I wanted to know the map. The lines of dots in the area meant it was marshy, though the terrain was generally rugged.

Passing Ardvourlie Castle I was in Harris without a doubt.

333

Down to my left in a newly changed scale was Loch Seaforth grandly widening southeastward, not a boat or tree or human body; and ahead of me was the first pass through the mountains toward Tarbert, and the rain began.

The map and the country seemed to try to alter each other's accelerations. Sixty meters south of the o9 grid reference, the road (as the map promised) came tangent with the electrical power line; I paced off forty meters from that point and prepared to leave the road; I estimated that grid west must be five or six degrees right of west on my compass.

I had come twenty-five miles, even more with my archaeological detours, yet I was not tired. I was impatient; I was still in Glasgow. My way would have been easier had I not determined to stay on the grid line. There'd been hardly enough gradation of light to show where the sun had been, and now there was no real light let alone sun. So I set my track at fifty-meter intervals on the peak of a bush or rock. I went down into a hollow tight with copse and surprisingly dry. I went up a spongy precipice and was wet to the knees.

Circumstance had held me up. You could not have conveyed my idea of that on film. You'd have needed, back in view of Callanish, to feel against your ribs last night's dark collision and the similarity Krish's tailoring bore to my own which had, so to speak, had a hand in my near-accident when I'd been pushed down the stopped escalator now perhaps three mornings the far side of this light pack and these strong shoes.

I shone Krish's lighter to see my compass and my watch. I held my breath to hear voices. I didn't need to breathe. Ned Noble—no, Andsworth—said you could master a way of breath-holding so that at a new limit of need you fell through an edge of your own head into an internal source of breath. I never believed in such miracles, but I didn't forget.

I'd climbed a thousand feet from the road. It wasn't possible.

Ahead voices were alight with feeling but ahead all I saw was a dark rise and over it a cleared space I thought was the rainy sky.

I heard *Frenchman* and *dynamite*.

I could tell something about the men talking but did not yet understand what they said. The deep, flatly unmodulated voice bored in: No sweat. The gentler intellectual voice given to ups and downs said, How's he going to find this god-forsaken place? He's no Sherman. The deep voice—which I took for Gene because I'd last seen Sherman the hiker from St. Louis in Gene's house—said, *God-*

forsaken! This hut's been a regular mecca from what I've heard, *I* had no trouble getting here. Oh, said the gentler voice—Paul's I thought (which if so made me the third brother, Jack), you've camped in the Northwest Territories, brother, you've trapped and portaged, you've strip-mined (haven't we?), you've killed, you've expanded, you're great, you've blasted craters for factory foundations with magnificent views, you've flown your own red plane out of the wilderness and home to Chicago, you've made a killing in real estate, you are a child in the fun warehouse of the profit system, you are a man, oh are you a man, never mind the Midwest, what do we have in New York City, Jack?

So the deep voice was Jack not Gene.

Jack said, *You* forget the Midwest, you're living over here. What do you mean what do we have in New York? You know what we have—a warehouse and a parking lot.

Oh a parking lot, *that's* new. And what's the price of natural gas?

Washington's had the lid on since the middle fifties, but you wouldn't know that.

I think you'd gladly liquidate Paul is what I think.

Jack said, Look, Krish planned to come and he would have come two weeks ago but he had to be in London; look, when he acts he doesn't leave anything to chance.

The other voice said, How come *you're* here, then? Oh you're just like Dad.

Thanks for the welcome, said Jack.

This isn't my place, said the other, who was obviously not Paul.

On the crest of the rise I wanted to check the compass. But I knew that if my steady stumbling steps were right, I'd come some 350 meters, close enough for Krish's lighter to be seen if Paul's hut was on target. So I should just be able to hear the voices.

But I'd heard them more than just.

But as I stood on the crest wondering if I had not heard the answer to the big question that the gentler voice had asked Jack because I had started going away from the voices, I smelled a peat fire and found a shape slightly to my left—and lower down (though I knew I was looking at Clisham's upward slope rising to a summit 1100 feet above me): and as I saw the shape, it gained uncertain light as if I had exhaled tentatively then with confidence into its stony window, and Jack's voice answering some inaudible complaint said, I don't know why he's not here yet but let's give him some help, and who's around except someone's sheep.

The dots on the map meant bog, possibly between me and the hut. The light barely curved out beyond the window frame but I imagined the roof was the thick gray-brown Hebridean thatch I'd actually seen little of today, that is held down with wire netting weighted at the edges with rocks and that can last as many as ten well-insulated winters. The hut's walls were evidently stones jammed together like the stone wall separating the cow pasture from the west side of the Callanish site.

Instead of descending directly to the hut, I moved westward along a sort of ridge and came to the hut from the southwest seeing into a window on this other side of the hut from an angle that did not let me quite see the speakers and then I went up to my knees in bog, and then I saw blond hair and on the other head a hat.

I leaned onto dry ground, scratched my hands, crawled, crouched head up, watching the man with the deep voice, Jack, till he moved and sat down. He wore an olive green bush hat and had a thick growth of dark stubble. The wind was all around me as if the influence of Clisham created a wilderness of currents. The voice I'd thought was Paul's came again, and then I saw him.

I wasn't paying strict attention. It didn't matter to my luck that I paid attention of that sort. I felt my automatic and wondered if its use last night had lightened it. Even if I hadn't killed Krish he might die in the ditch, he might turn into a new peat fraught with force, through a change accelerated by the fact that the moor had never had an Indian like Krish to absorb before. The automatic felt like about two pounds but maybe I couldn't judge now. Prolonged weightlessness shrinks the heart. I was powerful.

Well, I'm wasting my time too, said the gentle voice, and furthermore you didn't have to come.

But I did, said Jack, this thing's gone too far.

A chair scraped.

He was always dangerous, said the gentle one who was sounding not so gentle.

Krish? said Jack.

No, *Paul*, said the other, who was saying, Krish wouldn't tell us straight about the film.

Incremona asked him too many questions, said Jack. Krish doesn't go for that.

Incremona's up tight. I only know what Jan said—that Krish

was watching DiGorro's friend. Did you tell him to do that? DiGorro's friend was in New York.

My people had someone on him but it fell through.

Jan told Paul she was afraid of Cartwright because he expected something of her.

Sure, but Krish thought Cartwright was in London, and I said do what you have to. Then Cartwright *was* in London two days ago. And Krish gave me a rough schedule and with him a time-line's a guarantee. OK, so he was detained tonight. He's a perfectionist. Whatever he does, he does right.

I've never set eyes on Cartwright.

But you *must* know Cartwright: they were going to film your place? Something about a vicar down the road Len said preaches sermons on Marilyn Monroe?

It fell through, said Gene (it had to be Gene of the Marvelous Country House, the other brother of the absent host Paul—just as it had to be Krish they were waiting for who'd said he wanted my presence but not my company on the Stornoway plane back to Glasgow and who if he had risen from the neolithic muck to press onward rather than downward might at this very moment be watching me from behind, and not like some wet-wool-matted black-faced sheep).

I had to speak but couldn't. I looked behind me wondering if I was between again. I hoped that if the soft spots I'd crept over had been bodies I'd done them as much good as the Druid that politician.

As if they felt my field had impinged, the brothers had dropped their voices; but I could hear them, they were protesting that of *course* they accepted each other, Gene had nothing against the chemical business and he had always hoped Jack was an enlightened employer; Jack for his part had nothing against expatriate life or marrying money (he felt they went together) and by the way it wasn't just chemicals, it was natural gas in Michigan (had he told Gene?) and liquid fertilizers and pollution research, and government contracts—and Gene said he had nothing against fertilizers *per se* and I heard a clink and saw the dark dumb undersea green of a bottle, and Jack said just as well Gene had stayed out of the business, and when Gene said, All the better for you, Jack said he hoped Gene knew he had nothing against the film business, and by the way what was with the portfolio, kind of an odd thing to bring up here.

So Gene was *in* films. But whose?

Jack said Incremona didn't seem the best type of employee,

he'd heard he went around armed, he was certainly a transient. Gene said, Ask him, and Jack said, Maybe I will.

Gene said on the whole Len had confined himself to making arrangements like passports and taxi working papers—and Jack said quickly, I'd like to put Paul in a capsule and shoot him up to the moon. Gene said you've probably got just the capsule, and Jack said, I probably have, and Gene said, Take out some insurance on him and send him up in your little red Comanche, and Jack said, Help pay my alimony—must be nice to have a rich wife, Geney.

Mind you, said Gene, Len's been filmed at the gallery with me and Jan and Reid and Sherman, the boy from St. Louis. Sherman's the only one he trusts.

Well, said Jack, Incremona didn't ever take rainy-day pistol practice with your kids around, did he? Gene asked what that meant, and Jack seemed not to answer but said he doubted Jan's original idea was commercial enough, and Gene said they'd been through all that today and where was the Indian, and Jack said, No sweat, he'll be here—said it so soft I heard only because he'd said it before. Gene said, Noncommercial films are making money. Jack said, Aut must have been doing it for his crazy wife but anyway how had Gene and Nell and Jan gotten involved with characters like Incremona and Nash and this Negro genius Chad, and Gene seemed not to reply; then a glass banged the table and Gene said they'd been all over that this afternoon and Jack was hopelessly out of the picture, for instance had he ever in his life heard of Harry Pincus and what Harry Pincus had done to force into English politics the issue of Vietnam and the American exiles, and what did Jack mean about Chad? And Jack said, I know, I know—and Gene kept at him, *had* he ever heard of Harry Pincus? And Jack said he'd decided to act when he'd heard that Phil's man from New York had got some great night shots of Paul running out of a grove in Wales, yet at that point Jack had had it. Gene said Jack had acted already, and Jack said would Gene please drop that, if he'd really had the film destroyed would he be trying to get hold of the Bonfire now? And Gene asked who had told Jack that *Aut's* man had shot a bonfire, and Jack said almost inaudibly, Claire.

Upon which, Gene made some heavy noise on the table and, his voice moving around in its registers, he said, The Bonfire was shot by DiGorro.

It's in there? I thought Jack said.

Well no film could have caught both all this and my thoughts under the wind and the new rain wondering if last night's jeans had dried in my pack.

338

Clearly, Incremona was Len, the bald fractious presence of Corsica and the Marvelous Country House. Clearly Phil Aut had been shooting parallel footage to which ours might have been added as cut-in or complementary expansion; but Claire must have given Jack the idea that the Bonfire had been shot by Outer Film, not Dagger and me. It was moderately clear also that Gene was not acknowledging our Marvelous Country House footage, for though he'd been away that day, he must surely know we'd been there filming his kids and his dining-room pewter and his patio telly and his wife whose name I guessed was Nell. And it was possible, if not clear, that Jack knew about the Marvelous Country House: and if so, then he knew Gene was pulling a fast one.

It seemed to me they knew different things, and this might be why or how they were going round in circles.

But as I moved back from the hut keeping low and tried to get a sight through the west window to see more of the table than Gene's arm (but for a second purpose too), most interesting was Jack's answer now to Gene's saying why had Jack gotten Krish to come way up here: Jack said that there was a man who had a place and a boat on the other side of the island who had information Jack could get only directly and Jack had thought this man could give Krish a lift down here while Krish was pumping him.

Gene said, Do I know him? and I silently asked if he had a red mini.

Jack passed my window several times. He was talking *Geney boy* talk, big brother saying Gene had come up here for the same reason he had except Gene might feel even more responsible for little brother Paul because these people Paul was involved with had been some of them Gene's friends; my God there's Incremona armed, and Sherman armed, and now I hear Cartwright's armed.

I came up here, said Jack, to stop Paul, and I think you did too.

Gene said, Of course, Jack, of course, and Jack said he didn't like Gene's tone, and Gene said, How would you stop Paul?

He came into my frame, and suddenly with the words What *is* this? he picked off the table a black portfolio on which even at my distance of twenty-five yards I spotted blue at the corners which would be flowers Jenny had stuck on when I'd brought it to her from the States.

Gene went after Jack. There was a crash out of sight, probably Gene falling, he looked the type.

My second purpose came due, and projecting my voice away

from the hut I called dimly Hello! and again, Hello! and moved back toward the ridge out of the light. By the time I was around to the east side of the hut and the door had opened, and I had tramped in, a god from the bog, showing mad merry eyes above my sparkling beard and muddy jeans and saying Good-O a couple of times to limber up my English accent (which Geoff Millan has told me is a good imitation of a Portobello Road antique dealer) the portfolio with my diary indubitably inside had found its way back to neutral object-hood on Paul's rough-hewn table in the center of the room, and whatever I knew that they did not, they were right in not imagining I was primarily after the portfolio, for since Glasgow I had cared less about the film and some meager muddle of my past that it held, for what I wanted was information that would take me into the future.

Jack introduced himself and Gene, and as I felt in Jack's handshake his great breadth across chest and shoulders I introduced myself automatically as Paul Wheeler. Jack gave me a drink and said the name was familiar, and I stood in front of the small fire. Gene was sitting at the table, his arm across Jenny's portfolio. He was tall and slight and he slouched.

Paul Wheeler? he said.

You know the name? I said, bristling and jolly.

Jack asked if I'd come across anyone out there, and Gene, who grew tense, asked what I was doing and I said, Mad dogs and Englishmen, I'd come from clocking Callanish with a compass in my hand and hoped to find a shepherd's hut on the mountain before dark—check an alignment with Callanish at dawn—the stones? didn't know the stones!—I said I'd been taking bearings but couldn't write them down in the rain; I nodded toward the table, You don't by chance have some paper, I want to get them down at once. When Gene shook his head, Jack said of course, strode to the table, unzipped the portfolio, found a page with only a few lines of typing on it, tore it in half and handed it to me, leaving the portfolio open and his brother looking as if the manuscript were his mother's last poems. Gene said didn't I carry paper, and I said yes indeed but it was in my rucksack.

There was something wrong. I had it in my head, and you who have me may have guessed what it was. But floating free in front of the fire surveying the bed, the books, a pot, a kettle, I had too much in my head to be sure, and I was after all in the presence of so many of my own words that I needed a certain silence and economy, and feeling full of these last few dreamlike minutes outside in the dark I wanted to be sure not to know too much. I jotted numbers, I used a small book of French prayers to write on.

I observed the size of the manuscript there in front of sullen Gene, though a silly irrelevance looped lyrically through my new brain and out into the night, that Dagger had wished to cut the Suitcase Slowly Packed into the Marvelous Country House at the end to go with Len Incremona's restiveness and John's calling out to him asking if he was going anywhere just before Len entered with the pistol.

Gene asked how I'd seen my compass in the dark. Jack said, How's your drink?

I kept Krish's lighter in my pocket and extended my glass. I was a mile from that table, twenty years. The distance was temptingly great.

Got a sleeping bag? said Jack.

We're expecting some others, said Gene, it's going to be crowded.

Sheep-hunting party, I said.

Things are a bit confused, said Jack.

I said I was pressing on, and remarked that this didn't look like a shepherd's hut, with books on early Christian gnosticism and Hindu thought.

Who said it was a shepherd's hut? said Gene.

Jack inquired about my trip, he was a good host, and I had to dream up a theory that the Callanish Stones might be coeval with Stonehenge, even a model whose existence had been rumored hundreds of miles south so the Stone Age people who brought the Stonehenge bluestones from Wales may have been carrying on a tradition though the Callanish stones probably didn't come from far away.

I sat on the bed but I kept my shoes on in case I had to go fast. I didn't know what I could get from these brothers. Jack was diverting his irritation with Gene into cordial inquiries about my learned interests. I said Stonehenge was marvelous enough to look at—almost animate in the shapes—and easy to feel something about, and mysteriously suggestive to the mind—computer or calendar or some sun-worshipping lookout post or just a magnificent neolithic burial ground or a sacrificial site centuries after—I subscribed to all these theories in a way and had a private one of my own (which in fact I had just at that moment remembered, staring into the red wine) but to tell the truth (I said) Stonehenge was rather a typical American tourist stop and all the mystery had gone out of it with the car park and the souvenir stand and the barbed wire and I preferred Callanish up here in the lonely windy north because it was untidy and perhaps undramatic and left more to the imagination, like the difference between a movie and some overexposed family snap-shot you find in your suitcase unpacking.

Jack got another bottle and was pulling the cork when Gene said, What about Krish? and Jack nodded curtly. I said there'd been a missile base a mile north of Stonehenge, and then I couldn't think of anything to say and Gene asked rather pointedly where I was from and I said Wandsworth in South London.

Jack was walking around the room again and said the man who owned this hut was much involved in the study of Callanish and other such sites and I said what was his name, maybe I'd heard of him, was he also an American—but Gene said bluntly, He's not here.

I said, Oh you're expecting him.

Jack said, I'm just beginning to wonder.

He paused at the table and read from the page on top, *A lock to look at, a cross to bear, a memory to bring back.* Very poetic, he said.

I couldn't get up and look because I wasn't sure of Gene; but the last words were surely Jenny's.

Jack flipped a few pages. Gene sat upright and stiff.

I pretended to ease the situation.

I'd like to meet your friend, I said, find out what he thinks about the Celtic cross idea, the limbs that make the cross may be just as neolithic as the avenue and the circle—just other alignments. Mind you, Stonehenge might be a still more curious calendar if you link it in with the Maya, but Callanish leaves more to the imagination.

Jack came and stood over me. You said Maya? Maya Indians?

Why yes, I said, sensing a certain lack of concentration in someone who'd been drinking, and watching Gene as he carried the diary manuscript to the fire.

Thinking swiftly, I said that there were possible associations between two of the Maya calendars which turned upon each other like ratio gears in an analog computer (the first time I'd expressed it so persuasively to myself) and on the other hand the inner and outer circles at the Henge.

Jack heard the paper crackling and turned. Some pages were burning like a fan. Jack reached and retracted and reached again.

Gene said, Dynamite you said?

Jack asked why the hell Gene had done that, and Gene said Jack knew why and Jack knew something about destruction.

Jack said, I did *not* destroy that film and neither did Krish, and I'm suddenly wondering where you got the idea it was destroyed.

A good diversionary maneuver, brother.

Do you need some film? I asked from the bed, and as they turned to me, and the burning pages of my diary were visible past them at shin level, I was aware of having created an idea that had not been in my head prior to my lurch into the thin and broken areas of my knowledge, but there was no time to think about those circles or even about how *two* things that I felt in my head somewhere were wrong where there had been just one before; for I must see through Jack and Gene forward. I was already beyond this hut headed somewhere, and there was something wrong with the peat fire here.

That isn't *your* portfolio, said Jack, it has flowers on it. It isn't Paul's either.

What? I said.

It's Jan's, said Jack.

It's not her kind of thing.

But we know she was here.

I stood up and my new shoes felt like bones not yet filled with blood.

I said I had to go.

Jack the man of action stared at the fire thinking by some executive fiat he could run it backward and extract the diary. He put a hand on Gene's arm and asked who had given him this idea about the film.

Gene seemed easier with the diary gone. He said when you came down to it Dagger had told someone and it had gotten to Nell, and then everyone had been talking about its being ruined.

Jack said, Then you think . . .

Gene said, Maybe.

So the Bonfire?

Gene said again, Maybe.

They seemed still far apart but Jack with his warm Rotarian muscle thought he and his brother Geney were friends again.

And as I reached for my pack, Jack asked Gene how many pages it had been and Gene told him and Jack smiled and shook his head, and I thought of the 8-millimeter cartridge we'd shot the night we came back from shooting the air base, and I thought of Dagger's strange slowness in getting film processed and thought that in the end I'd seen only two and a half sections of film—the Softball Game and Corsican Montage, and a little joke of hands laying out TNT like a vertical xylophone; for Dagger had delayed the processing of several scenes, either because the man who was giving us a special deal was away or had too much regular work to fit us in, or in the case of the Bonfire in Wales and the Hawaiian Hippie in the Underground, something special had to be done to bring up the light because it turned out we'd shot in semidarkness; and what occurred to the two brothers in this hut in the middle of nowhere where you could be sure James Boswell and Dr. Samuel Johnson (of the clipping in Claire's Manhattan lav) had never ventured in their eighteenth-century junket to the Hebrides, occurred now to me: that Dagger DiGorro might have faked the ruin of the film.

If so, the film I'd found myself content to cross off, in lieu of something else I was finding, was now the future too.

Unedited. Possible.

But the reason it evidently *could* have been destroyed stayed with me. And whatever the protection of Paul had to do with this, the film, *my* film, had now been called Jan Aut's idea. Which hinged an eerie angle between my idea of the Unplaced Room and the actual room we'd used, which was hers.

I must get to her. Through her I might see Paul.

Through understanding, I might protect Dagger, though he was right when he'd told Jenny loyalty might not be the most interesting thing.

But as I bade goodbye to Gene and Jack thinking if I didn't run afoul of Krish I'd find a bed a few miles south in Tarbert and get to Glasgow tomorrow by steamer and plane, I was glad the diary was finished yet through this struck by the fact that the black leather case I'd brought Jenny as a present from America had yielded one copy not two.

And Jenny and Reid would have picked up at the Xerox her original closet carbon as well.

HINGE | Waves preceded me. Advance word framed my entrance into Jan Aut's flat, I couldn't simply go in. I must learn her idea for my film.

Did I like making waves? If I hadn't invented them, still they were made personally by me and conveyed something of me. The

344

cork among the molecules bobbed only up and down, but the wave-front advanced through both like spells of middling motives charging up a static slot.

Charging no doubt through the Indian and West Indian neighborhood where Jan's Notting Hill Gate flat placed itself: and through her to the Druid's busy phone south of the river: or miles southeast to the trees and the old gray stones of a Marvelous Country House that I could only look forward now to understanding better: beyond even these to whoever had thrust me onto that unmoving rapid-transit escalator back up which I then rebounded like a wave myself through an unmoved medium but found at the top only the moist smile in the change booth and her transistor enlarging itself with the mumbo jumbo of *You Are Everything and Everything Is You.*

Where the hinges are missing, saith the priest, I will spark the gap.

Ah *Mumbo Jumbo,* said Dudley Allott when I'd described from start to finish the shooting of what I'd thought was our final scene: but capital *M* and capital *J, Mumbo Jumbo* means among the Mandingo of Western Sudan a priest who keeps off evil.

Action, yelled Dagger, and for this early part of the six hundred feet we shot at Stonehenge that midnight in early August of this year 1971, I had the Nagra in its case on my shoulder strap and the mike on a short boom.

I moved parallel to Dagger across the interior of the Sarsen Circle northeast among the battery lamps and torches slowly as if *we* were the procession; for outside the circle the line of New Druids and others proceeded toward us from the misnamed Heel Stone some eighty meters off as Dagger and I inside the circle came to the central and misnamed Altar Stone with the huge pi-shaped trilothons either side of us southeast and northwest unbeknownst to our faithful Beaulieu whose focus on the New Druids was at this point narrowly framed through another arch on the far edge of the ring.

Dagger had shortened his depth of field, as we'd agreed. We would get an effect of some flaming conglomerate body back in the heavens clearing the horizon and getting bigger and nearer until it was persons singling themselves out of prickly light. Individuals from the void but coming communal, like parts of our film: the earth of Corsica yielding the brick and plaster of Ajaccio, the stone home which takes in and lets go yellow and olive and red slickers (and from which several communicants here tonight had come), and now

345

these windy megaliths built in circles and avenues, barest of dreamable forms.

Concentric circles of stones and vanished stones ring the half-fallen horseshoe of trilothons, once two horseshoes: all forms broken, some of the twenty-ton lintels gone almost as wonderfully as they came: one of the thirty-ton Sarsens fallen in '63, raised in '64: the mind completes the architraves, the eye describes the circles, no bloody gags about Druids and old doomed maidens can fill the gaps devised hundreds or thousands of years before the Druids, who nonetheless deserve this place too, no technical chatter about loop pans from Cosmo in his poncho off in the shadows toward the car park can rattle the Beaulieu's snakelike advance, and we will presently hear under one cloud-lit trilothon visiting statistics in an Alabama accent about a Stone Age computer whose spokes turning through fifty-six-year cycles predict the future of the sky.

I knew more about Stonehenge now than when I'd told Rose's friend Connie about Merlin; more than when Jenny (not here tonight) giggled at the bank clerk; and more even than when I told Tessa (tonight distinctly here) that a cremation barrow nearby yielded blue beads from Egypt, 1400 B.C.

The Indian from Kansas City came through the circle across our advancing path from right to left—as if heading for the trilothon through which one aligns with midwinter moonset—and as he grinned, I asked what he thought of the place, and he and his Hollywood cheekbones were off camera when he said: I wish my brother could see it!

Coming along the Altar Stone, I had for a moment no sight of the procession and Dagger's must have been through the 29–30 portal to the left of the one into whose alignment with the distant Heel Stone we now bent, for we were around the Altar Stone, it was behind us now, and stretching behind it through the great southwest trilothon was the alignment of midwinter sunset. And ahead—though I had to stay next to Dagger to keep our personal parallax from blocking my view—the procession we were shooting had come from the wide avenue and was passing the probably misnamed Slaughter Stone, and as we moved toward our trilothon picking up laughter, shouts, and the flat dry voice of the procession, its torches filled our frame ahead at a rate not fast enough to match our rate of nearer approach so there was more rather than less of the night sky in our portal as we came up to it and then went through, camera first, mike second.

346

In the glimmering dark just where the circle's outer circumference bent out of sight, a man was taking pictures with what looked like a very large double-lens reflex except he held it up in front of his eye.

We'd stopped moving here ten feet outside the circle. Into the mike I told Dagger's man from the Ministry of Monuments in whose charge we were that these were the New Druids. They were willing to stage an artificial rite to give themselves some exposure, and by my own Druid Mr. Andsworth these were neither sanctioned nor dismissed.

The bank clerk from Salisbury who had given me all the facts at the Altar Stone months ago, had got into the act too. He knew the man from the Ministry, and he interrupted to ask Dagger if this was in color. Dagger said no but he wished we were because black and white wasn't commercial any more.

The man from the Ministry was reciting to my mike the numbers of tourists for this year and last year and the year before that, but Dagger I am certain had focused past the man's shoulder to pick up Nash.

Nash was rubbing an eye with his ring hand and I recalled the silver, orange, and ruby rings from the Softball Game. Nash was watching the procession approach but he must have felt Dagger and turned at the camera and stared. Elizabeth of the Marvelous Country House greeted Dagger and shook hands, and said to me, Still in England?

Round the circle and frame of another portal I saw Tessa weightless in her open raincoat against a huge standing stone; she tried to pull a man apparently in our direction, pointed to us, then relented; I couldn't see the face, and when I mentioned him, Dagger laughed loudly and said he'd already gotten him. Nash had moved off. The procession was close. I said, We back away into the circle at their speed. Dagger said, Right.

I glanced behind through the portal we'd used once and would now use again and back at the Altar Stone with the largest hand-hewn prehistoric stone in the country—the lone standing part of the central trilothon—rearing up behind him, I saw the man with the camera and he had it trained on the portal where Tessa had been bugging that man, and the man with the camera who in his plastic mac and with a high forehead might have been the bank clerk but he couldn't be because when I'd seen the latter he hadn't had a camera, which I now saw was a cine camera not a double-lens reflex, and when I asked Dagger who he was, Dagger said Oh some friend of John's.

Dagger said Let's go, and we started backing up somewhat more slowly than the procession was approaching us. I asked what the man with the camera thought he was doing. Dagger didn't know; check it out later; his own was heavy enough.

The procession divided at the edge of the circle, one line came through 29–30, the other through between 30 and 1, the white robes brushed the stone. I looked back and the other camera was gone, but the Alabama academic we'd been put in touch with through Mary in Corsica (or through her brother whom we hadn't met) was on schedule waiting for us. I heard Tessa say, Oh go to hell.

I forgot my mike was on and said to Dagger that if that man had black-and-white reversal film he could film silhouettes of stones and people and after we shot our b & w negative film we could have the lab double-print so what we shot would fill the shapes of what he'd shot.

But the Alabama archaeologist in his broad, pale-colored hat was ready to talk, and that camera man with wide eyes disappeared. In my original account there were two full pages of third-hand stuff the archaeologist told about azimuths and alignments, the Z holes and the Y holes (circles lying between Sarsen and Aubrey), the relation between eclipses and the winter moon's rise over the Stonehenge Heel Stone, with anecdotes neatly inserted such as the ancient Chinese astronomers who failed to predict a solar eclipse and were liquidated.

Dagger tracked the procession past, while I kept the mike on our archaeologist who had just been asked by Tessa at my shoulder what was so important about eclipses and who had not planned to take that up and was now setting out to speculate on the positions of the fifty-six Aubrey Holes (the outermost circle way beyond the stones) and the rising and setting alignments through various arches, so he quickly disposed (he thought) of Tessa by saying priests in other cultures also used astronomical lore to hold power and Tessa asked if he knew the Maya observatories and he said, Much later than Stonehenge of course, and she as quickly declared that the origins were in ancient Asia and what about the thirty-six columns at Aké which Le Plongeon proved marked 180 years each, which came to more than twice the age of Egypt if you insisted on exalting measurement.

The man who had declined our Beaujolais at the Bonfire in Wales came by and the woman who had embraced Dagger in May and the Kiowa Apache who had a brother in Idaho and who in May had said he'd been in Britain for four months and wasn't looking back and who in my gathering uncertainties I thought uttered the word Māyā twice as he brought up the end of the procession.

A strange voice said, Oh is *he* here? but when I looked, there was only Tessa, and I asked Who she'd been playing hands with over there, but Dagger hauled me off toward the Moonrise or southeast trilothon, leaving the Alabama archaeologist pontificating to Savvy Van Ghent the UPI newsman and casting alarmed glances at the mike and camera retreating.

Only now, after Gene and Jack and the Clisham hut (weeks after Stonehenge), could I think the other filmer there may have been Aut's New York man who as far as I could see would have no edge on us since it was our scene he was shooting. I did not ask Dagger that night, *Which* John? because I was not to meet John of the Mercer Street loft till October. And a near-nausea like what I'd had in the New York camera shop due to photography I think and not the sewer fumes much less the sight of the stabbed man's chest blood, came into me now en route from the autumn Hebrides to London and Jan Aut—yet more a threat of sickness maybe not truly sensed by some crystal semiconductor whose outer-faceted solidity reveals its inner atomic form, but sensed rather in the other and peculiar and mingled attributes of liquid crystal—and looking back and forth among the boats and real estate and tall antique clear-glass Shell Motor Oil quarts so beautiful in shape and embossed imprint you might prefer to think that their origin (A.B.M.) meant something more probably transcendent than Automatic Bottle Machine—I hovered again near nausea that might swirl between me and a growth as dangerous as it was parallel and independent—or eyes (say, Stonehenge and Callanish looking out to space) dangerous as the idea I was to hear expounded dreamlike by that odd and genuine John in steel-rimmed glasses which I then drew into what was only in part my own form: to wit, that as capitalist ingenuity may save us at the very brink of its own imminent lethality, so certain digital manipulations John prophesied that you and I though not John know threaten their opposite (for they envision the thinker's mental state as if in some police act hooked by pulse rate and brain electricity to a computer) will find lo and behold a gated instrumentality that was always there by which to project (and here it is!) mind directly upon the screens of other minds—and maybe more even than this, which I might have to postpone seeing, for I had work to do; and from the Stonehenge footage, the altercations, the sweet burn of pot, and from our survey of views on Stonehenge voiced that August night accommodating themselves to the doorless doorways and roofless diameter of what Geoffrey of Monmouth calls the Dance of the Giants—and Dagger (off camera) called a symbol of British progress—I recollected only now what seemed to have a bearing on my search. I did not scout the spectrum of variously lighted opinions—interrupted to reload the magazine—the (now bearded) deserter's opinion that Stonehenge was like a mind-blowing sundial, his hard-nosed friend's (from the Unplaced Room) that Stonehenge was a chain of priestly shit to keep the people snowed, the Alabaman's that ultimately he would rather not say, a New Druid's (his upraised white-draped arm like wings) that these were petrified trees, the jolly woman in the blanket who had embraced and loved Dagger at the Bonfire in Wales that Stonehenge with its spinning circle and its open doors was a place where everyone could be everyone else, come out of hiding, come and go in love, and yet once more the Alabama archaeologist that he'd really rather not commit himself and did I have a light, I did and handed over a box with one match in it and he bent over the box as if already shielding a flame from the wind, and I turned away and caught Tessa watching and then she turned away; but I did defer two other views important now in the light of what seemed not quite to be happening. I had left Dagger and gone out of the circle to find a drink and Cosmo said, Did you see Tessa's green beret on that guy who's supposed to be a mute?

And seeing Nash with a half-gallon jug, I went near him and heard him say to the deserter (whom I'd not recognized in his beard), Well is he here or not? I heard he was.

The deserter's dark-haired companion from the Unplaced Room arrived, and I turned as if not paying attention. He *is* here, said the deserter. I heard nothing else and when I turned toward them Nash was turning toward me and the other two were walking off toward the circle where there was some physical activity. Nash had only his own paper cup, so I had a quick drink out of it. But on an impulse like self-preservation I said to Nash, That's OK. I know he's here. I saw him.

I returned to Dagger.

What energy in process were we tying into here? It was an energy constantly disturbed in its course or starting out again and again at new points.

The film might be a mess but we'd have to see. Tessa and I weren't driving back to London tonight. Dagger and I hadn't negotiated the centrifugal pan that with the processional reprise (plus chant) might climax the scene. But we still had plenty on the third spool. There seemed fewer people, but these were crowded around the Altar Stone.

Tessa was goading the deserter, Are you going to let him tell you to shut up?

This must be the deserter's companion. He looked at me keenly as I prepared to record. Gene's wife was there with two children who had climbed onto the fallen stone and were trying to push each other off.

Yeah, said Nash, don't tell him to shut up. I'll shut *you* up.

Look out you don't get a nosebleed, Nash, said the deserter's companion.

Again I wanted to ask Tessa whom she'd had by the hand before. She certainly wasn't missing her green beret. The man from the Ministry stood calmly embarrassed next to the bank clerk. Nash got pushed, and he and the deserter and the other fellow as they jostled each other toward the single upright of the Sunset trilothon were joined by Cosmo who was saying something and was told by Nash to stop shooting off his mouth. They went outside the Sarsen Circle and I heard the deserter say something like, You *did* see him.

Whereupon of all people little Elspeth of the long hair and stern visage was at my side introducing the Indian from Kansas City and telling me his responses to Stonehenge might be relevant, he didn't think the place essentially English.

This was now pounced on by Tessa (ah that curled lip!) who declared the *quintessential* Englishness of this place, the practical mysticism of the *land*. An English voice was heard to say, There, there! and I turned asking who had said that.

But Dagger was shooting the scuffle now intermittently manifest through the north northeast part of the circle, and I said, wishing to rescue our scene, Let's do the big pan.

Dagger agreed and called to the New Druids to line up and reprocess before the torches went out, and I suddenly asked if Reid was here, the guerrilla-theater actor, and Dagger said yes somewhere.

And though I couldn't enter it into my diary which Jenny was going to type, I felt that very much a part of this scene was her off-again-on-again relation with Reid who had got some hold over her but who had not been the reason I'd made sure Jenny wasn't here tonight. But the word *Reid* threw me out into the real successes of our silent Softball Game where *I* and he had appeared together, and the Indian Krish (now perhaps dead in a ditch).

And Reid had appeared (or *dis*appeared) with the red-haired woman, and as he'd crossed the grass beyond third base and headed off into foul ground and Hyde Park he'd had a glow about his body, almost an aureole, that had probably not come out on our film. But Dagger said, Wake up! and he was right and I found myself waking from some still further arc of time whose formula I couldn't frame but whose swimming materials I knew included Tessa's mouth and the cassette recorder my mother wanted us to write letters to her on, and a sheet of liquid crystals like a negative being peddled by the God Mercury Cartwright, and a rusty zipper between two sleeping bags in the light of moonlight wind upon a lake in Maine: and the arc whose formula these partly were, was the softly cadenced sigh of Lorna's sobbing in the late fifties that I could hear even when she was out of the house like a new motion of our Highgate things, a picture, a hunk of quartz, a piano, a Victorian couch, a refinished stairway, all for a long moment on loan and not after all ours—sobs that made me fear for my life.

And as I got with the reprocession but was still afield on waves of pointless past, I said Who *is* this that people are asking about—is he here, is he not here, who *is* it?

Probably not just one person, said Dag, maybe some of these Hindu mystics are your greatest sex fiends when you get away from the firelight, right?

In the dark, through between two lintel-less slabs, I saw Nash moving his hands in front of someone all in white whom I couldn't see.

We tracked the procession back toward the northeast portal on a route that led toward the Slaughter Stone again and the Avenue and the Heel Stone, but when Dagger said, Now! he swung past them counterclockwise and I kept out of his way as we made one revolution passing the procession, made a second revolution-pan so fast Dagger staggered, and a third even faster with Cosmo calling, Just loop that pan and run it as many times as you want.

But the fourth time around, the procession was just through the arches and outside the circle—the dark gaps had been run into the gray-lit stones and the stones into one whirling circuit of the continuous panning shot as if we had whirled the procession out a runway by centrifugal launch and made the circle an unbroken power once again.

A voice was saying, If you don't feel homesick, either you ought to or you ought to stop worrying about *not* feeling it.

Nash was suddenly in view holding a handkerchief to his nose.

Dagger spun us out toward the Sarsen Circle, and the bank clerk was standing at the 21–22 arch northwest from the Altar. I urged Dagger to follow, and we gave the man a chance to speak, I felt our climatic unifying pan had not held anything together, I was a long way away from what I had felt with Jenny here, the windy innuendo I'd felt here and then the crystal truths measured for us by this very man whom you might see tracing generations of craftsmen at the County Archives during his lunch break or poking about the Wessex barrows on the crest of some remote down with not even a bike to convey him home, only a thin ash plant and his knobbly-knuckled thumbs. He was saying now that he'd just heard someone nearby groaning, Graveyard, graveyard, just a graveyard; an interesting view, but he hadn't found the owner of the voice.

Dagger was pointing elsewhere but I had the mike close.

Yes indeed, said the bank clerk, for if it's just a burial ground—and make no mistake, it *may* be!—(and I half-heard the word *Is,* like a gust's mild buzz through the stones, yet there *was* no gust, no breeze) why then our main concern is the giant *work* of the thing. Now these Sarsens, the big ones, came overland from eighty miles away. A miracle. But the bluestones, which are much smaller but still run to five tons, were many if not all of them brought from Wales. Geology tells us that. Think of it! One hundred thirty miles by air—but in real miles, two hundred and forty! And this without the wheel, though possibly with rollers. But by water, more than halfway by water, from West Wales through the Bristol Channel to the mouth of the Bristol Avon—you know the gorge?—then up the Avon, then overland, and perhaps along the river Wylye, then overland again to here. Think of it. This is what Stonehenge means, I say.

And as the man took a deep breath and began to speak of the three other (but unlikely) routes the bluestones could have taken, a voice from outside the circle with a tremor of irony I thought, said, It comes to that, and that alone.

Who spoke? said our bank clerk, and stepped out through the arch.

Tessa was with us again from another direction: I walked over some bodies out there, she said.

Did them good, I said.

The bank clerk in his plastic mac was telling Dagger of the five kinds of rock the bluestones came from, but Dagger thanked him, and as we moved away and the mike and camera were off, the bank clerk tall and devoted called to us did we know the theory there may have been an earlier Henge these bluestones composed prior to their transport here, so just possibly these stones came as one completed monument from Wales and may have been—he called desperately—a *Blue*stonehenge.

Reid appeared in white blouse and white jeans. He asked how it was going. He was graceful and relaxed, he seemed to have moseyed over from his own acreage where he'd been doing some work. Hey, he said, is Savvy writing a piece on this?

I guess I'll be the only one, I said.

The man from the Ministry hoped everyone would be accounted for.

The small Elizabeth with a proper sense of order came pelting over to us to say that the fair-haired boy with beard had disappeared. Dagger and I knew this to be the deserter. Elizabeth pelted away into the dark. Dagger gave me the camera and followed her.

Behind me I heard through the openings of the ring we'd tried to blur closed, the American voice confirming the bank clerk's words about human effort. The moon was still cloud-bound, but I could see Elspeth and a pair of stragglers going toward the car park. I had asked Dagger to ask her. She had asked three friends and one of them had asked a friend with a car. Nell had come with two kids, plus two men I didn't know. There was a University of Maryland part-timer who had thrown a Thanksgiving party several years ago that Will and Jenny and I had gone to and who'd been greeted with open arms by Dagger tonight. It was a pretty eclectic coven. You make sacrifices in the interests of accident and naturalness. People had friends nearby. There was a party somewhere in a caravan.

Dagger and I had come separately, he in the VW with Cosmo and others, I in the Fiat. Tessa had looked at a cottage in Hampshire on our way down and wanted to see another tomorrow on the way back. We were supposed to be giving a lift to Elizabeth, who was staying with an aunt in Salisbury. Some of these arrangements were not in the diary.

I did include, though, that I wanted to change my life: for this, however light, was my reply to Elizabeth, who came back looking for Dagger and was most distressed about the deserter who hadn't yet been found and then asked with that English no-nonsense trick what *in fact* was the point of our film.

We had six hundred feet I knew would be better in the

processed print than my sense tonight of the muddled scene. But when I'd been here in March with Jenny, I'd felt like a giant. The hingeless doorways had unlocked their field of possibility and all those concentric fronts of memory had passed out the lens of my loved daughter's camera before she turned to me radiant and announced that Stonehenge was a message; and inspired by her I thought, That's it! Instant developing movie film! And I was even free (though not so great) when the voice behind began doling out distances and weights and I pictured proving myself by showing a hundred Stone Age huskies how to get the Sarsens into the foundation holes and, topping that feat even, lift the lintels let's say by rocking them on a log-staging till the lintel was high enough to roll onto the pillars, there to be fixed with my patent lock of mortise and tenon.

And I thought it was this passage, linking daughter and lock, that brought Jenny to me in tears after she'd proofread the typescript. Tears damped the lashes and shone on the cheekbones, I hadn't known her to cry in years, she's dry cork as the poet says, though not cold; and she wept again then, asking if I would show this to Mummy; and then I saw it must be the part about Lorna's sobs.

Materials for a life, I said.

It'll take a lot of editing, I was about to say, but Lorna had forgotten her key and I went to let her in. Upon entering the living room she took a Kleenex and dabbed at Jenny's makeup.

Dagger came back and I handed over the Beaulieu. I'd had the touch of an idea but lost it when he spoke, but maybe it was Tessa now quiet at my side. There were shouts and singing somewhere and cars starting. Someone called, Where's your torch? Dagger said he'd felt it needed something more and he now had had a thought for another scene which we could discuss when we got home.

The man from the Ministry came from another part of the circle. He said he must say these New Druids took rather an activist line.

I said somebody had to in this benighted country, and Dagger said Here here! and I said if you leaned on a stone and waited for something to happen, nothing would, and the bank clerk with a tremor in his tone said he wasn't at all sure about that.

Headlights beamed through us.

The other way, to the south, I saw a flashlight moving through a field. (A torch, these hoary English call it.)

I asked Tessa if her shoes were wet.

We were moving north toward the passage that went under the road and came up by the car park.

Dagger called back into the dark, Closing up!

Dagger's talk of a new scene had interfered with my thought of one. Or had it been Tessa, who might now be contemplating our hotel room in Salisbury a few miles away. It had been six years. She took my arm and asked if Dagger had seen my written account of this mad documentary of ours. And as I said No, my idea came cresting back: to film the boatyard in which I had an interest, and get the old man to put in a nice clear explanatory word about making things by hand.

It might help, said Tessa.

We turned and the others went on. I couldn't make out the ruined horseshoe, only the open wall of Sarsen monoliths. The moon was trying to come out.

To one side of the circumference I saw, at a distance I could not gauge, two silent flashlights. Tessa said, Good luck to them.

Priestly shit indeed, I said—think of the poor fucking Catholics being interned.

In London Dudley told me *mumbo jumbo* meant not just nonsense or obscure ritual but also a fetish; he got out a book to show me that *mumbo jumbo* came from Mandingo for a magician who makes the troubled spirits of ancestors go away.

Now what had been the Stonehenge message Jenny had felt in March? But she'd been looking *out* of the circle. Did that mean you only got it as it left? or if you stood in it and conveyed it out?

Waves aren't simple; they hit each other; they interfere, take each other's force, but also reinforce.

Ned Noble could tell you.

In the stillness of the Highgate house once I read about a scientist who made up a law about waves hitting particles so that every point in space becomes a source of spreading waves.

But Tessa was simply a good fuck in '64 and '65—and in '71 in a green beret and nothing else but some enigmatic chit-chat queries about our other film-scenes, was there one in Wales? one in South Kensington Underground? and what was the American blowhard professor really doing there?

But I was afraid time would stop if I didn't get to Jan Aut's and beyond.

I did not need to buzz Jan's flat to get in downstairs. I hadn't noticed the old house, its outside, what it was made of. I was in Notting Hall Gate.

Maybe *I* was the message.

Cartridges stayed hard when out of touch with other cartridges but when in touch opened and shifted—even to glows of high hue or even varying grays with a black as lush as Lorna's suede gloves so richly wrinkled, from finger to elbow setting out for our first and last Embassy cocktail party where a matter-of-fact madam's orange hat and blue-green eyeshadow or a patronizing young parliamentary secretary's machine-matched mauve tie and snotrag stood out like senseless data next to my Lorna with her gray wool dress that showed her wholeness, her high waist and her hips and stomach, and with her dark almost black hair alive around the gray-blue eyes. I was proud enough of her not to get mad afterward in a cab when she said, You like that crap more than you admit.

The door wasn't open when I reached the second landing. There was no key under Jan's mat. The last time I'd come with a friend, two others, a camera, and sound.

Lorna did not know how near I was.

There was a new lock on our door in Highgate. Had Jack had our house broken into? I couldn't tell on the phone from New York how badly Lorna had felt about it—scared, unready, sad. Her tears were never hot pools on the carpet (where Tessa had dropped her butt) but slow and steady as if measured out.

And as I heard a hand on Jan Aut's doorknob, I knew I was still between—for I knew (for how could I not have seen that) *lock* in Jenny's cryptic note had an *h: a loch to look at, a cross to bear*: whatever waves I'd made had traveled on ahead to here, but back as well to Callanish behind me where my American daughter had saved the other remaining copy of the diary.

14 | Which put me between again.
| But with what in front?

Godlike I saw through Jan Aut's door before it opened. She was fresh from a bath, a twist of towel round her hair. But she'd been up on Lewis with Paul. She might be anywhere, South Uist, Edinburgh, Wales.

The turban was still a towel, but no—she looked like Jenny; that was it. I was ahead of my own sound, I could have been still asleep three nights ago in my Glasgow hotel. I reached out to her still feeling for Jenny, and in the instant that I checked the impulse Claire accepted my embrace and I blocked the new wish to draw back, and was glad because I knew I could not help her. But no: Claire's dog had just come out of hospital and she hadn't settled her affairs at Outer Film and there was no reason to think Monty would want her here in London with him on business. But why did I think Monty was in London tonight—because he'd phoned Dudley? because if this system, whoever it was, was closed, the probabilities were that things should be beginning to come together?

But I was rehearsing; and, even irredeemably between, I knew my power lay in not rehearsing; and so as the door came open I would still proceed as if I had a plan even if I were no god.

It was Kate, the girl from the gallery. Her hand, the fingers of her tanned hand, went to her collarbone. She'd been in no mood to imagine me a god when we'd first met. I inserted myself sideways past her, bumping my pack, saying Jan expected me.

My pack stood next to the brown velvet chesterfield; my parka I laid over the arm so the pockets rested on the cushions.

Of course, said Kate.

The portrait of Jan's to which I had added leaned against the leg of a baby grand. The piano was a Yamaha, the firm that makes motorbikes and flutes.

There was no one here. I fell into the chesterfield. The room was full of things chosen over a long period of time one by one. It had not been right for what we'd wanted when we'd filmed here. I said this to Kate, who stood at the foyer entrance, one ankle almost touching my pack.

You filmed here?

Yet looking around at a delicate brown bowl, a solid red jaguar some ten inches by four, a silver belt of ornately worked links lain across a bright-woven shawl thrown over a table, I felt that this room impossible to unplace. May 24 was personal not local. That is, you would not have looked at it and said England. There was a turtle. There was a color photo of Jupiter on the music stand above the keyboard.

I got up and walked away from Kate to a doorway. It was evening. A blanket or two lay on the floor beside a large bed with dark green sheets twisted and draping. I turned away to a further door that was almost closed.

What did you film? said Kate.

I don't know any more, I said.

The Unplaced Room of our film was dark through a crack, and I did not go in. I remembered morning light through the top of a green tree. A bold bright portrait of someone with long lustrous hair leaning against the wall near where I stood. Large open windows with those peculiar screw locks at the middle and along the sash. The garden didn't appear in the film. Pale clouds were filling the early blue when Dagger and I and the featured performers arrived. The sky in New York is gross, it is a blue land that will get you.

She's not here, as you can see, said Kate. She was by the couch now. She started to lift my parka but I stopped her.

I said, Saturday night. I need a bath. I've just been up to Paul's.

Why had she said Of course when I'd come in?

She sat on the piano stool. It's Sunday, she said.

In the corner of my eye something moved, inanimate. Kate's small mouth dimpled, in a quiver not a smile. She did not point out that as of Monday I hadn't known Jan Graf. Either she thought I'd faked ignorance then, or she was doing something very special now.

I asked if she'd been at the gallery the day Aut's man filmed; I said I knew Jan and the four men had been in it, but I hadn't heard Kate mentioned.

When she shook her head—almost as if she couldn't speak— I put my head back and closed my eyes and intoned like a list of heroes the names of Reid, Gene, Sherman, Incremona. I sighed and said it was a sordid thing, this commercial competition, utterly cut-throat.

Take my film diary, I said, my eyes still closed; it was inciner-ated in Paul's hut on Mount Clisham yesterday. So that's that. A regular trade war. What's the use?

I sighed. Even Paul got demoralized, I said—he stopped caring about all the deserters coming through Norway and the islands.

I let myself seem tired. Kate nodded once. My mind played in a field of someone else's inventing, more than one someone, I thought. Maybe I was as tired as I was seeming. I rolled my head toward where the inanimate movement had been, and saw it again. The door to the Unplaced Room swayed. I said there was a draft, and with a groan I leaned forward but Kate was up, crossing to the Unplaced Room, saying she'd close the windows, but I said just shut the door, and she did, stopping short of it so she had to reach out for the knob, and pulling it to so quickly—as if she had other duties to pass on to—that I felt she'd never meant to go in there and close the windows. I asked for Jan; Kate said she was here looking after the cat while Jan was away. That was like a past part of the truth. Kate was being careful. I asked for a drink. I'd been dreaming in the plane from Glasgow, I said, I was wild, I had all the passengers looking back at me. What a dream! Could I tell Kate about it?

Please do.

It must have come from the daydream I'd had *before* I dropped off: to wit, putting Paul and Chad together; plus the deserter's dark-haired friend when we filmed here and Nash's nosebleed when Cosmo accused him of planning to blow up the Underground. Plus Len's angry trigger at Paul's brother's house.

Kate passed me a wine glass of whiskey and asked if that had been my dream, and I said it might as well have been. The door of the Unplaced Room was open a crack again but there was no draft, as if interrupting the current of air had lowered the windows automatically like the line-and-pulleys I'd rigged from my bed when I was twelve. I carried my parka into the bathroom, and Kate laughed but I didn't believe her. But I said, Got some plastic explosive I'm carrying around.

I unlaced my boots.

I asked if she had anything to eat.

I was into a stationary area again. But area might be so only by me. I wanted what Kate knew.

I said I had been launched down a dead escalator as part of an international power struggle. My words made my hands sweat.

Kate tried to speak, reached for her collarbone, decided to slouch with a hand on her hip.

Was that your daydream, she said, the power struggle?

I half-closed the bathroom door. I said she knew of course that Sherman was very dangerous. However, they were waiting for him in New York. Paul had had a strange violent effect on Chad. (I turned on the shower. A clear plastic shower cap hung over a tap handle.) Paul had opted out of the violent project and was in danger like me. Reid's plans went ahead. (I turned up the water and lowered my voice.)

I was easing into the water. I might have been standing in my Tuesday shower at Monty's.

Yes, I called out, it was my daydream, but I'm adding.

Outside the fall of my shower Kate's silence seemed not to be paying much attention to me. She wouldn't know much. Somewhere Mummy would be hoping she'd meet someone suitable.

As for Chad, I called out—and the phone rang and I turned off the shower.

I thought Kate said—the children.

I know she said, Can I give him a message?

I would let *her* bring this up. I flapped the shower curtain, sang a riff from a Brandenburg, ran water hard in the basin, flushed the toilet and soundlessly closed the bathroom door.

I didn't hear her speaking. I tiptoed wetly out and carried my pack back. I didn't see her. The phone was in the kitchen. How did I know that?

I dressed.

I called from the bathroom, As for Chad—and then came out to my sandwich—well I see Chad as the black second lieutenant in Heidelberg who helps that kid skip to Sweden and has work for him when they meet again in London a long time after. It was Paul's hut the kid stayed in—that's no dream either. Only one film now. Plus a piece of ours with Paul on it, a Bonfire in Wales. When we caught him there he was already backing out of the big one, the big project, and he'd gone down to Wales. To see Elspeth, yes. I suppose you don't know Elspeth. She was at Stonehenge. In my daydream Jan helps Paul escape from his two older brothers, who fear him. Jack has risky business up in the Hebrides anyway—yes, with a rich dilettante geologist who has gotten in too deep because the deserters and other Americans he's ferried over from Norway are involved in a little bit more than mere exile, and this rebounds upon him and he wants out, and at this point Jack can't afford to let that happen. Ditto the diary, so it has to be burned. I can understand. I'm not in arms about it. Nash was brought together with Krish in one scene and this could have led who knows where. Likewise Nash and the deserter at Stonehenge. Likewise in Corsica Mike and Incremona. The project will probably go through. But I've got to see Jan. She wouldn't be at the Community with Paul? You know the Community?

I don't, said Kate. I don't think she'll be back tonight.

You've been looking for adventure, Kate.

To you who have me, it may have been patent by now that I sensed a third person. If probabilities were as I imagined, this person closeted doubtless in the Unplaced Room would be someone who had already figured in my experience of the system. If it was a lover, even Kate was not so uncool as to hide him. If Jan, then why Kate's nerves? On Jan's behalf? Doubtful. If Paul, where was Jan? Why would this person wish not to be seen? And by me in particular? Or by anyone? But why would Kate not discourage me from staying? Either because she or the other person felt me to be dangerous or because the other person had signaled her to have me stay.

But what she said now did not fit: Be serious, she said.

She might well ask, I said, why these and others who had connections to hide should let themselves be filmed at all. Surely with what they stood to lose it was strange to consent.

Kate had to claim something for herself. She said that everyone knew how persuasive Jan could be.

I agreed with my mouth full, but having swallowed the last soft lump of grainy crust and held out my wine glass, I said there were things Jan could not understand. Nor Phil either. Did Kate know John? Ah well, John had a curious relation with Phil. John wasn't into this other side of the film either.

Kate did not ask what other side. She carried my plate out.

I had put on my parka, and in a second, with one eye on the crack of darkness showing from the Unplaced Room, I added the heavy red jaguar to my stock of other people's weapons. The phone rang and I moved to the foyer, looked suddenly at the Unplaced Room, lifted my pack around the corner out of sight, opened the front door—and letting it close hard I concealed myself beside the hall closet. Consequently I could not hear, except a word that sounded like *gallery*. I put my head around the corner; the door to the Unplaced Room had not stirred. I caught Kate looking at me around the door of the kitchen. She disappeared and closed the conversation saying, I'll tell her you called.

Beside the painting to which I had added was a large blue-red-and-umber cushion which had figured in the otherwise drab Unplaced Room.

I had proposed that we drop to eight frames a second here and there because when eventually projected these moments would introduce an agitation into Dagger's flat *verité*.

Kate had stalled me here without being one thing or the other.

What I could have told her—fast forward, sixty-four frames a second—was that the Unplaced Room was precisely the footage Dagger had not told Claire about; the letter I had left on Aut's desk left me no doubt about that. For Dagger there was something in the scene worth withholding. The scene held more for me. Jan's whiskey had spread to my shoulders and fingertips. What I could have told Kate at 64 fps was the precise color of eggshell-cream I painted a room in our first house in 1955 that was to be my study. There was a golden Goya guitar—not to be confused with the two twelve-string guitars I bought in Germany the following year and sold to Americans in London—and the door was closed and window open, and when I laid down my roller I would pick up the Goya and strum my four chords and sing a ballad. "Sir Patrick Spens" was one I sang. They are out of fashion now and in all these years in England I never met anyone not American who sang them. That room was where the children wouldn't come. Will was a baby, Jenny went half days to a play group in a church basement. I had a table and two chairs and only what I needed. Sometimes not even the paper. And Lorna had the balance of the house to herself. The old pub across the road hadn't yet been tarted up; the prefab panels and light cubes and chrome trim were three years off. But while I liked to make space, so to speak, by piling things rather than letting them spread, objects in quantity passed through that room and sometimes stopped for considerable periods. My father had unearthed in the country several old Shell Oil bottles 14½ inches high with fancy embossing, and because I'd been struck with the tall, thin beauty of these old bottles that had been used to hold a quart of motor oil, I had interested a young Portobello Road shopkeeper in having (on a percentage basis) a serious bottle corner. This corner soon acquired a name for its nobly seductive American wares, though the strangely reassuring Mason jars and blown-in-the-mold medicine bottles with the four indented circles embossed on the side, the cobalt-blue witch hazels and the whittle-marked Moxie Nerve Food bottles—long ball neck, strap-sided, and (a mark of pre-1900 work) the applied lip—were mingled as you'd expect with a deceptively large sampling of non-American work—free-blown Persian saddle flasks, aqua-colored Jamaican gingers, Italian cordials with embossed suns, French perfume and English gin. And there were times when such objects as these would accumulate in that precious room of mine where Lorna would always knock before she entered. She picked up the guitar overnight and now can really play but never does. She would sit down in the bare room and I would close my manila folder over my lists, plans, and letters and she would tell me the old lady in the furnished room on the ground floor next door with access to the garden (hence a view across into ours and up to my study window) had told her her life story this morning, Miss Topp, a sitting tenant whom the new landlord (an actor no one had ever heard of who had made some money on a film) was dying to evict along with Mrs. West on the third floor (who could barely move now, she was so fat), and Miss Topp after a tale of complaints and small revelations said, I see your husband up there busy doing his correspondence. But Lorna then heard that Miss

Topp had been saying that I didn't work, that all I did all day was correspondence, and the police-woman had come because I was living off my wife's immoral earnings. Indeed the police-woman had come, to check our green cards, but the old lady as I pointed out to Lorna gave us credit for more imagination than we probably had— Miss Topp had heard from old Mr. Sharpe the gardener that Lorna was English, which gave her the right to take a job without going through red tape, and from the dustman that there were a number of Americans resident in the area, just living. This was off the Edgeware Road a half a mile from Marble Arch in a little one-block street of neat, narrow, often dilapidated three-story Georgians in the borough of Marylebone since then absorbed into Westminster—and just round the block from a public baths with marvelous seven-foot tubs Lorna and I used in shifts during a water crisis our first winter, listening to the locals hollering pop songs from cubicle to cubicle. My room that I had painted off-white and at first kept free of possessions was not, as you may imagine, like an interrogation chamber—though at first it was as bookless as the early life of a 1954 draftee whose G2 loyalty check proves his mom and fiancée to have had no traffic with communists—and newspapers did pile up with occasional unread alumni reviews; and the security of that room, and of that rented house (and of that year 1955 in England featuring the autumn debate in Commons on the defectors Burgess and MacLean when Eden with Senator McCarthy in mind asked how far "we" were to go in pursuit of greater security) I see now was haunted by some secret and possible heroism, and a college friend Reb Needles from Chicago wrote that I. F. Stone had done a piece on the Watkins Committee report as a great antifascist event and in listing the Senate honor roll of Fulbright, Flanders, and Morse, Hayden, Hennings, and Hendrickson—not to forget Benton who first looked into that demented American's financial affairs—the writer had called them all (even Jenner) *Senator* but had singled McCarthy out again and again as just McCarthy, which may have seemed to say it all but said still more and left the man alone and distinct.

But a briefly fast 64 fps if you ever get it developed comes out of your 24 fps projector slow motion.

Babysitters were thirty cents an hour, chars sixty. Lorna began to want a job, but an interesting one. The children were still too young. We bought a better piano. By the time we moved to Highgate to a house that despite the corruption of its roses is worth nine times what we paid for it in '58, I was glad to leave that plain white room bare again, a possibility for someone else, and Dagger DiGorro on May 24 would not have understood my sense of the room we filmed—a room anywhere, a future.

Jan Aut's marmalade cat walked slowly out of the Unplaced Room and made its way to the kitchen. The phone had rung again, so I waited. Kate had said *Speak of the* . . . when she picked up; then she said, Her brother; then a succession of yeses; and then: I'll tell him.

When she came out she was the gallery girl again, and so, picking up her last remark before the phone calls, I said, Jan's persuasive all right but she needs a helping hand.

I nodded at the picture leaning against the piano leg. Kate looked pretty well through me, but found a smudge of foreign matter and could not look further.

Where are you off to now?

Back to New York, I said, some work that Paul's involved in. I've hardly been away.

Kate's hand found the collarbone, but no connection occurred, and I wondered if she had tried two glasses of warm water and a good vomit first thing before breakfast.

She couldn't quite let me go. What limit would my going put upon her? She ran her words together: Just as well this film was lost, p'raps you'll try another someday.

I took two steps to her, my hands at my sides: Who says it's lost?

Beyond her shoulder I saw the door to the Unplaced Room stir but it was only my angry imagination fueling the fire of my diary with a chair seat and a table leg or two from the absent brother's hut.

I had a hand on her shoulder and did not let her move. I asked what the devil *she* knew about an Unplaced Room, or Māyā, or a Hawaiian Hippie playing a guitar under the Science Museum and his little girlfriend from Long Island in a U.S. sergeant's jacket swaying from one boot to the other above a dirty yellow felt hat on the ground with a coin in it. What had such a thing to do with Kate's job in a gallery, with a green, stone-walled private school? What was West Hempstead, Long Island, to Kate? Not even a suburban town that supplied an entrant for the Miss New York State contest. Had Kate any feeling for a couple like that? the boy's father in the iron business in Honolulu County, the girl's father in the carbon business; the girl as American as a Duncan Hines brownie, the boy as American as a quart can of pineapple juice, a dropout on the move represented in the 1960 tattoo on Savvy Van Ghent's strong arm by one

star no newer than the star that stands for that ancient and funda-
mental signatory state Virginia. There was a simple power in the two
of them together that Kate could disparage as boring and American
and even unsavory—

Wait, she said without removing her shoulder from my hand,
oh wait, half my friends are Americans.

I said what could Dagger's rhythm of approach mean to Kate.
Without a dolly he had had to level his walk as if with a sort of slow-
motion gear astonishingly well-coordinated, the camera like a quart
of trinitro-glycerine—though the different speeds at which he went
by the two young people did not include actual slow-motion, though
after five or six passes we set up right in front of them so pedestrians
who'd been our camera point of view would now be separate and pass
between us and the two kids—

I may not know what you mean by Māyā but I do have some
feeling for fine things—

—and now at my urging (for two bowlers and two rolled
black umbrellas came bobbing and capering toward us respectively
down the passage) we went to 64 frames a second so in the print the
Hawaiian Hippie's fingers would be dream-slow and the girl's bending
and swaying might hint of girls in grass skirts and thick swinging leis
performing to make compatriot tourists feel right at home under a
sunny volcano just as the bowlers and brollies marched darkly past in
a sudden resumption of the sound of the hard authentic unsweetened
version of "Both Sides Now," and Dagger had made the preceding
series of approaches from the Science Museum end of the tunnel
with the South Ken Underground end facing us beyond the boy and
girl almost as if we were trying again and again to make someone
appear at that end and come toward us, but I had inserted a silence
without telling Dagger, just switching off the little Nagra we were
using while creating a silence between the music so the music would
ride on with its own momentum or the viewer could suddenly find
he'd been making his own music all the time, or silence would plunge
him into meditation. Dagger had said when we started out that
American kids playing in Undergrounds around London could be a
good little scene and Jenny you see had spoken a day or two before of
how she and I and Will used to go to the Science Museum and the
Natural History Museum and so I suggested that pedestrian tunnel
and there we found this boy and girl but they weren't there when
Reid and Jenny ran into Dudley and Jane in the same tunnel three
weeks later.

366

The same tunnel? said Kate, and I removed my hand from her shoulder. I was between her and something that was going on outside this flat.

Yes the same tunnel, I said, and Dudley Allott was wearing a black V-neck pullover under his mac exactly like one that was packed in a later scene of our film.

But wasn't it a coincidence their meeting?

They were bound to meet someday, I found myself saying. Like Dudley and your employer's brother-in-law Monty Graf who have been on the blower discussing Maya within the last seventy-two hours. Like Nash and the deserter at Stonehenge.

Kate backed away and sat down by the table from which I'd taken the red jaguar. That was Monty Graf just now, she said, and I had the sense (which I felt then that no formula could validate) that I'd drawn her into a moment of freedom where accelerations had equaled one another and she would give me anything I wanted, even the knowledge of what it was I wanted. The door of the Unplaced Room moved. The cat, having come out of the kitchen, walked across a rug. Put the two shots together, rig the illusion of an adventure, and the viewer like some attentive victim-to-be of terrorism could be made to see the cat as moving the door instead of the real event which was the wind from the window of our May 24 film scene which at that moment of increasing weightlessness and vision I in-clined to see as my own presence in that Unplaced Room plotting my way, glad of my young wife's willingness in the fifties to live abroad for a while, listening to Will somewhere in that first house screaming while I watched Miss Topp and blue-nosed Mr. Sharpe with his pruning shears in the adjacent garden standing like conspirators by the smoking incinerator into which he had stuffed refuse, and the two of them then turn to catch me watching from my study which in '58 I was to abandon for the Highgate house where my study had none of that free unspecified air in which as in our film much was possible.

Or for that matter (I said) me and Phil Aut's cameraman who wouldn't have understood the silence I inserted like a breath of seawater waxed in your ears.

The words came unchosen, and I added, Oh we ran him ragged at Stonehenge, he didn't have a clue.

There's not much John misses, said Kate.

For one thing, I said, he sometimes misses Incremona's moods. Which is about as risky as you can get. Now *that was* a coincidence, I said (thinking that that bumptious John of the Marvelous Country House had certainly not been the other man with the movie camera at Stonehenge).

What was? asked Kate.

Running into Incremona in Corsica, I said.

But the other coincidence, said Kate, as if not wanting to change the subject—who is Jane?

I was picturing John the man in glasses from the Mercer Street loft holding a camera in the lurid flashes of our Stonehenge night. That cameraman hadn't been wearing glasses, and this John of mine on the loft floor where I'd dropped him had been half-blind till he got his steel-rims back on. I told Kate Jane was the daughter of the man that Monty had been phoning for information, and I remarked that the real coincidence was that Jane knew Reid.

But my words were again almost too much for the occupant of that Unplaced Room amid the circuiting dark of many degrees of past: for hoping to look only out ahead, wherever I looked was back—the tunnel of pedestrians impeding our scene in static twilight while the boy from Honolulu banged his steel strings, the tunnel bearing me home from the fact of English twilight which that afternoon I had learned must preclude any undertaking to launch a Drive-In cinema in the Liverpool area, the tunnel of Beatle rock in my carriage drowsing me toward that mobile terminal the wheels of which are paved with peat but which recedes from what Ned Noble once called my pedestrian imagination, so maybe I will never except in daydreams catch it and patent it or in some weightless or depictured bare unsituated room plan it down to each revolution of each wheel, but there is no revolution, the wheel is at Yarner's Coffee Shop in Upper Regent Street and it is a huge elegant coffee-grinder wheel for show, and Jane to be precise had said merely that Reid had waved passing the window: but to Tessa? or to the other woman? what was her name? Hunt, Winston, she was American, Simpson, *Flint*, it was Flint.

Oh Reid knows everyone, said Kate.

You didn't know him when I asked you Monday.

Kate's hand skipped her collarbone and went to her eyes. She crossed her legs.

I would try one more thing, then give up here in order to preserve momentum. I was going to Dagger's to find out why he was holding the Unplaced Room out from Claire, why he'd wanted to put the Hyde Park Softball Game between the Hawaiian and the Suitcase; to find out if in fact the film I'd seen unwound and tangled on

368

Dagger's table (of even less value now than the strips of adhesive tape that had been used to seal the silver cans) had been our film, and if not, why not—and to find out where the sound was, that Monty outside my New York cab had suddenly thought of when the headless bike-rider whipped by. Also I had to cash a check.

I moved toward the foyer and asked, without looking back, if Kate would be surprised to know with whom Paul and Jan might be staying in Scotland.

Kate was close behind me, her steps left the rug and touched the floor.

You *knew* she wouldn't be here, didn't you! Why did you come?

I turned to Kate in the foyer and over her shoulder the crack of dark into the Unplaced Room flickered like a Highland chieftain's thigh or Tessa's, or like Dudley's detached elbow in the pool lane parallel to mine, or like my face retracting from the bare window of my room in the Marylebone house in '55 when Miss Topp and Mr. Sharpe the gardener looked around from the incinerator, or like the mystery snap packed quick as a blink between sweater and shampoo.

You don't know Mary's brother, I said, who used to be a force in the Scottish Nationalist Party.

I had the door open. I didn't feel the weight of my pack. I had been editing the film as if it existed. Did I want it to exist? In my dream, miles of film paid out of my abdomen into the light as someone walked away holding the leader.

I'd nearly run through the cash I'd taken from the Indian's wallet.

Kate had her hands crossed over her chest. Her eyes were wide. I had won her, if not her information.

Where? she said.

Mary's brother?

Kate nodded.

I leaned toward the open doorway and shifted my feet.

Kate's next words were barely breathed. Your daughter may be in weal twouble.

Jan before Jenny, I said, but pictured two heads on a motorbike and two hands signaling an impossible turn, and a diary cached at Callanish.

Even *I* am supposed to be tonight, she said. In danger.

England is not safe for me, I said. But neither is where I'm headed.

My voice sounded loud after Kate's. Will you be seeing the Flints? I have something for them.

Kate whispered in reply: That was Nell who *phoned*.

I replied in a whisper. I stroked the cheek of this English girl wondering if my heart had shrunk like the brave dismembered Montrose's into a secret cartridge: *Māyā*, Kate, means the world is not separate from me. It is color, it is black and white.

Kate and I talked low as if indeed there were someone in the Unplaced Room.

Your film, was it in color?

Some of it. The Unplaced Room was.

Oh, the paintings.

We took them down.

Where are you going?

Who was the third phone call?

Nash.

Whom were you going to tell what?

You never told me your dream.

My daydream will have to do.

What's your favwit color?

You ask as if you knew.

Orange Monday, red tonight, said Kate.

So in return for inadvertently identifying the Flints for me, Kate had noticed the jaguar's absence.

I thought of shadowing the building to see who went in and who left. But in return for the ten quid I borrowed from her, Kate said she'd phone me a minicab.

The driver was very young. I got hardly a glimpse of his face. His accent was not English, not European, a hint of Irish that he might have been hiding.

My pack was in the front seat and the pockets of my parka were lighter sitting down.

15 | The second-floor windows were dark, but it was early for Dagger and Alba to be in bed. On the other hand, the baby was less than two months old and Alba had been tired. The house in Belsize Park in which they had their high-ceilinged floor-through flat was fronted with pillars like Geoff Millan's. But theirs was part of a row of heavy cream-colored residences owned by the

Church, whereas his was a narrower brown brick with gray and red on either side.

The names by the bell were lighted. The downstairs door has had no lock for as long as I have known the house. I did not ring. The cab motor idled; under the dome-light the young man was studying his *A to Z* as if he was aware of me. There was a white stripe painted down the middle of the bonnet.

I climbed the two half-flights of carpeted stairs.

I looked around the DiGorros' door for a key.

When I went back downstairs I heard an engine fade. I found a ground-floor hall through to the rear and a door to the dark garden. The far end of the garden seemed higher than my end perhaps because of the mound of compost and junk that crested thornily above the low fence dividing it from the bottom of the opposite garden and two lighted windows at the back of the house beyond.

I got into a shed and hauled myself with surprising ease because it was dark onto a balcony. Behind me I heard a movement in the garden. The garden would be called a back yard in America. In the late summer sun I had had a drink on this balcony with Dagger and the baby and Alba nursing her. The French windows opened when I depressed the handle, and I was in the big room they used for everything except sleeping and entertaining. Dagger used this wonderfully full yet clear and open room to work in, but he often worked in the living room on the street side at the fatal table which you who have me may by now remember, if by now but dimly.

The familiar sweet and dairy-sour scent of the baby grew stronger in the hall. Yellowish light from a street lamp came through the baby's room to where I stood as if projected in the hall with the doorway of Dagger and Alba's bedroom behind me. Their bed was smoothly pale; a dial glowed, and by looking off-target I could tell it was ten twenty.

On a table in the balcony room my fingers found a coolness I knew to be a sheet of mica. I had bought some stained sheets cheap and had given Dagger two to try as makeshift insulation under the base of a living-room amplifier that was heating up. A strip of this flexible mica sensitively inserted could have sprung the lock of the front door for me. We had not been reimbursed for Corsica. A god does not think twice about an overdraft, but I thought again about the science-hobby exec Red Whitehead at this moment watching pro football at home in Long Island; my cut from him was small enough, but Nixon's devaluation which in itself mattered little more to me than to a rich tourist touched off familiar reflections on the cost of living and the rising price of land. There was apparently a cat in the garden scratching in the compost or fishing from the rim of a half-open dustbin. A car engine arrived suddenly on the street side and died and I was through the hall brushing some half-open door on the way and into the living room looking out, but in the street no one moved. Matters were not exactly crystal clear. But they were neither as distant nor as shifting as a week ago. In the dim gleam of the table by the window where I had seen hundred-foot and two-hundred-foot spools and their cans and lids strewn and film cork-screwed every-where and draping off onto the carpet, my fingertips hit a slender cigar and then picked up a sticky patch, perhaps a dried wine spill Alba had not seen late at night when she was in bed and Cosmo and Dagger were batting around the future of Allende or the death penalty or Ted Kennedy. Across the room in front of the round, carburetor-like slide-projector my hands found the red bowl of Jaffa oranges and soft leathery tangerines, and stiff-stemmed, hard, wax-paper-smooth apples green, yellow, or red, I couldn't tell, that Alba, with her fear of not having fresh fruit and vegetables, invariably overstocked. My toe hit something heavy, it was the offending ampli-fier which Dagger had moved down from its stand. I could see he had removed the lattice cover, under which, as I could feel, the tubes were not all bare, some had metal housing over the glass.

Back in the balcony room I lit Krish's lighter before a large glass-fronted cabinet of shelves. Inside were five cigarette lighters, three flashlights standing like the TNT that had got onto our film in August, a dozen little cigar-packs, and a cubic cache of Kodak and Agfa-35 film. In a lower shelf were four brand-new Japanese lenses in their boxes, four lens-dusting blower-brushes, a few flat yellow boxes of 4X movie film. In the shelf below—and as I bent, my pack slipped up like the yellow air tanks in the Gulf of Ajaccio—was a goodly trove of Beaujolais and Teachers scotch, and in front three Sony 110 tape recorders brand new in their boxes flanked by a stack of cassettes in theirs and a stack of typewriter ribbons in their boxes, a dozen or more.

Which returned me to the living room across from the pro-jector to look behind the turntable on a bookshelf that extended outward at knee-level; there had been a couple of the Nagra tapes there once, but now they were gone. In the dark it may be harder to get angry. I did not know if I was looking successfully forward. Can one be angry about the future? Alba's curtains were of fine Indian cotton, and the light that came through them sifted out the reds and oranges and purples but left the weave and the print as if on a shadow screen.

When the delicate splitting sound came from the back of the flat I went at once to face it. But in the balcony room I found nothing more than the draft stirring up the papers between the two type-writers across from the glass cabinet on the long work table that was in fact a hollow door. I closed the French windows and retrieved three sheets from the floor and one from the chair seat. A car stopped, but I did not go back where I'd come from to look. I lit Krish's flame and read a letter evidently from an American telling Dagger they'd been through all this before and if he was willing to take the movie projector right now he could have it for a low low rock-bottom price. The second sheet was a note from Monty Graf under the monogram of a London hotel dated Thursday: "If, as you say, you are counting on Cartwright's diary to *advertise* your film, perhaps I should see a piece of it." Between the lines there was a familiarity: off to see a man in Coventry; back Saturday; Claire unnecessarily worried; Jan in retreat between Art and social life; that little actor's to blame.

At that instant, like an axis, two sets of sounds joined street and garden: the slam of car doors; the clang of a dustbin lid; a voice I'd heard calling Hey Dag; and a cat's yowl like an arcing nerve.

On my way to the living room I again hit the open door in the hall and this time slid the pack off onto the floor. On the living-room threshold I heard steps on the stairs, but I continued to the street window and saw, just soon enough to fall away beside the semitrans-parent curtain, a man who was not Cosmo leaning against Cosmo's white three-wheeler in a heavy pale Faerile sweater, a man who I thought had a heavy, moustached cheer about him like a Games Master or like Dagger's when he carved up a high roast of PX ribs or ran his motorbike the wrong way up a narrow noontime street in Soho benevolently greeting outraged pedestrian definitions of the law—for Dagger in some highly developed sense of the warning above the bar of a Hebridean pub

> *Please do not ask for credit*
> *As a refusal often offends*

took credit.

When the upstairs bell rang, then rang again, I wondered who would wake the DiGorros. I moved halfway across the living room.

There was the soft crack of a lock. I let myself down onto the

373

couch and the papers crackled in my parka pocket when I curled up in a sleeping position. The hall light went on, and there was a bump of something being deposited on the floor which had to be near my pack which was against the wall by the hall closet. Before the front door closed again and the steps went downstairs, one of the stranger sounds I've ever heard came from Cosmo's voice: it was my name with a question mark.

The objects in this flat might yield the film.

Cosmo and the other went away and I turned off the hall light and went back to Dagger's table in the balcony room and with Krish's lighter looked through the letters and bills and notes to himself that Dag had accumulated. There was nothing explicit on the film unless Monty had written the note Thursday of this just-ending week, and Dagger had told the truth, and my diary was advertising a real film, in which event the film existed. But still only in part? The Softball Game. Maybe more. What more? Why more? The 8-mill. cartridge? The one we'd added the night we came back from shooting the air base? The Unplaced Room unmentioned to Claire?

There was too much here: too much between Dagger's pica standard and Alba's elite portable; too much between on my left the poster blow-up of Trotsky in his tortoise-shell glasses with a very young man with an open face beside him (as if photographed together when in fact there was a panel line dividing them) and on my right across above the glass cabinet Mercator's northern and southern hemispheres framed by Alba; too much between (at the balcony end on the far side of the French doors from me) a folded playpen (sandwiched between two suitcases) and (toward the hall door) several thigh-high piles of books and a stack of magazines staggering up from the floor; too much between (at that end of the room) the upright little oblong steel stove (about as high as the book piles) in which Alba (who would not have in her house one of the antique French stoves I'd been peddling) burned smokeless fuel— and (surprisingly yet somehow not awkwardly near the door to the hall) a huge white paper lantern ballooning down from the ceiling.

Too much even if you did not think of that playpen's history in our Marylebone house and then as mere clutter in the Highgate house when we didn't have a third child. Too much whether you knew or not that Dagger had once sold to a rich Swede a forgery identical to that framed forgery of that Map of the World executed by Mercator in 1538 just eight years before the set of observation instruments he had made for Charles V for his campaigns was destroyed by fire—the map lost for three centuries to be found in New York just thirty-six years after Catherwood's Jerusalem holocaust, a mental montage which in the dark of this room might be more visible than the object itself behind the glass of Alba's impeccably cut, narrow white frame.

Too much even if you did not place among the college youths who came down to Coyoacán to help guard Trotsky the New Yorker Bob Harte paneled with Trotsky in this poster visible to the eye of memory if not to the eye of Krish's flame from where I stood at the balcony end of the balcony room looking on a table for a film.

The stiletto button touched my palm and I pulled out of my pocket the papers which the draft I had caused by leaving the French windows open had blown off the table. The third letter was from an Air Force sergeant alerting Dagger to a special sale of Super-8 in minimum large lots. I blew out Krish's flame and strode out to the hall closet, Alba's closet; for one piece of our film was the 8 cartridge shot the night we came back from the base, and the 8 that Dagger said had burned was the cartridge Alba had taken of a friend's baby, but if Dagger was concealing the fact that the film had not been destroyed, and he'd slipped up somehow telling me the spoiled cartridge on the living-room table was the baby picture, why not put together the possible existence of our own Super-8 cartridge and the inviolate privacy of Alba's closet—where, as I lit Krish's lighter and pushed the closet door all the way open, I remembered Alba's flippers were kept, for the morning we departed for Corsica I had neglected to remind Dagger of them. This closet, with perhaps more of Alba in it than the balcony room or the master bedroom, was exactly between the box and the rucksack, and roughly (along the warped axis aforementioned) between balcony room (or garden) and living room (or street).

In the shelf facing me were boxes of Pampers and layers of baby clothes, the sleeved little vests (that Dagger called *smalls* and that are *undershirts* in American), the nightgowns, the Baby-Gro stretch suits waiting for Michelle, and all the other stuff I'd forgotten about, stacks of blankets the size of towels, more than she'd ever use.

Alba made friends easily in London. She said she could get excited by Dagger's absence, but the truth was she had many resources beyond her life with him, friends he hardly knew, a Milanese couple who designed furniture, a Greek engineer with twelve toes, an American golfer who had found life in England married to a Spanish girl congenial, several Italian, French, and Swiss *au pairs,* and an old Rumanian Yiddish poet more personally anarchist than his ideologue friends from the Whitechapel of 1914, a good poet who was said except when he was with Alba to speak only Yiddish, who drank anything and sang, and whom Alba had thrown out on one occasion for pissing on the bathroom floor.

She kept her stationery supplies here in this cupboard, not at the long and vulnerable table where her typewriter kept its distance from Dagger's. In the large lower space from waist-level down she kept her heavy equipment. An olive green tool box, planes, a drill, a level whose window blinked its bubble at Krish's flame, and hanging from the sides and from the underside of the shelf saws that glinted like swords—then right above a shellacked box marked BITS (and beside a hammer) a brace fixed angular on the wall, in shape like the zig-zag crank of the Angenieux zoom we'd used to shoot the naval engagement in the very bay for whose depth I had used flippers hired in the sight of Incremona's blond sidekick sitting with a girl in a port café across the cobbles from the *plongeur* van. Alba's flippers—bought for her by Dag—lay one on top of the other at the back of this neat dark closet forgotten the day we left for Corsica and recalled with Corsica tonight. Alba's Super-8 camera came into view at another cavelike level of her closet. The cartridges in their little yellow cartons were all unexposed, for you could not imagine Alba not having a cartridge developed as soon as she'd shot it; in fact, she rarely used the camera. The cartridge of baby film bizarrely burned by a brief ray of radiance through the atmosphere, through a bright clean windowpane, and through the lens of a magnifying glass had been on its side when I arrived in response to Dagger's call. There were burn marks on the sides; my feelings I had thought at the time were like the 16-mill. corkscrewed around the table but may have been more like the ruined 8 still acrid and even (I thought for a moment, visibly) smoking inside—a cartridge browned at the edges but not noticeably harmed.

I wheeled out of the closet mouth, three rooms and more distances in mind at once—the bedroom clock and cupboards (closets in American), the living room with Dagger's work table that must have burn marks from at least the first inches of leader I saw lying on the table that day, and the bathroom darkroom off the hall in quite another direction the thought of which staggered my already warped line so I kept turning and faced again this packed closet whose cartridges might be the heart of the matter somewhere in their

376

relative unimportance to Alba, and wheeling again I moved past Cosmo's heavy-looking carton and into the living room where I switched on a light and examined the table and found nothing on Alba's finish but the wine spill.

I switched off the light and saw parked five doors down across the street a driverless vehicle that had the same broad white stripe painted down the middle of its bonnet from windscreen to grille that my minicab had had—it looked like the same car. The silence of Dagger's and Alba's things seemed at this displaced time better far than to ask—to interrogate. Dagger's old cousin in Farmingdale, New Jersey, was a Trotskyite hanging on to a future that was the socialist nostalgia of his Jewish friends there. Bob Harte gave away the key to a builder who was working at Avenida Viena; Trotsky saw him do it and warned him; the young American was easy-going. Who else had a key to Dagger and Alba's? Lorna didn't have a key to Tessa's. I hadn't a key even to my own fresh lock in Highgate.

It was not ten twenty any more. I went for the balcony room and its cabinet, but passing Cosmo's carton and my half-full rucksack slumped softly against the wall and between them Alba's closet with the cartridge boxes that had made me wonder about those apparently unopened cassettes in the glass-fronted cabinet, I turned into the dark bathroom.

This was an impulse, a godlike move veering and light as if Red Whitehead had given me an expense account. Here baby flesh was overcome by the acid of urine and the foggy perfume of talc. I was getting closer. A red light went on beside the sink. I avoided the mirror. There were chemicals and two pans but no film cans or spools. I got a *shtip* in my gut—Tessa's Yiddish for *stab*—and I wanted a long hot bath. I got away from the smell.

The film if it existed might be in the bedroom where, as I passed it again, I could tell at a glance the clock didn't say ten twenty any more. Now the cabinet in the garden room; the shelf with the lenses and blower-brushes: the Kodak 4X movie film: three boxes open in the dark then under Krish's flame betrayed no images; I opened the rest—for why not hide old film in new cans?—but it was the same story. If Māyā as I had said to Kate meant the world was not separate from me, maybe (but I did not believe it) the film I sought had nothing to do with a world of mine.

If, as you say, you are counting on the diary to advertise the film, maybe I should see a piece of it.

But a piece of what? Monty had seen a piece of the diary. Did

377

he want more? I was between many people in many directions. The people I was looking out for may have exited through another part of the building site and the other people coming after the people of the first part may never come. And if so, will the site blow? The steps in the hotel pass Glasgow, Portland, Cincinnati—but a modest B & B where Lorna and I had a week just before American Labor Day is relatively hall-less and I had a chance to talk to my boatyard partner about ferro-concrete hulls and to his granddad about exactly what part of a wheel the felloes were and again about why the cleavage had to be so right, and in that B & B mopping up our egg and banger-grease with fresh white bread (for breakfast is what the second *B* stands for) the news came on the Irish landlady's wireless on a shelf up among some bric-a-brac and it was Nixon's devaluation, and Lorna said we could have feathered our nest even better and I said maybe now's the time to sell the house and transfer the money through Canada and go home, and Lorna drank her tea and looked at me: It's possible, she said quietly; I said Jenny would like that; Lorna said she wasn't at all sure because Jenny was English—and now by the cabinet in the dark amid Dagger, Alba, Dagger plus Alba, Alba in Dagger, Dagger in Alba, I had to try the bedroom. But then I wheeled away from the luminous clock-face far and dim, for there was a bathroom closet that might hold more than bath crystals and pumice.

Yet setting foot again in the darkroom where Dagger developed his black-and-white stills, my shoe hit something, and I bent and put my hand not first on *it* (a comb) but on the lino tile which Alba had laid and which I knew to be black and white diamonds, but whose cold I could not foresee: it traveled across the heel of my palm and the inside of my wrist close to my blood, straight to my armpit, and turned me blue: not blue with cold: for Tessa's *haiku* quoted to me in bed by Lorna emerged briefly along that vein of thermal action—some bare chill I could not recall the words for climaxed by: *my dead wife's comb under my heel:* Lorna's robin's-egg blue comb, and then I did touch what my shoe had felt, and it was a wide comb—Alba's?—with a tuft in the teeth—I had a hard-on, the two of them Lorna and Tessa in that smooth untouched bed in the next room—with me—and with the lunar intruder coming in at an extreme angle, a pilot's five o'clock, and the *shtip* came again and again like the film paying out in my dream, and amid the mere things of this household beyond which or in which I must find the film or its history, I could have lain in a hot tub as I did on the night of the Marvelous Country House and been fingered by Lorna while defining

378

Māyā for her and seeing the Southeast Asia of my sex enlarge and straighten and some time later swell and vanish like some multiple dream of achievement into the huge faded black towel she surrounded me with blotting out Dagger tooling away toward Hampstead with the boys and girls in the VW minus Sherman, and the Marvelous Country House in two cans and the Beaulieu—and no doubt using his talent to stir up a little friction if there wasn't any or calm things down if there was, though when he retorted to Sherman on the way to the MCH that Yucatan was just as tough as Africa, Sherman seemed to leave that for Dagger to explore—which he did not, for he told that tale of the dwarf which purported to be first-hand from his supposed wanderings in Yucatan but derived from my idea of tying into power possessed of momentum but undeveloped purpose which Monty Graf had pondered while I ate my New York fish, though out of loyalty to myself I would not have told him my sense at the end of June that some almost too adequate purpose of mine was being drawn into Dagger's new lack of momentum which was not his New Jersey Italian *dolce far niente* but his willingness to believe what his man the cine-film processor in Soho promised and his determination to use this man rather than someone who'd do the job for us at once, even though driving home from Wales in the early hours of Saturday, May 29, with (at that moving point in time) three scenes in the can (the May 16 Softball Game, the May 24 Unplaced Room, and the May 28 Bonfire) he had said it was possible but not probable we could get the man to do our work as early as Monday.

However, Stanton the charter man in London got after me to book some tours that were a new extension of our services to American tourists including hotel accommodations and tight time tables for visiting Stately Houses and Civil War castles, the American Museum at Bath and cathedrals up as near the Scottish border as bare towering Durham where the Venerable Bede seems to be interred—which was what saddled me with this chore in the first place, for I'd told Stanton I'd be away the first part of that week seeing a man at Union Carbide's plant in Durham, and Stanton had made it hard for me to refuse, and it meant money, so I didn't think about Dagger for a few days during which I was home just often enough to take Lorna to a party at Geoff Millan's and to have a discussion with Jenny about her social life interfering with her Latin A-levels—her social life being the guerrilla-theater actor—and when she spoke of the trips she and Will (then Billy) and I took to the Science Museum and the Natural History Museum in the old days to push the buttons and clock the

379

dinosaur, it stuck in my head and when I not Dagger suggested the Underground not at Tottenham Court Road or Piccadilly where you might expect to see kids banging guitars but the old long dusky tunnel under the Science Museum and the Natural History Museum connecting with the South Ken Underground and Dagger didn't say anything but looked through his supplies in a shelf of the glass cabinet and brought out two 100-foot-reel cans in their boxes and said absent-mindedly, How much of this are we going to need for sound track, and when I said That's *film*, I thought Alba's coolness might mean they'd had a fight and Dagger was going around in circles for the moment like me more than two months later in face of Lorna's coolness over breakfast in the seaside B & B getting Nixon's devaluation on the news but being more conscious of the first *B* than of egg and sausages.

Which made me hungry through my heat and through the pain in my stomach (which might well be less Kate's sandwich than a *shtip* of guilt which even a minor god can feel) and spinning from the bathroom darkroom past the comb of whatever color and in another direction away from the entrapping axis of living room/balcony room into the kitchen I found hanging near a window a salami in its unbreached skin, and to find a knife I switched on a light which set off a ventilator, and then grasping the knife I spun away again into the dark of the hall and the balcony room to the glassed cabinet, for Dagger's absent-mindedness put me in mind of what I now withdrew from the low shelf where the Sony 110 recorders were: and indeed three of the little cassette boxes, resealed so that in Krish's light I made out only a tiny almost imaginary line of slit, contained not cassettes but Nagra spools. These I put in the tight pockets of my jeans, turning involuntarily to lay my hand on some ordinary thing in that room that would tell me the truth about Dagger.

The sheets of mica in the indirect light from the kitchen felt very like Red Whitehead's plastic-encapsulated sample sheets I'd shown Dagger to illustrate the behavior of certain organic chemicals being developed for use in the display-panel numerals of cheap microelectronic calculators which like Mylar insulation for ordinary sleeping bags are yet another spin-off from space research. Dagger uncorked another bottle and said, OK how did I know what our warm fingerprints were *really* doing to what I had been calling liquid crystals encapsulated in that "there" plastic sheet, but this altercation differed from the one we had toward the end of June when Dagger showed me three spools of reversal film which, when he said these were the Softball Game, called up a cylinder of unspecific cinders, my grandfather in his can which the weekend of his death in a Maine hotel I saw only the outside of—I demanded to know why the Unplaced Room and the Bonfire in Wales were not here as well, and Dagger was visibly unhappy he couldn't divert me with his idea to shift the Softball Game to between the Hawaiian Hippie and the Suitcase Slowly Packed which we had just shot, so as to leave the Unplaced Room first—a far simpler opening, no? I asked *why* we had to do business with this lab; Dagger said again this was a fellow who'd give us a break.

I did not recall losing faith in Dagger, yet I had been quite capable of loosening Claire's faith in him when on Monday over drinks at Monty's I'd told her the only film developed had been the Bonfire—knowing that Dagger if he'd told her anything about developed footage would have mentioned the Softball Game but not the Bonfire.

Why did he never ask about the diary?

Even when I said Jenny was typing it.

I would have asked Jenny then and there the night she finished typing Hawaiian Hippie and Suitcase Slowly Packed—June 27—what she thought of my speculations on the snap so quickly shot; but she gave me the pages so glumly all I could do was look into her face and murmur, Is it Reid?

My words seemed to move Jenny's feelings into view: she said there was no telling with Reid, they'd been all around London that day and he had said they were going to the cinema, but after they left Jane and Dudley, Reid had decided he had to split—he'd call her—and Jenny said to me that if she was being punished she'd like to know for what. But when I prolonged that question, she kissed me and went up. And on the 4th of July a week before we set sail for Corsica, Dagger said his lab man had gone on holiday to America but it mustn't hold up, and when Cosmo who I'd never thought had a key to this flat drove me home in that three-wheeler that looks as if it would take off or tip over he asked if Aut had sold the film to TV, and the question (more interesting than I gave it credit for) passed by in my then strangely released exasperation: I said I was beginning to wonder if Dagger was ever going to get our film processed.

Would Krish have heard my gripe from Cosmo?

Could Reid have heard it from Jenny?

I had not found the film in the things of Alba's household; I had only three tapes and they could be Stonehenge, Unplaced Room,

HH, MCH—the minute hand of the bedroom clock had swept from the straight line of ten twenty round into the acute angle of ten fifty-five. I slid back the long door of the clothes cupboard and felt among neat-stacked boxes behind hanging wool and silk. Alba made a smooth bed. I was beginning to think she and Dagger had gone away. Again I tried the bathroom, stepped over the comb, reached behind some plastic bottles lined up in the window-inset—the tub had a puddle near the drain—the small plastic tub leaning against the wall under the sink was dry. That was the baby's tub. I had forgotten all that. I remembered Lorna standing legs apart on the pebbly strand, Lorna stroking steadily out through the dark damp sea. I saw her from the boatyard where my partner was trying to buy me out. Lorna stroked beyond the children and out past the pale fat breast-stroker with thick dark hair, Lorna's steady crawl learned in a New England lake thirty years ago was young and beautiful, and even you who have me would not have guessed that the night before at twelve thirty by my wristwatch she was demanding to know what Stonehenge had to do with "draft deserters" (from one sagging B & B single bed to another across a turquoise carpet on the second creaking floor of that B & B) and then demanded why I had not taken Jenny to Stonehenge. And I had to have something repeated by my boatyard partner, who then observed that I was distracted by the girls bathing, and when granddad the old wheelwright came up and remembered me I had to have something else repeated, being between in more ways than Reid's with Jan and Jenny (to judge from that curious scene along the gallery street in Knightsbridge, the kisses, the bus stop, the Underground): Jan and Jenny might have in common that he was less or otherwise interested in them than they in him. I sat on the tub-edge and looked at the comb so out of character there dropped on the lino and saw in the still gloam from the kitchen down the hall the tuft sprouting in a tiny languorous arc, and wishing to reach for it I felt the slippery porcelain under my new jeans, and Dudley Allott and I, bare thighs on the tiles of Swiss Cottage pool, shared an illusion of April intimacy that I now see was also intimacy's authentic shiver, at least for me who was between: for it was the closest he'd come since the night of his appendix forked saffron off a Jewish table into my jaws with (at differing gates and distances) Tessa, Lorna, and the pediatrician's wife who had not then done her children's book and who now (as I sat on Alba's clean tub and listened to Dudley naked the last day of April) sat conversing with animation at a small party at Geoffrey Millan's, and (as you

382

who have me may know if you can now lay your hand on and insert a flash-forward printed-circuit cartridge heartfelt or cryptic) before the night was over I was to put in an appearance at Geoff's party:

Catherwood, said Dudley. How odd! I took up Catherwood to interest Tessa. Can you feature that?

I'd known this as far back as New York in '64—the first flush of Dudley's interest. I told him so, and he looked at me. I looked down at his belly flapped over his bathing suit. He spoke at length, and I leave you who have me to imagine my occasional responses and the washing of pale green chlorine waves clearer in their refractions than hard crystal.

Whatever was between us, said Dudley (meaning himself and Tessa), it came to take solid forms.

Stones. Violence. Mexico.

The Maya, their sacrifices, their underground rivers in Yucatan, the noses and the lips, the legends. I made her come with me to the British Museum to see what she'd seen on her own before—the wooden lintel from a temple in Guatemala with the *halach uinic*, the religious chief, seated holding the round shield and the manikin scepter, one of whose legs ends in a serpent's head; and I'd read about Tikal, the ancient city the lintel came from, and I said someday let's go see its pyramid temples which are the highest man-made things in Maya country ranging from 143 feet to 229 measuring from the ground to the roof comb, and in fact she'd seen a painting of Tikal, an enclave of powerful structures shadowed by time and perspective into a forbidding scene held off from the viewer who feels he might lose out if he tried to enter—at which point Tessa says Dudley, do me a favor and stop trying to be a poet; she cared about the method of sacrifice and I was unable from my rudimentary reading to say for sure if the heart-excising ritual was common to Tikal or not and she wandered away to look at Egyptian antiquities. I took her to Switzerland, I know you remember, when she had a bad chest but principally to surprise her with the Maya lintels at Basel which are the finest. You can guess how I made the same bloody mistake over and over. I took her to Holland to see the Leyden Plate which is just a hunk of jade 8½ inches by 3 from Guatemala in a shape like a little chisel implement they call a *celt*—the Leyden Plate was unearthed in 1864 and of the highest importance though not for the ferocious sleepy profiles of animals or gods—the enormous-nosed, dollop-lipped, retreating-chinned profiles Tessa loved—and the captive under the warrior's sandal. I read Bishop Landa. I read

Stephens' *Incidents of Travel*. I gave it to Tessa. I tried to intercept her—you know her—but then again *I* know her. And if it was ever physical it had little to do with whether I took regular exercise or studied breast-beating in the *Kama Sutra*. For a time I virtually gave up European history except to lecture on it. I took up Catherwood (said Dudley) because I wanted a German Jewish refugee who was obsessed with her mother's disappearance in a death camp.

Catherwood was between us, the friend of Keats and Shelley, Prescott and Wilkinson, and no one except possibly Wilkie Collins in *The Woman in White* described him, and there the character Hart-wright goes off to Central America and is a draftsman and the rest of it may not be Catherwood at all—the star-crossed lovers (for he *was* married)—but the honesty and legality in Hartwright does seem right for the man I find in Stephens' *Incidents* and in the drawings; he was a great draftsman and the first to use daguerreotype to record Maya remains, but there is no picture but the self-portrait vaguely self-effacingly at the center of his picture of the Tulum ruins where he's either paying out or pulling in surveyor's tape, possibly the same reel they used for the ruins in Jerusalem.

Tessa would of course interrupt me (said Dudley) in the presence of her father and others when I would speak of my Catherwood inquest. She would say Dudley is counting the fifteen-foot-long rungs of the famous eighty-foot ladder that runs down the well of Bolonchén but the real current is the underground river that feeds the well; Dudley is working out what Catherwood's camera lucida was and just how he used it between his eye and the paper to bring Egyptian temples and obelisk carvings and Alexander's grand cock jutting along from wall to wall at Karnak down to the right proportions and perspective—while *my* Catherwood is finding in a ruined city his friend paid fifty dollars for, a Maya idol he instinctively knows is a blood relative of Egypt.

You know her. Why do I tell you all this? In '64 Catherwood instead of being a means to a juncture became a subtle passion. To me. Tessa begged off the Brooklyn Museum and the Natural History Museum. She reminded me that because of her in the Natural History in London I'd said I'd never set foot there again with or without her. On a mad detour en route to Yucatan she could fly around southern California looking out her window for the 167-foot man, but she wouldn't come uptown in Manhattan to see the vaults of the Museum of the American Indian, though on the other hand she always made me feel I'd done well when I took her to a restaurant as I did that night, there was a Mexican place in the Village, but you must recall it—and even as early as '64 I knew it was hopeless and at this time Catherwood got larger in my thinking, a mystery man, exile engineer, impromptu physician to the Indians—how much of Collins' Hartwright is Catherwood?

And Catherwood stayed between Dudley and Tessa but for Dudley as a memory of his need for her and an inkling of discovery. And when a lawyer was interested in Cabot and the rotunda burning of Catherwood's Maya drawings and the Jerusalem panorama, Dudley consulted him about a divorce.

Her disparagements ceased to touch him, he said. The Leyden Plate tells us how early the Maya calendar systems and the associated hieroglyphics and astronomy were developing in Yucatan: but Tessa turns away to tell tales of dwarves looking out of windows, and widows underground selling river water in exchange for babies in order to feed pet snakes—did Dagger really go to Yucatan?—not to mention the feathered serpent god, the exile Kokulcan, who seemed to go away but who landed further down the coast—or she confuses Kokulcan Quetzlcoatl with the extended snake-head foot of the manikin scepter somewhat as she confuses fourth-century Maya calendrics with animal cycles in Tibet.

I, Cartwright, sitting on an edge of the Swiss Cottage pool, had been following the stroke of a girl lap after lap. Dudley's unprecedented talk moved steadily ahead through a hotel in Merida, North Yucatan: Tessa suddenly got nice when they talked of going southwest to find the hundred-foot-high terrace where two giant cottonwood trees originally from India spread their great roots thirty yards outward to bind down the ruined stone structures—and Dudley didn't touch the water or the beans and still got cramps.

The swimming girl passed close, twisting her head to breathe automatically as if in a sleep, and Dudley passed through a Welsh farmhouse with two long-haired cats that filled his allergic lungs and itching chest and a gentleman farmer friend of a Scottish friend of Tessa's took her off on long walks and got drunk and amused Tessa with the jumbled tale of how Lord Cardigan of the Light Brigade had been responsible for the r-w defect politely imitated by his officers and bequeathed now to certain members of the upper middle class, and Dudley asked where in Wales Cardigan was and the gentleman farmer asked Dudley questions he'd asked a half hour before about what kind of sanitation they had in the stone castles along the Wye and the Usk and whether there were any castles in America, where the Allotts were about to return, and Tessa and their host were still up when Dudley was in bed asleep.

But on the round edge of Alba's bathtub I'd seen or heard through outward curves like someone else's fingerprint of my life Dudley fibbing to Jane: This man Dudley in the probities of resolved habit would not go to that museum in London any more; I'd heard him say so. It hadn't been the *museum* he wanted to stop at after they left the nearby air terminal. The museum was a pretext.

Reid had been in the pedestrian tunnel then with Jenny, had been recognized by Jane, and had suddenly changed his mind.

Jenny had wended her way home and typed two parts of my film diary, the Hawaiian Hippie and the Suitcase Slowly Packed.

In the hall I lifted the carton Cosmo had left; it didn't feel like wine, not heavy enough nor, in its lines of stability, vertical. Nor did it clink.

Cars passed. I switched off the kitchen light. Pushed in the drawer I'd left out. Switched on the light to see if I'd left a knife out. Then switched off.

The worldly goods of Alba and Dagger had conveyed themselves to me in my rounded fingertips and rising memory. Man and woman, let them together cleave. They might come back. The place had cloven itself first from garden to street:

at thigh level:	mica sheet to film table
	steel stove to fruit bowl
at knee level:	a letter blown onto a chair seat,
	a stereo turntable in a bookcase
at toe level:	unhoused tuner, fallen comb.

But was the comb along that axis between garden and street? No. It was in the bathroom: and it turned me: or I was turned to it by the leveled contents of Alba's closet which itself was off or barely on that axis that now rotated. Round and round I turned looking out to these dark things that were also all (especially in Dagger's "exciting" absences) Alba's. Well, Dagger had dropped into my house one day when I wasn't there and taken some magazines—Lorna didn't know which. At eye-level across from the forged Mercator, the fresh face of Bob Harte murdered in May 1940 (in part because he lent away the key to Trotsky's gate) thickened to the lips of Mick Jagger peeling down off Jenny's wall, blinding in turn into my own merchant mouth nosing Lorna's calf toward twelve thirty to confuse anger if not only to please the object of my desire, but having lost that axis to a turn

386

and having turned less clearly yet more smoothly borne past faces two, three, four, six times familiar, not just a father and a daughter approaching a daughter and an actor, but (cleaving watery distances) others, round through origin after origin, still the building site my people were wiring to blow up while I stood guard is alone with me, and the absence of them (for they have gone) and of the others whose approach I was to intercept but who now may not come softens the fore-and-aft axis where I stand between, to a conglomerate of foreign fields surrounding me on all sides belonging to other after other after other, hence seeming to decrease probabilities, hence seeming static, yes parts of a wheel I have not wholly made myself, in turn a conveyance I've also partly made, like the Nagra spools I've added to the weapons in my pockets, like ideas for a film whose idea was also Jan's, like my dream on the Glasgow plane which a preclassic Maya shrink deglyphs as a rueful record of Tessa who acted out for me the old Maya price of cuckolding a noble—the belly opened, the intestine coaxed forth into the temperate air loop by loop, a trout's dream of fish heaven, but here too the cuckold-executioner with his hand on the real inner thing which yet escapes him for under its belly-flesh it has so often turned over when stroked lightly by the adultress his wife. But what did Tessa ever say about Lorna? Nothing!

Not, Why do you fuck your wife's friend?

Not, What would she feel if she knew? or feel if she did not know?

Between rucksack and carton in Dagger's hall I felt the slow thump of steps. Not many. As many as the steps behind me Wednesday in New York (though they were odd) and as I went to the living-room couch and curled up in a self-defense Napoleonic or godlike in the casual will to really sleep for plausibility's sake, I was still deeper into the wheel which was a new, less violent between.

So that I was an axled part not just of objects where I'd hoped to find the film, not just among objects which, in proper light, film they say can best reveal, nor of a wheel merely solid; for the things in this flat swelled my head like a lung or the ripples round a disturbance, out through what the objects meant in the DiGorros' life, beyond to Catherwoods and Cartwrights that abandoned such darkly solid household effects as these to pass so far out in this cycle as to reach then an inner not an outer vacancy to be filled with words which (let me finish) may yet turn up bodily parts like the Maya limbs hired machetes unearthed while John Lloyd Stephens "leaned over [them] with breathless anxiety" not knowing what he'd got hold of—in fact a city he would presently buy for a record fifty dollars still not knowing what he had.

Red Whitehead watched a fourth-quarter screen-pass unfold on his TV and reached blindly for the pack of filters on the table between a beer can and a hand-painted plate of crumbs. I must abandon my subservience to minor moneys, and make my fortune in America. My mind was a live liquid. A Xerox lay under a wet stone at Callanish. OK, let it advertise the film. Phone the Indian-boned Calvinist widow and ask her to retrieve it. Let Jack and Aut, Reid and the boy named Sherman who had helped roof Reid's dome in Ridge-field with Reid's parents' phonograph discs, let Incremona and Gene and others fear the film through the words of mine that lay between them and it.

A piece of flesh in Lorna's firm fingers.

Pachisi, the backgammon Hindus play with cowry shells—which is like Mexican Patolli.

From Prescelly, Pentelicon, Aswan, the Copan quarries, the great stones (how, one does not know) sometimes without the wheel, moved through the four ages of the world, Maya, Hindu, other.

So that the world comes to be believed in, between us and the truth.

An illusion the Hindus call Māyā.

Felt even more in the partly separated blocks that never quite made it out of the mountain-top quarry and that Stephens and Catherwood scratched their names in.

Catherwood with his hand moved column-idols thirteen feet high all over the world. Stephens arranged the digs, studied the finds. Catherwood went on sketching.

Māyā is the world this side of the truth.

Dudley did not make it up to the Museum of the American Indian that Monday to look at the Catherwood drawings in the vault. The place was closed. On that Monday, Catherwood grew between Dudley and Tessa. In the evening he took her to a Mexican restaurant and they ate baby cactus, and it is quite likely that Tessa did not think of what she had had that afternoon. Dudley knew.

I am Catherwood.

I am Māyā.

Why not use the film to push the diary.

As if still in Glasgow, but now with more weapons, I had nearly willed myself to sleep and knew the comb on the bathroom floor did not belong; for Alba was too careful.

Hands pinioned in the new raincoat now packed in a suitcase checked at the West London Air Terminal, I heard through that static escalator field down which I had plunged, two men angrily arguing, their voices receding.

Between this and what happened next, I knew myself to be adequate.

16 | Dag, she called, and a light came on and she got no answer. I was half there.

I contemplated my absence. Nothing happened.

More light thinned my lids, and a rustling preceded a second silence unlike the first. Then above me very near, the baby moaned.

You who have me may see on the far side of my shut, untrembling lids, the tight-bunned contour of Alba's hair silvery in this light.

She went away.

The baby squawled.

Would Alba change her in the bathroom?

Alba, I called, as if I had just woken.

Alba didn't speak.

After a while she was nearer.

The baby at first crying as she was at last put down was not sung to but told some nonsense tale that she could not understand at two months but that in some sound of the words stilled the cycles of her energy.

Alba was in the living room, the light behind her.

I told you to take care of Dag, she said. And what have you done?

A woman with a baby, a woman with a closet full of tools, a woman with a husband she had introduced me to ten minutes after she had met him herself and five after she'd met me, in November of '63 in the hotel room of an American acting as adviser to engineers who were about to introduce a computer into the London traffic mess, and this American Lorenzo kept hugging Dagger and calling him an untrustworthy bastard and when Dagger invited among others me and my "wife" over on Saturday and I accepted, Lorna came up behind me, said we had tickets to *Uncle Vanya* Saturday, and introduced herself to Dagger and Dagger said her dark hair and blue eyes were sensational and demanded to know when our show let out Saturday. Six of us that Tuesday night (for Lorna had a sitter) went

389

off to Alba's for spaghetti, and it was clear that she and Dagger clicked. She kept her aphorisms demurely few but sharply apropos.

Here cut in ten seconds of Dagger's applause record, a particular favorite with Cosmo, who taped it for his own collection.

Add: Dagair, Dagair, I will geeve you da Croix de Guerre, crooned by Alba's Paris pal, the model, kissing him once on each lip.

Or if maps came with sound, think of Bourguignon d'Anville the eighteenth-century cartographer clearing away the false lakes of Africa and shrinking the Antarctic continent he refused to believe covered half the southern hemisphere.

If you have filmed Alba with sound, but failed to change the aperture when shifting up to slow motion, you who knew her and had seen her would have the efficient voice still more sequential. With it you could call up the turn of one shoulder toward you with the dip of the neck as she introduced between (a) your curious question (Did you recently refinish the table by the window?) and (b) a simple reply (which would have been No) the counter-query to you, Why did you have to keep a diary in the first place?

Anyhow facing you she was so gently still that slow motion would have singled out only her lips: unlike the night Dag and I came back from the final shooting at the air base and I insisted on our filming with Alba's 8 their flat and the three people we found there, and suddenly I knew how to do it—in slow motion with the sound later slowed also—a fitting end for our film and for me a private recollection of a dream I'd had a week after Lorna and I fought our one and only first and last physical fight, and after trying to dream my lookout dream I was stuck instead with our fisticuffs and wrestling falls and crabbed fingers slow motion as if we were running down, or approaching the state of stills or being analyzed in someone else's purview plan we'd no say in, and the dream turned words and grunts into some unheard-of madness or underlying real structure that in my dream I was merely impatient with though I'd heard in these disintegrated sounds evidence that Lorna was Jewish —and Alba the night we came back from the base was so restless, up and down, smoking, cocking her wrist, jumping to change a record-band, that she would have constituted a struggling current in the ultimate footage: but Dagger yakking on about Cartwright's unique plan for a moving terminal had not changed the aperture, and though he said he'd send the film in, there was no hope—as it turned out—at that speed apparently you need much more light. And since I was going away mad, Dag decided to be funny describing Phil Aut, a tense abstemious man, who had told Claire a rule of thumb for 16-millimeter production was a thousand dollars a minute, but the three fellows in Alba's Swedish chairs either were tired or didn't find our film venture droll, and neither did I till I was in the minicab Alba called for me and was away from her living room watching white-framed windows flicker down a quiet sturdy street and then saw we were wrong and told the driver to turn, and then was sorry, as if a univac's fingerprint of micro-rectangles had switched us to a more logical route at the end of which was the chance I had always fore-seen that the film would come to nothing, and a gate swung open upon the nuclear family if in fact you got past omens along the way and reached the gate and inside the gate slept wife and hilly seaside village a week hence—son and maybe daughter—who were *not* coming to the seaside village—and the memory of two helium bal-loons Dagger gave them the first Christmas we knew him, 1963.

Tell me, Alba, why did we even go there? I asked her now in October in answer to her challenge that you who have me will recog-nize echoed her light parting plea to me in July to take care of Dag during the Corsican trip. But I added that I had not needed to go to Ajaccio to know that Mary-the-Scot's brother had helped to influence Paul to disentangle himself.

I got my feet onto the floor. Would the lady like me to go? I asked.

What did it matter? she said.

Very tired I was, I said.

Had I been locked out then? she said. Surely *Will* was at home?

Dagger's plan to put the Softball Game between HH and SSP would bring into linkage or collision with the mystery snapshot and the tunnel I'd more than once traversed with Jenny and Will as children, the top of Will's head: for the camera as I'd thought (and Dagger confirmed) had scalped Will—for Dagger panning behind home stopped to get a long shot of Krish, Jan, and the other Indian sitting on the grass, and Will was under the Beaulieu's path and we got his hair. But what could it matter, editing a film that was possibly as Claire had said nonexistent—said so bleakly I'd wondered that first noon in her flat if after all she did indeed care; no, it was Monty who cared, and in part because of his sister Jan whom I assumed Alba knew, though I asked not about her but (yawning) whether Monty had got back from Coventry, I'd meant to phone the number there, did Alba have it?—which drew from her then, You mean John? and I at once though casually said yes that bumptious florid chatterbox ego and she said well he was very intelligent and was always going off to America but she hardly knew him and had *I* involved Dag with him? he was in munitions. Monty, I said, was responsible for that, and if Dagger was going to have secrets from me with Claire I could not very well be held responsible for his involvements.

I rose—still profound with my brief half-sleep—and followed Alba into the kitchen. My rucksack seemed even more in evidence as if Alba had lifted it and let it slump back lower against the wall.

She filled a kettle and did not look at me. She said she should imagine Lorna was home by now if I wanted to phone.

To ask, Is the film destroyed, and to hear, Dag *told* you so, why ask me?—was like going back to September yet like drifting into November—Guy Fawkes pennies dropping boom boom—Thanksgiving harvest—Christmas cassettes from the U.S. But Alba was less tired than she claimed, for when I said I'd never really *had* the film so I could not really discard or lose it, she cited the Sufi sage who retorted to a man lamenting his penniless state, My son, perhaps you paid but little for your poverty.

But my diary was gone too, I pointed out; and in the instant now before Alba's startling answer I saw the dilettante geologist in his red mini combing Callanish for Krish, and maybe Jack with him, for Jack had sent Krish to pump the man, which might mean Jack was not sure of the man, yet were one of them to find Jenny's cache and Reid were then to know, Reid might pay her back, assuming I was right that Reid was merely using her for information, albeit information on how much information I and possibly Dagger and others had on him and others associated with a project I now had to assume went well beyond the mere harboring of Vietnam exiles and drug-pushing in the Underground.

I *know*, said Alba, and took a plate down from the closet and automatically ran water on it, and it's just as well for all of us your diary is gone.

She would like *me* gone.

She and Dagger served each other, and also by absence.

Jenny looked up from her hard concentrated typing and when I gave her a peck on the forehead she asked what I'd meant in what I'd written about the Corsican waiter and the Italian who imposed his will on all those shrimp, and I said that if Dagger or Alba were ever to read the passage they'd laugh.

French for *revolution* is French also for *revulsion*, the Corsican waiter (looking daggers at those shrimp) serves the affluent

392

Italian's bald power not quite satisfactorily cloaked just as the Italian's smug will serves the waiter's energy—this on each side in lieu of wishing real change.

Dagger that first night in Alba's flat after drinks in Lorenzo's hotel room, reached an arm round Alba's shoulder to slide in another box of spaghetti. He ordered her around. She opened a bottle of Chianti which of course she would have in her larder. Lorna asked the computer man if Kennedy was in trouble and he said Jack was doing better with the girls than with Congress, and I shut up because Lorna had recently condemned me for talking for her in public.

But go back to '58—the eve of Tessa's disappearance—and I'll tell you Lorna wanted more than that: she wanted me silenced, wanted me in some subtle or tentative embodiment dead. We would speak not quite loud enough: What? The words would get said again. Lorna often didn't hear when she should have heard. And she guessed wrongly all I heard in her silences, conceded me a power.

Which might be like what Alba was coldly to concede later tonight as I was leaving when she said, I do not *want* to know what you know. But Alba conceded in another stubbornly obeisant way now and a moment before, by hinting Lorna's whereabouts, a party (which could not be Geoff Millan's, that I now recalled we had been asked to, for he did not know Dagger and Alba)—and hinting she'd heard my diary had been destroyed (which meant that Kate or someone who'd spoken to Kate had routed the knowledge to where Alba was).

So Lorna let the cat out of the bag tonight, I said.

Of course it wasn't Lorna, said Alba, it was Savvy.

But he heard it from Lorna, I said.

No, someone phoned him in the bedroom, Michelle woke up and was crying, and I was sorry I'd come, I'm very very tired, he hung up and asked me where Dag had *really* gone. He asked if I knew your diary had been burned.

But Alba had not been too tired to lift Cosmo's carton out of sight.

She simply wanted to get rid of me.

She hadn't even asked how I'd got in, maybe thought if Cosmo had a key why not Cartwright. Yet it wasn't tiredness that made her try to stop me as I went on to tell her how Jack had told Gene that Incremona was armed and Sherman was armed, and Gene had lied to Jack about the Marvelous Country House (chosen, I added, by Dagger not me) and Claire had told Jack that our Bonfire in Wales had also been shot by Aut's own man—well, there I'd been in Paul's hut telling Jack about the Maya when Gene had slid my diary into the fire, and on top of that, Kate (for I assumed Savvy's news had come from her direction) had told me Jenny was in danger, and I was about to go on to tell Alba that Gene had let Jack think the portfolio was Jan's—but Alba brought the needlessly rerinsed plate down into the sink hard and cracked it, and said Stop!—but meant to stop my giving her what she didn't want by (it now seemed) stuffing back at my voice any information that came into her head. She said, You are powerful; you were powerful the morning you picked Dag up to go film the Hawaiian boy in the Underground; Dag was deeply disturbed by that, and he is somewhere I don't know where now because he is deeply worried and Jenny is part of it and I want you out of here, please, you are armed.

But before I'd arrived the morning we went to film the tunnel under the Science Museum, Dagger and Alba had been having a little battle in my opinion.

And that would be at least as good a reason for him to be disturbed.

I'd sensed it when he said would she be in all morning in case of a phone call; I saw it in her blank look when I found her in the balcony room stacking two suitcases on the glass cabinet, thus partly blocking the framed Mercator; it was in their manner of parting: no loud call from Dag out of sight, nor a joke and a kiss; just his pause and an exchange of times and places at ten paces, her belly beginning to show. But if Alba said Dag had been disturbed by my suggesting that particular tunnel, what of the fact that when Jenny and I had talked about A-levels, continuity, and museums, it had been Jenny who brought up the tunnel?

And *because* Dag had been disturbed (said Alba) he'd let her go over to France to see her parents that weekend alone, though I knew he didn't much care for Seine suburbia, the French language, or all that tennis.

Well, had she talked all this over with Dag?

Actually to Cosmo. But only about filming the Hawaiian boy in the Underground, and how (said Alba) Dagger was afraid of you now because he did not know all you knew and didn't know what you'd do.

I said I was armed only with other people's weapons. Alba asked if I had disarmed Sherman. I asked if he was with Reid. Alba said that was why Dag had gone off in a hurry—someone was going to get hurt, someone had already been hurt. What do you need *me* for in this war of yours, said Alba.

Tessa was taking apart the pieces; she was saying that blood and cruelty are to the Maya the source of what is good, and that the famous Maya blue, the color of sacrifice even more than the red magic that was bled from some poor penis, draws the horror up into a blue hole in the blue sky. But I needed Alba's defenses here, for she defended herself against me by telling me things: Incremona was dangerous; I must not ally myself with him.

But I had found myself to be helplessly a collaborator, mingling beyond mere will with the mixed obsessions of others. It had been months *before* our first friendly fuck in New York that I'd gratuitously daydreamed a safe way to write Tessa in London: I'd just write her London address on the envelope's upper left, stamp it with insufficient postage, and mail it to a fictitious New York address. But the daydream: why was it painful? how did the Maya punish adultery with wife's one-time best friend? Answer: Reid and Sherman dividing Jenny.

Why did we go to Corsica? I said.

Alba did not know.

What had been Dagger's real reason?

Alba fended me off: Nash had been at Savvy's tonight all dressed up with his rings on trying to make Nell Flint laugh and when she went into the bedroom he followed her. Could you see Nell fancying that bundle of nerves? They were talking about a car, no doubt all he could manage.

Why did we go to Corsica? I said.

To get away, said Alba.

Was Incremona at Savvy's?

The handsome bald man?

Yes, Incremona.

No, he was not there, but his name was spoken by the man with the rings, Nash.

To whom?

To the black man.

Chad?

Yes.

Would Alba like to hear my views on Nash?

Nash? No, please, please. Please go. Incremona and the man with the rings, said Alba, as if she were saying something. Chad does not like the man with the rings.

Nash? I said.

Yes, he suspects Nash was looking for Bobby's friend the deserter at Stonehenge. Chad looked angry at Nash.

I said, Krish wasn't there—did Nash get a nosebleed?

The question infiltrated Alba, as if its far origin had built up a force too strange by the time it arrived.

What killed Krish? I asked myself. John's pistol? The sight or idea of it? The Great Menhir?

I'll go, I said, if you'll tell me why Dag deliberately kept from Claire the fact that we had shot the Unplaced Room.

Alba could only answer unasked questions. Krish was in rebellion against his father who belonged to the Mahasabba and claimed (though Krish did not believe his father) to have been involved with the Mahasabba people who supposedly were behind Gandhi's assassin. He believes he has personal power and perhaps he has; he has control over Cosmo and the man with the rings; they tell him everything. So in a way Krish is very different from Jan. But don't think Jan was helping Paul escape from his two brothers, she simply wanted to know why he was dropping everyone now, I don't know what that means, I don't want to know. She is interested in Reid, not Paul, she's had such trouble with Aut, so has Claire, poor Claire, this cut-throat thing of the two films, what do you know of Claire. Aut found a letter in her desk and phoned Jan in London to find out if Claire was in cahoots with Monty or Dag to steal Jan's idea, and Jan went up to the Hebrides to see Paul purely for information, not for what you think, and she is disturbed about her son as well, she did a beautiful picture of him, maybe you've seen it, the son is the one thing she and her husband have together, he adores the boy, who hardly ever sees him, but if Jan wanted to stop anyone it would be Reid.

Alba leaned her elbows on the sink, her face in her hands.

You're afraid of me, I said.

Only for Dagger, she said.

That why you got him out of Corsica in a hurry?

Alba shook her head, did not look up.

I phoned home. Will said Lorna had said she was going to Geoff's.

I asked Alba for the taxi number.

I had nothing to do with his coming back from Corsica, she said. He was a day early; I wasn't even here.

It was a minicab. It would come in five minutes. The voice sounded Irish.

The overhead light was on in the bathroom. I bent down to look at the comb on the floor. Alba would have been carrying the baby when she came into the bathroom.

Alba had disappeared.

I would be drawn into a past as paralyzingly elusive as the crystal receiver set Ned Noble designed and soldered all by himself and promised to give me. As pointlessly elusive as that weekend in '63 when we had tickets to *Uncle Vanya* with Redgrave and Olivier and Plowright and had promised to drop in on our new friend Dagger DiGorro after the theater. But we gave away our tickets.

The sequence is not clear. Ned Noble's now nonexistent crystal set may help. In the hotel room, I was asking the American computer man's friend, an ex-serviceman who'd stayed in Europe, whether he did much mutual-fund business here in England or confined himself to the Continent. There was a large elderly English woman in a permanent who totally obscured Lorna, but it was Lorna I heard and she was telling how an actor who wrote children's books had asked two sculptors to design a cat to go on top of the Whittington Stone on Highgate Hill because in a story he was writing the Queen stopped to talk to Dick Whittington's cat at the spot where the boy who was to be thrice Lord Mayor of London turned round three times—and there *was* no cat.

At Alba's after the cocktail party Dagger told of his search for his lost brother in Mexico, not a real brother but close enough. Lorna was with Alba washing up in the kitchen. The computer-traffic man and his friend the ex-serviceman selling mutual funds to servicemen in Europe, listened to Dagger digress upon those instruments called *raspadores* made of bones human, deer, or tapir which made a grating sound and if a player in the Maya orchestra did not keep time he was punished painfully though not (like the hapless captives of war) sexually mutilated; there was no "pure" music, but songs that told old tales, and dances to bring new rain.

But the World Tiddlywinks Congress at Cambridge did not occur in November '63; it was in June of '58 after Lorna and her new friend Tessa attended the Festival Hall recital of Menuhin, who lives in Highgate not far from the house we'd recently bought. And a clergyman had urged the world to look to tiddlywinks as a way of recapturing primeval simplicity.

I remember because a week later came the execution of Nagy in Hungary.

Which was the day (yes) before Lorna and Tessa took the children and Dudley to the Dominion Cinema to see *South Pacific*.

Macmillan had been in Washington with Eisenhower, which would have been impossible in November of '63.

Thursday Lorna and I had a fight which would have been impossible in June of '58 when I still treated her as an invalid.

At the end of our fight I told her Dagger's music story about punishments for not keeping time, and we laughed ourselves to sleep.

She did not want another child.

Ned Noble had promised me his crystal set even after he knew he was dying.

Lorna phoned Tessa Friday morning, November 22, even though we were going to see them that night. Lorna told Tessa Dagger's story—the Maya orchestra, the *raspadores*, the punishment.

At 6:45 P.M. when I began to smell onions, I switched on "The Archers—An Everyday Story of Country Life." I had been listening to it since '54: Farm talk about markets and new methods; Dan Archer's good sense; hired man Ned Larkin's south-country accent with its rounded American *r*'s (and a measured something like my grandfather's Maine cadences that he never lost even when he found himself removed to a city as foreign to him as if he had gone to live abroad); pub gossip; the antique dealer's love life; the new entrepreneur in the village; Doris Archer's nerves; more farm gab; for me the ripe soil, the thick-tufted pasture grass, great sheltering trees by a group of graystone barns and sheds and dwellings with the small square parish church tower in the background so the whole scene reminded me of some famous painter's paintings I'd seen years ago at the Met; the sweet rotten odor of silage, the petty and poignant preoccupation with annual events, the village of Ambridge (for Americans who do not know "The Archers") ridiculed by Geoff Millan but not by Lorna. (Why does a hen lay eggs, said Jenny at six or seven, the riddle stage, when I would sometimes want in desperation to tell her what her intimations about her parents could not quite reach, but she would have to wait, for she was too young, but even if she had not been, I could not clearly have said what was wrong with Lorna and me.)

At the end of one episode of "The Archers" when Mr. Grenville the local gentry had his car crash destroying his leg and killing John Tregoran's fiancée, the BBC did not close with the theme music, a heart-warming jig: there was just silence, which even I felt—and then the seven o'clock news.

But the music did play at the end on Friday the 22nd, and I turned back to the front page of *The Evening Standard*.

And then came the news from Dallas.

Where it was only one o'clock.

Which made me feel that I'd been missing something all afternoon, yet there was a chance to catch up.

Lorna was already weeping before I had understood the chance Kennedy was dead.

The other couple who were coming to dinner with Tessa and Dudley phoned to ask if we would rather not, and I do not recall what I said as if underwater at a very long distance—I thanked them and I must have given them a rain check, and I could not say goodbye because the waterworks exploded unexpectedly in my head and Will materialized and he could not for a moment think of the words in which to ask who had died.

I do not remember Alba saying much about Kennedy Saturday night. The French liked Jackie. The story had not yet come out that the blood-stained wife in the open accelerating car had been reaching back for a piece of her husband.

Lorna was saying she wanted to go back.

Johnson! she said.

Then at eight thirty we were finishing our drinks with Dudley and Tessa and I remembered having spoken on the phone to our other guests.

Lorna said I might have told her.

I put my glass down in a hurry and raised my hands to my face.

My mother phoned from New York.

Geoff Millan phoned, distraught.

I kept the radio on in the kitchen and got up from the dinner table once to go and listen.

Dudley was subdued in any case, but tonight partly because he did not feel what Lorna and I did. He said it was too soon, the death.

We let that lie. But Tessa said, Dudley will have an opinion on this by 1980 if you can wait till then.

Can *you*? I said.

Lorna and I had triple helpings of lasagna.

Dudley said to Tessa that after all it wasn't as if he'd ever been a Republican. But Tessa went beyond that: Kennedy was beautiful. Unusual beauty draws secret violence toward it.

I could not believe he was dead, and I said Rubbish.

Ned Noble's crystal set means more than if he'd been faithful to his promise. There was a red stripe across the base of a condenser and blue numbers on what he said was a rectifier.

Dudley agreed it was rubbish and he and Tessa argued but as if soundlessly, for Lorna and I were stuffing our faces and looking at each other. Dudley got up in a huff and I followed him into the living room still chewing, where I found him inspecting a photograph of my sister.

I went back to the table. Lorna was weeping. As Dudley returned I daydreamed a way of posting a clandestine letter to Tessa. Now it looks like a long-term plan.

Sub's letter was the first of the American letters to reach me after the assassination. He said that that weekend several of his friends had screwed like crazy. He and Rose even, and they weren't getting along.

On Sunday there were queues clear round the Embassy. Cabdrivers parked their cabs and got on line. BBC radio interviewed people waiting to sign the book.

On Saturday Mr. Jones in the dairy said, Mr. Cartwright I want you to know that Mrs. Jones and I sympathize with you and your family. This is a sad time for all of us.

Jenny picked up our purchases. I couldn't answer. My mouth was nowhere. I just nodded.

We gave Tessa and Dudley our tickets to *Uncle Vanya.*

Saturday we went to Dagger DiGorro's for the first time.

A very bright and sexy Pole taunted Alba. He said Ho Chi Minh's father, a mandarin scholar whose knowledge of Chinese was said to be at least as good as that of anyone else in Vietnam, had lost his job because he refused to corrupt his language by learning French.

That's something he and I have in common, said Dagger appearing magically and sweeping Alba against him so that I wondered what had happened since the computer man's Tuesday night hotel room and Alba's spaghetti.

Alba could only beam at Dagger and say—in answer to some unasked but implicit question—Yes.

That weekend receded. Alba emerged from the baby's room. She had told me not to think Jan was helping Paul escape from his two brothers but she *had* said Paul was dropping everyone now and she *had* almost echoed me in her reference to this cut-throat thing of the two films, and she had brought Nash and Chad and a deserter together, and I believed my daydream on the plane was largely true and this was why Kate or someone she had spoken to had got on the blower to Savvy Van Ghent's party (which in turn reminded me that Lorna might now be at Geoff's).

The bell rang. The downstairs bell. The minicab. Alba opened the door for me. I had my pack in one hand.

She said, You weren't really asleep. The lights went out just as my cab rolled up.

Tell me who Bobby is.

The one who talked to the deserter in your film.

Alba wanted to close the door.

I was half in, half out. Tell me, I said, why the hair in the comb on your bathroom floor is red.

Alba tried to close the door on me.

Failing, she spoke: Dagger was afraid Phil Aut would find out about the portrait of his son. It shows up in your scene of the Unplaced Room.

I remembered the palette-knife-thickened face with the lustrous hair, to my right against the wall. And on my left Dagger turning the Beaulieu briefly on me, panning downward as if to show the equipment or study my feet.

I said: You would never leave a comb lying on the floor. It's Jan's hair in the comb. She was here this evening.

My words weakened me, like the stomach-turning sight of all that equipment in the camera shop in New York just after the stabbing accident.

Do you blame her for fearing you? said Alba; Dagger has feared you since the day you proposed filming in that Underground tunnel. And this time Alba did shut the door.

But as I passed out of the house and into the very same cab with the stripe down the bonnet that had let me off here at 10:20, Alba's words made me powerful again.

A power of destruction?

Her words seemed to say Dagger had seen a print of the Unplaced Room.

17 | Once upon a time I dismissed our film, but told no one, for I am a secret noncollaborator.

I could not see what Phil Aut would want with it. But I went ahead and it began to make sense.

My life reflecting a larger life. Not your usual formula documentary.

Dagger talked of editing it this way and that way, but it was still only an exposed emulsion. He talked about control over the final product.

Why did I begin a diary? Did I foresee the film's ruin?

I learned to look more closely in order to see what Dagger was seeing through the viewfinder. But later to recall what ought to go into the diary. But perhaps always to take for myself a depth that was in our film if not on it.

For instance, a leader and reputed beautiful person preceded out of his grove into the light of our camera by a sacred beast.

Or a thick apricot bob above a green blouse, in turn above my son's just visible chestnut hair—the whole preceded by a forty-eight-state flag-tattoo blown up in my chosen words.

Or, say, a Church of England vicar among his rainy roses and photos of Marilyn.

The depth I refer to was also harsh Corsican hills praised by Boswell, touched with scrub pine whose contours might have looked at dusk like children's mountains or the evergreen armies in my grandfather's New England but in fact were sparse and crabbed and were seen hazy from a warm sea where I lay buoyed by the nearby wave-rocked words of Mike to Mary: Your brother is a bad influence on Paul.

The film, or some pause it gave my life, made me sit at Sub's window in New York and contemplate a high window-washer for his own sake.

Only hear Sub mention the Bronx or Staten Island and you still sense that in Manhattan you don't think of yourself living in the whole city. (Not even in the now capsuled forties when the Heights was barely within Ned Noble's Brooklyn and for Sub and me the Broadway theater district under the river and twenty minutes away from Brooklyn by Interboro Rapid Transit was in the true New York which we could contemplate like its harbor from our residential stoops like early Dutchmen.) But in London even with its villages you do live in the whole city. Never mind Geoff Millan's velvet-legged friend Jasper languidly claiming not to know what lay "south of the river," or, in that evening circle at Geoff's (which you who have me must recall cartridged in relation to our present position not so far back or forward that you'd have to stretch to put your finger on it like the other icepick point of a draftsman's compass) the bearded intellect with puffy eyes who said that he ventured south of the river once a year.

My cab with the stripe down the hood rolled toward a fictitious address. But when we paused at a Belisha Beacon for a car to
cross I realized we were going the wrong way. I leaned forward and
in the amber which outside was the foggy glow softening the dark
terraced houses to an aura of privacy but inside the cab gave things a
lurid point, I knew my driver's profile. I said to him that we were
going the wrong way. I got no response. And if you who have me are
way ahead here and know already that my driver was Mike, the
quarterback of my imagination who at a table under the stars of
Corsica and under a string of festal lights in Place Foch had asked
me if I could kill, you will be glad I now move under my true colors,
and shoot and twist among layers of distance as if they were mere
liquid films or gelatin, and not forth and back but out and in at all
angles sanctioned by my sphere. But as soon as I've said that, and see
the sphere opened flat on a bed bounded by east and west like cliffs at
each edge of the world—and recall the stopped escalator, and recall
my legs and feet that would survive apart from me if need be and
hence slowed their motion to fit my plunge—I find my position resists
the formula I've sought; for my position belongs also to that shove in
the back whose force dies near the foot of the escalator yet turns then
into my own heart rebounding up those grooved stairs after the
shover who recedes into an elastic field not mine yet not wholly his
since he was moved to push me by a great love including him in its
reach like a larger plan. And if John's white-nosed automatic did not
let me very far into Mike's life as I now lifted it from my parka
pocket, changed hands, and laid it along the leather of the driver's
seat near Mike's head with the magazine-grip away from me and
asked Mike if he recalled his question to me in the restaurant in
Place Foch—and another car came up behind us and beeped as Mike
looked along his shoulder at the white barrel and asked if I was really
a lefty—there was no gloved window between me and him.

The cab advanced but Mike and I hesitated.

I said, Ask away. He said, What? (as if surprised that he was
to do the asking when I was the one with the gun). Why wasn't I
looking out for my daughter, he said, she was looking out for me.

Was she looking out for me by letting my diary go? I said.

Listen, said Mike, we know what Jack told you. But suppose
he burned one copy for Gene to see but kept the other?

Mike had turned back toward the fictitious address which if
we ever got there was a ten-minute walk from Geoff's.

They were all acknowledging my power. Could I solicit information they thought I already had? And did Mike know what the Highgate burglar had taken?

Furthermore, Jan in New York two days later told me Paul's story not only as if her openness might deter me from further aggression, but as if its meaning was beyond secrecy. On the other hand, Dagger's new sense about me the morning we filmed the Hawaiian Hippie had made him not more frank but more secret.

But now—in the cab with Mike, or forty hours later in New York alone in John's loft with Jan—I had to question what the full tale could be worth if it came to me as easily as the bedtime freedoms I once took with "Puss in Boots" or "Beauty and the Beast" when Jenny and Will were small. For Mike (who voluntarily identified the pistol at his neck as Chad's) assumed I knew that Jack felt the vagrant astronomer who'd come out of the island murk into Paul's hut was an equal. And Jan forty hours later seemed to assume I knew that Jack the eldest of the three Flint brothers was cobacker with her husband of her film plan. And both Mike and Jan—as if joined in some mind of mine that had never left the Glasgow hotel room— asked humbly, yes humbly, if there was another Xerox of my film diary in the case I'd checked when I left Glasgow for Stornoway.

Mike asked why I'd wanted to get Incremona all stirred up with hints of a link between Phil Aut and John, for after all John only knew Phil through Gene: why had I had to go and do that? first thing we knew the whole thing would blow up—didn't I know?—I *must* know—how crazy Len was? ate deep-fried shark for breakfast stuffed with Roman sausage—I must have known his temper, otherwise I wouldn't have been so careful not to flush him out of Jan's studio when I was talking to Kate tonight, which must mean I knew John was giving two lectures in the New York area—

To all of which there was no need to reply that the John I'd meant was the other John in New York (who I now saw must have acquired this pistol from Chad some time before my last visit to John's or Jerry's Mercer Street loft). I merely said that Incremona was so stirred up that my contribution hardly mattered. And Mike, as we neared my fictitious terminus, asked in vain if Gene had known that John was involved with Phil Aut, and I could not ask the key question: *what* thing would "blow up"?

I could have asked Mike and Jan who they thought I was.

She said she had known I would come. I did not tell her (what she might well know) that there was a chance I'd been set up. I had phoned June from Monty's house saying I was at Sub's and she'd said that's where she'd thought I was, and when I asked at once if she knew Jan, she told me Jan would be at John's loft in the afternoon. The shades were drawn as before. I wondered if she would mention the space of hair colored in—an open message like a signed blank check.

A heart-shaped face, thick pale eyebrows, eyes dark, red hair not long but in denseness of growth and hue not to be equaled even by Jenny's magic marker.

This was the first time I'd seen her in a skirt—it was white and hung barely above her sturdy knees. A well-made not tall figure of a woman perhaps just out of her thirties who stood composed upon her feet, the workbench behind her, as I pushed the door further ajar and entering and seeing her green blouse felt the jaguar's red weight in the pocket of the parka I had left at Monty's.

I let her talk. I did not break in to say (what would have been a lie) that I knew all this. I sat in John's straight chair and stroked my beard and hoped to seem patient hearing what she would think I largely knew.

So (she said) I wanted to stop whatever was happening, right?—but in the process I had stopped her plan too and whatever had been good about it. Hear her out, please, even if this was old stuff. Oh we do not know enough!—That was what a friend had said months ago and it had crystallized her idea and then her husband Phil my associate (she said) had strangely not turned it down. His interest was a pretext financial or other, but the end sustained itself and could even transform her husband's motive.

What was the end?

I did not ask.

I had left the door open a crack to listen for steps on the stairs. John and others might wish to stop me.

But from doing what?

Mike seemed to fear not my stopping something but starting it. (Over again?)

Jan said her idea for the film was no secret but I mustn't assume I understood Paul who to her was even more a hero now he'd opted out of the plans she knew I'd set out to stop. Paul was someone she would like her own son to emulate.

It seemed to me best she think me thoroughly acquainted with her film idea.

She even seemed to try to shock me with her knowledge of what she assumed I largely knew. Paul had opted out, she said, but not because of the big projects discussed—a symbolic war on children waged against school buses; or slowly, through many collaborators, assembling the parts of two bazookas in a Washington rooming house with a roof and shelling the President during a scheduled lawn function; or simply bombing the White House in order to precipitate martial law and with it consequences leading to change. No, on the contrary, Paul had made a mystic parallel between public political action and the family firm now so complex in its indirect holdings that possibly not even Jack had it all in his head. And since effective political action no longer seemed feasible, Paul had conceived a small community in New England which would be neither as remote as he had felt himself to be in that Hebridean hut nor as socially involved as he had really been both through his power in a movement and through his location so useful to certain American exiles.

Mike in the cab two nights before is likewise concerned with Paul. Not Paul some magical youngest brother in a tale of fortunes bequeathed and abandoned—but a man dangerous in his purity, and in danger like a Weatherman who doesn't know enough but sets out to make an impact-bomb by turning TNT back into nitroglycerine. If you go a degree too hot, forget it.

Why did you take the red jaguar tonight? said Mike.

It made me think of Nash's nosebleeds.

Did you expect to find Paul at the painter-woman's?

These minicab drivers don't know London half so well as regular cabbies, I said.

But Mike was getting close to the fictitious address I'd given him.

Could he think I was reviving the film?

Jan forty hours later said that on hearing I was interested in filming Stonehenge she'd thought that after all maybe she and I were not so far apart.

But why had she ever thought we were far apart? I said; was it some suspicion roused after Dagger and I accidentally found the Hawaiian hippie and his girl from Hempstead in that Underground tunnel?

The only accident, said Jan, was Dagger assuming his businessman friend Cartwright was just along for the ride. Well, I might see Paul from more clever angles than anyone else, she said, yet miss his core of personal vision, deeper than an island, than color on canvas, than violence, deeper than dynamite—(deeper than her words or mine?)—deeper than restructuring custom by blowing up cops.

Downstairs in the Mercer Street loft building a Bach chorale opened fire in mid-cry and at once stopped.

I said there were businesses and businesses, and before dismissing me, even if I lacked a core of personal vision, she should learn about liquid crystals which are organic chemicals having the uniform molecular patterns of crystal systems, yet in the way they flow to conform to their containers they seem not solids but liquids. Now when an electric field is played across an area of liquid crystal the molecules are upset and light is scattered which in technological application can be controlled so as, for instance, to create displays of numbers or letters.

Jan thought her husband and Jack Flint were producing a science film for children. Science was impersonal. There were no right angles in nature.

You see, I said, they bond together two glass plates but keep between the two a space one-third as thick as a human hair and fill it with liquid crystal.

She wasn't interested in micro-spaces and mere completions. She had passed on lots of ideas. Many from Dagger, who tossed out too many ideas, some jokey. No, what was needed was life, growth. Afeni Shakur who was said to have planned to blow up the New York Botanical Gardens desired life and growth. Ahmed Evans whom Jan had met found energy in systems of the occult. She would like to meet Erika Huggins, and ask her one question.

The Bach blew on, was turned lower, but still would cover any but the nearest and heaviest of steps.

In earlier scenes Jan Graf Aut had receded over and over again vivid and possible. The friend of Krish and Dagger; sister of Monty, wife of Phil; mother doubtless of Jerry; intimate of Reid, rival of Jenny; intimate of Paul. Now she leaned back against the workbench as if against the one source of light in the dusky studio; for her head came between me and the green-glass pool-table shade hanging in front of the poster displaying formulaic sequences.

Gene the middle brother had been swayed (she said) by Paul to have nothing to do with the family business; then of course Gene had married money so he was free though Nell was giving him trouble; she had been to Wellesley and believed power most corruptible when it lay unused.

Gene, however, had grown. Phil had approached him no

doubt at the urging of Jack, but Gene had turned down the substantial offer to come in with Phil and consented only to cooperate on a scene or two for Jan's pan-human film. Gene disliked business because of the people, and film because it tended fatally toward entertainment (as Paul had often said) and so could not be used to convey a rigorous theme like Jan's, i.e., in one ninety-minute peace-montage to bring together clashes of practice, doctrine, color, and geography among (and here, as I knew, for she assumed I knew, was the point) certain revolutionary groups: interviews, glimpses, faces sometimes only half-seen which Jan believed would say implicitly not just that their human aspirations were more kin than foe to each other, but more (and this to the ordinary audiences who would see the film if only on their television sets) that such groups were full of passionate love which might lean toward violence but only in answer to what there was no point in her spelling out. It was to be the deed of her life, plain black and white, Aristotle had said Man was a political being and a being endowed with speech—so a film of silent faces would not do—she left the execution to Phil and John and (though she had not pressured him herself) her son. A greater deed than a painting, or being a parent, or abandoning your family. It was this deed that I had stalled, from motives she said that even with her limited information she could guess had something to do with large amounts of cash rumor said Jack was handling lately—I had contaminated her vision and in spite of what I might think of the scene filmed in her studio, I had actually increased the chance of violence knowing full well that on camera Jim would speak of Paul and be hushed up and thus pushed even further by Bob, and she would like to have only pity for me but confessed to fear as well.

My words—the groaning afternoon on the Mercer Street side of John's window shades had passed into an early evening of such dingy delicacy under the lush sky that the air looked crystal clear.

In Mike's London cab the questions are nearing an end two days earlier.

OK, I answer, say I give filmmaking a rest and leave you and Len and Sherman and Reid and Nash's nosebleeds alone, what sanctuary have I? Any number of Xeroxes won't safeguard me from Len Incremona or for all I know—

Don't pretend you *don't* know, said Mike, then whipped his head away toward his right-hand window having said the reverse of what he'd wanted.

—or for all I know I could be hit by Nash or you or Bob—

408

—No, Bob's not with us any more, he got sentimental—

—or Sherman, I guess Sherman's in the States with Reid by now, and Krish may find it harder to intimidate Nash than before.

Mike wants to know what I hoped to add to my leverage by shooting Len and himself and Marie (the fortress girl) in the setting of Ajaccio; they were there and even the action originally planned was not going to take place in Corsica—nothing happens there.

I answer that I was concerned with the ecology seminar the Americans were running at the école, for in my own view it could emerge in our film as a revolutionary though tenuous theme of displacement; however, his Edinburgh friend Mary had been an unexpected dividend.

The automatic stirred up off the seat back. The ammunition was in my head, film or no film. The gun had a moment of weight on the end of my bent arm like our damned camera hand-held or not hand-held threatening to drag down all it framed: down would go 2-D slides of Hyde Park and the English country, and down also the screens of dusty fort and Mediterranean crag; down would go gaps in the Stonehenge circle filled for a moment with new Druids or a lurking American voice or Nash angry with Bob the dark-haired late co-star of our Unplaced Room who bickered with him outside the Sarsen ring: so that the literal weight of that Beaulieu dragged down out of sight even the hand of my wife touching me and the borrowed breath of Tessa in my mouth turning to words and out of words until (as you who have me may say) through manipulation, not real courage, I saved that New England drive-in movie screen by the waters of the Atlantic by placing at the base of that land-slipped clay cliff (cartridged long ago for later thought) Tessa's uncle who was struck in middream thus not by a cruel-faceted quartz paperweight a German cat pawed off a high night-time ledge but by the very screen 60 by 100 that I couldn't sell the merchant-investor near Liverpool. Hit but not killed, for in his early old age Tessa's Uncle Karl became, for all his blindness, a Zionist settler dictating to his wife and her long, comforting fingers epistles from a Tel Aviv suburb to Tessa's half-envious father in Golders Green which expatiated greatly and with Talmudic pomp upon the age-old zone of mystic In-Between carved like a moat of insulation (in Uncle Karl's prose) to guard a Jewish self prior to actual territory, yes the inner and spiritual claim to separation from others and claim to a place that was a claim that created that place (that beautiful place) by fiat of communal will. Tessa's father would tell his neighbors in their well-watered gardens about Karl's commitment as if he and Karl were collaborating, and about Karl's theory that despite a permanent eclipse of his main sight, he had intimations he was recovering of all things *peripheral* vision.

Now Jan might disdain "mere completions," but I with my parka-full of others' weapons and my Druid's counsel on how to make my body breathe had never laid claim to any kind of completion. I had more than once in recent days found myself poised weightlessly mighty like a god, held in a field of my own generation or finding, in a space between impingements of other fields like the short moment between forces when I snatched the autographed ball flung up by Ned Noble (who when he would jauntily take leave of us would say, I shall return). Yet now from either of two random parallels—the minicab in London Sunday night, the loft in New York Tuesday, each ending with offspring, the ominous mention of Jenny by Mike, the queer allusions to Jerry by Jan—I was now being situated in an independent power way past even what I had pretended.

Perhaps it was true, the god bit.

Yet no: my hero the Franco-English engineer, Isambard Kingdom Brunel (in whom my own beloved and neglected Will may not have been so intrigued as I hoped) was much struck by the collapse of a bridge near Manchester in the late 1820's: the steady tread of troops across it one day set up a harmony so deep it shook loose a pin in one of the suspension chains and the bridge at one end let go. Fields impinge. You must build yourself into the life around you. Which sounds so like good advice I must find another way to pass it on to Will.

Paul was misconstrued, you see. His views these last months had grown apparently more abstract, not less. But Mike, Chad, John, Nell, Incremona, Sherman, even Gene at first (until then likewise suspect) saw Paul defecting because of the target. This target, which no doubt I knew the logistics of even better than she, touched the Flint family enterprises, and she did not want to know more than that. And John, with his English sense of sinister unity within great families, insisted Paul himself had proposed the target. But Chad and Len believed Paul planned to join Jack in the business at last; Mike and Gene believed Paul had found a new strange reverence for the father who had founded the firm, but Mike thought Paul wished only to safeguard the firm while Gene believed Paul had learned to love his brother Jack. Sherman and Len believed Paul would blow the whistle, and so did Reid, who did not otherwise agree.

410

Jan said Paul had gone to Wales in May to see the Prescelly Mountains whence the Stonehenge bluestones had come heroically by land and sea and hand, and Paul had been thinking in a new way about Stonehenge from a new distance.

And Callanish?

Jan did not know the name, she said, and I neither challenged her there with my superior evidence from the dilettante geologist in the red mini that in fact she had been at Callanish nor let her know other dates I believed she did *not* know: that Paul was in the Hebrides sometime before May 24 when we shot the Unplaced Room and heard the deserter's half-squelched words of praise for Paul, and in South Wales with Elspeth the Bonfire night of May 28 by which time, to judge from Jan who saw him in Edinburgh in June, he'd made up his mind to break with the group.

Mike said, for we had arrived, Who lives here?

Near here, I said.

At the next crossing stood a policeman. Lorna had mentioned Geoff's party over my Glasgow phone when, on the verge of my lookout dream, I had found myself between her and some northwest passage which on my cartogramic variant of Gerardus Mercator's flat map curved an unheard-of new great arc remarkably between two seemingly contiguous virtually congruent parallels through Callanish to fields of people compassed by their secrets from each other. I would chance Lorna's being at Geoff 's party. I had no key to the new lock at home.

What if we aimed for that cop? said Mike. This cab's got pickup.

That would be the end of one callow revolutionary, I said.

But you'd be stuck in England for years, said Mike.

I'll call in a good lawyer; at least *I'm* within the law.

The lawyer Mary's been talking to?

Why not?

The New York State Bar doesn't cover London. What was his business with Allott?

Maya business, I said (and did not add "undoubtedly," for I knew on some cooperative current of instinct that this was the lawyer Dudley had consulted on international divorce, having been in touch with him first about Catherwood's New York holocaust).

I needn't shoot you, I said, you don't have working papers unless Len got you some, and I think we'd find something at the dispatching end of your two-way radio, which by the way may be on, that would be at least as interesting in its connection to Paul Flint as you are yourself, maybe Bob, maybe Nash if he's back from Savvy's party.

Well Mike came around in his seat so suddenly I almost shot. Then, too calmly, he asked if I knew where he could *find* Bob.

I haven't seen him since Stonehenge, I said.

I was on the pavement, my hand on the roof.

Why was Mary a dividend?

Her brother sent us a touring archaeologist from Alabama.

At Stonehenge, said Mike.

For comic relief when more important things were happening.

Like a film, Mike murmured.

People threatening to appear, I said, or rumored missing. The Alabama academic replying with coy caution, I'd rather not say, really—as if he'd been asked if Mary Napier had actually got her hands on the Montrose heart.

Mary's crazy, said Mike.

On the contrary.

On the contrary, eh?

You didn't hear when Mary described Montrose's dismemberment the night Marie's blond costarletto of our fortress footage was mad at her for being with the dark-haired local in the guitar bar. Mary's brother put the Alabama archaeologist on to us. A good courier.

The policeman was looking.

I knew I would have to fly to New York. Mike slid suddenly along his seat to the left-hand window, but then did not say anything, then said, You're wrong about Sherman; he's not in New York. I would know.

I shrugged, I deeply did not care, I turned away—and beyond the street lamp that lighted the policeman who now moved off I nearly saw Ned Noble (on a Brooklyn stoop) from whom I also turned away on the singular occasion of his last departure—as also I turned away from the crystal set he'd promised and broken—toward something I could not see in front that I swore would replace it.

Mike's cab came alongside like a perpendicular coordinate to his violent sideways slide along his seat when I linked Mary's brother to our Stonehenge. And I held Chad's gun at arm's length toward the window, a headless pedestrian. What else have you in your jacket? said Mike's voice, and I told him I had good reason to know they would kill to keep the lid on.

In that case (said the voice from the far side) think about Reid because you're right he's in New York; and even if you're planning something yourself and you know like day by day where Paul Flint's been since Stonehenge-night-at-the-film-festival, it doesn't matter, Reid's in New York, you know who's with him; you know what she tried to do, and you know that as of right now she doesn't have to have done anything, she's Cartwright's daughter.

A loch to look at, a cross to bear, a memory to bring back. Now she was in America, I in England. Nonetheless, by some oscillant continuity I was still on the American trip with its many centers, the second tenor bidding my Highgate wife goodbye, the three against the fortress wall, the stabbing, the escalator plunge, the sullen death of Ned Noble in Brooklyn Hospital in '45, the portals of Stonehenge with their emulsified night, the cruder stones of Callanish where Jenny hid my words and whose widow's face has Indian bones (or as the insular English with their lurid distinctions say, *red* Indian).

And the Kansas City Indian last seen at Stonehenge I had first seen the night Paul scampered from the grove in Wales.

Which Jan seemed to comprehend now not by receiving but only by in response demanding if I'd done violence to her jaguar—bored a hole maybe.

To house a bomb? To bomb a house—a structure, say, like an inveterate dream-plan where a dark watchman tries to wake and I a lookout on double watch (the squad within, the threat without) may have to cosh him so he stays coshed. Certainly I have not inserted anything in her jaguar, I've barely touched it since I took it two nights ago and, traveling under true colors shortly after leaving Alba, put less confusion than evidence into Mike, to wit (which then seemed true as I said it) that I'd taken the red jaguar because it made me think of Nash's nosebleeds.

But there is someone whom I make see red, I learn from Jan.

Oh who is that?

But Jan's answering that it is not Paul (for Paul has found in stones and stars a calm beyond revolutionary purpose, beyond even peace and contemplation, that she wishes he could pass on) turns my words back to me to the hearsay tale Sunday night told by the splendid woman who left as soon as I came: the nod she gave me: her face like Lorna's, her name something like Lana: her tale diffused in her absence into a terminal colloquium on violence guess where: but her tale: the man cartridged backwards of so many long pages: a

413

committee of one to undermine a network of violent exiles by sowing confusion among them: is that man me?

If all this is in fact my lookout dream at last and has been since Glasgow (where in that case I am still and where a hotel bed once holding a map now holds me), then I find myself not simply defending the squad inside the target building nor yet excluded from the squad of approaching pursuers: but am instead some crystal semiconductor whose designed impurity draws the two together.

The two? The more than two. As one who once entering Paul's hut in his absence assumed Paul's one-time alias, Paul Wheeler, to deal with brothers Jack and Gene who were in the presence of my daughter's present from me containing a copy of my words that are parallel to the film that was Jan's idea, I at once now three days later reminded Jan that Paul had indeed been able to pass on to others something of the genius she felt in him.

Witness the deserter Jim and what he found. He came down from Norway and the Faeroes to the Western Isles, the outer and northern parts, and he could have stayed, he said; the low, leaning peatland where a dilettante geologist who owns a small red car put Jim ashore is like the endless Sundays of the crofters' faith, the dense tablets of fuel dug and handled slow as that Calvinist gravity they were dried to warm; and Jim, next heard of south at Paul's hut on the slopes of prickly damp Clisham, could just have stayed there: for Paul's power seemed to Jim to draw an imaginary space where before there had been none so there was now no need to pass on along the line of ostracism from one center of exile altogether by finding an elsewhere in between—

Oh I see, I see what you mean, said Jan.

Which was why Bob his mentor-to-be tried to make Jim's potentially incendiary words mean something else, for Paul who on our sound track of the Unplaced Room was never named was powerful enough to seem to Jim to change Jim's life, which is what Jan seemed to hope could be done for someone she was thinking of before—as indeed Paul changed Claire's life—

Claire! said Jan, blinking twice automatically.

Drew Claire into an idea for amending a world, but she need merely arrange a few introductions, not actually grind an idea into a camera.

You can't mean Phil Aut's Claire.

What did Paul say to Jim? Stay on in the hut? No, Paul would not say that to anyone then, not even Claire. Did he tell Jim not to get

414

in touch with Gene, whose name had been given Jim by the dilettante geologist who'd ferried him from Norway to the Hebrides but knew only Paul's first name and not that Gene and Paul were brothers (only that Gene was the brother of Jack, the dilettante geologist's periodically profitable connection)? No, Paul was already breaking with the London group but he wished not to have any influence on anyone; he remembered what he had done to Chad at a time when Chad was contemplating a peaceful academic career. At the time Jim left Paul, hiking to Tarbert, buying postcards in the little Harris tweed shop and thinking again that if he could not be a fisherman or a weaver he might just go on walking, Paul was about to leave too: to see first-hand the bluestone quarries in Wales and visit rose-cheeked serious Elspeth and her Hindus and their grove near the two rivers.

Are you sure?

I was there. Near the two rivers the Usk and the Wye along which Dudley Allott on a map as if it were all real could point to where in Wales stone castles had stood long before those rivers were conveyed to Dagger—

The rivers came to Dagger?

—and this influence on Claire rousing a glamorous amateur to cloistered action occurred even before her rendez-vous at Callanish when Claire sought Paul's hut by figuring alignments but also bringing to bear an interest unconnected with any mere use of Callanish, say to get someplace else. Which is worth remarking, for what did she find after taking her compass readings (which she could have avoided with a map)? She found the man himself in the flesh come all the way up from the south to Callanish to meet her.

Not Phil Aut's Claire?

It is a refrain Jan can't help inserting into her alternating protection of Paul with Jerry, and Jerry with Paul (though never the two protected at once). Like my Transatlantic Saving Time that holds in one liquid crystal a Tuesday loft, a London Monday.

After four hours' sleep I'd woken in the middle of a dream about Lana, and Geoff surprisingly got up when I did—I might have been a condemned man.

I phoned my charter associate.

Geoff and I could not decide between us exactly where Lana had picked up her tale last night of undermining the ring of violent exiles by sowing confusion among them. We discussed the tale but not its link to me. My feet were sore, my daughter now quite near.

We decided after all not to drink last night's coffee. Did the Corsicans drink coffee at the time Boswell visited the revolutionary Republican Paoli? Paoli took him at first for a spy, while the people took him for a British envoy, while Boswell himself (warned on arrival that seducing Corsican women would mean "instant death") spoke grandly of an alliance between Great Britain and Corsica. I put away half a narrow loaf of last night's French crust with preserve whose slippery thickness of real apricot I could not bite through as neatly as the small rounds of rewarmed bread. I had to phone Lorna.

And she was asleep but at once began to talk of visitors she had not asked in, she felt guilty now—the parents of a young American. God, she'd never known I was mixed up with deserters, the name is Nielsen, the boy is Jim Nielsen. The father seemed to apologize for his son's staying in Sweden on some American farm not facing the music, and Lorna asked why Jim *should* face it, and then a strange and sad thing happened (and Lorna still seemed as if my phone call had plugged into her sleep, and I knew she'd been at Savvy Van Ghent's and probably out late and Will gets his own breakfast and I wanted to crawl down through that line to her and so almost wasn't paying attention when she told what the thing was) as she and Mr. Nielsen in his lightweight beige waterproof windbreaker stood at the top of the steps Saturday: a woman tall as he and thin and round-shouldered wearing the same new windbreaker came along up the street as if flat-hunting, and it was Mrs. Nielsen and she came along up the steps to stand beside Mr. as if through indigestion she'd fallen behind in the tour but had caught up and was going to get as much out of the guide lecture as she could; she looked down at each step as she came up and didn't look at Lorna till she got to the top.

But what was the sad thing?

They had come for Jim. Lorna said God what if he doesn't want to go, or isn't here? The father said that was really why they'd come. In case he wasn't here. That is, because he ought to be here. They knew that much. And Lorna said why did they think Jim might not be in London; she said she couldn't stop smiling. At the end Lorna went back inside, having not asked the Nielsens in, and she could have cried on Will's shoulder if he had been there, not for her rudeness that had been genuine enough, nor for their tour of inquiries perhaps subtly budgeted; but for their matching windbreakers. My husband is not at home, Lorna had said—it was just an accident I was, she said to me. The Maya, I replied, say there *are* no accidents. Lorna laughed and said, You and Tessa.

Mr. Nielsen looked toward the line of great trees shrouding the houses along what's called The Grove, where Menuhin lives, and Nielsen had no camera nor the stomach to take a picture. He asked how high Highgate was, and Lorna said the highest spot in London.

Maybe, said Lorna, the son didn't believe in the war. Mrs. Nielsen put a patient hand on Lorna's wrist: Jim used to believe in God and in his heart of hearts he still does. He was in our Youth Fellowship his junior year. The Army shouldn't have had such a bad influence on him. He liked Germany. We told him he would.

I asked Will's whereabouts.

Away for the weekend.

I said I was sorry to ring so early. She said she was wide awake. How could she be so sentimental first thing in the morning, I said, and about windbreakers?

She thought I had gone right back to America from Glasgow.

Why the hell should she assume that? I said too fast.

Geoff was slowly counting spoons of fresh-ground coffee.

You going back?

Why?

Geoff dragged a black terry-cloth sleeve over some pale Danish butter to get to the small Aladdin's Lamp dripping fresh-ground Milano that would be too harsh for me at this hour.

Just so I can tell Jenny and Will.

Will's away, you said.

At Stephen's.

And Jenny's in New York. So enjoy yourself.

I did not wish to discomfit Lorna.

New York!

That's also why I have to be there. How did the Nielsens get my name?

Someone named Bob said you might help.

How?

Find Jim.

Why *were* you in, by the way.

Waiting for a phone call.

Jan after hearing this a day and a half later nonetheless said: *Claire? Did you mean Claire?*

Claire Wheeler, I said. The astronomer-painter. Not the girl at Outer Film.

Jan walked away, as the movie heroine does when in turmoil. She now recalled her Callanish alias. If, as she now said, there was something too much in my knowledge, she herself was adding to it.

Well, she said, she was through protecting Paul; she would leave that to Elspeth and Mr. Andsworth; even that poor idiot Jim, who could not begin to know the size of Paul's abdication, had gotten into the risky bit of protecting Paul and what with my own involvement with Jim perhaps I was in the business of protecting Paul too, but what could I know of Paul—mere information—business—and she would not hold that against Paul. He did what he could with his gifts . . . and yet he didn't.

I suggested Jan introduce Jerry to Paul, Jerry could use help.

Which here Ned Noble, even on his death bed up to the very time he told me I was not getting either his crystal set or the plan for his time machine, would have called a pedestrian trick to learn more of Paul. Yet Jan coming back close to me turned now to the son and not the hero, maybe because it struck her she knew where Paul was and I did not.

If only Jerry would come and live in London. I have so many good friends; an Indian—but you know I'm sure. Jerry is so gifted, so resentful. John has been good to him, Jerry has been good to John. Phil hates me probably. He did the film to lure Jerry, though Jerry says it was to get me. If Phil was corrupting John, as Jerry said, how could Jerry reconcile that with my film itself when John was more than glad to shoot some scenes? Jerry wouldn't come over when John and June shot the air base. Not even and stay with me. He would do anything to help me. He hates his father owning my gallery. Phil imagines it will keep me in London, but it isn't the gallery. And here I am: I'm not even *in* London. Phil doesn't know I'm here unless you told him. But Jerry knows.

My suitcase was at Monty's, the case that in the minds of Mike and Jan might still be checked in Glasgow, and of whoever had spread word that in Jan's Mexican jaguar was hidden after all not Mary Napier's Montrose heart (conveyed to me, it was said, Stonehenge night by the Alabama archaeologist) but a bomb no less. Which, when I learned this shortly after leaving Jan, might have explained why, when I put my hand in my raincoat pocket, I said in answer to her question (What is left if all copies of your diary are gone?), Rub a whiff of nitroglycerine on a table-top, drop a book there and Bang.

Highgate, I might have told Mr. Nielsen, is at its highest 423 feet above sea level. Decomposition sets in more slowly than at peat level.

Jan would like to go shopping with Jerry, she said. Silly of her. She was too bohemian to miss that side of marriage, wasn't she?

Bohemian? I said.

Get him new boots, or get the ones he was wearing resoled. You never knew what he'd show up in. He had beautiful hair. Why wasn't it red? His was fine, hers tough.

Where had she gone when she left Alba's? I asked. I got up; but I couldn't go, as if she were painting me into her picture.

Jerry wants to do things for himself. He installed two new locks in his loft. He started resoling one boot but that was as far as it went. You're not as bad as Jack. I didn't mean to imply that. Just that without you the film could have come off. Paul said there should be some right-wing revolutionaries in the film too. We do not know enough; from that to a series of quiet interviews, and some close-face, calm exposures of some people telling what they want and why; it might have spread a spirit of relenting. But everyone not knowing enough wasn't the only point; another was just not tricking up some neat script-story but taking power in process, other people's ongoing energies and tying into them, that's the way I express it but I got the idea from someone else and that's appropriate too. I think Jerry understood. But for him as you know Phil is an exploiter.

Jan and I getting together to talk about our kids. Her son the locksmith. My daughter the photographer. Jerry and Jenny. Each child defending its parent. Oh the joy of Jenny discovering American comics. Not in America but in the funnies my mother wrapped the children's presents in. The inner wrapping waits while Jenny who used to be too polite about presents stops to read the outer.

I've really talked to you, I said: and Jan nodded vigorously and showed a small but pleasant gap between her broad front teeth; and so saying, I understood: not what Mike said I was wrongly igniting or what Jan said I had stopped: but through telling Jan what Lorna had told me of the Nielsens, its meaning: Mike had said Bob was not with them any more and did I know where he could be found, and Jan had said the Unplaced Room increased the chance of violence through Jim's being squelched on the topic of Paul: now Bob referring the Nielsens to us and then like ancient history Elizabeth at Stonehenge running up to report the boy with the blond beard missing: well, the meaning was this: that Jim, having taken steps to end his war and having (from place to place, mainland to island to studio to Stonehenge) thought his war was over, had now had it ended for him: Jim had been removed, and probably by Nash.

That was my reading.

But if Jim had been killed, was it for protecting Paul or advertising him?

Tessa had said she had walked over some bodies.

Jan had never had much interest in comics. Slick drawing. Cheap color. The English have a wonderful sense of humor. Sly. Droll.

I said they felt it was a national asset.

Jan had narrowed her nostrils. She is about the age of Gilda the florist, and of Renée whose hot copper hair had come all the way from the kiss-proof rouge of a Brooklyn Heights tease through the romance of the Golden Gate.

I am out of my chair. I had forgotten the chorale downstairs which now ends.

If, now that my diary is thought defunct, I myself am the hit, will they bother to find out what is in my head—whether, say, I'm trying to stop something or pull it off? Jan is telling me how I have too much power; her vagueness is convincing because she is trying not to weep, and I point out that I am under surveillance—witness Wheeler, who might have stabbed me instead.

But he knew you—that's why he was hired.

I tell her to tell me where Paul is, but I am deeply and privately wondering whoever said Wheeler knew me, for Wheeler never knew me except as someone in a poli-sci class or playing tennis two courts down.

Tell me where Reid is, she says.

Reid for Paul, I thought.

A god has no morale, needs none. What if they got hold of me and hooked an amplifying system to my heartbeat? What might come out? How could I be a god? An emptiness or semi-conductor at the heart of their system.

Reid is with Paul, I said. Jan cocked her head. Not with Sherman? she said.

If I am a god, it is precisely because I am not independent.

There came steps on the stairs below the chorale, but their seeming familiarity may have been the music they rose to. Jan urged me to the loft's far end.

There were quantities of time as the steps came on. I was behind the curtain where John's slit-scan track ended, and Jan may have told me more now when she touched the empty pocket of my new raincoat touching at last upon the most intimate and least rational connection between us: "He" would not forgive what had been done to her picture—stay out of sight.

But wait: did Jan think Kate had been in the main room when the blank hair had been colored? Did anyone imagine Kate knew what hung in Aut's gallery well enough to walk out into the main room and see at once the white space absent in the flat orange freshly laid on? Oh no indeed. And indeed even if I paid the bills, I could not be held responsible for my daughter's magic marker.

A look from Jan's dark eyes brightened her heart-shaped face and she said in a whisper, *Jenny* then!—the Suitcase snapshot!— and receded swiftly toward the center of the room rented for John by the growing boy who I heard now bash open the door and exclaim, I knew you'd be here! Guess where we're going?

Tell me on the way, said Jan his mother, and at once took him off downstairs.

I wanted to take home a tale to my family they could understand. But it might be too late. They were dispersed.

Who had recruited Wheeler, a mere acquaintance at college years ago?

I wanted time to myself.

I wanted to know for sure the film was destroyed.

Cooking came up to my mind from the direction of the Bach chorale—oil, tomato, even cheese, even the pale slick filling steam of pasta, a bland blend doughy and delicate: I could see a pan of lasagna being layered. And I tried to recall which of Paul's two brothers back in that northern hut had said Sherman was the only one of the lot that Incremona trusted.

CARTRIDGE | Cut to an idea: initial system highly improbable moves toward increasingly probable states: the bog will seep into Krish and thus equalize pressures either side of his thin skin: with Krish gone, the next Nash nosebleed will have fewer probable causes: Phil Aut (legal spouse of Jan, the film's apparent source) and John (whose loft is rented for him by their son Jerry) will prove to be still closer: pairs of namesakes crop up: two Jims— the newly bearded lately departed deserter, and the lunchtime stabber of the man in the target T-shirt; beautiful *Mary* who told her tale of a dismembered heart to my secret cassette, and pretty *Marie*, who crossed our Corsican field first at the fort and then at the *Son des Guitares* café; *John*, the Coventry munitions expert, transatlantic technologue, bumptious debunker of our film, and owner of a house near Portland, Maine, and the other *John* whose glasses I'd knocked off, whose friend June had helped me, and whose loft conveyed an authenticity beyond the sum of its video-synthesizer, slit-scan gear, and formulaic poster with the computer code-word NAND in a lower part: further probabilities are that Len Incremona, who disliked the English John enough to blow a bullet through a dartboard, will if given cause to think John a private opportunist act upon it, though Len would not fly to New York just for that: and probabilities are that the package of pages typed by Jenny Cartwright and left by her under an ancient megalith in Callanish where the great stones are like petrified tree-shards is less and less likely to stay a secret, for the dilettante geologist now possibly joined there by Jack may spot it while seeking Krish, or I could phone the crofter widow to retrieve it (which forty years ago you could film with that trick of the diagonal wipe bundling two distant talkers into one magic frame), or I get Dagger to drop everything and go collect the package—or Jenny is made to talk, in which case anyone (if anyone truly operative is left on that side of the watery world) could zip up to Glasgow, Stornoway, and Callanish and grab what may now be the single copy of a diary whose interest seems increasingly to be in what it yields about its manufacturer and his life and less and less in what it hints of certain schemes.

Does Jenny grow more like Claire or less? Claire lacks that fine detour like a wave or illusion in the bridge of the nose where Jenny's new camera came up to hit her after Will backpedaled into her, teasing a friendly neighbor's hound that had in turn been excited by a turtle, and she fell, both hands clutching the camera. Jenny and Claire will approach each other, probably.

Yet on the other hand how *im*probable the procession now to come.

But this idea is cut from me, or I from it: not to a timeless scheme of parted window shade, doors ajar on two floors, dark stairs tapped into cadence; nor to a course laid out as on a map projection where curves and zig-zag turn into one bearing, straight from the slit-scan track to a blue air letter typed in red on the workbench beside the video-synthesizer thence to a dark corner three flights down where I Frederick Dudley Jack Paul Monty Mercator held my breath till two unlikely fellows and one voice tiptoed past on the way up: instead cut from that glimpse of conversely increasing *im*probability to what I merely did.

In the loft I opened the shade to the city and outcroppings of sky. Mother and son came into Mercer Street below. The fine billowing brown hair and the shorter, coarse red lost some of their color in the aisle of shade northward. The air letter was from Dagger DiGorro postmarked London, and it was addressed to me in New York but not at John's loft. There was grit on the stairs. On the floor below, the spitting of oil in a pan covered my steps. The letter in my pocket was another weapon, this time mine though already used by others though not therefore useless to me.

At the last instant before I would have emerged into the street and been seen, the ground-floor door opening made me find, in the luck of its deepening shadow, a corner to stand in, but just in time to find only a mass of trouble which seemed to have no bearing on American society or international commitment, on the poster in Dag's living room of Trotsky and his American aide Bob Harte in Mexico or in the Sorbonne courtyard in May '68: TAKE YOUR DESIRES FOR REALITIES. But the mass of trouble bore not merely on the cross-hatched plots and the faces heart- or cartridge-shaped and sounds (dry wet soft hard) excised from tracks, and parallel beards and that strong swimmer Mary's two missing finger joints, my wife's underwear, my son's Chartres, the characters of Dudley and his daughter Jane, and endlessly inescapable informations beneath if not a god maybe a man, such as Jenny saying she and Reid had been in the pedestrian passage leading under the museum to South Ken tube station, which moved me to urge that site on Dagger who it turned out was planning to find the Hawaiian boy and Hempstead girl precisely there that morning, which is where they had been the day Jenny passed through with Reid. No, the mass and waves of trouble I found in this dark dusky ground-floor corner of a New York Manhattan loft building bore not just on all this but (I swore) toward a formula for how such power could be ascribed to me at the very moment my own field seemed less definite than ever.

The one voice spoke: Believe me, somehow that bastard knows we're coming, he's got Chad's gun, remember.

And when I saw the speaker's long concave profile and short coiled body of prowling legs and shoulders and arms and on his hand, for it was Nash, those three colors that in the glance of late light from the street flashed like sound being heard somewhere else, I found not the formula but the red that Jan said I'd made a certain someone see. I felt it in Sub's address red-inked under my name on the typewriter of the much-connected man my friend, collaborator, and protective deceiver Dag in whose Hampstead flat I'd met the other of these two the evening of the day we filmed the air base.

Yes, the man with Nash was the big Frenchman with a shock of prematurely white hair. He and the other two waiting in Alba's chairs had been glum or contemptuous when they heard my brainstorm. I said two new minutes of them now slow-motion would beautifully top what Dag and I had just filmed at the air base thinking it would be the end—namely, men sending trained hawks to kill starlings so the starlings from the fifties deployed like the regular trees along avenues administered with street signs and speed limits like those in U.S. bases and towns anywhere—then (and here had been our finale) the bombers themselves in quick repeat (like the Hawaiian hippie approach shots) again and again stiffly lifting off into the sunset which to an audience wouldn't be necessarily northern or August—on the way back to the stationwagon the U. Maryland part-timer we'd run into at Stonehenge asked if I knew John, and when Dag said, No, he doesn't know John, I at once said, Sure I know John, was it John I was going to be introduced to? and the U. Maryland part-timer who was our host because he taught here though Dagger had done one term a few years ago, said No, unfortunately he changed his plans at the last minute. Dagger was not amused.

But now beyond this, my new idea: three men lifting their hands in parlor talk so slowly that the audience (if Phil Aut would distribute us to one) would feel the endless distance from those real and rising bombs just as Alba's reappearing wrist and long American cigarette and solo activity would flute the edges of the room with nerves—a woman's service, her unease, the seeming ceremonies of men. Add sound at too few revs per second slow-motioning small talk into garbled agony, and Lorna if her blue eyes ever saw the film would see the struggle of our years, the reach from somewhere less real to something more, which might be less likely the cadres and secret councils of terrible change—CONSUMER SOCIETY MUST DIE A VIOLENT DEATH—and more the unchecked wages of Sub's days at home and at work, unchecked actuality of a small-claims suit and his lack of a divorce, a historic Bach sweatshirt on a heap of spin-dried sheets, hamburger the color of crushed strawberries on a table near an old blue cut-glass tumbler that holds the water Sub washes his deep-yellow-urine-producing Stress Supplement vitamins down with while on the sink beside the steaming kettle his red-white-and-blue Japanese mug stands ready with its teabag damp from the film of water left in the bottom (for Sub washes last night's late teacup first

424

thing in the morning) while Tris is drinking orange Tang seeing in the middle distance floating astronauts squeezing their breakfast into their mouths as he and Ruby spread their white toast with grape jelly that comes in a jar with a picture on the side which Ruby will use to drink her skim milk from when the jelly is gone—and Ruby anticipating opposition announces over the radio news that Sub some time in the past ruled that tonight she may stay up late for a TV program because today is Monday (which she turns to Tris to confirm), and then the news on this good-music station ends with the weather and a calm commercial for stereo systems and Sub tells Ruby also calmly that he would like to drop the TV set out the window (the new smaller portable I haven't reimbursed him for), but at that instant his Japanese radio slips off its band onto another with those hermaphrodite voices singing "*You* Are Every*thing*, and Every*thing* Is *You.*"

But the steps of Nash and the Frenchman went up the loft stairs toptoe in unison drawn by the prospect of Cartwright. The escalator was in my pocket in red ink. From two things Jan had said, I knew I had been unjust to John; he had not been the breaker of Sub's TV and Sub's window, nor had he pinched the pennies out of a recycled tin. And the hands that had shoved me down the escalator likely belonged to the person whose fingers must have found my letter on Sub's kitchen table beside the phone pad this morning (the letter itself having come yesterday Monday) because Sub on his way to work at 9:15 digging in his jacket for a token so as not to have to stand in line at the subway change booth might leave some of his mail where he found it in the postbox in the lobby—though lately it is never distributed until ten—but he would never go back upstairs just to leave, say, a letter that had come for me. The unison toes passed above me. I had the ponderous street door open and my other hand in my raincoat for Dagger's letter. Mother and son were into the next block north, still on Mercer; once I got past two trucks parked pointed south with their right-side wheels up on the sidewalk, I could see diagonally ahead of me on the other side of the street also walking north and looking it seemed diagonally ahead to Jerry and Jan who were on my side of the street someone I should have been seeking but was not, yet someone who did not act as if she might be in danger but was trailing two people I thought would be willing to harm her.

I wanted to catch up and ask her the whole sense of her note on the top page of the manuscript Gene had burned in the peat fire Saturday. If I quoted the Sorbonne poster TAKE YOUR DESIRES FOR

REALITY in order to ask Jenny what she took mine to be, she might know at once, better than I. I had dismissed our film yet made it what it was, composed a parallel diary yet incited its theft, suffered this girl ahead on the other sidewalk (this Virginia Ginny Jenny in a U.S. Army corporal's tunic and a high-crowned blue denim hat Lorna had had made by a theatrical hatter in Soho) to become my English hostage, yet I'd let her be drawn toward the claws of a confusion that could use her as a hostage against me.

In turn the four of us turned west and when Jan and Jerry hit a light and he started to dart across but she wouldn't go he stopped and waited, and when she turned to look back I was already in a phone booth hoping Jenny had not seen me.

I dialed June who at once complained that her brother Chad had been using her; I told her she had set me up for Nash but Nash was by now sorry he'd tried to jump me.

The light changed, the sky was clouding over, I turned away and as Jan looked back in the corner of my eye I felt a figure stop or turn or in some way change; June was saying it was Paul's fault what had happened to Chad and she only wanted to help me, not harm me, and she didn't know anything except about taking the heart out of the red jag and putting a bomb in instead and she didn't know what that meant but had heard it only when Chad asked what she knew about it.

I said I was slowing things down and was getting several pictures different from before and would ask her and her nice friends to my Halloween slide show. Meanwhile, I said, find out more about the jag, it would help Chad—and Chad needed help, I had come back from the Hebrides and I knew. Stay there, I said, and hung up.

The four ahead were moving.

Jan turned south, then west, then north, then west again. Three trucks got tied up and I could not see Jenny.

At a light Jan looked back and I stepped into a café that was closing. A headline said the U.N. had seated Peking. I phoned June. She had gotten new information awfully fast, it seemed to me. Gene had told Chad only what sounded to her like a riddle, that Paxton had passed the heart at Stonehenge and that I had hidden it in a hole I'd bored in a red jaguar but I had taken it out and inserted plastic but the way he said it it sounded like a trade name.

I think someone's coming, I said; stay there. I hung up; but folding back the booth door, stepping out and pulling back, I knew I had made a prophetic projection in what I'd said; for through the café's plate-glass front I'd seen passing at a slow springy tread the figure of Reid across the street who if he had been watching me might have lost me when the trucks got tied up. So we were now five, and I in possession of the rear and no longer between Reid and Jenny though now forced further behind Jan who was leading me to Paul.

But from Macdougal and Bleecker I saw her cross the cobbles of Sixth Avenue chased then by the sudden northward swarm of cars and trucks, a blue bus full and a green right behind it empty, and a wildly high-slung old gypsy cab skipping the potholes. Jan and Jerry turned south.

Jenny waited at the light, which held up Reid who was half-way between Bleecker and Sixth in the doorway of an electrical shop eyeing me. The expulsion of Taipei did not affect the flow of cheap umbrellas from Hong Kong.

That Paul was holed up in the same house as my parka and my suitcase was so improbable I accepted it, and when Reid looked away I ran south on Macdougal to the corner of East Houston where I followed the high, wire-mesh playground fence and saw that my right-angle shortcut parallel to Jan's course on Sixth and risking a loss of visual contact had left me closer than Jenny and Reid, almost too close, for as Jan and Jerry increased speed (and just before they turned into King) Jan looked round again but I automatically like a soldier given the order "To the rear, march!" reversed my direction and was approached without enthusiasm by two old Italian ladies, all in black. Then I crossed East Houston and pursuing Jan and Jerry from my own angle I reached a phone in a cleaning establishment across Sixth from King Street whence I saw what my daughter and her boyfriend were not in time to see but what I'd imagined and did not need to see: Jan ascending with her son the stoop of her brother Monty's house, the address Dagger had expressed the air letter to.

June asked where I was. A helicopter came from the Hudson so slowly the distance seemed greater. IMAGINATION TAKES POWER a Sorbonne poster said in May of '68. I could only think of my posterity yet not as that but as my daughter and my son to whom I had probably done little. They are English, and there is something and nothing in that.

What was Will doing at Stephen's? Lorna urged him to go. Did he and Stephen speak of Ogg the mapman? of Chartres and its 176 windows? No more likely than of the New York Botanical Garden with its 70,000 panes of glass. Less likely than of cricket. I didn't know.

Now, under this helicopter, I was less certain I'd brought him back the Wall Street brochure than that Lorna had got him out of the house for a reason; less certain I'd given her the Joni Mitchell *Blue* than that on July 18 when the DiGorros had met the Allotts and Dudley had embarrassed Tessa by asking persistently about someone named Nash, Dagger had mentioned Mary Napier from Edinburgh; more sure that Will left the bath soap smeared with gray than that Gene had picked up his astonishing statement about me and the red jaguar in part from Nell his wife who to Jan was a Wellesley girl but to me had been the mistress of a house I was let into like a mover come to pack the best bone china and de-leg the ancient grand; but I was less sure what my son had in mind when he eyed Lorna's behind as she bent to reach into the fridge and he spoke of a pulley-block hoist maneuver to check in Chartres some cryptic stained glass, than I was sure that it was through that muscular mystery Savvy Van Ghent who ran into Dudley in the British Museum that Nell knew Tessa, who would have told Savvy anything or nothing (you never knew).

But of course: I had indeed gotten Will's Wall Street material; for I'd said so over Sub's phone some time in the last few days, and Will had asked if I had any enemies and if I was going to Lorna's choral concert, which I had forgotten more than once.

He closed his door a lot lately. He did it the night I sat down to write the Softball Game. He was brave; he had prowled through the dark house with his new metal tennis racket and had been disturbed only that his mother took him for a burglar though he had taken her for me. Did he think of Jenny when he masturbated? I thought of my sister Stonehenge night in a creaky hotel room with a naked lady in a green beret whose great concern with real estate during that trip may have spread the passion of her fantasies that night, but nothing like the reluctance of the man she tried and failed to tug through the Sarsen Circle into the light of our camera (and who knows whence else) and who she (like most of us there) may still not know was the youngest of the three Flint brothers, Paul, come imagining he'd find there his uncertain middle brother Gene the integrity of whose life Paul rightly believed was in danger. So Tessa's unnamed Paul (who stumbled over his lines and could only say with stammering grace and amusement that he was a *tourist moved* by the *distances these ssstones had come*) met my sister (her round cheeks and happy hungers so unlike Tessa) in a new bed of an ancient room over the road from Salisbury Cathedral Close. Children were near my phone and the proprietor of the cleaning establishment

flung open his door and snapped his fingers at them to get, express-
ing his impatience with the alleged emergency that was my excuse
for using his phone. June asked where I was.

Jenny turned into King Street, hesitated as if under direction,
and began to run up the north side, receding, as June said, Please.

Jenny had run beyond Monty's house (which I, even more
than you who have me, remember is on the south side) when I saw
Reid, and when he reached the corner of King she had turned the far
corner at the end of the block no doubt wondering where Jan and
Jerry were.

Where's Chad? I said into the phone.

The English guy John said he's supposed to be in the city.

Did you set me up?

I *like* you. Don't I *like* you?

June was more visible than Reid. I heard the helicopter flap-
ping somewhere and asked June if I could have an overseas call from
a pay booth charged to another phone, and I realized as I said the
words not mentioning the dreaded Hebrides that Jack with his
connections could tie me up royally if he found Krish dead in the peat
bog.

June had asked where it was I wanted to call.

I said, Incremona hasn't caught up with John yet; so maybe I
can help Chad.

June was complaining warmly that this morning I wouldn't
tell her where I was, and I wouldn't now. She'd said she worried
about me like Claire worried about Monty.

Reid reached Monty's and vanished into the areaway.

June said, Please, baby, all I know is what I said—someone
blew the whistle and John said my brother was to do nothing but
nothing except contact John.

I said I was meeting Claire and was phoning from near
Claire's (which in fact was thirty blocks north and east of my present
position). I looked behind me but saw only children.

You know I love Claire, said June.

I said I'd get John's number from Claire, but then June said
please not to ask Claire, she didn't want her getting into Chad's problems, she had enough of her own—was that a deal?

As June said the number—slowly, twice—Jenny reappeared
at the end of the block looking back down in the direction of Monty's
house and me, and Reid popped out of the areaway and ran up the
front steps, probably seen by Jenny.

I told June she had set me up.

The helicopter swayed back toward the Hudson but it looked bigger. The blades have to swivel to develop horizontal thrust and they could not swivel without a swash-plate that wobbles on the rotor shaft. Prince Philip is a competent chopper pilot.

June was protesting that when I'd asked her this morning to find Jan, she had phoned Claire and Claire had quietly flipped out and said Monty didn't like her dog and what was she going to do, her uncle was out walking the dog right now and she felt she had started something she couldn't finish.

Jenny had started back down King toward me, and I felt the lower circle of the phone receiver beaming on my Adam's apple, and I observed to June that Claire wasn't the only one who felt that way and I for one was trying to just go with events, and Saturday night in the Western Isles I had not foreseen that forty hours (clocktime) later I'd be here in New York.

Her uncle thought you were still in London, said June.

I said I'd call from Claire's, and then instead of asking how she had known where to reach Nash and his nasty companion, I hung up just as Jenny turned around and started running back to the far corner; but now too late I caught the sense of June's last words. The helicopter swung off up the Hudson like a glider tuned at will to any wind in a field of winds, and as I made my move wondering if in the twilight Jenny with her fine pale hair and broad-brimmed blue hat had been seen from Monty's house when she'd stopped opposite it, I saw in simple form that it would be harder to make my move than I had registered looking west along King and glancing behind me here and there at children vaguely aware of me; and the simple form was a right angle whose two lines meeting at me came east from Jenny, who had run now almost out of sight, and south from (speak of the devil) Nash's white-haired Frenchman who had stationed himself near the playground. The chopper slid sideways and lower, lower, it may not have been the same one, it made a great clatter that would have competed with the northbound traffic had that not by now thinned.

I recall hearing on BBC a witty speech Prince Philip gave to some science body and wondering who'd written it and being smartly put in my place by Tessa who said all his speeches were written by Philip himself.

Prince Philip with his engineering and nautical interests may remember enough cartography to know the law of deformation: which is that there will always be at least two pairs of directions

430

perpendicular to each other at a given point on the globe that will reappear when that curved surface is turned into a flat map.

Monty Graf when he and I caught up with each other Thursday found this law less urgent than the right angles that gave rise to my memory of it. But persisting, I said that Tuesday opposite King Street I suddenly had not known whether I'd moved from sphere to plane or plane to sphere, which was a discomfiting application of my Druid's thought—

But Andsworth's not in this, said Monty on Thursday; not deep anyway. Or is he?

Less than I, more than you, more than he knows, less than he fears.

Yes, but what was his thought you mentioned? He helped set up Stonehenge for you. He wasn't on the film was he? And who was Marie's boyfriend?

My knowledge of operations seemed to go unquestioned; it was my knowledge of policy that seemed dubious to me and others. There comes a point at which one wants to compute no more of these facts. Still, as my Druid says, in each age arise unlikely tongues which nonetheless may help us: the gods of the body's warm organs may show themselves now not through a burning bush or a martyr's funny bone on fire or in the mysteries of appetite, but along intangible electronic canals where slippery loops joining pancreas and lung, bowel and eye, become, for the sake of a diagram's current, straight lines and right-angle transits, and clarity's pulse waits for the gate which if open may flip whole futures of gates drawing that pulse like a spasm of the greater body through gods who blink and gods who do not blink (for Andsworth ever was a closet polytheist) until at some crux near the analogic cog or digital core a twinge of harmony is heard like someone else's pain. But at that moment Tuesday I was not clear if those right angles had survived from true sphere to projected plane or from plane to sphere.

But when you saw Andsworth before you took the train to Glasgow, said Monty Graf, was he disturbed that you tried to pass as Jack Flint to get by the housekeeper?

If the merchant deforms himself seeking the direct route, credit him at least with not knowing till he gets there what the project is he is merchandising. It might be a film, might be words, or from Red Whitehead's science-supply firm a gross of liquid crystal newly marketable in a cartridge that approaches the condition of music; or it might be the Montrose heart discovered like Mercator's

1538 map of the world—famous, lost, then rediscovered in New York thirty-six years after Catherwood's panorama burnt. If the deformation from sphere to flat yields you straight-line bearings from here to there, the fact that your trip is expedited by an illusion costs you no more than the way taken by Raleigh to vast and undefined Virginia or than the routes abstracted to a straight line in the partial Underground map Dudley Allott stares at traveling with dear Jane (for like the Druid, Dudley seldom takes a cab, though unlike Dudley the Druid drives everywhere—an ancient English Ford).

He wasn't on the film? asks Monty Graf again, not knowing that at least since Tuesday night (diary or no diary, film or no film) there has been a hunt on for my life.

Oh Andsworth calls film evanescent.

But he wasn't on your film?

He *isn't* on it, no.

You say isn't! How much *is* there, then? More than you said?

There's so much a film can't find. It catches the dull gleam and choppy chill of the sea when the dilettante geologist was bringing Jim Nielsen into a Hebridean cove; but not the sea's curve over the horizon, for you have to reflect upon that, formulate it, imagine it. The film catches the look of Paul's shoulders so narrow they seem to have been framed in a vise which simultaneously heightens him. Film claims his shaggy moustache, frames the lanky hint of ungainliness when Paul stumbled and braced himself as Tessa tried to tug him through a portal toward the light. You could catch that on film, but not the posthumous alignment on the one hand of Paul's widely suspect conversion from violence which he'd come to believe was not authenticity but the mere figment of change, and on the other hand (*his* hand that's being tugged!) Tessa's long fling with Maya blood, and the heart-excision atop the priestly pyramid, and some half-chewed creed of cruelty whose roots plot their length through the other violence of a tame marriage which was in turn one yield of a wifeless father (seeking angrily, fearfully his wide-eyed daughter hiding in a bombed house) and of a mother crystallized into ash or bone-meal or, at best, thought. Catch even on a sound track as if from under a stone in response to the bank clerk's account of how far some of Stonehenge had to come, these words: It comes to that, and that alone—Paul Flint's words, as you who have me may have guessed.

But take the film in daylight or night light or from the air even if—action!—we restage the wheelless haul from Wales by neolithic land and water with bare brawn and animal hides and at the end on Salisbury Plain log stages for raising the lintels—and instead of a star in the lead a blond or swarthy tall unknown—think of all an emulsion, a lens, a drive motor, and a mind running the contraption can't convey. There's so much more.

I suppose you've seen your swashbuckling friend Dagger since he arrived, said Monty. If there's more, did he bring it with him? Claire said all he sneaked in was a carton of audio gear he's going to sell.

So much more: not only the idea of the sun cutting across the eyeball as if its vitreous arc were a gate giving a million alignments to that other energy the brain—oh not only the hot god or mere star or grid-fixed force passing from parallel to parallel across that useful fiction the celestial sphere (not parallel—*declination,* blinks Ned Noble from someplace in my system which is not only *my* system, for I have grown into the impingement of other fields on mine and this sense should in theory mean I'm in less danger than, say, Incremona, Jerry, or Claire) each day each year each 26,000-year cycle of the whole solar system. (Whole? Who says it's whole? blinks a light which may be Ned at an outpost of my lung or may be just my thought of what he'd say.)

What is this danger Claire is in? asks Monty Graf fresh from England, continuing to smoke to keep his weight in hand, and now less clear what it is that he and his young beloved are trying to salvage for themselves.

But Monty old friend, having like you and Claire set too high and narrow a hope upon the film, I then let the contrary occur, let its scenes come between me and it, so what I valued was not the film at all but the fog at the edge of the bonfire ring, the fog becoming something else gassy to jump and bend (I told Claire) through the forms of a boy in overalls, a big woman in red and yellow swinging across the circle, her glad tantrum of head-wagging, two burning branches bearing a gray label—all that was left of a carton—not the label even but letters once on it like some instance of Hindu Māyā that lets us believe in the rest that may not really be there.

Then was it you who destroyed parts of the film or let people think parts were destroyed?

Instead of the film as all or nothing (which is dangerous) let us conceive something else: beyond the Druid's circuitries with Yes or No gods at the gates of our bodily systems which in the idiom of computers become newly strange and finely limited and whole and, hence, beyond Jenny at Stonehenge stepping back inside the circle but facing out with her back to me taking a picture through a linteled arch then turning radiant to me as if she were my transit outward or my charged gate and calling to me (where I stood by the altar stone with the bank clerk behind me), It's a message!—while he, rustling in his clear plastic mac coughed and the cough turned into hard facts about two circles (not one), sixteen Sarsen stones left out of thirty, exact measures of consistent distances from midstone to midstone—

Did you take your daughter to the Stonehenge filming? asks Monty, who fears me now and in a moment will ask the waiter first for another gin and milk, second for the Men's Room, and go phone Claire instead.

No, instead of the film as all or nothing, which is dangerous, very dangerous, Monty—something else: something beyond the straight routes the globe's arcs become when opened flat upon Mercator's grid, something beyond the mere choice of flat to sphere or sphere to flat.

I happen to know, said Monty, that you and Dagger DiGorro do a little quiet trade in rare maps.

Beyond, to what Andsworth has hinted are new modes of mind that likewise will do violence in order to pan from state to state, but benign violence by which a mind that has become whole with the personal body it is part of can project force into other minds without the medium of plotted motion or verbal circuits, to live with others in a new privacy of collaborative process in which getting there or back here has become so minor as to be forgotten—

Monty is almost angry: Claire had nothing to do with the rare maps or the electronic equipment, and she does not know Andsworth. Do you recall when you introduced him to Dagger?

—and there won't be Time in the old sense of resistance that impedes what in some old sense of Space is unresisted or unlimited, and hence there will be no motion in the old formula synthesizing the two—

One hears that in Andsworth's macrobiotic community there is an American girl quite hung up on him. Why do you speak of danger to Claire? From what John said to me in Coventry, your daughter Jenny is the one who is in danger.

—which I only now see may yield, through the old man's prophecy and then my intervention, a formula for those still more distant futures loosed in 1945 by the bitter shrug of an adult who seemed in that corridor of Brooklyn Hospital to be neither breathing nor holding his breath, Hy Noble, with the olive pallor left like some helpless health below his tan from a month at the Jersey shore. I had come from Ned's private room where Hy's young-looking wife (if she was now jumping up to crank Ned's bed) sat with her horn-rimmed glasses in her lap across an open book. I came out into the corridor, and my future like Lorna's at fourteen when she asked an intern in the middle of the night if her father would live would hinge on the question I now asked Ned's father: Is there any chance Ned was kidding about the crystal set and the plan for the time machine?

Mr. Noble's shrug holds very still now, as I look out across two empty glasses at Monty Graf—the shrug so still that the shoulders and their anguish sink into a negative to which the son Ned undying might well have conceived an entry that would interest if not ravish old Babbage with his skeleton key (given to the world as naturally as Bob Harte lent away the key to Trotsky's gate or, Monty, you gave Paul Flint a key to your house in King Street), and behind Babbage, Lord Napier the inventor of logs, with his early computer, bits of wood or ivory, Napier's Bones.

Paul never had that key from me, said Monty Graf.

A duplicate cut from mine maybe. But probably cut from Claire's, though who knows what Nash will think—or Incremona or the Frenchman?

You mean the boyfriend of this French girl I hear about? said Monty. Is he in New York too? Look, if we pooled our information—

But in the crowded restaurant our waiter saw Monty's hand at last and came, and as he made his right-angle turn into our aisle I wondered if it was by guess or false report that Monty thought me part of Dagger's traffic in old maps and audio gear.

Another Frenchman, I said.

Look, said Monty, it wasn't Claire, it must have been my sister got Paul into the house—she could have waited till I arrived. But what's it matter, he's gone now, isn't he?

It's known he was there. But if Claire was the one who got him in you shouldn't stop trusting her for not telling you.

Don't tell me how to treat Claire.

What do I know of Claire? What she tells me. What Dag tells me. What he does without telling me, like not telling Claire we filmed a scene in Jan's studio.

What do you know of Claire?

A weightlessness I felt in your basement bedroom partly through Claire's presence.

She's such a giving person, said Monty.

I have no formula for this weightlessness as yet, any more than the secret of peat or how to build mobile terminals with it or change it into power I can use but may not then be able to see or touch—like what Ned Noble did not in the end leave me.

Claire doesn't know any Ned Noble. Was it from the Jersey shore?

At school Ned said that the real spelling was N*obel* and that they were related to Alfred Nobel's family through a maverick uncle who set out from Stockholm to visit the torpedo works in St. Petersburg that Alfred's father had started during his sojourn in Russia. But this uncle trapped bear in Finland and around the time of Lincoln's assassination found himself on the southern coast of the Baltic being taken for a Polish Jew because of the company he kept and for some reason he never protested. My friend on Parents' Day asked Ned's mother and she said no, Ned was wrong, it was N*oble* with an *le*.

The Nobel prize for gunpowder, said Monty.

The waiter had paused along the way.

The crystal oscillator Ned built by himself at thirteen was deliberately old-fashioned, not just pre-radio but subtly primitive he said with uninsulated connections and a second-hand crystal diode but more than one station if you knew how to turn the tuning condenser. He told his parents they were stupid to praise it like it was some epochal invention; he'd gone back to a proto-tuner, in order to sense the thinking by which sound-wave reception had developed, because what he was interested in was a new volume to be created out of nothing—or nothing more than the imaginary boundaries between volumes that already existed. I think it was during his first stay in Brooklyn Hospital when he had a semiprivate room that he sketched a rough plan for his time machine (as *I* called it) which was less a device to go back or forth than a pictured formula for slipping between and creating a space that was not there before.

Sort of a fluid concept, said Monty Graf.

I described it once to Ned's parents and his roommate the first time Ned was in hospital with jaundice and from what little he'd said about it weeks before, I could fill in the blanks.

From crystal set to liquid crystal, said Monty as slyly as he was able, which a film-frame might or might not have caught, depending on whether it could show how Monty under duress was between me, the waiter, Claire, and something I was sure had happened to him in England.

436

Not quite, I said, though I am not sure how much of what follows I said and how much I thought (or thought because I had said): for no matter how subtly my drift takes me from Mercator to computer to some as yet unformulated future mode where I believe old Andsworth's intimation touches young Ned Noble, I am (as Ned said during that first illness) of pedestrian imagination, yet (as he did not say) even more fit therefore to poach upon, understand, and (with a patience Len Incremona once but no longer had with the radio-telescope nitty-gritty he'd been on the verge of real involvement with in New Mexico) underwrite the marketable futures of power-systems already in existence and more or less under way, as Graf in his efforts to tie himself and Claire into our action clearly saw himself, though the error he and, to her peril, Claire made was to meddle in what they imagined was a single or closed system but in which really let's say Jack Flint's mercantile angle might well remain the same vis-à-vis Gene, Jan, or Aut, yet figure in systems very different whose peculiar open impingements must be sensed, else violence might befall Claire, let's say, and possibly as a direct result (and here I reached out on impulse to last weekend at Coventry) of Monty's interrogating that bumptious voluble John who was in danger himself from Incremona, but Ned knew something about me, which led him to tell me just enough and then do the terrible thing he did.

I, said Monty Graf, did not interrogate *John: John* of his own free will told *me,* and I've known him much longer than you.

But Sub disagreed. He said that what Ned had done was not terrible, that my question to Ned's already grieving father Hy was not heartless, and that Ned's mother following me out into the hospital hall still holding the book Ned did not want her to read to him and hearing my question to Ned's father and then her rebuke to me, was reacting as helplessly to the messages coming in as Ned was himself in that high bed she smoothed every hour, or as I was myself, coming out of Ned's private room to ask a question that meant I did not want this undependable friend (whom Sub never liked) to die, but in words as clear as the messages in my head were scrambled.

Look, said Monty, if you want to know exactly what John—

But the waiter asked if we were ready to eat.

Ned had promised me his crystal receiver. He had done so on the day I reached far out my window in Brooklyn Heights to grab between its upward and downward course (like two gravities) his vertical throw. But when I visited him in Brooklyn Hospital the autumn of '45, he said he'd destroyed the crystal set precisely because he'd promised it to me, and having committed the plans for the other thing to memory (I called it a time machine but Ned never labeled it) he'd soaked the page in rubbing alcohol blurring the ink and when it had dried and what was flammable had (so he said) evaporated, he had burnt the page, though not the logo he had designed for the formulas. And since the night I came home to Highgate from Liverpool having failed to sell the drive-in movie project (and all the way to Euston toyed with the vision of mobile terminals for trains or new conveyances) and arriving home heard the climax of Tessa Allott's tale of Uncle Karl who was blinded by the same blow that woke him up, which in turn was to Tessa first of all an intimation of some other (or after-) life rooted in her vision that a thought properly held just before and during death carried into timeless survival with it the person whose brain (no doubt, as I suggested to her, tuned and integrated to the whole bodily life) had for its part helped to crystallize the idea and then had flickered out hundred-cell-parcel by hundred-cell-parcel (heca-cell by heca-cell if you think of Welsh cows offered up as unsacrificed accidents to a would-be god), I have seen Ned's act as another kind of gift and as a model for futures even further than Andsworth's vague next stage, which may be really like what I felt after Mrs. Noble came to the door of Ned's private room (now awful again, its colorless door ajar at my back) and heard me ask Mr. Noble if Ned was kidding about the crystal set and the time machine—she said, You are heartless.

But Hy Noble said no he was afraid his son wasn't kidding, and then he stuck out his hand to shake mine. He said, You understand.

I said, Yes.

He said, I think you've helped. You've helped me.

How? said Monty.

Monty was afraid but cool. A camera could not show what I state: If I wouldn't tell about those right-angles Tuesday and operations he assumed I was at least mentally in command of, then he would think of Ned and try to compute digital trivia.

The hand of Ned's father held mine for several counts as if the hand-to-hand connection was still on the way. Time held. I looked behind still holding Ned's father's brown hand; the door was shut.

Always after that, I felt between them.

And I never saw them again, though Christmas of my freshman year in college Mrs. Noble phoned my mother to say they had an extra ticket for *Streetcar* and later on I heard Ned's sister had graduated from Chicago and gone to Germany. Ned read my mind;

438

but during these years in England perhaps he's read it even more truly.

Wait—said Monty; he's alive?

He died a routine drugged death in the fall of '45. Hy founded a scholarship at our school. There's no telling what Ned might have achieved. My father heard in Wall Street that Hy had talked to his partner about changing his name back to what it was in 1920 when his father had changed it to Noble, but Hy's wife was against this. Hy was an expert doubles player. His feet, he said (though I never saw for myself), were almost perfectly flat, but there had been something else as well that had kept him out of the war. Why do I call him by his given name Hy?

How close are you and Dagger really?

Close enough to have read his letter to his niece about the project she contemplated behind Aut's back. Close enough to have in a pocket of mine hidden at this instant in the King Street house a note Dagger had from you, Monty, in which you say that if he is counting on my diary to advertise his film, maybe you should see a piece. A piece of the action, Monty, your thing.

The waiter is thinking mainly that we haven't ordered, and to judge from his permanently raised gray-tufted eyebrows and creased forehead and his skeptical eyes, he is not interested in what at first glance he or a camera would see in Monty's now suddenly quite undivided face, a fixed look that could be dislike, could be rage, a hot antipasto that wasn't sitting well (but the waiter knew we hadn't eaten), or a coldly intelligent fear much more clearly coherent than its nearest cause, which was what I (in my hypothetical field of multiple impingements) was doing to him and to myself. I did not have to have the sharpness of a god to know that he did not wholly mean to let go his next words: Who put that letter on my brother-in-law's desk.

I answered, A sequence of footsteps, phone rings, bucket clanks, lights, darks—words which reminded me that, godlike or not, my strength was in knowing what these others mistook: that all I had was my place in a multiple system. So I was not wholly responsible for now saying to Monty (what I knew would worry if not scare him) that Jack Flint wouldn't like that letter, he wouldn't like it one bit, and neither would the man who had almost shot John in my presence—did Monty happen to know Incremona?

Monty, whom a cine camera of any water would have shown to break his pose as soon as the waiter limped off, and a sound track would have voiced in cadences heavily ironic, now softly pounded out such words as Power already in process, right? like someone else's crystal prototype? someone else's formula? like some other boy's baseball you happened to catch? someone else's film idea you steal without understanding? isn't that what it's all about, Cartwright? like someone's lighter which those who have not handled it before had better not reach for in your pocket?

There was no beer in the stein I tipped back to my mouth—tipped more calmly than a camera could see. Monty had heard about Krish, so Krish had been discovered. And Monty had heard I was suspected. I saw him through the stein like an old forgotten hypothesis, then set it down and looked for the waiter and waved, while Monty said how he cared about that girl and nothing must happen to her even if I was the one as he now began to think who was at the heart of the whole thing—and even if I already had the information he was about to give me, I was not going to have the chance to sneak it, he was going to give it to me free and then he was going to get up from this table and he hoped I understood where he stood.

Over your head, I said.

He said that taking me into account Dagger DiGorro was wise to distribute his chances so now he had H.E.W. and a carton of audio gear to fall back on.

Which gave me, as Tessa's father would say, a *shtip:* Dagger then was really serious about that vita sent to his old friend in Washington, and he was busy too with a carton of audio gear like an extra suitcase or a box of softball bases and bats and balls or of Nikon lenses (the Nikon *system* you're urged to commit yourself to) bought through the U.S. Air Force or Navy or from the woman in Amsterdam or the man in Antwerp with pounds sterling acquired in bulk the week after the Marvelous Country House when (as I learned from Jenny) he'd had advance word of devaluation by that revolutionary Republican Nixon and unloaded all the dollars he could get his hands on. But I had no time to trace that *shtip* from side to back to stomach to calf, chest, and shoulder, a node of warm mercury lurching like some bulk of liquid around my body when I smoked Geoff's friend Jasper's hash.

For, extending the waiter's course, my eye reached the bar and there just leaving was John the man in glasses—friend of Jerry who paid his loft-rent, friend of June whose voice I'd last heard at the moment Tuesday that I discovered the two right angles Monty now seemed to have foregone—and there, too, were the steel-rimmed

440

specs I'd knocked off, which was nothing to what Incremona, that lithe, otterlike personal and impatient revolutionary might do to the other John if John was in cahoots with this John's boss Phil Aut (though I could not then on Thursday have said exactly why). And yet, whatever Hy's wife might think of me to this day when she is beyond the first shocks of that twelve months during which her son Ned died of a lung cancer as swift in its race to self-destruct as it seemed mysteriously untraceable, and during which she had news of her mother's cousins and her husband's Nachbush cousins spirited into an ultimate statistic whose increasingly rhetorical melody rhymes with *ill, will, kill,* and *pill* (*pillion* indeed) as readily as it calls up my bedtime variant of the witch shoved into the oven or echoing chatter in the soap-strewn steamy concrete showers after swimming practice the winters of '45 and '46, and may even twist the unable mind to dollar dreams (but what's six million worth today?), say some law-making appropriation so those who find technology cold and soulless might suddenly think (if they could) of that early European computer made of one hundred human beings—this *shtip* or stab seemed a thought crystallized as at the fork of a nerve cell, yet in my whole body too, whose heart was hard to find because pointless to seek since now so open to the lines of others in this petty system I had had a hypothesis about but forgotten.

Having lived something like the story of his life, Dagger had moved on to fatherhood; he had a daughter. It was not clear if the English schoolmaster had lost his job in the Bahamas because he had sat by Dagger's driftwood fire watching a cube of pink meat with certain wartime associations drip and spit on the toasting prongs that belonged to the lady who had the guest house; but the island's Church of England vicar to his deep joy and satisfaction (though not his wife's, in her pink, broad-brimmed, locally woven hat bending over a large lush garden having issued two of her three servants their day's easy instructions) was transferred back to England not long after he had told a commissioner that the schoolmaster drank bor-rowed hotel rum with an American beachcomber who had been a comfortable spectator one Sunday while native boys offered mild violence to a small tourist from Toronto, a white female child. And (if you wished to be suddenly very clear) Dagger was almost Monty's age; and even with various kinds of American money (even after the Nixon devaluation) and at London prices (even with inflation), and even with the pleasure which a French wife named Alba took in wheeling a pram just a few blocks to the Heath (which reminded

Lorna Cartwright not at all of Central Park and its dream-fence of high-rise stone to the east, west, and south, but of real country far from smoke, lunchtime mobs, and the press of motors, not to mention amenities like the Indian physician who was Alba's devoted friend and so gave that extra attention to her minor ailments, to the baby's skin, and to Dagger's gastric pangs, that compensated for the shortcomings of the English Health Service)—there were measurable respects in which between life in London and life in America the differences had begun to deteriorate. So how did you figure the big money at this stage? A way had opened for Dagger and it was through Claire, who would do almost anything for him, and through Phil Aut, who would do almost anything for his son Jerry (who in turn would do anything for his mother Jan, whose dreams of world rapprochement included her dark-haired preoccupied husband only as a block of flats includes a plumbing system or a democracy includes other people). And Dagger's way—through Claire and Aut and Jan—had lain from London through New York to London, to Hyde Park and its Sunday bases and to wild Wales through an Unplaced Room that by identifying son and mother could suddenly change Aut's estimate of all that came before or after—and Dagger confessed to me the Saturday morning after the Thursday evening of my interview with Monty that shooting Jan's wild portrait of Jerry had been designed to ensure a little last-minute leverage if only to sustain Phil Aut's concern with a film which to his strangely inhibited but intense protectiveness might thus seem to implicate in left-wing activities the two human beings he told Jack Flint in a rare moment of frankness he would make any sacrifice for. And I with my diary and my daughter had intervened in Dagger's simple sequence of acts and maybe thrown a monkey wrench into his chance of the big money.

For me the film was just one speculation. I had some irons in the fire and I expected to be solvent no matter what happened. But it seemed on Saturday with Dag, on Thursday with Monty, and on Tuesday listening to June while watching Reid, Jenny, and the Frenchman—that my film could not have developed parallel to Dagger's without disturbing it.

His had been one open and neat part of Aut's exploitation of Jan's plan. Like getting rare maps from one part of the world to another. The serial route of some man-made automaton. Background footage for insertion, a piece here a piece there, in something else.

I, however, had deliberately used this thing as a point through which attention might be distributed. But whatever the film now meant to me, I must succeed in selling it, I must get us both a decent return on our parallel inputs.

I thought, That's it! My *shtip* is simply that by not letting Dag's film alone, I've cost him some money.

But at once that line of thought lapsed like blips on a weather scope into new blips as the radar pulse sweeps full circle but never quite full because never through quite the same weather, though from sweep to sweep the blips may seem as stable as a map or a fleet at anchor. No, my *shtip* had no neat equation in cash or rueful credit. You would not exactly measure it as a Hyde Park home run stretched for years of Dagger's extra bases to a right-angle two-phone desk at H.E.W. in Washington, where he had been recommended by the English schoolmaster whose Bahama contract had not been renewed. Nor would you exactly measure my *shtip* in the two U.S. Coast Guard weather balloons Dagger picked up through an Embassy attaché inflated now almost eight years later not by the local or imported American helium inside the sheer white elastic that Will and Jenny got their hands on and bombarded briefly the day they got those gifts from their father's jolly new friend, but rather by regret—inflated so to constantly enlarge their equally lessening size loose over Hampstead Heath—adrift yet not moving, not moving, and yet the Heath itself was retreating.

Nor would you trace my *shtip* one thing at a time as fast as a gun crew's range computer in a sequence of digital trivia thus: (1) Precisely because I had mentioned my dream of a moving terminal (for monorail or other unspecified conveyances) to Dagger in the car coming back from filming the air base, it was the moving terminal that occurred to him that August evening at his flat as a topic calculated to keep me quiet when I was about to shoot the little group including the three men and I inspected the exposure ring on Alba's Super 8 and challenged the f-number and Dagger said, It's all set, man; (2) but set wrong (and at the cost of a cartridge): because he did not trust me: had not since that morning two months before when I amazed him by urging for our location the very Underground passage he himself had planned for us to use; so he automatically judged my motives dangerous even if akin to his own; and (3) of at least as long standing: or so I learned in this terminal week in October from my no longer so jolly swashbuckling pal forty hours after my talk Thursday with Monty Graf: for, driving the old Volkswagen with its faulty windscreen wipers to South Ken that June morning (to film, as Dagger thought I must know, the Hawaiian and his girlfriend), Dagger's swift, mechanical hindsight now credited me with having known of this pedestrian passage under the Science Museum even before he—indeed as far back as Nash's nosebleed precipitated by Cosmo as if Cosmo's indiscreet taunt from the pitching rubber were a valve flipped by Krish's watchful silence across the diamond behind third, a taunt which had led Dagger that night of May 16 in a redecorated Hampstead Village pub to bribe out of Cosmo the following facts: (1) that Savvy Van Ghent had been followed from his health club in the Finchley Road, watched at his flat in FitzJohn's Avenue, phoned by his UPI superior in New York and asked if he'd had dealings in hash or with Americans lacking passports, and had since then smelled reassignment in the wind: which, he'd told Alba, had just plain disoriented him, he'd always thought he could just pack up his books and his banjo, his shrunken head and his catcher's mitt (which he was ruining playing softball) and sell his motorbike and weigh anchor on as short notice as a University of Maryland "regular" on a two-year contract (who, unlike the resident part-timers who took what they could get from the U.K. director at 3rd Air Force H.Q. South Ruislip at the start of each of the five eight-week terms, had to be ready from term to term to fly off whenever courses had materialized and a teacher was needed— Madrid, a base in Verona, or a mountain vale in Germany); (2) that Nash had been instructed to use as a point of contact the Hawaiian Bill Liliuokalani whose cover was his guitar and his emaciated girlfriend from Hempstead, Long Island, whom you glanced at if you could bear her pallor and bad posture so fast you never lost sight of the end of the tunnel; and (3) that a U.S. Army deserter named Jim Nielsen from Heidelberg via Sweden had slipped into London and found help through the Hawaiian, and had been through hell, and Krish could not tell Cosmo how to go about meeting this cat (because Cosmo would like to rap with him) but when Cosmo named a pub in Camden Town where Nielsen had been seen, Dagger rose to go to the bar for two more pints of best bitter and privately guessed that Nielsen knew a certain American with dark kinky hair, who lo and behold as if from the magic print of Dagger's index finger dialing one two three local or trunk calls the following day became Nielsen's co-star in the Unplaced Room a week later on May 24.

Cosmo's silence at the outset Sunday night, May 16, had drawn from Dagger like a warm little confession an offer of a carton of blank cassettes on which to record some collector's-item jazz Cosmo

444

had said Dagger was holding out on him. But Dagger's silence when he came back to the table with two more pints drew from Cosmo a blank, blanched stare and a stammering announcement that he did not want the cassettes after all.

No, the *shtip* I felt at Monty's words went beyond your ordinary schemer's adrenal spurt blinking at danger.

It went beyond my blow to Dagger that June morning that set off some servo-circuit beeping him back to what we had seen and done in Wales: back to the Notting Hill Gate flat that he wrongly thought I knew was Jan's: back to May 16 and Nash's nosebleed: back to New York, Claire, and Aut where the servo having found no resolution could only loop, and my blow to Dagger signaled him also instantaneously then forward to all he did *not* know about Bill Liliuo-kalani and Bill's Long Island girl Ronnie. But Dagger betrayed nothing except to Alba who confided in Cosmo who told Krish while Alba crossed the Channel alone that June weekend of her seventh month. Now these were the days which marked Monty's first involve-ment in the films, for Claire phoned him to report her Uncle Dagger's alarm call from London and to ask of Monty what she'd never asked before—his advice on a business matter. Which may have joined (by warmly mingling) the two divisions of his face, for as he told me about the moving moment of Claire's call, the pocks seemed to fade from his cheeks into some vibrancy received from the black eyebrows and his voice, and the chin deepened and the mole made its cleft seem as ample or sensual as the area above his lip beneath the nostrils of his fine nose; yes the parts seemed to join now, warmly mingling, but not gently—for whether or not he had felt from the bar the flash of young John's steel-rimmed glasses whom Monty in this restaurant two weeks ago had taken prophetically for my associate, Monty now faced not Claire but a strange antagonist.

Oh cash, credit, regret, nostalgia—my *shtip* was more than these. It was more than computable gossip tracing Nash's nosebleed in its causes and effects or sampling Cosmo's cold sweat under the eye of a lean-chopped sun-burnished man in a beret staring through the window of that pub on Hampstead High while Dagger's large, broad shape stood at the bar bending its brown suede elbow patches and making the barmaid laugh—and my *shtip* was more than some measure of Reid's utter coolness in the pedestrian tunnel running into a young girl he didn't really know who gaily linked him to the wife of Gene Flint and asked Reid to sign her cast just where it curved between Dirk Bogarde and W. Cartwright.

No, my *shtip* might seem to you who have me to have been merely sparked by what you could afford to lose sight of (knowing I would not)—to wit, Graf's news that Dagger was diversifying in a survival program designed to maintain some of his established ventures (the carton of audio gear and no doubt old maps) yet pushing also to a new job at H.E.W. in white, monumental Washington, and toward new chances in a declining land or at any rate a very tricky economy: but Graf's words were not themselves the cause of my *shtip* (not an unexpected absence that like a NAND valve's zero sets off in the South Ken tunnel conversely a positive pulse in Reid's temple, for he'd expected someone who is not there); no, these words concerning Dag came as some mere percussion.

Like Savvy or Dudley pasting a Sunday fastball to deep center.

Like Gilda depressing automatically the keys of her brother-in-law's old cash register (to complete a transaction which went on ending for two or three minutes more between her brother-in-law and florid Father Moran come in person on this Wednesday to face up to what he called after all the one-to-one relationship we so rarely enjoy with the people we do business with, and to complain about the price of glads and chrysanthemums which he said might necessitate breaking his church's long tradition with its neighborhood florist [such as the neighborhood was] to buy instead from the wholesalers on Sixth Avenue—and then suddenly he was not at all amused despite himself by this Jew from Kew Gardens way the hell out in Queens who expressed the belief that when it came to the flowers of the field not even the Pope could work an economic miracle), but Gilda had sensed as she rang up the priest's post-dated check that the pair now entering the shop as if in response to the cash register weren't after flowers—the much heavier man in the beret with bristly thick silver hair who didn't say a word, and the much younger man, tan and totally bald, with a short sharp nose and fleshy lips, a mean sinewy attractive man who shoved some folded newspapers into the hands of the white-haired man and spoke softly but could never have persuaded Gilda the man they knew she knew whom they were looking for was a *friend* of theirs—only that the man was Cartwright (she believed that) and she was known to have visited him (she guessed that) at the apartment with the big unmade bed (*I* guessed she recalled *that*) and he had said he was meeting a mutual friend yesterday but—(Claire, I said) and as Gilda looked at the long brown hand (of Incremona, no guesswork) gripping the top of the register

446

with the thumb-nail so short (news to me) the thumb seemed to be missing half an inch and the fingers coming down over the four white numerals of the priest's bill, Gilda had a sensation of falling: and not down but forward: and the priest said But you people gild the lily, and her brother-in-law went to close the door left open by the big man in the beret—and when I said to her Wednesday night with a pronounced intimacy pushed into the phone by my lips, Did it give you a *shtip* (and she said, Where do *you* know Yiddish), I was saying more than I'd known how to.

For my *shtip* exemplifies the multiple and parallel sorties which raise our brain above the digital computer to which it is akin; the digital computer works its yes and no operations faster than the brain yet is confined to serial single-file one quest-at-a-time circuit-seeking; but the human natural Body Brain (as my Druid terms it) sends countless of these single files not one at a time but all at once circulating down the deltas, through the gorges and moving targets and (like parties of Indians—Brooklyn, Hindu, Maya, Hollywood or, as the English call the American, *Red*) athwart the axes of all pulsing fields.

When the phone rings, Tessa's father waiting at his dining-room sideboard steps away. Queenie Stone brushes her well-corseted front by me where I stand hungry and dumb at the kitchen doorway. But before she can answer the phone, Jane has come from the living room. At the first ring Tessa has turned from a pot of thick vegetable soup and she pauses at my face which has turned from her father to her; she cannot see her father.

The third ring completes her move to the kitchen table. It wasn't my face ringing, but the phone. Jane gives her grandfather's number. The call is for Tessa. Tessa is lifting onto a china platter pieces of mackerel in a jellylike sweet-and-sour sauce. She tells me to tell Dudley to take the call. Across the table set for lunch, I tell Jane this. She has heard her mother.

Leaving the dining room Jane murmurs, It's Edinburgh.

Will calls out from the living room, We give up!

Jane with her strong oval face and straight hair seems older.

Queenie Stone lays a gold-brocaded white cloth over the chala. Its crust is glossy along glazed arcs of the plaited weave which will seem to disappear when the first slice shows the inside. It is our contribution. Lorna picked it up at our Highgate bakery where the very cheerful women—one of whom is as phony as the English lower middle-class can be—have never sold us a chala before; they are very busy Saturday. Tessa's father does not answer the phone on the Sabbath. I pull in my stomach and Queenie Stone's bosom brushes my chest.

Tessa's father points at the phone receiver on the sideboard. Whoever he is, he's talking.

Dudley strides into the dining room and without looking at anyone reaches for the phone before it is quite within reach. Tessa's father does turn the lights on and off on the Sabbath, but when he goes to *shul* or to Dr. Zeidel's for tea on the rare Saturdays the Allotts are not here, he travels only by foot. Dudley turns his back to us and says into the phone, Yes?

I did not see Tessa's father place his black silk silver-brocaded yarmulka on the flat, fine hair that covers the back of his head behind the high receding forehead like a larger yarmulka silver-white. He calls toward the hall that leads to the living room but actually right into Dudley's neck, We're ready!

Dudley turns his head as if he has heard something strange. Lorna is heard laughing in the living room.

Dudley puts down the phone, comes around the dinner table to the kitchen door: It's the chieftain, he says, from Edinburgh.

Tessa says without looking away from the mackerel platter, I'll call him later. Then, feeling Dudley's tread move away, she says, It isn't as if it's been so long.

Which makes him halt and turn, but he's several feet into the dining room so it's me he looks at, not Tessa.

A huge green-and-blue kilt swings in a breeze of Hassidic beards dancing to bells full of wind and whiskey. I move to a place at the table and Dudley brushes me returning to the phone.

When we are all at table, Tessa's father blesses the bread in Hebrew he learned from Queenie after the war. We are Will, Lorna, Jane, Dudley, Jenny (who is not saying anything today), and now Queenie Stone and Tessa from the kitchen. Tessa's father uncovers the bread and folds the white-and-gold cloth. He cuts two slices and cuts them into little pieces. He salts each and passes them one by one on the end of the serrated bread knife. We take a sip of Israel Tokay, after all of us except Jenny and Will say *l'chayim*.

Tessa's father nods at Dudley. He says, My son.

At the end of the meal Tessa's father recites a long grace in what sounds like precisely articulated Hebrew. Then he and Queenie, with Tessa singing some of the words, sing the end of the grace, and Lorna hums along.

Later we find ourselves in the living room. The children are in the garden. Their fathers are non-Jews—or almost, though Dudley disputes his father-in-law's pleasantry to me that all born New Yorkers are Jews. I am a wandering New Yorker, I say, but Tessa disputes that (with a finger on my knee): You don't wander much.

How would you know? says Lorna. She turns away from the window. Will turns in the middle of the front garden as if cogged to Lorna; the knees of the man who is flat on his back under his red Humber across the street don't move. He doesn't travel just to New York, says Lorna, and he doesn't always have married friends to organize him.

You are a jack of many businesses, says Tessa's father.

His interests are diversified, says Lorna.

Maybe I am not more than she thinks.

Jane enters. She and Jenny and Will are going to Golders Hill Park. Queenie Stone hears this entering behind Jane with a tray of stacked saucers and tilted cups. Queenie has wanted to marry Tessa's father for years. Once after Tessa had been sightseeing in New York, I speculated about her father and the firmly corseted Queenie Stone. Tessa said, Nothing in it—she plays the viola and she cooks.

Queenie purses her lips and turns down her mouth. She shakes her head at Jane: Jane doesn't want to go to the park now, does she? Is her grandfather's house a sinking ship that Jane and her friends have to go off when people are coming for tea? Queenie touches Jane's cast.

I imagine (for in my time I have seen) the prams elegantly sprung like eighteenth-century carriages standing as if empty beside the green benches—the grandmothers of Golders Hill Park—privacy—three conspiring schoolboys hastening across a path. Dudley has an absent look. Queenie has gone back to the kitchen. Jenny is in charge of Will and Jane. Jane promises her grandfather not to do any running. Dudley turns a Granny Smith round, examining it. You want a knife for that? his father-in-law asks. Dudley slowly shakes his head—then as an afterthought, the quick English No thank you. I blink at an illusion that it is '58 or '62 or '64 or '68.

Tessa's father says, You did so well the first time, you should try for another.

Tessa says she could strangle Queenie for talking like that to Jane.

Dudley says he knows she could, but it isn't as if Queenie was drawing the kishkes out of Jane.

449

Tessa's father laughs, Ah your Yiddish, it's getting good.

It's all Queenie's, says Dudley, and where she got it who knows.

He takes a bite.

Tessa's father, instead of taking issue, subsides. Lorna starts at once to tell Jane's riddle that stumped them in this living room before lunch. This was what made Lorna laugh.

The phone is ringing. Tessa's father leans forward in his seat as if to get up.

Tessa says Oh, and gets up and goes to the living-room door. Dudley echoes: Oh?

Queenie Stone, whose father was German, has the blood of her late invalid Polish mother in her somewhere. She opens the door from the other side as Tessa grasps the knob. Doctor Zeidel has phoned (No, don't tell me, says Tessa's father) to say his wife has one of her migraines, he'll come on his own—(ah, thank goodness, says Tessa's father). Queenie removes herself as Tessa goes to the window, but Queenie opens the door again to refuse Lorna's offer of help, then returns presumably to the kitchen where she is doing violence to the different sets of pots and dishes and preparing the small thin sandwiches of smoked salmon, and cucumber almost liquid thin, and cream cheese, and a nice brown Hovis. She is such an overseer here that you forget until you can't see her any more (except—in the mind's eye—for you've never actually seen this except in the mind's eye—weeding her famous garden of parallel beds four houses down from Tessa's father across the road which is Park Way) that her blue eyes are set wide apart and are oddly touching with her faultless brown hair, but only in retrospect. She has been known to have a ham roll at the Victoria and Albert Museum, but alone with Tessa not with Tessa's father.

There is a western all the Cartwrights are going to see tonight. Except me, for I have a business appointment.

Tessa says to her father, Why don't you change your mind and come *with* us.

The trip to the States is discussed.

Somewhere in the deeps of the afternoon a Polish widow whose son is farming on the edge of the Negev, recalls how for a time during the war her late friend Mrs. Edelbaum had sent her husband with a cheese sandwich off to Hampstead Heath each morning in case they came looking for Germans to intern.

There is a general discussion of the Health and of when each of the elders present had a walk there recently. I observe that where we live in Highgate it's just down our hill. Dr. Zeidel compares Central Park unfavorably to the Heath and asks me where I'm from in the States. He names three people on the upper West Side of Manhattan.

It gives me a *shtip*, says Tessa's father, when I think of those days on the Heath. A *shtip*.

Shtip, shtip, says Dr. Zeidel looking out the window where beyond the garden and the low wall and across the street the legs under the Humber are now stretched flat.

To be taken for a German at a time like that.

But you *were* a German, says Tessa.

A German Jew, says the Polish widow whose name I didn't catch or can't recall but won't ask Lorna later, who would bawl me out for not listening.

It is no longer an interesting question, says Mr. Rivera—there are the eastern European Jews and the old Spanish Jews, and the Germans are in between somewhere.

I thought you said it wasn't an interesting question, I say.

To be taken for a German pure and simple at a time like that, says Tessa's father. To find a real countryside set in the middle of the greatest city in Europe—real country with hills and lakes and none of these child molesters standing in the trees—the city invisible all around you. Hills, streams, thickets.

Gemütlichkeit, says Dudley.

Why the hell not, Lorna retorts.

Shtip, my dear friend, says Dr. Zeidel, starting a slow cycle of finger-shakes, means first of all a push—*a shtip in di tzen*, a push in the teeth in the sense of a bribe to keep the mouth shut; then *shtip sich nit arahn*, don't push in where you're not wanted; and *shtip* of course in the sexual sense; and you have also *shtip un sha* when the mother says to her child at the table stuff and hush, eat and shut up.

Does that make me wrong, Zeidel? says Tessa's father.

Lorna says quietly to Dudley, Why the hell *not* a little *gemütlichkeit*?

Zeidel, you are a pedant, says Mr. Rivera.

A baker's dozen of blue harrows like they don't make any more turn the earth, hand-made, hand-held, furrowing parallel up over a hill. I put this room on the map. It is my closed-circuit scope. There is no occulting sweep hand. I monitor the empty distances between the bright blips—from the moment (reported to me by

Tessa but also by Queenie who said he became like an Old Testament prophet) when Tessa's father capitulated, breathless and palsied, the water twinkling still in the corners of his eyes, and said to Dudley, My daughter tells me you are circumcised—thence a decade, a cloaked decade and more, to this well-aired room and its weighty white floral molding round the ceiling and the electric heater's parallel rows of dark coils framed by the marble fireplace itself framed by a marble mantel with a dark bust of Tessa at fifteen and photographs of Tessa and her mother, and color shots of Jane—from words about a circumcision thence to the same room years later where the blood trouble between Tessa and Dudley which threatens to spread into an indifference beyond divorce seems so far from any trouble which the blood let out of some child's penis thirty-odd years ago could have stanched, that I see a cluster of blips between; and they say, I Cartwright of London and New York lessen these distances and bind these troubles. All is still. I see it all, I seem to protect it by seeing it my way. Scots time cogs into the slower teeth of the Jewish calendar. Lorna's riddle joins the flow and instability of my blood to the name of my son and to my daughter's stanched but septic arm from Kew. My princely helicopter swashes here the groping hand of Dudley, there Lorna's pearly stretch-marks, yonder the absence of pulse in her father's wrist, arm, breast, throat, and mouth that will gnash no more, hither the contemplative lingo of Andsworth within earshot of his French vegetable slicer with which his housekeeper is doing violence to onions, aubergines, and the great baggy red peppers Lorna buys in Highgate Village from a green-grocer who does not get on with his mother-in-law, peppers like huge rich cells. I draw all together in someone else's house. Less like micro-slivers of bone that the dentist's high-speed drill sprays through some lung as like as not his own. Less like the flicker-flash of radiant particles in night space that get through the capsule and the helmet and into the eye of the astronaut's brain. More like the character of a liquid crystal. I will find a formula for (in the phrase of Boyd's father) that Brooklyn Indian Ned Noble. Someone's car radio rides by in the quiet street. But crystal scope or not, have I even a god's limited control over this field of force affirmed, like a NAND valve's zero, by nonforce? The street would be quiet even if it were not Saturday in Golders Green. I am omnipotent.

The phone rings. *A shtip in hertz*, says Queenie, putting her hand there and smiling a tight theatrical smile.

Hartz, says Zeidel.

452

I rise.

A heart attack, says Lorna brightly and looks to me.

A *pang* for goodness' sake, says Tessa's father as if from long familiarity.

I'm at the door. My interests are diversified. A new smoking device still on the drawing board which a small design-research firm of young people fresh out of Central School want to sell to an American tobacco company. I'm holding acreage in the Norfolk Broads. There are still boutiques. Boats. Liquid crystals. And now kids' marbles, the old kind.

When did your father take his digitalis, the intern asked Lorna, and Lorna turned to her mother.

I wish to stay in Tessa's father's living room, but I wish to go. I have had help in my omnipotence. My hand is on the door knob.

What, says Dudley to Tessa, is *shtip* in Scots?

It doesn't mean pushing in where you're not wanted, says Tessa.

And then there's *shtip a goy*, I say, and leave the room closing the door.

It is Dagger on the phone, and now with Monty on a Thursday in October I recall not wishing to speak with Dagger. He's two hours late phoning.

He can't make it tonight. Got to pick up a carton of stuff and take it over to Cosmo's. It crosses my mind to tell him there's a big market for American kids' marbles in England, but I say nothing.

I tell Dagger Lorna's riddle. I shorten it. A boy and his father. A terrible accident. The ambulance takes them to the hospital. The father is dead on arrival. The boy is rushed to Emergency. The surgeon takes one look at him and says, I can't operate. He's my son.

Dagger can't make it tonight. Why does a stop at Cosmo's take so long? Well, Dagger's got to see the man he knew in the Bahamas whom he wants to fix up with an introduction at H.E.W. but who is meanwhile exploring the feasibility of an American-style alumni mag to serve the Old Boy network—oh by the way, says Dag, I gave him a couple of copies of your alumni review that Lorna let me have one quiet afternoon, did she ever mention it?

A door opens, I think the living room. The steps are familiar.

Also, Corsica is off, says Dagger.

Diversity in the other room collapses into one tiny prick of light fading.

I may have to go anyway, I find myself saying. I sound convincing.

There is a pause in which Tessa soundlessly appears at my side.

Dagger doesn't seem to know if I'm kidding. He says slowly, by rote, You may have to go anyway.

Yes, to Corsica, I say, holding my hand out. Tessa licks my palm.

There's more than a film in Corsica, Dag. You know me.

My scrotum tingles. I turn my palm to Tessa's cheek—oh tell the schoolmaster from the Bahamas he can keep those alumni reviews—I hang up on Dagger who's saying, I'll tell him when he gets back—

When I'm halfway down the hall I hear her placing a call to her Scottish chieftain. It is much less perhaps than Dudley thinks. The front door swings in, and Will is not with the girls. They go ahead of me into the living room. Dudley has made Lorna unhappy. Jane shows Lorna the autograph of a stranger on her cast. Dudley asks me where Tessa is. Will appears, and he is furious. Lorna says, You're bleeding.

His accent which I felt all over again at the Softball Game is so deeply London it screws around into Cockney now and then, no doubt colored by school.

It is a nasty scratch above Will's nostril; the blood is red. Queenie Stone observes that it could be dangerous if it goes septic.

I say, without thinking, Goodbye, Mrs. Ashkenazy.

And there it is—that's her name.

Having created a new Corsica out of anger, I might go there.

Dudley is explaining patiently that German Jews on the whole cared nothing for Yiddish; if it had depended on them Yiddish would have died. Zeidel is tense, no doubt because it is Dudley.

A tiny child scratched Will's nose when he bent down to return the child's ball that had rolled away. But this is not why Will is furious. Jenny is pale and the trouble is there.

But the formula?

Monty would not let me push through to a formula. A formula for mutual fields. Do you hear me peddling mutual fields up under the casements of Lincoln's Inn lawyers? John the young man in the glasses I'd once knocked off stepped away from the bar, as if to leave.

I had to be at Sub's in case Gilda called again; she would not let me call her in Queens.

454

A *shtip* in time, says an old Māyā proverb I adapt from the Hindu, may well have to be its own reward. And like a *shtip* within a *shtip*, or like teeth meshing the small and large wheels of the short and the long Maya calendars so that even Tessa's beautiful violence of the sacred cardiectomy atop a Yucatan pyramid waits upon the mechanical program of named and numbered cogs, I was drawn by Monty and the thought of Dagger away from multiple sorties ex- emplified in my sense of that Sabbath Saturday in Golders Green, away from what you'll by now have seen to be my fitful trip toward an emptiness in order to fall ahead to where Ned Noble would by now have been, and drawn away into the one-track trivia of a dangerous plot I was supposed to be near the heart of. But what was this *shtip*, this sense of other people's lives? Was it not also a word in someone else's language? And on the point of seeing if not my formula the meaning of my power, I was cut short by Monty and the thought and threat of Dagger's letter—but suddenly thereby received a gift.

And this was the thought that I had indeed dreamt my look- out dream the other night, Tuesday night in this terminal October week, the night I'd last seen Jenny. The night of the afternoon I'd found her between me and Reid and found myself between her and the Frenchman.

But I saw now it might not matter if those perpendiculars had survived from sphere to flat or flat to sphere, any more than it mattered if I could sense some rendezvous between Andsworth's armchair globe with its crackling shellac and Dagger's facsimile Mercator hung directly across the long axis of his and Alba's balcony workshop from the poster of Trotsky with his pointed beard and lofty brow and the young American of good-will the hapless Bob Harte— any more than it mattered that I had forgotten all about that lookout dream I'd had at last except that I'd had it.

My words go single-file, but many files which if blessed by the right angle are others' words in other times, a future Monty phoning transatlantic Thanksgiving Day just to talk, and still seemingly sleepwalking because he had no one to sleep with, blinded by pas- sion, or in a terribly special sense its absence, found therefore the attention to tell me in case it might somehow matter two facts he now recalled he'd had from his dear dear Claire: that the man she later learned must have been Wheeler had been accosted by a driver while shadowing apparently me on foot, had had words with the driver then passed on leaving the driver stuck in that thick traffic, had walked suddenly past me when I stopped to look through a coffee shop window, and moments later had been overtaken and cut off by the same driver.

My words go single-file, but Monty's this Thursday before Halloween had not stopped. But in the interlude of my *shtip* no time had elapsed. Next time I might not be so lucky. With John's housekeeper in Coventry Monty had left word that he was coming in the late afternoon; the housekeeper had said only that John would be in for dinner, not that he was leaving for the States—maybe Monty had dialed Coventry direct and she did not know he was coming from London. John was talkative and tense. He must stop in London to persuade a lady to come along to the States with him this time; he must eat; and he could not stand train food. He and Monty talked. They dined. They continued their talk in the London train. The long and the short of it was John's fear of Cartwright, whose name he hadn't even noted when they met on the day of that silly filming.

He was aware he had dismissed our film to my face. And after Len Incremona had fired a "ball" through the dartboard as if he'd missed his real target, and we had left, and John had pulled himself together with a third plate of Nell's buckwheat spaghetti which the black man Chad had made the sauce for, John recalled my face bearing him as much ill will as Len's. John did not remember what he'd said to me except who the hell would pay *us* to go make a film in Corsica. But now John had heard from Nell's husband that Cartwright was running about with explosives on him. Nell had told Gene that Len had told her Cartwright and his friend were not to be trusted, Cartwright was trying to unload a famous shrunken heart or head, a French girl who'd tried to convert Incremona to macrobiotic food had told him this and she had it from an American whose name John said wouldn't mean anything to Monty (which Monty did not push, though now across the table from me he said *I* of course would know who the French girl and the American were). And John said since he regarded Incremona as a dangerous opportunist (precisely because, from decathlon to radio-telescope maintenance to political adventure to, one suspected, quick and surreptitious cash killings, Incremona was not a patient *enough* opportunist) and since Incremona regarded Cartwright as dangerous, Cartwright became dangerous raised conceivably to the power of Len. The man's anger was like nothing John had seen before except in two Hungarian Catholics who as it happened had been married to each other. Oh Incremona fell out with anyone, even one who revered him.

Nash, I said.

456

That's the one, said Monty glancing away.

John-of-the-loft was off his bar stool.

Monty said no doubt I knew Nash had been beaten up by Incremona in South London two hours and more after Incremona had apparently gotten over his anger. Nash had acted independently, which was bad enough; but he had arranged a meeting in an Underground station with a woman supposed to know Cartwright, Paul Flint, and something important, and she never showed, but others did, and Incremona led Nash away berating him. But finally calmed down. Or so Nash had thought.

John-of-the-loft was leaving. There was no doubt of it.

I was up feeling for my trenchcoat, my eyes on Monty.

He now made a pretense of keeping me: The grub at John's is better than here, he said. You'd expect that. John's a gourmet, his housekeeper's Austrian; he's opinionated: what does macrobiosis mean anyway but longevity? he says, and only a fool measures that in mere years. He says macrobiotic food takes the spring out of the capillaries.

OK, I said, you went to Coventry. You had a meal. You heard some gossip.

I don't know some of these people, said Monty—Len, Nell, Gene, Nash.

Graf, I said (and he put a hand to his ear), you spoke of liquid crystals, there is no question that you spoke of liquid crystals, you said from crystal set to liquid crystals, right?

John again, he said.

I turned away into the dim aromatic tinkling and a waitress's laughter, but Monty said, Jack Flint was responsible of course.

I turned and nodded slowly, though John might be getting away.

So they investigated you, said Monty. I gather it's been mutual.

But Graf, I said, you haven't said why you had to see John in Coventry in the first place, nor why he passed on to you all this trivia. The truth is, you haven't begun to talk.

Monty's last words, against the laughing of the waitress, were a comedown from his earlier challenge about the letter left on Aut's desk—for now he said, Take care of Claire.

A bicyclist passed on the far side of a panel truck, I saw her head. John-of-the-loft was halfway into the next block. I'd been holding my breath, a habit Andsworth says is dangerous. John stopped and half turned as if to see me, and in that very instant a bottle came out across his path, missed him, and split in the gutter. John-of-Coventry's irked and rubicund words pursued John-of-the loft's intention that I follow him. I had crossed the first crossing when a cab passed. And I had reached the vicinity of someone's deep chuckling when a second cab crunched over broken glass and stopped at my curb just as the cab ahead stopped for John. The chuckler leaning back against a stoop was black, but he was not the asbestos-watcher I'd given a dollar to so long ago. I opened the cab door as John did the same ahead, and the person on the stoop said, We all part of the system, man.

I did not understand why more people didn't drop objects out of these high buildings.

The history of Gramercy Park as in an essay by some private-school student veered away at right angles (its brownstones, its large central iron-fenced garden for residents, venerable clubs with newspaper rooms, mediocre food, and domineering darky servants), plaques outside showing say a pair of masks (tragic? comic?) and overhead two pre-Civil War black-iron entrance lanterns with curved spikes like fierce horns crowning a vacant-faced warrior. I was at the southern edge of midtown Manhattan within striking distance of Sub's icebox and Ruby's coloring book and a curiously imprinted amber pinch bottle I'd had my eye on and a telly glowing gray on Sub's face and a jack-o'-lantern on the sill facing the heights of New York but directly across the way a clipped white dog watching in a window. I hadn't seen a headline since Monday. My life was in danger, my suitcase at Monty's, my parka likely discovered, my daughter on her own.

We turned sharply again and drove downtown, a high-slung gypsy cab able to move more than one way at once. I'd told my driver to follow the other cab. This simplified things for him but also, as he did not know, for me. It gave us both a certain illusory freedom between ourselves from the consequences of coercion. Our fields impinged in ways I knew more about than he, with his narrow hunched shoulder blades as if he did not know this city or his vehicle though his moustache was in the current younger mode of college cabbies if without Bach for background though his aerial was up. I saw the shaggy tip of his moustache aligned above the window-wiper beyond it and on my side between two signs on the steel screen dividing front and back seats ("Please do not smoke. Driver is allergic" and "This cab can be hired for trips of any distance. Ask driver for rates"). If he had sat up straight, his hair might have brushed the roof. If he was who I thought he was, what could I say to him? Which side are you on?

We were on Broadway down among the blocks of dark and comparatively low commercial buildings; we were between the East and West Village and we must soon turn if we were headed for Mercer. I could not say to him what did it feel like when Tessa on Stonehenge night said Go to hell? I could not say, What blame do you take for Jim Nielsen's death? Was Krish correct in saying yours was the picture filmed in the Suitcase Slowly Packed? Knowing that my driver did not guess I knew him was too much for me to lose—but most of all I wanted to ask him what my last cabbie Mike had meant on Sunday night in North London when he'd said that if I went on as I was going on, the first thing "we" knew the "whole thing" would blow up again.

No: even more, I wanted to ask Paul Flint—for even if the moustache and the shoulder-blades that were hunched as if they'd been jammed into a vise have not told you what you would have known all too soon in a film for having already glimpsed him in Tessa's grip framed by a Stone Age trilothon, you have me and my ordinary probabilities and you might hence have guessed this to *be* Paul Flint, though as for me (between blind coghood and that sinister hint of godhead or godbody in me issuing from my place in a field of multiple impingements) I was amazed but could not ask— What did you mean when from the darkness behind a Stonehenge stone and echoing the bank clerk's claim that Stonehenge meant simply the distance and the work in moving those stones, you said, it comes to that and that alone.

But my life was in danger. I was hungry. If my parka with Chad's gun and Krish's ten-inch blade had been found under the bed in Monty's basement, no telling where the red jaguar was by now. Or the three sound-track tapes I had taken from Dagger's cabinet.

We ran a light to keep up with John's cab.

Ahead at our next light, cars were crossing and we would have to stop. I could not stop. I'd said to Mary in the *Son des Guitares* (but not in the diary pages Jenny typed), Suppose I've got the Montrose heart, what would it go for? And Mike heard me, and our last morning at the école (bowls of café-au-lait, a dish of apricot jam, three big American girls in yellow curlers and cut-off jean shorts) he was confirmed in his contempt and suspicion when Marie appeared and took him outside the dining hall and must have told him Incremona had said I was dangerous and Mike mentioned the famous heart spirited into the moving hand of an American merchant-adventurer named Cartwright, and Marie relayed this to Len urging him quite possibly in the same breath not to order coffee and croissants at the port café but to eat some local yogurt laced with the granola she'd brought from London or an orange she produced from her bag which instead made him think of the open market at the bottom of the Cours Napoléon with slabs of tuna dark almost as whale flesh, though in reality there at the port café Len was staring across the hot cobbles to the *plongeur* van and its entrepreneur the tough brown bawdy half-naked Neptune as bald as Incremona but a happy man, a Paris watchmaker half the year, the other half down here in Corsica on his own southern time with his dials strapped to his wrists and his yellow air-tank on his back taking the tourists diving where weightless they could move in any direction at will, sighting an ashtray's glint below or the endless translucent green cushion far above.

Information theory? I had none. Only these circuits of addition two by two—Marie and Mike—Nash and Incremona—false labor or no, had Alba truly phoned Dagger in Ajaccio that last morning? And now Jack Flint's investigation: how could it turn up me and liquid crystals without Red Whitehead's help?

Information, and the prospect of more dragged me toward some final grid no grander than this one here and stuck to it the regular driver's two signs declaring a man's cab is his cab and he would move it any distance for a price: a final grid like this protective mesh that had changed the New York taxi not to a London cab's class-comforted hackney carriage but to a squad car's compartmented coop: the wipers now slowly swinging against a film of rain.

Monty Graf never learned about those Tuesday right angles; he moved one track at a time, by the numbers: *which* Frenchman? (And was I trailing Jenny or Jan? Did Reid have a key to the house in King Street?) Yet there was no time to broach with him the Other— the rule of cartographic deformation, and which way those two right angles had survived—from sphere to flat map, or from flat to sphere —and I would have liked to broach this with him, for Monty is a humane man, not just out for a buck or a slow killing, and apart from the loud mechanics of a mysterious action that seemed to have shifted to New York, Monty and I might have emptied many a dram and had a good long talk between these two imagined poles of globe and map, family and fortune, the friendly chill of London rain and the coordinates of American danger; he might even have known why Incremona and the Frenchman had called at the florist's Wednesday morning.

460

The *shtip* of my Māyā proverb might have to be its own reward. It seemed to have less than nothing to do with macrobiotic diets ordained by Andsworth for his community in South London or urged by Marie upon Incremona.

Why not find Jenny and take her back to Highgate to Will and to Lorna even if I found Lorna with that young second tenor? But what if Jenny would not go? She believed Reid had followed her to King Street because he needed her.

I abandon the burly white-cropped Frenchman and by an indirect route along Charlton south of King I catch Jenny at the corner of King and Hudson where she keeps a lookout for a boy she admits to me now dismissed her that day in the South Ken tunnel as if he didn't like her any more and she dragged on home to Highgate to type Hawaiian Hippie (or most of it) and my Suitcase Slowly Packed (including the moccasins just like the ones she had been shown in Jan's case opened in the Underground and held by Dudley). But now on a Tuesday in October when the diary recedes I tell her she must stay away from Jan's son Jerry with the long hair who is in Monty's house at this moment, and she says, But why?—with that defiant gentleness of her generation, to which I say, He will do you violence.

But why? says Jenny.

His mother, I say.

But, says Jenny, she's stopped running after Reid.

I ask my daughter how many other times Reid ditched her. She says, It was a funny day, he'd said he had to meet a couple of blokes in the South Ken Underground and he wouldn't mind introducing them to me and when we got there I said Oh my father and I used to come through here when we went to the museums. And at that moment I saw Jane and her father and I said Oh there are two friends of mine—and Reid seemed to look beyond them and then said he'd split and go home; but it was too late, Jane had seen us.

I've distracted Jenny from her post. How did you find me? she says. You think I'm here because of you, she says. That is the mood she's in. I spotted your hat, I say. She's back at the edge of a building where she can see most of King Street. Maybe she has missed him.

Merely helping would be dangerous.

I raise my voice in hope, in gratitude: I got the message on the diary.

You know the woman, she says. I was afraid of Reid. But I've changed.

This must mean she wants Reid. What do I know of Reid?

Wears a bush hat. Friend of Sherman's. Roofed a dome with his parents' LP's. Tried street theater in South London which I was invited to see but couldn't make.

She isn't herself. There's something odd in what she said. She's back at the edge of the building watching Monty's house and hoping I will go, I can see it in the settled way she lays a khaki sleeve along a black iron fence, two parallel chevrons, corporal, U.S. Army.

She comes back. She says, I would have been in it anyway.

I don't believe her, there's something wrong in what she's said. Come on, there's a Mexican place a few blocks up, I'm probably staying at Sub's if she wants to bunk in tourist there, surely she remembers the Bach sweatshirt, the man with the two kids?

I fall flat.

He may have to go into hospital tomorrow for tests.

She doesn't know what to say, but she does not smile.

Look, I say, it's not fair to me: and this makes her look toward her lookout post seeing Reid's face with its premature lines from the corners of his mouth up to his wide nostrils: or did she hear me? Her silence refutes me better than Dagger's words in the domestic scene my words call up when she and he had been out to the hardware-housewear shop where I bought Andsworth's French vegetable slicer run by (if not owned by) the white girl and the man from Ghana who always closed for a long lunch even on Saturday so Dagger and Jenny came back without the wine glasses Lorna had sent them out for and in response to Dagger's later toast to not taking Jenny seriously she downed a whole old-fashioned glass of Liebfraü- milch Dagger had got us a case of cheap, but the toast arose from Dagger saying fairness was the great empty virtue, Jenny saying fairness was one reason he stayed in England, Dagger answering with his mouth full of veal and rice that fairness was like loyalty, Jenny saying he didn't take her seriously, Dagger choking on rice and laughter, reaching for his almost empty glass.

Jenny's silence leaves fairness in my mouth but she comes back from the edge of the building and she tells me my life is in danger. Her phrase is solemn, she is a child again for me—my life— manageable.

Oh she could tell me some things but for God's sake now go, go—please go.

I say she's in danger too and it's my fault. A police car parks across the street, both cops watching us.

At least get Reid to get my suitcase out of Monty's.

462

She will call me at Sub's—she promises—what's his surname? What's his address?—go.

I say she hasn't told me anything new, I am in danger from many sides.

She asks if I looked at Jane Allott's cast when she came in from the park and showed it to Tessa.

To see Dirk Bogarde's signature and Reid's?

And Nash!

Nash from the softball game?

Oh that little bloody softball game!

Sweat off a Sunday hangover.

Well Hyde Park wasn't the only park in London. Nash was at Golders Hill that Saturday we had lunch at Tessa's father's. Nash came up to the bench. Jane was telling Jenny about the signatures, and Will was pretending he wasn't interested. A clan chieftain (serious, slow, extravagant with money I guessed; pan downward to bare legs spread at his desk in Edinburgh on which Jane's moldy cast lay like an independent object); Dirk Bogarde (eyebrows raised, kindly scribbling in the middle of a city); Reid—Reid's handsome! said Jane.

That hippie! said Will, and Jenny said Reid was an artist and a man and Will could learn a thing or two from him about political consciousness, and Will said it was Dad who'd mentioned that hat. Jane reached her cast across: Look, you're right here with him, Will—my Daddy said he's in the theater. And then Jenny said Will's signature was a carbon copy of his father's, and at this Will got up and walked away down the path, though here standing over Jane was the man with the colored rings who asked if he too could sign—and had trouble getting his byro to run ink into the fibers of Jane's cast, saying, If at first you don't succeed—and then, Show that to your mother when you get home; and when he walked off he had an odd lean, like a limp you couldn't quite pinpoint.

Jenny is back to her post. I follow just to where looking east one can see enough of the south side of King Street to see Monty's house.

I talk to her again: But Will recognized him surely—Will was the one who called out your nose is bleeding at the softball game we filmed. And you yourself must have known Nash.

I step further to see clear down King to where I phoned June, and Jenny steps back and I grab her arm and she tries to pull away, and the cops are watching and I try to shush her, though her voice is low, and it is appearances I'm trying to save, as she was when she hid a snapshot I now knew must be of Paul and Reid together.

Her accent is native London: Oh you imagine I know him just from your baseball game—well who do you think Reid in fact was looking at down the South Ken tunnel the day he signed Jane's cast?

The burly Frenchman like me bare-headed has turned into the far end of King (where Jan and Jerry and Jenny turned and near where I kept watch under the one or possibly two helicopters and phoned June). I duck back.

Behind me the cop in the right-hand seat which in England would be the driver's seat (as in Sweden till recently) gets out and stands up into the street. I raise my free hand and there is a cab which overshoots me by just half a length, and as I get into it I say over my shoulder, But I bet you don't know who Nash was *with* that day.

Incremona, the answer came, but not from Jenny.

Oh the retreating scene through the cab's back window! Jenny alone, the cop looking at Jenny, then easing back into the squad car—*Incremona!* I answered myself: *Incremona:* Incremona had been the one in the South Ken tunnel with Nash: Incremona: the man at whose command Kate rang up Savvy's farewell party to pass on to Gene the news that Jan's red jaguar had been pinched by Cartwright but Kate passed the news to Nell, who did not tell Nash (hovering on Savvy's bedroom threshold) but did later tell her husband Gene, the middle Flint brother, the uncertain one who in his younger brother Paul's hut on the slopes of Mount Clisham could commit my diary to the fire with Jenny's strange phrases on it more than clues when but a few moments before he had grimaced as if at some violation when his older brother Jack tore off a blank half-page of it so I could have a scrap to jot down compass bearings.

No matter where it took me I would go to the end. Even if only to find myself alone then with someone else's profit system, or state of mind, or shrunken heart. Or opening at last an air letter I did not trust, that a friend named Dagger DiGorro had expressed to Monty's. Or far from Jenny (who must have known about Len anyway but did not know about the Frenchman). Far from family and from our insulated though not friendless life in England. Far from things warm or even serious. Far from gray film or dry froth left on the soap by my son Will. Far from Isambard Kingdom Brunel fresh from nearly drowning his head in an unforeseen pool during a fire on the maiden voyage from Bristol (but not by a long shot to New

York) of a great ship he had designed, the *Great Western,* whose boiler laggings had been laid on so near the furnace flues that, being of felt and red lead, they had ignited. And far from the interesting differences between a stand-up shower with its advantages of moving water and quick and thorough rinsing, and a lie-down bath. There one can speak to one's dry, attendant wife on many subjects, the space program, the Vietnam war, the concept of Hindu Māyā, even if three weeks before as a bitchy *bon voyage* to Corsica she called the film half-baked, though in fairness to myself I had so vividly foreseen screw-ups in shot-selection, in cutting, in the issue of color and black and white, and in our story-line, that, as far back as May, I had said to Cosmo that if we didn't watch it we could get into trouble—which I at once saw was misplaced frankness with a person of Cosmo's insecurities, for he nodded sagely with a twisted grin glad to let me seem to put down our film when in fact all I was doing was politely *not* putting down his own grandiose advice that we use cartridge loops and kindred tricks.

And so instead of trailing Jan Tuesday right on into her brother's house to find Paul at last, I had instead been found by Paul on Thursday and been picked up with John in what was clearly someone's plan. As systematic as Jack Flint checking me out by inquiring of that Sunday armchair quarterback Red Whitehead what territory I worked and what my work was like and what my interests were. And Red "So call me Red!"—though he answered the phone "This is Mr. Whitehead"—welcomed the chance to tie into the great multiple field of impinging informations to dump his bit into the memory bank, manila folder and all, shredded for better digestion, complete with my having failed to exploit the Bristol liquid-crystal market.

But it's Jack's! I cried, and Paul Flint flicked his head around, then back to the red light that has been oncoming through the swash of three cabs Tuesday, Thursday, and Saturday this terminal October week.

But wait: I didn't mean this was Jack's taxi; I meant that Jan had told me her erstwhile husband was doing a science film for young people and he was doing it with Jack Flint, and I meant that Red had said he was now into audio-visuals for schools and that Red had tried to put me on hold when I asked if he knew Phil Aut: so that, improbable as it seemed, I would be surprised if Jack Flint did not have a controlling interest in the very science firm for which Red provided executive noise and I was the erstwhile U.K. rep. So I had been working part-time for Jack perhaps. But if he and Phil were doing that film together, why wasn't Jack behind my film too? Jan did not have the imagination to take that further step—she had been busy saving the world or bringing understanding to it. You might as well try to convey my *shtip* of understanding to Tessa's father: Lorna gets up to leave, depressed by Dudley more than his nastiness; and so it turns out we're leaving with the Polish woman I've been saying goodbye to, while Tessa, who didn't get through to her clan chief, examines Jane's cast so closely she does not even say goodbye to us, and in the front garden, half of which Queenie Stone faithfully weeds each damp English week, I say to Lorna Oh I *am* going to the film after all, and she says Dagger can't see you after all, and I say You didn't put anything on Will's nose, and she says Jenny's date was called off too, she can come, but Jenny says I'm not sure: and Tessa's father's front door unlatches and swings in and Tessa runs out toward us as if we've stolen something, but only to ask if she and Jane can come to the cinema tonight.

But the cast! the cast!

I didn't say this out loud and still Paul looked round.

Something was wrong with Paul's cab. Less swing and swash but no increased structural tightness. A shock gone? A waterbed losing water? Brunel would have the door open at once and be two-thirds out hanging under the body, the back of his brain six inches off the street whose potholes, ridges, and cracks at this speed had a liquid flow of which in turn the great man pushing through cave-in, shipwreck, and fire to success would be unaware, giving his un-divided attention now to this cab's under-carriage, not (or not yet) the larger related problems of paving material and traffic stress, or the soluble and insoluble problem of his own gravity, for I am inside the cab's passenger compartment holding his feet.

Now my own Māyā proverb may be 75 percent right—a *shtip* in time must suffice to be merely its own reward. However, that Sabbath stab in Tessa's father's front hall reached also some system of attention that felt less my own than borrowed or shared—whereby the message on Jane's itchy cast came to me through others: and the message was that the woman Nash and Incremona had come to meet on June 27 in the pedestrian subway leading under the Science Museum to the South Kensington tube had been Tessa Allott, and by some improbable accident she had been proxied unknowingly by Dudley and Jane.

This was a message fleeting enough; for the cast had hardly

any future: two days after our Sabbath lunch July 3 and within hours of Dagger's call to say Corsica was on after all, Jane's cast was hacked and scissored off in Dudley's presence while Jane pretended agony at every cut. But she did not pretend when she looked at last at her mended arm. She ran a finger over the crease in the soft flesh above the elbow where the cast had reached, and she looked at the diaphanous pallor against the warm color of her other arm that had been exposed to London sun and Edinburgh rain and the Channel winds of the Kent coast where she had visited a schoolmate whose parents had a cottage in Deal. You see, Dudley talked to me. I would sometimes guess why, but I didn't know; and he'd have been embarrassed if I'd asked.

Tuesday, July 6, we rested in the water at the far end of the pool, an elbow lying on the tile, feet idly treading for pleasure, and Dudley told me how he had not liked the doctor's rough handling of Jane's cast but when she looked at her arm he had felt something else, a *shtip*—he stopped, he smiled the scholar's quick mad smile to himself—a *shtip* indeed, a *shtip*—for her reaction hurt him, her arm was a thing the way it is when circulation gets cut off and you have to pick your arm up and hold it while you shift your position in bed, and what hurt her hurt him.

But even more idly than I was treading, I was staring idly at his pale and hairy stomach enlarged in the tile-blue-tinted water, a lens for Corsica—not so much Dag's call the night before to announce that it was on again he was glad to say, but more what I'd proposed: the women looking ten years older than the men, a woman flogging Napoleon souvenirs, a university student in a café explaining in English to an American the meaning of the '68 slogan THE MORE I MAKE LOVE THE MORE I WANT TO MAKE THE REVOLUTION, American dropouts living in the coastal caves, sharp CUT to a construction crew wiring sticks of dynamite apparently (because of the sharp cut) on top of the very cliff that housed the caves, and finally (or as far as I had gone with Dagger on the phone) a Corsican breaking open his fowling piece and cleaning it and laying it back in the boot of his car.

Thus preoccupied, I wondered only later if my reason for not asking Dudley why he talked to me openly the way he did was that I was afraid he would reply in his direct way something that on the contrary would embarrass *me*, or lead if you will beyond the inherent reward of Dudley's candor on certain accepted subjects.

He is an honorable man.

There in the water he said, Well I couldn't let her go to the doctor on her own with Queenie, could I?

But he would never have said, That bitch of a wife of mine had to pick yesterday morning to go to the British Museum to try to identify the person on whom the romantic hero of Wilkie Collins' *The Woman in White* is based who also may well have given his name or most of it to the heroine of that book.

But Dudley—as a combination of waters now washed glimmeringly into my view—could embarrass Tessa when he wanted. Yes, that Sabbath *shtip* apart from its inherent reward had its 25 percent of incremental information gossiping through gate after gate like a digital sum to the hot and nice but (because Will had not washed the tub) faintly scummy bath water from which I delivered to Lorna my two-part definition of Hindu Māyā and she for her part told how Dudley had angered Tessa at that party by asking Dag and interrupting to ask again and yet again who was this Nash, eh? who was Nash?

A query I now saw came from Jane's cast, destroyed to reveal the true limb it had been made to mend—first inspected—inspected rather casually I should have guessed that Sunday, July 3, while Tessa washed the teacups and Jane looked up the movie they would see with us that night.

But Jenny did not go after all. She phoned Reid, and they met, and the *quid pro quo* of their meeting I imagined now in Paul's cab that had gone strange on us this October Thursday in New York just as accurately as Jenny herself told me when I got it out of her Saturday.

But why did Nash want to call himself to Tessa's attention?

Mike! I exclaimed.

Mike indeed. Mike who had heard me answer Mary Napier that the name of my friend who visited in Edinburgh was Tessa Allott.

But Mike had heard this in Ajaccio, whereas on the Sunday Nash autographed Jane's cast Dagger and I had not even been to Corsica. A valve had opened with a blink like the Mercurial god of film, cutting some prefigured Corsica into a Marvelous Country House as yet unshot, and some coordinate part of me had leaned naturally toward that vacuum blink, but must say No, and in lieu of an answer ask the question Why did Dagger change his mind and say on Monday night, July 5, that we were going to Corsica after all?

I knew only what others knew.

As you who have me know, I did not seek top secrets from the bottom of my heart. But that is where they seemed to fall, and I had no hard-hat to leave above the grating's grid. I become all these data shredded into their oscillations. A Zen voice from Lorna's crisis of the late fifties comes home with her: it is late at night: she stands over me still in her coat, I look up at the smell of her soap and the damp rain on her shoulders: I love her: she smiles a brave matinée smile that asks for an understanding no man can give, no real man, or maybe just not me: she quotes her koan: Open yourself as wide as the sky: she laughs silently.

Open myself as wide as the sky?

But that was not Brunel's way. Consider the astronaut. Unlike those wartime shipyard workers who now know that the asbestos they breathed a generation ago may yield a fiery carcinoma, the astronaut cannot know what lesions of the eye or breakdowns of the head may hit him in his earthly autumn from those flicker-flashes radiating by night through his helmet and out the other side into the unresisting space of his late youth. Meanwhile we do what we can. We look at the unmediated glare of the sun in space and devise a visor and rethink certain properties of imperviousness in gold. We look at the fact of heart shrinkage in the weightlessness of space where it works less; and it is possible to do something; we measure stress in the elevated levels of activity of a nerve-transmitter called catecholamine related to hormones. And Brunel with his banged head sunk in an overflow that has collected—Brunel breathing air and water and fire—will think not of the devoted waiting wife, or his centrifugal solution to the threat of suffocation by a coin caught in his throat in the bosom of his family, or his dawn horseback ride to Bath thence to survey the valley of the Avon and the soft hill clay along a canal, but thinks rather at once about what caused the fire on the *Great Western*—and the clear answer in his new *Great Britain* is David Napier's new feed-water heater, not to stop the excess heat around the funnel but to use it. I do not wish for a technology of wedlock. Still there are times—a problem could have been stated, a pain received as a message. Dagger got Alba's phone call at the école in Ajaccio and at once saw that even if her false labor did not last, she had to know he was on his way back to London—though in Paul's October cab I wondered if Dagger had used the false labor (which must have been nerves because Alba took methodical care not to overtax her body) to get us out of Corsica before I poked into something that was not our business. Now Brunel's *Great Britain* had another problem on her maiden voyage to New York. She lost her way and ran aground on the coast of Ireland, and at daybreak the skipper looked for the Isle of Man and saw the Mountain of Mourn, but this was because there were errors in a new chart that had not existed in the old. More important, this was a mishap that Brunel's unprecedented longitudinal iron girders (like his earlier timber viaduct that survived the head-on collision of two trains) could withstand but not forestall. And so in the transfer from the old chart to the new the *Great Britain* (51 feet broad, 289 feet long between perpendiculars) survived, and so did Brunel's name, which was enhanced.

I was on the verge of a formulation. Ned Noble's terminal breaths lay ahead but near, and Andsworth's Integrated Breathing beckoned me on past my concern for a shrunken heart and my concern about why he did not urge me to attend macrobiotic meals at the Community though I would have declined. He kept his activities in compartments, as Geoff Millan did his friends, and as once in those long drizzly safe winters in London I had thought Dagger did not.

Speak of the devil!

I said it aloud.

We were bumping to a stop at the red light and John's cab ran on ahead.

It was what Dagger had said coming away from our preliminary visit to Stonehenge.

Slowing down to help the Druid, Dag had said Speak of the devil, as if recalling negotiations through Andsworth and not our present dispute about what film we'd used for the threesome against the fortress wall in Ajaccio. But Dagger had been stubbornly attentive; and now I understood.

But I had no time; two of that threesome were Marie and Incremona, and John-of-Coventry said she had been after Len to go on a macrobiotic diet, and Dagger's stomach had been kicking up after breakfast at the école and I'd told him to change his diet, and he'd been reaching with his free hand for a Tums when the three appeared, and whether or not it was at Andsworth's in South London that Incremona had beaten up Nash after the South Ken fiasco, it was clearly Andsworth's Community that drew the Druid into the fortress scene in Dagger's mind as we sighted the old Ford on Salisbury Plain and slowed down to help him fix his flat.

But I had no time, because that was precisely what Paul's cab had—a flat.

No time to figure Andsworth's collaborations with friends, enemies, and neutrals; nor for the unlikely prospect that my train of thought had caused this flat.

Guiding Ruby and Tris across the islanded double road of Park Avenue South at 7 A.M. for breakfast at a coffee shop, I saw Incremona and a blond man half turned away at a postbox on the southwest corner, I could have raised my voice in song and no one would have heard, for the sound around us was that great; I could have been one of those street singers of yore who materialized out of Atlantic Avenue and wandered the fine enclosed streets of Brooklyn Heights on a Sunday morning and looked up to our windows for a couple of buffalo nickels tight-folded in a chewing-gum-sized scrap of the Sunday *Times*—and no one here in Manhattan (perhaps even including Incremona who at that moment tracked my physical presence only) would have known much less taken me for a mad yeller attacking the system diagonally from some corner—the sound around us was that great.

But now as I bolted from Paul's cab and ran after John's, thinking if nothing else I could ascertain that he was not after all leading me where I thought, Paul shouted into a quiet that can be a city's powerful charm at night be it London, New York, or somewhere in between—a humming quiet like an afterglow of glare, a field just out of sight voicing a guarantee that something has happened and will again: Paul shouted, I only wanted to help!

In the last word the deep voice out of that narrow tall chest contained still like an obscure unvoiced quiet surrounded by all the windy vacuum of other answers, those words It comes to that, and that alone.

Two hundred and forty miles without the wheel.

But where then was the calm Jan said Paul had found beyond stones and stars, beyond contemplation? But hell, here he'd been driving me into a trap.

To help me?

I could not find John's cab. It turned west where I expected but did not then turn into the block of Mercer that I'd thought I was being drawn into. I was out of breath. There was no light around the shade in John's loft.

When I got back to Paul's cab, it was empty in the middle lane with its lights on and the traffic light ticking from green to red, and John-of-the-loft seemed not to have come back. I ran my hand around the tread of the tire that had gone, and I found what I was looking for.

Rose had Ruby and Tris till Sunday. Sub's tests would be over then.

Should have kept the cab, said Dagger on Saturday—fixed your flat, hundred percent mobility, drive and park till the city towed you away, could have had it as our first car for weeks.

I was curious, said Gilda on Friday; you're not responsible for me. She had at last got a call through to me at Sub's to report that the man who had called himself Cartwright had come again and she had got into the spirit of the thing, couldn't help it, and had told him a scary bald man had told her Cartwright was meeting Claire—at which this impersonator of me had been strangely shaken.

I walked from Paul's cab to Monty's house, which was dark. Later I phoned Claire and got her answering service.

Paul would not knowingly kill me.

I must find out what it was I knew that was so important to these people.

I would have to ask.

The black man who'd said We all part of the system, man, had chuckled when Paul's cab crunched the glass of a bottle the black man would have hit John with if my steps or the inevitable field of my presence had not made John stop and look back, and the bottle crashed in the gutter instead, there to insert some of itself into the arriving tire of my cab.

Friday I waited in Sub's apartment.

For Incremona, Nash, the Frenchman, Jenny, Chad, June—I wasn't sure.

I phoned Claire's answering service and said I'd be seeing her.

Nothing happened.

I found if I waved at the TV from a distance of four feet I could stop the picture rising.

In the evening Sub phoned from the hospital. Keep the sound down, Ruby had bad dreams. Then Sub remembered the children were with Rose, and I heard him breathing erratically.

At home he watched the news and thrillers, thrillers with the sound off. Educational TV was starting a series of good films, old films, no interruptions.

What are you doing in? said Sub.

At ten the phone rang but the caller did not speak.

At eleven and at twelve the same.

No one tried the door.

Incremona had seen the children with me.

I tried to get you, said Dagger Saturday.

But in fact it had been Claire who'd phoned Saturday morning just as I was leaving for her apartment, and when I told her it was a pure accident my leaving the letter from Dag on Phil Aut's desk, Claire did not know, she did not know—she had not been told—she had not been to her office.

Why did I believe her? I let her talk. I could not stop her. But something stopped her, after she had told me Monty was not a fool no matter what our meeting at the restaurant might lead me to think. In London he'd told Dagger I'd be staying at the King Street house, I was extraordinary but Monty was afraid of me; but I must not, please, think him a fool.

Her goodbye came so fast then that it seemed cut off; I had not answered his challenge about the letter on Aut's desk, so Monty must have heard from Jan.

But there was so much he had not asked. Like the sound. The sound tapes he'd asked about like a madman outside my cab the first time we parted so long ago it seemed. Why didn't he ask this time? Three of those tapes were in a parka under a bed in his house. Where were the others?

But here was my friend Dagger who at length had opened Claire's door on a beautiful October Saturday in New York and was jollying me along about "our" taxi whose flat I should have fixed, and my secret visits to his wife, and was I trying to put Jenny through a survival course, man, and Dagger had come very close to flying up to the Hebrides looking out for her.

He wore an Army jacket and a Castro cap; he took the dog's leash off the closet door-handle. I was about to ask where Claire was and why Dagger had wished to put the Softball Game between the Hawaiian-in-the-Underground and the Suitcase Slowly Packed, but I reached down without looking and touched the familiar bulk of an untouched Sunday *Times* and was glad the film was probably destroyed, maybe I could conquer my weightlessness and sell the destroyed film to Jack Flint who must not wish his brother Gene's wife and house on view, nor his agent Krish in the Softball Game, nor his brother Paul the guru in transit at the Bonfire in Wales (near where Brunel's timber viaduct over the Usk burned and was replaced by him with iron)—nor would Jack want his brother, his youngest his magnetic brother Paul's voice on a Nagra tape or his face in a stone doorway at the probable scene of Jim Nielsen's liquidation. For

you could never tell how someone would make use of film footage—
U.S. Air Force planes acquired for a moment to illustrate power
possessed of momentum but insufficient focus like Cosmo's Sunday
fastball; America and England mingling in some dream of action and
peace; Brunel's great Clifton suspension bridge across the Avon gorge
failing to convey me, my son, my dreams, my daughter, my wife (so
that one might almost agree with Ned Noble's late conviction that the
finished thing, contrary to Kelvin's belief in demonstration, was
inferior to the concept); an American couple making music in a
passage I used to walk along with my children; the use of my life as
background for something else; the nervous wife fluttering in anti-
climactic 8 mill. stronger than she looked.

Strong enough to lift that carton out of sight last Sunday
night.

Claire's big black retriever lay across the living-room threshold while Dagger fumbled for the ring to snap the leash. The dog
seemed very calm if it was really about to be walked.

Dagger must have been telling the truth that Claire was not
in, for he was taking the dog out. Asking me to wait.

To wait?

Claire's expecting a delivery man.

I don't believe you, friend, I said.

That's your fault, friend.

If Claire's absence and her unexcited dog did not show I was
being once again set up, all other signs pointed inward at me. All the
reports.

I placed a call to Highgate. While I waited I reread Dagger's
letter. It had come from London to Monty's house in King Street,
been conveyed to John's loft probably by Jan, read by Jan or Paul or
John or Monty or some or all of these or more; so whatever of me
Dagger had sent was there for them as well: H.E.W. (on recom-
mendations from, among others, a behaviorist friend of the English
schoolteacher who'd been sacked from his job in the Bahamas) will
take Mr. DiGorro on for pilot study to determine if the government
wishes to get into sleep-teaching at federal level; and Dagger says in
the letter, All bets are off with the film, sorry man you pushed too
hard but you surprised me man and I'll always wonder what you
would have done in Corsica without me, right now the heat's on and
this heat confuses me but you know all about it—be good to Claire,
we'll be in touch.

It would work; it was not the piece of that retreating dream he'd had the morning of that little b & w crucifixion on the beach with the Bahama sand in his eyebrows and California sticking to his eyes and he'd been asleep enough to hold the thought that dreams are a species of sleep-teaching with a key difference that Dagger was just awake enough to lose; but now, what the hell—for peat's sake—plain sleep-teaching would pay the bills—it would work, it would keep millions of kids away from violent schools during peak hours and Alba would work and transfer her closet to a new set of equally clear axes, Dagger did not get bogged down.

I said Cancel the call.

A man's voice with an English accent said, No reply, sir.

Just as well. She would have asked where Jenny was.

Right, sir.

Well, Tessa had never except literally had her teeth in me, and I thought Lorna knew this by instinct, even if she did not know what she meant when on that July Sabbath that my own Hindu-American *shtip* had set off she'd said I had friends—married friends —to organize me on my travels.

I ran by others' times and, cogged to one another, they by mine—which brought me near again to a formula but shunted off again at the memory of being shunted this terminal Thursday of October by Monty's information and the thought and threat of Dagger's letter but by being shunted given a gift, namely that on Tuesday night when Sub had already entered Roosevelt Hospital for tests and I fried cheeseburgers and told the kids the story of the Three Brothers and of how Dagger got his name, and watched a thriller in which everyone talked softly and walked loudly, and I waited for Jenny to phone and wondered if the Frenchman and Nash had gotten to her—I had dreamt my lookout dream, and now recalled nothing of it but that fact. But as if sound had been time, no time had passed while for me Monty had been soundless—and when my Sabbath *shtip* had ended I listened as closely to the dinner in Coventry as I had to the trivial news that had caused my *shtip*— Dagger's H.E.W. and a carton of audio gear to fall back on.

A *heavy* carton? Dagger had surely swung a hop from a U.K. base and skipped the excess-weight charges. Alba loved London. She was excited by Dagger's absences, but she would not like Washington. But they would find a flat or something larger and there would be room, and they would have another child. And Alba would be careful. And have I lulled you who have me?

Well I was over Claire's living-room threshold in a second as if the room were a thought and from that clear pale indefinably oriental order I carried in my eye in another second back to the bedroom door the living-room blow-up of Claire's grainy arm, and as I opened the bedroom door knowing what I wanted in her closet, I feared I would find something awful between it and me. But the king-size low expanse was flat as a motel bed and I whipped open her deep closet and hauled out from under the longer hems of dresses and the shorter limits of pants suits what Alba would never never have made the mistake of lifting Sunday night in London if she had not feared I would find out what was inside.

I clawed at the seam.

Tore my right index nail.

Two amplifiers a snug top layer.

Below were Nagra tapes.

And the rest was 16 mill.

Ours.

Dated and Placed. In my hand.

Developed or not I could not easily tell.

My blood was on the amplifier carton.

I gathered all the tapes.

I put them down on the bed and left blood there too.

I laid the amplifiers back in the carton.

A picture of Claire on the night table reminded me of how Jenny is like my sister.

In the incinerator room shared by the other tenants on this floor I unrolled our black-and-white Stonehenge and it was a developed negative, tiny and lurid.

Near the hundred-foot mark of the second Stonehenge reel I looked for Paul being tugged through a portal by the witch Tessa in her green beret but found Nash instead and remembered that not Dagger but the other man in the plastic mac had probably shot Tessa tugging Paul, and then I gave up unrolling the cork-screw celluloid and took the reels out of their cases and dumped the lot and heard the rattle halfway down fifteen floors to the basement furnace, then read the white letters on the black plastic plaque telling what not to put down the chute, and wondered if in fact film was still made out of celluloid.

Liquid assets you say?

Not liquid enough.

I took last Sunday's *Times* from Claire's hall table. I opened the pages and scrunched them as if to start some kindling and filled the top of Dagger's carton and found some Scotch tape (called one of America's signal inventions, by a famous English writer with famous scientific forebears who himself died an American citizen in California taming his terminal throes with LSD).

I sealed the carton, shoved it into the closet, realigned two pairs of slippers in front, and went to answer a buzz that proved to be not the door but the housephone.

Dagger had been told by Claire all right.

Delivery man.

Two: a tall old man in bell-bottoms, a red bandanna under his chin; and a woman my age or older whom I felt I knew from a negative somewhere—platinum shag, a plump pretty face matured by comfort.

O.F. pick-up, the man said.

Had Claire known Dagger would be out?

O.F.? I said.

Outer Film, the woman said.

Your key, the man said, and handed me the key to Claire's flat.

Now where would it be, I said, thinking of Peter Minuit and the Indians.

Bedroom closet, said the woman. Which is the bedroom?

So Claire's triple game had now been left to simplify itself for safety's sake.

I thought, There goes a box of newspaper; but the old man in the bandanna asked what the hell was in here, couldn't be just film.

I pocketed Claire's key, as her door closed.

I imagine that if you (who have me) cut me open at the right points you'd find Will, Lorna, Jenny, some others, each in motion in some way but you would find them. Yet there is something in what Jan and Tessa said of me later; and I wonder if, in the trap that I presently had to choose, my morale could have been worn down by an amplifier tuned to my heartbeat: the thunder thud: a closed system growing conscious of itself till it thinks itself into pause as if it guessed some lightning ought to have preceded it: and it waits breathless: and sometimes it waits too long.

Dagger didn't come back.

I answered the phone.

I had to go.

The scene shifts and I with it.

Heartless they both called me—Jan, angry, then fearful;

Tessa weirdly tremulous then angry at herself: heartless it was of Cartwright to gamble Jenny's life.

Ah Tessa, there's more than one way to gauge hormone levels (mine, Dudley's, or a kilted chieftain's in orbit). The two wheels cogged to each other turn their calendars toward one special day in the mesh of Maya teeth, the sacred cardiectomy proceeds upon a sunny pyramid, no sutures needed but the stress is real, four priests spread the victim on the stone, the fifth so marvelously brings down the knife and up the beating heart in his free hand that watching from below you know the heart came up to meet the hand; but not today, for here, my dear Tessa, the victim has no heart—that's right—the breast is parted, blood goes on, there is no heart; the priest must improvise—but dares, since only the four can really see him stick the beautiful knife here and there hunting the heart the people want, who if they get to see the frantic hack-marks may go after the surgeon.

Kill him, he can disappear, said Incremona who'd been looking beyond me, and so saying he looked away from me to the doorway of a larger room that had been dark when they'd whisked me through.

For you see, Jan had said Cartwright could make people appear; and Incremona listened when she said she felt in her bones that I had made Reid appear Tuesday for I had said he was with Paul and yet when Reid entered Monty's house Jan could see Reid was stunned to see Paul.

Skip the magic, said Chad, who was the last person I'd looked at as I was struck in the chest downstairs (if in fact where I now was was upstairs and not the basement). In the dark room that we'd come through to reach this red-and-blue room there were two great square metal housings, a TV screen, a typewriter-like keyboard, a light-pen attached to a console by a telephone-type cord—other hard edges. There were voices there now, and Chad shut the door. I knew where the building was but not where in it I was.

I was there they thought because of Jenny. I had not really expected to see her and I was not disappointed in my expectation. The blow sent my breath away and the word Stupid occurred but whether said by someone else or me or merely thought, I didn't know, and when I could see again and think what I was seeing I was being helped through a hall to that dark room by Chad and Mike and it had not been Chad who'd hit me in the dilapidated marble vestibule, for I had turned toward him where he stood against the wall, and the

478

blow, the fist, the arm into my chest had come from someplace else.

In the empty red-and-blue room there were newspaper head-lines on the carpet.

I did not ask where Jenny was. When Chad sat down on the floor, that is where they all were—Gene, Mike, Jan on a bright cushion, Nash in a half-lotus kneading his lips with a knuckle, beside him the white-haired Frenchman leaning back on his hands shifting his legs, Incremona kneeling back on his heels at the far end by the other door, Chad's tribal cuts seeming both more raw and more leathery in my state of altered alertness after the blow to my chest—all of them on the floor except John-of-Coventry leaning against the wall and he later went out through Incremona's door to find a chair.

I moved above them, moved about the room. No one stopped me. I passed between Len and John, Jan and Mike, and therefore Chad and Mike, between Chad and Nash and therefore Chad and John.

I had brought them together. The headlines were medium big. I didn't let John go further with Len than the curtest rebuke before I broke in. After all, I said, Len had never liked the film except as a cover, and after we caught him in Corsica with the girl Marie who could be traced to the Druid's macrobiotic community in South London, the area where on a certain summer Sunday Len had given a pal of his a beating without visible injury in particular that tell-tale bloody nose, Len had liked me less and less; so John-of-Coventry should not stop Len from saying what he felt, any more than John should stop knocking our film which was for us, if I might speak in a pedestrian way for myself (and here my words threw up an improbable idea) an ongoing form of communication whether with Beaulieu 16, later Kodak Super 8, or now in New York (and here was the idea) slides, slides shot with an Olympus-Pen brought in from the other side by Dagger DiGorro—so, from first-strike U.S. bombers taking off, to our burly French operative in Dagger's flat in August betraying as much with his uncomfortable face as with his taped voice (but betraying exactly what?), to a blank momentum of white screen, the plunge now to slides would be like a movie's ultimate still—like Morse code for Beethoven, eh Lorna (dot dot dot daaa) better yet 3 (dot dot dot daaa daaa)—or a heart, Gene, which having raced like a bomb beats easier transplanted to a fresh system; listen, Jan, in this growing work of ours this jump from movie through blank screen to slides feels like a jump between two rates of Maya time that bypasses the cogged tangent where the sacred and the solar calendars, great circle, small circle, move each other meshed; so this communication grows, Nash, from Stonehenge, where you thought one rite concealed another wrong (which Jim Nielsen's folks would have paid to hear from you in their new windbreakers if you had stood at my door in Highgate a week ago today), on up to Callanish, Chad, where by a miracle your gun helped kill the Indian agent Krish who after all was not hired to break in and destroy the film, though was indeed employed by Jack Flint with whom I've on occasion been inseparable as Elspeth's mother will attest. So all in all, John, it isn't surprising Incremona wants to liquidate me, for he's quite right—I and this film that never says die and is worth quite a lot of cash are no good as a cover, for the cover doesn't cover, it reveals.

CUT to CLOSE SHOTS, mostly reaction shots where THE FACE IS NOT THE SPEAKER'S:

Chad (mouth open as if singing, while the speaker who is not Chad says): Don't listen to him, he had the gun in my cab Sunday night in London pointing at my head—the gun isn't in Callanish.

Nash (looking over his shoulder, but at whom? while the speaker who is not Nash shakes his head and snaps his hand with its finger stuck out like a conductor's): Had *I* known what was going on I wouldn't have merely disparaged your half-baked ideas, I'd have had the film destroyed. And that is what, Gene, you should have done. Power unfocused in process, Graf told me last weekend. Balls, I say! Sow confusion.

Gene (blue eyes into the camera, while the speaker who is not Gene says): *I* never called it a cover. What cover? Sherman called it a cover, not me. Cartwright lost his job with Whitehead. You didn't know Whitehead, but I know Whitehead. Cartwright needed money. You should see the bills stuffed in the desk in his living room. I say we hit him *and* the girl.

Jan (slowly shaking her head while the speaker who is not Jan says): I have it on good authority through June that Callanish was not in the film. Or is it in the diary? But the film was liquidated, and so, I gather, was the diary (CUT to CLOSE SHOT of *Gene*). So what we need is your head, Cartwright, that is to say, how serious you are about (*a*) blowing the whistle and/or (*b*) using the original plan as Mike alleges but which seems to me strange indeed if you are working with Jack Flint.

Incremona (the decathlon star tilting as if to spring through Chad's verbiage—but in the direction of no one, while the speaker who is not Len says): My brother didn't find Krish. So how do you

480

know he's dead? And would you mind telling us (CUT to CLOSE SHOT of *Jan*) what you've done with a red jaguar.

John (who is about to remain silent but—this time the face in the close shot—speaks): Don't speak, Nash. Suck on a ring, but do not—

Nash (automatically bringing ring hand up to mouth, then dropping it while a familiar voice that conjures up its own narrow, tan, virile face speaks in answer to John): Don't you tell anyone shut up. Nash can speak. Speak Nash.

Frenchman (looking at his watch while speaker not the Frenchman blurts): All I say is your sister June speaks on authority too damn much. I never heard of any windbreakers. So don't talk to me about windbreakers.

Incremona (rocking on his own private axis as we hear the Frenchman): Za Catwight gell.

Incremona (forestalling a CUT, by speaking): We got her.

Cartwright (halting on the side of the room opposite John-of-Coventry and between Mike and Jan as she suddenly says): You are heartless.

But what Len said is close to the bone. Bills in pigeon holes. For a piano. For the builder. Doctors. Magazine renewals. Bills on the floor in riffled sequences, in swirls, little white frames with names and numbers, strewn by Incremona. He's unmarried. Jenny wants a proper shower. Lorna likes a bath; the scum gurgles down the drain, never a problem though in the winter of '63 the outside pipes clotted, but I always paid the bills and they were there in the desk for Incremona to go through two weeks ago because Lorna saves them like the yearly New York Metropolitan Museum of Art calendar richly colored oriental medieval Moslem what have you, that my mother sends us that as Lorna looks back through our code of names, phone numbers, times, can tell her what we did. But you who have me know what Incremona doesn't, that it looks like not one lost income but two or three, the charters, the boatyard, add to that the perqs through Dag, cheap booze, a blender, and for Will for Christmas though we sing our carols live a Sony 110 cassette recorder (like a policeman's walkie-talkie in lieu of his traditional whistle), toss in a brandied plum pudding you can't even buy at that Knightsbridge landmark Harrod's where according to Queenie Stone the Queen and Philip have a charge—and American smokes though those I give or sell away. Yes, Mike, I could kill—kill Len for going in my house. Forget the diary he burgled.

481

Not a marvelous country house; a city house. Not a revolutionary life; a plain life. Where suitcases are packed and unpacked (never mind if Tessa says to Lorna Let him pack his own bloody case). Where the soap opera of our marriage has serialized itself in cartridges I've packed away in a hole in my study wall behind a picture. And where a park is near, and if we wish I and my wife may let the grass grow under our feet and the garden walls decay and title to the turtle grow as communal and friendly as the weatherman's crystal-clear forecast of bright intervals for a hungover Sunday. Our children grow up.

A house at London's highest point (Y'don't say, murmurs my father, affable once standing on our Highgate stoop)—near park and pub and bus, outdoor summer concerts, history, tennis courts, near a good school for my son with Mr. Ogg and the digressions he spontaneously maps.

I lost my temper and asked Len if he found the five-pound note in the far-left pigeon-hole, and Len too quickly said that when he knew where he was going to pick up twenty grand cash, no sweat. Len rocked back, and John grumbling about a chair got out the door to the other room that I probably had not seen.

My answers came out of nowhere. These people did not quite know, but I was one with them, and like a pedestrian accosted in the New York subway I wasn't sure whom I could protect by giving them what they wanted.

I said, I keep the red jaguar with my weapons, but what if you do find out if I'm going to blow the whistle or revive the film which I don't even know myself?

Cut it out, came a voice from Corsica, Mike's, cut it out—*you* know Chad didn't mean the film.

But Incremona (a face from Corsica as stiff as its eyes are bright) speaks (and rocks, as if to give the words a secret beat): Who said the film was destroyed?

Depend upon it, I said, and heard our spools clanking down Claire's chute.

But Jan, now kneeling, hands clasped, said: Oh yes, oh yes, more than I knew when I first said the word, oh Christ yes! *heartless*—he doesn't even ask where she is.

Heartless! I said. I fell to my knees. What about these people around you? I bet you don't know who Nash was *with*, that day—

The words go on while Jan and I retort.

The words go on down fifteen floors to Claire's furnace, then

482

back up like a loop, and they're not quite the right words, for here captive in a room and speaking of cruelty, I'd meant to say *Len* and said instead my very words to Jenny Tuesday.

Which day? said Jan.

That summer Sunday, the fiasco, Nash, Len, Reid, my daughter—

Nash?

Incremona, the one who bashed him up—And what's it matter? The film's gone, your idea's safe.

Oh I used it like a weapon, said Jan.

Len stood aside as the door opened. You were a long time finding a chair, he said, and John brought in a straight chair and puffed himself down.

And it wasn't original, said Jan.

And I—I had found out that what threatened to be revived was not the film.

So: if Flint but not film (and if Len flaunted Whitehead before me)—

What fiasco? said Len. He had come toward me from his post by that door and was standing above Mike.

The jaguar, I said, and stopped.

At Graf's, said Gene.

You were there Teeyoosday, said Chad, you phoned June.

Balls, said John. Get him back to London, put him under house arrest. Simplest thing.

At Graf's, said Incremona, and turned his back to me and faced the door he'd knelt by. Chad at the other door seemed to have forgotten me.

It was Dagger DiGorro, said Jan.

House arrest? said Nash, house arrest? Where do you get house arrest? He blew Bill and Ronnie at South Ken. How many copies of the diary are there? He's got connections, connections.

Shut up, said John.

Like the telephone, said Len, looking at John.

Krish got it from Cosmo, said Nash, Cosmo got it from Di-Gorro's wife: DiGorro didn't know what his own partner might do.

Shut up, said John and Len looking at each other.

Len's fist clenched and unclenched again, the same knuckles that as my breath like a brain swashed here and there in some equal time had gripped Gilda's cash register; and I said Stupid (the English way, *steeyoopid*), why *should* Nash shut up?—does him good to

483

talk—like autographing Tessa's daughter's cast in Golders Hill Park to contact Tessa—like acting independently—so don't shut him up, he's getting it out of his system and I know all he's saying anyhow.

But like a cartridge track without its containing cartridge, Jan was saying that the idea had been that none of us know enough—that was the idea, and it wasn't original because it came from Dagger and Dagger was good. The thick pale eyebrows frowned, the heart-shaped face finds me dangerous and tries to look through my impurities that bring this group together, and the face can't understand how I could wait patiently to hear about Jenny what I do suddenly hear from Incremona clenching and clenching the fist, says *Stupid* eh? which he probably did not say after Chad with his English pronunciation called him (I'm now sure) stupid downstairs or upstairs for delivering that blow to my chest (for it must have been Len)—Stupid, eh? We make you disappear, how about that? You and your girl, she's with Reid and he's with Sherman and you know where they are just like I know where your little weapons cache is, right, Cartwright?

It was true. But only when he said it. I now knew where Jenny was held. Incremona's door opened a crack and John was called to the phone by a voice that was John-of-the-loft, and as John-of-Coventry went out he was saying God save us from bourgeois adventure.

Incremona pulled shut the door. Who's Lana?

Nobody knows her, said Mike.

A friend of a friend of a friend of mine, I said automatically (meaning Millan's Jasper). You drove me to her Sunday night.

It was true, as if by my saying it.

The idea wasn't all that came from Dagger, said Gene. The jaguar did too.

You knew that? said Jan.

My brother told me.

Paul! cried Chad like an explosion.

Jack, said Gene.

You been talking to Jack? demanded Incremona.

Don't get onto *my* loyalty, said Gene. This whole thing started as a test of that, and I passed the test, right Len?

Jack, mused Len.

Jack of course, I said—old money bags, eh Len? was twenty thousand the figure you mentioned?—and I shook my head and smiled, and Mike said to Gene, Mary Napier is in New York.

484

But the pain came back through my chest and the name I'd said *Jack* instead of was Dagger, but the *shtip* right through to my back was too bony and bodily to be out of a mere intelligence report about Dagger that seemed to place me again outside some system that in the past fortnight I had on the contrary felt at the crux of.

Again outside, though near.

Will has made a six-year-old movie out of cards each subtly different from the one before so you riffle them and there's a motion picture—it's Little Red Hiding Hood. Incremona riffles my doctor bills.

I look at Jan. I shouldn't have let her think Jenny magic-markered the self-portrait.

I look beyond her to Len who is staring at Gene who (mouth open) is pointing at Mike as if to let follow his finger the memory inside his body of what Mike has reminded him of to do with Mary.

Where are you going? asks Jan.

Like Len now vanishing in fury through that door, waves of improbability pass outward: Lana and the woman John is traveling with are probably one and the same; *sow confusion,* her phrase at Geoff's was likely taken from John; Mary is here in New York for the heart of Montrose, but Gene recalls her brother the one-time Scottish Nationalist Party activist who urged Paul to retire; Gene knows about Dagger and the jaguar from Jack who used and may own Red Whitehead who was in turn the object of some further attention here that was less improbable than potential or, like liquid crystal Red sold through me, shifting and mysteriously double-duty; and Dagger the donor I can hardly believe—and Dagger the source of Jan's film I can't or won't: In June I send my aged parents a pre-release carbon of the Bonfire in Wales, in June I send Sub the Unplaced Room, in July I send Dudley the Softball Game, in August only now in this receding room I recall dispersing Corsican Montage at his request to the only hard-nosed pro among these likely readers the horny one-time world-traveler Savvy Van Ghent, and to complete this impulse-distribution there's Lorna closeted in the October night with yet another part of the film record, unsure why I insert our friend Tessa into the Marvelous Country House, but curious only for a moment because then comes the tread in the dark Highgate house which she takes for an intruder, the very thing that the intruder, her dark-haired blue-eyed son Will prowling with his new aluminum racket, takes for her.

I breathe away the pain, the room is in my blood, breathing.

Gene squints as if in pain, he doesn't dream it's the Montrose heart Mary's here in New York for. Nash bites on a ring staring at Len's empty door.

I say to Nash: It was Nell—it was through Nell that Tessa's daughter knew Reid.

Nash to Gene: Tessa knew Nell!

Gene to me: Savvy knew the husband Dudley.

Nash to me: You were balling Tessa. Nell told Savvy.

Gene to no one: Tessa got him into Mexican stuff, she said.

I'm queasy. The uninterrupted expanse of pale carpet looks new. Headlines say 2500 to 5000 are dead and there's a follow-up on what seems now recent news I've missed—Britain has opted for the Common Market.

There's talking outside this room from beyond each door, but then also around—like an axis turning into motion.

What Mexican stuff? says Jan.

I believe Dagger the source of Jan's film no more readily than myself the source of the Marvelous Country House described by me to Dagger then really found by him—nor the source Tessa either, who in March described to me that very house known I see now through Nell Flint, but Tessa did not meet the DiGorros till mid-July.

System probably moves toward increasingly *im*probable states: Cartwright's Law?

My *shtip* Thursday with Graf is now far off as the point of its twinge, to wit Other Life at some harmonious remove from me— which is my power that I'm on the point of formulating in front of Monty when I remember having had my lookout dream; but power about to burst in through Chad's closed door and Incremona's open door plunges me again, in mid-formula, beyond its knowledge, and the body that Andsworth's ideas have given me is mine but not mine: pulses swash more ways at once, there's a chopper coming apart in my future, the Dagger-loop blinks through evenings of discussion and through the Beaulieu's advertised featherweight six and a half pounds but greater far through a growing diary now marked by a megalith near where Krish's body if unfound by Jack may have risen with the aid of a dilettante geologist in a red mini whom Jan must know—Dagger-loop parallels other pulses, loops or not loops: red jaguar darting (Mexico, Jack, Dag, Jan, me): plot against *Flint* that Jack seems himself part of; and (near, yet tracked apart from, John-of-the-loft's authentic care for his real work surrounded but not touched by Aut's cash) the Druid's holy sobriety leads near but past a cache of organic exile hash, near but past a quiet downstairs bedroom where Nash was sorely beaten, near but past more of Andsworth's survival economics—a Napoleonic fake of the French cartographer Nicholas Sanson's 1658 map of the British Isles with two delicate scroll *cartouches* and thickish yet delicate outlines that make the land look singed out of the sea, survival economics—near but clear of the undevalued strait gate of the one flat map thence through the strait-jacket of the body's network to Ned's sixteen-year-old face not to be saved by any bell the despised Lord Kelvin rings from his demonstration models yet not marked by a cancer frantically circuiting within to carry the message out, petulant sixteen-year-old futures leaving a go-Dutch-yourself blank for a Brooklyn Heights Gentile hand of pedestrian invention to fill in with its own magic *shtip* reaching between gravities but not in time for an autographed sphere along a flat shelf that exists only in that hand's instinct.

I'm hungry. Sub's children are with Rose for the weekend.

Nash eyeing me laughs and speaks; but it has no more to do with his real thoughts about Nielsen and Stonehenge and me, than on the day of Boyd's autographed ball my stabbing reach was conscious of a meaning in it that Ned and I later tacitly shared without benefit of demonstration. Nash is telling me of all people that Incremona's been in a rage ever since the cops towed his taxi off day before yesterday, and I ask if he's planning to blow up a few police tow trucks, and when Jan (behind me as if behind my eyes) asks if Len had the necessary cash to bail the cab out, Nash and I laugh in such a way that I know the cab was stolen whether or not they knew Paul had it—and now the Frenchman lets go with a great laugh like the ground rushing up to meet you, and I am sure the twenty thousand is some deal Len has with Jack.

Gene says, You don't know what you're doing. Mike says, He *knows* all right, but there'll be no *doing*.

Between the two truths a space occurs, a new volume there was not room for.

I get out my pen and search my pockets and say, Oh *Jerry's* got the address book. And I reach down and tear a corner of newspaper just above the headline. I put it in my palm and draw spontaneously a logo for Ned's lost time-machine.

There is a space I'm trying to use, having seen it come into being. Mike is questioning Jan.

Chad is saying that I gave parts of the diary away.

To my wife, for instance.

That doesn't count, says Nash (and then irrelevantly but with relish), she was holding hands Sunday night.

At Savvy's of course—whom I told to look up Dudley Allott in the North Library when Savvy had to use the British Museum one week long ago.

But the space that I have reached into existence fills with the memory of a stabbing pain due to past or future hard to tell—(a) a train ride up from the south coast, a boatyard mentioned to a Frenchman who kept saying, Correct, and would not discuss the May événements ("CONSUMER SOCIETY MUST DIE A VIOLENT DEATH"—"TAKE YOUR DESIRES FOR REALITIES") or (b) the prospect of a drink with Lorna, Dudley, Tessa, and Tessa's father—or some jellied eels in between that may have been as pivotal as the depressing old man in the bog (English for john) who kept my hands wet and bent my ear about his dream of a wheel-shaped radially compartmented pub to please everyone—yes after him my stab dissolved and I went back upstairs to have a drink and hear about German Jews wandering the wartime Heath.

Why not, says Nash—you took his wife to Mexico.

And the space I have reached into being fills on the eve of the Allotts' sailing for New York with Tessa's suitcase and with the stone she gives me, then, hearing Dudley and Jane, takes away to give Lorna.

I've never been to Mexico, I say to Nash. I've been to Stonehenge.

And before I can do the job myself, the space fills up with something other than Tessa's third moment: it is survival politics, stop-gap, and crass, a curtain of flesh and failure, both the Māyā Lorna had her hand on firming it up so it didn't look like Southeast Asia any more, and the purpose Dag and I in an old Volkswagen receding from the National Film Theatre settled at last, a film-to-be, settled in words.

But there is still space, and for Uncle Karl who finds in his wife's fine-fingered hand space for a postscript to Tessa's father who phones me when "the children" are in Massachusetts to ask what is the matter with Dudley and to share with me Karl's P.S. (you know he's blind? yes, I know): that the early nomad Hebrews living "between the desert and the sown, between the most fertile of lands and the total negation of life, which in this remarkable corner of the earth lie cheek by jowl" may have developed a "tension . . . be-

488

tween a desire and a contempt for what is desired": interesting, I agree, and the Dudley question fades, very interesting indeed; and is Uncle Karl still enjoying his dream house? Oh no, they moved to a flat in Tel Aviv. Still sleeps till ten in the morning? It's possible, the voice turns uncertain. And have they a cat? Always a cat. A new cat? An Israeli cat.

By luck Karl is prepared; he dreams of a house he has often designed, bombs turn to rain showers and garden flowers spring up faster than mushrooms or the house itself; there is not even pain, or so he can't recall—he has a bump later, and of course he is blind, but the dream house swung back and disappeared like a shooting-gallery target but then swings back up and Uncle Karl is awake: the German tabby dislodging an old heavy wedding present was four feet above him, so not even his cat's paw did he feel, much less claws at a throbbing eyeball like body meat ripped out from under a river turtle's shell by a jaguar unlike either the red jaguar throne at Chichen Itza near an ancient Maya observatory, the Caracol, with its square wall-holes giving sunset and moonset lines-of-sight which Dudley himself checked on March 21, 1965, nor the jaguar's Maya name *balam*, hidden thing, which in Tessa's troubled passion was just right for the camouflaged violence that reached its thirsty teeth down from the dark, and Dagger told me he wished he'd known all this before venturing into the heart of the jungle in search of his friend because he could have used a cultural rest-stop even a detour from time to time—he looked up the Mayas later in New Orleans.

I did not in so many words offer Lorna the Marvelous Country House. Was it Tessa I was offering?

You say my face betway? Betway what?

Oh at last the Frenchman's come out of his visiting bulk.

Betray? I laugh to Gene. Well if this thing began as a loyalty test Len laid on you, it might end out of all your hands, so don't sweat the loyalty angle, Geney.

Geney! says Nash. *Geney!*

In my mouth Jack's big-brother name for Gene surprises me, it comes from the east and the north, from invented compass bearings scribbled with a wet hand on borrowed paper in a Hebridean hut a week ago tonight, and Gene grabs for the scrap in my palm and misses, and the Frenchman demands my answer and Gene in some collaboration that is out of my hands says low to me, Do you think Incremona would ever have settled for a *Flint* warehouse, do you think that? you know damn well the idea wasn't Incremona's just as

Jack knew damn well your name wasn't Wheeler with that fake accent coming in out of the rain—*he* knows Wheeler—but Incremona! forget it! the idea for a *Flint* warehouse—

Fingers jerking my arm are French and the question comes again, *Betway? betway? betway what?*

I shake my head with a pitying grin for Chad who has darted over behind Gene and grips Gene's arm, but Gene thinks the grin is for him.

Nothing like sharing information, I say, you've told me *where*, why don't you tell me when?

You *know* when, says Nash—we know that from Van Ghent.

I say (and laugh), Oh you guys are incredible, aw Chad boy you should never have visited Paul in the Hebrides, June told me all about it.

Nash moves close, he wants to hit me with those rings, he's raised his voice to a pitch of purposeless energy: OK so it was Chad's idea, man, but it came out of the group, man, and did you know you're through, man?

Yet none seems to see me.

Chad has swiped Nash to the floor.

Gene eyes the other door. I know what Incremona will say. He is through Chad's door and I am saying, Don't worry about *me*, Nash, it's Nielsen's friend Bob Coronelli you better look out for, but the Frenchman yanks me around, and now Incremona is calling across the room as if across a considerable distance: how did Gene know about Jack and that jaguar? was Gene in touch with Jack? and whose friend was DiGorro anyway?

Not mine, says Gene—

Because (calls Incremona slowly) I don't know the answer to that one—because "your" friend DiGorro pulled a fast one, right?

I was on the carpet, the Frenchman had shoved me down; but I've spun up to face Incremona, who stares through me as through a gap and says, not across the room but close, You were right there's no film; you knew he wasn't going to come across.

I was up; but hands from behind held me. So Dagger planned to sell the film. But who to?

Voices evoked by me pass through me:

Jack didn't know him at Paul's last Saturday so they've worked fast.

Paul's behind this!

Paul's gone to Chile.

What do you mean Chile?—that's where I'm going with Jerry.

Cut it out. So *what* if there's no film?

Don't give me Bob—*Bob* knew Nielsen had to go.

Twisting to be free of the arms, I want to know whose. The other door where Incremona left to take his call now shuts. Incremona's right behind me, and he has himself shut the door he reentered by—Chad's door. Ned Noble is dying in a movie theater, the children's section smells of peanuts and warm chocolate, there's a rustling arithmetic of nickels and dimes dropped in the dark of the St. George Playhouse on Pineapple Street on Brooklyn Heights—and in the darkness the starched white matron leans over my sister and me to tell Ned to stop groaning; I can't quite see the movie, can't quite hear whose words in Dagger's VW receding from the National Film Theatre, key words—but all that opens is Sub's ripe fridge, a snowdrift round the freezing compartment, semisoft Birds Eye cardboard thus insulated from subfreezing temperatures; and Ned, dying, can say only that Kelvin was a jerk; and while I want to dream of peat wheels and hand-hewn oak subway carriages and the Brunel-Cartwright memorial moving terminal founded on that original Maya system using twenty and the breathtakingly original concept of zero, and a hand claws a scrap out of my palm, I feel but cannot understand a law that lies beyond increasing improbability and the more I feel it the less I can claim it as let us say Cartwright's Law; but not quite hearing the words in Dagger's car I am ready to be at home with the unexpected which is a concussion that inserts itself like the *Om* of an overhot stereo in a space in my body not previously there, an emptiness eased in with dry oil of whispers:

The gell.

Tourists have accidents.

What are you doing? What's that?

Lighter fluid.

Where are you going?

Back to Taos, New Mexico. How about that?

He's going to blow up a few police tow trucks.

The Bay of Bengal tidal wave blobs like a fingerprint that didn't hold still, the dead align along mud terraces that I see now too late were the isobars of my fingerprint, reaching for the strings of two helium balloons my wife has just yanked from the ceiling and punched out the garden door. Through a crystal clarity equaling a kind of silence, a hand in glove reaches to you—you are dangerous, worth study, valuable, and what seems at first to be Tessa's word *twenty* disperses itself into Tessa saying, So what, *twenty*? so what, *zero*? the Maya got that from China—that's not what matters about the Maya!—but no, the word *twenty* cut off so it turned into an absolute or an idea was my word, my last word.

I do not know what went on inside me while unconscious if I was unconscious. I know what happened outside.

But my head filled the dark closet where I was slumped. The voices outside plus the thought that I was at last ready to be launched into the dream so as at last to control it led me to see myself still in that room with the newspaper, but the vivid faces that belonged to the voices I now heard did not belong to Len, Nash, Chad, Jan, Gene, Mike, or the big Frenchman, but to John-of-the-loft and someone else, and their faces were vividly visible because I was blind.

I reached for a Beaulieu sync button thus though unfilmable to record on the attached Nagra my remarks which I rehearsed in my body as if these remarks were to be my lookout dream. But as fast as I could evaporate the irrelevances with which this rehearsal filled the closet up to and beyond liquid level, more came.

But I needed the practice—my head felt inside a cartridge lined with training electrodes and was getting bigger to where it would fill the cartridge imbedding those electrodes in my head, and as for the readiness I had felt, it now needed just a quick rehearsal, but Lorna kept breaking in yet it was somehow I doing the talking and she didn't answer when I said did she buy her new comb in London or New York, I could get two of those French tortoise-shells for the price she'd paid for one—but this one dyes, she said, and sure enough she took off her bluejeans and her hair was red in the form of Corporal's chevrons.

But there's a different darkness in a line across my feet; I'm not blind; whatever I was ready for has passed and I don't feel it and I'm now not sure I had any lookout dream Tuesday, let alone just now.

I'm in a closet. It's empty. The voices are about to stop. One of them is sorry to be late—held up in traffic. (On a Saturday? Is it still Saturday?) I smell something. A chemical used in the room where the voices are, or used on me. I'm the watchman of that lookout dream recovering consciousness, but what do I watch? It's clear the man I haven't heard before knows this equipment and this room but has only just arrived and is failing in some way; he can't get John excited about the random possibilities. Of cartridge loops. John is saying Well that's straight sixteen-mill. It's John-of-the-loft.

John says he would follow Whitney's early analog work complete with rotating discs, multiple axes, that whole multimovable table thing, and feed the patterns in and come out with flower targets and kaleidograms and concrete words exploding into galaxies—beautiful things, right; but now we're going to have plasma crystals and that's a digital system that changes the whole future for us, analog computers are antiques.

Not yet, the other says; plasma crystals don't give you motion; you got 480 lines of resolution with 512 points per line and you need six bits of information for each of your quarter-million points all for just one single static image, man, and where you going to get that kind of computer capability?

John: Real-time projection direct—that's what I'm after. We need two-megacycle-a-second capability in a computer to generate motion with the plasma visual subsystem, but we'll get it. Progress is exponential now. Used to be subsystems weren't up to the computers; now the shoe's on the other foot.

Other: You got the subsystem?

John: My boss's boss if we play it right.

The other is explaining plasma crystals and how you sandwich a layer between glass plates, and one plate has a mirror-conductor on the inside against the crystal and the other has tin oxide, and when you charge the crystal in between, you disrupt—

I know, says John. You know too.

But inside a headache that seemed like an old vacant idea, I knew too!

For they were talking about my product.

For these were *liquid* crystals, and to get motion what you do is lay on your conductive coatings in a collective mosaic like colors in successive silk screenings to produce one multicolor print and as you go along you electrically charge the tin coating and so the liquid crystal molecules are disrupted in just the patterns out of hundreds of thousands of picture elements that you want, and your preset mosaic is affected precisely as you want with your scanning signal.

Crazy turn-on, the other has said, but John says, Well, no.

The other: A visual, right?

It's past words, says John.

It's something else! says the other (and I could hardly hear).

No, says John. I don't think that's it. The liquid crystal—it's going to be . . .

Exponential, the other says quietly.

Let's not talk about it.

Like a new circuit? But not *real*-time projection, John—don't give me that.

Steps, receding steps, supplant the voices.

My hand tries the knob, a button snaps into my palm. The lock works from inside too.

I see the room clearly. It's dark. There's a red light on a console. There's a light somewhere else. I close my closet behind me.

My headache is the price of my power.

The footsteps slide along the light that widens as I reach another corner and two doors. I open one, I draw it closed behind me, I've picked wrong, I'm in another closet, and it has things in it, I fall back but sit down on metal that rises to my upper thigh.

A chance I'm still dreaming.

Because I recall no dream.

Just young John's voice calling John-of-Coventry to the phone offstage long ago.

A new voice, an older voice, says something was terrible and someone won't die of old age and this someone wouldn't talk but is crazy and can be traced everywhere, England, here, France, the Flints, that crazy diary; but Jack is pinning it on someone else if that someone else stays lost.

You'd need a dozen x-ray helicopters to trace Incremona, says John. What about Mercer Street? What's the matter with you?

It was terrible. He had trouble with her. She looked all chewed up. I don't know what I saw, John. She looked wall-eyed. Think of it. When he got through with her.

Was she before?

And her hands were crossed on her chest and one knee was still raised. The house was OK but a windbreaker was on the floor in the basement. There's a bedroom there. Right after she called out, the door banged and someone in the next house heard steps on the stoop, so Incremona must have gone through the house first. It was terrible.

Can I still use Mercer Street?

They thought it was an aerial. Then they found a stiletto. It springs out of a lighter. Oh God her neck, John, her front. She had the beginning of a black eye. Her hair was pulled out, John.

Who did she call for?

She just called. They said it wasn't a scream. The steps on the stoop couldn't have been more than one person.

I never met her.

That hair. Not exactly blond, John. They thought rape but it wasn't after all. I never had a daughter. It was the color of wheat.

You never saw a wheat field in your life.

We'd be better off with rape. No motive problem. Why did he go after *her*? They didn't close her eyes, John. Brown eyes with that light hair. They didn't close them.

Just like a movie.

I never saw a dead girl, John. I felt responsible just looking at her. You know you can get a black eye after an extraction. You know she closed her mouth tight, can you imagine that? You know you always think of them with their mouth open.

I don't.

Just a kid.

This spring-loaded lighter . . .

Can't be traced to Incremona.

Will anyone come here?

And that picture on the wall. My God! This mess makes me see her in a whole new way.

A cartridge flies like a wingless bus into the future. I must get away from these words. Three overhead rotor blades sweep their segments of air, they do the work; but perpendicular to their plane there is at the tail like a light wheel feathering its own gleam a smaller vertical prop that checks the main rotor's tendency to rotate the fuselage.

Static gravels the voice on the police frequency. We slide left like a diagonal vector-product. Under the two sets of blades perpendicular to each other, what am I, as I look below me, looking for? Under that grid lie bones and for that matter flesh of New Netherland, sixty guilders or twenty-four dollars worth of 1626 goods.

We are rising, but (down by the Battery where the grid turns into a fingerprint if you could just see the streets) I can't find the tavern founded by the black man whose daughter Phoebe saved Washington from a bodyguard's poison. The story was told to us at a lunch there by our retiring American history teacher Mr. Johnson, John Paul Johnson, who having told us that we will presently go up to the third floor to the museum now stands above our empty ice cream dishes as if we were Rotarians or utilities analysts; and Mr. Johnson as he does when he's caught up in what he's saying brings his hands together under his pink, dimpled chin and round, rimless glasses as if he's praying or giving a Zen goodbye—he's saying farewell like Washington in this very tavern to his troops who when he suddenly says, How many Presidents came from Virginia? answer (as one) Eight! and who laugh when Ned Noble who's been here before with his father drawls irreverently from a far corner of our oblong circle, George left his hat here.

Not up to Ned's usual standard—for he'd told me during the main course. Also I'd seen it coming in the doodle on the tablecloth.

And Lafayette his pistols, Noble, which I'm sure you also know, said old John Paul, who completed his remarks and was applauded and made his way round to Ned just in time to offer him (improbable as it seemed) a light—because Ned had produced from under the sleeveless sweater he wore under his camel's hair jacket a pack of Raleighs with a book of matches inside the outer cellophane and had tapped out a cigarette and put it between his teeth, the only time I saw him smoke.

As we climb higher, Ned Noble is not at the controls.

Nor am I.

New York approaches the condition of a map. Nothing comes through.

The pilot in a turtle-neck looks over his shoulder and shrugs.

I'm responsible for our being here.

Want to keep your friend out of trouble, meet me: Nash deftly delivered this on June 27 not knowing Tessa was in Scotland. Dudley was not expected to see the note.

Dudley felt responsible. He knew that passage under the museum. The Maya hated empty space.

Problems may have solutions.

The pilot slides off toward the 40 Wall Street tower—pauses. Our swash-plate leans and straightens.

The things way high in Chartres Cathedral meant only for God may perhaps be reached by diagrams. I didn't tell Dag I meant to pay a visit to Chartres. When I said on the way up from Marseilles and the car-ferry that he could drop me in Paris, he merely named a hotel I should stay at, he didn't register surprise. In Paris he offered to wait until my affairs were completed, but I reminded him of Alba's false labor. He left me at a small hotel near the Odéon Métro. He went on to Dieppe. French roads in that area are to Paris what a system's electrical power is to a main "bus" or distribution terminal. I took an early train.

Dagger would be waking up in London.

I walked from the station.

I stood under a windowbox in my sturdy, shoe-backed English sandals and looked up at the western front.

Knowing the heights of the two so different spires, I reckoned as something under thirty meters the average distance between the taller sixteenth-century north (fine, decorated, obvious) and the twelfth-century south (a steeple strangely steep, a wizard's hat, also isosceles), though as I went closer and away from two women with knapsacks chattering about Americans who say *châtre·* (castrate) —this great flat-sided tower became octagonal.

Entering, I can't see for a moment. I peer to the left where they're selling pictures, and my eyes adjust.

Where are the things up high meant only for God toward which Will would hoist himself by means of his mother's behind bent at the open fridge? I'll get back my feeling for the Corsica footage. I have bought a guidebook and it is in my hand open to a title-page photo of a twelfth-century sculpture of Pythagoras writing. God knows what is on that Corsica footage. Mike having a long silent chat with the student who lent me the cassette recorder who I'm told (by the woman who identified the date palms) has a great deal of money in his own right. I will think about it when I get to London. Daylight stands beyond the crystal green hills and the still waters and the crudely outlined sometimes leaded heads of cartoon martyrs. I'm sure there's bearded Noah, and some craftsmen at the bottom and a wheel and much higher a rainbow and some man, and below the rainbow maybe Noah and his wife. I go east and south. Light slides past noon. I am between two groups and two languages. Is it a cloud passing, that for a moment invests with motion all the compartmented colors of a window like a sound wave made visible? I am in Chartres. Time is light. My son was here. A tear films my vision. There is a huddle of some kind to the west, and as I pass, an English guide grabs me. I am to give my hands, arms, shoulders—he's explaining Gothic vaulting—my arms are crossed, hands gripping other hands, I lean, I look away and over on the north side several yards away almost in shadow I catch the eye of a man with a moustache who looks like Dagger, and I grin but he turns away toward the photo and postcard place no doubt thinking this demonstration mad; I am part of the vault of our Lady the Virgin's mystic city, it is a surprise.

We should all breathe together, I say, and suddenly I want a cigarette.

And the guide, a good English schoolteacher type, parental, clear, brisk, interrupts himself to say to me, Good, good, yes indeed, that's the idea, one body co-laboring for the Lord.

This isn't London Bridge he's playing now. He's inside.

Now knees up he is hanging from the vault to show us how miraculously strong its structure is.

The man with the moustache looks out from behind one of the piers of the north tower as if he can't believe what we're doing, and in my semiconductive cartridge slung forward above New York on Sunday, October 31, that instant of cool cathedral twilight in July borne by some rhumb and random constancy in me from Corsica to England via Chartres yields almost those words said on Waterloo Bridge in Dagger's car receding from the National Film Theatre in March but instead not quite, for they are the words right after, which are (from Dagger) We'll use Claire, (from me) and Jenny too, (and then from Dag with a casualness that made his next words seem merely part of some larger harmony) They *look* alike (which I hadn't myself seen on meeting Claire the preceding fall, but saw now).

The vault broke up, pack it and send it air freight to Arizona, I found a cigarette, I saw the moustached man and called Hey and moved toward him to ask for a light, but he was out the door into the sun and as I reached for my matches and put my cigarette between my lips and caught sight above me again of the West Rose, an affable English voice said, Mustn't smoke in *here,* and I turned suddenly but the wrong way and saw not a red double-decker which could not have squeezed down the nave aisle between the flanks of folding chairs, but at the east end an intricate shine of color overpowering my ignorance of the tales told in all the compartments.

You see even now I can't be in that closet simply, but must flash-forward into some known future, for what do you think about when you're eavesdropping on someone's revelation of your daughter's body? I kept my cigarette in my mouth, sauntered to the north side to the cathedral shop to look at pictures. In Seward's day you could leave your daughter a little town house on Madison Park but there is no refuge in history; John Stephens may have given for the Maya city Copan, whose plunder Catherwood was to preserve in his drawings, twice what the Dutch paid for Manhattan, but twenty-four dollars was a lot of money and look at what the Dutch got fot it—real estate inflation—always depressing—and I look down over an area near City Hall Park and some warp of air or temperature from the overhead rotor makes the grid nine hundred feet below bulge slightly, the pilot is looking where I am looking, and I have more than one picture of the man who looked like Dagger in Chartres.

What picture? says John, and my hands are colder than the

steel I sit on in the closet I chose by mistake. I have missed nothing. But am I Tessa's Maya god Kokulcan who was exiled yet at once relanded and never really went away? Not quite.

My wife's, says the voice. I see her in a whole new way. The gallery was a mistake. I was measuring her with something she couldn't resist. I should have let her go. But instead I gave her presents.

Why did Incremona do this?

You don't want to know.

Why did she have nothing on?

She lives there half the time.

Why did the cops call *you*?

They found a letter from my secretary telling her to come in and clean out her desk. I got nothing against her. It's my brother-in-law.

John says, Can I use Mercer Street?

Incremona hangs out in that area.

But can I use Mercer Street?

Aut says he has to go.

John asks if Flint is doing anything on the real-time project, and did Aut contact U.K.?

Aut says he'll see John tomorrow.

A famous hotel is mentioned.

The last I hear as they recede is Aut: so what's the matter with your eyes? *You* didn't know Claire; you wear glasses, don't you?

Data from Chad and Nash tumbled into the absence of my lookout dream, and with them two contact lenses dropping in search of a soft slot and shimmering now between two Sarsen stones, for John in contacts had been the strange photographer, Aut's man at Stonehenge. Now if Jack planned to frame me for Claire's death and to do so not just with the lighter-stiletto but by means of my absence, how had I got away? I went from one closet to another closet of that detached room, I clipped my knuckles on a steel corner somewhere, I plunged down the service stairs.

In a cab up Tenth Avenue I was thrown forward and braced my hand against the back of the front seat next to the pivoting V-shaped fare-receptacle marked PLEASE PUSH and PAY HERE. The meter clucked, I found blood around the nail I'd ripped at Claire's and blood on my knuckles, and as if at some consequence I made a quick stop at a corner booth to phone the florist, and told Gilda I'd nearly been killed and in fact my head *was* killing me—she'd heard nothing more of Incremona. Then it was crosstown from red light to red light and to a news dealer with a gray fedora who could not see what his hat made me feel in my shoulders, that I'd left my expensive trench-coat behind—and who sold me a paper that had no news of the war.

I went through Sub's unmanned lobby and up to his empty apartment which had something to tell me but not in answer to what I wished to know of my daughter whom I might have been respon-sible for killing if she had been where I had thought she was, and now, assuming Claire had been improbably killed by Incremona who had set out to kill Jenny, what I wished to know was this: when the Frenchman had said, The Cartwright girl, and then Incremona had said, We got her—who was *we* and why hadn't Incremona known where to go?

And there was an emptiness here in Sub's place I could not put my finger on. It was an absence I might have believed was watch-ing me (to see, say, if I picked up Sub's phone before it stopped ringing). I was looking through it, and I left the living room and lifted the receiver and said Yes, and I felt an emptiness grin, except if I was looking through the emptiness the smile might be my own.

Can a god have a religious experience?

Can a god be isolated?

It was Jenny and she said thank god I was all right. She'd been told I would probably be killed if she didn't tell who else had installments of my diary. Sherman had found Incremona's copy at Mike's apartment and had thought the best thing was to liquidate it. Incremona had found out.

Crescendos of highway cars behind her were between us. I'm in Connecticut, she said.

I could not speak.

You who have me may put some construction other than clinical on my inability this Saturday, October 30, 1971, to speak to my daughter who was alive. I must warn her Incremona had missed once and wouldn't miss again. But that is what she now said to *me*. And because I could not bring out those or other or any words, she said nothing more, except to ask who this was.

The first thing Sub's wife Rose did when she moved out was get an answering service.

It had been more than probable that Incremona would go after Jenny. However, Claire, who looked like Jenny though wouldn't be taken for her by anyone who knew them both and had not been taken for her by Incremona because of looks, had improbably been hit *as* Jenny.

In part because of me.

But did I know why Incremona had gone after Jenny?

Incremona (who had stared at me as through a gap beyond which was his object) couldn't know that through the scene of Claire's killing, Aut had seen Jan in a whole new way. And as for Phil, she didn't know (what Jan just might) that that moment of insight had required me.

Was there a dream looking into my head while I was out cold in the closet? All I recall is emptiness but also way out across it like punctures in a dartboard words said in the red-and-purple room with the headlines on the carpet: You *know* when; we know that from Savvy—It was Chad's idea, man, but it came out of the group, man.

On the phone one may lose some sense of where places are. But I'd never even had June's address to lose, though it would have been as easy to find out as it was hard to stop her from saying as she did again and again that whatever the idea was and no matter what Nash said, it wasn't Chad's idea, it was Paul's, it must have been Paul's.

Hard to stop her—for this was said not quite direct to me but to Claire's answering service since it was Claire's number I automatically gave June when upon feeling the special pressure I applied she said she couldn't talk and I said call back at eight—I didn't want June to know I was at Sub's.

I may sit in a hired helicopter and see what was not quite there when I had the real chance at it. But by now I've lived through the thing.

From Savvy it had been learned that I knew *when*.

Yet how could he know this from me?

From Tessa maybe other things (she butted in between Dudley and Savvy and toyed with Savvy because she sensed his secret, that he wouldn't lay a hand on her), maybe other things. But not this.

I could not quite see why Jenny hadn't tried to save me when she could have. She knew where at least two other parts of the diary were, and could have mentioned one. Not the Bonfire, for even if those pages were still over in Brooklyn Heights, why jeopardize her grandparents (if they were home?). But why not mention Corsica? By now Savvy Van Ghent's dustman had probably carted it off.

My headache was gone but my neck was stiff.

I lit the pumpkin when I left Sub's at seven thirty.

When I came back later I blew it out. It scared me. I was by then no longer alone.

By then I knew when: but not till I'm in the chopper the next day Sunday noon swashing gracefully hither and yon do I see that what I finessed from June Saturday I could have known in Sub's twilight flat even before I lit the pumpkin and saw it on its window-sill against the dark slots of Manhattan and made out among cool dry American clouds what looked like a stretch of virgin white screen and was a close-up of one of the two big weather balloons Dagger gave my children that rose above Lorna's rage one Sunday years too soon for the Beaulieu to catch their flight and together floated toward the Heath. On page three of the *Times* by the light of Sub's TV and next to Webster's open at *mania, manhunt, man-hour, manhood,* and *manhole* is former Prime Minister Macmillan, old hound bags under the eyes, coated, scarved, moustached, an overexposure behind him which the caption identifies as a bonfire on the Dover cliffs set by the old Tory himself to mark Heath's Common Market victory in Parliament—old hound who knew the cause would overcome.

As far back as '65 Savvy had called it inevitable but said England wouldn't get in until it cost too much. But Savvy did not talk shop. He filed his dispatches and he lived his life. July 25, while batting, I heard his voice behind and below me saying, I hear I'm a star in your journal.

Dudley it seemed had mentioned the Softball Game when they ran into each other on Bastille Day at the British Museum, but I hadn't turned up to play last Sunday. (Still in France, said I—Sightseeing again, said he—How did you know? said I) and well, said Savvy, the diary sounded almost better than the film (I swung and missed) and was it for public consumption, said Savvy, hunkering down behind the plate again (but now dark hair and bluejeans, there was Lorna first time ever at a Sunday softball game come unexpectedly on her own having slept late, now fingering a shy wave from the third-base coaching box if there'd been one); oh I use all the help I can get, I said (and Ball! called Umpire Ismay, for Cosmo's bomb had risen high outside); I wouldn't presume to help, said the voice behind, but I wouldn't mind a peek at the next installment, and by the way how do you concentrate with that incredible creature giving you signals at third? (So blame it on Lorna's not wearing a bra that Cosmo now spun a drop-ball by me at the knees) but it's more than insurance, Bill, said the husky voice behind me, it keeps the record straight, makes the film open-ended, nothing like hearing someone tell it like it was in words—hey take your time. I signaled a change-up, said the voice below and behind (and Cosmo snapped furiously through but then at the last micro-second let up like some silent-comedy Jock calmly turning away into Jekyll), and the Air Force softball floated in and a slot was open I'd thought was closed and I hit that change-up with a waiting rhythm thanks to Savvy's warning and felt the ball soften at the meat end of the bat and by the time I was rounding first it was just coming down over the left-fielder's head and I wound up with a triple and a pat on the ass from Lorna and in the next fortnight Savvy who in what he'd said about open ends had touched a pulse connecting my knees and shoulders, fingers and head to a body of salt water where my heartbeat had once enlarged, dispersed, then vanished into the co-labor of other organs, received in his voluminous mail a Corsican Montage which I now at the end of October see through (past bits of a power station on the east side of the island blown up like burnt strips of Aut film)—through a hired face-mask to a far open end where immigrant sandhogs brave the bends to build the Brooklyn Bridge, and where beautiful Mary's Montrose heart draws forth from my cuckolded Swiss Cottage swimming friend doubt about the Faeroes but fact that that matchless Scot had Germans among his water-borne troops—(for by a method Andsworth would judge well short of telepathic) the mind that made that Corsican Montage was secretly admitting further forces which the fine-printed channels of a daughter-typist's finger-pads might pick up even more truly at a hundred words a minute where love may now be sheer energy of attention and the person typing knows in some new unbroken instinct the person typed. And so at half past seven I opened Sub's door to go, and there was Gilda with some pale streaks through her hair saying she almost had not answered the phone because they were closing when I phoned, and she shouldn't have come—and I kissed her and she touched my ear and said there was blood, and I took her with me. For, amid my fruitless survey of Savvy—his barbells, his parties, his lack of response to Corsican Montage (except to say he liked the diving), his flying lessons, his soft hand-made low boots, his drunken fag nephew who came to London for the theater once a year and was Savvy's only connection with his own family, did I know Savvy any better than I knew Gilda?—a desperate though mechanical and trivial problem had struck me as I put my hand to the knob, and Gilda was the answer.

Such a hand, she says, a hand like a face!—but think of

Savvy's horny hand spearing Cosmo's high outside bomb saving the wild pitch with a bare-fingered stab, for why did he say *sightseeing*? because he knew the man who looked like Dagger under the street lamp who came with Cosmo to deliver the carton but stayed outside? the man who shadowed me at Chartres?—such a hand! my God what a hand! she says again (and I put mine on her), it was like he would crunch the cash register like a beer can, such a hand (mine jumps an inch, for this is another bad cab, we're all over the road, coming apart at every crossing, plenty of time, bullet-proof plastic divider completely plastered with notices in more than one language, some nearby religion its address lost in the shadows but its theme as clear as the formula I'd barely mined in Monty's presence—You will not have both power and the understanding of it)—*Estamos temprano* I call from our compartment but he accelerates so there seems still more time for Gilda to speak of Incremona's hand which she says is like a face and I say they're planning new very thin beer cans that squeeze like foil; while I'm thinking around Savvy and getting no answer, and I should find a neutral corner on a flight to London but I'm increasing the improbability of a system at whose increasingly empty heart I am by being too well dressed for the service entrance twenty-five yards west of Claire's gray awning and dressed too evidently for outdoors to be Claire's next-door neighbors we'd pose as, if a cop answered Claire's buzzer and I am too probably wanted in Claire's death to be softly with a valid key letting myself into her dogless flat together with a woman I know only through a stabbing I don't understand who must wait a plausible number of rings (for June knows about answering services) but not so many that Claire's own service picks up—and a woman whose breath I've just breathed who laughs a familiar laugh and says the dog's been playing with the Sunday *Times* and whose shoulders I incredibly could make time now to undress (even as I note on the *Times* a letter whose letterhead U.K. means Universal Kinetic—the film distributor) and who says to my fingertip on her hip where her hip extends from her waist to meet her green flowered raincoat, There isn't time, just as Claire's phone goes fifteen minutes early and as I turn the other way Gilda recedes into the bedroom and the name of parents who never fought in front of Claire because they never fought—or never fair—and left the blood to be shed by her from her own thirteen-year-old womb without warning when Dagger brought her back to Philadelphia from a day at the races and a night in Freehold's American Hotel to a home that in her absence had at last been broken, and a living room that had

504

always seemed large, and she sent Dagger (uncle or cousin or what-ever he was) a pair of slippers for his birthday which never got forwarded to him and a year later asked him in person never to tell her mother about the onyx elephant from the gift shop in Freehold, unlike the red Mexican jaguar which she broke her promise and told Monty her fond employer Phil Aut had asked her to secretly pass on to DiGorro for Jan, which I did not know at the moment Gilda hung up in the bedroom and I in the living room pocketed the cloisonné cross and left the living room.

Was Claire—unlike Gilda—wearing lipstick when Incremona killed her? I can't ask Monty, for on Sub's phone answered first by Gilda at dawn Sunday, Monty sounds blind except that the eyes staring at a wall in his King Street house do not know what even to imagine out of the zero that has been inserted behind those eyes, and as if from that absence of pulse I find an idea which he assents to—he knows a man on the west river—easy enough to rent a chopper on a Sunday but do it through Monty, when did I want it?—I had not even thought until his call came, I had been asleep in Sub's bed my skin on someone's hair—Monty will phone, will phone—nor can I ask if Claire had on *no* lipstick—I look 900 feet down hours later from a hired crow's nest and June's frantic words said to Claire's late answering service come to me in Gilda's voice in a delayed trans-lation: Leave Chad out of it, it wasn't his idea it couldn't have been, you said you know where and when but not who, only that it's Chad's idea. But I don't even know the idea but it's not my brother's please believe me it isn't Chad, for Christ's sake it takes a sick mind to blow up a bunch of children Halloween morning—and something makes the surface of Manhattan bulge and instead of the green which city or barren land or industrial area shows up in an infrared aerial photograph there is a blue of Claire's lips snapped directly without box or emulsion into me like thought.

Whose open end betrays across the East River Brooklyn Heights where trees soften the edge of the promenade below which cars flash softly along that stretch of the Belt Parkway; the St. George Hotel sticks up; I know where there is a wood-frame house, and on the top step of its stoop I tried my tongue upon the corner of Renée's closed mouth and when she at once turned her head my tongue-tip ran all along the fold where her lips met until my mouth was in her russet hair which we found we liked and under the angled light from the street lamp the russet took on a less soft sheen though hardly that hot San Francisco copper I have made so much of somewhere here—her parents' house not original New Amsterdam though like it, as the Dutch wood-framing was like the New England and the New England like the Virginian, itself a recollection of Tudor half-timbering—but what those great brick-layers the Dutch thought up was stone masonry construction, first rubble laid in straw-bound clay but ultimately oyster-shell-mortared stone-block walls which with wood-framing inside came to be your common combination in taverns and warehouses; and I know if I can't quite see where there are a hundred stoops, I know one near my parents' old apartment house where we played stoop ball which was in those days a matter of angles (unlike London where in any case they don't play stoop ball) but now is a matter of wide cars oncoming between parked cars like a transistor's printed circuit. The kids, said Gilda, as we listened in Claire's foyer and heard steps in the hall and now the phone again, you won't let anybody blow up some kids.

Alba's false labor was false. Why did we leave Corsica when we did? Not because she phoned, because she didn't phone. But why in the first place did Dagger change his mind again and go?

Have I asked that before?

In the long cozy trench of English life I say that the tortoise has come back and Lorna who has got into the habit of not hearing says, What? and I (as they say in the military) say again; but the next day when I say the man from the County Council is coming about the tortoise and Lorna says What? in a servo-circuit which threatens to loop until Doom's Day, I interest myself by saying the County Council man's coming about the grass, which exits me even excites me out of that forlorn loop—a service to us both.

LIBERTY, the '68 poster said in another language, IS THE CRIME WHICH CONTAINS ALL OTHER CRIMES.

I was at liberty, a framed killer of Claire, but only so long (Aut said) as I stayed lost. But how could he call me "someone" and say "lost" if he knew I was collapsed right there in a closet?

What are you doing, said Gilda, for I had sprung into Claire's room, fallen across her bed and speared the phone on the eighth or ninth ring.

June sounded farther away now than the message Gilda had related.

Did I have the news?

Tragic, I said.

Had I been at Claire's long?

Two minutes, still out of breath, just long enough (I said) to call the answering service and find out its log was impounded, so it was lucky I hadn't missed June.

Oh. Did I know their name? the answering service?

I knew where, I knew when, but I didn't know who (remember?)—only that it was Chad's plan.

Oh. Yes.

Gilda snuggled her ear in, but for a moment there was nothing to hear; then June asked for the name of the answering service and I said *quid pro quo*—and I heard nothing, not a breath. I pointed to the bed-table drawer and Gilda moved over and pulled it out so she didn't hear June say with a matter-of-factness that was not like her: It's tonight.

But I know that, I said without thinking, at least I figured it out before your brother or someone hit me on the head. But I want to know *who*.

June got nice. She pleaded. She honestly didn't *know* who.

You could say for her that she loved her brother.

I looked in the bed-table drawer and saw the name of the service. I gave it to June, she gave me the time, I said I was going to be held up downtown just south of the warehouse till nine thirty and tonight was in fact more convenient for me. I hung up.

What am I doing here? said Gilda when I blew out Tris and Ruby's jack-o'-lantern. A light moved one-way between two dark towers and it was a helicopter or a plane. Former Prime Minister Macmillan was on Rose's indestructible acrylic-fiber carpet which by the light from the new solid-state TV which came on at once and which I hadn't reimbursed Sub for had changed color from what I recalled as orange and magenta.

George Washington Carver and me—peanuts and peat, for Christ's sake. I lit a cigarette.

She touched me and I spoke to her. All these things I knew that others didn't. Gene in effect lied about the Marvelous Country House letting Jack think it didn't figure on the film. Aut's so-called man who Claire told Jack had shot the Bonfire was really Dagger. Gene let Jack believe the portfolio on Paul's table was Jan's. Gene did not dispute Jack's assertion that Jan had been at the hut with Paul just before Gene and Jack had come. My eyes caught smoke as if this were my first cigarette and I touched Gilda and I wondered where Aut and John as Aut had said were meeting tomorrow. But all these things I knew that others didn't left me feeling like a rat whose brain has been somato-mapped so you can predict which cells will show electrical response when a given limb is stroked.

Hair-thin pages of mica flipping now fast as Will's hand-made movie—

Digital mosaic compounded through liquid crystal techniques but impounded from me—

So what good was what I knew?

She said and was still saying the next day 900 feet high above Manhattan (but by then only in her mind), I think you have to go to the end, I think there is an end.

Too high to see Incremona inflating with mad rage, say, his own taxi Paul left to be towed off. A yellow taxi balloons between buildings, squeezes out into the air.

Something is about to happen. Is there an anti-Lenin demonstration? From here I could never see into the Ukrainian neighborhood north and far east of where I watch—and just south of that ancient and dilapidated and only theoretically open-ended street of chipped stone and greasy fire escapes and chilly mattresses and busted glass where that junkie you remember having (through me) not met, hides in the fourth-floor toilet to count the stolen wallet's cash he doesn't know is hot.

Something else is making Manhattan bulge.

It probably isn't the Flint warehouse. This turns out to be a grab-bag full of things left over or waiting—surplus acupuncture models; surplus science treasure chests with magnets, one-way mirrors, materials for many experiments a ten- or twelve-year-old can do; 25-foot surplus weather balloons (for holding up swimming-pool covers, facilitating aerial photography, marking scuba divers' descents); a dry-chem component of a surplus experimental liquid fertilizer destined for Cambodia; thousands of rounds from a Minnesota cartridge firm now lobbying to weaken the '68 gun control law; and to plug the ears, cartons and cartons of Swedish Wool made of glass down best for frequencies of 2000 to 4000 cycles per second. Don't forget also surplus Science Fair projects, geodesic dome kits, Digital Counter Kit with integrated circuits, and water that goes uphill.

Where are the armored vests found by the forces in Vietnam to be defective? Are there any left? Or the 40,000 emergency artificial respirators sold in the U.S. though known to be badly designed and ineffective?

Don't forget also acres of thin plastic sheets that change color

508

because of the liquid crystals inside them but compared to other liquid crystal displays will have uses far more sophisticated (to use a term from weaponry, confides the man himself, J. K. Flint, approaching a flagon of Scotch during an encounter so fatally fortuitous Saturday night very late that now these five moments of October 30 and 31 turn slowly at different speeds in an equilibrium more spatial than genuine: attempted ambush earlier Saturday night; attempted helicopter-watch Sunday afternoon; the bombing of Incremona Sunday at twilight; the eye of all this terminal action Sunday morning, and the midnight chat with Jack Saturday). I said we had talked about women and the Hebrides and my various accents, and speaking of liquid crystals Jack must know that our old associate Red Whitehead would shift his ground at the drop of a toy bomb and kept his mouth shut only at home watching color TV (though it wasn't, said Jack, just the TV that shut him up at home and he might be *my* associate but he wasn't *his*), and (I got up, I went on, I could capitalize on what lay behind the affability) I couldn't trust anything now except cash, I said, Dagger had set me up never guessing what *I* wanted out of the carton in Claire's closet of which I could make interesting use, though what I really hoped to get into was the digital mosaic capability with John who had the real-time-projection ideas (mind through machine direct, though he was getting a bit irritated at delays) while I had as Jack knew a certain commercial acquaintance with plasma crystals, as I suspected so did Jack (who now again grinned affably saying Commute from London but my only tie with Whitehead was what Len got out of him about you and as I moved to the window-seat he leaned to take up the decanter again with the smooth coordination of an alumni fullback whom the pressures of domestic life have not kept from staying in shape), so since I said the footage showing the revolutionaries was just going to get in the way of my work with John whom I was going to see first thing tomorrow after he got through with Aut, the footage was for sale and—(and recalling some Yucatan or Hindu and in some way Māyā proverb about plunging ahead without too much thought if you're going to get what you didn't know you wanted) I slipped something in Jack's trenchcoat lying on the window-seat beside Sub's black navy mac and gray forties fedora, returned to put my glass on the desk in this hotel room and after he asked if first thing tomorrow meant Monday, for it was now past midnight and it was Sunday, I said, Twenty thousand cash tonight would almost do it.

Give Jack credit for madness, my God.

Almost! he laughed, and never spilled a drop of that old Scotch and pulled out the desk drawer and produced four green, white, and black stacks of hundreds.

He asked if I knew what Incremona was capable of if I didn't come across, and if I knew that Krish had not been found. I said I knew whose weapon Len had used on Claire and who Jack was framing which I didn't like at all, and this was the rest of the deal I'd meant by *Almost*.

I've got an *almost* too, he said, but don't tell me you know Wheeler (and for a moment Jack thought back but couldn't reach it, and was interrupted by me to hear the name of a New England college, one of the Little Three)—don't you worry about Wheeler, he said. What the police know and what they can do are two different things, but that depends on you.

Why don't you frame *me* for Claire, I said.

I like your style, he said.

Where's Wheeler—South America?

Jack gave a stiff smile in my general direction and then and there could have killed me if I could have vanished. Then he laughed. Then he laughed again.

Mexico of course, he said. You could have figured that out for yourself. Hunting jaguars bare-handed. Maybe he'll disappear.

Your *almost*?

The one remaining copy of the diary—arriving by mail from Callanish yesterday, tomorrow, immediately.

Jack did not know quite enough. And I leave it to you who have me to conclude that this one of the aforementioned five moments has its dreamlike features.

Like the strange collaborations early in the summer arising out of the London subway.

Like the liquid crystal warehouse elsewhere in this other city.

A warehouse not exactly central to the Flint enterprises but associated by multiple systems under the normal levels of commerce and product research which are coded not to make Manhattan bulge. What is that bulge seen from a hired chopper? Black kids move weightlessly from subway car to car. So do black men.

Although Incremona was given cause to think John-of-Coventry a private opportunist when Red Whitehead told him John had made inquiries, improbably Incremona won't act on these suspicions.

And whereas the diary is less and less likely to stay secret at

Callanish since the dilettante geologist (joined or not by Jack Flint a week ago) will probably spot it while seeking Krish, improbably this doesn't appear to happen.

The chopper pilot looks back at a middle-aged businessman and shrugs. We have circled, but I recall this only later, staring at a smashed pumpkin, seedy and moist upon Sub's sidewalk.

Wait for me, I said at eight thirty Saturday night to Gilda.

Not funny, she said, as if answering something insulated in my words.

After midnight Jack says It's who you know.

I'm to wait for a call tomorrow, I give Sub's number, no address; Jack has a car, a man gave him a left-over Opel unexpectedly yesterday, someone will pick up the carton tomorrow (wait for a call); a gift car? I say; oh that, says Jack—the warehouse janitor deserves it and will get it.

But twilight comes Sunday and still no call from Jack, yet no less risk to Ruby, Tris, and Sub whose new solid-state color TV with an unprecedented minimum of horizontal linearity I'm on the point of extracting four bills to reimburse the cost of, when the plug is yanked and the set is being lugged across the room and Tris is protesting and Ruby's *Daddy!* sounds a crystal clear reproof.

But Sunday morning at either empty end of the warehouse street in lower west Manhattan on the edge of a market area, there is no one, and no one in the empty lot opposite. But I turn, feeling a presence, and at the double door to the warehouse I check all axes: up the street, down; up to lenslike windows adjacent and diagonally across; up to a sky where a plane heads slowly into Kennedy; across to the cement lot and its alley invisible from here—then sense a change. It was probably behind the windshield of a parked car up the block. I put my hand on the knob of the warehouse door, the left one of the double doors, and then my case twitches and almost tugs and simultaneously there's a shot like a dry back-fire. And above me inside this warehouse a familiar man's voice uninterrupted by that shot that hit my case is telling children's voices something too broken up to be a story: they're working for him, it sounds like.

But at one on Sunday afternoon 900 feet up I seem to see out my window the pounding of a new tempo: it's as if my optic nerves through the new vacancy made by the absorption of my former heart into the co-laboring of all my other body parts are now tuned to that tiniest muscle that operates the stirrup bone in the middle ear's drum—itself a slot in the temporal bone guarding the inner ear's semicircular circuits that compute my balance—and so Lower Manhattan bulges, or bulges in some inflationary sign to me that weightlessness may make those canals come unplugged and Terminus the god of boundaries and property may be subject to Mercurial delusions because of insecurity arising from the fact that his post was created to take some of the work-load and even responsibility off Jupiter's back but the liquid stir of that city aggregate there below may be my post-Terminal sense that I'm at the center but overcommitted and underconnected. A plane makes its way above our new tempo and can it be we cannot go forth and back now?

But it was June not I who changed the time from Sunday morning to Saturday evening—whoever ordered her to, after that first explosion into my answering service's willing ear. June did not guess who Gilda was, and the forces at June's end did not see that I'd gladly settle for two times in place of one knowing that surviving the first, an ambush, I might be better covered to control the second, though surviving that first visit to the warehouse Saturday night I might risk seeming not to have come at all and so to be an even more vulnerably probable visitor on Sunday morning, the time June had originally divulged to Claire's supposed answering service.

What's happening to the helicopter? What would Philip do?

But the night before, I'm just in time to spot from my doorway two blocks north within range of music and talk emanating from a hole-in-the-wall theater where it's intermission time at a multimedia dance recital, two figures coming from the south who suddenly disappear.

When I get there it's not the Flint warehouse but one abutting it on my north side. I am early. A helicopter blinks by quite low, I can't see its skis (if it has them) or its silver side—only a red light—so Incremona would see it before it saw him.

The door is locked. This is not the door that was my destination. The Flint is the next one down. A car races in behind me from the direction of the theater and parks at the Flint doorway and the man who bursts out of the back seat is Chad, and a man with Gene's voice steps out looking over the car roof across the street. Both disappear into the Flint doorway but I hear only a murmur inside my own door and the car moves off, makes a U-turn, and parks across the street and fifty yards to the south and I can't see who the two in the front seat are but though they drop down now, I think they could have seen the movement of my hat sharp gray in the extreme north corner of the wide old doorway—the dark is shadowed on the sidewalk and street by light only from the theater just round the corner two blocks north and from the south one of the experimental anti-mugging street lamps that with their dayglow have forced or persuaded certain trees in residential areas to drop their leaves in July or betray no signs even of color-turn by mid-October. My voices are now nearer but no louder, but Chad says, Nothing, so he and Gene have not gone inside the Flint warehouse and I wonder if Gene would have a key. My hair is light, but I take off Sub's hat and hold it behind me. My voices are even nearer but not louder and the south half of the great steel double-door creaks inward and the voice of Jack Flint says, Just between you and me it's going to be an interesting bit of work in its own right, money's secondary of course. The other, a high foreign maybe Scandinavian voice says, You've had experience, have you, Mr. Flint? and Jack says Oh enough to manage one of those things, and listen: Thanks. And the other voice says OK Mr. Flint, any time. And suddenly Jack's broad back is to me, the peajacket and glimmering white construction worker's hard-hat, and as he turns he seems to have on goggles. He crosses into the lot and is gone. There is more talk in the next doorway. Nothing to do with us, Chad says, but Gene's reply is lost, except the word *newspaper*, but Chad says, Who was he going to pass it to? and Gene says Jan and some other words, and Chad says I guarantee it's your brother. And presently steps from inside bear down on my door and a man with a flashlight that is turned off as he emerges walks south right past the Flint doorway. I extend a foot but my door has already closed. I wish I knew what to do. Time of some kind passes.

And then a long way away I feel the uneven grain of familiar steps, closing fast yet slow; there is no one in the street, the steps are inside and my door is about to open and the steps are those of the person who pushed me down the escalator but I already know, and what matters is that I not be seen and that I catch the door. In the middle of the street far down, the Scandinavian cups his hands to his face. My door is opening bit by bit and if I'm not seen it's a miracle. But the car starts up and without lights pulls on up past me. It makes a U-turn and comes on back and keeps going, and when it turns out of the street at the south corner where the Scandinavian janitor is turning, my door opens.

And in the lookout dream that I once thought I must, by design, dream I am in motion across Ned Noble's sunny sick room and its threshold, his mother behind me fixed in a chair, his father before me with a sitting alcove and a window behind him and on either side of him the corridor opening like oversized arms toward either end of the floor, and he's waiting for me to tell him something about his son he doesn't know—that Ned will live, for instance—and I am about to ask again about the time machine and crystal set but know tonight as I enter the warehouse next door to the Flint and hear the door crank closed that that bequest of nothing from Ned Noble (a terminal miser as if those mere possibilities, which is all they were, were chance transistors that might by some unknown system shunt the cancer messages out of him like waste) was really what I wanted—yes wanted—looking down either end of the hospital hall to recall where the elevators were but knowing I must speak to Mr. Noble, and even asking if he'd been to the beach (he looked so tan), upon which he said he was just buying a place on the Jersey shore at a very good price—but Manhattan's bulge lets go a flash of light as if in some coordinate ignition with the new broken beat of the chopper blades which shakes us as if the cabin hangs on the tip end of a blade, and elsewhere on the circuit of revolution a peajacket is slung over the TV though the other item of Jack's costume, the white hard-hat, is not in evidence for Jack would probably not wear it into this hotel, and elsewhere in this flat map of times is the hole in my case, a bullet hole not big enough to leak paper money I'm safeguarding against a search of Sub's while I'm gone and still elsewhere is Sub's fury bearing the new TV across the room and as it reaches the sill my hands get under it, Tris grabs the rotating base of the aerial, Sub, Tris, and I collaborate, and Jerry (whom the last figments of flexibility in the helicopter enable me to say I am to see twice more—Sunday morning at the warehouse and Sunday noon watching me lift off the helipad) darts forth now Saturday night turning south toward the street lamp where the car he heard has just turned, and before I quite know it I've moved to block the door from latching shut.

But what does Gilda want?

And what will she want at dawn Sunday passing me the phone with Monty on it who with a strange dead mechanical energy says he wants to arrange the helicopter I'm asking about out of my sleep, for though I don't say so to him I hardly know why I'll need it later in the day.

But if he thinks I made probable Claire's death in this system that so many think I engineer, did he arrange to have our swash-plate loosened?

We can go only down and forward, it feels, but not fast-forward any more, and can a god evolve?

Lorna speaks her Zen koan out of earshot, Tessa calls me heartless but that is in the future and all the open ends I might use to escape some other sequence come so near telling me something I seem once to have known that I gladly take that sequence down to earth.

Though not below all there is.

Not below Gilda's digital manipulation: of my hair, my ear, my fingers.

Nor what followed the crank of the door (whose lock Jerry had picked) and his familiar slow-fast heterodyne tread dissolving as he now from what I could hear sprinted for the corner, but nothing followed him but Chad saying *That* wasn't him.

The steps that had proved to be Jack and his Scandinavian employee had been descending, so I would take the stairs, yet I felt here on the first floor a great space.

There was no watchman. That was him, the Scandinavian. More a janitor. The car had turned that corner just as he did. I was the reason the car was here, perhaps why Jack too, therefore probably the janitor.

Who had what to watch? A great area of floorboards.

Would Chad and Gene have heard the last creak of the door and thought it came not soon enough after Jerry's exit? What if they thought I hadn't come? What had happened in the red-and-blue room came back gradually but not a bit of what was in my head while unconscious. Chad had said it would be strange if I was both with Jack and in the original plan.

I heard nothing. The south wall was bare brick. I tripped over a stool and then another.

The car came back and stopped and I went to the window. I could see no one in the car. Chad and Gene had been in front of that other door to the Flint warehouse designated as the place.

I moved my ear slowly along the south wall toward the rear or west and then there was a hole just below eye level. A square. There was no sound in it. I put my hand in, and I kicked over what felt like a chair.

I picked up a tripod. I put my hand in the hole again. There was a square metal housing inside with a square cap. I raised the latch and the cap opened out and there was an oblong tunnel maybe eighteen inches long I couldn't get my hand through. I felt the top of the tripod. It was a big one.

On my hands and knees I felt around and along the wall and

there was a case maybe a foot and a half by two feet which I snapped open.

I lit a match and wanted a cigarette.

An oblong camera lay packed with some accessories, in compartments. It was a videotape camera. My head contracted on the left side where the blood had been. If I was still lying in a Glasgow hotel preparing my lookout dream, where was a skeletal building in process of going up? Instead, this turn-of-the-century warehouse complete, and across the way the lot, empty.

What did I look like from that other Flint warehouse through this hole? What would I be doing there?

Through a third-floor window I saw a pale movement under the car windshield. I went over to the south wall and moved my ear along the cool rock.

Halfway west there was a square hole again and the square housing and the cap and a stool and a tripod I didn't kick over this time, but no case.

The car started and I went back to the east wall to see it move up toward the theater. The case was under the next window.

On the fourth floor I found what I foresaw.

On the second, third, and top floors, then, Jack had the means of shooting what went on in the next building, or for that matter in the street. In Paul's hut in the Hebrides, Jack had mentioned one warehouse.

I couldn't see the roof. At each window on my way down I checked the street. I waited at the second floor, and the car came by twice from south to north, and a third time parked, then moved off.

It was eleven thirty. The car had gone north. I'd have to go that way probably, for if I went south I'd pass Chad and Gene in the doorway. I saw Jenny's abdomen spread-eagled spinning on Reid's dome with someone else at the controls.

At the ground floor with my hand on the door knob I let go as if by instinct; I called out over different distances: Take the roof! Claire! Jack! (I opened the door a crack.) She was killed by more than Incremona. What Len doesn't know can hurt us. (I let the door close.) Incremona! Cops! No no no. (I opened the door.) Jack can't frame me: he needs me. Get finished fast and leave by the roof, ten to one they'll send a squad car. No!—(I closed the door. Then I opened it.) OK. Good luck tomorrow. You're on your own. See you in London.

But struck in the corners of my eyes by two figures on my

right out on the sidewalk not in the recessed doorway and on my left up near the theater corner by headlights swinging round, I looked neither way but without knowing where I was going hastened like Jack Flint in his peajacket and white helmet into the depths of the dark lot directly across the street and found a moment later that I had disappeared.

We meet again, said Jack Flint holding out his hand, but at my touch he seemed to reach back for something he couldn't quite find. And when we shook hands on my departure forty-five minutes later, same thing—but by then there was more for Jack to reach back *with*.

By then I had his Scotch in my system and twenty thousand dollars in Sub's pockets and mine, and Jack didn't know he had Claire's cloisonné cross left by my unaccountable impulse in his raincoat on the window-seat, and both of us had new information.

I had said my head ached but (I said) whether from the whiskey or the shot his brother's crowd had given me I wasn't sure, and Jack had said, Which brother, the good one or the bad one? and I had said, Maybe neither. That's the one thing I don't know.

That, and one other thing, I went on: since red was Jack's favorite color—the jaguar, the plane—had Jack in fact given that dilettante geologist the red car that he was tooling around the Hebrides in?

To which Jack replied, He's got money. But it was easier to buy his services than for Aut to please his own wife. And that was the exact thing she didn't even know she wanted so much, even more than dashing up to Clisham to protect my little brother.

But was it so easy to buy the geologist's services? I said, and wondered again as I looked at the peajacket on the hotel TV why Jack had needed the disguise, and I didn't understand the money I was taking with me, I had to reach closer; and I said as for reimbursement Paul would never have approved of the geologist taking Krish's lighter, if he was lucky the crofter widow didn't see his car; and Jack said, she couldn't have seen what was in it but it wasn't there for long and isn't it like you to take the lighter which was useful and leave the body; but when I said What body? *You* didn't see it, Jack shot back at me Just goes to show how efficiently your dilettante geologist served me—and if I was under the illusion his brother commanded undying loyalties etcetera, that guy was on his way to Chile; and when I said did he mean his brother, he said no, the dilettante geologist as I called him—and by the way I was funny; but Jack's square-boned face that resembled some police photographer's reconstruction had a haggard tuck around the mouth and there was deep and genuine anger in his throat—so I asked if the d.g. knew Gene, and Jack said, See you tomorrow, Cartwright, and I said, Is Wheeler really out of it, and Jack couldn't quite let me go and it wasn't the twenty grand and he said, So you and Wheeler went to college together—well, he had a checkered career, that was the other reason we picked him, and Jack at once (so I didn't believe him) added, Actually I never met Wheeler.

So I said, Like the geologist never met Gene.

Jack reached at me and instead put a hand on my shoulder: *You* know who your geologist was under the spell of, Cartwright, you must surely have found that out, for God's sake.

I reached out for what I was supposed to possess, and turning away into the long carpeted hotel hall said without any question in my voice, But the spell is over, eh Jack?

The strong hand like a steel automaton pinched my bicep and I felt it in my heel, and I smelled the greater alcohol on Jack's breath as he said, Oh the time's they are a changin', man, and Christ it's *about* time.

So turning upon our separate axes Jack and I had met for a moment, and I had to get away in part to think how he'd known Wheeler and I went to the same college, and I said over my shoulder that I was still suffering from jet lag, or maybe the bang on the head, and I wished I'd had one of those construction worker's hard-hats.

When I let myself into Sub's apartment the jack-o'-lantern was burning again, and Gilda was reading. Sub had phoned to ask me to get eggs, milk, and bread, because they'd all be back in the apartment tomorrow; and did I want to get arrested?—a friend had mentioned a peaceful occupation scheduled to take place tomorrow at a base in New Jersey, a bus was leaving Manhattan at 10 A.M. Someone had phoned and hung up—the usual, this time of night. Well, on the way back from Claire's we had already bought all that Sub would want and Gilda had told him exactly what we'd bought, and it sounded as if they'd had quite a pleasant conversation.

Gilda put her novel down.

Later a loop rang all around me and I was not really dreaming of Monty in color on top of an affectionate pastel Claire; I woke to black and white shades of someone else's skin and hair which moved, and then Gilda was speaking far away and said Graf? but I was trying to deliver a speech on my American trip in the Highgate Literary and Scientific Institution Reading Room while at the same time trying to pull some tight-folded old collector's-item newspapers out from under the arms of Incremona for I wished to have in my conclusion some headline violence I knew was there; and to a group of old parties on folding chairs, one of whom had on the greasy old mac that had inspired Lorna to make me go buy a new trenchcoat, I was saying, We are in the grip of forces—but also of their absence, and I tried to make Paul Flint appear, but an empty London cab rolled up with a motor like an outboard and then Gilda handed me a smooth warm phone and I was not in bed but hiring a helicopter, at least through Monty the middleman, and as an afterthought asking how well and from whom he had known my old college acquaintance Wheeler, and Monty could only say I'm so tired, so very tired, but he roused himself to answer (what I hadn't asked) that Claire had known nothing and that he had known only that Wheeler had wanted out, whatever he was in, and had been following me at the time of the stabbing and had dropped out of sight.

I had gone too far with Monty.

The more I make the revolution, the more I want to make love.

Later Gilda and I had breakfast.

She borrowed the novel.

So what was with the suitcase, she said, where was I staying tonight?

I said I didn't know.

The Sunday streets were solemn and poignant. You could think of slave-catcher Clare—for that was his name—arriving quietly on horseback, hiring a carriage and making arrangements, then kidnapping James Hamlet to Baltimore, there to become (according to my son's research) the property of one Mary Brown. You could hear lone roaming cabs rattle the manhole covers. It was a pleasure to see a long way. I dropped Gilda at her subway and she made me wait and bought two copies of the only paper sold at the newsstand and shoved one through the window onto my case which I had put on my knees when she got out.

And fifteen minutes later I left that paper wrapped in its funnies in the cab untouched.

I went toward the warehouse from the east through the alley that ended in the lot. There were four cars parked along the old street, one a VW microbus—no Opel.

I looked straight at the left-hand warehouse as I went. There came a glint above and to the right, in a window of the right-hand warehouse where I'd been last night.

A change occurred as I set foot on the west sidewalk. It

seemed to be in the late-model Ford parked down the block which looked like last night's car. My hand was on the knob of the left-side door of the double-doors of the warehouse that I'd had only described to me by J. K. Flint, and then my case twitched as if someone had kicked it, and as if by coincidence a dry back-fire like a shot acted through my shoulder and arm to yank the door open and I was inside, and far above me John-of-the-loft called to the voices of children, and there was a second adult voice, and it was Aut's.

I silently climbed the first flight, and John was saying into an acoustic slot I shared, OK when I say Action, really bend it, OK? then lay it on the table and talk into Mr. Aut's mike, and then when he nods, light your match and talk into the mike again.

Experiments were being filmed. This one was low-density Nitinol, a spin-off alloy from NASA advertised now to hobbyists as "Metal with a Memory." No one had reopened the front door below me. At the head of the stairs I saw the vast second floor, and crouched. There were stacks of cartons, aisles of shelves, detachments of great paperboard cylinders.

Somewhere below me the ground-floor door was opening and I slipped down between two four-by-four boxes made of some tough gray composition material. I listened to more instruction and to a light, low child's voice.

Steps were coming up. Did Brunel apply engineering principles to delicate situations at home? The Clifton bridge was over-designed. There was a new shuffle of steps above me and I thought the filming must be not there but on the fourth floor. The steps overhead moved across from south to north, and then I knew the other person climbing from the ground floor had arrived and was with me here on the second floor—but hidden where I was I saw only across to the north wall.

I was unarmed.

I wasn't thinking.

OK, sweetheart, called John, have your scissors handy so you can cut the flow after you show what it can do, right?

Hello? called John, and there was silence except for a child.

Then there was more talk and Action! and a girl's voice was clearly though with indefinite loudness (but with my help since I knew the product) telling how what she put in the glass of water was an antigravity additive that had such a long molecular structure it reduced friction and the water would now . . . flow . . . uphill!

There was a silence and after a time John was asking a boy to tell how his dad had once made one of these (and here I found myself witnessing such an improbable coincidence I reached back for an old but unused, even surplus, hypothesis perhaps as Jack last night had in his own way tried to put his finger on something I'd said that in fact would have told him that earlier last night I'd seen him here, or—to be precise—in the next warehouse, or coming out of it) and John said explain how the high-Ω tuning coil worked and the variable condenser and germanium diode and then play your station, man, play it right into Mr. Aut's mike. (For this must be a kit-facsimile of the old crystal receiver that Red was trying to get because he said it would sell in England.)

But a soft pop was heard now. Then rapid steps. Then John from beyond the steps called Hello? and the presence that had been near me moved and I looked out from behind a box and Nash with stubble merging with a bruise turned away then and had his back to me and said Jesus! and Incremona in a beret plunged the last half-flight to the second floor three-at-a-time, and he knocked Nash down in passing and ran into my big room with a long pistol. He had on the hooded olive-green parka I'd bought in Glasgow ten days ago, his pistol was longer but I couldn't see if there was white; he squeezed and darted along the wall as if there were someone else here that he was hiding from, and then there was.

For Incremona clambered between two cylinders along the north wall and shoved the pistol into a hole in the bricks, an oblong hole in the bricks that was wider than it looked which I'd been staring toward without recalling the old hypothesis I'd posed but neglected and was on the point once more of not remembering, and there was a pronounced pop like what I'd heard above and Nash and I stared at each other for a moment whose miraculous length Ned Noble would not have scoffed at and during which I wondered what the one question was that Jan wanted to ask the black revolutionary woman Erika Huggins—and Incremona knocked Nash down and made off down the stairs and Nash got up and plunged after him calling, He didn't do it, did *you* do it?

Upstairs John said, What happened to Flint?

Must of had a hard night, said the other voice.

I risked time and ran to the windows on the east side, but Incremona was not waiting for me.

What had they thought I might be going to do here, and why had Jack wanted to film the children's science filming secretly?

Nash was down on the right in the middle of the street

looking north, and Incremona was running up toward the theater corner; then Nash was running to the Ford and I made out the Frenchman's hair, Chad's face, and someone else. And I was as sure Incremona had meant to kill Jack as I was that Jack had been possessed by the deepest hatred of his younger brother Paul who was not here. John called Hello?

The work resumed upstairs.

I was on the sidewalk. I crossed and paused. Nash at the driver's window looked as if he was giving directions.

The front door on the other side of the car opened but no one got out; Nash set off toward me and I ran west across the lot and into the alley. Then around its first sharp turning I waited to hear how many feet came after me. I set my case down, and I wondered if a bullet hole through a pack of hundreds inside my case would be easier to trace than a finger-mark on a busted aerial.

The steps were light enough not to be the Frenchman.

My pursuer veered right and with both hands I grabbed his right arm and used his momentum to swing him out against the wall, and it was Nash.

He was on the ground under my knee, his eyes were choked, and when I demanded to know who had fired at me his nose began to bleed, and he said no it was the suitcase, the suitcase. And when I said what about the suitcase, I was told by this now receding figure whose colored rings might have done me damage if he'd tried to hit me but whom my own madness might cure of his loose tongue, that they had thought I might hit the Flint warehouse, they didn't know who I was working for, Chad had shot at the suitcase.

I couldn't hold Nash. But it was not his strength. He receded.

Len let you down, I said.

Krish sold his boss old information.

I didn't know if Nash was armed. I slapped him, it didn't seem to matter, increased deep in his being a certain resigned determination to get away.

Was that Chad's gun Len had?

Nash mustered last-ditch contempt: You don't fit a silencer onto a recoil.

What little he then said I took with me. We ran in opposite directions.

I had to talk to John. Nothing to save a soul. But a proposition.

I was in a helicopter level with the tops of buildings.

522

I was nothing.

A godlike thought.

What had I lived through?

Would Incremona liquidate me if I didn't keep after him? But it had been Wheeler Jack planned to frame, not me; and they had let me get out of that closet—maybe because they thought I wouldn't leave without my trenchcoat.

Back through the vacuum of unremembered lookout dreams in a closet near a display console, I recalled the red-and-blue room, a paper on the carpet, Mike's voice just before or after I got slugged saying of Incremona, He's going to blow up a few police tow trucks, and saying it with a quiet scorn that I heard the more clearly for seeing it in Corsica, it was like his scorn for Paul's pastoral archaeology that had led to some dumb mysticism of distances and muscle enslaved in a pre-proletarian dream of big stones dragged from here to there, and the night Nielsen was killed at Stonehenge there were those who might have killed Paul Flint not just because of Jim's renegade devotion to Paul nor for what Paul knew about them all or a plan of theirs he'd helped to put in Chad's head which was about to be called off (and which two months later they had begun to think a London-based American who'd come almost out of nowhere or out of some film was going to pursue on his own) but might have wished to kill Paul on account of what he'd given and then disowned for reasons more numerous than some formula that real revolution in America was as unlikely through violence as it was just plain unlikely.

But here was I with strange detachment recalling my daughter who would do whatever she was going to do; here was I pondering Minuit's famous payment to the savages of Manhattan (*menahanwi*, isolated thing in the water, in Sub's Webster), pondering Stephens' fifty-dollar Maya city his gifted English friend Catherwood was to draw wearing a hat like the broad-brimmed high-crowned affair with a buckle Ned doodled on a cloth at Fraunces Tavern down to my right, and a logo not Ned's, not wholly mine, I scrawled for myself alone on a scrap torn off a newspaper in a red-and-blue room— pondering real estate inflation only suddenly to see as if evoked by me Manhattan bulge below me, bulge as if to split—but the bulging I saw below was in fact an illusion due to wave cadences from the changed blades of our helicopter, and the flash below was an explosion but not antiaircraft, and there was not at this moment of radio static and altitude-loss any way to be sure Monty held me accountable for Claire or therefore had got his locksmith nephew with the one noiseless and one organic nonnoiseless shoe to unlock the overhead rotor's swash-plate before lift-off, but I was now, through another (an orange) emptiness, sure that my Jenny could not have helped save me by revealing Savvy's receipt of Corsican Montage, because she knew those people had read in his copy probably as long ago as early August my recorded swimmer Mary saying once not overloud to Mike, as they floated and flirted between me and the naval engagement he had left, the word *Halloween*, though who besides me knew that Savvy would probably never have received Corsican Montage had Lorna not come to the softball game that Sunday after our Saturday night fight and appeared just as Savvy behind his catcher's mask was speaking of open ends.

But Jack, I now knew, had received from Krish old information: the time of the hit, Halloween morning. Inaccurate because canceled, but when Mary (with the Montrose heart on her mind) had phoned Dudley's lawyer friend at the Westbury (when?) to ask if he knew a link between a Maya jaguar and a New York bombing and Mary mentioned Halloween, the lawyer (the New York history buff whose services Dudley had decided he did not need) had mentioned to Dudley the phone call from the Scots woman, and from Dudley the connection had reached Tessa (now faintly impressed by his protectiveness), thence Alba, Cosmo, Krish, Jack.

Seeing—yes seeing seeing seeing but what was seeing—smoke flow from the flash that had now vanished (though was the emptiness in Sub's flat yesterday before Jenny's call merely the pumpkin grinning or was my cockeyed idea right that it was an emptiness that belonged to me like a grin I might grin through that emptiness appropriating it)—I weighed what Nash had said: they had feared I would go ahead with what had been called off; and Nash and the Frenchman had learned from the janitor last night that Jack Flint had cameras going right through the walls of the north warehouse to make a scientific film of what went on in the south warehouse.

And to get what I thought I otherwise couldn't get I'd asked a question of this dependent and erratic Nash which was of zero value to me (for I knew the answer), namely had Len left a time bomb in there? but which stirred one small pulse in Nash who began to splutter breathlessly that he'd finally gotten a phone call through to Len at five this morning to tell him there were cameras in the other warehouse and a Norwegian watchman and Cartwright and Jack

Flint, so Len knew but he had said merely have you seen the newspaper, and hung up.

The change in rotor rhythm had sounded like a flat. The pilot was edging us left or uptown toward the nearer of two East River helipiers. He had called in the explosion.

As Nash had receded and begun to run I had called out, What did you tell Len?

Meaning just now at the warehouse.

I was a second-story witness.

The way does not belong to things seen, nor to things unseen, or so says Lorna's koan. It does not belong to things known or to things unknown. Do not seek it, study it, or have it. To find yourself in it, open yourself as wide as the sky.

Was that why she'd had a plug-in phone installed upstairs?

I did not expect to see my address book again.

The clouds were rising and we were wobbling down and Manhattan did not look like a surface now.

That initial system highly improbable would indeed have yielded increasing probabilities, things coming together, the bog seeping into Krish to equalize pressures either side of his thin skin, the dilettante geologist finding the diary—but only if that system had been to begin with one system and not many systems which I had to forget in the living, and whose multiple impingements I had easily imagined operating through me in the chance of my life but operating through this impure semiconductor like many parts of *me* or as through one terminal albeit moving. But that was not the case. For look at the life of Jenny—so far from me I could be a collaborative cause of someone else's accidentally dying *for* Jenny; look at Dagger and his health, his education, his canny welfare, and the jaguar and the idea he gave to Jan Aut; look at Jan the rival of Jenny twice her age, look at Dudley all by himself entering to safeguard Tessa—or was it pure systematic curiosity?—and look at Claire and at Krish whose unfound body still eventually yielded the name of the lighter-stiletto's owner who thus came to share Claire's half-solved murder with J. K. Flint in whose hotel room was found a cross of delicately compartmented enamel in a technique Monty Graf identified for the police as cloisonné.

But that was then some future or past beyond what we had to go on. And what we had to go on was a certain forward capability like a plane's and enough lift to get us down before we hit the veterans hospital or that main peripheral artery FDR (or East River) Drive, where traffic was light to medium on this autumn Sunday and moving at a good clip. But then as if our advance was merely added to and overweighed by the vector force of that traffic north and south, we were not moving forward now, we were hovering, and I went forward to see why, for the rotor system maintained its slowed and laboring cadence and we were in trouble. The pilot verified my guess about the swash-plate but said there was more to it, he was testing our turning action, that was why we had momentarily stopped going forward, and he said go back and sit down it could be worse we could get flipped by a cross-current and come down in the river upside down and as I turned away he asked what I made of that explosion and he said he never worked on Sunday, and was this something special?

At the East River pier I gave him a hundred dollars which was on top of what I'd paid on the Hudson side.

A cab let me off near City Hall Park.

I could ascertain from two Sunday strollers only that a police tow truck had been badly damaged by an explosion that had destroyed a car the instant the tow truck started to tow it away.

I phoned Jack Flint's hotel, and was asked who I was. I said we had an appointment tomorrow but I had to be in L.A. and wondered if I could see him today. My name? James Wheeler.

Mr. Flint died this morning.

That is incredible, I said.

I phoned Sub's hospital. Incremona knew Ruby and Tris by sight, and I was concerned. Sub's doctor couldn't see him till late afternoon and Sub wouldn't come home till suppertime, which was when Rose his gifted wife was bringing Tris and Ruby.

I went to Mercer Street.

I pressed the top button beside the nameless slot and got no answer and pressed the next one down and was admitted. I passed the door behind which the music was playing and from where I was sure I had been buzzed in and went on to the top, where over the door of all places was a key and I opened the massive metal door and walked between the two TV sets, once more facing each other, to the work bench where I left a note which read *Real-time projection is still financially possible* and wrote my last name.

The music volume rose and there were steps but going down.

I phoned Lorna and she was home. And she was cool enough for me to sense anger, which was all to the good probably. I asked her to find out if one could open an "external" account at a bank for someone without the person's signed approval or at least without the person being there. I said I would try to catch a plane by tomorrow or Tuesday, I had two pieces of unfinished business. You don't say, she said sounding like my father, and added that a package had arrived from the Hebrides.

I stared at the word NAND in the corner of John's formulaic poster, and Lorna asked again, and the twitch or pulse or whatever it was in my shoulder went away into the mystery of my body and I said under no circumstances even touch it and that goes for Will too, and Lorna said she already had touched it and Will was at Stephen's but due home any minute, and what about Jenny, and I said Jenny was OK.

I locked up and left the key.

I did not walk into King Street. I found a phone booth a block north—the one Jenny and Jerry and Jan and Reid had all passed—and I got the deep gong you still got for a quarter and dialed Red Whitehead.

No, he said, the bald man who'd asked about me had identified himself as an Immigration agent and had nothing to do with any higher-up at Red's end because there was no big holding company controlling "our" operation, how did I ever get that idea; it was independent. I said I was leaving and did Red have anything for me.

Leaving? You hardly got here.

He had his stuff at the office and he was busy right now. He would be in touch.

I went looking for John in Chelsea in the building where I might have been killed or dreamed my lookout dream. There was a pane missing in the street-floor hall door. I plodded all the way up. The service door was not locked, but the inner room with the display console was, and I didn't have a loid.

In the red-and-blue room there along the wall was my trenchcoat.

I tore off a bit of newspaper and wrote John another note and stuck it in the door to the computer room. I packed Sub's coat and hat in on top of the money, put on my trenchcoat and left.

The last piece of the sun was visible down an aisle of high buildings. There wasn't a car in sight. I was in the shadow of Sub's apartment house and I went in carefully.

I did not answer the phone.

I phoned Mercer Street but John was not there.

I raised the window all the way, it was a beautiful late afternoon despite the clouds.

I leaned out over the pumpkin and there was nothing to see

except a cab passing and a cab parked twenty feet past Sub's entrance. No Opel.

The package was from the crofter widow of course. That was what Jenny had meant when she said, You know the woman.

I could see Jenny get off Reid's motorbike and plod up to the widow's door with the pack on her back. I could see her as far as the door and hear her ask for a glass of water and see her step inside and the door close. But I could not see or hear her produce three or four or five quid and ask the crofter widow to wrap all these typewritten pages and mail them to Highgate, it was an emergency.

Again the phone rang and I looked out at the twilight, and the cab was still downstairs. I could hardly describe to John my experience of digital trivia, my sense even now that even if mine had been a gloved hand at last programming its way through a deep transparent wall to handle dangerously contaminated substances much less administer justice, bring peace, or transform my own oscillations into something more fixed (that would nonetheless then demand motion in the observer to be understood), I would still feel short of that direct current I had envisioned if not dreamed of.

And again the phone rang, and digital mosaics leafed over one after the other, and I saw John with the money I would provide thinking directly through a machine to something visible and new which might be no nearer Andsworth's prophesied telepathy than my own *shtip*-like sense of other people's pain but might be revolutionary, profound, and (who knew?) even profitable.

I answered. It was Gilda. Had I read the news?

It was probably in a cab somewhere.

The girl Claire who had been killed and whose answering service Gilda had been honored to impersonate had been murdered for a reason that had not been guessed till new information received just before press time, and this new information was that she should have had twenty thousand dollars there in cash in payment for a film deal she'd been mixed up in and it was missing: Twenty grand! said Gilda, where did she get twenty grand? The police had other leads.

The door came open and it was Sub with a suitcase and a huge, loaded brown paper bag of a kind almost unheard of in England, though one can buy a sturdy shopping bag with a handle if one has not brought one's string bag or other bag with one to the shops.

His energy had risen. He stood as if waiting for me to disappear. He looked toward his bedroom. He said he was ready for a vacation.

He had gone way out of his way to find corn candies and a "revolting" Halloween cake, and I said, Look man, *we* bought bread and milk and a lot of other stuff—and Gilda was saying the same thing in my other ear as Sub took a deep breath through his genuinely wise gray beard and smiled bravely and said, You should know by now I am programmed to act in a certain way and I hope at some point in the future to be able to look back and say I have come through.

He put on some water, he carried his suitcase into the bedroom and put it on the unmade bed, he went into the living room and I heard him talking to his plants, he bumped me coming back into the kitchen, he laid out plates and forks and spoons and knives for three and put a cake on a plate and the candies in two orange-and-black dishes, and put a transparent package of hot dogs into the undefrosted icebox, poured water onto his tea bag, took the hot dogs out of the icebox, dipped his teabag several times, turned and added a fourth place to the table, and I said I'll be in touch, I've got the florist shop number, and hung up.

I went into the living room and looked out over the pumpkin and the cab was still there twenty feet beyond Sub's entrance.

But where should I go?

My case lay on the day bed.

Sub said the icebox was the story of his life, it would take two days to defrost it.

I asked when Myrna was coming.

He said at least no one had broken in again—had I finished my business?

I said I would be out of his hair by tomorrow or Tuesday. I opened my case and the gray hat was squashed to one side of the money, but Sub in the kitchen was saying No and again No, and then he said No, that wasn't it, and he sounded odd and I felt I had put too much strain on the friendship but also that I was out of place yet also not even wholly here, and I wondered if the strains of convalescence had made Sub a little crazy.

I heard the elevator and then steps and voices and I was going to offer to defrost the fridge tomorrow but the buzzer went three times fast and I wondered if Sub (who now strode from the kitchen) still wore that gray hat—but the children burst in before Sub quite got to the door. They were alone and excited. Ruby said Oh Daddy, Mommy made us turn off the TV, and Sub said where is she and Ruby said Connie brought us home, and Tris put down a small suitcase, said Hi Dad, how are you, and followed Ruby to the TV which being a solid state started making noise instantly and the picture was two or three seconds coming. I think my going now to the window where the pumpkin was and looking out infuriated my friend as much as his children ignoring him on the Halloween of his home-coming from the hospital and Ruby saying Fix the picture, but it was his laying hands on the TV that made Ruby scream and made me turn from my dreamlike vision of the sidewalk ten floors down and two yellow cabs and the brief gleam of a bald head bending beside the first cab; and as Sub with a hand on the top handle which enables the maker to call the set portable and a hand underneath bore an unreimbursed telly toward me past a day bed and a suitcase and his gray hat and dark Navy raincoat and a lot of money, I knew that right to the last moment Jack Flint had figured the south warehouse was going to be blown up by his hated brother's people, and knowing this I wanted to protect with my own life these children and my friend who had just said the box was going out the window and seemed to mean it.

I met him halfway but seemed only to help him or to support the set which was small but heavy. Tris had his hands on the rotating base of the aerial, as if in response to Ruby's request he were going to pull out the rabbit ear, I staggered back and recovered my balance and staggered again jamming my back on the windowsill and Ruby screamed and I seemed only to have helped Sub get the TV set to the sill and now I held it also back but Ruby screamed and I looked away toward the door and because of what I thought but did not see I relaxed my grip and Sub's suddenly unrestrained force sent the TV set over the edge, yet—since my belief in the multiple and collabo-rative impingement of many systems beyond my own had suffered a new relapse sensing like a *shtip* that I and no one else had been the one to tell Dagger about Maya jaguars and to speak in his car the idea he gave to Jan, namely, that none of us knew enough, and to mention long ago to Jenny that the Hebridean crofters were utterly depend-able and generous—I thought, Is it insured for this kind of thing? and in some final force as if one outer or inner system comprising all our mysteries blinked open for a micro-instant in me an instinct of collaboration—I think I gave the set an extra push.

I was higher for a second seeing the black-and-brown object pass strangely like a space capsule through an alien medium turning with slow force, but then I dropped five or six inches it seemed, as the set hit the hood of the first taxi and headlights speeding north through this most treacherous time of day could not have seen the figure in the hooded parka jump automatically to the cab's front bumper as if released by the concussion of the TV set and spring past into the path of those headlights and flashing grille that sent him twenty feet through the air so narrowly missing the fender of the second parked cab that one might have seen some diagrammed triangulation of impulses Incremona had no control over.

The pumpkin was smashed on the carpet under my foot.

The driver of the taxi that had almost been hit by Incremona had him under the shoulders and was getting him into the back.

Incremona was dead, I knew it as surely as I knew that even if the police acquired the three filmless tapes the words would be an impenetrable if interesting surface, and it was as unlikely that the authorities would get the tapes from whichever part of the group now had Incremona as that they would get the random letters I'd taken from Dagger and Alba's and stuffed in my parka pocket.

A high street lamp had come on. There was something in the street that looked red.

The woman who got out of the first cab looked up, and it was Constance. Her driver stood by his door on the street side. The driver of the car had stopped half a block up and was coming back; Incremona's cabdriver closed the rear door, got in, and drove off past the man in the street who was yelling and gesturing. Incremona had seemed to become motionless as soon as the car hit him and he had passed through the air as if fixed between times.

Everyone was looking up at me and Sub, and I was not sure what I had seen but I knew what we had done.

A NOTE ON THE TYPE

The text of this book was set on the Linotype in a face called Primer, designed by Rudolph Ruzicka, who was earlier responsible for the design of Fairfield and Fairfield Medium, Linotype faces whose virtues have for some time been accorded wide recognition.

The complete range of sizes of Primer was first made available in 1954, although the pilot size of 12-point was ready as early as 1951. The design of the face makes general reference to Linotype Century—long a serviceable type, totally lacking in manner or frills of any kind—but brilliantly corrects its characterless quality.

Composed, printed, and bound by American Book–Stratford Press, Inc., New York, N.Y. Typography and binding design by Virginia Tan.